THE **TEXAS**

Brides

COLLECTION

9 Romances from the Old West

THE **TEXAS**
Brides
COLLECTION

DiAnn Mills, Kathleen Y'Barbo,
Darlene Franklin, Darlene Mindrup,
Tamela Hancock Murray,
Lynette Sowell, Michelle Ule

BARBOUR BOOKS
An Imprint of Barbour Publishing, Inc.

Serena's Strength © 2001 by DiAnn Mills
The Reluctant Fugitive © 2001 by Darlene Mindrup
Saving Grace © 2001 by Kathleen Y'Barbo
An Inconvenient Gamble © 2013 by Michelle Ule
Angel in Disguise © 2013 by Darlene Franklin
Reuben's Atonement © 2006 by Lynette Sowell
The Peacemaker © 2006 by DiAnn Mills
Outlaw Sheriff © 2006 by Kathleen Y'Barbo
A Gamble on Love © 2006 by Tamela Hancock Murray

Print ISBN 978-1-68322-732-8

eBook Editions:
Adobe Digital Edition (.epub) 978-1-62416-088-2
Kindle and MobiPocket Edition (.prc) 978-1-62416-087-5

Scripture quotations marked KJV are taken from the King James Version of the Bible.

This book is a work of fiction. Names, characters, places, and incidents are either products of the author's imagination or used fictitiously. Any similarity to actual people, organizations, and/or events is purely coincidental.

Published by Barbour Books, an imprint of Barbour Publishing, Inc., 1810 Barbour Drive, Uhrichsville, Ohio 44683, www.barbourbooks.com

Our mission is to inspire the world with the life-changing message of the Bible.

Member of the
Evangelical Christian
Publishers Association

Printed in the United States of America.

Contents

SERENA'S STRENGTH

by DiAnn Mills

Dedication

To Troy and Barbi Tagliarino.
Good friends are special gifts from God.

Chapter 1

San Antonio, Texas, 1841

Serena Talbot lifted her gaze to the open road and waded a wooden spoon through thick venison stew, now bubbling over an open fire. From a distance, she heard the deep throaty laughter of her pa.

"Serena, your pa's riding in," her ma called from the cabin. "Looks like Mr. Wilkinson is with him, too. They're gonna want a cool drink of water."

"Yes, ma'am. I'll draw a bucket now."

Standing, she wiped the perspiration from her reddened face with her soiled apron. Texas heat in midsummer proved unbearable, but at least the cooking could be done outside.

Serena caught sight of the two men and waved. Snatching up the water bucket and ladle, she headed toward the well.

Ranger Chet Wilkinson. She'd just been thinking about him. In fact, he occupied quite a bit of her thoughts lately. His smile, well, it seemed to take her breath away. Good thing Pa didn't know her fancies. He'd be lecturing her about the wild ways of Texas Rangers.

If Ma married a ranger, then why couldn't she dream about one? But Pa knew the dangers of his rugged life and the hardships it placed on families. He didn't want his daughter to suffer through the anguish of loving a man who risked his life each time he rode out.

"Hey, Little One," her pa said, "you cookin' up something good? We smelled it five miles back."

Serena grinned at the rugged, broad-shouldered man. "You want to guess?"

"Nope, it's venison stew, and I could eat it all myself." He rode his red dun mare alongside the well and rested on his saddle horn. "I think I could drink up that whole bucket of water, too."

"I'll bring it to the barn as soon as I draw it up," she said and turned her attention to Chet. "Evenin', Mr. Wilkinson. We're pleased you're joining us for supper."

Chet's lopsided smile sent her pulse racing faster than Pa's prize mare. Even in the late afternoon with shadows of evening stealing across the sky, she could see his pine green eyes peering out from under his weathered hat. Or maybe she simply envisioned them. Sometimes at night, when sleep evaded her, she wondered if those green pools ever searched her out as she did them.

"I'd be much obliged, Miss Serena. I'm mighty hungry. Your pa hasn't stopped riding since sunup." A tousle of sun-colored hair fell across his forehead. Hard to believe his slight frame and boyish face followed the rough road of a Texas Ranger.

"We have plenty cooked up, and Ma's just made biscuits with fresh-churned butter."

"I'll be hurrying along then," Chet said with a nod. "Won't take long to tend to the horses and wash up."

He's too pretty for a Texas Ranger, she thought. *After riding with Pa for over two years, he ought to be looking hard.*

Her pa reined his horse in the direction of the barn, and Chet followed. "Hurry on with the water, Little One," Pa called over his shoulder.

A moment later, she untied the rope around the bucket and dropped the ladle inside. The deep springs below their land—not far from the San Antonio River—hosted the clearest, coolest water around. At least that's what Pa always said.

"Serena, ask your pa if anyone else is expected for supper," her ma said, stepping back inside the cabin.

"Yes, ma'am. I'll ask him now."

Serena noticed her ma had smoothed back her pecan-colored hair and changed her apron. Ma always fussed with her looks when Pa came home. Serena hoped someday to find a special love like her parents'. They'd been together since Pa rescued Ma from a renegade band of Comanches when she'd just turned sixteen years old.

She glanced down at her worn green dress. At least she'd brushed through her hair before Pa and Chet rode up.

Toting the heavy bucket, Serena slowly made her way to the barn. She'd given up on adding a little meat to her bones. Ma called her frail; Pa called her skinny. In any event, she still looked twelve years old instead of nearly eighteen. She had height, but no outward appearances of a woman's figure.

By the time Serena made it to the open barn door, her shoulder and arm throbbed. No one would ever hear of it, though. She felt determined to do her share of the work.

With a sigh, she stepped into the barn, and her ears perked at the sound of men's voices.

"We ridin' out again in the morning, Cap'n?" Chet asked.

"The following morning," her pa replied. He seldom talked much, seemed to be always thinking on something.

She heard the *whish-whish* of the grooming brushes gliding across the horses' sleek coats. Just as she decided to make herself known, Chet's voice caused her to linger a moment longer.

"You know, that little girl of yours is going to be a beautiful woman one day. Why, she's right pretty," Chet said.

A little girl, Serena fumed. Pa's nickname coming from Chet's lips didn't sound at all endearing.

"Well, I'd just as soon keep her around for a long spell. I ain't in no hurry to have her married off." Pa paused. "Leastways to no ranger...even one who carries a Bible in his saddlebag."

Pa, I'm a grown woman, she fumed. Chet had a reputation for being a Bible-prayin' preacher man, another reason why he favored her attention. A man who loved the Lord and the Rangers ranked at the top of her list.

"Yes, sir. I just meant for as young as Miss Serena is, she's bound to be a pretty woman. But when I get ready to settle down, I want a round woman, real tall, too. Good and strong."

Silence. Serena sighed, realizing Pa had no intentions of telling Chet the truth about her age. Frustrated, she kicked the side of the barn to announce her arrival.

Shortly thereafter, while inside the cabin and helping Ma finish supper, the matter still picked at her—like a whole patch of chiggers.

"What's wrong?" her ma asked, studying Serena with pale blue eyes. "You've been frettin' over something since you came back from the barn."

"Oh, nothing," Serena replied, pulling out tin mugs for the coffee.

Her ma set a jar of apple butter on the rough-sawn table. "Serena, you can't keep anything from me."

She gazed up into her ma's flawless face. No hint of lines around her eyes or streaks of gray in her light brown hair. She looked young, too, but not as skinny as Serena. "Mr. Wilkinson thinks I'm a little girl."

Her ma glanced up, surprise clearly lacing her face. "And it bothers you?"

Serena lifted her chin. "I'm a grown woman."

Her ma's laughter rang about the kitchen. "That you are, and don't you have a birthday coming up soon?" She gave Serena a hug, forcing a laugh from her.

"Another month, and I'll be eighteen. Ma, most girls, I mean women, my age are married with children of their own by now. Besides, any single men around here are afraid of Pa."

Ma crossed her arms over her chest. "Your pa does have a way of intimidating a body—especially if he thinks a man has his sights on you. Do you have someone in mind?" Her ma studied her curiously. "I haven't heard you mention anyone."

Serena took a deep breath, but the door creaked open and Pa and Chet walked in. "I'll go get the stew," she offered and slipped out the door between the two men.

When they all sat down to supper, Pa invited Chet to ask the blessing. Serena bowed her head and closed her eyes, eagerly anticipating Chet's deep voice. No matter how hurt she felt, he did have a way of making prayers sound meaningful.

"Thank You, Lord, for helping the cap'n and me get here safe. Thank You for this fine family and their hospitality. Mrs. Wilkinson and Serena have cooked up some good food, and we thank You for this and all of Your many blessings. In Jesus' name, amen."

All during supper, Chet's reference to Serena as a little girl bothered her. In fact, he'd succeeded in making her downright mad. As she ate, she conjured up a good plan to let him learn the truth.

"Would you like more coffee?" Serena asked her pa.

He handed her his mug, and she rose from the table to fill it. "Pa, you know my birthday is coming up soon."

"Yes, Little One," he replied, leaning back against his chair. "And I plan to be right here with you when it happens."

"Thank you. I was hoping you wouldn't be gone. Do you mind if I ask Moira to join us for supper then? She is my dearest friend."

"Fine with me as long as it's all right with your ma."

Her ma nodded approvingly.

"Birthdays were always special to me when I was growing up," Chet said, reaching for the jar of apple butter.

"And this one is more than special to me," Serena said, swallowing the irritation of Chet's earlier remarks and tasting the sweetness of revenge—or rather nursing her pride.

"How old you gonna be?" he asked, spooning a healthy dollop between the layers of a biscuit. "Oh, let me guess. I have a fifteen-year-old sister, so give me a moment to think on it." He peered at her with a mischievous look in his eyes.

"You might be surprised," Pa said between mouthfuls of stew.

Ma glanced curiously at Serena then picked up the basket of biscuits. "Have another, Chet. Might help your accuracy. Although I've been told never to question a woman's age."

Serena cringed and her pulse quickened. Ma knew she pined over him. Hopefully, she wouldn't tell Pa.

Chet thanked her ma and gathered up two biscuits, adding a generous slab of butter to each. He popped one into his mouth and chewed slowly as if considering her reply.

"Hmm. Since this one means a lot to you, I'm guessing. . .say thirteen."

Pa coughed and reached for his coffee. "Ah, Ranger Boy, you might want to rethink your answer."

He grinned, the same earth-shattering smile that always melted her heart. "Tell me, Miss Serena, how old will you be?"

She allowed herself the privilege of hesitation before staring into his handsome face. "Eighteen."

Chet's mouth flew agape, and he dropped his knife. "Why, why excuse me. I thought. . ."

"Surprised?" Serena asked sweetly.

His face looked as if he'd worked all day in the sun without his hat.

From the corner of her eye, she saw Pa's wry smile. *Good, Pa isn't mad at me.*

"Would you like to come to my birthday, Mr. Wilkinson? You'd probably like Moira. She's a bit bigger than me, but the same age. Funny thing about Moira, she works hard as a man—strong, too."

This time, Chet choked. He sputtered and reached for his empty tin of coffee.

"Oh my, let me get you some water," Serena said and scooted to the water bucket. For the first time she regretted embarrassing Chet. He looked miserable, and his face had reddened even more with the choking episode. There wasn't as much joy in seeing him squirm as she originally thought. Perhaps she should ease out of the topic and let him regain his composure. For a moment she considered apologizing, but she didn't want to own up to overhearing Chet and Pa.

"Pa, I know what I'd like," she said, handing Chet the water and avoiding his reddened stare.

Her pa raised a brow. "The palomino mare of Dugan Niall's?"

"You mean it?" Her voice quivered in anticipation.

A smile widened his dark bearded face. "Did you have something else in mind?"

She slid onto the bench beside her ma, feeling her delight nearly burst. "I was going to ask for your old rifle, but. . .no, Mr. Niall's horse is the finest gift anyone could ever want. Oh, Pa, thank you."

He pushed his plate back and rested his elbows on the table. "What do you say, Little One? Want to go pick up that palomino in the morning?"

Serena did not hesitate. "Yes, sir, and I'll fix you the best breakfast before we go."

He eyed Chet. "Why don't you come with us?"

He'd slowly begun to recover. "Dugan does have a good-looking stallion for sale. Yes, Cap'n, I'd like to ride along."

Pa pushed his chair back from the table, its legs scraping the floor. "Now, Serena, you owe Chet here an apology. No need to explain why. He's our guest."

Chapter 2

C het felt hotter than if he'd been branded across his face with the letter S for stupid. The truth burned clear to the pit of his stomach—and worse yet, he deserved it. All of his big talk in the barn about James's pretty "little girl" blared across his mind. No wonder Serena wanted to get even; she'd heard every word. Eighteen years old. Bewildered, he looked up into her angelic face. He'd landed in a heap of trouble with one skinny girl, rather woman.

Oh, Lord, I need a muzzle over my mouth.

Serena rose beside her ma from the bench and folded her hands at her waist. She brushed thick, black hair from her face. He inwardly grumbled why she didn't wear it up. Maybe then he'd have guessed her right age.

Eyes the color of nearly ripe blueberries gazed coldly into his. He saw a tint of anger, a mirror of pride masked behind softened features and pink cheeks. Yes, she did look young. . .and furious.

Lifting her chin and wearing a sweet rosebud smile, Serena addressed him. "Mr. Wilkinson, I'm sorry for humiliating you. I don't have an excuse except I heard you talking to Pa when I brought in the water. Will you forgive me?" She tilted her head like his little sister used to do when she needed understanding. "I know I didn't behave like a Christian woman."

The word *woman* poured thick as honey from her lips, and the sound of it sent little prickles up and down his arms.

He gulped and took a swallow of water. "Miss Serena, I most assuredly forgive you, but I believe the fault is mine. You can be sure I will address you in the future according to your. . .your rightful age." He stuttered through the last of his speech as the proper words escaped him—something that seldom happened.

"Thank you, Mr. Wilkinson. I appreciate your tolerance of my bad manners. Will you still be joining Pa and me in the morning?"

He swallowed hard and attempted to gather his wits. "Yes, ma'am. I'd be honored."

Serena glanced at her pa, and he nodded his approval. She sat down to finish her meal, but Chet noticed she picked at her food. Odd, he didn't feel so hungry anymore either. He sneaked a peek at James's daughter. Yeah, she looked way too skinny for him, but she did have a right pretty face.

Serena gave up trying to sleep. Chet's words echoed through her mind like a herd of horses stampeding across the dry plains. He hadn't noticed her as anything more than James Talbot's little girl. Even worse, when he got ready to settle down, he wanted a big, strong woman. Humph, strength didn't necessarily mean size. Hadn't Pa taught her those things? Strength meant courage in the face of danger or when she needed to stand for her beliefs. It meant trusting God to see her through bad times and thinking things through with her head and heart—not her muscles. Just because she didn't have much meat on her bones didn't mean she lacked gumption. It would serve Ranger Chet just fine to saddle himself with some huge woman who'd run from her own shadow.

Oh, Lord, could You make Chet see I'm strong enough to be a ranger's wife? Amen. And Lord, You probably need to change Pa's mind about me marrying up with a ranger.

Tossing on the straw pallet in her tiny room, she heard Chet snoring in the kitchen.

Good for him; glad he can sleep.

She cast aside his dismissal of her and tried to convince herself he didn't matter. But he did. Fighting the urge to cry, she focused on the following morning and Dugan Niall's palomino.

Staring up at the darkness, she couldn't help but feel excitement about the mare. What a wonderful birthday present. She'd never dreamed of such a fine horse. Pa and the other rangers took special pride in their mounts. A good horse often meant the difference between living and dying. Although she treasured the love from Pa for his generous gift, it didn't stop the ache in her heart for Chet.

Serena finally found a few hours' sleep before she woke to fix breakfast. Staring out the small window of her room, she saw a glaze of pink and gold ushering in the dawn. She quickly dressed, then remembered Chet was sleeping in the same room where she'd be cooking.

She told herself she had nothing to be wary about. He had insulted her, not the other way around, and, besides, he didn't know her feelings about him. Still, they were both bound to feel uncomfortable around each other, and Serena realized she needed to make things right.

Stealing into the kitchen, Serena tied an apron twice around her waist. Someday she would pile enough weight on her bones to secure it in back like a normal woman. She studied Chet sleeping on the floor and struggled with wanting to kick him or allow him to rest peacefully.

Pulling her gaze from the blanket-clad figure, she mentally calculated what she needed for breakfast. Due to the quickly rising temperatures, she welcomed the task of frying bacon, baking biscuits, and boiling coffee outside over an open fire. They might eat there, too, which would be a refreshing way to start the day. On second thought, Pa shared enough meals under an open sky. He'd prefer sitting around the table inside. After all, she'd promised him a good breakfast.

The idea of eggs floating in a pool of bacon grease would be an added treat, and the chickens had been laying good. Ma told her she could use all of the eggs she wanted.

Grinning with satisfaction, Serena collected matches, the coffeepot, and the empty water bucket before moving outside to gather dry wood. Not long afterwards, a fire crackled and spit. She loved the smell of wood burning and the sight of sunrise faintly splitting the darkness. A rooster perched on the well top and crowed. He peered about as if to make sure every living creature had heard him. Serena laughed as the birds seemed to sing a little louder in answer to the rooster's call.

A trip into the cabin produced a skillet filled with thick slices of bacon and peeled potatoes ready for her to slice into a second skillet. She'd already mixed up the biscuit dough and silently kneaded it before cutting the huge rounds.

"Can I help you, Miss Serena?" Chet whispered from his position on the floor.

"No, thank you, I'm fine," she replied in the same soft tone and immediately felt her heart race with the low sound of his voice. "Sorry to wake you."

"I've been awake. Hard to sleep in when you're used to rising before dawn."

She said nothing else but took the bacon-filled skillet outside, knowing she'd be back inside the cabin at least two more times to bring out the other skillet and biscuits. While at the fire, Serena checked the coffeepot and inhaled the aroma of freshly ground coffee.

"Here, I brought these for you," came a voice from behind her.

Startled, she whirled around to see Chet carrying the other items she needed. "How nice of you," she said and smoothed her apron before taking the skillet and the pan of biscuit dough.

He stood barefooted with his suspenders resting haphazardly on his shoulders, and he'd buttoned his yellowed white shirt wrong with something bulging at his heart. His sun-colored hair lay every which way but flat against his head, more like a boy than a grown man. A second later, his dimpled smile gripped her senses.

It ought to be a sin for a man to affect a woman so.

Embarrassed and grateful for the dim light, she pulled a paring knife from her apron pocket to slice the potatoes.

"Sure I can't help?"

"You can eat later," she said, "and maybe have a little coffee now."

Chet produced a tin mug from inside his shirt. "I hoped you had it ready. Can I sit and talk a spell?"

"Of course." While he settled down into the dew-covered grass and leaned back on his hands, she prepared her words. "Mr. Wilkinson—"

"Chet. My friends call me by my given name."

She took a ragged breath. "All right, Chet. I did a bad thing to you last night, and I am truly sorry."

"Naw, it's me who wronged you." He shook his head. "Funny how a man can earn a reputation as a Texas Ranger or a preachin' ranger or a big talker and still make a fool out of himself in front of a woman. Leastways, I never meant to hurt your feelings."

"I know."

"So can we go back to being friends?"

How could she refuse? Masking her sinking spirits with a flair for teasing, she eyed him suspiciously. "Aren't you afraid I might poison your coffee?"

"Would you do that to me?"

She lifted the pot from the fire, and he held out his mug. "A skinny little girl like me has to fight back any way she can."

He grinned and it eased her ruffled feelings.

She slid the coffeepot back onto the burning embers. "You know what Pa used to tell me?" she asked, poking at the fire with a thick stick and sending sparks into the slowly lifting blanket of night.

"Hard to tell with the cap'n."

"He told me if Indians attacked the cabin while he was gone, that I could hide myself behind a fence post."

Chet laughed heartily. At least she could lighten his morning with a little humor.

"Be back in a minute. Got to get my eggs." Serena headed toward the cabin.

"I can tote 'em out here for you," he called after her.

"No, sir. I don't want them broke before I fry them."

He chuckled, and she felt better since supper the night before. A lot of truth in freeing a body from sin.

Inside, Serena found Ma bustling about the kitchen, placing plates and cups on the table. She stopped and watched Serena. "Honey, you don't need to be fixing breakfast all by yourself."

"I told Pa I wanted to last night."

"I know, but I slept a mite longer than I intended."

"Good," Serena said. "You don't rest well when Pa's gone." She picked up the egg basket along with a platter to pile on the meat and eggs.

"Serena?" Her questioning voice sounded soft and tender.

She glanced up into Ma's face in reply.

"Why didn't you tell me you had feelings for Chet?" she asked, placing a hand on Serena's shoulder.

Avoiding Ma's eyes, she shrugged. "Seemed like a secret thing, and I needed to keep it to myself."

"But we've always been able to talk."

For a moment, Serena felt like releasing all of her pent-up emotions in her mother's arms. "I didn't mean to hold anything from you. It just seemed too personal to tell anyone—not Moira or even you."

"Can we talk after he and your pa leave?"

Serena felt unsure of her answer. Talking about it wouldn't change a thing. "Are you going to tell Pa?"

"Not unless he asks, and he's said nary a word." She offered a smile, and Serena returned the gesture. "Certain things only a woman can know."

Only a woman can know. She spoke the right words. "All right, Ma. We can talk."

Serena turned and opened the door. She gasped. In the pale daylight, a huge, wild boar stood between Chet and the cabin.

Instantly, she set the basket of eggs and the platter on the rough-sawn table and reached for Pa's rifle leaning against the fireplace. Pulling it up to her shoulder, she rushed outside.

"James, come quick," her ma said. "Serena, wait on your pa."

Chet waved his hands above his head. "Serena, don't come any closer. It'll tear you apart."

Ignoring first her ma's warnings and now Chet's, she knew exactly what to do. Suddenly, the boar took an unexpected turn in her direction and barreled forward.

Chapter 3

The boar raced straight toward her. Serena faintly heard her mother's cries and another shout from Chet, but she had her focus dead center between the animal's eyes. She squeezed the trigger. Rifle fire echoed and the boar fell six feet in front of her in a puddle of blood.

Instantly, Chet stood by her side, clearly amazed. "You got him right square between the eyes." His face had paled, and he looked a bit angry.

Serena blinked. "I know. That's where I aimed."

He poked the boar with his boot. "Who taught you to shoot like this?"

"I did," James boomed from the doorway of the cabin. "Good shot, Serena. You didn't flinch once."

Serena beamed. "Thanks, Pa. I tried to remember everything you taught me, but it took me by surprise when it barged forward."

"Couldn't have handled it better myself."

She adored her father's praise. "You hungry? I just about have breakfast ready."

"Nigh starved," her pa replied. A grin spread across his full face, as he wrapped his arms around Ma's waist.

Serena glanced at her ma, trembling beneath Pa's firm hold. Her grim expression left no question as to the fear she'd felt.

"She's fine," Pa said, obviously realizing Ma's apprehension. "She can handle a rifle better than most men."

Ma nodded and sniffed, blinking back tears. "There's a few things about our daughter, James Talbot, that I wish she hadn't gotten from you."

Chet cleared his throat. "Ma'am, I can understand your fright, but I'm glad she has her pa's eye and smooth pull on the trigger. Thank you, Miss Serena. I've been in a lot of dangerous places, but taking on a boar didn't rank among them. Praise God for your shootin'."

His words broke the tension flaring around them, and Ma laughed and cried at the same time.

"I'll get this overgrown pig out of the way so we can eat," Pa said. He released her ma and walked toward the dead animal, passing along a wink to Serena.

She handed his rifle to him, and he squeezed her hand. Fighting the urge to take a quick glimpse at Chet, she moved toward her ma, still quivering in the doorway.

They held each other without uttering a word. Ma had been right; certain things only a woman could know, and Serena had just earned a note of admiration from Chet.

Once breakfast and chores were completed, Serena rode with Pa and Chet to Dugan Niall's. She felt completely immersed in the hill country around them—the cedars dressed in blue-green leaves and gnarly post oaks with an occasional mesquite tree. She admired patches of orange trumpet-shaped wildflowers, purple wide-leafed petals, and a host of yellow beauties. She listened to the singing insects and calling mockingbirds as they offered their lulling songs, but Serena knew the dangers of the land—more powerful than any wild animal.

Three races of proud people claimed Texas: the Mexicans, despite the war for independence; the Apache and Comanche Indians; and the proud Texans. She'd long ago decided whoever fought the hardest would have the vast land. Pa told her once if he'd been Mexican, he'd be fighting for them, and if he'd been born an Indian, he'd be warring alongside the red man. Lucky for Texas, James Talbot was a white man and believed in the Rangers.

"God did a pretty good job out here," Chet said, squinting as he stared up at a robin's-egg-colored sky. "No wonder the land's restless; everyone wants a piece of it."

"No matter the cost," Pa said. "He made Texas for those willing to die for it—or defend it like we do."

"Some folks claim we rangers are of the devil," Chet said, "but they sure call us angels when there's trouble."

Pa chuckled. " 'Cause we aren't afraid of anything—leastways, nothing we show. The only thing I hate is leaving my family so much. Guess I'm lucky Rachel knew my commitment to the Texas Rangers when we met. Sometimes it's right hard to push thoughts of her and Serena away when we're in the thick of things." He lowered his gaze at Chet. "You listen to me, now. God's done me a fair amount of blessings, but this is a life for a single man. Your head can't be clouded with anything but the job at hand."

Serena listened intently. Pa seldom talked so freely, and she knew every word meant something important. The only thing was she didn't like what he had to say. Oh, he spoke the truth about wits and clearheaded thinking keeping the rangers alive and winning, but the yearning in her heart for Chet couldn't subside so easily. If Chet ever decided to look her way, he'd have to deal with Pa. Some said the devil could be more obliging than James Talbot when he was riled.

Lord, if me and Chet are supposed to be together, then let it happen. I'm already a Texas Ranger's daughter, and I can be a good ranger's wife. With Your help he could be right proud of me.

Dugan Niall met them as they rode up. He grinned from ear to ear. Most likely he anticipated the sale of his palomino and a stallion to Chet. Moira accompanied him along with a dozen other rusty-headed siblings.

"Aye, James, Chet, and Serena. Ya do me pleasure by stoppin' by. Is it the palomino you came for?" Dugan's Irish brogue sounded musical, and his wild, fiery-red hair and beard were a colorful match to his character.

"We sure are," her pa replied, lifting his hat and wiping the perspiration from his brow. "I want to give the mare to Serena before her birthday." He waved at the Niall clan. "Mornin', all you rooster tails."

They loved Pa's teasing and greeted him all at once.

Dugan's eyes twinkled, and he laughed till his round belly jiggled beneath his suspenders. "And you, Chet, do ya still have an eye for me stallion?"

"I'm just looking today, but I'm looking hard."

Dugan's mirth roared above the treetops. "First let's have some coffee. Me wife has just made a fresh pot."

Serena and Moira stayed outside, knowing the men would be talking awhile. The two walked to the corral, where a half dozen fine horses grazed.

"Why's Mr. Wilkinson with you?" Moira asked, her brown eyes dancing.

"He and Pa are riding out in the morning," Serena replied, hoping her friend thought Chet's presence meant nothing to her.

"He's a mighty handsome man," Moira continued, her gaze lingering on the cabin door then back to the horses. "I'd give anything to have hair as yellow as his."

Serena frowned. "Your pa would skin you alive if he knew you were contemplating a ranger."

"Yours, too. But they're right. Rangers live too hard a life for us. Besides. . ." She clasped her hands behind the back of her green print dress and teetered on her heels.

"Besides what?" Serena asked, feeling a giggle rise in her throat.

"Aaron Kent's been calling."

Clasping her hand to her mouth, Serena tried to stifle her enthusiasm. "Since when? How long has this been going on?" Aaron Kent had been widowed about a year, and he had two small young'uns to raise.

"Three times now—and I'm not saying another word."

Serena couldn't help but laugh at her friend's serious face—the same round face as her pa's, beautiful skin, and huge brown eyes. "Oh, you have never been able to keep secrets from me. And Aaron Kent is a good man, Moira, and easy to look at."

Moira blushed from her neck to her eyes. "He wants to talk to Pa."

The two girls hugged and, with no one in earshot, began to plan Moira's wedding.

An hour later, Dugan and Chet settled on a price for a chestnut stallion to be picked up after the ranger's next pay, and Serena rode her palomino home. Pa paid a fine price for the mare, and the horse acted frisky enough to please Serena.

She patted the mare on its neck. "Pa, I know I said this before, but I really appreciate this horse. I'll take good care of her."

His dark blue eyes peered into hers. "I know you will. That's why she's yours."

Serena treasured the proud look in her pa's eyes. As a little girl, she'd lived for his special look and smile meant only for her. Now, she wished Chet would show some kind of affection. Certainly, she wouldn't have to save him from a wild boar again to get him to notice her.

Chet shifted uncomfortably in the saddle. James's little girl had gotten under his skin. First she surprised him with her age, next she shot a charging boar between the eyes without a flinch, and now she handled Dugan's newly broke mare like she'd been born in the saddle. Why hadn't he noticed these things before? It rightly embarrassed him. He needed to have shown a little more foresight or at least paid more attention to the Talbot household.

A Texas Ranger prided himself in his good judgment and intelligence. Many times he'd heard a good ranger needed to ride like a Mexican, trail like an Indian, shoot like a Tennessean, and fight like a devil. Nothing was ever said about sense with a woman. Good thing only the Lord knew his thoughts.

Ever since he learned about Serena's age, being around her made him feel rather peculiar, and today he found himself admiring her spunk. Of course, being the only child of James Talbot meant she knew how to handle herself like a man. He should have figured that out when he noticed she refused to use a sidesaddle. Scary thought when Chet had already angered her the night before.

He glanced her way, not really meaning to, and she smiled back at him. Her innocent look made his toes numb, and a chill raced up his spine. He'd never reacted like this to anything in his whole life. . .until now.

How many times had he thanked God for giving him a steady hand and a clear head? He prayed every time a bullet or arrow whizzed by without so much as piercing his clothes. Those qualities, vital to a ranger's way of life, kept him alive and able to defend his beloved Republic. In addition, he owed his life here and in eternity to the Lord. Jesus rode with him everywhere he went, guiding and giving him courage to complete the task of defending the people of Texas.

Chet prayed and studied God's Word every day of his life. He'd learned life didn't always happen like he figured, but he couldn't dwell on it. A man had to wait until the smoke cleared and see how God worked. He'd learned to expect the impossible and not flinch when trouble came knocking. But nothing had prepared him for these new findings about Miss Serena Talbot. The little lady kept amazing him everywhere he turned.

God must be chastising him for his prideful talk when he hurt Serena's feelings. Well, he'd never do it again. This strange feeling unnerved him.

"Pa, where are you headed tomorrow?" Serena asked, breaking the silence.

"Rio Grande," he said with no emotion creasing his rugged, lined face.

"How long are you going to be gone?" She knew Mexico and Texas were in heavy dispute over the border. The Republic claimed the Rio Grande, but Mexico insisted on the Nueces River.

"Couple of weeks, Little One. I plan to be back for your birthday."

Serena sighed. "It's not my birthday bothering me."

"I know." He sounded tired.

"I'm not complaining, Pa. I just love you."

Chet felt as though he shouldn't be hearing James and Serena's conversation.

Rather too personal for his liking.

"Oh, if God would only let peace come to Texas," she said with a sigh. "Can you imagine Indians, Mexicans, and Texans all getting along like friendly neighbors? I mean, I know the Tonkawas, Choctaws, and Delaware sometimes scout for you."

Her pa nodded with a grim smile. "We've had some real good Mexicans help us out, too."

"But I'm dreaming and talking like a child. As long as men walk the face of the earth, there will be war," she said. "And I do respect your commitment to Texas."

Her pa cleared his throat. "It doesn't matter who's threatening the lives of folks, they have to be stopped. If the Rangers don't step in, the innocent will die."

"I understand, Pa, I really do." Serena said nothing for a few minutes, then asked, "Do you believe we'll one day be a state?"

Her pa shook his head. "Hard to say. A lot of folks would like to think so."

"What would happen to the Rangers then?" she asked.

He chuckled. "Chet, you answer that one."

Serena turned in the saddle, her deep blue eyes penetrating his soul—trusting and seeking an answer.

Suddenly, Chet couldn't remember his own name.

Chapter 4

James slowed his horse to keep pace with Chet. The older man peered into his face. "Didn't you hear me?" he asked.

Again, Chet felt color burn his skin. "Ah, I reckon my mind went to wandering." Why did the cap'n have that angry glint in his eye?

James chewed on his lower lip, a sign indicating he contemplated a serious matter. "Serena wondered what might happen to the Rangers if Texas became a state."

Chet swallowed. He sure didn't like the hard look on James's face. He must have riled him, except the cap'n didn't get provoked too easily. "Hard to say," Chet began, determined to give the popular subject his best. "Statehood might be fine enough, but I don't think we'd get along with the army—have a hard enough time with the Republic's army. Too many rituals and regulations for me. I don't see any purpose in wearing uniforms or keeping my boots and buttons polished. And I couldn't ever take orders from a man I hadn't ridden with. Texas Rangers earn their rank by showing they have guts and use their heads. I can't respect a man simply 'cause he wears a fancy uniform."

Serena turned in the saddle to address him. The late morning sunlight fairly glistened in her dark hair, giving it a copper cast. "So do you think Texas could get along without the Rangers?"

"Texas will always need rangers," he said, sitting straighter in the saddle. "I guarantee you the US Army or our Republic's army would not consider any fighting without first sending us to clear the way."

She smiled, and he noticed her sparkling white teeth. "Thank you, Chet. I agree with you. Nobody can keep us safe like the Rangers." She reverted her gaze back to the path ahead, leaving him feeling plumb foolish. And he had no idea why.

"You and me need to talk," the cap'n said under his breath. He spurred his horse forward to ride alongside his daughter, leaving Chet short of bewildered.

—⁂—

Serena wondered what she'd said to embarrass him. He looked akin to a ripe tomato. Then she had a thought. He must be sweet on Moira and seeing her must have gotten him flustered. Serena supposed it didn't help matters any with her bold statement about him probably liking Moira. Her dear friend filled his requirements and looked comely, too.

Pa had picked up on Chet's discomfort. Of course, Pa had a way of knowing what people were thinking long before they said a word.

A knot settled in Serena's throat. If Chet had eyes for Moira, Serena might as well forget anything ever blossoming between them. Her sweet friend would make a good wife. But. . .Moira said Aaron Kent had come calling, and she'd rambled on and on about him. Surely she'd rather have Aaron than Chet. At least the widower didn't live a dangerous life. Good thing she hadn't shared her dreams with Moira, especially with Chet possibly interested in the pretty redhead.

Lord, help me not to be selfish and jealous. I know I've given this to You, but it doesn't help this ache in my heart.

Maybe she did need to talk to Ma about Chet. Like Ma had said, some things only a woman understood.

By the time the three made it back to the cabin, Ma had a noonday meal almost ready for them. She'd pulled one of the hams from the smokehouse and cooked it with a bunch of fresh green beans. Ears of buttered corn boiled on the fire with a pan of corn bread baking beside the pot. Ma always cooked hearty meals when Pa came home.

Outside the barn, Ma admired Serena's palomino. She patted the mare's neck and let it nuzzle against her. "Beautiful horse. No wonder your pa had to have it for you. Have you a name for her yet?"

Truthfully, Serena had been thinking on it. "I like the name Fawn. The palomino's color puts me in mind of a baby deer."

"Sounds real fitting," her ma replied, giving the mare another pat, "and I don't recollect hearing a horse called by that name before."

"Would you like to go riding tomorrow evening?" Serena asked.

"Yes, I believe I would. Might be nice after your pa's gone."

Pa leaned up close to Ma and kissed her on the cheek. Tears welled in her pale blue eyes, a sadness seen much too often. Serena felt compassion wash over her. For a brief moment she asked herself if she really wanted the same heartache and separation in her life.

"Let me finish in the house," Serena said, gathering up her skirt. "I've had Pa to myself all morning, and now it's your turn."

Pa took Fawn's reins, and she left her parents to a few stolen moments alone. Chet tied his horse to a post and wordlessly followed Serena inside.

"Shall I tie an apron on you?" she teased. Odd, he looked uneasy. "Something ailing you, Chet?"

"No, nothing." He looked like a bull calf at a quilting bee.

"Why don't you sit down while I finish here?" She went about her business, trying to shake herself of his disturbing presence. What had happened to the free-talking ranger she'd known and grown to care about for the past two years?

Once Chet eased down onto a chair at the table and removed his hat, she ladled him a tall mug of water. He murmured his thanks and watched while she placed butter, dewberry preserves, and sliced tomatoes on the table. All the while, his piercing gaze increased her nervousness. While filling a huge bowl with the ham and green beans, she dropped a big wooden spoon on the floor. Snatching it up, she slammed the spoon on the table a little harder than she intended.

Exasperated, she began, "Chet Wilkinson, we've known each other for quite a spell, and you have never acted this way before. So why don't you just tell me what's wrong? Are you sick? Did you and Pa have words? Are you still mad about last night or me shootin' the boar this morning?"

Chet raked his fingers through yellow hair. "You could pester a man to death with your questions."

"Oh," she said, raising a brow. "You certainly have gotten mean-spirited all of a sudden. I was only trying to help."

He narrowed his pine green eyes and lifted the tin mug to his lips. In a huff, Serena covered the bowl of vegetables and ham with a clean towel and pulled out the plates and utensils. Realizing the corn must be ready on the cook fire, she grabbed another towel and bowl, then stormed outside.

What made her think Chet Wilkinson could possibly be the man God intended for her? The man had suddenly become intolerable and sullen. She didn't need a moody man, leastways one who couldn't answer a little question without getting sour as day-old milk.

She didn't need him, and neither did Moira. . .or any sensible woman. And he claimed to be a God-fearing man. He needed to spend more time in his Bible and less time on himself.

"Miss Serena."

She startled and dropped the towel, narrowly missing the fire. "That's the second time today you've scared me," she said, ready to take on the devil if necessary. Her gaze flew to his eyes, and she clearly met the contrite ranger. He held his dusty hat, toying with the brim and standing as though he'd been riding for a month without a stop. The pleading look in his eyes softened her. . .a little.

"I apologize for snapping at you. Don't know what got into me, and. . .I didn't mean to ruffle your feelings," he said, then expelled a heavy breath.

Serena bit back a curt remark. Maybe he had the Rangers' next job on his mind—or the one they'd just come from. Pa rarely talked about the perils and circumstances about his work, and sometimes he was short when he fretted over a matter.

God instructed her to forgive.

"It's all right. You have your own feelings, and it's none of my business anyway." She bent to lift the kettle from the fire.

"I'm not used to women," he continued and bent to help her.

Serena smiled. That word sounded better all the time.

"Haven't seen my little sister or Ma in quite a spell. Guess I'm not used to y'all's ways."

She nodded. "I think we got along better when you considered me a little girl."

His eyes brightened, and he took the kettle of corn from her. "Oh, but then

I learned the truth and got into trouble."

Serena laughed, and the two walked toward the cabin. "I'm glad you're coming for my birthday."

"I think I'd like it. . .very much. Will I get in the way of your friend?"

"Moira?" Serena's heart suddenly plummeted.

"I didn't remember her name, but you might prefer having her all to yourself."

Her insides relaxed. "No, the more the better. In fact, Ma mentioned having all the Nialls come for supper. They're a wonderful family who care about each other and love the Lord. Mrs. Niall visits a lot when Pa's gone—makes Ma laugh and tells her stories about Ireland."

"I reckon being the wife of a ranger is real hard," he said. "Not too many women could handle it."

"Depends," Serena replied slowly, as a bushel of answers raced across her mind. "If a woman loves a man, she can't be happy unless she's a part of his life."

He opened the cabin door. She turned to thank him, but his gaze peered into hers and sent an unsettling chill up her spine.

"Imagine you would know." He hesitated, wetting his lips. "I mean, since your pa's a ranger and all. You'd know what kind of woman it took to marry up with one." His face reddened again, and she felt her own grow warm.

"I suppose," she said, placing a jar of honey on the table. "I don't know any other way."

He cleared his throat. "Would you be interested in taking a walk this afternoon and leaving your ma and pa to some time alone? Your ma looked real upset when we left them out there."

"I'd take kindly to your offer," she said. "The river's a nice cool spot."

"And I haven't been wading for fun in quite a spell."

Silence permeated the room. *Oh, Lord, are You making progress?*

Standing in the small room, arranging the rest of the meal about the table, Serena felt Chet's gaze studying her. Oh, for a woman's figure. She didn't relish the thought of Chet staring at a fence post. Her nose stuck out farther than her bosom.

She decided to sit across the table from him. With everything ready but the corn bread, they'd eat as soon as Ma and Pa came in from the barn. In the meantime, she had the handsome ranger all to herself.

Searching for a topic that steered away from her fragile emotions, she remembered he and Pa would be leaving in the morning.

"I'll be praying for you and Pa's trip to the Rio Grande," she said, wishing her voice sounded stronger, more encouraging.

"Appreciate it," he said and laid his hat on the floor beside him. "We need all the prayers we can get."

Silence filled the corners of the cabin, and Serena wished she had something to do.

"Blueberries," Chet said, breaking the quiet surrounding them.

She lifted a questioning brow. Did he have a hankering for berry pie?

"Your eyes," he said, picking at a loose thread on the sleeve of his shirt, "are the color of ripe blueberries."

Before Serena could respond, the sounds of Ma and Pa laughing met her ears. Her parents entered. Ma's hair had slipped from her tightly wound bun, and her cheeks were rosy.

Pa's wide smile quickly changed to a frown when he saw Chet and Serena seated at the table. "After we eat," he said to Chet, "you and me are gonna have a long talk."

Chapter 5

C het had been hungry before James made his announcement, but his appetite soon disappeared. Second time today the cap'n announced a need for them to talk, which meant he planned to do the chewin', and Chet would do the listenin'.

Now he sat across from the cap'n, who cut his gaze at him sharper than a bowie knife. He was in a fine pucker about something. He'd been around James Talbot long enough to recognize a bad mood.

Serena already made him feel peculiar, and with her sitting so close beside him, droplets of sweat rolled down his cheeks. Fortunately, Mrs. Wilkinson still acted normal, and she smiled comforting-like while passing him the corn bread. Every bite of food hung in his throat, worse than his own cooking. The meal seemed to take forever.

Awhile later, James cleared his throat, rattling Chet's nerves. The cap'n stood and downed his coffee.

"Good food, Rachel," he said with an appreciative nod. "Chet, you coming?"

"Yes, sir," he replied, sliding off the other end of the bench he shared with Serena. "Thank you, ma'am, for a fine meal."

Rachel smiled. "You're welcome, but you didn't eat much."

Chet noted a glimpse of compassion in her eyes. She must know what had upset the cap'n. He stole a look at Serena. She looked as confused as he felt.

Outside, he fell into step beside the cap'n. "Don't recollect what I did to anger you, but I reckon you're about to tell me."

"I am." His tone reminded Chet of the many dismal times on the trail when they'd be riding into a dangerous situation against the odds.

They strode away from the cabin and toward a huge post oak shading a corner of the pasture. Chet had enough of waiting, but the Bible had a lot to say on patience. So he leaned against the tree, first kicking up a mound of fire ants and then daring to peer into James's blue eyes, almost as intense as Serena's.

"We're leaving in the morning," the cap'n said, standing square in front of him without a trace of friendliness. He looped his thumbs in the waist of his pants.

"Yes, sir."

"And I want you to forget everything about Serena."

Chet raised a brow. "Serena? What are you talking about?"

"Don't be acting like you've lost your senses."

Suddenly Chet felt anger race through him. "Well, maybe you ought to explain yourself, 'cause I have no idea what you're talking about."

James's jaw tightened. "You've been looking at her all day like some moon-sick calf. And I've already told you that no ranger is going after my daughter."

Chet couldn't believe his ears. "You're seeing things. I'm not interested in Serena. I've only been making polite conversation."

James shook his head in disbelief. "For one ranger—a lick smarter than the rest—you sure are acting stupid."

Then it hit Chet. The uneasiness around Serena, the way he liked to see her smile, and those eyes. Maybe the cap'n did know something he didn't. He glanced at the cabin and back to James.

"I had no idea," Chet said, shifting from one foot to the other.

"Well, take notice," James said, jamming his finger into Chet's chest. "Don't be putting any fancy ideas in her head or dreaming up any of your own." He peered out over the horses grazing in the pasture. "I'm fixin' to promote you to lieutenant. You're a good ranger and you have the respect of the other men. Being a single man is the easiest way to do the best job."

Chet expelled a heavy sigh. "I understand about Serena, and I appreciate the promotion."

"Good. We've settled this little matter, and now we can head back and get us some more corn bread and honey."

Wonderful, Chet thought. *Something else to stick in my throat.*

Back inside the cabin, Chet couldn't bring himself to look at Serena. What had happened to him since he learned Cap'n James Talbot's skinny little girl had grown into a woman? She still looked the same, didn't she? He'd noticed her pretty face before, but he'd never really talked to her until today. Or experienced such unnerving thoughts about a woman.

He swallowed hard. Flashes of last night and today darted across his mind. He admired Serena, and she'd surprised him a time or two, but he thought he kept those notions to himself. Obviously not. He hoped she hadn't sensed the same thing.

"Chet here just got a promotion," the cap'n said after a few moments. He'd piled his plate high with corn bread, added a hill of butter, and poured honey over it. "He's now Lieutenant Chet Wilkinson."

"Has a good ring to it," Serena said, flashing him a smile.

"A lieutenant has to deal with a lot of responsibility," Rachel said, refilling his coffee mug. "But I'm sure you've earned the title."

The cap'n offered a wry smile. "You earned it last August at the Battle of Plum Creek when we fought Buffalo Hump over his prisoners and loot taken at Linnville. You demonstrated real grit, and I haven't forgotten it."

Chet remembered how the Tonkawa Indian scouts had assisted the Rangers in tracking down the Comanche warriors who had attacked and destroyed an entire

Texas town. "They would have made off with it all, if Buffalo Hump hadn't been so concerned about saving his loot, especially the nearly three thousand head of horses."

James is right, Chet thought. *My life is too risky to ask a woman to share it with me.* Suddenly Chet startled. When had he begun thinking about Serena as a wife? He felt himself grow increasingly uncomfortable. No doubt he looked as red as a ripe tomato.

"I'm committed to the Rangers," Chet said, knowing the cap'n expected him to share his beliefs. "God first and Texas second."

"As it should be," Serena replied, folding her hands on the table in front of her. "Your folks will be glad to hear the news. I know I'd be proud if we were kin."

The cap'n cleared his throat, and Chet felt an invisible bullet pierce his heart. *Lord, help me. I think I've fallen in love with Serena Talbot. How does a man prepare himself for something like this? I haven't been looking, and she isn't the woman I thought You wanted for me. Worse yet, I'm bound by my pledge to the Texas Rangers and her pa to do nothing about it.*

—∞—

Serena hummed her way through the chore of clearing the table from the noon meal. Pa and Chet were outside, probably talking about what awaited them along the Rio Grande.

"The palomino sure has made you happy," her mother said, gathering up the dishes to wash them outside.

"Oh, yes. Fawn is a beautiful horse." Serena remembered again Chet's likening her eyes to ripe blueberries. "Some other things besides my birthday gift have me feeling good."

Ma stood in the doorway with her hands full. She paused and set the load back on the table. "Chet noticing you?"

Serena couldn't help smiling. It seemed to start from her heart and burst through to her face. "I believe so. He asked me to take a walk this afternoon so you and Pa can have some time alone. Maybe I'll know more before he and Pa leave in the morning."

"Your pa knows."

Serena felt her stomach twist. "He does? Did he say so?"

"Yes, and he's not pleased."

She sighed and peered into her mother's eyes. "With me or Chet?"

"Both."

"So I imagine Pa will talk to him about it on the way to the Rio Grande."

Her mother shook her head. "He already has—right after we ate."

"So that's why Chet didn't say much," Serena said, thinking out loud. She blinked back a single tear and focused her attention on covering the honey jar.

"You know how your pa feels about you taking up with a ranger." Ma's words sounded gentle, not chiding or finding fault.

Serena nodded, avoiding her mother's gaze. "Yes, ma'am, I know. But I think I should be able to choose how I spend my life."

"I felt the same way, too. I was younger than you when I fell in love with your pa—your age when I had a baby in tow."

"Have you ever regretted marrying Pa?" Serena asked, wringing her hands and turning to face her ma.

Her ma smiled through her own tears. "Never. I love him more now than ever. I fret and I miss him, but he's the man God gave me. Loving a ranger is hard, but I wouldn't have it any other way."

"And what if I have the same feelings for Chet?"

Ma tucked a loose curl behind Serena's ear and slowly nodded. "I understand, but we both have to respect your pa's wishes."

Serena considered the matter, not ready to relinquish her heart so easily. "I've already given the matter to God. If Chet and I are to be together, He will change Pa's heart and mind."

"And I'll ask God to give you the peace and courage to accept whatever He deems proper," her ma said. With a quick hug, she gathered up the dirty dishes and stepped outside.

Serena caught a glimpse of Pa and Chet walking across the pasture toward their horses. The two men looked as different as day and night—Pa with his nearly black hair, like hers, and Chet with his sun-colored, wayward locks. Even beneath his hat, Chet's hair tended to stick out every which way. But they were a lot alike, sharing characteristics neither would most likely own up to. Both had a stubborn streak, a unique way of thinking things through, a strong sense of values, and a love for the Lord.

She sensed Pa would deny a walk to the river, unless he really wanted to spend time with Ma. Odd, Chet hadn't even mentioned being interested in her, and already the thought had been dismissed. Pa must have picked up on something she didn't know about, but then her pa had a way of reading a person's mind. He simply knew things before anyone else did.

A smile surfaced through her low spirits. *Blueberry eyes.* She wondered how long it took Chet to think up such a sweet description. Serena hoped a long spell. She'd like to know he'd been pondering over her during the long nights on the trail. Impossible. He'd just found out about her age last evening.

A wave of sadness blew over her, much like the foreboding wind sweeping through the trees before a thunderstorm. Serena knew she could do nothing about Pa's bidding, but only pray and trust God to work things out for good.

After Serena finished cleaning inside the cabin, she joined Ma outside to finish washing and wiping the dishes. Squaring her shoulders and pushing away her pride, she resolved her ma wouldn't see the ache in her heart. Maybe she could fool Pa, too.

"Everything will work out for the best," her ma said. She dried her hands on her apron and wrapped her arm around Serena's shoulders.

"I know," she replied more confidently than she felt.

"If it makes you feel any better, when your pa came calling, my pa ordered him to never set foot on his property again."

"What did you do?" Serena asked, curiosity gaining the best of her.

"Well, James isn't going to like me telling you this. . .but I reckon I will. He showed up at my door and told my pa he wasn't leaving until he got permission to marry me. My pa threatened him with a shotgun. No daughter of his was going to marry a wild Indian fighter, but your pa got off his horse and stood there until Pa gave his consent."

"How long did it take?"

Her ma laughed. "Close to seventeen hours. My pa said later he figured an hour for every year."

Laughing with her ma, Serena finally sobered and asked, "Would Pa be that stubborn about Chet?"

Ma gazed into her eyes. "Since your pa decided beforehand to stand there a week if he had to, I'd say he'd be even worse now." She kissed Serena's cheek. "Better stick to praying."

Chapter 6

Before Serena and her ma could speak any further, Chet and her pa ambled toward them. One reminded her of a mountain cat, the other a bear. Pa laughed about something and Chet joined in. Maybe things between them weren't so bad after all, unless Chet had agreed to her pa's demands.

"Rachel," Pa said, "Chet has volunteered to keep Serena company for a spell so you and I can have a little time together. He first suggested a walk along the river, then decided fishing sounded better. What do you think?"

Ma beamed and flashed Chet an approving glance. "I think the new lieutenant has a wonderful idea."

"I like it, too," Serena said, trying to hide her eagerness. Could it be her pa had changed his mind?

Pa frowned, narrowing his dark blue gaze. "Well, I expect plenty of fish for supper."

An inward sigh coursed through her. She guessed nothing had changed. "Of course," Serena said. "I'll fry them up tonight."

"And I'll clean them," Chet added.

Ma rose from the ground and handed Pa the pan of clean dishes. A flush of pink tinted her cheeks. She whisked off her apron and smiled with a special smile meant only for him. "We're finished here, and it looks like supper is taken care of."

A broad grin slowly spread across Pa's face. "Are you still of the mind to see those mustangs I spotted a few weeks ago?" he asked, heading toward the cabin with Ma right beside him.

She slid her arm around his waist and leaned against his shoulder. Serena didn't hear what she said. Perhaps the words were only for Pa's ears.

Serena glanced at Chet and found him staring at her. The glint in his eyes didn't look like anything she had seen from him before. It made her feel downright fretful.

"I reckon we'd better gather up what we need," he said, kicking at the dust. "Suppose it's all in the barn?"

"Yes, on the wall opposite where the bridles hang." She clenched her fists to control her nervousness. "Which one of us gets to dig for worms?"

Chet chuckled. "Oh, I suppose if you bring a couple of canteens of water, I'll get the bait."

She relaxed slightly. "You have a deal. Do you want me to pack any food? You didn't eat much."

Chet studied a spider crossing over the toe of his boot. "Most likely so, especially since your pa is expecting us to catch a mess of fish. He must have a powerful taste for them."

"And we wouldn't want to disappoint him."

"Or rile him."

All the while she busied herself with food and water for later in the afternoon, she wondered if Chet might mention Pa's ultimatum about her. Of course, nothing had ever been said to her anyway. . .except the comment about her eyes. The color of ripe blueberries. She simply couldn't get his words out of her head, simply because Chet hadn't said anything else to give her hope.

—⁊⁊—

Chet stomped the shovel into the ground with such force he feared breaking it. Snatching up a couple of worms, he pitched the wiggling creatures into a wooden bucket. His thoughts spun with James's instructions about Serena. He understood the reason why the cap'n didn't want him seeing Serena, and given the same circumstances, he'd most likely feel the same way.

But something had happened to him, and now a whisper of her voice sent a funny tingle up his spine. He liked the way she wore her thick, dark hair down, the healthy glow of her skin, and the sprinkling of freckles across her nose. Most of all he liked those huge eyes. He could drown and go to paradise in them—nearly had this morning. He did wish she had a mite more meat on her bones, to make her a little stronger. A woman needed strength in this Texas wild to hold up with the hard work.

Chet sank the shovel into the ground again. The cap'n would skin him alive if he knew his thoughts about Serena.

Oh, Lord, You've pulled me out of more scrapes than I care to mention, but this one is the worst. I don't know whether to ask You to take away my feelings for Serena or show me a way to convince her pa.

Within the hour, Serena and Chet wandered nearly two miles up the riverbank to the fishing hole. Tall oaks and cypress trees kept them cool while the quietness of nature soothed Chet's racing mind. Now and then a crow called or the distant drum of a woodpecker broke his musings. A snake with familiar coloring slithered across his path.

"Watch out, a copperhead just raced in front of me."

She laughed lightly. "As long as he doesn't head back this direction, I'm fine."

Her laughter reminded him of a Mexican guitar on a still night, when the only sounds were singing insects and the crackling fire. Easy and soothing.

"We're almost there," she said and pointed to the river. "See that fallen tree where you can walk across to the other side? It's right on past where the river widens."

In a short while, they dipped their lines into the gently rolling water and sat down on a grassy knoll beside a cypress tree.

"Isn't this a pretty spot?" she asked, barely above a whisper.

He cradled his head in his hands and leaned back on the green earth, crossing his ankles and balancing his pole between his boots. "I like the peacefulness. Makes me wonder if heaven could be like this."

"I hope so. I mean, I can't imagine any place more lovely."

"Tennessee's pretty and green like this."

"Your family lives there?"

He nodded. "Ma, Pa, and six sisters."

She laughed. "I can't imagine you in a house full of girls. I suppose all those sisters made life interesting."

"Don't know if *interesting* is the word I'd use to describe it. But I did my share of pestering them."

She gazed out over the smooth river. "Do you miss them?"

"Oh, sometimes. We had good times, and my pa is a preacher."

"So he led you to the Lord?"

Chet chuckled and stared up at the sky. "Not exactly. When I was fourteen, I got chased up a tree by a bear. I figured that was as good a time as any to call on the Lord. Been calling on Him ever since."

"Well, I'm sure your family is proud of you."

He shrugged. "Suppose so—never thought on it much."

"Oh, I'm sure they are. Did you happen to bring your Bible?"

Her question surprised him. "No, I'm sorry. Left it in my saddlebag."

She plucked a purple wildflower and let it rest on the skirt of her deep green dress. "I've been thinking some of the Psalms would sound good now."

"Yeah, they would." He hesitated. "Serena, do you believe God has a plan for us? I mean all of us."

A bit of pink touched her cheeks. "Oh yes, and I also think we can make big mistakes by not listening to Him."

"Do you think rangerin' glorifies God? With the killing, it makes me wonder if I'm living like I should."

Tilting her head slightly, she appeared to ponder the matter. "We both know God hates killing. But if a man does nothing while his family and friends are murdered, then who's the real murderer?"

"Yeah, you feel the same way I do. I'd sure like to see this country safe for folks to live peaceful-like. Seems like it won't happen in my lifetime, though. The Republic is having a hard time getting established, and peace with the Indians and Mexico is afar off. Makes a man tired thinking about it."

"You're just the man to help tame Texas, and I'm praying for you," she said and offered him a smile so sweet he wanted to pull her into his arms and protect her forever.

"Thanks. You know, sometimes I think I'd like to be a preacher, but. . ." He laughed aloud. "I'm afraid I'd rough up anyone fallin' asleep during a sermon."

Serena continued to smile. "Well, folks would be more apt to pay attention."

"Imagine so." He pulled himself up from the grass on his elbow and rubbed the back of his neck. "I like you, Serena."

"And I like you."

"I mean, a lot."

"And I like you a lot, too."

They went back to fishing then, neither saying a word while Chet felt perfectly content sitting beside her. An hour passed and they hadn't caught a fish, not even one small enough to toss back in.

Serena deliberated upon her pa's words. He wanted a whole string of fish, and right now they had nothing. The thought worried her. She was his only child, and her pa could be stubborn about some things. He seemed to forget she'd be eighteen years old soon.

"Chet, we haven't caught a thing," she said.

A furrow creased his brow, and he expelled a heavy breath. "The cap'n is expecting fish for supper."

"I know. He'll be disappointed."

"No, he'll be wrathful," Chet said.

"Pa wouldn't get mad because the fish weren't biting."

"He's more concerned about things other than what we pull out of this river."

Serena's heart pounded hard against her chest. "Your job along the Rio Grande?"

"No."

Silence seemed to deafen her. She couldn't think of anything to say or ask. So he lay back down on the grass, and they sat for another half hour waiting for the fish to bite.

"Are you hungry?" Serena asked when she heard his stomach growl.

"Yeah." He glanced up at the sky. "A little food would be nice."

She stood and walked over to the leather pouch containing leftovers from earlier. Refusing to dwell on Pa's anger when he would find out they hadn't caught any fish, she pulled out biscuits and corn bread left from breakfast and chunks of smoked ham and laid them on a cloth. The canteens held plenty of water.

"Here we are," she said, doing her best to sound cheerful. Spreading the cloth between them, she urged him to eat, but she had no appetite, no fish for Pa, and no endearing words from Chet.

"Aren't you hungry?" he asked, after downing a thick biscuit with a layer of ham tucked inside.

"No, go ahead. Can I ask you something?"

"Sure."

"Will you still be here for my birthday, like you said last night?" She held her breath, almost afraid of his reply.

Chet wiped his mouth with the back of his hand and took a swallow of water. "Serena," he said softly.

She peered into his face, and if somebody had asked her, she wouldn't have known her own name.

"We both know why the cap'n is expecting a whole mess of fish."

She took a deep breath and nodded. A noisy blue jay chased a squirrel up a tree, reminding her of Pa chasing Chet.

"So what are we gonna do about it?" he asked.

The gurgling sound of the river hitting the rocks masked her fluttering heart. She wet her lips and tried to form her words. "I don't know."

"I've been praying for what's right—not saying a word to you and abiding by your pa or speaking my mind."

Her heart pounded so hard, she could barely breathe. "Since you spoke up, what have you decided?"

"Aw," and he tossed a pebble into the water, skimming it in wide circles. "Both."

Stunned, Serena gazed into his eyes, then hastily glanced away. "Then say your piece."

He leaned on his side again, still balancing the fishing pole with his boots. "I need to tell you how I feel. Not sure why, except I'm about to explode like a hundred shotgun blasts." Taking a deep breath, he continued. "I believe I've fallen in love with you, Serena, and your pa would have my hide for saying it."

She felt herself trembling. How many nights had she lain awake dreaming of Chet telling her those words? Did she dare reply? "I. . .I feel the same," she managed.

He snapped off a blade of grass. "Might be easier if you didn't. I didn't mean to stir up any more trouble than I already have."

She fidgeted with the petals of her wildflower. "So you believe there's nothing we can do?"

The tension between them could have been split with an axe.

"Well, I certainly hadn't planned on this, and life with me wouldn't be easy. I reckon I could give up rangering. It might ease things with your pa."

Serena shook her head. "You belong with the Rangers. It's your life, like breathing. I wouldn't ever ask you to give it up. There's bound to be another way."

He chuckled and squinted up at her with the blade of grass sticking out his mouth. "Sure wish God would tell me what to do."

"Me, too."

"Funny how I've known you all this time and never thought about you as more than a friend. . . ."

"James Talbot's little girl."

He grinned. "And now I can't seem to get you off my mind."

About then his pole jerked, and he grabbed it. Sure enough, Chet had a fish. "By golly, look at the size of that bass," he said, pulling in the line.

"And there's bound to be more." She studied her line. It wiggled and bobbed up and down. "Chet, I've got one, too."

A moment later, she pulled in a huge bass, bigger than his.

Suddenly they both started to laugh. How utterly ridiculous to become so excited about two fish, yet they were. They both quickly baited their lines and tossed them out again. Before she could consider what was happening, Chet swooped her up into his arms and whirled her around.

That started the trouble. The moment his hands touched her waist, she felt her arms chill and her toes grow numb. Chet must have sensed her feelings, for his gaze softened and he lowered her to the ground. His fingers reached to brush across her cheek, then trace her lips. He lifted her chin, and she felt her pulse race faster than she believed possible. Staring into his pine green eyes, she believed her dreams had come true.

"Serena, I have to kiss you this once. I may never have a chance again."

When he bent to lightly touch his lips to hers, she encircled his neck and allowed him to draw her closer. His kiss deepened, and she gladly melted into his arms.

"Oh, Serena," he whispered, "I shouldn't have done this, but I can't help myself." He drew his fingers through her hair.

"What is going on here?"

Serena and Chet instantly stiffened. James Talbot stood before them, pistol in hand.

Chapter 7

Serena instantly tore herself away from Chet's embrace. With a gasp, she felt a tinge dizzy and her knees weakened. Pa stared at her as though she'd done something terrible. And he looked at Chet as though he'd done something worse.

Ma dismounted from her bay mare and touched Pa's shoulder. "Easy, James. We talked about this," she said, but the scowl on his face could have carved out a mountain.

"Pa," Serena said, lifting her chin. "Nothing's going on here. We..."

Chet touched her arm. "This is my fault. I'll handle it."

"Like you handled my daughter today?" her pa asked evenly. He handed Ma the reins to his horse while his finger rested a hair's span from the trigger.

"I'd like to explain, Cap'n, if you'd give me a chance."

Chet's words relayed confidence, but a sideways glance at him told Serena he felt anything but self-assured. Serena refused to move, believing her silence might hold Pa back from ending the dilemma about her and Chet once and for all.

"I have eyes," Pa said, slowly nodding his head to emphasize each word. "Didn't I tell you what wouldn't happen between you and Serena?"

"You did the talkin' and I listened," Chet said. "I understand how you feel about your daughter, but you don't understand how we feel about each other."

The surroundings grew oddly quiet. A few insects braved the tension, and a mockingbird seemed to mock them. The air grew hot and humid.

"Maybe you need to calm a bit, James," Ma said, breaking the silence. "Serena's old enough to know her mind."

Thanks, Ma. Lord help us. We've got ourselves in a fine fix.

"Not when it comes to Texas Rangers," Pa said. His voice sounded cold and steady. "Rachel, you and Serena head back to the cabin. Chet and I have business right here."

"Please, Pa. You're sending me away like a child."

"Serena." His voice rose.

She stopped herself, knowing better than to defy her pa when he had his mind set. She glanced at Chet, and he motioned for her to step toward Ma.

"Cap'n, forbidding me and Serena to see each other isn't going to help the situation at all."

"I'll be the judge of that, since I'm her pa."

"By filling me full of holes once the women are gone?"

"I might."

"James, you and Chet have no business fussin' with each other right now. Won't solve a thing," Rachel said, slipping her arms around Serena's waist. "You two have been friends for quite a spell, and this is not the way to end it."

"You're right," her pa said, not once glancing at Ma or Serena. His fingers still rested entirely too close to the trigger. "So I'm a fixin' to send him on ahead to meet the other boys. You two head back to the cabin, and I'll give the *lieutenant* his orders. He might need special instructions, since he appears to be hard of hearing."

Serena saw an angry spark in Chet's eyes. How could the two men she loved be at such odds with each other?

"Cap'n, this won't work," Chet said, crossing his arms defiantly and standing square. "You can send me on ahead, but you can't stop me from having feelings for Serena."

"Feel what you want—but you ain't touching my daughter again."

"You make it sound like I've done a bad thing here."

Ma urged Serena to take Pa's horse. Grasping the reins, she climbed on the saddle, braving one last look at Chet. His composed expression gave her the chills. No wonder he was one of Pa's best rangers. She wouldn't want to face either one of them knee-deep in trouble.

Brokenhearted, she pulled Pa's horse behind the mare. How could he not understand a man and a woman in love? As they passed the men, Chet made a comment, but Pa bellowed about God intending for a man to respect another man's words.

The horses clipped along at a trot, single file along the path she and Chet had walked hours before. Behind her the muffled sounds of the arguing men churned her insides, and before her lay nothing but loneliness without Chet—before it had even begun.

When Ma slowed her mare to ride side by side with Serena, she could no longer contain her sorrow. "Ma, how could Pa be so mean?" she asked, her eyes brimming with tears.

She sighed and slowed her horse to a halt. "Oh. . .he simply sees too much of himself in Chet," her ma replied. She gazed at her through pale blue eyes and smiled sadly. "I hate this for you because I remember all those same feelings."

"But you two made it just fine."

"Yes, we have. Your pa loves you, Serena, but he doesn't want you spending night after night alone and worrying over the man you love."

Serena stiffened, her heart beating furiously in righteous indignation. "Ma, I'm a full-grown woman. I know my heart and mind, and it's with Chet."

"Then you best be praying God does a mighty work in your pa 'cause his mind is dead set against any ranger courtin' his daughter." She sighed and glanced up into the treetops. "I ought to know, I spent the better part of the past few hours trying to convince him."

Gratitude entwined with love washed over Serena. "Oh, Ma, I'm so sorry. You didn't have to use your time with Pa discussing Chet and me. He and I will figure this out."

Her mother raised a brow and peered into Serena's face. "That's what I'm afraid of."

"Ma, you know I mean we're expecting God to work out this problem with Pa."

"And He doesn't need your help."

—⁓—

Chet expelled a heavy sigh as he reined his horse away from the Talbot cabin. The orangey-red shadows of evening clung to him, reminding him a portion of his life was fading into a memory. He'd found love and lost it in two short days. He'd known Serena better than two years and liked her as a little girl—and loved her as a woman.

The cap'n had sure enough wanted to blow a hole through him. Never had he seen him so mad, and nothing Chet said could move him. Not once had the cap'n moved his hand away from his gun.

"I'm not out to hurt her," he'd told the cap'n.

"Don't you think being away from her all the time is gonna hurt her? It ain't just hard, ya fool. The pain in a woman's eyes stays with you all the time."

He realized then how much James loved Serena. Maybe Chet needed to do some thinking on it. Maybe the cap'n made sense after all. He didn't want to be self-ish or come between a man and his daughter. Swallowing his pride, he had walked back to the barn, packed up his gear, and left, not once seeing Serena inside the cabin.

Now he rode alone to meet up with eighteen rangers who served under Cap'n Talbot. They'd be anxious to head for the Rio Grande as soon as they could. God have mercy on anyone who got in James's way on this job, be it the enemy or a ranger.

Lord, I don't want this to be hard on Serena. She looked powerfully unhappy riding away with her ma. Her sweet face seems to be branded on my mind and heart. What choice do I have but to turn it all over to You and let You work on my heart and her pa's? So I'm trusting You with my love for Serena and whatever is best for her.

He felt better. A sense of peace settled upon him like a cool breeze on a hot day. No need to fret over the matter because God had already handled it. Chet would simply do his job, think about Serena when night folded in around him, and wait for the good Lord's answer.

For a moment, he wondered if God had any idea how intolerable James Talbot could be when upset.

—⁓—

Days later, after a bloody battle with a gang of Comanches, Mexicans, and white raiders, scattering some *bandidos* by the wayside and others racing deep into Mexico, the cap'n approached him.

"You're a good ranger, Chet, and I've always been able to depend on you."

Surprised, since James hadn't spoken more than two words to him in three weeks, Chet stuck out his hand. As the two men grasped calloused hands, he stared into the cap'n's eyes and saw respect, nothing more.

"I hate this difference between us," Chet said. "Wish we could talk it out."

The cap'n expelled a heavy breath and released the handshake, as though contemplating Chet's words. "Someday you might have a wife and family. Until then you won't understand what I have to do to protect mine. There's no changing my mind. You know my Serena is a frail thing. She couldn't handle this life."

Chet said nothing. God had already spoken to him about the cap'n's daughter. In his heart, he knew God had a plan for him and Serena. He felt certain they would end up together.

—⁓—

Serena pulled a brush through her dark tresses, as always, her mind on Chet. Today marked her eighteenth birthday, and he'd promised to be there, but Pa had come in late last night alone. She'd been foolish to think Pa would allow Chet to visit.

Her pa had refused to talk about Chet before he left the last time, and their good-bye had been strained. She remembered her and Ma's words.

"Why does Pa have to be so muleheaded?" she'd asked, digging her fingers into her palms as she and Ma watched Pa ride just beyond earshot.

"You'd be the best one to answer that," Ma said, smiling and waving although she could no longer see him. "Since you're both just alike in many respects. You, James, and Chet...stubborn and lovable."

The reply stung and brought a well of tears to her eyes. She turned away and headed back inside the cabin. The truth always hurt more than she cared to admit.

She even confessed to Moira about the whole thing with Chet. Her dear friend listened and held Serena while she cried. Neither of them could think of a solution but to seek God for the answers.

They didn't hear from Pa for nearly four weeks, and when he'd ridden in last night, Serena felt uncomfortable. Oh, she hugged him and welcomed him home, but uneasiness rested between them.

She wanted to tell him about the palomino and how the horse responded so well to her commands, but the words wouldn't come.

She wanted to tell him how she'd worried he might have been hurt, but her heart ached to hear about Chet.

She wanted to cry on his big strong shoulders and tell him how miserable she felt since their parting, but she wanted Chet's arms around her, too.

Serena knew she needed to talk to Pa and had prayed about it more than once, but the words refused to come. As the beginnings of light filtered through her tiny window on this, her birthday, Serena felt miserable. She wanted her relationship back with Pa and Chet. Had God forgotten her?

Rising and dressing in her favorite sky-blue dress, she attempted to concentrate on the Niall family coming later on in the afternoon. Yesterday she and Ma had cooked most of the day for the birthday dinner. It would be a wonderful celebration, and Serena vowed to cover her broken heart with a smile. No one would see how she truly felt about Chet Wilkinson, and she knew he dare not be there today. Pa had probably threatened to shoot him on sight.

As was her custom when Pa first arrived home, Serena went about making breakfast while her parents slept. But her determination did not stop a few tears trickling into the coffeepot.

All too soon she heard the murmuring of voices from the other room. Determined and inhaling deeply, she pasted on a smile.

"Mornin', Little One," Pa said, standing barefoot in the kitchen.

He sounded cheerful and it nearly broke her heart with the differences between them. "Mornin', Pa. I've got coffee brewing outside."

"Sounds good. Happy birthday."

"Thank you, Pa." She smiled into his eyes, the same color as hers. "I'll fetch you some." She snatched up a mug and started for the door.

"I'll get it," he said, his eyes searching hers. "I'd like to take a look at your horse."

"She's a fine mare." Serena felt like her words were memorized from some book. She hurt all over.

"Would you go with me to take a look?"

She fought the urge to cry and tried to suppress every semblance of her emotions. "Sure, Pa, but breakfast is almost ready, and I don't want it to burn."

"We won't be gone but a minute."

They stepped through the door and saw Chet sitting atop his horse, leaning on the saddle horn.

"Cap'n, I told Serena I'd be here for her birthday."

Chapter 8

H ave you no more brains than a stunned mule, Wilkinson?" Pa asked, his fists clenched as he stepped toward Chet. "We settled this weeks ago. You're not to see Serena, not now or ever."

Chet's gaze didn't waver. He straightened and pushed back his weather-beaten hat. "I told her I'd be here, and I aim to keep my word." He paused. "Although I discovered another matter over the past few days that should interest you."

Pa's eyes narrowed. "What might it be before I run you off?"

"You've been followed, and it might be a bit serious."

Pa leaned against the door, disbelief pouring from him like a swollen water hole. "Do you want to take a look at the tracks or blow a hole through me?"

Serena held her breath. Chet spoke calm, quiet-like, causing her to shiver. He had yet to glance her way, but then again, she didn't expect him to.

Pa licked his lips. "You'd best not be lyin' about this."

"I don't have a reason to."

"All right, show me. Serena, get my rifle and boots."

She felt riveted to the wooden step beneath her feet, but a second look from Pa spurred her after his things. A moment later she emerged from the cabin to see Chet had dismounted and tied his horse to the hitching post. Still, he avoided her.

"Let's see those tracks and hear you out before you get going," Pa said, reaching for the firearm and his boots. He glanced back at her and scratched his stubbly cheek. "You wait inside."

"Pa. . ."

"Tend to breakfast, Little One. This ain't easy for me either." His gaze softened before he turned and ambled toward Chet.

Resigning herself to obey, she allowed one glimpse of Chet's face. She met his smile and saw the love she'd dreamed about every night since she could remember. Her spirit soared, and without a word, she whirled and walked inside.

Ma stood in the cabin, still dressed in her nightgown, sleep etched on her face. "Chet's here?" she asked, combing her fingers through tousled brown hair.

"Yes, ma'am. He and Pa are talking outside. Not all of it about me. Chet said someone trailed Pa here last night and—"

A rifle shot split the air. Serena's gaze flew to her ma's. Color drained from her

45

face, and Serena felt her heart seemingly leap from her chest. They scrambled through the door. Fear for Pa and Chet ran deeper than anything awaiting them.

Not forty feet from the cabin, Pa lay on the ground, one hand clutching his side and the other wrapped around his rifle. Blood oozed through his fingers, forming a crimson pool beside him.

"James, no!" Ma's screams pierced the air.

Serena lost any thoughts of danger, and despite her ma's and both men's protests, hurried to his aid with her ma close behind. She and Serena bent behind his head and each grabbed under an arm to pull him from the blood-caked earth toward the cabin.

With one hand on his rifle, Chet peered in the direction of the barn and helped drag Pa on to safety. Another shot clipped Pa's leg.

"We got you, Talbot," a man's voice called in a heavy Mexican accent, "right where we want you."

Raucous laughter rang from the barn, enough to tell Serena more than one man lay in wait. Terror ripped through her body. For a moment it paralyzed her thoughts, except for a need to help get her pa inside. She caught his dulled gaze before he closed his eyes with the pain obviously wrenching through his body.

Chet snatched up a pistol then his gun belt and powder horn from his saddle. He fired again just before another shot zinged over his head. Stepping inside the cabin after Serena and her ma, he slammed the door shut.

Ma gathered up clean rags and pressed them against Pa's side. "It's gone clean through," she said, her features rigid and her hands trembling. "Good, I guess. . . no bullet to remove."

Serena lifted her pa's rifle from his arms and laid it on the table. "His leg's not bad, Ma. I'll wrap it."

"Cursed *bandidos*," Pa managed, biting his lower lip. "We should have chased them into Mexico and ended it."

"They'll wish they'd stayed there by the time I'm finished with them," Chet said, staring out the window. "I counted three of them, Cap'n."

Ma used her apron to wipe the sweat trickling down Pa's face. She took a clean piece of muslin from Serena and dabbed at the blood running down his leg. "Who are they?" Ma asked.

"What's left of a murdering bunch we chased across the Rio," Chet replied, searching the area between them and the barn.

"We got two bloodthirsty Texans," the unseen man called out, his boasting echoing around them. "You both come out and the women go free."

"Do they think we're stupid?" Serena asked, picking up Pa's rifle and toying with it in her hands. *God, help us. I'm scared, real scared.* Bloodstains on the wooden floor tore at her senses.

"Give me my rifle," her pa said, his words raspy and labored. He lifted his arm, but his strength failed him.

"No," she replied, feeling a strange mixture of anger and courage. "You aren't in any shape to help Chet. Besides, I'm a ranger's daughter, and I know how to use this." She turned her attention to Chet and hoisted the rifle into her arms. "Pa knows I've beat him a time or two at target practice."

"Sere—" But Pa couldn't finish. He'd passed out.

"All right," Chet began, still keeping watch through the window. "We can handle this. Mrs. Wilkinson, I need you to keep the guns loaded for Serena and me. Looks like three apiece." He glanced about him. "Do you know how to measure the powder and load them?"

"Yes," Ma managed, not once taking her sights from Pa's face. "I. . .I can keep them loaded."

"Serena, take the window in the other room." He motioned to Ma and Pa's bedroom. She grabbed a pistol. The two guns were heavy, but at least she knew how to use them.

"What do you think they will try to do?" she asked.

"Shoot at us until they get tired, then most likely set fire to the cabin."

Her gaze swung in his direction. "So what do we do?"

"Prayer would help." The look he gave her pointed to the seriousness of their position.

Another rifle shot pierced the air and lodged in the side of the door. Thankfully, Pa had insisted on a heavy piece of wood.

From her position, Serena saw Chet haul a chair across the floor to the window and balance one of the rifles on it and through the window. Snatching off his hat, he propped it atop the trigger.

"I'm going out the back," he said, grasping a loaded rifle and a pistol. "Keep 'em busy."

She nodded while a hundred warnings darted in and out of her mind. She tried to pray, but all she could muster was a plea for deliverance.

Serena's mind raced. *Lord, I've never shot a man before. It's killing, but if I don't, they'll kill us for sure.* Meeting her ma's gaze, she saw fathomless sorrow. Regret. Fear. Both of them had jobs to do. *Help us,* she prayed repeatedly. *Pa looks terrible, and he's losing blood. Ma's as scared as I am. Lord, keep us safe. I can't do this without You.*

"Go, Serena," Chet instructed, touching her arm. "Time's wasting, and we don't know what they will do next." He followed her into the bedroom and pulled back the tiny flowered curtains she'd help Ma sew. "You have a clear shot of anyone coming out the barn. Don't be afraid to hit them."

She swallowed hard. An attacking boar looked a whole lot different than a man. Serena and Chet bent beneath the window, so close she could feel his warm breath against her face. Another time, another circumstance, she'd have welcomed his nearness.

"Serena," he whispered, "we only have a few moments, but something needs to be said."

She tore her concentration from the barn and into the beloved face of her ranger. Biting her lip to keep the tears from overcoming her, Serena waited for him to speak.

His finger traced her lips. "So many things I'd like to say, but I can't. Pray without ceasing—like the Bible tells us to do. I love you. No matter what happens, remember that."

"I love you, too," she murmured. "God will deliver us. I know He didn't bring us together to die today."

He cupped her chin in his hand as if memorizing every feature about her. His ineffable glance spoke volumes. "Do not let them take you or your ma," Chet said with deadly gravity. "I have an extra pistol." He pulled the gun from his side. "If they get inside. . .use it on you and your ma. Don't let them take you. . . . Promise?"

She hesitated. Taking her own life and Ma's went against God's commands. How could this man of God ask her to do such a terrible thing?

"I've seen what they do to women," he added, as though reading her frenzied thoughts.

And she clearly understood his meaning. "I'll do my best."

"You have a special strength, Serena, one God doesn't give everybody. You are going to need it."

He touched her lips with his and offered a faint smile. Without another word, he left her alone to ponder what manner of sin she dare commit—murder those men in the barn or take her and Ma's life. Confusion and fear raged through her, leaving her stunned and cold. *Your will, Lord. Whatever You want of me, I'll do.*

She watched the empty barnyard, blinking back the stinging tears. Chet loved her, and if she died this morning with him, the thought would help her take Jesus' hand into eternity.

The rooster took his station on top of the well, calling in a new day. Then it grew quiet, not like other mornings. Pa had always said the waiting proved to be the hardest. He'd spoken the truth.

"We smoke 'em out," a voice called, breaking the stillness, "kill rangers and have women for ourselves."

Chapter 9

Serena aimed the rifle and fired into the dark shadows of the barn in reply to the Mexican's threats. She laid the firearm aside and snatched up a loaded pistol. Glancing at the one left by Chet, she shuddered. *For Ma and me.* She refused to let it happen.

Within moments, her ma had carefully measured the gun powder and slipped a bullet into the rifle. Laying it on the floor beside Serena, she stared at Pa, still unconscious.

"How is he?" she asked, studying what she believed to be the figure of a man lingering close to the barn door.

"He's doing fine for right now. When this is done, you and Chet can help me get him into bed." She sounded more optimistic than Serena knew Ma truly felt.

"Good. Soon Chet will have them sprawled out there in the dirt."

"Serena, I've never heard you talk this way," her ma said, shock edging her words, "but. . .In all the nineteen years your pa and I've been married, we've never had danger at our door, either."

Serena refused to let her emotions overrule good judgment. "All I know is we have to stop those men out there." She stole a glance at her ma. Nothing else needed to be said, for reality cut deep.

Ma nodded and paled again. "Praise God, your pa taught you how to shoot. I wish I'd taken the time to learn. Then I could do my share now."

Serena steadied the pistol. "Simply keeping these guns loaded is help. And please pray I won't lose my nerve when the time comes, 'cause I'm scared."

Ma brushed an errant strand of hair from Serena's face and tucked it behind her ear. "I will. . .I am, but you'll do just fine. I'm sure of it."

"Thank you." Serena waited for a wave of emotion to pass. "I love you, Ma. We've had lots of good times together, haven't we?"

Ma nodded, sorrow etching her smooth features, and her hand touched Serena's arm. "And we'll have years more. Someday your babies will crawl on my lap, and I will tell them what a beautiful, brave mother they have."

"And how I spent my eighteenth birthday? This isn't how I pictured today." She nodded toward the cook fire. "And would you look at breakfast? The eggs and bacon have burned." She wanted to make light of their precarious situation, but instead tears stung her eyes, and she hastily wiped them away.

"I'm proud of you," Ma said, ever so gently. "We'll make it through this thing. . . and work out your and Chet's problem, too."

Before Serena could reply, movement from the side of the nearest corner of the barn caught her attention. At first she thought the figure to be Chet, but the man wore a sombrero.

She stared at the far corner, where a second man, dressed like a Mexican but more closely resembling an Apache, studied the cabin. Chet had said three men followed Pa. Then she saw a third lurking inside the barn, near the entrance.

Dear Lord, I'm so scared, but I can't let them get to the cabin.

She realized then what they planned. She figured while the two men rushed and covered the man in the barn, he would head for the cook fire and a burning log. In the dry heat, he'd toss the log through a window. A simple plan for three ruthless men who thought they dealt with one badly injured ranger and another single man. A lot they knew about the women inside. If only she knew what Chet wanted her to do. But what God wanted of her ranked even higher. The Indian raised his rifle.

"They're coming," she said, wanting to shout. Her heart pounded more fiercely than before, and she clenched her fists in an effort to dispel her shaking hands. Every breath became a prayer.

"We have God on our side," Ma said, "and He does not forsake His own."

Serena refused to think of Goliad and the Alamo. The brave men who died at the hands of the Mexicans believed God had been on their side, too.

"Yes, of course we do," she replied.

Raising the rifle, she took careful aim at the man wearing the sombrero, hoping Chet had his sights on the other. The Mexican stepped into the sunlight. He made a dreadful mistake.

He raised his pistol. She held her breath and squeezed the trigger. The two shots fired simultaneously, but the Mexican fell. Still holding her breath, she wrapped her fingers around the pistol and moved to the other window, where Chet had leaned his rifle to look like another stood guard. It occurred to her then. Chet only had one rifle.

Another shot fired, and the Indian fell. The third man stole around the barn entrance in the direction of the fallen Apache. Serena didn't see Chet, and a new set of tremors raced up her spine.

The third man stood in the clearing for a mere second before chasing around the side of the barn. Serena could wait no longer. Unlatching the door, she hurried outside. The man must have sensed her, for he whirled around, pistol aimed.

With a loud groan, the man fell face down with a knife in his back. Chet raced toward her.

"You crazy girl," he said, his voice hoarse. "He would have killed you." He caught her and pulled her into his arms.

Serena could not hold back the sobs. "I was afraid he'd shoot you. And you lied to me; you only had the rifle. I couldn't sit by and do nothing."

For several long minutes, he held her and stroked her hair. "It's all over now, sweetheart."

Finally he released her and they looked behind them. The men were dead; no doubt entered her mind. Reality sickened her at what she'd done...they'd done. Chet stepped in front of her, blocking her view of the fallen men.

"Let's go see about your pa," he said, slipping his hand around her waist and urging her to the cabin. "You're still shaking."

She nodded, unable to speak until she garnered enough breath to calm herself. "I feel horrible, dirty, and yet relieved," she said.

He brushed a kiss in her hair. "I know. I feel the same way each time I finish a job. You did real well, Serena, but you have to put it past you. Think about what they'd done if you and me had not stopped them."

"Oh, Chet, I know, and I'm grateful God spared us." She took another glance behind them. "Would you pray with me?"

He turned her to face him and grasped both of her hands into his. They bowed their heads; even so, tears still trickled down her cheeks.

"Thank you, Lord, for delivering us from those men," Chet began. "They won't be hurting any more folks. Lord, I still don't understand the ways of war, but I know You protected us today just as You have done for me many times before. The cap'n is in bad shape, and we ask Your healing powers to mend his body. Amen."

"Thank you," she whispered, gazing into his treasured face. "I think we need to give them a proper burial."

"I will," he said firmly, "right after we check on your pa."

Hand in hand they walked into the cabin where Pa had gained consciousness. His head lay in Ma's lap, and she held his face in her hands. His side had been bandaged, but his leg still needed doctoring. The agony of pain layered lines upon his face, causing him to look years older.

"Go ahead and tend to my leg, Rachel. It won't get any better like it is," he said through a labored breath.

She bent and kissed his brow, then glanced up at Serena and Chet. "Would you bind it? I don't want to let him go." Ma picked up his hand and wrapped her fingers around it, her lips braving a tender smile.

Together Chet and Serena cleaned the wound and bandaged it. Pa said nothing but gripped Ma's hand all the harder.

"There, it's done," Chet announced. "What do you say we get you into bed?"

"Not yet," Pa said, wetting his lips. Perspiration dotted his brow. "Let me rest just a minute. Besides, there's a thing or two I need to say."

Serena suddenly grew numb. Surely Pa would not run Chet off after he'd saved their lives.

"Chet, you saved my family today," Pa said, struggling with each word. "And I owe you."

"I didn't do anything you wouldn't have done for me."

"I know, but you and I haven't been on the best of terms lately."

Chet kneeled on the floor beside him. "Just some misunderstandings, Cap'n. We can put it behind us."

"Guess we can."

"You'd be proud of Serena. She got one of them," Chet replied, placing an arm around her waist. "I couldn't have licked them without her."

Pa attempted a smile. "She's a ranger's daughter. . .and I reckon. . ." His face distorted in pain, and he paused before speaking again. "She'll make a fine ranger's wife."

Serena gasped as the words graced her ears. "Oh, Pa, do you mean it?"

"Don't think I have much choice. You already know how hard this life is; I won't be disguising it." He grimaced and sucked in his breath. "Both of you got the best, so I'm giving you my blessing."

Chet squeezed her lightly, and she laid her head against him. "Thank you. I'll love her good and proper."

Pa raised a brow. "I know you will 'cause you won't want to tangle with me."

Chet chuckled, sparking a lopsided grin from Pa.

Pa peered into Serena's face. "Happy birthday, Little One. Guess you got a little more than what you bargained for."

"A husband, a blessing, and a palomino," Serena said, bending to touch his whiskered cheek. "Best birthday I ever had."

~~~

The Niall family joined them in the afternoon, with Dugan returning home for an Irish cure to soothe Pa's pain. By then, the three men were buried, but the tale only needed telling once. None of them felt boastful over the morning's happenings.

"I have an announcement to make," Pa said, long toward evening with the effects of Dugan's elixir easing the burning in his body. "Chet and Serena are fixin' to be married."

"When?" roared Dugan.

"I reckon as soon as we can get a preacher here to do the ceremony," Pa said. He cast an approving glance toward Serena and Chet. "Guess I'll have me a son and a lieutenant. Seems to me, I'm one lucky man."

Later on, after the celebration ceased and Pa slept, Serena and Chet sat on the porch and watched the stars break through a night sky.

"I need to ask you in a fitting way to marry me," Chet said, his hand clasped firmly into hers.

She said nothing—but waited.

"You aren't going to make this easy for me, are you?" he asked with a nervous chuckle.

"No, I plan to savor every word, so speak nice and slow." She drew her knees up under her dress and rested her chin on them. She had long anticipated his endearing words and a promise of a life together. Now, at this moment, she wanted it all to last forever.

He cleared his throat. "Serena. . .what's your middle name?"

She straightened up and gazed into his face, wishing she could see his eyes. "Hope."

"Hmm. I like that; it's right pretty."

Another long minute passed as they were serenaded by a family of locusts and purple martins.

"Serena Hope Talbot, I love you—imagine I have for a long time, just didn't have sense enough to recognize it. I used to have this peculiar idea of what I needed in a woman. *Strength*, I called it, and I thought it meant physical strength. But I made a terrible mistake, for in many ways you are a stronger person than me. I need you, Serena, for now and always. I know God planned for us to be together as man and wife. So I'm asking if you will marry me—be a Texas Ranger's wife."

She sighed and formed a smile she could not conceal. "I've loved you since the first day Pa brought you home and introduced you as a new ranger recruit over two years ago. I knew I wanted to marry you then, and I've not changed my mind since. Yes, I'll marry you and be a ranger's wife."

He pulled her closer and lightly brushed a kiss across her lips. "Our lives won't be easy. Trouble is always springing up somewhere, and this feud between the Republic and Mexico over Texas's boundaries isn't going to be settled without fighting."

"I know. You're a ranger."

"And you'll still marry me, knowing I'll be gone for days at a time?"

"Yes, Chet. I agree to it all. I love you, but. . ."

"What?"

"Please don't call me skinny."

He kissed her again. "I will never call you skinny, just my precious Serena."

"You've got me, Lieutenant Chet Wilkinson, and I'm never letting you go."

THE RELUCTANT FUGITIVE

by Darlene Mindrup

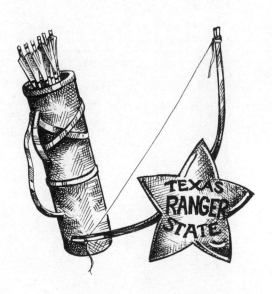

Dedication

For Rowan, grandma loves you.

Chapter 1

West Texas, 1859

April Hansen set a glass of milk next to her twin brother's plate, then took a seat across from him. She studied the hard lines of his face and wondered just what had happened to him over the last two years.

The chilly November wind whistled eerily outside the cabin, the mantel clock above her fireplace chiming the hour of midnight. She shivered, waiting for the heat from the Franklin stove to warm the air around her.

"So tell me, Ted, what you've been doing with yourself. Did you find the gold you were looking for?" she asked, pulling her robe tightly around her to help ward off the chill.

He grimaced, tucking into the plate of stew, seemingly oblivious to the cold around him. "Not really. How about you?"

She pushed a strand of coal black hair behind her ear and shook her head slightly. Her sky blue eyes met an exact replica when they collided with his.

"Not really. I *am* making good money as a seamstress, though."

He smiled slightly, pushing the cleaned plate away and downing the glass of milk. "That doesn't surprise me. Mother always said you had real talent."

For a moment, his face darkened. He turned away, looking out the paned-glass window of her kitchen. The wind found its way through cracks in her small cabin where the chinking had dried and left small holes, causing the hurricane lamp to flicker slightly.

April laid her soft white hand on his darker, harder one and gently squeezed. "They're with the Lord now, Ted."

His blue eyes were like chips of ice when they met hers again. "Why? Because He needed them more than we did?"

Seeing the pain he caused her, he relented. "I'm sorry, April. I just can't help wondering if my life would have been different if only they had lived."

"We were sixteen when they died, Ted. If you didn't have their beliefs embedded in your heart by then, what makes you think you would have if they had lived longer?"

"It wasn't their beliefs that I needed!" He jerked his hand from hers, glaring a message she refused to heed. She hadn't seen her brother in two years, and she wasn't about to miss this opportunity. He needed to come back to the Lord if he wanted any hope of a normal life.

"You can't blame God for the way you choose to live your life."

He jumped to his feet, his hands clenching into fists at his side. There was a haunted, unhappy look about him that touched her sisterly heart.

"Can't I? Can't I just! Keep your God. I don't need Him!"

She got up and reached out to touch him, but he jerked away from her. Her hand fell uselessly to her side.

"Don't you, Ted?"

For a brief instant his eyes were filled with an intense yearning. April seized the moment.

"Don't you remember how good it was to go to church every Sunday and sit together as a family? Remember, too, the day you accepted Christ into your life?"

His lips twitched slightly. "I remember. It was October and the water in the river was *extremely* cold."

She smiled. "That day you were baptized, you said that God would be the master of your life."

The smile fled from his face, and he turned angry eyes to her. "Have you ever heard of the slavery in the South? When a master is mean, the slaves sometimes run away."

April's face paled. "Don't say that. God is never mean!"

She could see that her brother was rapidly losing control. He closed a fist and shook it at her.

"I *needed* them, and He took them away!"

"Ted..."

"No! I don't want to hear any more. Say another word and I'll leave!"

April closed her lips on the angry torrent of words begging for release. Tears threatened her composure.

"What about me, Ted? *I* needed *you*, and you left me."

She couldn't read the expression that flashed across his face. "You've never needed anybody," he disagreed, his voice lacking inflection.

How wrong could a person be? Had she seemed so self-sufficient to him? After her parents had died of the fever, she had quickly taken charge of their lives. Having been apprenticed to a wonderful seamstress at the age of twelve, by the time her parents died four years later, she had developed quite a reputation of her own. She had an uncanny knack of mixing just the right colors and styles to make women look their best. Her business had thrived, bringing in the money they needed to survive.

It was only when Ted had started getting into trouble that she had listened to the advice of one of her customers and come west to Abasca, Texas. The woman had told her that it was a growing, thriving area yet still free of many of the vices of larger, more settled towns. Thinking to remove her brother from the temptations to which he had so readily succumbed, she had quickly made arrangements and left Chicago far behind.

She had hoped to influence her brother to make the right decisions, but somehow or another, she had failed miserably.

Having lived on his own in Chicago for four years, the constraints placed upon him by the remote location of Abasca had finally gotten to him. After two years here and thinking that he was man enough at the age of twenty, he had set out on his own to make his fortune. The loss of her parents had been devastating enough, but losing her brother as well was almost more than she could bear. Still, she had survived, though her lonely heart often ached with the need of someone to love.

That had been over two years ago, and she couldn't help but wonder what had brought her brother back now.

"Does it ease your conscience to believe that?" she asked quietly. He looked away, and for the first time, she noticed the Colt revolver holstered on his hip. Her eyes widened, lifting quickly to meet his enigmatic look.

"What do you need that for?" Her voice squeaked. "What have you been up to, Ted?"

Taking her by the shoulders, he tried to calm her. "It's for protection, all right?"

She wanted to ask him if that protection included killing people, but she didn't have the courage. Seeing the set look on his face, she was afraid to find out.

"I need your help, April."

The very words she dreaded hearing. How many times had she heard them in the past and lived to regret it.

"What. . .what do you need? I have a little money."

Tenderness filled his eyes, and he smiled. "I don't need your hard-earned money, sis."

Releasing her, he pulled a handkerchief from his pocket and began to unwrap it. When he held it out to her, she drew back, gasping at the beautiful diamond necklace nestled among the blue and white folds.

"Where did you get that?"

"A friend gave it to me to keep. I want you to keep it in the bank for me."

April threw him a suspicious look. "This *friend*, why couldn't she keep it herself?"

He chuckled. "You sound almost like a jealous wife." The smile slid from his face and he became all at once grave. "She had to go somewhere in a hurry. The only thing she has left in the world is this diamond necklace, and she'll need it when she gets back."

April wrapped her arms tightly around herself, her teeth chattering with the cold seeping into the cabin. "W–why can't she j–just put it in the bank. . .herself?"

Seeing her shivering, Ted pulled her close, holding her against his warmth. She snuggled closer, as thankful for her brother's love as for the heat from his body. She had missed him terribly, even though he was forever causing her pain by his crazy shenanigans.

When her teeth finally stopped chattering, he told her, "I'll make up the fire and we'll talk."

They huddled around the cheerful blaze, neither one looking very cheerful themselves. There was something serious on her brother's mind, and April's suspicions were rising by the minute.

Ted told her that his friend, Darcy, was being hunted by a man who thought she owed him money. Since the man practically owned the town, she couldn't put her jewelry in the bank where she had been living. Afraid for her life, she had fled, leaving Ted with her necklace and a promise to reclaim it.

Though there were holes in Ted's story, April's heart went out to the young woman.

"So you want to put it in the bank here?"

He nodded, his look fixed intently on her face. "I know it will be safe with you."

"What about you?"

He shrugged, looking away. The rocking chair creaked when he rose, the only other sound the crackling of the fire as he added more wood and the soughing of the wind through the pine trees outside.

"I'll move on, too, once the necklace is safe."

"Why can't you just stay?" she asked him softly.

He lifted his head slightly, still not looking at her. She could see his shoulders tense. "Maybe I will."

April felt a little thrill of hope. If only she could reach her brother and remind him of the boy he had once been. The boy whose sole hope was in Jesus Christ. Surely he could still become the man the Lord meant him to be.

She dropped her gaze to the gold-and-green braided rug between them. "You are more than welcome to stay with me."

He looked at her then, something indefinable in his eyes. Again, there was that look of desperate yearning. He opened his mouth to say something, then quickly closed it.

"Thanks," he told her, his voice lacking emotion. "And thanks for letting me stay tonight and feeding me."

"You're welcome. Anytime, Ted. You know that."

His shining eyes smiled into hers. "Have I ever told you just how much I love you?"

"No, but there's always a first time," she told him, grinning impishly.

He got up from the chair and knelt beside her. Lifting a finger, he stroked her cheek. "Just in case anything happens to me, I wanted you to know."

At the husky tone of voice, April felt a prism of fear clawing its way up her stomach. What was he trying to say? Just exactly what did he expect to happen?

"I'll get my bedroll," he told her, "and camp out here in front of the fireplace."

He left her sitting there worrying over what he had just said like a dog worrying over a bone. When he returned, she pulled chairs aside so that he would have ready access to the floor in front of the fireplace.

She opened her mouth to ask him about what he had just said, but she noticed the weary lines graven into his face. She decided it could wait until morning.

" 'Night," he told her, and she heard the sluggishness in his voice.

"Good night. See you in the morning."

She went to the other side of the cabin, and placing her robe on the wall peg at the foot of her bed, she climbed beneath her double wedding ring quilt.

Though she had much to think about, the rattling of the shutters by the wind soon lulled her to sleep.

———

When they entered the bank the next morning, Mr. Dice, the bank manager, saw them coming and quickly rose to his feet. He looked immaculate in his business suit, his dark hair parted in the middle. It had surprised April when she had first met him to find out that he was so young yet held such a responsible position.

She exhaled softly. For several weeks now Jason Dice had been paying marked attention to her. At first she had been delighted, never having had much attention from the male set before, but then she had overheard Jason talking to another gentleman when he didn't know that she was just around the corner.

"Marry April Hansen? Sure. A man can overlook a woman's lack of good looks when she has a sufficient bank account."

His greediness had repelled her more than his thoughtless words. Since she knew that she was not pretty like other girls, his remark had left her unfazed. She had enough confidence in her abilities not to worry about good looks. What were good looks when you had to make a living? Though she had never mentioned the conversation to Jason, she had studiously avoided him as much as possible. The trouble was, he didn't take subtle hints very well.

Now he crossed to their side, assessing Ted as he came. There was an ambiguous look to his face when he finally stood before them.

"Miss April. What can I do for you?"

April motioned to her brother who was carefully scrutinizing the other man. She could tell by the look on his face that he had appraised Jason's character in that all-inclusive look and found him lacking.

"Mr. Dice, this is my brother, Ted Hansen."

Looking relieved, Jason held out his hand. At first, April thought her brother was going to ignore it, but then a sudden sparkle lit his eyes and he suddenly crushed the banker's hand in a mighty grip.

Rubbing the offended appendage, Jason quickly moved to April's side and out of Ted's way. April gave her brother a reproving look.

"Mr. Dice, my brother has something he wishes to place in your vault."

"Indeed?" he glanced at Ted doubtfully, slipping his fingers into his vest pockets and puffing out his chest pompously.

Ted pulled the handkerchief from his own pocket and held it open for the banker to see. An avaricious light entered Jason's eyes. His demeanor changed instantly, becoming almost fawning in his attempt to please.

"Come this way. I'll help you fill out the paperwork myself, since April is such a good friend of mine."

April barely kept from rolling her eyes at the ceiling.

"If it's all right with you, Mr. Dice," Ted interrupted hastily, looking suddenly uncomfortable, "April has a few things she needs to attend to at home."

Both Jason and April glanced at him in surprise. "They can wait, Ted," April disagreed, frowning. "I'd like to spend time with you."

He looked from her to Jason, and April sensed his nervousness. His jaw tensed, the muscles working convulsively.

"That's all right, sis. You can go ahead. I'll come straight home when I'm finished, and we can have that long talk."

The bell jingled over the door and a tall man came in. His dark, stringy hair looked like it hadn't seen a washing in many a long day. April saw her brother's face pale. He tried to push her toward the door.

"You go ahead."

April resisted. There was something mighty strange going on here, and she wasn't about to leave now.

"I think I'll just wait," she told both men inflexibly.

Quick anger fired in her brother's eyes. He gave Jason a forced smile. "Perhaps you can convince her, Mr. Dice."

Ignoring the undercurrent of tension between brother and sister, Jason smiled at April, his white teeth gleaming. "Oh, don't ask me to try to persuade April to leave. Her very presence adds sunlight to an otherwise drab day."

April hastily averted her eyes from the banker's proprietorial look. She noticed that the stranger caught Ted's eye, flashing him a message, and April wondered how they knew each other.

Biting his lip, Ted tried once more to get her to leave. Again, she refused. Though she could tell he was angry with her, he said nothing more.

April sat quietly while the two men transacted their business, her gaze wandering around the bank. Few people were there this early in the morning.

Jason got up, motioning them to follow. There was an edginess about Ted that communicated itself to April.

"This way, please. Your trinket will be safe here, Mr. Hansen, I can assure you. Our safe is the finest quality steel. We have never been robbed."

Fumbling with the tumbler on the safe, he puffed out his chest proudly, turning to retrieve the necklace. He found himself looking down the cold barrel of Ted's revolver.

Chapter 2

Things happened so fast, April was caught totally unaware. When she finally realized what was happening, she grabbed for Ted's arm.

"What are you doing? Put that gun away!"

Wrapping a large arm around her shoulders, Ted pulled her to his side and held her firmly.

"Be still, April, and no one will get hurt."

The stranger had his gun out as well and was glaring menacingly at the bank's occupants. He waved his Colt threateningly.

"That's right. Everyone just take it easy and no one will get hurt."

The look of betrayal April gave her brother caused his lips to turn down at the corners. His returning look asked for understanding.

"I'll never forgive you for this, Ted," she told him coldly.

Jason stood frozen to the spot, his angry gaze flashing from sister to brother. "Don't try to make it seem as if you had nothing to do with this, April. You brought him in here."

Ted's look became more threatening, and the banker's eyes filled with fear.

"My sister had nothing to do with this. She knew nothing about it."

Though Jason said nothing, his expression was skeptical. April realized that she might possibly go to jail for something she had no control over.

The stranger pushed past the trio and entered the vault. "Let's get the stuff and get outta here."

After filling a bag with cash, the man motioned for Ted to take it. Ted released April and took the bag from him, avoiding her accusing glare. He reached across and grabbed the diamond necklace from Jason's unresisting fingers.

"I'll see you hang for this," Jason hissed. The hatred in his eyes filled April with alarm. Instinctively she knew that having his pride dented would make him a lethal enemy. It was obvious that his anger was directed at April as well. There was no way that he was going to believe that she had nothing to do with this fiasco. He had quickly changed from ardent suitor to impassioned foe.

"You'll have to come with us," Ted told her grimly, recognizing the threat to his sister.

"I won't," she answered defiantly. "Unlike you, I'll take my chances with the law."

Ted exchanged glances with Jason, the look in the banker's eyes bringing a swift frown to his face. Ted shook his head, never breaking eye contact.

"I said you're coming with me."

"We ain't taking no woman along," the stranger interrupted angrily. "She'll only slow us down."

Throwing the man a blistering scowl, Ted set his shoulders uncompromisingly. "She's my sister, Amos, and I'm not leaving her here to face the consequences alone."

So intense was their argument that neither man noticed Mr. Harris, the bank teller, lift a rifle from behind the counter. He pointed the gun at Ted.

"Drop them revolvers," he told them, his voice shaking slightly. His beetling eyebrows lifted to his receding hairline as he waited for compliance.

Everyone went still. A split second later, Amos whirled to fire at the teller. Seeing his intent, April lunged to stop him. The Colt revolver went off, the bullet missing Mr. Harris's heart, but imbedding itself in his shoulder. A woman screamed and fainted to the floor.

Amos looked shocked, then turned an accusing glare on April. "Let's get outta here!"

Grabbing April, Ted lifted her and threw her over his shoulder, striding out of the bank behind Amos. He unceremoniously dumped her on her stomach over his saddle. Climbing up behind her, he quickly turned the horse.

"Let's go!" Amos shouted, and from her upside-down vantage point, April could see a flurry of horses' hooves kicking up the mud. It was then she realized there were more men than just Amos and Ted.

As they thundered out of town, April heard shouts behind them. Bullets winged by her head, and for the first time in her life, she felt the very real presence of death.

When they were far enough from town, Ted briefly stopped his horse and helped April to sit upright. Her stomach was still heaving from the pummeling it had received from their fast escape, and she glowered at her brother.

"I'm sorry," he told her, and there was true contrition in his eyes. "I never thought this would happen."

"You never thought, period," she snapped. "You never do."

April heard a chuckle and turned to find Amos and two other men watching them with interest. The other two looked as disreputable as Amos.

"Shoulda left her behind," Amos smirked. "Women ain't nothing but trouble."

"Aw, now, Amos," one of the others disagreed. "They have their uses."

Gleaming eyes studied April thoroughly, and she cringed closer to her brother. She could feel him tense against her.

"Watch it, Chauncy. She's my sister."

The other man lifted his hat slightly, surprising April with his courtesy.

"Ma'am." He smiled. "I'm pleased to meet you."

April's reproachful silence met this greeting. Amos frowned. "Enough of this. We gotta keep moving. They'll be after us by now."

The others waited for him to take the lead, then rapidly set out after him in a quick gallop. April clung to the saddle horn, wishing that she would wake up and find herself in her nice cozy bed.

She tried to button her blue wool coat, but her fingers felt frozen, whether from cold or fear she wasn't quite certain. Only the fact that it was her brother's arms wrapped around her kept her from giving in to sheer hysteria.

Several hours later, Amos pulled to a stop. April's teeth were chattering with the cold, but it was her bones that felt like they had been jarred out of her body.

"Al," Amos commanded, "go back and see if you can catch sight of a posse. We'll head for the canyon. Be sure you take the back route to find us, just in case anyone spots you and follows you."

Al nodded once, turning his horse back the way they had come. He raced away like the hounds of fury were after him, his speeding horse churning up mud behind him.

They traveled on, but at a much slower pace. April was thankful for the reprieve from the bone-wrenching ride. Her mind was as numb as her body, and both refused to obey her will. Ted leaned forward so that he could whisper in her ear without being heard.

"I'll get you out of this somehow."

She said nothing. She heard him sigh in exasperation.

The sun had set hours before, and now April noticed that they were descending into a small valley. Entering it, the cold wind suddenly decreased. The freezing temperatures caused frost ringlets from their breath to swirl around their heads in a light mist.

Finally, they stopped at the entrance to a small cave. It was well hidden from view by the scrub brush around it and therefore made an excellent hiding place.

Ted helped her dismount, holding her while her shaky legs became accustomed to the ground beneath her feet once more.

Amos led the way into the cave, lighting a lantern near the entrance. April wrinkled her nose at the smell of unwashed bodies mixed with rotting food. How on earth had her brother gotten so low in his life?

He cleared a place for her and motioned for her to have a seat while Chauncy made up the fire. Amos came and stood next to them. He grinned down at April, his tobacco-stained teeth making her stomach churn.

"How's it feel to be an outlaw?" he wanted to know.

Ted glared at him. "That's not funny, Amos. She wasn't supposed to be involved."

Amos shrugged his shoulders. "Hey, I wasn't the one offered to get us into the bank."

Flushing, Ted had no answer.

April glanced from one to the other. "So what happens to me now?"

"Well now, that kinda depends on you. You be a good little girl, and I'm sure we'll get along just fine."

He gave her a warning look then turned and left them alone. April shivered.

"How could you get mixed up with someone like that? He's awful!"

Ted knelt beside where she sat stiff-backed on a wooden crate. The pleading eyes that normally wrenched her heart had no effect on her now. She deliberately ignored that tender spot in her heart that only he could touch.

"April, I can't explain now."

She studied his face. "What explanation could you possibly give for using me to commit a crime?"

His eyes flashed. "If you remember correctly, I tried to get you to leave."

Her brows lifted, hiding beneath her dark bangs. "And that's supposed to make a difference?"

There was a rustling at the entrance, and Amos and Chauncy spun, their guns already drawn from their holsters. Al came in, stopping short at the sight of the two gun barrels facing his way. He lifted his hands, palms facing forward.

"Hold on, fellers. It's just me."

Slowly they replaced their guns. Al joined them near the fire.

"So what'd ya find out?" Amos queried.

Squatting down next to the fire, Al held his hands out to the warming flames. "Well, since no one saw me in town this morning, I just moseyed on into town and hung around the saloon for a spell. Figured I'd hear the news better there." He grinned, his gleaming eyes speaking clearly of what he had done while in the saloon.

"And?" Chauncy interrupted impatiently.

"I guess it's just too cold for them town folks. They decided not to send a posse out after all."

Amos leaned back, sighing with relief. "That's good news."

Al shook his head. "Not quite."

Ted frowned. "What do you mean?"

"I mean," he told them, "that they called for a Texas Ranger instead."

Amos's face paled. Chauncy threw his coffee into the fire. "Blast it all!"

April glanced up at her brother and caught an odd expression on his face. "Who are they sending?" he asked quietly.

Al looked at each man in turn, his own face rather pale by the light of the fire. "Yellow Wolf Jackson."

—⁂—

April settled down under the blanket her brother had provided for her and tried to sleep, but the sound of the hushed voices of the others unsettled her nerves. She could hear the conversation as clearly as though she were sitting among them. Her eyes were fixed on her brother, sitting quietly like a statue.

"He's like a wolf," Al muttered. "He slowly, methodically stalks his prey until he's ready for the kill."

"Learned his tracking skills from his Comanche father," Amos said, spitting into the fire. The hissing of it had barely faded before Chauncy took up the refrain.

"Everyone knows a ranger can shoot a fly off a fence a half mile away, but Jackson uses his bow better than most men use their gun."

Amos nodded. "Yep. That's what makes him so deadly. Leastways if you hear a trigger cock, you have time to draw, but you never hear that bow twang until it's too late."

A long silence followed this pronouncement.

"Why's he called Yellow Wolf?" Ted asked, his quiet voice startling the others.

"His ma was white," Al answered, "but his dad were Comanche. He's got his mama's hair, yellow as sun-ripened wheat."

The more she heard, the more alarmed April became. What if this Yellow Wolf caught up with them and killed her brother? She might be angry with him, more than angry even, but she would never wish him dead.

Chauncy sighed loudly. "We're in for it, that's for sure. He has a reputation for always getting his man."

Amos answered this with a snort. "There's four of us, ain't there? And some of us is pretty good at trackin', too."

"Did you ever hear of the Walton gang?" Chauncy asked without lifting his eyes from the fire. "They was ten of them. Jackson caught 'em all. Killed four of 'em with that bow before they had a chance to reload."

April's eyes widened. The man must be some kind of savage.

"Let's get some sleep," Amos commanded. He motioned Ted toward the entrance. "I need to talk to you."

When her brother returned, his face was pale and strained. He glanced her way, then quickly turned aside. April could hear him stumbling about for some time before he finally settled with the others for the night.

Exhausted from the torturous ride, she felt the tug of sleep's call, and too weary to do any more thinking, she finally succumbed.

She dreamed of galloping horses and a faceless man with golden hair chasing her across the hills of West Texas.

When she opened her eyes in the morning, the man sitting Indian style across from her was not her brother. His yellow hair hung long to his shoulders, and the two Colt revolvers strapped to his side gave away his identity before he ever said a word.

Chapter 3

April lay immobile, frozen with shock. Numerous thoughts chased themselves through her mind finally settling into one cohesive idea. She had to warn her brother.

Jumping to her feet, she ran for the entrance to the cave. She never reached it. Strong hands latched onto her upper arms, whirling her around. Her eyes were level with a broad chest housed in soft buckskin. She struggled against the restraining grip, pushing her small fists upward until she was able to pummel the intruder in the chest.

"Let me go!"

Grabbing hold of her wrists, he twisted them behind her until she was effectively pinned against his chest. She lifted frightened eyes and was surprised to find a smile on the man's face, although the smile was a decidedly nasty one.

"Just where did you plan on going?" he asked, a snicker in his voice.

Chocolate brown eyes roved her features, and April stilled beneath his careful scrutiny. He was a big man, tall and powerful. She felt a tremor of fear run through her when she remembered the comments of the others.

"Unhand me!" she commanded. She wanted to hurl the word *savage* at him, but realizing his size and power, she didn't dare.

As though he could divine her thoughts, his eyes darkened until the only thing she could see was her own reflection in them. His face turned grim.

"Where are the others?"

Glancing around, she realized that they were truly alone, just she and this savage. Her own brother had deserted her, leaving her to face this man alone. Pain unlike any she had ever known rose up to choke her. Although she was angry at her brother for deserting her, she was relieved that he had gotten away.

"I don't know." She could barely speak past the obstruction in her throat.

Again he searched her face, delving deeply into her eyes. A puzzled frown crossed his face, and suddenly he released her.

"So they left you here to divert me from the chase, huh?"

The nasty smile had returned to his face. He cocked his head slightly, assessing her critically from her tousled black hair to her black button-up shoes. Blushing profusely, she wrapped her arms defensively around her waist.

"I must say, I'm tempted."

The color multiplied in her cheeks until they resembled overripe cherries. "You, sir, are no gentleman."

The smile turned into a full-fledged grin. He folded his arms over his chest, causing the buckskin to strain against him. April's eyes followed the line of his figure past long, lean legs wrapped in the same buckskin to feet encased by leather moccasins.

"Not like your brother and his cohorts, huh?"

She had nothing to say to that. If the truth were told, this man had a strong magnetism that reached out to her even from the distance she had removed herself to. If he was a savage, he was unlike any she had ever heard about.

"What are you going to do with me?"

His eyes flicked over her briefly. "Well, I've got to hand it to your friends, their little ruse worked. I can't very well take you with me, and I can't leave you here alone."

He went to the fire and lifted the coffeepot from the coals. Surprised, April watched him pour a cup and hold it out to her. She hesitated before crossing to where he crouched and took the offered cup.

"So, I repeat, what are you going to do with me?"

He glanced up at her from under a lowered brow. "I'm going to take you back to Abasca and then come back and follow the trail again."

April pulled her lips in between her teeth, pressing them together. She sat down on the crate she had vacated the night before. When she finally looked at him, she found him watching her.

"Look, Mr. Jackson." His eyebrows lifted at his name, and she stumbled to a halt. His eyes grew dark and stormy.

"How do you know my name?" he asked in a quiet voice that was frightening in its intensity.

She explained about Al's returning to town. His eyes began to gleam, and April felt real fear for her brother.

"So, it *is* Miller's gang."

Confused, April tilted her head slightly. "Miller?"

His eyes narrowed to slits. "You're good, I'll give you that. The perfect picture of innocence."

April felt her temper begin to rise. Trying to keep it in check, she took a deep breath before continuing.

"Mr. Jackson, I *am* innocent. I have no idea who this *Miller* is that you're talking about."

"Mm hmm."

Throwing all restraint to the wind, she snapped back at him. "Fine, then take me back to town. I'm certain no jury in the world would convict me if they knew the facts."

"And the facts being. . . ?"

She was sorely tempted to smack that smug look off of his face. "I was unwittingly involved in that bank robbery." Something occurred to her, and she gave him a hard look. "How did you find this place so fast anyway? Surely you weren't just passing through the vicinity when they called for you."

A quick look flashed into his eyes and was just as quickly gone. "Hoping to have more time to get away?"

He was obviously going to ignore her question. "I told you. Just take me back to town and be off on your search."

His slow smile made her insides tingle. "No can do," he told her softly. "It's been raining for the last hour, and with the temperatures dropping, we're going to have an ice storm."

Panic robbed her of speech. To be lodged inside this small cave with this big. . . *man* suddenly shortened her breath. Her chest rose and fell in alarming rapidity.

"We can't just stay here," she finally managed to whisper.

"Woman," he told her in aggravation, shifting away from her until his back was against the cave wall. "If I wanted to do something to you I could have done it long before now. I've been sitting here for the past three hours."

The thought of him sitting there watching her sleep left her slightly rattled. She didn't know what to say.

"By the way," he said, lifting the steaming cup to his lips. "Did you know that you snore?"

Affronted, she forgot to be afraid. "I most certainly do not!"

He grinned, nodding his head. "Yep, you do. It's kinda cute, though."

Of all the compliments to receive, this had to be the worst. He was unlike any man she had ever met, savage or otherwise.

"Look, Mr. Jackson."

"You can call me Wolf. Most folks do," he interrupted.

With his slanting eyes gleaming at her, he certainly reminded her of one. The wolf from *Little Red Riding Hood* had been a sweet talker, too. It was an analogy she would rather forget.

"Mr. Jackson," she reiterated and watched the slow smile curve his lips again. If she didn't know better, she would believe him capable of reading minds. "I don't mind a little rain and cold. We can't be that far from town."

His amused look made her feel like a foolish little schoolgirl. "We're a good forty miles."

Her mouth dropped open. "That can't be. We made it here in one day."

"Yep, hard, long riding will do it. I made it in six hours, myself. I'd say it probably took you the better part of fifteen."

She went to the entrance to the cave, but he didn't try to stop her. Peeking out, she watched the rain falling in torrents. The river at the floor of the canyon was already rising. She turned back to Wolf.

"Will we be safe here?"

He shrugged, refilling his cup. "Safe as anywhere, I expect."

Restless, she wandered around the cave noticing things she hadn't when she had arrived last night. This cave must have been used by Ted and the others for some time. There was a load of supplies in one corner, along with extra kerosene for the lamp that hung from a nail pounded into the wall. Ted had been so close yet hadn't come to see her until he was ready to use her in his crime. Her heart felt as though it were breaking into a million pieces.

She felt Wolf watching her and turned. He was regarding her warily now, no smile left on his face.

"You say you're innocent. Tell me what happened."

So she did.

Wolf noticed every changing emotion on her face, every nuance of her body language. He was tempted to believe her, but he had been this route before. It wasn't often his intuition failed him, but it *had* been known to happen. Especially where the *weaker* sex was concerned.

He studied her earnest face, noting the freckles speckled across her nose. She was neither attractive nor unattractive, but she *was* interesting, though he couldn't put a handle on why he thought so. He hadn't been attracted by any woman since Moonwater, and he didn't relish the idea now.

But then maybe that's why this woman was so attractive to him in the first place. She had the same coloring as the Comanche. If anything, she looked more like an Indian than he did, though her skin was much fairer and her eyes were the color of the summer sky. Even her scent was unlike any he had come across, soft and fresh like the spring rain. His mouth twisted wryly at his decidedly poetic thoughts.

She finished her story and stood looking at him, expecting him to believe her. And strangely enough, he did. Still, he wasn't taking any chances.

"That's all very interesting," he told her. "Now when you tell it to the judge and jury, maybe they'll believe you."

She glared at him. "But you don't, do you?"

He leaned back against the wall of the cave, one eyebrow lifted upward. "It doesn't really matter what I believe, does it?"

April got up from the crate and stormed across to her blanket. For some reason, it bothered her that he held such a low opinion of her. Throwing herself down in a huff, she shifted the blanket to make herself more comfortable. If she was going to have to stay there with this giant of an Indian, she might as well make herself as cozy as she could.

She heard something rattle, and lifting the blanket, she found a piece of paper lodged between two rocks on the floor of the cave. She picked it up and unfolded it, recognizing her brother's handwriting at once.

Sis,
I had to leave you. It's for your own good. I'll be back for you as soon as I can.

Ted was coming back. Her heart leaped with joy at the realization that he hadn't deserted her after all, but just as suddenly she was seized with fear. If he came back now, he would come face-to-face with Yellow Wolf. She had to get the ranger out of there somehow. Crumpling the note in her hand, she casually crossed to the fire. When she reached out to drop it into the flames, a large hand wrapped around her wrist. Though the hold was gentle, she knew he could crush her bones if he wanted to.

Prying her fingers open, he retrieved the paper. After reading it, he glared at her. "So you're innocent, huh?" He placed the paper carefully in his pocket, noting her attention. "Evidence," he told her coldly.

"It's not what you think," she argued.

"Sit down."

She wasn't certain why she felt she had to justify herself in his eyes, but she couldn't let things stand the way they were.

"Mr. Jackson. . ."

"I said, *sit down.*"

April sat. If other Indians looked that ferocious when they were angry, no wonder they were called savages.

Wolf rummaged through the supplies stacked in the corner until he found what he was looking for. Using his knife, he pried open a can of beans, his silence profound. He wasn't exactly sure why he was so angry, although maybe *disappointed* would be a better word.

He dumped the beans into a small pot and set it over the fire. This woman might look like a Comanche, but it would seem she hadn't the honor.

"As God is my witness, I am innocent," she told him clearly.

He lifted one eyebrow arrogantly without looking up from his work. "God? What would you know about God?"

She knelt on the ground across from him, her eyes beseeching. "I'm a Christian, Mr. Jackson. I don't lie nor do I steal."

He dumped half of the pot of beans onto a tin plate and handed it to her. His enigmatic eyes met hers.

"You ever hear of John Brown, Miss Hansen?"

She had. The man was a notorious abolitionist who wasn't beyond killing to further his cause, and all in the name of Christianity.

"I'm not John Brown," she told him scathingly.

He took up his own plate of beans and began to scoop them into his mouth. He politely chewed and swallowed before answering.

"Maybe not," he told her, his eyes traveling over her slowly. "But in my eyes you're about the same caliber of Christian."

Hackles rising, April set her plate on the floor untouched. Her appetite had deserted her.

"And what exactly would a man like you know about Christianity?"

His look was so dark she shivered. "A man like me? You mean a half-breed?"

Horrified at his train of thought, she shook her head vehemently in denial. "I didn't mean that at all! I meant your profession."

He got up, reaching for her plate. He scooped the contents up with his own spoon until the plate was empty, then took both and disappeared outside. When he returned, the plates were clean. He set them with the other supplies.

Coming close, he knelt beside her, and she shrank back from the anger in his eyes.

"I'm a lawman, Miss Hansen. I keep and uphold the law. What about you?"

"I'm the same," she told him, her voice softly supplicating. "I'm telling you the truth."

He pulled the slip of paper from his pocket. "This tells me otherwise."

They stared at each other for a long time, searching for the truth in each other. The atmosphere between them grew tense with suppressed emotions. Nostrils flaring, Wolf moved away first.

The thought that April could so move him that he wanted only to believe her, to deny the evidence, made Wolf angry. Being close to her clouded his thinking, and he didn't fully understand why. It wasn't like him to accept a woman so quickly.

She returned to her blanket, sitting cross-legged across from him. Dirt streaked her face where traces of tears had been the night before. Something wasn't right here. He couldn't believe that his judgment was *that* faulty.

For three hours he had watched her sleep, her face innocent in its repose. Back and forth, his emotions had surged. Something about her touched his icy heart, and he felt it slowly begin to thaw. And that was before she was even awake. Now, after talking with her, he was even more confused.

She had been more hurt by his denial of her Christianity than by anything else he had said. It was there in her face, as plain as day.

The day passed with turtlelike slowness, their cramped quarters making them both edgy. They made desultory conversation some of the time, at others falling into a silence fraught with unanswered questions. Each of them thought of what would happen when the rain stopped, but neither broached the subject.

When April next spoke, her words scattered Wolf's thinking to the four winds.

"Did your mother love your father?"

April regretted the words as soon as they left her mouth. What on earth had possessed her to ask such a personal question in the first place? The anger in his voice when he had said the word "half-breed" told her clearly that it was a sore spot with him. Maybe she had wanted to hurt him as badly as he had hurt her, but then, she really did want to know.

Wolf's body went so rigid, it seemed as though he had turned to stone. His dark eyes glittered dangerously.

"He didn't rape her, if that's what you mean."

April dropped her gaze to the floor. "I'm sorry," she whispered contritely, knowing that if her purpose had been to give him pain, she had succeeded.

"My mother was the daughter of a missionary to the Comanche people. She was a child when her parents came to try to teach the people about the white man's God."

April lifted her head at this. "He's not a white man's God," she interrupted.

"I know who He is," he answered harshly. "My mother taught me all about Him. How His people love and care for one another."

His biting sarcasm caused April to flinch. She remained silent.

"When my mother's parents died, the Comanche took her in and raised her as one of their own. She and my father fell in love, and he chose to marry her."

Curious in spite of herself, April leaned forward. "Do you have brothers and sisters?"

She could see him tense. He got to his feet and walked away from her, as though her very presence disturbed him. He stared out at the wet landscape, watching the sun slowly sink below the horizon.

"No. My parents were killed when a group of white settlers attacked their village in reprisal for an attack on their own town by renegade Comanches."

Appalled, she could think of nothing to say except to tell him that she was sorry. He smiled at her, a smile that didn't reach his eyes.

"Don't be. If what you believe is true, then they are with your God."

Chapter 4

April awoke the next morning slightly disoriented. It took her a moment to get her bearings, rubbing sleep out of her eyes as she did so.

She glanced around the cave and noticed that it was empty. Her heart plummeted to her toes. So Yellow Wolf had gone after her brother after all and left her there alone. Would he come back for her? She had no horse, and the thought of the long walk to town in the freezing cold was a daunting one.

But maybe he hadn't gone far. Maybe she could still catch him. And then what? He had already said that he wouldn't take her with him, but could she possibly get him to change his mind?

Stumbling over her blanket, she got up and rushed out of the cave. She hadn't taken more than two steps past the entrance before she found her feet flying out from beneath her. She would have plunged over the edge of the trail and catapulted to the rushing river in the canyon below if not for a long arm snaking out and pulling her back to safety.

Her back was against Wolf's chest, and she thought surely he must be able to feel the pounding of her heart against his arm. He bent his face forward until their cheeks almost touched.

"Going somewhere?" he wanted to know.

She tilted her head back slightly, bringing her face even closer to his. The fresh scent of the cold outdoors clung to him, but he seemed totally unaffected by the cold. Her heart slowed its thundering pace.

"I. . .I thought you were gone."

One corner of his mouth tilted up on the side. "What, and leave you here alone?" His eyes twinkled down into hers, laughing at her. "But then, I'm not a *gentleman,* am I?"

He slowly released her, keeping one hand on her arm to give her support. Only then did April notice the landscape around her. Prisms of rainbow light were reflected all over the small canyon from the ice clinging to every surface. She caught her breath sharply.

"Oh! It's beautiful!"

He nodded, watching her carefully. "Beautiful and *dangerous.*"

She moved slightly, and her feet slipped again. His hold on her arm tightened fractionally until she steadied herself.

"I see what you mean." She peered over the edge to the canyon below. "We'll have to be very careful leaving here."

He lifted one brow, the twinkle back in his eyes. "We're not going anywhere. At least not for awhile. It would be suicide to try to make it out of here just now."

Her eyes flew to his. "When can we leave?"

Wolf shook his head, picking up the cup of coffee he had sitting on a rock beside him. He took a swallow and grimaced. In the short time April had been out there, it had already grown cold.

He had been standing there drinking his coffee and marveling at the beauty around him when she had come plunging out of the entrance to the cave. Only his quick reflexes had averted a near disaster.

He had felt her heart drumming in her chest and knew that his was pounding in equal rhythm. He looked at her again. It was odd, but he wanted to take her back into his arms just to feel her nearness, to know that she was truly safe. She aroused every protective instinct in him that he had thought long ago dispelled.

With his feelings in such chaos, he knew that it was not a good idea to stay there another night, but he also knew that he had no choice. Were he alone, he would manage it, but with April in tow, he couldn't take the chance. His horse would have to pick his way carefully back up to the top of the canyon as it was, but he couldn't walk his horse and hold on to April, too. And he couldn't let her ride, just in case the horse did slip.

"Mr. Jackson."

He brought his attention back to the matter at hand.

"I said, when *can* we leave?"

He threw the cold coffee over the ledge. Without looking at her, he told her, "Another day or two, probably."

Her appalled look brought a quick frown to his face. "As the day warms, the ice will melt, but by then it will be too late to travel. We can't camp out in the open in this kind of weather. It would be foolish."

Her throat worked convulsively. She crossed her arms, shivering against the cold, and met his look. He could see the fearful uncertainty in her eyes. What was she afraid of, anyway? Hadn't he proved himself trustworthy?

"You mean we have to stay here?"

Without realizing it, his face took on the immobile mask that the Comanche used to hide their thoughts.

" 'Fraid so."

She carefully pulled out of his grip and moved cautiously toward the cave. She threw him one last look before ducking back inside. Wolf lifted his head upward, closing his eyes. Somehow, he just knew this was not a good idea.

April stood in the entrance to the cave, her lips pressed tightly together. Closing her eyes, she rubbed her forearms to relieve herself of the chill. She couldn't stay there another day. She just couldn't. There was some kind of force at work here, and she was very much afraid it wasn't godly. Why else would there be such undercurrents of emotions between her and a perfect stranger? *Well,* she thought wryly, *not quite perfect.*

Her eyes flew open. Could it be that God had brought her to this point to show this heathen the way to Him? He knew about the Lord, but she sensed that it was an area of his life he wished to ignore. Much like her own brother.

She shook her head slightly, frowning at her thoughts. Wolf was no heathen. She could tell that it bothered him not to be considered a gentleman in her eyes, but she no longer believed that to be so. He was everything a gentleman should be, more so than her brother's friends.

He came into the cave, bumping into her from behind. He grabbed her arms to keep her from tumbling forward.

"What are you doing standing here in the doorway?" he asked, his voice laced with exasperation. "You'll catch your death."

"Sorry."

He dropped his hands, and she moved quickly away. He went to the fire, and picking up the coffeepot, he lifted it enquiringly in her direction.

She retrieved her own cup and held it out to him. While he poured, she studied his face. He had the high cheekbones of the Indian, the proud tilt to the head. His skin was darker than most men she was used to, but he was definitely handsome.

He caught her staring at him and lifted a brow in inquiry. April flushed brightly, dropping her gaze.

"Thank you for the coffee." She managed a smile. "You make it rather well."

He grinned. "For a man, you mean."

Her smile came more naturally. She seated herself on the crate, lifting her gaze to meet his eyes.

"Tell me more about yourself," she encouraged.

He met her look, and both found themselves unable to look away.

"Why do you want to know?" he asked quietly.

"Because I'm interested," she answered softly, realizing that she really was. He fascinated her more than anyone had in a very long time.

He glanced away. She thought he was going to ignore her request, but he seated himself in his usual spot, leaning back against the cave wall. He turned to her, but it was some time before he spoke.

"I told you about my mother and father. What else do you want to know?"

April shrugged. "What was your childhood like? Where did you live? How did you become a ranger?"

His mouth tilted into a half smile. "I lived as a child among the Comanche. My mother was a typical wife—feeding her family, caring for her child and husband, visiting with other female friends. For the most part, it was a good life." He stared vacantly at the wall opposite, and April knew that his mind had gone back to that world so different from her own.

"I was taught to hunt and track and kill. I made my father quite proud of me with my prowess with a bow. When they were killed. . ." His voice tapered off. He glanced at April then, his eyes dark and haunted. She saw in him the same yearning that she had seen in Ted. They were so very much alike in their pain.

"I was never accepted by the Comanche as one of their own, nor by the whites either. I found it better to become a Texas Ranger and live my life alone."

April's heart went out to him. She could picture the lonely little boy he must have been. What agony it must have caused his mother to watch her child being shunned by others.

"You said your mother was a missionary's daughter?"

He nodded, staring deeply into her eyes. She wondered what, exactly, he was looking for.

"She taught me of Jesus and His love, and for a time I believed. Maybe that's why the Comanche never accepted me. When they danced to their gods, I sat aside. When they gave offerings, I only watched."

April wet her lips, hesitant to ask. "Did you ever marry?"

Wolf jerked his gaze back to hers, wondering what had provoked such a question. Just idle female curiosity? Somehow, he doubted it. She didn't seem the nosy type.

"No, I never married."

The set look of his face warned April not to further probe that area of his life. He tilted his head to the side. "It's your turn," he told her, smoothly changing the subject.

"There's not much to tell. Actually, we have something in common. Both of my parents died when I was young, too."

His face became inscrutable. "At least they weren't murdered."

"No," she agreed softly. "But my mother also taught me about Jesus and His love."

"What about your brother?" he asked, refusing to be sidetracked into a theological discussion.

"We were both raised to believe the same things, but somehow he's gotten away from them."

She didn't like his smile. "Life has a way of changing us."

He got up and went to the cave entrance. He took a deep breath of the clean air. April joined him, and he glanced down at her briefly. Again, there was something strange that seemed to be pulling them closer together. They could read it in each other's eyes, though neither would mention it.

"The ice is melting," she suggested cheerfully, turning away from his look. He said nothing, continuing to watch her.

"I need to go outside," she finally told him in embarrassment. "Is it safe yet?"

He nodded. "But don't go far," he warned.

She went past him, staying only as long as necessary. Although the temperatures were rising, they were still too cold to stay outside for very long.

When she returned, she found Wolf bent over the fire with a fry pan. He took some flour and water, mixed it together, then poured it into the sizzling hot lard.

"Can I help?"

He shook his head. "There's not much to do. I'm just making some fry bread to add to the beans." He grinned up at her. "Not exactly hotel cuisine, but it'll keep us from starving."

She was surprised by his reference to a hotel, and she had noticed that his English was as proficient as her own. Again she found herself wondering about his life.

"I think I'll go crazy if I have to stay cooped up in here much longer!" she exclaimed, dropping to the seat across from him.

"Solitude is good for the soul."

The look she gave him spoke volumes. "Well, I'm not exactly alone, am I?"

"Bored with my company, huh?"

She could tell he was laughing at her. His eyes crinkled at the corners, though his mouth merely twitched into a smile.

While they ate, Wolf told April about attending college in Boston. There was much he left unsaid, and she thought she could read between the lines. After living among the Comanche most of his life, city living must have been very difficult for him. Although he didn't mention it, she suspected that being half Indian had probably caused him much grief at school.

After they ate their impromptu meal, Wolf rummaged through his saddlebag. He brought out a small piece of wood with an intricately painted design on it.

"How about a game?" he asked, and April narrowed her eyes at him suspiciously.

"What kind of game?"

"Well," he told her in a wickedly amused voice, "actually we'll have to modify it somewhat. It's usually played by a group of people."

He explained how the Comanche used the piece in a game both men and women alike enjoyed. "There are two teams. Each one takes a turn trying to fool the other by passing, or not passing, the wood. Someone from the other team will finally call out which man he thinks has the piece."

She watched him warily. "Then what?"

"You keep score. The one with the highest score wins."

"Just what exactly does he win?"

His look made her grow warm all over. "That depends on the bet," he told her softly.

Her eyes widened, and she drew in a shaky breath. "I don't gamble," she finally told him in a quavery voice.

He looked disappointed. Sitting back, he smiled ruefully. "That's all right. We can play the game anyway."

"How?"

He closed his fist around the wood, then began shifting his hands back and forth. When he stopped, he grinned at her.

"Pick one."

She returned his grin. "This is like hide the button." Her forehead puckered in concentration as she studied his hands. Finally, she reached across and tapped his left hand.

"That one."

He turned his empty palm over. "Wrong. That's one for me." Reaching over, he drew a mark in the sand with a twig.

He handed her the wood. "Your turn."

Giggling like a child, she followed his example. He tapped her hand, and she turned over the palm with the piece in it.

She frowned at him. "How'd you do that?"

Ignoring the question, he took the wood piece again. After almost an hour, he had far more marks in the sand than she did. She looked at him, clearly puzzled.

"How do you always seem to know?"

His eyes roved her face slowly, and she felt her stomach begin to churn.

"It's your face," he told her softly. "It gives you away."

Her eyes widened until they were so large Wolf thought he could walk right into them. He smiled slowly.

"You're wondering what thoughts I can read on your face."

April sucked in a sharp breath. That was exactly what she had been thinking. Over the past hour she had found herself wondering what his bet might have been. The look in his eyes made her breathless, and she had wondered if he would have demanded a kiss. Paradoxically, she had hoped that he would.

He leaned across, placing one large hand behind her neck and pulling her gently forward.

"I'll take my winnings now," he told her quietly.

She placed her hands against his chest, pushing firmly.

"I told you, I don't gamble."

"But I do."

His lips closed over hers, and she forgot every reason she had for refusing him.

Chapter 5

Wolf stood outside the entrance to the cave castigating himself severely. That kiss had to have been the stupidest thing he had ever done in his life! What on earth had gotten into him anyway? He had only known the woman for two days.

He pulled the slip of paper from his pocket, reading it yet again. He tried to use it to bring his anger to the surface, but somehow, he just couldn't do it. No matter how hard he tried, he couldn't reconcile April's innocent face with a desperate gang of outlaws.

He was confused by the strange rush of emotions she invoked in him. This was something far beyond his experience, especially where women were concerned.

Most white women shunned him, though there were those who followed him with longing in their eyes. Those women he avoided. Indian women were more lenient, but he was too white to fit into their way of life. The education his mother had insisted upon set him apart from most.

Being around April just that short period of time had set him yearning for things he wasn't even aware that he wanted. But she was far too different from him, also. She had a faith in a God he had long ago abandoned. Though his parents had served Him almost their whole lives, He had chosen not to protect them when they needed Him most.

The sun was setting and it would soon be dark. An eagle screamed high above the trees, circling ever downward toward its nest and its young.

Would he one day have a nest of his own, with children and a loving wife? Was it possible any woman would want him? And even if it were, could he do that to a woman that he truly loved? Could he subject her to the same kind of prejudice his mother had faced all her life? The same kind of prejudice *he* had faced all *his* life.

Gritting his teeth, he forced himself to return to the cave. Though the cold air had cooled his ardor and his thinking, the tense atmosphere remained.

April watched him warily, sitting cross-legged on the blanket she used as a bed. Her blue dress had long ago taken on a dusty hue, leaving her looking a bit bedraggled. He lifted an eyebrow slightly.

"An Indian woman would never sit like that. It's not considered proper," he told her, hoping to lighten the mood. It had the opposite effect. Her forehead twisted into a frown.

"I'm not an Indian woman," she returned coldly, her frosty eyes raking over his beaded buckskins.

He sighed heavily. "I'm sorry. I was only teasing." He crossed to her side and knelt on one knee before her, careful to keep some distance between them. "I'm sorry, too, for kissing you." He reached out to touch her, the fringe on his buckskin shirt swishing with the movement. He saw the trepidation return to her eyes, and he dropped his arm, his hand curling into a fist. His lips tilted into a half smile, and a twinkle entered his normally serious brown eyes. "Well, not really. I guess I'm sorry I kissed you without your permission."

April stared at him, confounded by his honesty. "Do you always go around kissing women you've known for such a short time?"

His look became at once sober. "Only when their eyes ask me to."

April's mouth dropped open. Snapping it shut, she turned her eyes away, unable to deny what he said. "You think too highly of yourself."

"Maybe," he agreed, unruffled by her sarcasm. "Anyway, I wanted to tell you that you needn't be alarmed. It won't happen again. I give you my word."

She gave a small sigh of relief, which quickly fled at the temerity of his next words.

"That is, unless you want me to."

She got to her feet, glaring down at him. Dark tendrils of hair that had escaped her bun hung around her face. She brushed them back with an impatient hand. "Don't hold your breath!"

He rose to stand before her, towering over her by at least a foot. She prudently moved backward a step.

The emotion in his eyes caused her heart to start fluttering irregularly.

"We'll see. In the meantime, you might as well get some sleep. We'll be leaving in the morning."

April was surprised at the reluctance she felt at this disclosure. When her eyes met his, she found the same feelings reflected there. Nodding, she began to prepare her bed for the night.

They ate their supper in silence. After Wolf had again cleaned the plates, they settled down on their respective bedrolls. The crackling of the fire was a soothing sound as the darkness and cold descended outside the cave.

April leaned up on one elbow and looked across to the other side of the cave where Wolf had his back to her. "Wolf?"

"What?"

His testiness did little to encourage her, but she had to know.

"Did you turn from God when your parents were killed?"

By the dim light from the fire she could see his back and shoulders tense. "That was part of it," he finally replied.

"And the other part?"

He rolled over to face her, his dark eyes glittering through the dimness. His voice was filled with anger. "I watched people claiming to be representatives of

God murdering, stealing, and lying to a race of people they thought inferior. Many thought they were doing it in the name of God. *Manifest destiny* they called it," he spat. "I saw little children lying in the dirt, shot through the heart, their mothers lying beside them, dead. Their last act one of motherly devotion in trying to save their children."

The images his words elicited filled her with horror. She didn't know what to say.

"Grant you, the Indians have dealt with the whites just as badly, but at least they don't do it in the name of God."

"Not all whites are that way," she rebuked softly. "Just as not all Indians are."

His eyes met hers. She found it hard to read the message in them.

"So I'm beginning to find out."

She lay back down, turning her back to him. She wanted to say more, but she didn't know how. It was hard to share a faith that she didn't understand herself. Hard to explain *why* she believed the way she did.

"April?"

She looked over her shoulder. "Yes?"

"What has God ever done for you?"

She turned fully toward him, wondering how she could put into words such a feeling.

"It's hard to explain, Wolf," she told him softly, "but I'll try. When my parents died, I had to take care of myself and my brother. There were times when things were bad, but no matter how bad they got, I knew that God was there watching over me. Crying with me. Laughing with me. It gave me strength to go on. Perhaps that's the best way to explain it. He gives me strength and courage when I need it most. Even if I die, I know I'll always be with Him. It's like the Apostle Paul once said. 'To live is Christ, and to die is gain.' If I live for Him, I have everything. If I die for Him, I still have everything."

He seemed to be pondering what she said. Again, there was that longing in his eyes.

"I wish I could believe that," he whispered. Turning back to the wall, he effectively ended the conversation.

—※—

The next day dawned bright and clear. April joined Wolf outside, her eyes darting away from him in embarrassment. After yesterday, she found it hard to look at him without remembering that kiss and his words about her wanting it reflected in her eyes.

Though cold, the air was fresh and invigorating. April crossed her arms and rubbed them vigorously.

"It's a beautiful day," she greeted cheerfully.

There was a frown on his face. His head was tilted to the wind, and his eyes scanned the blue expanse overhead.

"Something's not right," he answered absently.

Suddenly frightened, she glanced all around her but could see nothing. The hair prickled on the back of her neck at his mantic voice. "What do you mean?"

He took a deep breath, letting it out slowly. "There's something in the air. It might not be wise to leave just yet."

Now April was really frightened. To stay here with him in such close proximity was unthinkable. "The ice has melted, and the sky is clear. I think it would be best if we left now."

Wolf's eyes met hers then. He could read the uncertainty and the fear. Was she so afraid of him that she would risk her life, and *his*, to be away from him? Or was it something else? Perhaps she knew more than he believed about her brother returning for her. Maybe he was on his way even now.

Still, she had a point. The way his feelings were escalating, it wouldn't be prudent to remain there much longer.

A crackling in the underbrush brought him whirling around, his Colt whipped from his holster. A small rabbit came from the bushes, startled at their presence. It froze in fear, then turned and skidded away.

Wolf turned back to April and found her staring fixedly at his gun. She lifted terrified eyes to his, and he quickly holstered his weapon. He could read the questions racing across her uneasy features.

"Get your things together," he ordered gruffly. "I'll get my horse."

She watched him walk away and saw what she hadn't noticed previously. A small cleft in the side of the canyon formed a natural indented shelter. Wolf had lashed pine branches together to form a covering against the wind. He pulled them away, and a beautiful pinto was revealed to her eyes. It nickered softly when it saw Wolf.

"Hey, boy," he responded, patting its sides. "Ready to go?"

He carefully moved the horse backward out of the little shelter, turning him until he faced back up the canyon.

April stared at the two of them, wide-eyed. "Has he been here the whole time?"

"Yep."

"But I never saw him or heard him when I came outside."

Wolf grinned at her in amusement. "Not very observant, are you?"

April ignored his comment. She came closer, stroking the animal's soft nose. "He's a beauty. What's his name?"

"Sky Dancer. I call him Dancer for short."

Wolf entered the cave, returning moments later with their packs. He glanced at April's shoes.

"I hope you can make it up the canyon in those."

Surprised, April studied the trail they were about to take. "Aren't we riding the horse?"

He shook his head, strapping the packs to the horse. "Not until we get out of this canyon. There's still ice clinging to many of the surfaces. It's too dangerous." He took the horse's reins and began moving forward carefully. "Watch your step."

April took one last look at the cave. It had been a refuge of sorts for the past two days, and she was suddenly reluctant to leave its comfort.

When they reached the top of the canyon, the wind hit them with its full force, taking April's breath away. Her blue wool coat did little to dispel the cold. She shivered.

"It seems colder up here," she yelled.

Without turning, Wolf yelled back at her. "It is. There's nothing to block the wind."

When he attained a safe distance, he turned and reached to help April into the saddle. Climbing up behind her, he settled himself comfortably, stretching around her to hold onto the reins.

April tensed at his nearness, then slowly relaxed against his warmth. "Are you sure Dancer can carry both of us?"

"He can, but not as quickly as he can carry one. We're going to have to camp out tonight."

She jerked her look back over her shoulder. "Outside? But we'll freeze!"

His intense eyes met hers. "It was either that or stay until the weather warmed."

Unable to hold his knowing gaze, she turned forward.

"Although leaving might just have been the second stupidest mistake I've ever made," he continued, his voice dangerously low.

"Why?"

The question barely left her mouth before the sun was blocked by moving clouds. She looked up and saw the sky growing leaden gray.

"It's going to snow!" she said in surprise.

His look flickered around the sky, his face growing grimmer by the minute. "I'm afraid so."

As they plodded along, April sucked in a deep breath of the cold air. The distance between them and the cave increased, and she became more relieved with each passing mile.

"A little snow won't hurt us," she encouraged.

His silence made her curious. She looked over her shoulder and caught the quick frown on his face. Her heart began to hammer with dread. "What is it?"

"This isn't going to be a little snow." He shook his head in disgust. "I knew this was a bad idea."

Wolf stopped the horse in a stand of trees. Getting down, he pulled April off after him.

"We need to make a shelter."

April looked around at the forest of pines. "Can't we just go back to the cave?"

He shook his head, retrieving a small ax from his saddlebag. "We've come too far. It would take too long."

He started hacking away at small pine trees. "Help me get these over there to that spot beneath those three large pines."

They worked together as quickly as possible, but even so, by the time they had cut enough saplings, the snow had started to fall.

Using some rope from his saddle, Wolf made a crisscross section using the three large trees as poles. He then wove the saplings between the rope until there was a small lean-to, while April gathered their blankets and some of the supplies.

Finding some dry kindling, Wolf started a fire in the middle of the area and motioned April to have a seat. She hurried inside, watching as Wolf began putting more saplings against the front, finally closing them inside.

"What about Dancer?"

He shook his head. "He'll be fine." He scooted over until he was close to the fire. "We should be all right here 'til the storm passes, though I'm not certain how long that will be."

Although it was far from warm in their little shelter with the wind blowing through the cracks and branches, it was much better than being outside. April was thankful that she was with Yellow Wolf. His survival instincts would keep them alive, she knew without a doubt. Oddly enough, despite his earlier amorous attitude, she felt remarkably safe with him.

"How far did we come?" she asked.

"About five miles."

Amazed, she turned a shocked face to him. "You mean we still have thirty-five miles to go?"

He looked at her, laughter in his eyes. "Yep."

"How long do you think the storm will last?"

"I'd say until tomorrow morning, at least," he told her, without looking at her.

April swallowed hard. If this man was so attractive inside the cave where she had some room to move around, what was he going to be like sitting three feet away?

She caught his glance and saw his slow smile. He knew what she was thinking, she was certain of it. If he was dangerous in the cave, she decided, here he was going to be absolutely lethal.

Chapter 6

For two days, they were buried by an avalanche of snow. Periodically Wolf would push his way free of their shelter and check on Dancer. April stayed huddled near the low-burning fire.

During this time, they were able to talk. The tension between them crackled like the burning embers of the fire, but Wolf kept a respectful distance. April wasn't certain if she was grateful or disappointed. She had never experienced such a strong attraction to anyone in her life, and she didn't know what to do about it.

Periodically, April caught Wolf studying her and wondered what he was thinking. His thoughts were hidden by his set, immobile face.

April shared with him the story of her life. Whenever she talked about her brother, Wolf could hear the love and devotion in her voice. He wondered again if she was as innocent as she claimed. Perhaps her brother had used that devotion to convince her to help him. Still, it was hard for him to believe.

When they finally rose from their shelter, snow had fallen to a depth of several feet. Wolf had never seen anything like it in his life. He'd lived most of his life in these parts, and while snow was common, this one was definitely out of the ordinary.

He was lashing what was left of their supplies to his saddle. He glanced over his shoulder at April.

"In my saddlebag is some twine. Could you hand it to me, please?"

April hurried to do as he asked, anxious to get moving. Her feet crunched through two feet of snow, the cold seeping up her legs and into her already numbed feet.

She delved into the bag, her fingers encountering a small, hard object. Curious, she pulled it out. She stared at the Bible in surprise.

Wolf glanced up at her, his mouth open to hurry her. He stiffened when he saw her standing there, his Bible open in her hands. He crossed quickly to her side, his long legs making short work of the distance.

He jerked the Bible from her hands. "I said *twine*," he grated, moving to put the book back in his bag.

She placed a detaining hand over his. "Wait!"

His set look was forbidding.

"Please, there's something I would like to show you."

He didn't stop her from taking the book, but the glare he gave her was uncompromising.

"It was my mother's. That's why I keep it, no other reason."

"Wolf," April countered, "you and Ted have something in common besides the death of your parents. You both blame God for their deaths."

He lifted a supercilious eyebrow. "And I shouldn't?"

She looked into his eyes, trying to impart a small measure of her faith. He recognized the sincerity behind her look and stilled.

"For two years I've wanted to show my brother two special verses in the Bible, but I didn't have the opportunity until just lately. I missed that opportunity." Her blue eyes were serious. "I don't want to miss that opportunity with you."

She flipped the pages of the Bible to the book of Hebrews. Sliding her finger down the page, she finally stopped at chapter two, verse fourteen. She lifted it for him to read. His eyes skimmed it, then lifted to hers.

"And?"

She then flipped the pages until she reached the book of Matthew. She had him read the twenty-eighth verse of chapter ten.

"Wolf," she told him, "Satan has the power of death. You blame God, but there is another entity with the power to destroy lives. It's Satan you should be angry with, not the Lord."

His eyes darkened in anger. "The book of Job talks about God allowing Satan to use that power. He could always say *no.*"

Surprised, April studied his tense face. He knew far more of the Bible than just a casual reading would allow. It was obvious that at some time he had studied it.

"Tell me," she asked him sharply. "Are you angry with God because He didn't serve *your* purpose instead of His own? Maybe you think you have a better understanding of the universe!"

Her sarcasm stung. Wolf's nostrils flared. He pulled the twine from the bag and turned to leave. April called after him, desperation in her voice. She *had* to make him see.

"If Satan killed your parents, then why do you serve him? *He's* the one you should be angry with, and you should be doing everything in your power to deny him instead of following after him."

He turned sharply, his face unusually pale. His hands folded into fists at his side.

"Get your things together, and for your own sake, *shut up!*"

April's eyes widened at his ferocious look. She swallowed hard, staring at him in impotent fury. She turned quickly and disappeared inside the lean-to.

Wolf released his breath slowly, his hands uncurling at his sides. The thing that bothered him most was that she made perfect sense. One could only serve two masters, either the god of the world or the God of heaven. And it was not the God of heaven who had brought sin into the world.

He finished his preparations to leave in heavy silence. April came and stood next to him, her look wary. He lifted his gaze to her face.

"Don't worry. I'm not about to scalp you."

Her lips twitched slightly. "I *had* wondered."

Ever so slowly his lips curled into a smile. The darkness of his eyes lightened as the anger drained from him.

"Are you ready to go?"

She nodded but said nothing.

"We're going to have to walk. The snow's too deep for Dancer to carry us through." He lifted an eyebrow. "It's gonna be tough going."

April looked around, then sighed. "Well, we can't stay here, can we?" Moving past him, she began trekking forward. Wolf's sharp whistle pierced the air, and she turned to him in question. His hand snaked out, his forefinger pointed in the opposite direction.

"That way."

Flushing, she raised her nose slightly and headed in the direction of his pointing finger. Grinning, he followed her.

It took them a whole day to travel only a few miles. That night Wolf once again rigged them a small shelter.

"Tomorrow we should make it out of the snow, then we'll be able to travel faster."

April laughed, though she felt no humor. "Can't wait to be rid of me, huh?"

His eyes met hers, and at the look in them, her breathing grew labored. She ducked her head, sorry that she had spoken.

"What will happen to me?" she asked quietly.

Folding his tongue behind his teeth, he glanced away. "You'll have to stand trial."

The color drained from her face. "But I didn't *do* anything!"

Still not looking at her, he told her, "That'll be for the jury to decide." When he finally looked at her, she could see uncertainty in his expression. "Would it help if I told you that *I* believe you?"

She smiled slightly. "I'm glad for that, but somehow I don't think it's going to help me much. Jason will want to see me hang."

He frowned. "Jason?"

April told him about the banker. He glowered at her. "If he's any kind of a man at all, he'll want to see justice done."

"Maybe."

The unrestrained fury in his eyes unnerved her. She settled down to try to sleep, exhausted by the day's travels. The snow had been brutal to try to travel through, and even Dancer stood a few feet away with head hung down.

Wolf lay a short distance away from the fire listening until he heard April's deep breathing. He turned his head slightly until he could see her by the light from the fire. She lay on her side, her blanket clutched tightly against her. Her dark hair spilled in a mass around her head, and he found himself wanting to run his fingers through its silkiness.

Shaking his head, he forced himself to concentrate on his next move. Within two days, he would hand April over to the sheriff at Abasca. His insides went cold at the thought. Was it possible that she would really hang?

He glanced back at her sleeping form. For the first time in his career, he wanted to take a prisoner and run. Get her as far away as possible. But he knew that was not the way. He had to trust in the law to make things right.

April, he knew, trusted in God to make things right. But what if it wasn't in His will to let April live? She knew the possibilities, yet she seemed so secure in His love. What if He chose to let her die, just like his parents? Pain lanced his heart at the thought.

How could one woman so consume his thoughts and feelings in such a short time? Was it just the fact that they had shared hardship and danger together and so naturally grew closer by doing so? He thought not, for April was not the only woman he had ever been sent to capture. The problem was, she had instead captured him. Whatever happened, he was irrevocably tied to this woman in his heart. He sighed heavily, rolling away and forcing himself to crawl into the arms of Morpheus.

—⁓—

Three days later they topped the ridge that led to Abasca. Wolf pulled Dancer to a stop, suddenly reluctant to continue.

April's quiet voice startled him.

"Wolf, do you think we could go by my cabin first so that I might clean up some?"

She glanced up at him over her shoulder, and his mouth went dry. Could he do it? Could he actually turn her over for trial?

"Sure," he answered gruffly, thankful for the reprieve.

They plodded into her yard, and April sensed the emptiness. Had it only been six days? It seemed more like a lifetime.

Wolf pushed himself backward over Dancer's rump and came around to help April dismount. His hands rested on her waist long after her feet touched the ground. Their gazes were locked together, and April found herself unable to look away. She placed her hands against his buckskin-clad chest and felt his heart racing against her palms.

In a few short hours, this man would hand her over to the sheriff. After that, he would be gone. If he caught her brother and his cohorts, he would bring them back for trial, but what if he was killed? Or what if she was hanged before he returned? Despite what he said, she had no faith in seeing justice served when so much was stacked against her. Still, with God, she knew that she was loved and protected. Whatever happened, He was there for her.

"Wolf?"

He said nothing, continuing to stare into her eyes. She knew he would never break his promise. She surprised herself with her boldness.

"Please kiss me."

His eyes grew so dark, they reminded her of her mother's black onyx stone necklace. He pulled her close, crushing her into his arms. His kiss told her that he felt the same, as though this might be the last time they saw each other again. The kiss went on and on until April's legs grew weak beneath her. She finally pushed away, but Wolf refused to release her. His fingers grazed her jaw ever so lightly.

"As God is my witness," he told her roughly, imitating her own words, "I will *not* let you hang."

She lifted her hand, allowing her fingers to stroke the several day's growth of whiskers on his chin. "Trust in Him," she whispered. "Just this once, trust in Him."

His look moved over her face, imprinting its picture on his memory. "I do."

Wolf flinched as he heard the door of the jail cell clang with finality. April curled her fingers around the bars, looking out at him. Such faith shone in her eyes that it softened his heart.

The sheriff glared at her in disapproval. "Miss Hansen," he barked, "I never would have thought it of such a fine upstanding young woman like yourself."

Anger rose up in Wolf. "Sounds like you've appointed yourself as judge and jury already. Are you going to be the executioner, too?"

The sheriff's cheeks turned ruddy with embarrassment. "She'll get a fair trial," he snapped.

"She'd better."

The sheriff's eyes grew large at the softly implied threat. His face lost some of its color. There wasn't a person in the territory who hadn't heard of Yellow Wolf Jackson. The sheriff's eyes slid to the Colt revolvers resting at his sides.

April's cool voice lifted some of the tension in the room. "It's all right, Sheriff Baker. I know you'll do your duty and do it well. You always have."

Disconcerted by her show of faith, the sheriff coughed slightly. "Yes, ma'am."

Wolf glared at Sheriff Baker. "I need to speak with the prisoner alone for a few minutes."

Glancing from one to the other, the sheriff nodded and left the room. Wolf wrapped his hands around April's, leaning close against the bars.

"I'll be back, I promise you."

She moved her mouth through the bars, and he kissed her again.

"I believe you," she told him softly.

Reluctantly, he turned to go.

"Wolf?"

He turned back.

"Please don't kill my brother."

His expression clouded. "I never kill unless there's no other way."

"Then I'll be praying for you both."

Her quiet words hung in his mind long after he had departed the jail.

Chapter 7

The judge's gavel rapped twice on the desk. Silence finally settled down over the room with only a whispered comment rupturing it from time to time.

Since Abasca didn't yet have a town hall, the trial was being held in the one-room schoolhouse. There was standing room only, and it seemed as if the whole town had turned out for April's trial.

Jason sat to the side, his dark look filled with malice. If anyone hoped she would hang, it would probably be him, April decided.

The attorney seated at her side gave her hand a reassuring squeeze. She smiled at him, relieved that Mr. Cord had decided to stand in her defense. He was a well-respected member of the community, and what was more, he was firmly convinced that April was innocent.

He pulled his watch from his vest pocket, frowning. He might be in a hurry to get the show on the road, but April was certainly not.

The circuit judge from San Antonio glared out over the courtroom, and April felt her heart sink. Mr. Cord noticed her frightened expression and smiled reassuringly.

"It's all right, April. Judge Bonner is a very fair and honest man."

Relaxing slightly, April sat back and allowed the lawyer to take over. He rose to present his case to the court, his well-groomed appearance giving him credence as an esteemed member of his profession.

He brushed a hand back through his iron gray hair and cleared his throat. "Your honor and members of the jury, my client wishes to plead not guilty to the charges of aiding and abetting a robbery."

There was a brief tittering in the room. The prosecution counselor, Mr. Myers, rose to his feet also. Giving Mr. Cord a slight nod, he suggested to the court that he would prove beyond a shadow of doubt that April Hansen had, indeed, participated in the robbery on Abasca's bank.

When Mr. Harris, the bank teller who had been shot, was called to the stand, he walked by April and gave her a shy smile. April smiled back. She had always liked Mr. Harris. Not only was he the teller in Jason's bank, but she sewed dresses for his wife.

Mr. Myers tucked his hands into the armholes of his vest, his grave look making him rather intimidating.

"Now, Mr. Harris, tell us what happened on the morning of November third."

Mr. Harris related everything he could remember from that morning. He motioned to April with his arm in a sling. "And if it weren't for April Hansen, I'd be plugged six foot under right now. She saved my life!"

The crowd broke out into excited chatter, and Mr. Myers frowned. Obviously, that was not what he wanted to hear. The judge rapped his gavel to quiet the crowd again.

"Be that as it may, Mr. Harris," Myers continued, "she was there with her brother, was she not?"

Mr. Harris agreed that she was. Myers ended his questions.

Mr. Cord rose to his feet to cross examine. "So, Mr. Harris, is it your opinion that Miss Hansen was trying to thwart the robbery?"

Myers got quickly to his feet. "Objection, your honor. Mr. Cord is asking the witness to speculate."

"Sustained." The judge gave Mr. Cord a warning look. He apologized.

"Let me rephrase the question. Mr. Harris, did Miss Hansen's quick action help to thwart the robbery?"

Wrinkling his face, Mr. Harris cocked his head to the side. "Well, the robbers got away with the money, but no one got hurt. So I'd say, yeah, she did."

When Jason was called to the stand, April's heart sank. His malevolent look focused on her, and she shivered.

Mr. Myers crossed the room and stood next to Jason's chair.

"Please tell the court your name."

Without taking his eyes from April, Jason answered, "My name is Jason Dice. I am manager of the Abasca Bank, the one *she* helped rob."

The crowd came alive again. Mr. Cord frowned at Jason. "I object, Your Honor."

"Sustained." Judge Bonner glared at Jason. "Kindly refrain from making any more of those suggestive remarks, or I will have to declare you a hostile witness and remove you from the courtroom."

Jason subsided, his lips curled out into a childish pout. He answered the questions of both Mr. Cord and Mr. Myers, still trying to implicate April with the robbery.

Mr. Myers called as his final witness the woman who had fainted. She made her way hesitantly to the front of the room and, after swearing on the Bible, hastily seated herself.

Mr. Myers smiled reassuringly. "Now, Mrs. Winston, suppose you tell us just what you saw and heard on that morning."

She basically confirmed the stories of the others, but she added one final clause.

"I heard Miss Hansen try to stop her brother. She told him she would never forgive him for what he was doing."

The silence was once again disrupted. Mr. Cord refrained from questioning, knowing that Mrs. Winston had already made his point for him. The judge dismissed the jury and told the room that court would resume after three o'clock.

April was returned to her jail cell, where she quietly prayed, not on her own behalf, but for Wolf and her brother.

When they returned to the courtroom several hours later, the judge asked the jury for its verdict.

The jury foreman stood to his feet. "Well now, Judge, the law says you don't condemn a man unless there's no shadow of a doubt about his guilt." He glanced at the other members of the jury. "We all feel that Miss Hansen is a good, upright young woman. We have our doubts about whether she's guilty of such a crime. Therefore, we find the defendant not guilty."

The room erupted in cheers. April sank bank into her chair, exhaling her breath in relief.

No one noticed the tall figure clad in buckskins who exited the room at the back.

—⁂—

Wolf slipped out of the courtroom, his heart light with relief. Through the whole trial, he had been praying that God would spare April. Now he realized that if God had done so, it wasn't because of him, Wolf, but because of April's faith in the Lord Himself. Still, she was right, and he was through serving the devil who had killed his parents. From now on, he would give his all to fight Satan here on earth in any way he could.

He had found the trail of the Miller gang. Three had gone in one direction, one had circled back. Hansen was in the vicinity, he knew, and he had no doubt that he would be waiting to talk with his sister. Wolf would be ready.

—⁂—

April climbed down from the buggy, turning to smile at the man holding the reins. "Thank you, Mr. Cord."

He returned her smile. "You're quite welcome. I knew you were innocent."

"Well, thank you again for having such faith in me."

She stepped back from the buggy, but Mr. Cord didn't move on. He frowned at her. "Are you sure you won't come and have dinner with Mrs. Cord and me? I hate to think of you spending this day alone."

Her lips tilted wryly. "Solitude is good for the soul," she quoted. "Right now, I think I *want* to be alone."

He nodded in understanding. "Well, don't be a stranger. You're always welcome in our home. Besides," he grinned, "you owe Mrs. Cord a dress."

"Are you sure you don't want more payment than that?" she asked softly. "I *do* have some money, you know."

He lifted a brow. "Not until that Texas Ranger gets it back, you don't."

At the reference to Yellow Wolf, April felt her breath lodge in her throat. Where was he, anyway? Had he found Ted and the others? Was Wolf alive, and if so, had he had to kill Ted? These torturous thoughts had been with her the entire past week since Wolf had left. She longed for him to finish his job and return to her as he had promised, but she also knew that to do so would more than likely be to condemn her brother.

"Good-bye, Mr. Cord, and thank you again. Tell Mrs. Cord to let me know when she wants to start on her new dress."

He nodded, tipping his hat. "Will do."

April watched him leave, then slowly turned and headed for her small cabin. She entered the house, dropping her bonnet by the door. Her whole body was filled with lethargy from the anticlimax of the past two weeks. The whole thing seemed like some surrealistic dream.

Jason's glare when he had passed her on the way out of the courthouse had left her just a little shaken. His look promised retribution. She shook her head sadly, going to the fireplace to ready a fire.

She stopped short. The logs and kindling were already set, just waiting for a match. Who would have done such a thoughtful thing? Mr. Cord? Glancing quickly around the room, she froze when a figure rose from her bed in the corner. She could barely make out the figure in the dim light coming through the small glass windows. With a glad cry, she flew across the room.

"Ted!"

She ran into his outstretched arms, and they folded close around her. He laid his cheek against the top of her head.

"Oh, April, April! I thought you would never speak to me again. I'm so sorry for the hurt I've caused you."

She pulled away slightly, staring up into his face. "How could you, Ted. How could you leave me like that!"

He pulled her over to the bed and sat down next to her. Taking both her hands in his, he squeezed gently.

"I had no choice. Amos told me that we either had to leave you behind or kill you. Since there was three against one, I was afraid to take a chance on you getting hurt." His hold tightened. "I've never prayed so hard in my life."

"Oh, Ted! Then it was all worth it."

He pulled back, looking into her face. He stroked his fingers down the side of her face. "I'm so sorry for all the pain I've caused you. I realize how much I've hurt you, especially by rejecting God." His smile was rather lame. "But I never could get away from Him. He wouldn't let me go."

"He never will," she told him softly.

He noticed her shivering and crossed to the fire. Striking a match, he soon had a roaring blaze and motioned her to join him next to it. The look he fixed on her was intent. "I take it the ranger found you?"

Flushing, April watched the fire flickering in the stone hearth. "Yes," she answered him quietly. "He found me."

"Did he. . .were you treated good?"

She swallowed hard, still not looking at him. "Yes, he treated me well." Her voice softened on the last word, and her brother's brows rose.

"What aren't you telling me?" he demanded, pulling her around to face him.

"She's not telling you that we fell in love."

April spun around at the same time as her brother, his hand instinctively reaching for his gun. He pulled it from his holster so quickly, April stared in amazement. The only problem was, Wolf stood in the doorway, his gun already pointed at Ted's heart.

Chapter 8

W olf!"

April barely got the word out of her mouth before Ted shoved her behind him. Neither man was willing to drop their weapon.

"You don't want April to get hurt, do you, Hansen?"

Ted glanced over his shoulder at his sister huddling behind him. She lifted terrified eyes to his face. Slowly he dropped his Colt to the floor.

Glowering, he glanced up at Wolf. "What do you mean you fell in love? In a few days? That's impossible!"

"It's been known to happen before," Wolf replied, still not holstering his own weapon. He moved carefully across the room until he could pick up Ted's gun.

"Wolf, please!"

April tried to push past her brother, but he snaked out an arm to hold her in place. He glared at his sister. "Is what he says true?"

For the first time, Wolf totally ignored Ted. His dark eyes were fixed intently on April. "I knew it as soon as I left you," he told her softly. "I didn't want to love you, but I do."

Ted's angry voice lashed out at April. "You can't be in love with a...a..."

"Half-breed," Wolf supplied, his eyes glittering angrily, and he heard April's swift intake of breath.

Ted turned to him, anger rising in his own eyes. "I wasn't going to say that. I don't want my sister involved with a ranger. That's no kind of life for a woman."

April was staring fixedly at Wolf. She knew she had been attracted to the ranger, but she hadn't realized just how deep those feelings ran until he walked out of her life. She looked at her brother standing defiantly against Wolf, still trying to protect her. She loved him, too.

Her gaze clashed with Wolf's. "Let him go, Wolf, please."

What did she see in his eyes? Disappointment?

"I can't, April. I have a job to do, and I've given my oath."

They both were surprised by Ted's soft voice. "You know he's right."

April turned a pale face to her brother. "They might hang you!"

He shook his head. "Not for robbery. That's just jail time."

Wolf studied him closely, his thoughts hidden behind a granite mask. "Amos

Miller's gang has killed eight people. April's right. If convicted, you'll probably hang."

Ted flashed him a look. "She didn't need to know that."

April didn't know what to do. She had always gotten her brother out of his scrapes, but this one was beyond her. "Oh, Ted," she lamented softly. She didn't know what else to say.

"Where are the others, Hansen?" Wolf demanded.

Ted gave him a strange look. "I think you already know, Jackson."

Wolf's puzzled look moved over Ted slowly. "I only tracked them as far as Hilton's ledge, but you're right. I'll find them. But it would sure save me a lot of time, and possibly help you, if you cooperated."

April tugged on his sleeve. "Tell him, Ted."

Ted shook his head, still watching Wolf intently. "I don't think so. Let's just see how good you are, Jackson."

Wolf sensed a double meaning behind the words. His lips pressed into a tight line. Without saying anything, he fastened a pair of handcuffs to Ted's hands, while Ted watched him impassively.

April looked from one to the other, wringing her hands in agitation. She tried to get her brother to see reason one last time, but he still refused.

Wolf found Ted's horse where he had hidden it behind the cabin. He helped him to mount, then mounted Sky Dancer.

April laid a hand against his saddle, and he frowned down at her. Her blue eyes pleaded with him, and despite himself, he felt his heart soften.

"I want to come, too," she begged.

He looked like he was about to decline, but then giving a quick nod, he reached down and lifted her to the saddle in front of him. Wrapping his arms around her securely, he noticed Ted's uncertain look flicking from one to the other.

Wolf led the way back to town, reluctant to open April up to any more censure. Still, Ted was her brother, and she loved him. It was only natural that she wanted to be with him.

He glanced once more at Ted, and the other man met his eyes. There was a message in them that he couldn't quite interpret. Wolf pulled April closer, thankful for the time he could hold her in his arms.

April's silence made his heart ache with sympathy. She loved her brother so much. What would it do to her if he did hang? And how could he live with himself if he was the cause of that pain in her life? At times like this, he almost hated being a ranger.

He handed Ted over to the sheriff, leaving April alone with her brother. He filled out the necessary paperwork to submit to his captain and quickly left the building. The sooner he got on the road, the sooner his job would be finished. And when this job was finished, he was coming back for April.

Although he had wondered if he could make any woman go through the prejudice his own mother had been through, he knew that he couldn't go on without at least offering April the chance to give them both a life full of love. After today, though, he was no longer confident of her feelings in the matter.

He had just mounted his horse when April hurried outside. The cold wind caused her gray wool dress to wrap around her legs. Shivering with the cold, she wrapped her arms tightly around herself. "I need to talk to you, Wolf."

His hands tightened on the reins. He thought he knew what she had to say, but he wasn't certain he wanted to hear it. After consigning her brother to almost certain death, how could she help but hate him?

"Not now, April. When I get back."

"No! I have to say this now."

Staring into her determined blue eyes, he slowly dismounted. Taking her arm, he pulled her to the side of the building, out of sight and sound of others who might be passing by.

He folded his arms across his chest, his look wooden. "Go ahead."

She studied his face for some time. Sighing, she laid a hand gently on his arm. "What Ted has done, he has to pay for. He made his own choices."

Slowly, his shoulders relaxed. "April, I—"

She placed her fingers over his lips. "It's all right, Wolf. You did what you had to do. I don't hold that against you." A sad smile curled her lips. "If you hadn't, you wouldn't be the man that I love."

He pulled her close, his large hand pressing her head against his chest. She could hear the thundering of his heart against her ear, and her smile widened. She looked up into his face, and blue eyes filled with love met brown eyes filled with adoration.

"I'll be back," he told her huskily, and she knew he was making her a promise.

"You better," she agreed just as huskily. Her eyes grew solemn. "Be careful, Wolf."

He kissed her with a kiss so full of promise, her legs threatened to buckle beneath her. She watched him climb back on Dancer, and giving her one last look, he wheeled about and headed out of town. Heavyhearted, April watched him leave.

She made her way slowly into the sheriff's office, not certain she was up to her brother's upcoming interrogation. The look in his eyes told her that she had a lot to answer for.

The sheriff allowed her into his cell, and she seated herself on the bunk next to him. His look roved her features, and lifting one dark eyebrow, he asked, "Jackson gone?"

Flushing, she dropped her gaze to the dusty floor. "Yes."

"Do you really love him?"

She looked at him then, her eyes sparking with resolution. "Yes, I do."

He sighed heavily. "I hope for your sake that you're not disappointed."

"Why should I be?"

Reading the look on her face, his own face darkened. "Don't even think that! I am not referring to the man's race. If you remember correctly, mother hired a black nanny for us when we were younger, and we both loved her. You're not the only one who can see beyond skin color. I have no problem with his race." He got up and curled his hands around the cell bars. "But there are things you don't understand."

"Such as?"

Instead of answering, he yelled for the sheriff. Sheriff Baker took his time answering the summons, and when he finally meandered into the room, Jason Dice was with him.

"What do *you* want?" the sheriff snapped.

Jason's look was nasty. "He wants to hang, don't you, Mr. Hansen?" The look he threw April was full of loathing.

"I have something for you," Ted told the sheriff, surprising everyone. He reached down and took off his boot. Turning it over, he pried open the heel with his fingers and pulled out a piece of paper. Unfolding it, he handed it to the sheriff.

Curious, April joined him at the bars. She tried to see past his broad shoulders, but all she could see was the stunned expression on the sheriff's face.

"What is it?" she asked.

The sheriff looked at Ted, his face a curious mixture of disbelief and awe. "It's a letter from the commander of the Texas Rangers, Mr. John Ford. It's cosigned by the president of the United States, James Buchanan."

April's startled gaze flew to her brother.

"It says here," the sheriff continued, "that Mr. Ted Hansen, Texas Ranger, is acting under the auspices of the federal government and the State of Texas, and that he is to be afforded every vestige of legal rank."

Jason grabbed the paper from his hand. "Let me see that!" He quickly scanned the note, his face blanching. "It's a forgery," he declared vehemently.

The sheriff took the paper, studying it. "Not with the president's seal, it's not."

The color drained from April's face. "You're a ranger? But. . .but why didn't you tell Yellow Wolf?"

He avoided her searching eyes. "I need out of here, Sheriff. Now!"

Sheriff Baker hastily retrieved his keys and opened the door of the cell. Ted quickly exited, April following more slowly. Jason followed behind, his manner suddenly subdued. He stalked past them angrily and left the office.

"I need my guns," Ted barked at the sheriff.

"Ted!"

He turned to her then. Taking her by the shoulders, he bent until he could look into her eyes.

"Listen to me, April. I don't have time to explain things now. You'll have to wait until I get back."

"*If* you get back!"

He cocked her a grin. "Have a little faith, will you?" Strapping on his holsters, he returned the paper to his hollowed-out boot sole, tapping the leather back in place. Putting his boot back on, he told her solemnly, "Pray for me."

He dashed out the door, jumping to his horse tied to the rail. Whipping the reins loose from the post, he turned and galloped after Yellow Wolf.

April watched him leave, her heart in her throat. Swallowing convulsively, she decided that he was right. It was time to pray.

Amos Miller had been decidedly sloppy in leaving a trail to follow, and Wolf was more than a little suspicious.

He watched from the confines of a green shelter belt of trees as the trio ambled around their shanty in preparation for leaving. They were tying bundles to their horses, and he suspected it was probably the loot from their recent escapades. That they were cold-blooded killers warranted caution.

He pulled his bow up, knocking an arrow onto the string. Two other arrows sat on the ground beside him. He would have to be fast, because Amos was a notorious quick draw.

He located each man, and with quick precision let fly three arrows, one right after the other.

The first pinned Chauncy to the side of the shanty, his gun arm arrested by the piercing of the arrow. The second arrow struck Al in the right arm, effectively ruining his gun hand. The third arrow missed its target, Amos's quick reflexes causing him to drop to the ground to allow the arrow to fly over his head. Still, it gave Wolf the time he needed to get quickly to his feet and draw his two revolvers.

Amos, reaching for his holster, froze to the spot. The other two did the same. Seeing Wolf clad in buckskins, his bow slung over his back, reminded them of all the stories they had heard about him.

He carefully descended the hill until he was on level ground with them.

"You're getting sloppy in your old age, Miller. You left a trail a child could follow."

Amos cursed, spitting on the ground. "That's a lie. We took care to cover our tracks."

"It were that pup, Hansen," Al growled. "You told *him* to disguise our trail."

"That's right, you did."

Wolf tensed, recognizing the voice from behind him. He could hear Ted climbing down the hill at his back. If he let off three shots at the others, would he have time to turn and fire on Hansen?

With his mind off center from his opponents, Wolf missed Amos's quick draw. A shot rang out from behind him, and Amos's gun fell with a thud.

Ted drew up beside Wolf, his cocky grin a bit disarming. A wisp of smoke from his gun added the smell of burning powder to the air. "Hi ya, Jackson. Glad we're on the same team."

Snarls from the men greeted this statement. Puzzled, Wolf threw Ted a quick glance.

"I'll explain on the way. Right now, let's get these desperadoes behind bars where they belong."

Ted passed him, going to the others and cuffing them. He then searched the saddlebags and bundles. "Looks like it's all here."

Wolf waited passively while Ted got the three hoodlums onto their horses. Ted turned to him, shifting uncomfortably under his steady regard.

"You don't have much to say, do you? Aren't you curious?"

Wolf crossed his arms over his chest, feet spread apart. His look was enigmatic. "Ford sent you, didn't he?"

Startled, Ted turned to him, his mouth slightly agape. "How'd you know?"

Wolf took Dancer's reins and swiftly mounted. Though his face was inscrutable, his eyes sparked with anger.

"It doesn't take a genius to figure it out. Rip Ford hates Comanches, and I'm half Comanche."

Ted had to hurry to catch up with him. "It's not like that at all. Rip found out that there's a bad ranger, one who is helping robbers for a piece of their profit. Since Miller and his gang have been so hard to track, he knew they must be getting help somewhere."

Wolf cast him a wrathful glance from the side of his eyes. "And since I'm part Indian, of course it had to be me."

Color mounted to Ted's cheeks. "I'll grant you that probably had a part in his thinking, but you aren't the only one who is under suspicion. You *have* been trekking around out here where we knew Miller's hideout to be. And since the Comanche have been giving settlers and reservation Indians so much grief this past year trying to implicate them in crimes, well. . ."

"You needn't explain. I understand perfectly." Wolf glanced at him again. "I've been tracking Miller for some time on my own. I knew if anyone could find him, I could," he suggested, totally without conceit. He tilted his head slightly. "What about you? What changed your mind about me?"

"April."

Wolf jerked his head upward. "What about her?"

The look Ted gave Wolf spoke volumes. "My sister couldn't love someone the way she loves you if they were bad. It's just not in her."

"She deserves better," Wolf growled.

A small smile tilted Ted's lips. He reached forward, patting the neck of his gelding. "She couldn't find better, and I'll be telling Rip so."

Wolf's features hardened. "You can also tell him that I'm resigning from the Rangers."

Ted sighed heavily. "I can't blame you, but are you sure you want to do that? The Rangers need men like you."

"I'm doing it for April."

—⁓—

April heard hoofbeats outside her cabin and hurried to the door. She flung the portal wide, breathing a sigh of relief when she saw her brother and Wolf come cantering into the yard.

Though Wolf dismounted, Ted stayed seated on his mount. April's eyebrows lifted in question.

Ted smiled wryly. "I have some things to do. I'll return in a few days."

"What kind of things?" she asked, coming across the yard to his side. Looking up at him, she studied him to see if he was well.

"Well, I have to return that diamond necklace to the bank in San Antonio, for one thing. They only let us borrow it with a guarantee of return."

April placed her hands on her hips, her forehead wrinkled. "There was no Darcy, was there?"

He shook his head, smiling. "I'm sorry about all the lies. It was necessary." Seeing the questions about to come, he told her, "Wolf can fill you in on the rest." He leaned down and touched her cheek, his eyes meeting hers. "He's a good man, Sis. Keep him if you can."

She smiled, quick tears coming to her eyes. "Come back soon."

He returned her smile then gave Wolf a quick nod. Turning, he trotted out of the yard. April watched him until he was out of sight.

"I like your brother," Wolf said, his hands coming to rest on her shoulders.

April turned slowly until she was facing him. His arms wrapped around her.

"I'm glad," she told him, placing her palms against his chest. "And he likes you."

Wolf smiled wryly. "It always helps if you can get along with your in-laws."

He looked deep into her eyes and saw the answer to his question before he ever asked it. He asked it anyway.

"Will you marry me, April Hansen?"

"In a heartbeat," she returned quickly.

His smile turned into a full-fledged grin, but it slowly faded, his eyes becoming serious. "It could be difficult."

"Aren't all marriages?" she quipped.

He frowned. "April—"

She stopped him with a quick kiss. "People have survived it before. I suppose we can, too. I love you, Wolf. Like Ruth said so long ago, wherever you go, I'll go." She wrapped her arms around his neck, waiting to see if he would break his long-ago promise.

His eyes grew darker with each passing second, but he still refused to move.

Realizing that he would never break his oath, no matter the incentive, she sighed. "You're a very stubborn man, Yellow Wolf Jackson! Would you please kiss me? Now and every day for the rest of our lives."

He readily complied.

SAVING GRACE

by Kathleen Y'Barbo

Dedication

This novella is dedicated first and foremost to my heavenly Father who reigns on high and to my earthly father who now lives with Him. Also, to the men in my life: Robert Turner, my Texas-born hero in combat boots, and Josh, Andrew, and Jacob, the source of much inspiration, irritation, and indescribable joy. And finally to all the strong women before and after me who, through their courage and convictions, have been the roots out of which my family tree has flourished, especially Mom, Mimi, Granny, and of course, Princess Hannah.

"For by grace are ye saved through faith;
and that not of yourselves: it is the gift of God."
Ephesians 2:8

Chapter 1

Texas, on the trail between Santa Fe and the Brazos River
October 1854

Nine times out of ten, Ranger Captain Jedadiah Harte listened to the Lord and acted without questioning Him on the finer points of His plans. Today, however, he felt like maybe he'd misunderstood.

Many times on the ride from San Antonio, he'd been tempted to slide his trusted matched Walker Colt revolvers from their resting place beneath his King James Bible and slip them back into his belt where they used to belong. Always he'd felt the strong pull of the Lord's hand keeping his fingers on the reins and his heart on the straight and narrow.

To the surprise of everyone but the God who knew him well, Jed had turned over leadership to his second in command and hit the trail. The talk around headquarters gave him six months before he came riding into town and reclaimed it, but Jed knew better. A part of him would forever love being a ranger. The thrill of the chase and the triumph of good over evil never failed to satisfy.

In nearly fifteen years with the Rangers, "Heartless Harte," as he'd become known, had amassed an impressive list of criminals dispatched to the afterlife, a testament to the deadly accuracy with which he could aim his Walker Colts. He'd been proud of his record, and more than one newspaperman had trailed Heartless Harte to write about it later in gory detail.

Then last spring he'd been tracking a couple of rustlers when he came across a camp meeting south of Gonzales. Normally he would have steered clear of the place in favor of a warm bedroll and a shot of red-eye, but something he later realized to be the hand of the Lord caused him to stay.

First thing, the circuit-riding preacher asked him where he planned to spend eternity. The question left him madder than a peeled rattler, and the answer left him frightened for the first time since he'd been out of knee pants.

Right then and there he gave his life over to the Lord and promised Him He'd be first in command. Baptized in a little creek in the middle of nowhere, the infamous Heartless Harte became just plain old Jed Harte, citizen and soldier for the cross.

No more killing and no more use for the Walker Colts; he'd promised the Lord. His rifle would shoot all the game he could eat and his bowie knife would skin the carcasses. He'd lived by his senses before he'd become a ranger, and he sure could do it again, although with fall nearly past and winter coming on, he had his doubts on exactly how.

Besides handling a firearm, he'd been pretty handy with a hammer and nail. If carpentering was a fine enough profession for his Savior, it sure was good enough for him.

His prayers had led him to believe his true calling came in winning souls, and someday he hoped to do just that. Heading for Galveston by way of the Brazos River, he felt he might have some luck gathering a following for Christ amongst the roughs on the dock. After all, those were his people; the ilk from which he'd come. What better place to finish his life than where it all started?

Jed shifted positions in the saddle and stretched to loosen the kinks. With an eye to the fading sun, he urged his mount into a gallop. A little luck and he'd make it by sunset. He'd camp there, maybe near a landing owned by a fellow he knew from his ranger days.

A decade ago, he'd helped him build a house to bring his bride home to. Now maybe Ben Delaney would return the favor by putting him up for the night. Tomorrow he'd catch a passing steamer downriver at first light and be off on the mission the good Lord had created him for.

Ducking his head to pass beneath the low limb of a spreading pecan tree, he thought about what he'd be doing right now if he were still back in San Antonio. The Lord knew what lay ahead, but Jed would never forget what he'd left behind. Someday, though, maybe he'd bring enough souls to the Lord to earn His forgiveness.

A lazy butterfly teased the rust-colored mane of his sorrel mare and landed on the horn of his saddle. For a few minutes they rode together in companionable silence, only the hoofbeats and the gulls' cry breaking the peace.

Then, from out of the blue came a loud crack, and his whole world went black.

~⚬~

"So much black."

Grace Delaney looked down at the yards of black muslin covering the rise in her belly. It spilled across the quilt and gathered in a dark pool at her feet on the chilly wide boards of the oak floor. Two months, three at the most, and her child would make an entrance into the world. A world filled with a future just as black as the widow's weeds its mother wore.

Only five-year-old Bennett and little Mary-Celine, her precious children, kept Grace from shedding the prison of her widow's clothing to disappear for good into the muddy swirls of the Brazos River. She fingered the heavy muslin of her skirt and banished the awful thought.

How little time had passed since she'd worn crinolines and whalebone corsets and attended the French Opera House in New Orleans and danced at the finest plantations along the river? Could it be less still since she'd come to Texas and settled at Delaney's Landing as the seventeen-year-old bride of the dashing Ranger Ben Delaney?

Some days it seemed like just yesterday. Other days, it seemed like an eternity had passed since she and Ben had taken up farming together and built the landing that now supplied foodstuffs up and down the Brazos.

From the ruins of a burned plantation, they built a farm big enough to meet their needs and feed the family they planned. Bennett Delaney, Jr., came first, a strapping boy with a shock of dark hair like his mother and a fierce streak of stubbornness like his father. Three winters passed after Bennett's birth, and with each one they buried a small blanket-wrapped bundle together and mourned the loss, only to find in the spring another child would be on the way.

Her husband loved babies, as did she, and what Texas took from them, they bore with the knowledge that the children were in a much better place. Finally, two summers ago, Mary had been born. Theresa, the former slave who now served as Grace's friend, confidant, and house help, presided over all the births with concern. At the last confinement, she had stood toe to toe with the oversized Irishman and declared to Ben that Mary should be the last of the Delaneys.

No more babies or Grace would suffer for it.

Grace let the folds of crisp cloth slip from her fingers and slowly squared her shoulders. As much as she would love to give in to the bitter tiredness in her bones and the inescapable pain in her heart, she had no time for such luxuries. The steamer *Lehigh* would arrive at the landing midmorning tomorrow. With only Uncle Shaw and the day help to fill the order, time would be tight. She and Theresa would have to see to the garden, a job that would make for a long afternoon under the best of circumstances.

Today, with the ache in her back and the heaviness in her belly, it would be downright unbearable. And yet, she would manage.

She always seemed to manage.

"Oh, Ben, why did you have to leave me like this?"

A question she'd asked a thousand times, of him and of God, and yet no answers had been forthcoming. Dead men don't speak, and obviously the comforting arms of the good Lord didn't reach as far as Delaney's Landing anymore.

He hadn't been with her husband the day lightning struck him and knocked him off his horse to die alone in the dirt at the age of thirty-two. And now, with more work to do before tomorrow than half a dozen men could perform in a week, He couldn't possibly be with her either.

No, the Lord of Theresa and her husband, Uncle Shaw, was not the Lord she knew. Their Lord showed patience and kindness and offered them peace and comfort. Only the blackness of exhausted sleep offered Grace comfort anymore.

Shaking off the thought along with the chill that had gathered in the small room, Grace stood slowly. Theresa met her at the door with a wool cloak and a tin cup filled with hot coffee.

"You tell those folks they'd best be treatin' you right, Miz Grace, or they'll have the Good Lord and me to deal with."

Grace mustered a weak smile and shrugged into the cloak. The faint scent of wood smoke still clung to it from yesterday's work in the fields.

Unfazed at her lack of response, Theresa slipped the tin cup into Grace's hand and frowned. "Now don't you mind what they say about a woman running Delaney's Landing. Womenfolk, they's a lot stronger than men, anyhow." Her dark gaze settled on the curve of Grace's belly. "Just let one of them try and push a young'un into the world."

With a nod, Grace pressed past her to emerge onto the broad front porch of the home Ben built long ago. The door shut with a resounding crack, and in an instant the thick, cold air swirled around her, almost visible in the first shimmering lights of dawn.

As she'd done every morning since Ben's death, Grace left her coffee untouched on the porch rail and made the trek down the path along the edge of the fence until she reached the giant pecan tree that marked the southeast corner of the Delaney property. Beneath its spreading limbs stood four simple wooden crosses, one newly planted and bearing the name Bennett Delaney, Sr.

Ignoring the protest of her sore muscles, Grace knelt at the edge of the fresh soil and smoothed the edges of the ragged blanket covering the mound. The quilt had been Bennett's idea, a way to keep his pa warm when the weather turned cold a few weeks back. Already the sky blue blanket had begun to dull a bit, and the edges of the white lamb Grace had embroidered on the center square showed evidence of fraying.

She leaned forward a bit to touch the corner of the quilt and allowed her mind to tumble back in time to her son's birth. The baby inside her shifted and pressed against her in protest. A moment later, the familiar pains shot up through her back and settled there. With difficulty she sat back on her heels to seek a measure of relief.

"Be patient, Little One," she whispered. "There's much to do before you come."

And there was much to do. A garden to tend, orders to fill, and books to balance—these were just a few of the items she knew she must attend to before she could sink back into the blissful oblivion of another night's sleep.

If only she had help. Uncle Shaw and Theresa had both become indispensable, each in their own way, but neither could ease her burdens completely.

Already news had traveled up and down the Brazos, and more than one captain had bypassed Delaney's Landing in the mistaken impression that without Ben Delaney in charge, the landing would be closed and the warehouse shuttered. Those who did stop were surprised to find Ben's widow had taken over the running of the warehouse and the filling of orders.

None of them were pleased.

Many refused to deal with her. Some made lewd comments or ignored her outright when she tried to conduct business as she'd seen Ben do. A captain by the name of Stockton had even suggested she pack up and leave Delaney's Landing, offering her what he called a first-class deal for the property. She'd called it something else entirely and sent the man on his way with a few choice scalding words and a request never to return.

Only afterward did she give any thought to the danger she would have been in had the captain not gone willingly. Uncle Shaw, while strong of body, was getting on in years and could have done little to stop a man who didn't want to be stopped. The day help, a dozen during harvest and less most of the time, were hired out from neighboring plantations and held a loyalty that was doubtful at best.

"Oh, Ben, what am I going to do?"

The silence rumbled thick around her, broken only by the occasional call of a gull. Her gaze skipped from Ben's grave to the three others lined up beside him. Her husband and her babies, all waiting for her in heaven.

Heaven? Since when had she given the mythical place any consideration? Surely Ben's death had caused some small bit of concern about it, but to give it any serious thought?

There had been no time.

Nudged by another insistent kick in her belly, Grace shifted to her knees and bowed her head. The north wind teased her hair and lifted the edge of her cloak to blow a chill air across the black muslin she wore.

It would be so easy to give up, to let the land win and let Delaney's Landing become a thing of the past. Her family in New Orleans, if any of them still remained, had never quite forgiven her for leaving polite society to marry a Texas Ranger. Ben, on the other hand, had no family left on this side of the ocean. Besides, she could never leave Texas and the landing Ben loved.

On the wind came a thought, one more frightening than the threat of an angry steamboat captain. "Face it, Gracie, old girl. You're on your own. At least as long as you're able."

What about the children? Like it or not, she had a family to take care of. Bennett and Mary depended on her, as did Theresa and Uncle Shaw. If she gave up, what would happen to them?

Too soon her time of confinement would come. Theresa already looked at her with baleful eyes, concern brimming on her face when she thought Grace couldn't see.

And if the unthinkable happened and Theresa proved right?

"What will I do?" she repeated.

You will pray, came the soft yet insistent answer.

"Pray?"

Surprisingly, the idea seemed to set right. She tugged at the strings holding her cloak together and tried to conjure up just the right words to speak to the Lord. After all, it had been quite awhile since she'd made the attempt.

"God," she finally managed, "I'm not asking this for me, because I can handle whatever life gives me. I'm asking for the babies." She touched the gentle rise of her belly. "This one included," she added.

Her eyes searched the sky, now fading from dark gray to a silver blue as the dawn gave way to morning. The distant whinny of a horse alerted her to the presence of a rider coming up the main road, most likely one of the day workers.

"Lord," she whispered, "if You're up there, I'd be mightily obliged if You'd send me a man to give me some help."

Her boldness surprised her, and yet again, it felt right. She touched the back of her hand to the sky blue blanket.

"He'd need to be strong of health and a dead aim with a pistol. A ranger like Ben would be fine if You've got one. Just to keep the babies safe and the landing going until I'm up and around again. Amen."

She sat back on her heels once more and waited for the answer. The limbs of the old pecan tree rustled and a squirrel skittered across the clearing ahead, but nothing earth shattering happened.

No answer came.

"Silly, I suppose," she said as she rose with difficulty and shook out her aching limbs.

Grace wrapped her cloak around her and turned to take the long, slow walk back to the house. In a few hours the sun would stand high in the sky and the steamer would dock at the landing. No amount of wishful thinking would get the ship loaded and the bill of lading in order.

She looked up at the sky, barely visible through the canopy of dark green leaves overhead. A profound sadness settled around her like a mist. With a weak wave of her hand, she attempted in vain to push it away.

Mindful of her tender state, she stepped gingerly over a fallen limb and headed toward the fence line and the grassy path. What had seemed like a short walk earlier now felt like an almost impossible hike.

If only she could go home and fall into the soft feather bed she'd only just left. If only the Lord heard her pleas and answered.

"What did you expect, Grace?" she asked as the sound of horses' hooves grew louder. "Did you think the Lord, if He exists, would hear your pitiful prayer and send someone just like that?"

Of course not, came the answer. *First you must have faith.*

"Faith?" She shook her head. "Lord, if that's You talking to me, You ought to know I'm trying. For the babies, if not for me."

A moment later, a sorrel mare stepped out of the brush into the path in front of her. Its rider, an oversized dark-haired man in dusty, trail-worn clothes, lay slumped over the saddle horn, a ribbon of blood flowing down the end of his outstretched arm.

As she crept closer to the horse and recognized the man in the saddle, she realized the Lord had sent her a ranger. Unfortunately, it looked like He had sent her a dead ranger.

Chapter 2

The morning sun had climbed over the porch rail and now brightened the front parlor with ribbons of gold shimmering across the flowered needle-point carpet. At the center of the light lay the ranger, silent, solid, and most likely bound for his reward at any moment.

Matted hair covered one eye and a dark purple bruise the other. His skin wore a paleness even the many layers of Texas trail dust couldn't hide.

Grace tried to remember what Ben had said about Ranger Harte. They'd ridden together as new recruits, and Jed had stayed on at the landing long enough to see to it that Ben Delaney's New Orleans sweetheart, should she agree to marry him, would come home to a real house and not a tent, like so many ranger wives.

He'd fussed over the porch rail so many times Ben had declared him soft in the head. When she arrived at her new home, she had been greeted by a hand-lettered note on the back of a reward poster asking them to please be careful of the rails until Ranger Harte could return to finish the job.

True to his word, he'd come back a week later to mend a wobble in the posts only he could see and ended up staying until past the last frost. Harte had claimed it was the carpentering that kept him there, but Ben had declared it to be Grace's cooking.

Grace smiled at the memory. She hadn't seen Jedadiah Harte in almost a decade, although Ben had spoken of him on occasion. While her husband had been content to stay near the landing and nearly give up the life of a ranger altogether, Jed Harte had pursued justice and glory until he reached the rank of captain and led his own group of men.

"Oh, Ben."

Why could she go for hours, even days, once, without feeling the grief, then out of nowhere, it would return? She felt it now, the blinding abyss of dark hurt chasing her, threatening her, nearly engulfing her. Only Theresa's sudden movement kept her from tumbling in.

"Let's git him comfortable, then I kin see what's what." Theresa eased a rolled blanket beneath Ranger Harte's neck, then began matter-of-factly to undress the lawman, starting with his boots, which she handed to Uncle Shaw. "Wonder who he is?"

"Harte," Grace said, almost numb with grief. "Jedadiah Harte."

"The ranger?" Uncle Shaw whistled softly and held the boots at arm's length. He wrinkled his nose. "Been on the trail, awhile too, I'd guess."

Grace nodded and took the coat from Theresa. Waves of nausea threatened at the smell of the trail-worn woolen garment and the sight of the blood staining the collar and sleeve. Quickly she draped it over Uncle Shaw's arm and stepped back to sink onto the stiff cushions of the rosewood settee.

"See that these are taken care of, please," she managed. "If we don't have enough to feed him, we can at least make sure he's clean."

"Shame on you, Miz Grace." Theresa bent over the patient and eased his blue flannel shirt off a broad shoulder caked with blood. "You can't be worrying about whether we can manage. You know the Lord'll provide."

Grace looked away, suitably chastised. Still, concern bore hard on her. When she petitioned the Lord for a ranger, she thought she'd made it clear she needed a healthy one who could wield a revolver and maybe scare up some game or plow under a row or two in the garden. She certainly hadn't bargained for the one now lying half dead in her parlor.

"Looks like it went clean through." Theresa lifted Mr. Harte's shoulder and examined his wounded upper arm, causing him to groan softly. "Sure did, and that's to the Lord's glory, I'll say for sure."

Grace handed a strip of clean cloth to Theresa. "So he's going to live?"

"He might. I 'spect the chill air's hurt his chances a bit, though."

Theresa began to bind his wound, lifting his arm each time to reach beneath it. Throughout the process, he showed no indication of noticing.

"It don't take but one bullet to stop a feller, even one as big as this 'un." She made a soft clucking sound. "Looks like he hit his head on somethin' and near put his eye out. Probably done it after the bullet got him."

The ranger's good eye flickered, and his lips, parched and cracked, began to move as if he were trying to speak. With strong hands and soft words of comfort, Theresa settled the man and covered him with several layers of quilts. She reached for a cloth and the basin of water warming near the fire. A noise above made her look up sharply.

"Them young'uns are awake."

Grace sighed and climbed to her feet. Too many things demanded her attention—the landing, the farm, and the complaints of her tired body—but her children came first. They always would.

"I'll see to them, Theresa," she said slowly. "You'll let me know if there's any change with Mr. Harte."

Theresa shook her head. "I'll get the babies. You don't have no business climbin' those stairs no way. When I get back we gonna talk about the help what's comin' this mornin'."

"Help?" Her hopes rose. "With the landing?"

Theresa shook her head. "With the chilluns, Miz Grace."

Yet another mouth to feed; not what she'd had in mind when she asked the Lord to send help. Grace opened her mouth to protest, but Theresa waved it away with a sweep of her hand. Handing her the cloth and a razor, she pressed the basin in her direction.

"I love those babies like I birthed 'em myself an' you know that, but your time's a comin'. I can't worry about them and take care of you." She hefted her bulk off the floor and started toward the staircase. "The Lord's so good, Miz Grace," she tossed over her shoulder. "I asked Him for help, and out of the blue He answers my prayer by sending my grandbaby, Ruth."

Grace nodded meekly and eased to her knees beside the patient. It was hard not to compare whatever help Theresa got with the help He had sent her.

While Theresa's heavy steps sounded on the stairs, Grace set to work on the ranger, determined not to allow her stomach to rule her hands. She did not have the luxury of illness.

Resolutely, she lifted his head into her lap, or at least what remained of her lap, and began to shave away the dark beard. As she worked, a ruggedly handsome face began to appear, first with the firm, square jaw and finally with the soft curve of a set of cheekbones that could have been chiseled in granite. When she dropped the razor in the basin, his features contorted into a tight grimace and a lovely amber-colored eye flickered open only to disappear once more beneath a frame of thick black lashes.

"Pray for me," came in a thick whisper between cracked lips.

"Pray?" She wrapped the muslin over his injured eye and settled his head gently on the blankets. "Is that what you said?"

Wouldn't the Lord be surprised to hear from her again so soon? What would she say? She shook her head. "I don't know if I can, Mr. Harte."

His good eye opened again, and after a moment, his gaze settled on her. "You must," he said with what sounded like the last of his strength.

"Of course," she said. Lowering her head, she cleared her throat and cast about her somewhat addled brain for the appropriate words. "Lord, I ask You to come and help the man You sent us. I know my aim was to ask for a body to protect us and see that the babies do fine no matter what happens to me. I'd be much obliged if You would see to it that this ranger—"

"No." He began to thrash about beneath the blankets. "Not ranger. . ."

His declaration startled her, and only her hand on his forehead stopped the man's movements. "What is it?" she whispered.

"Pray," he said, obviously struggling to keep his eye open. "For Jed Harte."

"I tried," she said, exasperated. "I asked the Lord to take care of you and heal you so you could ranger again and maybe—"

"No," emerged from his lips like the howl of a wolf.

"What in the world is going on here?" Theresa appeared at the door with Mary on her hip and Bennett at her side. At the sight of her, the children wriggled away and ran to her.

"Mommy, why is the man on the floor?" Bennett asked, wide-eyed.

"Big man hurt?" Mary added.

Ranger Harte settled into a quiet calm and stared at the children. The children, in turn, stared back.

Grace glanced up to see that Uncle Shaw had returned. In place of his usual bland expression, he wore an uncharacteristic look of worry.

"S'cuse me, Miz Grace, but you be needed real bad down at the warehouse."

The story unfolded on their walk to the landing. Ruth had arrived only moments earlier. Sadly, trouble had tagged along in the form of the obstinate steamboat captain Stockton, the same man who'd given Grace trouble a week ago. Shaw told him of the lawman's arrival and led him to believe Harte would be running things soon. Stockton left in a hurry, although Shaw had a suspicion they hadn't seen the last of the man.

Grace responded with a nod and a word of thanks, seating herself behind Ben's desk to begin yet another long day of work.

When she finally pushed away to begin the short walk to the house, she wondered where the day had gone. Her stomach complained at the emptiness and her muscles ached. Only a meal and a few hours' rest stood between her and repeating the whole process.

She thought about the ranger's Bible, retrieved from his saddlebags, and the words she'd seen circled there when she opened it. "Create in me a clean heart, O God; and renew a right spirit within me," she whispered as she trudged the last few steps to the back door.

Shame flooded her as the meaning of the words emerged. Should the Lord come today, neither her heart nor her spirit would stand the test of His all-knowing mind. Right there in the middle of the dusty path, Grace knelt and opened her thoughts to the Lord.

"Oh yes, Lord, I do need a clean heart. Forgive me for losing sight of You and blaming You for all my troubles. Ben and my babies are in a better place, and I know I've got a long way to go to get there." She paused and lifted her gaze to the purple twilight as Ben's child shifted and squirmed beneath her ribs.

"I love You, Lord, and I love my Ben. Don't let me forget him, but please, if You could, teach me how to live without him."

The back door slammed and Grace looked over in time to see Theresa running her way, skirts held high and her petticoat rustling. Grace's blood ran cold at the wide-eyed look on the older woman's face. "What's wrong, Theresa? Did something happen to the babies?"

"Oh, Miz Grace, I done thought your time had come, and you couldn't make it t' the door." She fanned her ample bosom despite the chill air and seemed to have trouble catching her breath. "I declare you scared the life right outta me."

"You mean that's why you came running out of the house?" Grace stifled a grin as her racing heart slowed to nearly normal. "I thought something had happened to one of the children."

"Oh, lands sakes no," she said with a chuckle as she reached to help Grace up. "My Ruth, she's already got those sweet angels fed and nigh t' sleep. Don't you worry about them, not at all."

Grace took the hand Theresa offered and stood gingerly, allowing her body to settle and the baby to stop moving before attempting to walk toward the house.

The mention of Ruth caused her to remember the Bible she'd forgotten on Ben's desk. This sent her thoughts reeling to the ranger, and a stab of guilt reminded her she hadn't given his health any concern. She'd only thought of herself and the selfish pity she'd wallowed in. The shame of it burned deep. *A clean heart,* she repeated to the Lord. *Please teach me, Father.*

Theresa slowed her pace to allow Grace to catch up. "You worried about Mr. Harte?"

The question pressed further the point of her guilt. "Any improvement?" The baby shifted positions to jolt her insides.

Theresa gave Grace a sideways look. "No," she whispered. What a cruel irony that she'd asked the Lord to send this ranger to her, and now he, too, could die. At least it seemed that way to her.

Grasping the stair rail for support, Grace shook her head. "I'll tend to the ranger tonight."

Theresa opened the door and held it wide so Grace could enter, then closed it softly before hurrying to the stove to stir the pots left simmering there. "I've known you too long to argue, Miz Grace, so I won't even try. Set yourself down and see to that baby of yours with some supper afore you tend to the ranger. That's all I ask."

Grace nodded. Satisfied, Theresa reached for the sassafras root and began to chop it into the mixture bubbling in the pot. Grace inhaled a deep breath of the exquisite smells of Theresa's cooking and sank into the slat-backed rocker by the fire, resting on her elbows to relieve the pain in her back. It would be gumbo tonight, Theresa's way of using the last of yesterday's hen in a meal along with the meager contents of the pantry, but it would be good. It always was.

As the flames licked and jumped beside her, the tiredness seeped into Grace's bones and settled there. The baby protested her bent-over position with a swift kick to her insides, so she accommodated him by shifting to a less confining position.

Instantly the little one stilled, although Grace's back muscles began to protest. Stifling the complaint she wanted to voice, she turned her thoughts back to Ranger Harte while Theresa began to slice the corn bread.

How could she consider offering to spend her precious sleeping hours taking care of a man who might die before morning? Yet, under the circumstances, how could she not?

"Renew a right spirit." The verse from the ranger's Bible came tumbling back to her, along with the surprise that Jed Harte even owned a Bible, much less read one. What had happened to her right spirit? Had she ever had it in the first place?

A shiver of guilt snaked down her spine. She and Ben had a Bible, a beautiful book Ben had brought in his trunk from Ireland. She'd accepted the Lord based on that book. Now she would be hard-pressed to know where it was.

A forlorn wail punctuated the silence, followed by a crash. Grace struggled to her feet despite the screaming protest of her muscles.

"Oh, Lord preserve us, that's the ranger." Theresa bustled out of the kitchen. "He done hurt hisself, I just know it," she said as she disappeared into the hallway and headed toward the parlor with Grace trailing more than a few steps behind. "Sakes alive, would you look what he's gone and done?"

Grace pressed past her to see Jedadiah Harte half sitting and half lying across her rosewood settee. The blood seeping from beneath his bandaged arm had already begun to stain the cushion a bright crimson. Her rosewood side table, now reduced to splinters, lay in a heap beneath one long leg.

"Lands o' Goshen, Ranger Harte," Theresa said as she eased him into a sitting position on the settee. "You done gone and made a mess of yourself for sure. Why in the world you wanna be a doin' that?"

Chapter 3

Why indeed? Jed took in his surroundings through one eye, in a haze of pain and a swirl of faces. Two faces, one dark and the other light. He blinked and the pain sharpened. His head tilted and the world went with it.

"Whoa there, Mr. Ranger," the dark one warned. "You ain't gonna break yourself along with the missus' table. Not if I have somethin' t' say about it."

"Break?" He caught the word and tossed it around in his addled brain until he made sense of it. Beneath his feet came the crunch of the most perfect piece of rosewood he'd seen this side of New Orleans.

"Excuse me, Mr. Harte. How do you feel?"

Jed blinked again, and the lighter of the women came into focus, robbing him of his thoughts. She touched his forehead with the back of a pale hand, and he nearly reeled backward with the cool relief it offered.

"Mr. Harte? I asked how you felt."

He licked his lips and shut his eye, then thought hard to make out the words and understand them. Formulating an answer seemed to take forever. "Weak as a newborn calf," he said slowly.

When he opened his good eye, the woman smiled and removed her hand from his forehead. "The fever's broken."

"Praise the Lord," the dark one exclaimed.

Jed nodded, confused. The pain swirled around him in a thick fog with his shoulder and left arm at the center. Atop the source of his discomfort lay a thick pad of muslin and a wrapping of red-stained bindings.

"What happened?" he asked, attempting with clumsy hands to investigate the situation.

The woman's pale fingers stopped him. "You've been injured," she said softly in the honeyed tones of a woman of culture. "Shot, actually." Her hand led his to the spot of greatest irritation and gently set it upon the bindings. "The bullet went through your left arm just below the shoulder."

In a few simple words, the woman told him of how he came to be in her parlor. Understanding dawned along with a white-hot burning beneath his brow. The events began to roll back in a slow progression beginning with his ride out of San Antonio and ending with a shot, which must have taken him down near the Delaney property.

"Ben's wife," he murmured.

She acknowledged the fact as if it pained her. Worry etched lines across her face where age did not. When she pulled a chair next to him and sank into it, he saw the evidence of the babe she carried.

"Well, well, old Ben's gonna be a daddy," he mumbled, a mixture of envy and pain flooding his heart. "Grace, isn't it?" he managed.

She nodded, stiffly rising to accept a bundle from the dark woman. "And this is my friend Theresa." She began to tear off a length of fabric. "You'll need to let me change the bandages now, Mr. Harte."

Jed watched Grace Delaney as the bindings loosened and the bandage fell away to reveal a decent bullet wound. What kind of ranger was he to be blindsided by a stray bullet? Then it came to him. He was no ranger at all; he'd given himself over to the Lord and promised to put away his weapons. The Lord had made him clean.

How long ago now had he given up the life that had carried him off the docks and into the law? Not long enough to put the past behind him. Straining to fight the blackness chasing him, he leaned forward, then fell back when the blinding pain hit him between the eyes like a runaway steer.

"God bless you for coming to save us, Ranger," were the last words he heard before he gave in to the dark waters of sleep.

—⁂—

He'd come to save them, beckoned by desperation and prayer. Many times during the busy daylight hours, Grace felt a pull of worry concerning the ranger but could do nothing about it. The duties at hand kept her mind tossing back and forth between the patient in her parlor and the never-ending chores.

Morning work in the garden had given way to afternoon work at Ben's desk when the pains began. She pushed away from the desk and stood in the hopes they would leave as quickly as they arrived.

When standing didn't alleviate them, she began to walk, first a few halting steps around the desk and eventually, after tucking the ranger's Bible under her arm, across the warehouse and out into the remains of the daylight. Still the discomfort chased her. Grace held a hand to her brow and squinted into the sun to find the distance to the house.

"You're an impatient one," she whispered through gritted teeth to the child in her womb. At least her other two children were not a worry tonight. With Ruth and Theresa, they were safe and well taken care of.

Grace lifted her gaze skyward and said a word of thanks for the two women, telling the Lord just what they meant to her. Later, when she managed the trek to the house, she made a promise to tell Theresa and Ruth at the first opportunity.

Ignoring the plate left warming on the stove, she left the Bible on the kitchen table and went upstairs in search of her children. To her delight, she found them sitting at Ruth's feet, eyes wide and listening to a tale about two birds and a squirrel in a pecan tree.

When Ruth saw her standing in the hall, she ended the story with a promise to tell another in the morning after breakfast. The children began to protest but squealed with glee when they saw Grace.

"These children sure love their mother," Ruth said with a smile.

"I love them, too," she said as she eased onto the floor and gathered Mary into her arms, then settled Bennett beside her. The children smelled of soap and sunshine, a heavenly combination. "And I couldn't manage without you, Ruth," Grace added.

The girl offered a shy smile. "It's me who's blessed, Ma'am," she answered softly. "And it is you and the good Lord who should be thanked."

Unable to answer, Grace sent Ruth downstairs while she took over the duties of readying Bennett and Mary for bed. After listening to the stories of adventures they had during their afternoon walk in the woods, she kissed the children good night, tucked them in, and read to them from a book of their favorite tales from Ireland.

Mary fell asleep first, her two middle fingers planted firmly in her mouth. Grace kissed her daughter once more, gently removing the tiny fingers from her pink, bow-shaped mouth. Quietly, she moved to Bennett's bed, where, true to his nature, the boy lay awake.

Grace sank heavily onto the bed and kissed his forehead. Sometimes it seemed as though the Delaney men had perfected stubbornness. Tonight this one wore it all over his face.

"Mama, Ruth says I can't sleep in the parlor." He pronounced his dislike of the statement with a face intended to convey the sentiment.

As she had done so many times before Ben's death, Grace climbed onto the bed next to her son and stretched her legs out, feeling the strain of her muscles and the pull of her belly. "You've got to listen to Ruth," she said while she fussed with the blanket then smoothed her son's curly locks. His nose wrinkled in protest, and she pressed it lightly with her fingertip. "Go to sleep, precious."

Grace curled her arm beneath her head and reclined, feeling the baby inside her begin to dance a jig in protest. At least the pains had stopped. For that she could be grateful.

Silence fell in the little room, only the usual chatter of the forest to keep them company. By degrees Grace felt her eyes slide shut and her body become heavy. Even the babe settled. Just before sleep overtook her, Bennett tugged on her arm with a soft whisper of "Mama."

She blinked and shifted positions to see him better, then instantly wished she hadn't. In the long shadows, with only the flicker of the lamp to light him, Bennett bore so much resemblance to his late father that it made her want to cry.

"Mama," he repeated.

She gathered her memories into a tight ball and shoved them into the corner of her mind. Later, in the privacy of her room, she might take them out again. Better still, she might not.

"Yes, darling," she answered softly, hoping her son missed the catch in her voice. "What is it?"

"It's about Ruth."

Ah, the Delaney stubbornness again. She sighed. "Remember how we talked about her being in charge when I'm out at the landing or working in the garden?"

Bennett nodded, but his frown told her he remained unconvinced. "The ranger's sleepin' in the parlor, and if I'm gonna be a ranger someday, I gotta learn how to make do, too."

"Boys belong in their beds, darling," she whispered. "And I'm sure that if the ranger had a choice, he'd be sleeping in a soft bed like yours."

"Your mother's right. A man always picks a mattress over a bedroll if he gets the choice, ranger or not."

Grace nearly jumped out of her skin as she turned to look over her shoulder at the doorway and the man who filled it. She stifled a gasp and scrambled off the bed, covering her legs and her embarrassment as best she could. To her horror, she nearly stumbled before she caught hold of the bedpost and righted her ungainly body. A shaft of pain sliced across her abdomen and nearly buckled her knees.

"Mr. Harte, what in the world are you doing up?" she said, when she could manage words.

Bennett bolted upright, and his cry of glee caused little Mary to stir in her bed. Grace limped to her and smoothed the blankets beneath her daughter's tiny chin, hoping to send her back to dreamland without the drama an early wake always caused. Despite her best efforts, Mary shook off the blankets and frowned while Bennett began a barrage of questions directed to the ranger.

"Mama?" she asked in a sleepy voice. "Is the big man all better?"

"I'm just dandy," Ranger Harte said quickly.

Too quickly.

She looked over her shoulder to see the ranger sway, then catch hold of the door frame to remain upright. Intuition told Grace something was very wrong, something beside the fact the ranger shouldn't even be up and walking, much less all the way upstairs.

Proper folk didn't go exploring a house without an invitation. Ben had always said she had an active imagination, and she gave it free reign as she worked to settle the children as quickly as possible.

"You two hush now," she said. "Our guest ought to be plenty tired."

Mary began to complain, while Bennett put his stubborn look back on. The ranger leaned forward slightly, and the dim yellow glow of the lamp illuminated his features. Like Mary, he wore a frown. Unlike her, his looked to be etched with worry.

Imagination gave way to intuition. Something was definitely wrong. His uncombed hair and disheveled clothing gave him the look of a man up to no good, but his reputation as a ranger said otherwise. Even in the semidarkness, she could see the glint of amber in his one good eye and the promise of it in the other. It sent a shiver up her spine.

Lord, please protect the babies from whatever harm might come, she prayed, as she firmly slid the blankets over Mary's kicking legs. One look into her eyes and the child lay still. A glance at Bennett produced the same result.

"Mr. Harte, I suppose you'll be wanting some supper since you missed yours. Why don't I go and see what Theresa has left on the stove?"

He nodded. "That would be just fine, ma'am."

"I'm hungry too, Mama," Bennett said. "I didn't get to—"

"A ranger learns to make do, son," Mr. Harte said as his gaze met Grace's. He slowly cut his gaze to the right. "Your gut might be telling you to eat, but your instincts are telling you there might be somebody right behind you that you'd miss if you were set on having vittles."

"That happen to you much?" Bennett asked.

"Occasionally," he said as he looked first at Bennett and then to his right again.

Grace's gaze followed his, and she saw the shadows. Where there should have only been one, there were two. It seemed as though the second person stood even taller than Mr. Harte. Her sharp intake of breath did not go unnoticed by the ranger.

His lips curved into a smile that didn't quite reach the rest of his face. "If you hombres don't mind, I'm going to borrow your mother for a minute," he said, his voice laced with a deadly combination of calmness and coldness. "You just close your eyes and dream about breakfast, little man."

She opened her mouth to refuse, to tell him she would never leave her babies no matter how many men he'd brought with him. Before she could protest, a silent warning passed between them like a chill in the night. Almost imperceptibly, he shook his head. Slowly, he lifted his index finger to his lips in a request for her to remain silent.

"Father, forgive me," she thought she heard him whisper.

The second shadow moved, and Grace jumped in surprise. Split seconds later, the ranger slammed the door. The sound of men scuffling in the hall echoed through the room, and Bennett cried out in surprise.

"Climb into the bed with your sister and stay there," Grace ordered as she pressed her ear to the door in an attempt to hear something, anything, over the pounding of her heart. Out of the corner of her eye, she saw Bennett race for Mary's bed.

As the sounds of struggle continued on the other side of the door, Grace spied the rocker and made a grab for it, one hand still firmly on the doorknob. With the last of her strength, she pulled the heavy chair toward the door, while the babe in her womb kicked in protest.

Wedging the back of the rocker under the knob, she stood back to test her handiwork and a spasm of sheer agony knocked her to her knees. Like flames licking at her nerves, the pain sharpened and splintered, then came to rest in her abdomen. Something wet and warm spilled onto the hem of her gown, and she looked down to see a deep crimson stain had begun to form at her feet.

Outside, the men had fallen mysteriously silent. Behind her, Grace heard the rustle of bedcovers and the soft voices of her children.

"Mama?" Bennett whispered. "What's happening?"

Then came the ear-splintering shot.

Chapter 4

J ed looked down at the body slumped against the door and waited while his breath caught up with his mind. With his heart still thrumming a furious beat, he kicked the Colt—his own stolen revolver—away from the dead man's hand.

"Thou shalt not kill," he said under his breath as the gun slid across the slick wooden floor and landed with a crash against the opposite wall.

His arm ached where the bandages wrapped his wounds, and in the semidarkness of the hallway, he could see a tinge of pink had begun to stain the fabric. At least he still had a cool head and a clear mind.

Clear enough to see that, even with only one eye, he'd sent another one to the undertaker.

Disgusted, he turned away and knelt in the shadows, closing his good eye and covering the other with a trembling hand. "Heavenly Father, forgive me. I didn't mean to shoot him. It was. . ."

He paused, the truth too horrible to repeat. But the Lord knew him inside out. He knew what lay in his heart. Jed Harte might have been washed in the blood of Jesus and bathed in the cold waters of a creek-side baptism, but inside he was still the same Texas Ranger who'd learned with pride a thousand and one ways to deliver a man to death's door.

"It was instinct," Jed finished, knowing the full depth of his sin was that he hadn't changed one bit from the man he used to be. "I shot him because that's what I do. I kill people."

In the silence of the hallway, with the smell of death bearing down hard on him, Jed Harte knew he would forever be Heartless Harte, the ranger who let no man live who'd crossed him. He was a sorry sinner and not worth spit.

Never would he be worthy of the grace the Lord had bestowed upon him. Never would he earn the forgiveness He so generously had offered on the banks of that creek such a short time ago.

"For by grace are ye saved through faith; and that not of yourselves: it is the gift of God: Not of works, lest any man should boast."

With a cry of anguish, Jed pushed the familiar verse from his mind. He'd contemplated the meaning of it once too often on the ride from San Antonio and had come up with nothing more than a headache.

How could the Lord send His Son to die for a man who made killing his business? How could He forgive a man who seemed to keep on running back to the old ways like a baby to his mother?

"Mr. Ranger," a child's voice called from the other side of the closed door. "My mama needs help."

Scrambling to his feet, Jed pushed the dead man out of the way and yanked on the knob. It refused to turn. Focusing his good eye on it, he tried again.

Still stuck tight—not a good sign.

Jed swallowed the bile climbing in his throat and assumed the amiable tone he'd perfected on the job. The last thing he needed was to be on the wrong side of a door with a scared kid on the other.

"What's wrong with your mama, little man?"

No answer.

Jed struggled to remember what Ben's wife had called the lad. "Bennett, is that your name?"

"Yes, sir," the wavering voice responded.

"Well, that's a fine name." Again he tried the knob and found it locked tight. "So Bennett, do you suppose you could come on over and open this door?"

"No, sir," the boy answered.

Sending a prayer for patience skyward, he eased his good shoulder into the door and pressed, hoping the door would budge. It didn't.

Perfect. He scowled at the dead man, the busted knob, and finally at the weak shoulder, which kept him from knocking the door down.

"Bennett?"

"Yes, sir?"

The panic in the boy's voice slid under the door and lodged in Jed's heart. Irritation took a turn toward uneasiness. "If you want me to help your mama, you're going to have to open the door."

He waited, hoping the kid would cooperate. Once again, nothing happened. A thousand anxious thoughts converged and separated in his mind. Shaking his head to clear the noise, he tried again.

"Little man, open the door."

"I can't," he finally said. "I tried and I can't reach it."

Jed leaned against the door and listened to the scampering of feet across the carpets. Obviously the boy was busy doing something. "Yes, you can."

"Nope," slid through the door on a loud whine.

The situation threatened to slip out of control. Just as he'd done countless times before, Jed met the situation head on and demanded results. "Open this door now before I shoot it open. Do you hear me, kid?"

Bennett Delaney's wail echoed across the hallway. So much for taking control of the situation.

"Your mother," Jed called when the boy had settled some, "where is she?"

"By the door. Mr. Ranger, you have to help my mama," he said as he dissolved once more into tears. Moments later, a second set of cries joined the chorus, most likely the little girl's.

Now neither of them could hear him, nor would they do anything to help him get the door opened. Frustrated beyond description, Jed sent a prayer to his Maker.

Lord, this isn't working out like I planned, so do You think You could step in and give me a little help with these young'uns?

When no answer seemed forthcoming, Jed returned to his investigative training for a solution. Kneeling once more, he leaned over until his ear touched the floor and peered into the space between the floor and the bottom of the door.

Through the opening he could barely make out the shape of a woman's foot partially covered by the same sort of white linen as his shoulder. By shifting positions, he could see more of her. She lay on her side with an arm beneath her head as if she'd fallen asleep or possibly been knocked to the floor.

Then he saw the blood.

"Mama!" came the plaintive cry from the other side of the door.

"She hurt," the little one added.

"Hang on to your sister, little man," he shouted over the din. "I'm going to save your mama."

He stood and brushed off the sense of foreboding along with the lint decorating his shirt. "Once a ranger, always a ranger," he said as he stepped over the corpse to fetch the Colt from the corner of the hallway.

Retrieving the matching gun from the belt of the criminal, Jed took a second to get his bearings. The mantle of ranger settled easily on his shoulders, although the prick of his conscience was something he'd have to settle later.

The throb in his shoulder had long since ceased to matter, and the meaningless hum in his brain had refined and shaped itself into a command. He was a Texas Ranger, always had been and always would be. Maybe there was a way he could please God and the great state of Texas at the same time.

Right now, he had to worry about Ben's wife. Later, the Lord willing, he would take the rest of his dilemma up with Him and see what He had to say about the matter.

Taking the steps two at a time, he hung on to the stair rail for dear life. At the bottom of the staircase, blackness met him and brought him to a quick halt.

"Lord, I can't do this in the dark," he said as he felt his way around the carved newel post and stumbled over something hard and immovable. His toe ached and he longed to say the scalding words that had once come tripping so easily off his tongue. "I'd be much obliged if You would shed a little light on this for me."

"Mr. Harte, that you?"

Jed blinked at the brilliant light accompanying the familiar voice. "Thank you, Jesus," he said under his breath. "Follow me," he commanded to the dark-skinned woman he'd come to know as Theresa.

With the light of a single candle, Jed managed to navigate a path through the fancy parlor, across the center hall, and out the front door. On the porch, a chill wind blew out the flame and sent Theresa scurrying for another.

"Forget the candle. Go upstairs and wait by the bedroom door," he shouted. "Mrs. Delaney will need you."

Theresa stopped short, one hand on the door and the other clutching the dark cloak at her throat. "What's wrong with my Grace?" she asked.

Jed stepped out into the yard and looked up at the window where the woman and children waited. He reached across to test the porch rail, pleased his work had lasted all these years.

"If the Lord wills it, there won't be anything wrong with her that can't be fixed," he said slowly. "But I reckon I'm gonna have to get to her first to find out for sure."

The door slammed shut on Theresa's cry. Bracing himself for the return of the pain and weakness that had dogged his days and turned his nights into a string of foggy memories, Jed climbed the steps to the porch and threw a leg over the rail. His shoulder complained a bit when he threw the other leg over and stood, but by the time he'd caught the edge of the roof and begun to pull himself up, the pain disappeared.

Somehow Jed climbed onto the second floor roof and slipped the window open enough to climb in. As he slid inside the bedroom where the children lay crying together in a small bed, he could only give thanks to the Lord he'd made it that far.

Jed whirled around to see Ben's wife in a heap on the floor beside a rocker. He deduced the woman must have wedged the chair under the knob to keep the door from opening, most likely thinking it would serve to protect her babies from the ruckus in the hall.

A small pool of blood had begun to darken the flowered carpet and her gown had soaked up much of it. With a harsh glance over his shoulder, Jed pressed a finger to his lips to silence the racket, and to his great surprise, it worked. He turned his attention back to their mother.

"Mommy sick?" an angelic voice asked.

Jed turned to see the wide eyes of the youngest Delaney staring at him from her brother's lap. All freckles and curls, the little girl seemed to be holding up better than her sibling.

"She'll be fine," he said to both of them, hoping the fear he felt hadn't seeped into his words.

It wasn't right, this situation. He'd only rejoined the Rangers a few minutes ago, and he'd already been forced to climb a building, let himself in through a window, and comfort a couple of scared kids.

Next thing you know he'd be delivering babies.

"Ranger Harte, you in there?" Theresa asked. She knocked on the other side of the door to punctuate the question.

Shaking away the absurd thoughts, Jed shoved the rocker out of the way and knelt beside the bleeding woman. Her eyelids fluttered open, and she stared at a point past him. The stare of a dead woman, he thought with a shudder.

He'd seen it before.

"Open the door, Theresa," Jed said, easily lifting Ben's wife into his arms. Stepping back, he waited for the door to swing inward.

While the woman outside fumbled with the knob, Jed let his gaze wander to the beauty in his arms. Under other circumstances, if he'd seen her walking down the street in San Antonio or sitting in the pew across the aisle at church, he would have given her a second, more discreet look. Now he just stared.

Her hair cascaded over his shoulder and lay in a dark, shimmering curtain against the worn flannel of his winter shirt. The eyes that had peered back at him before were now shut, and the color he remembered from her face had drained away.

A knot wrenched in his gut when her lips parted and released a soft complaint. Jed shifted her to lean against him, sliding her head to rest on his shoulder. The door swung open with a protest from hinges in need of a good oiling. Theresa stifled a gasp as her gaze traveled from the woman to the carpet, then back again.

"Ruth, come quick."

The girl slid past the older woman into the circle of candlelight. Thinking on her feet, she pasted on a smile and strode across the room to gather the frightened children into her arms. "We're gonna finish that story now," Ruth said with a cheery brightness.

Theresa turned her attention back to Jed. "You aim to help or just stand there gawkin', Ranger?"

He peered down at the feisty female through his good eye. "I thought I was helping, ma'am."

"Not unless you know how to deliver a baby," she said, worry etched along the lines in her face.

In his time, he'd delivered his share of calves, foals, and even a set of piglets once during a lightning storm, but babies were out of his realm of experience. "I believe I'll leave that up to the womenfolk, if you don't mind."

"Then git her downstairs and don't you be hurtin' her, you hear?" she declared.

For the first time in his adult life, Captain Jedadiah Harte willingly took orders from a woman.

Chapter 5

Ben's wife felt as light as a feather and delicate as the good china at the capitol building as he carried her down the hall toward the stairs, Theresa a half step behind him.

"Watch your big feet goin' down them steep stairs. She ain't no sack of corn."

"You just keep the light where I can see, and I promise I won't drop her," he said with a glibness he didn't feel.

Her husband ought to be told about whatever was going on here. If he knew his old buddy Ben, he most likely wouldn't stray farther than a day's ride. Two at the most.

One thing about Ben Delaney. He'd never liked leaving his wife for long, even for the Rangers. Jed hadn't understood it then. He envied it now. Given the fact he'd spent the better part of a week under the man's roof, he ought to be seeing him directly.

"You expecting Ben any time soon?" he asked as he turned the corner and sidestepped an especially ugly chair.

"I don't 'spect you heard 'bout Mr. Ben." She stepped ahead of him through the open door and readied the bed. Arms folded, she turned to face him with a softer look. "We ain't expectin' Mr. Ben at all, Ranger." She looked away. "Lightnin' kilt him nigh on two month ago. He layin' under the pecan tree at the corner of the property."

The weight in Jed's arms began to slip, and he realized he still held Ben's wife. Ben's widow, he corrected, as he adjusted her in his arms.

"Jest set her nice and easy on those pillows. I don't reckon you can hurt her much more than she's already done been hurt, but see if you can be gentle."

Jed complied and watched helplessly as Theresa handed him a length of toweling and indicated for him to use it to wipe the blood off himself. "Now git," Theresa said when he'd done the best he could with the toweling. "This ain't the place for menfolk."

Numb, he shuffled toward the door and mumbled something in agreement. The least he could do was to make himself useful by removing the vermin in the upstairs hallway. If he had to dig all night, he'd make sure Ben's place didn't carry the stench of evil come morning.

127

It was the least he could do.

"Ranger?" Theresa called softly.

He cast a glance over his shoulder. "Yes?"

"Thank you," she mumbled. Her voice strengthened, and even in the dimness of the candle's glow, he could see a tear fall. She wiped it away with the corner of her apron and straightened her shoulders. "You're the answer to a prayer. More'n one, actually."

Jed ducked his head and made a quick escape as the walls threatened to close in on him. He attempted a prayer of his own several times during the night's work—work he did with the help of Theresa's husband, a fellow by the name of Shaw—but mostly he busied his hands and tried to keep his mind as empty as possible. Once they had the dead man buried, Jed said a few words of prayer but kept his own thinking out of it.

At daybreak, the thoughts finally caught up with him. He walked with them swirling around him to the river, where he watched the Brazos until the first of the day laborers arrived along with Shaw to open the landing. Jed's shoulder pained him and his good eye scratched with the lack of sleep, but he could find no reason to rest.

Instead, he watched with interest as the first of the barrels were carried to the dock. Soon he joined the workers, handling small repairs and filling barrels—all he could manage with only one good shoulder. He continued laboring long past the time the others had stopped for water. At midday, Theresa found him and saw to his wound, fussing as she changed the bandage, then handed him his lunch.

"How is she?" he managed to ask, all the while pretending to concentrate on the chicken leg he held in his hand.

"Same," she answered as she pressed a cold cloth to his useless eye.

His nod met her gaze, and no more words were necessary. She walked away and left him with the food still held in his fist. Unable to muster an appetite for anything but work, he tossed the best fried chicken he'd ever smelled over his shoulder and went back into the warehouse.

Over the next few days the pattern continued. While Jed worked his worries into submission, Grace Delaney lay behind a closed door Jed dare not open.

For all he knew, his idiotic plan to get rid of the intruder by luring him upstairs into what he thought were empty rooms had put Ben's wife in that bed. Womenfolk were delicate and confusing creatures, and what went on in that hall probably caused her troubles.

Just another cause to believe he should do something to make up for his sins. To his mind, working his way out of the trouble at hand was the only thing he could do for her, so he spent all the time he could making himself as useful as a one-eyed man with a bad arm could.

The man called Shaw now ran things at the landing, although few along the river realized this. Most thought Jed had assumed the job, and the traffic began to increase. Men who refused to deal with a woman now returned, perfectly happy to do business with a man, especially one who happened to be a Texas Ranger.

In the back of his mind, as Jed hauled what goods he could and worked the small garden behind the house, he held out the possibility of making things right with the Lord and returning to the work he felt that God had called him to do. Someday he'd take care of himself, but for now he could only do this for Ben.

He spent Sunday morning in the ugly chair by the stairs reading the Bible and contemplating those scriptures that didn't affect him personally. The others he skipped over, promising the Lord he would return to think on them soon.

Returning to the passages proved to be more difficult than he thought. Before the noon meal could be placed on the table, Theresa left to see to the missus, then returned to Jed and sent the family out of the house with a warning not to return until Ruth came for them.

Giving thanks to the Lord for the unusual warmth of the day, Jed led the children to the garden plot and set them to the task of pulling weeds. As he knelt beside the boy who bore his father's stubborn expression and his mother's good looks, Jed felt the urge to pray.

Not just the simple words he'd said over the past few days, phrases he'd once knew meant something but now doubted. While his fingers worked the loose, dark soil, his mind turned over the ideas he'd once believed in so strongly.

The Lord. The Bible. His call to ministry. His duty to the Texas Rangers. Each was given much consideration. Finally, he formed the words to speak to God about them.

Lord, I'm coming to You a broken man. I had You written all over my heart, but then I went and killed a man. I took his life into my hands and I shot him dead. Even if he did mean to hurt Ben's wife and those babies, he was one of Your children and I ought not to have passed judgment on him. That's Your job, not mine and I was wrong.

"Somethin' wrong, Mr. Ranger?" the boy beside him asked.

"Wrong, little man?" He cut his glance to the side. "Naw."

"All right, then." The kid nodded and moved farther down the row to continue pulling weeds while his sister busied herself stacking twigs and leaves into some sort of creation.

Jedadiah Harte, you are one of My children, too, came the soft answer without warning. *It is not up to you to pass judgment on yourself.*

"But Lord, I. . ." The children both looked up in surprise and he shook his head. "Don't pay any attention to me."

Mary, the angel in muddy red curls, toddled toward him and settled against his side. "I talk to God, too." Smiling, she messed up his precise lines with a chubby hand.

"You do?" he asked as he tried to repair the damage.

She nodded. "Sometimes He talks back." Walking away, she took an oak leaf and buried it under a rock at the edge of the plot.

"Yeah, He does, doesn't He?" Jed asked under his breath.

"Mama says I'm 'sposed to listen when He tells me somethin'," the boy commented as he tossed something over his shoulder that looked more like a vegetable plant than a weed.

"Do you?" he asked.

To his surprise, Bennett Delaney, Jr., smiled. "I try," he said slowly. "But Mama says I'm stubborn like my daddy."

"Mine used to tell me the same thing," Jed said, remembering the words of loving chastisement that would trail him until his dying day. "You need to be more like your heavenly Father and less like your earthly one," his mother had said. Always, he'd pretended he hadn't heard her. Never would he forget, though.

With those words in mind, he bowed his head and squeezed his good eye shut. *Father, let me be more like You. Change my contrary nature and fix my heart so I can be the man You intend.*

"You gonna stay with us, Ranger?" the boy asked, interrupting his prayers.

"I don't rightly know," was the only answer he had, and it surprised him. Until that moment, staying had been the last thing on his mind. He'd come to Delaney's Landing on his way to go to work for the Lord. After he'd broken his promise to the Lord and turned his gun on a man, he'd pretty much decided he'd go back to San Antonio as soon as he was able and take back his captain's job. Suddenly a third option loomed large. He could stay.

Lord, I need to know what You want me to do, so I'm going to need a sign. Tell me who needs me more, You or these kind folks.

Jed ducked his head and rubbed at his good eye. When his vision cleared, he saw Ruth running toward them across the field.

"Come quick, Ranger. Miz Grace be a needin' you bad."

Jed raced back to the house, unable to believe the Lord would make his path clear so soon. He burst through the door and down the hall, slowing only when he arrived at the closed bedroom door.

"Lord, make me ready for this," he said under his breath as he resolutely pushed on the solid wood door.

Theresa stood beside the bed, hunched over a figure he hardly recognized as Grace Delaney. "He's here, honey," she murmured as she adjusted the wrinkled blankets and smoothed the woman's hair away from her face. "I'll be close by if you need me," she said softly.

Like a man walking to the gallows, Jed approached the bed. He stood near enough to touch her, near enough to watch her breath catch and her eyes close. Despite the chill in the room, beads of perspiration dotted her forehead and turned her hair slick and shiny.

She opened her mouth, possibly to speak, but instead began to make faint sounds, little whimpers like a child. Eventually her eyes opened. She fixed her gaze on him, making him feel like he'd just trespassed on a private moment.

"Ruth said you were in need of me," he said, painfully aware of just how inadequate those words were.

This time she managed a complete nod. "Yes," she whispered. "My children. Send word to my father."

"Your father?" Jed shook his head. "About what?"

Grace shifted onto one elbow and made a swipe at the table beside the bed, knocking a paper to the floor. Jed bent to retrieve it. In a shaky hand, someone had written a name, The Honorable Thomas Edwin Beaudry, and a New Orleans address.

Jed offered the paper to her, but she waved it away. "You want me to see that this gets to your father?"

She reached for his hand and caught his wrist. He stared at the pale fingers encircling his arm, then slowly shifted his vision to her eyes. Feral, that's what she looked like. Once on the trail Jed had run across a mama bobcat in the middle of birthing a brand-new litter. She'd worn the same look.

"If I die, you see to these children, Ranger." Panic seemed to lie just beneath the words. "Don't let my babies be orphans."

Pure terror struck deep in his soul. His heart clutched at what he knew he had to do. He was a ranger, first and foremost, and a missionary of God to boot. He still hadn't worked out how he would hold onto both these jobs, much less add another to it.

"Ma'am, I can't—"

"You must. And if my father or brother refuse to come, you have to raise them. Theresa and Shaw will help. Ruth, too." The grip tightened. "Before God, you have to swear it."

Chapter 6

Jed closed his eyes, terror swimming like ice water in his veins. *Father, I can't even figure out what I'm supposed to do with myself, much less with a mess of strangers.*

Instead of a clear answer, Jed heard the laughter of children in the distance and felt a deep peace descend, only to leave a moment later. He opened his eyes. Grace Delaney looked back expectantly.

"I'll stay," he said, unable to believe he'd voiced the words.

"Thank you," she whispered. For a moment, she lay back on the pillow as if all her worries had left her.

Something poured from those eyes besides the tears shimmering there, and whatever it was, Jed felt the impact right down to his boots. It seemed as if this woman had curled up behind his heart and settled there when he hadn't been looking. A crazy thought, considering the only thing he knew about her was she'd been a mighty fine cook in her younger days.

He felt the need to say something, anything, to shift the focus from him, possibly to keep her from thinking he meant what he'd said. "But you're going to be just fine, so there's no need to worry about those babies of yours. Come spring, this one here's going to be running around, and you'll have three underfoot."

"I can tell…" Her words trailed off as a wave of what must have been pain washed over her, tightening her features into a nearly unrecognizable mask that seemed to remain in place an eternity before it slowly ebbed away. "You haven't been around many babies," she finished.

"No, I haven't," he said, instantly grateful for the change in conversation. "See, I was the youngest of a mess of boys, and my mama said if I'd been first, I'd have been an only child." Grace almost managed a smile, so he continued. "We were a lively group, and I'm sure we sorely tried my mother's patience."

"Your mother," she whispered through parched lips. "Is still alive?"

He shook his head. "The fever took her back in forty-one."

"Mine, too." A gut-wrenching scream tore any further conversation from her mouth.

Theresa came running, and he fully expected to be sent from the room immediately. Dashing his hopes, the woman ordered him to a place near the head of the bed.

"Grab her by the shoulders and shove hard when I say the word. This baby's got to come or else we're gonna lose her."

In his lifetime Jed had seen many a man suffer. Never had he seen anyone in such a shape as this woman. Never did he intend to see it again, not even through one eye.

"The children," she managed. "You promised."

He slid into place behind her and rested his hands on shoulders too thin and delicate to bear the weight of her present troubles. The position pained his own shoulder a bit and made his wound ache, but he knew it was nothing compared to what the woman bore.

From deep within his soul came the urgent call to pray, which he answered with a desperate plea for help. After a moment, Theresa leveled a hard stare at Jed, interrupting his prayers.

"What did you promise about those babies?"

Grace's cry of agony prevented his answer. What came next robbed him of the power to do anything but breathe, and he almost forgot to do that. From beneath the heavy quilt emerged something wet and bloody. It looked to be about the size of a fair to middling puppy, but without the hair and tail.

It was still and colored a pale blue.

Theresa swirled a length of toweling around it and thrust it toward Jed, her face without expression. Grace's eyes slid shut, and her body relaxed as if all the life had gone out of her. Easing damp shoulders onto the mattress, Jed accepted the bundle and followed Theresa's silent direction to take it and leave the room. On his way out, he slipped the letter in his pocket.

He met Shaw on the porch. "Ruth fetched the children down to pick pecans," the older man mumbled.

Jed nodded and shifted the bundle to rest against his chest. Instinctively, he wrapped the jacket he realized he'd never taken off around the lump of toweling.

With his free hand, he fished out the letter and handed it to Shaw. The elder man's dark gaze scanned the writing, then looked up to lock with his. A wave of recognition passed between them.

Shaw looked away to study the porch rail. "I believe I'll saddle up and ride to town," he said as he placed the letter gingerly in his coat pocket. "Ain't no boats today, and the hands can manage what might come. Lord willin' I'll be back by breakfast."

"That's a fine idea," Jed answered. "Did you say Ruth had the children down by the pecan tree?"

Their eyes met, and understanding dawned on the gentleman's wrinkled face. He allowed his gaze to fall to the bundle in Jed's arms.

"I believe I'll have her fetch them back to the house. They can busy theyselves upstairs here jest as well as they can play at pickin' pecans."

Jed passed by the elder man, studying first the ground and then the horizon as he went. It looked to be a few hours before sunset, plenty of time to lay this soul to rest while there was still light left in the day.

Pulling his coat a little closer against his chest, Jed set off. From his wanderings, he knew where to go with the child, and from his dealings with the inquisitive Bennett and Mary, he knew to be careful to stay out of sight lest they be nearby.

The wind blew across him then abruptly shifted and stalled just as he entered the clearing where the pecan tree stood. Warmth flooded his bones and made his weary heart want to lay down his burdens right where he'd stopped. Instead, he clutched the bundle of blankets tighter to his chest and hit his knees like a preacher late for church.

"Lord, I aim to give this little one over to Your care." The prayer seemed lacking in something, and frustration brought tears to his eyes. Or maybe it was the body in his arms. He cleared his throat and tried again. "You took him before he even got started, but if You could, give him a warm bed and a full belly tonight in heaven because he's a scrawny little thing."

Carefully, he unwrapped the bundle a bit to show the Lord. Shock rendered him speechless when he saw two dark blue eyes looking back at him from a tiny face just as pink as the evening sky.

The war whoop he'd perfected riding with Jack Hays's First Texas Division during the Mexican campaign back in forty-six echoed across the trees and seemed to shake the very ground on which he knelt. The babe he held in the crook of his arm began to cry, and so did he as he raced toward the house and the woman busying herself at the stove near the window.

"You hush yourself. Can't you see Miz Grace is trying to—" Theresa flung the back door open and froze when she heard the baby's cries. "Oh praise the Lord! Ranger, you done saved us again."

"I didn't do anything," he said, though he knew she took no heed of his words as she collected the child and ran to reunite him with his mother.

Bone tired and weary beyond description, Jed sank into the rocker beside the fire and let the warmth seep into his soul. A floor above him, the children played, while down the hall, women wept aloud.

But there in the kitchen, Jed sat alone with his thoughts. He'd promised the state of Texas to be a ranger, the Lord to be a mouthpiece of the gospel, and Grace Delaney to be the keeper of her children until her father came to claim them. Only a miracle would allow him to do all three.

And if anyone could be counted worthy of a miracle, it sure wasn't him.

—⁂—

It was a miracle, pure and simple. Through the agony of childbirth, her baby boy had been taken away, and through the grace of God and the work of a single Texas Ranger, he had been returned.

Grace blinked back the tears to focus on the man who'd brought her son back. Every evening for more days than she could count, he had come to her room bearing his leather Bible, just as he carried it now.

At first, he merely sat quietly in the corner, dragging her favorite Empire chair from the parlor to sit quietly and read. Theresa said he'd maintained the habit of guarding her door during the dark days following Adam's birth, a birth she had little more than a dim memory of.

As she improved, he continued to visit, always bringing the Bible and the Empire chair. Nearly two months later, they still held evening visits, only now they spent the time talking across the kitchen table. The one topic they never seemed to cover was how long Jed would continue to visit her table or how long he would carry on the charade of running the landing.

Soon the new year would dawn, and on its heels would come the spring. Grace smiled and gave thanks for living in Texas, a place where the icy winds of winter merely teased but did not linger. If only she could be certain the ranger would be there to share in the joy of it. He'd become a part of the family in the months since his arrival, and even the baby sometimes quieted to the ranger's touch when Grace's did not satisfy.

She pictured the dark-haired ranger with the children and smiled. For such a big man, he certainly had a way with her babies. He'd begun to teach Bennett tales from the Bible, and Mary, ever the tagalong, had insisted he teach her as well.

Indeed, they'd all become quite attached to Captain Harte. He would never replace her precious Ben—nothing ever would—but he had somehow managed to carve a tiny spot in her heart and a huge place in her life.

This evening, as Jed settled across the table from her, she noticed a paper half hidden in the pages of the Bible. It looked to be a letter, although only closer inspection could say for sure. If Jed noticed her interest, he gave no indication.

Resolving to put curiosity out of her mind, Grace threaded a needle and picked up one of Mary's gowns from the mending basket. Now, if she could just keep her attention on her task and off the ranger. She cast a quick glance beneath her lashes.

Tall and arguably easy on the eye, Jed Harte made a figure to be reckoned with, despite the lopsided grin on his face. Lately, although she took great pains not to let it show, that lopsided grin had begun to set off butterflies in her stomach.

As he'd done so many times, Jed began to thumb through the pages. "Grace, I've been giving a lot of thought to something, and I'd be obliged if I could ask your opinion on it."

She nodded and continued with her mending.

"I'm wrestling with something I can't get a rope around. That ever happen to you?" He removed the paper—definitely a letter—and let the Bible fall open.

"Of course," she answered, looking away with a start when he caught her staring.

"Well, this is new territory for me. I reckon it all started back when the Lord caught up with me." He reached for the knife and cut off a large slice of fresh pecan pie. "I figured my ranger days were behind me." Pausing to eat a bite, he gave her an expectant look.

"Why?" was all she could think to ask.

"Because when I took the Lord into my life, He washed me clean." Jed cut a slash through the air with his fork. "No more killing; just preaching."

Grace paused and rested the needle in the cloth. "But now?"

"But now I've gone and made other promises." He paused to chew another bite of pie. "And I've killed."

She winced at the reference. "You shot a man to protect us, Jed."

They'd never spoken of what happened that night, and Grace sensed now was still not the time. She searched her mind for another topic to discuss.

"Did I ever tell you that the day I found you I had just asked God to bring me a ranger to help?"

To her surprise, Jed closed the book and pushed away from the table. With his big feet thundering across the floor like a herd of elephants, he stormed out the back door and into the night, leaving the Bible and his plate of barely eaten pie on the table.

Grace dropped her mending into the basket and picked up the Bible. The temptation to open the book and read the letter tugged at her, but she refused to give in. On a whim, she grabbed the plate and set off to find the ranger.

He'd taken to sleeping in one of the empty shacks behind the house, or at least that's what she'd overheard Uncle Shaw telling Theresa. As soon as she rounded the corner past the summer kitchen, she saw the light shining in a derelict dwelling some distance away.

Bypassing the cozy cottage Theresa and Shaw called home, Grace headed toward the dim light, holding the plate of food on top of the Bible. Before she could knock, the door flew open and the ranger appeared, gun drawn. The Bible, the plate, and the pie clattered to the ground, and she whirled backward, landing in a very unladylike heap on the soft ground.

"What are you doing here?" Jed stuffed the gun into his belt and lifted her easily to her feet, retrieving the Bible as well.

A chill danced across Grace's spine that could be only partly blamed on the temperature. "Well, I, um—" she began.

"I could have killed you, Grace," he said on a rush of breath smelling faintly of sugar and pecans.

"Oh, I hardly think so." She attempted a smile. "Besides, you didn't even have time to aim."

In an instant, the chill went out of the air. Suddenly there were only two people in the world, and one of them could have melted into a puddle at any moment. The other, the ranger, looked rightly aggrieved.

"I don't miss," he said evenly.

"Oh," she said, which came out sounding more like a squeak than a word.

For a moment, time stopped while the night sounds swirled around them. Her mind raced to put words to the conflicting thoughts, only to realize they could all be summed up in a single prayer. *Lord, what am I doing here?*

Abruptly, he released her. "I appreciate the pie," he said. Without so much as word of good night, he disappeared inside the cabin and promptly extinguished the light.

"I appreciate the pie," she grumbled under her breath. "I don't miss," she added in a voice several octaves lower than her own. "Well, neither do I," she said as she tossed the remains of the dessert, plate and all, into the pig trough and stormed inside the main house.

The next morning she still fumed about it, although her anger had been tempered by the fact she'd very nearly had some quite unacceptable thoughts about the testy ranger. Well, tonight when he came to sit and discuss the Bible with her, she'd be ready.

"Let's just see what Ranger Captain Jedadiah Harte has to say about the Golden Rule," she whispered as she placed a sleepy Adam in the rush basket where he slept.

Through the kitchen window, she noticed the ranger working in the garden, and she longed to be recovered enough to do the same. "I may still be mending, but I don't have to do it all indoors," she said to Adam.

She fetched her sewing and took it outside along with the baby and his sleeping basket. Settling into the rocker, she ignored the ranger and resumed her sewing until the sound of a horse and rider coming up the road drew her attention. She watched as the dark-clothed rider dismounted near Jed, and the two men began to speak in earnest before turning to walk toward the house. Putting aside her needle and thread, she cast a quick glance at the basket where her angel continued to sleep soundly, then straightened her skirts and went to meet them.

"Grace, this is Reverend Spivey." Jed paused to smile at the stranger. "The man who led me to the Lord."

Jed's gaze locked with hers, and Grace felt the collision straight down to her toes. Despite her anger over his unexplainably rude behavior last night, the familiar butterflies threatened to return.

"Reverend, this here is Grace Delaney," Jed continued.

The slight, well-dressed gentleman stared at her with the brightest blue eyes she'd ever seen. "Welcome to Delaney's Landing," she said.

"Thank you, young lady," he answered, removing his dusty hat to reveal a thick shock of gray hair. He turned his attention to Jed. "So this is the woman you wrote me about."

The woman you wrote me about. Grace swallowed her surprise and replaced it with a smile, while Jed's discomfort showed plainly on his face.

"I reckon," Jed said slowly, studiously avoiding her gaze.

"Captain Harte indicated you might be amenable to allowing me to intrude on your hospitality."

"Of course," she managed.

"I'll not be a bother, and I don't plan to stay but one night," he added as he turned to place a hand on Jed's sleeve. "I've got business in Galveston, and I must confess I had hoped you might make the ride with me, Captain. Especially in light of the fact the Rangers have offered to let you operate out of the office there while you preach."

Chapter 7

W ell, now," the ranger said, although his face spoke volumes more. Obviously he hadn't intended for her to know this, although he'd certainly been busy making plans. She gave him what she hoped would be an I-don't-care look. The lopsided smile she'd come to love emerged, and Grace felt what little breakfast she'd eaten threaten to rise at the sight of it.

"It would be my pleasure to have you here," she said quickly, hoping the numbness she felt couldn't be heard in her voice. "You're welcome to stay as long as Mr. Harte does."

Grace plastered on a bright smile and watched Jed's fade. If the ranger could consider leaving, then at least he would leave with no idea she would miss him terribly.

"If you'll excuse me, I'll just go have Theresa set another place."

She turned her back on the men and concentrated on walking slowly toward the house until a hand on her wrist tugged her backward. Whirling around, she came face-to-face with Jed Harte.

The lopsided smile had vanished completely. Hers disappeared as well. Even the satisfaction of having him think she wouldn't miss him had left, replaced by a yawning cavern of emptiness. Not since the dark days after Ben's death had she felt such a sense of dread.

"I'm sorry, Grace, I know you're surprised but—"

She held up her free hand to stop him. "Your friend seems like a nice man. I'm sure the two of you will do just fine in Galveston."

He nodded. "I reckon he is, and I'm sure we would but—"

A sharp tug released her hand, and she turned to take the first of five porch steps. "But he's going to be hungry after his ride," she tossed over her shoulder. "Why don't you show him where he can stable his horse?"

"I already did," he said. "Stop, Grace," he added, then picked her up by the waist and set her on her feet in front of him. "Stand still and listen, woman," he said roughly. "This is important."

Shading her eyes from the sun, Grace bit back on her anger and disappointment and said a quick prayer for the right words to come. "All right," she said slowly as she watched the preacher lead his horse toward the barn. "Speak your mind, Ranger."

He ducked his head and glanced toward the porch and the basket where Adam had begun to make little cooing sounds. Sunlight danced on the inky darkness of Jed's hair and turned some of the strands a deep golden color. The gold, she realized with a start, matched the amber of his eyes.

Slowly, he turned his gaze on her. A sane woman would have walked away. Grace stood stock-still and stared.

"I'm a man of my word, Grace Delaney," he said in a low voice. "I told you I'd take care of things around here until your family could show up to claim you, and I don't reckon that's something I'd walk away from."

As his meaning penetrated her heart, it threatened to soar. *Lord, please give me the words to answer him,* she again prayed.

"Say something," he said, his voice ragged and laced with what sounded like a thread of desperation. He caught her wrist once more. "Say anything."

Say good-bye to him, came the answer she hadn't wanted to hear. She took a deep breath and let it out slowly. With care, she pulled out of his grasp to take his hand in hers. "You were forced into that promise, and I'll not have you bound to it."

"Doesn't matter how I agreed to it." The lopsided smile returned. "Until I know you and the young'uns are taken care of, you're just going to have to get used to having me around."

Happiness bubbled to the surface and emerged in a broad grin. "Is that so?"

"Yes, ma'am, that's so." The ranger dipped his head as Adam's whimpering increased. "You'd better go fetch the little feller."

"Miz Grace," Theresa called from the kitchen. "We be havin' company for lunch?"

She cast a quick glance over her shoulder at the woman in the doorway. "Set one extra place at the table, please."

"Just one?" she asked. "Then what're you gonna do 'bout those other folks?"

Grace turned to question Theresa, then caught a glimpse of the riders coming toward the house. Her heart sank when she recognized the well-dressed gentlemen. It had been more than a decade since she'd seen them, but she would have known her father, Thomas Beaudry, Sr., and her brother, Tom, anywhere.

Before she could catch her breath, the two riders reached the clearing and the house. "Father," she whispered, "it's really you."

"Grace Mary-Celine Beaudry," Thomas, Sr., said in a rush of breath. His face paled, and for a moment he looked as if he might slip off his horse. "Your letter said. . ."

"You're a sight for sore eyes, Gracie," Tom said. "And seeing you for myself sure beats a letter."

Her gaze shifted from the stiff-backed silver-haired judge to her brother, seated casually in the saddle. From Tom's thick shock of dark curls to his stubborn jaw and soft brown eyes, he looked much as she remembered him at age fourteen. The difference came in the breadth of his shoulders and the length of his legs.

He'd already eclipsed her height before she left, but now, as he climbed out of the saddle, she could see he'd continued to grow until he'd passed the judge as well. The judge.

Grace swallowed her fear and stared directly into the eyes of her father. Still seated atop a bay mare, the look in those eyes seemed to match the feelings in Grace's heart. True to his nature, Judge Beaudry returned the stare without comment, leaving Grace to finally look away.

Never had she expected to see him alive. Obviously, he felt the same. Her mind raced as she watched him dismount and stand uncomfortably beside her brother. His eyes scanned the landscape as if he were looking for something.

She cast a glance over her shoulder to the little basket where Adam had been fussing only a few minutes ago. Thankfully, he seemed to have settled back to sleep. When her gaze returned to the men, she saw Tom studying her intently.

"I sure missed you, Gracie."

Knees weak, Grace tilted to look into her brother's eyes, and her whole world went with it. With a firm grip, the ranger she'd forgotten stood at her side righted her. He offered a weak smile, one she couldn't manage to return.

"Jedadiah Harte," he said, thrusting his hand toward her father. "Pleased to meet you."

The judge's eyes narrowed to slits as he slowly acknowledged the gesture. Tom's handshake bore a bit more enthusiasm, but the wariness he wore like armor could not be missed. "Tom Beaudry," he said, "and this is my father, Judge Beaudry."

Jed seemed to be doing a little sizing up of his own, and when he'd finished, he offered the Beaudry men a smile. To Grace, he offered a protective squeeze of her hand, which he quickly released.

"I believe you and I have met, Judge Beaudry," he said slowly. "Couple of years back I ran into a fellow named Collins. Bart Collins, I believe."

"Collins?" He shook his head. "Doesn't sound familiar."

Jed nodded. "I reckon you see all kinds in your line of work."

This time her father's eyes turned on Grace and rested there for a moment. "I suppose I do," he answered, focusing once more on Jed.

"This Collins fellow, he'd done some dirty work down toward New Orleans, and he was right reluctant to go back. Once I explained it a different way, old Collins up and changed his mind. I believe you tried his case."

The judge's wrinkled face softened slightly and a look of recognition began to grow. Numb, Grace smoothed her skirt and watched in awe as her father actually began to smile. What she wouldn't have given just once during her girlhood to have him smile at her that way.

At least she'd learned her heavenly Father had no such limits to His compassion. Reminded of Him, she quickly lifted the uncomfortable situation to the Lord in prayer.

"So you're Ranger Captain Heartless Harte," the judge said, admiration lacing his words. He cast a glance at Tom, who seemed as surprised as Grace at their father's reaction. "You know who he is, don't you, boy?"

Tom nodded. "Anybody who reads a paper knows about Heartless Harte."

Jed grimaced but said nothing. Finally the clang of the dinner bell broke the silence.

"Perhaps you two would like to wash up before we eat," Grace said unevenly.

The ranger led the men away while Grace raced to the porch to snag Adam and his basket and escape to the kitchen. Today the comforting smells of sweet potato pie, ham, biscuits, and a mess of fresh collard greens only made her stomach hurt. The baby must have sensed her nervousness because he began to cry.

"Sounds like someone wants his dinner," Theresa commented. "You go on and feed the little mite, and I'll see t' the gentlemens."

Grace nodded and lifted the baby out of his basket. "Where are Ruth and the children?" she asked as she bundled Adam in his blankets.

"Gone t' have a picnic." She gave Grace a sideways look. "Don't you 'member? You helped those angels pack the hamper last night."

She did remember, barely.

Adam's wails calmed as he began to look for his dinner. Scarcely had she carried the baby into the bedroom and begun to nurse him before the sound of heavy footsteps thundered through her parlor. Low, deep voices spoke in even tones, preventing Grace from hearing what they said.

Having so many men in the house at once discomfited her. Even when Ben had been rangering, she'd never had to play hostess to more than a couple of extra men.

Ben.

The thought of him surged like a knife through her stomach as she looked down on his peacefully nursing son. The son he would never know this side of heaven. Tears shimmered but did not fall.

Her memories of Ben, while they could never be forgotten, had begun to fade until they seemed to fit neatly into a corner of her heart. Now she could safely revisit them without feeling the blinding ache of his loss. Now she could see that she could go on living without Ben Delaney, and while life would never again be perfect, it could still be sweet.

Especially with her three precious babies.

And with the ranger, came the errant thought.

Grace gasped. Had she really come to think of Jed in that way? She shook her head. Of course not. He was her friend, her helper, and of course, a source of constant irritation and amusement. He would never replace Ben in her life or in her heart.

Never.

"Adam, your father would have loved you so much," she whispered. "You're not going to meet him in this life, but I intend to love you enough for both of us."

While the sounds of dishes clanking and men talking drifted under the closed door, Grace shifted the baby to burp him then settled him to finish his feeding. A short while later, he fell asleep, full and satisfied, and she placed him in the center of the feather bed with pillows on all sides to prevent him from falling.

One last look at her sleeping son and she fell to her knees to pray. "Father, I know I'm becoming a real pest, but the ranger says You don't mind if we talk to You a lot, so here I am again."

A lone tear gathered at the corner of her eye. She blinked hard, but it fell anyway. Laughter trailed the sound of scraping chairs and shook her already frazzled nerves. She swiped at her eyes with the back of her hand and swallowed her frustration.

"Lord, You know what's in my heart. I just don't know what to pray for anymore. I won't leave this place Ben and I built, and I can't give my babies to my father to raise like he raised me and Tom. I don't want Jed to leave because I will miss him something awful. I don't know what to tell You to do." She took a deep breath and let it out slowly. "Father, You are a mighty God, and You can work all of this for good. I turn over my family and the ranger and this whole mess to You and ask it in Jesus' name. Amen."

A calm descended, lifting Grace to her feet. With a newfound confidence, she opened the door and headed for the kitchen, ready to take on all three men in her life. Unfortunately, she found the kitchen empty, although just outside the door she could hear the laughter of children and the soft, deep voice of her father.

She crept closer to the window and watched in utter amazement as the stern man she knew lifted little Mary to his shoulders and carried her around the porch at a slow gallop. Bennett played the bottom of a copper pot like a drum and sang along with words that made no sense. Ruth stood in the distance holding the picnic hamper and smiling while she spoke in soft tones with Tom.

Things that had once seemed so confusing now seemed crystal clear. She knew exactly what she had to do.

—⁓—

He knew exactly what he had to do. After speaking to the preacher and the judge, and rereading the letter from San Antonio he'd been holding for the past month, Jed's path seemed crystal clear. He slipped the paper back into his saddlebag and placed his Bible on top of it.

The judge, he decided, was a decent sort, even if he had committed the error of cutting a perfectly wonderful lady out of his life for following her mind and not his. He and his son would take good care of Grace and her children, of that he'd assured Jed. Tom, the brother, seemed a bit more enthusiastic about staying at the landing until it could be sold, but the judge had given his word the Delaney family would receive his finest care and hospitality in New Orleans.

And if you couldn't trust a judge, whom could you trust?

With Grace Delaney safe in the arms of her family, Jed was released from his promise and free to move on. Surely the Reverend Spivey's visit had been a sign that the Lord meant for him to be on his way.

After all, he had a long way to go before he felt like he could stand before the Lord and answer for his sins.

Jed cinched the saddlebag and made one last trip to his cabin. His gift to Grace sat just inside the door, and he gave it one last long look. Unhappy with what he saw, he knelt beside the bed he'd made for Adam to make absolutely sure the rails looked straight and the finish was smooth.

The cradle had been made of the finest rosewood scraps he'd seen this side of the Mississippi. Shaw had laughed when he told him how the table had been broken, and Jed had hated that he had been the one whose clumsiness had reduced the once beautiful masterpiece into something less than furniture.

He'd planned for a month how he would take those scraps and build a proper bed for little Adam, and it had taken him the better part of another month to actually build it.

The boy needed a bed in the worst way, so all the time he spent was well worth it. It irked Jed when Grace carried the boy around in a basket that made him look like Moses hiding in the rushes. A boy deserved a proper bed.

He also deserved a man around to teach him how to grow up right. All three of those children did.

Saying good-bye to Bennett and Mary this morning had broken his heart. He'd already decided he'd have to find the time to help with the planting come spring, but another visit before then just might be in order.

After all, the Rangers had put him in charge in Galveston, and he could run the office as he saw fit. He'd just have to look up a few of his more trusted men and hire them on to help. That would free him up for more time to do his preaching and his visiting.

He began to tally a list of potential candidates as he used the back of his sleeve to polish the post to a soft luster. Two or three good men came to mind right off, and he made a note to write to them as soon as he got settled in Galveston.

This decided, he stepped back to give the finished product a critical examination, then frowned when he noticed the side rail on the left looked a bit uneven. Perhaps he should put off his trip to Galveston until tomorrow to give him time to fix it. He could write his letters tonight and send them the first chance he got.

"It would also give you another night to sit and eat pie and pretend you're not all starry-eyed and foolish over the boy's mother, too," he said under his breath, as he spied his hat on the cot and made a grab for it.

"Captain Harte," the reverend called. "Are you ready?"

No, he longed to say. *I'll never be ready.*

"I'm ready," he answered, wiping a speck of dust off the carved headboard with the tail of his shirt. "Just came back for my hat."

Chapter 8

Grace stood on the porch and looked to the east, shielding her eyes from the harsh glare of the morning sun. As the ranger rode slowly toward her, she couldn't help but be reminded of the first time he'd approached her on horseback. She lifted her gaze skyward and gave thanks to the Lord who'd seen fit to bring him back from death. She stepped forward to meet him, stopping at the edge of the clearing.

"I reckon I'll be leaving," he said.

"I thought that's what you were up to." She shook her head. "You take care now and don't forget us country folk once you get to the big city."

"I'll never forget you, Grace," he said slowly, his voice as rough as pine bark and his face half hidden beneath the brim of his hat. "Would you mind if I come back for pie and a visit with the young'uns once in a while? At least until you pack up and move to New Orleans."

She smiled and hoped her sadness didn't show. "I'd like that a lot, and so would the children." A gust of north wind tossed her shawl and made her shiver. "But I don't intend to leave Texas. This is my home, and you're welcome here whenever the trail leads you to it, Ranger."

Jed nodded then looked away, trouble etched among the fine lines on his face. "I wish you'd just call me Jed," he said. "Ranger is what I do, not who I am." He extended a hand and caught her fingers with his. "I aim to be a lot of things besides just a ranger, Grace."

The warmth of his fingers surprised her, and so did the softness in his face when she stared up at him. "What do you aim to be, Jed?"

"I'll do whatever it takes to earn what the Lord has given me," he said with a shrug.

"We receive salvation as a gift." She paused. "It's something we can never deserve." She took his flinch to mean she'd reached a nerve. " 'For by grace are ye saved through faith; and that not of yourselves: it is the gift of God,' " she continued, the words seared on her heart and their meaning forever impressed on her mind after a night spent in seclusion pouring over God's Word.

Jed allowed his fingers to slip away from hers and wrapped them around the rein. "Have you spoken to your brother or the judge?"

She shook her head, as much to answer his question as to catch up with his abrupt change in conversation. She'd hidden herself away from her family, claiming ill health, but truthfully, she'd needed the time to face them properly. There were things she needed to discuss with her heavenly Father before she took them up with her earthly one.

"I'll do that this morning," she said slowly.

Her answer seemed to satisfy him. He nodded and pressed back the brim of his hat to reveal the bright amber of his eyes and the inky darkness of his hair. She focused on these, the little things about Jed Harte, rather than to see the whole man, the man she would miss desperately. Although the Lord seemed to give her plenty of guidance on how to handle her father and brother, He had been virtually silent on the subject of Ranger Captain Harte. Every time she asked Him to lead her, He sent her to the Bible and the verse she'd just repeated to Jed.

It had been most frustrating.

"Would you mind if we prayed before I go?" Jed asked, gently leading her attention back to him.

"Of course," she whispered, as she watched him swing a leg over his saddle and land on the hard-packed earth in a single smooth motion.

As the horse protested with a whinny, Jed led the mare to the rail and tied the reins. Grace memorized it all, the length of his arm, the quickness of his hands, and finally, the look on his face when he turned to take both her hands in his. She drew nearer and closed her eyes, assuming he had done the same.

"Father," Jed began, "bless this fine woman and her family, and hold them in Your loving care. Keep them safe and help Grace to raise those young'uns in Your Word."

His voice stumbled, and he paused to clear his throat. Grace's eyes remained shut tight, sealed by tears she refused to allow.

"If it pleases You, give me and the reverend a good ride and a safe passage to Galveston. Always lead me to do Your will and be sure Grace finds the surprise I left for her in the cabin. Amen."

Grace lifted her head and their eyes met. When he gave her the lopsided smile, she thought she would faint. "Surprise?"

And then he kissed her.

Right there in front of God, the Reverend Spivey, and all of His creatures, he kissed her good and proper on the lips. Well, it was good, if not proper.

"Surprise," he whispered in a ragged voice. Then, before she could recover, he rode out of her life just as abruptly as he'd ridden into it.

"He's a fine young man."

She whirled around to see her father sitting in a rocker on the porch. "Yes, he is," she answered, still a bit unsteady. Knowing he had witnessed all or part of their kiss made her feel worse.

The judge's eyes narrowed, making her feel like a child instead of a full-grown woman with three children. She shook off the emotion along with the urge to delay what she knew she had to say.

"Mr. Harte and I had quite a talk last night," he said, patting the chair next to him.

She squared her shoulders and said a prayer for strength. "I would like to apologize for my lack of hospitality."

"You felt unwell." He made a slash through the air with his hand. "Perfectly understandable. I enjoyed the time spent with your children." His face softened. "Bennett's a brilliant boy, and Mary is a delight. You've done a fine job with them, Gracie."

"Yes, they. . ." She looked up in astonishment. "You haven't called me Gracie since—"

"Since you were a child." He rose slowly. "I know. Just one of the mistakes I made in raising you."

"Mistakes?" She shook her head. The Honorable Judge Thomas Beaudry did not make mistakes, at least none he would admit to.

He took a step toward her. "When your mother and little brother died, part of me went with them." Gripping the porch rail, he looked beyond her rather than at her. "I suppose it might seem like I didn't care for the two of you, but I can assure you nothing is farther from the truth. Believe me when I say I loved you and your brother more than life itself."

Grace tried to swallow the lump in her throat but couldn't quite manage the feat. "I never knew."

The leaves began to rustle as the north wind danced through them. "I wanted to protect you and keep you to myself, and when I realized I couldn't. . ."

His voice faded as he beckoned her to come to him. "I'm so sorry. I was a stupid, stubborn man," he said, enveloping her in his arms. "Forgive me."

It took a few minutes, but Grace finally found her voice. "Yes," she whispered. "Of course."

Too soon, the judge pulled away and motioned to the rockers. "Sit down, Grace. We've got ten years to catch up on."

They settled beside each other, Grace's heart still pounding at the feelings coursing through her. "Thank you, Lord," she whispered, her face turned so her father could not see.

"I suppose you'll be coming back with Tom and me," he said casually. "I'd be honored to have you and the children home again."

"Father, Texas is home now." She paused. "For my children and for me. Someday I hope Bennett will take over this place and love it like his daddy did."

"His father was a good man, Gracie," the judge said slowly. "Another of my regrets is that Ben didn't live to hear me say so."

Grace smiled. "Life's too short to hold any regrets."

"I suppose you're right," he said as he leaned back in the rocker and gripped the arms. For the next few minutes, he told the most amazing story of how Jed had come to him demanding certain conditions for Grace and the children. Before he finished, her father had agreed to all of them. Asking forgiveness, he added, had been the one stipulation the ranger did not demand. That, he stated, would have to come from the judge's own heart.

"So you see, after I got over the man's impertinence, I saw the point." He gave her a sideways look, then reached over to cover her hand with his. "He was right and I was wrong. I just hope someday I'll earn your forgiveness."

Grace studied the unfamiliar blue veins and dark spots decorating the back of his familiar hand, then slowly dared a look in his direction. "My forgiveness is something you don't have to earn, Father. It's always been there for you."

This truth, discovered in the wee hours of the morning, had set her free. She'd released her anger for her father to the Lord, and He'd taken it all away, replacing it with love.

—⁂—

Unfortunately, none of the Scriptures helped her to release Jed. All through the winter, even after the judge left for New Orleans while Tom stayed behind to help Shaw run the landing, she felt the ranger's absence. The children often asked of him, but she refused to allow them the hope he would return as he'd promised. While she rocked Adam in his beautiful cradle, she waited for letters that never arrived and dreamed of a life she would never have.

Then one day, while she was turning the soil for her spring garden, a lone rider approached. Jedadiah Harte had returned. Dirty hands and all, Grace ran toward him, laughing like a child. Jed slid off the horse and met her halfway. "I missed you, Grace," he said as he wrapped her in his arms. "I'm a poor excuse for a letter writer. Thought I'd tell you in person."

He smelled of soap, sunshine, and trail dust, a glorious combination. She could only nod before the first tear fell. When he released her to hold her at arms' length, he wiped it away with his sleeve.

"How long can you stay?" she asked, unable to think of anything but silly small talk with him staring at her.

"Well, now," he said slowly. "That's a good question. The fellows I hired to work the ranger office in Galveston are good hands. Don't have to worry about that part of things. As for the preaching, it's something I can do just about anywhere. I'm a right decent carpenter and figured someday to build a church of my own." He paused and looked unsure of himself for a moment. "I had a mind to ask you if I could stay awhile."

"Oh?" Her hopes soared. Could he possibly mean what she thought he meant? "How long is 'awhile'?"

Jed smiled his lopsided smile and her heart began to pound. Her fingers sought his, and when they entwined, she felt a deep peace settle around her. "I bothered the Lord about us all winter, Grace, and He kept sending me to the same verse you quoted the day I left. The one about the Lord's grace."

"I didn't think you were listening."

"I tried not to." Jed shook his head. "I have a mind to stay and grow old with you, Grace," he said softly. "If you'll have me to wed, that is."

Out of the corner of her eye she saw two riders approaching. "Jed, who is that?" He smiled. "The reverend offered his services if I could convince you to say yes. And the other one's your father. He intends to give away the bride."

"Is that so?" She stifled a giggle. "Seems like you were pretty sure I'd agree to take you on."

"I don't miss," he said with a grin. A moment later, with the riders fast approaching and her still silent, his grin dissolved and worry crossed his handsome face. "Grace," he said slowly, "you didn't answer me."

"I didn't, did I?" She allowed another moment of quiet to pass between them before allowing her happiness to show. "Oh yes, I reckon I'll marry you."

Jed threw back his head and let out a yell, one she'd heard Ben imitate many times. Lifting her gaze skyward, she smiled. The little part of her heart where Ben's memory lay was full to overflowing with love, and now the rest of it would be filled as well.

AN INCONVENIENT GAMBLE

by Michelle Ule

Dedication

For my girls:

Carolyn, Angela, Alisha
and
Ashley, Shayna, and Emily

Chapter 1

August 1867

Jenny Duncan pulled her father's shotgun off the wall and hoped she'd not have to use it.

A stranger on horseback ambled toward the house from the dirt road to town. He wore an army slouch hat and carried a full load in his saddlebags. A long shape, maybe a rifle, stuck out behind him as he gazed about the property.

There had been too much death lately; she couldn't risk appearing vulnerable on the isolated farm, even if she were as strong and tall as a man. Out of the corner of her eye, she saw a coal-black crow light on the split-rail fence to ruffle feathers and caw. Jenny tightened her grip.

The horseman stopped the handsome chestnut mare and tugged a canteen off the saddle horn. He took a long pull, wiping his plaid shirtsleeve across his mouth when he finished.

Jenny waited by the front door, glancing toward the south pasture where her teenage brothers were supposed to be working the ripening summer hay. Tom's no-good yellow dog, Sal, lay with her head on her paws, just watching. Curious, that; they didn't get many visitors five miles outside of Nechesville, Texas. Jenny nudged her. "Go get the boys."

The lazy mutt flicked her ears. Her husband used to say his dogs didn't need any training, they knew instinctively what to do. Jenny blew out her cheeks. Maybe how to hunt but not how to protect the house, much less her. Where were her brothers?

The stranger rode forward into the yard, and Jenny stepped out on the porch, shotgun to her shoulder. "Don't come any closer."

The hat's brim shaded his face, and she couldn't get a good look at him. He put up his hands. "I'm a surveyor, traveling with Colonel J. S. Hanks. Put down your weapon."

"I don't see Jimmie Hanks anywhere." She nudged the dog. "Git."

Sal looked up with tired eyes and dragged herself down the two porch steps and lifted her nose to the air. Jenny smelled the sweet clover from the nearby pasture but doubted the dog savored the same scent.

"Come here, pup," the man said in a deep voice.

The traitor dog picked up her floppy paws and jogged to the stranger. The man slipped off his horse and squatted to rub her belly. The horse whinnied.

"Don't come any closer." Jenny steadied the gun against her body.

"Nice place you got here. Are you Mrs. Duncan? Could you maybe put your shotgun down? It makes me feel a mite nervous." He faced Sal, but his voice carried in a clear commanding way.

"How do you know my name?"

"Is your husband home? He'll remember me. I'm Charles Moss, surveyor. Colonel Hanks stopped down the road and told me to come ahead and get set up. We're surveying out here."

"What for?"

He pushed up his hat and scrutinized her. A young man with clear blue eyes and a stubble of dark beard, his face bore a thick scar twisting from temple to jaw. She'd seen a wound like that before. Bayonet cut, most likely from the war.

"It's my job," he said.

"I know how Jimmie Hanks works. He rides all over the county picking out the best property and when he gets the chance, snatches it up at the courthouse door."

Moss shrugged. "I don't know anything about that."

The late August sun bore down on the farmyard, and the hot air magnified the scent of cut hay. Weariness swept over Jenny. She tried to remain calm, but the end of the shotgun shook.

Moss saw it, too. "Why don't you put the gun down? Even your dog likes me. I'm not going to harm you."

"I don't trust dogs or soldiers," she said.

He flinched. "I'm not a soldier."

"Maybe not now, but you were."

Moss scratched Sal's belly harder. "The war's over."

"Which side were you on?" she demanded.

He shook his head. "There's no good side in a war."

Jenny agreed. The war had stripped the land of young men, sent them far away and returned them broken like Tom or scarred like this man before her. Life was still turned topsy-turvy with no end in sight to normal.

Moss stood up and squinted toward the road. "I don't know where the colonel is. He said he needed to check on something."

"Where?"

"Down the road near a stand of trees. He tied off his horse and hiked up. He didn't say why."

The graves. He'd seen them and stopped to count. Maybe she should tell Moss the truth and scare him away.

"Tom will vouch for me," the ex-soldier said. "He's the reason I'm here."

Jenny nearly dropped the gun. "What do you mean?"

"I met him up North. He said I should come out to Anderson County and make a new life after the war was over. Beautiful country, all right, with these rolling hills and piney woods. Is your husband here?"

She slid the shotgun to her side. "Where did you meet Tom?"

Charles Moss took a step forward and met her eye. "Fort Delaware, ma'am. We were in the prison camp together."

A wave of nausea hit, and she trembled. Jenny shut her eyes to fight it, to remain in control. She dropped the gun, plunged off the porch, and lost her breakfast corn-bread in the bushes. Her face flamed with heat, and her body ached from the cramping. She sputtered when cold water doused her head.

Moss had turned his canteen upside down over her. "It was a bad place, ma'am," he said. "That's how I usually feel about it myself."

Jenny put out her hand to lean against the porch pole. Her mouth tasted foul, and her knees could scarcely keep her upright.

"Can I get you a chair, ma'am, or maybe more water?"

Jenny lowered herself to the porch. "There's a tin cup at the well. Water, please."

She rinsed and spit, not caring if it wasn't ladylike. She finished the cup and handed it to Moss. "More, please." Jenny leaned forward, shading her eyes from the noontime glare. Exhaustion poured over her; she'd been tired for weeks. If Moss had planned anything, she'd be too weak to fight.

"You okay, Jenny?" Another deep voice, this one with the rich slur of Tennessee, spoke from far away.

Colonel J. S. Hanks rode up on the splendid stud stallion her father once owned. Jenny sighed. She had nothing suitable to serve them for dinner as country hospitality required. "Yes, sir, just feeling a little peaked."

"I haven't been this way lately, and with school out for the summer, we haven't seen your brothers. Tom or your pa around?"

"You just saw them, sir."

The fine leather saddle creaked as he shifted his weight. She could smell the sweat on his horse, and her stomach turned again.

"How's that?" he asked.

Jenny jerked her head in Charles Moss's direction. "He told me where you were. That's Tom and Pa lying up there in those new graves with Ma. Yellow fever got 'em."

Chapter 2

C harles stepped away. He'd been too close to a vomiting woman who had a burning hot forehead. He knew the symptoms of the deadly disease.

The colonel, however, got off his horse and handed the reins to Charles. "Tie him off." He removed his hat. "My condolences, Jenny. How long ago did they pass?"

She waved her hand wearily. "A week, ten days, maybe. I wrote the date in the Bible under Ma and the boys' dates." She made as if to get up, but the colonel indicated she should stay put.

"Where are Caleb and Micah?"

The pale woman pointed to the south. "They're trying to work the hay. Storm may be coming, and we need to get it in." All three scanned the western horizon, the direction weather came. Charles saw tall white billowy clouds, but nothing appeared dangerous. Of course, he'd not been in the county very long.

"Are they well?" Colonel Hanks asked. "How about Tom's mother?"

She nodded. "We feared we might get sick, too, but didn't." She sniffed. "Pa wouldn't let us stay, told us to take Ma Duncan and return in three days. We left 'em here and slept in the old dugout. They were dead when we came home."

"I'm sorry," Colonel Hanks said. "Your pa was a fine man. Tom fought hard in the war."

The woman stared at him.

"I'm sure Tom would've found peace in time and settled down."

Charles watched her reaction. Her pretty face blushed, and he saw she wanted to believe the colonel. She pushed back tangled mahogany curls with a large, strong hand. "Thank you for your kind words."

"You want the preacher out here to pray over the graves?" Hanks asked. "Why didn't you send notice? Rachel will be troubled you didn't let her know."

"None of us have been feeling too good." The tall woman leaned against the porch rail.

A curlew bird swooped from the rooftop toward the thick woods on the other side of the road. The colonel watched it fly then indicated Charles. "This here's Charles Moss from Lexington, Kentucky. He's helping me survey and will teach at the Stovall Academy come fall."

Charles stepped forward. "Sorry to hear about your loss, ma'am."

"Jenny Duncan." She introduced herself in a murmur. "Thank you for your sympathy."

The colonel put his hat on and waved at the neat farmyard. A fenced-in pasture contained several yearlings and their sturdy dams. A roomy wooden barn separated the farmyard from the pastureland. "Jenny's pa and her husband ran this farm. How many horses have you got?"

"Two dozen head," Jenny whispered. "Do you need a horse?"

"Not right now. I tell you what, we don't need to complete the survey work today." Colonel Hanks slipped off his black jacket and loosened the string tie around his throat. He tossed them across his saddle. "We'll help the boys bring in the hay. You're right, a storm's brewing."

Charles's jaw dropped. Sure, he knew all about feeding horses, but he hadn't harvested hay in years. "We're not dressed for hard labor, sir."

Hanks's eyes narrowed. "You're not willing to help a widow lady and some orphans? I thought you were a Christian man."

"Mr. Moss is right," Jenny said. "This isn't suitable work for you, Colonel."

"I can't think of any better," Hanks said.

She frowned. "I can offer you Tom and Pa's old clothes. I don't know if they'd fit so well, but you wouldn't damage yours."

Charles didn't fancy wearing a dead man's clothes and particularly not Tom Duncan's. "I'll be fine. Where are we headed?"

"They're in the southern fields, at the bend in the river," Jenny said.

The colonel tipped his hat. "We'll be on our way."

"I'll take you." Jenny toted the gun into the wood framed house and returned wearing a black sunbonnet.

Charles secured his horse then followed them through a split-rail fence into tall grass. The dog, Sal, trotted after him.

Swallows and wrens sped through the grass heads and whisked overhead in smooth movements. Scores of butterflies fluttered in the warm sun, and they surprised several black-tailed jackrabbits.

"Mighty fine property your parents settled," Hanks said. "Your pa loved this land."

The woman straightened her lips and a line appeared between her eyebrows. "Yes. Land grants to Pa."

"I remember."

The property included large stands of woods to the hilly east, and fenced pastureland dotted with ponds and weeping willows from the road to the wide river. Two young men and a small woman worked with rakes beside a laden wagon several acres away. "Your pa and older brothers worked hard to clear this land by the water."

"He dreamed of horses," Jenny said. "This farm meant everything to him."

When they reached the wagon, Colonel Hanks removed his hat and murmured condolences to Tom's mother. Her white hair stuck out from the sides of the faded red sunbonnet, and her rheumy blue eyes filled with tears. She seized Colonel Hanks's left arm. "I've lost 'em all now. My family is gone and dead. What'll become of me stuck here on this farm with these children? I'm lost, I say, lost. We're doomed."

"Come now, madam, all is not lost. Your daughter-in-law is here, and the Lord will not allow you to be tested beyond what you can endure."

Charles noted Jenny didn't look happy with the colonel's answer.

"You took my boy, Colonel, and I never got him back until after the war. I never wanted my Tom to marry into this family and make me live so far from town. Now fever took him. What'll I do now?"

"He thought you would be safer out here," Jenny murmured.

Colonel Hanks drew himself tall and removed her hand from his arm. "Tom signed on with me of his own choice. He was a man. He made his own decisions."

"But you came home," the woman pointed her finger at the colonel. "My boy sat in that prison camp and up to near died. And look where he ended up!" Mrs. Duncan jerked her scowl in Jenny's direction.

Sal barked, and Mrs. Duncan backed away.

"We're here to help today. The future's in God's hands." Colonel Hanks beckoned to the boys. Charles saw they were mere teenagers. He glanced at the young widow. How would she manage if the old woman and these two boys were all she had?

"Do you have any hired hands?" he asked.

Jenny shook her head.

The colonel rolled up his shirtsleeves. "The older boy here, he's Caleb. How old are you now?"

"I'm fifteen come September." The russet-haired boy's gawky elbows and legs seemed to be growing while Charles gazed at him. "Micah, he's thirteen."

The brown-headed boy patted the dog, only looking at the adults through the corner of his eyes. He still carried baby fat, though it would melt away if he worked the fields the rest of the summer.

Colonel Hanks examined them in the manner of a commanding officer. "This is Charles Moss. He'll be your teacher at the Stovall Academy. You boys coming to school in the fall?"

They looked at their sister.

"If I can manage the fees," Jenny finally said.

"I'll see you at school," Colonel Hanks told them. "Let's get to work. Mr. Moss and I will help you today." Hanks gestured for Charles to take the scythe, and he picked up a hay rake.

Charles hadn't used a scythe in a long time, but the sweeping cut of the blade at the grass returned easily. He quickly adapted to the rhythm of sweep, step, sweep, step. Once the dog got too close and he nearly took off her ear, but a cry from Caleb saved her.

The boy raked after him. "You serve in the war, Mr. Moss? Is that where you got the scar?"

"Yes."

"Who with?"

"Second Kentucky. I was one of Morgan's Raiders." He waited for the reaction. Even from this Texas teenager, it came in a breathless rush.

"Did you ride with him? With the Thunderbolt of the Confederacy? You knew him?"

"I rode in his cavalry." Charles felt the pull of unused muscles across his back and shoulders. He continued his sweep, walking slowly and deliberately in a straight path so the hay fell smooth about him, thus making Caleb's raking easier.

"What was Morgan like?" Caleb asked.

"Brigadier General John Hunt Morgan was a charismatic, well-meaning officer," Charles said. "He was a good leader, a lot like your Colonel Hanks. Everyone liked him."

The boy frowned. "Colonel Hanks? He only lasted a year in the war."

"But he came home," Charles said. "Morgan died during the war and left a pregnant wife to raise a baby by herself."

Caleb picked up a stone and tossed it away. Sal sat up to watch it fly but didn't follow. "That would be tough, raising a baby by yourself without a husband."

Charles agreed. "How will your family manage without your father?"

The boy shook his head. "Jenny'll figure something out; she always does. Maybe I won't go to school."

So much for Charles teaching them. "What would your parents want?"

"Ma's been dead eight years, and now Pa's gone." He raked up a pile of hay. "Might not matter what they'd have wanted."

Charles paused in his swing and glanced toward the figure of a determined young woman trying to reason with an agitated old lady. "Someone's going to need to help you."

A thought flitted through his mind: Did he want to help her?

Charles swung the scythe.

The last thing he needed was to gamble away his peace of mind on Tom Duncan's widow.

Chapter 3

Jenny didn't know whether to feel surprised or relieved when Colonel Hanks drove his buggy into the farmyard several days later. His saddle horse trailed behind and Charles Moss followed after, but Jenny's eyes went to the one person who really mattered: Rachel Hill.

Tears started in her eyes. It had been so long since Tom warned Rachel to stay away. She'd missed her friend so much, but for both their sakes, they'd avoided each other the few times Jenny got to town.

Colonel Hanks reined up, and Rachel handed him the bundle from her lap. She adjusted her straw hat, climbed down, and opened her arms wide.

Jenny ran to meet her. She hadn't cried since Pa died, but when Rachel hugged her, the tears poured. She felt Rachel's hand rubbing her back and smelled her lavender scent.

"There now, cry your eyes out. I'm here to help," Rachel whispered.

By the time Jenny used her apron to mop away the tears, Charles Moss had unhitched the horse from the buggy and led it to pasture. Colonel Hanks handed the now crying bundle to Rachel.

Jenny's eyes widened.

Rachel's sweet laugh rang out. "Look who I brought to see you. Meet my baby, Elijah."

Jenny peered into the blankets where the red-faced baby wailed. "I didn't know you were expecting."

"You've been hiding out here for more than a year. Elijah was born four months ago." Rachel's cornflower-blue eyes shone. "It's been far too long since we visited."

"We're surveying nearby today," Colonel Hanks said. "We'll return this afternoon to escort Rachel home."

"I know this is an imposition, but when Pa volunteered to bring a message, I thought I'd just come." Rachel lowered her voice. "Is it okay I'm here?"

What could Jenny say? A crying baby, a dear friend, and a dead husband who could no longer protest her friendship, made it easy. "I'm so glad you're here."

Her mother-in-law scowled from the porch, but Jenny turned away. She watched Sal squirm under the fence to where Charles Moss ran his hands down the front legs of a piebald dam.

"What is it?" Jenny asked.

"Her legs look swollen. If you don't mind, I'll walk her a bit."

"Please."

She saw his point as he led the horse around the inner paddock with the foal trotting after. The mare walked fine, but her legs didn't seem right.

"You feeding her much grain?" Moss asked.

"The usual amount."

He patted the horse as he led her to Jenny. "Is she spending a lot of time in the barn?"

"There's so much to be done, I often let the horses out later than they're used to."

Moss rubbed his chin. "I'd start with this one in the morning. She may need to move around more."

"Is something wrong with her?" Jenny bit her lip. Pa always doctored the horses. She had no money for a vet and couldn't afford to lose the mare.

"No telling. Cut back on the grain and give her more exercise. That should do it." His confident voice reassured her.

Jenny fingered the rough wooden fence. "How do you know?"

"You can trust him," Colonel Hanks said. "He's spent a lot of time with horses."

Moss slapped the mare's rump and chuckled as the foal nuzzled close to its mother. "She's a beauty, and her foal looks promising. What'll you do with her?"

"Jenny's family supplied mounts to the Confederate Army during the war," Rachel said. "My husband rode one of their horses all the way to Chickamauga. Jenny's pa trained him."

"What happens now?" Moss scratched Sal's ears while Jenny opened the gate for him. At Colonel Hanks's nod, he swung into his own sleek horse's saddle.

"Pa was negotiating with the Army out at Fort Griffin to buy more horses. We're training them for army work." Jenny needed to find the army paperwork in Pa's office. Her heart sank.

Colonel Hanks patted her arm. "Let me know if you need help with the Army. We're off now."

Jenny nodded. "Thank you, both." She turned to her friend, pasted a smile on her face, and gestured to the house where Ma Duncan barred the door with her thin arms.

"I hope you brought food, 'cuz there's none to eat here," the old woman declared.

Rachel adjusted the baby. "I brought dinner to share."

Jenny carried a heavy basket from the buggy. She set it on the porch, stepped indoors, and watched Rachel take in the parlor.

"My goodness," Rachel said. "I'd heard about this piano. It's magnificent."

The Brazilian rosewood Schomacker upright piano took up most of the parlor, leaving room for two chairs and a small round table beneath the window. Heavy with metal filigree legs and panels on the front above the keys, the elaborate instrument had a padded stool covered in thick red velvet with gold fringe.

Jenny frowned. "What have you heard?"

"Everyone in town heard about the trouble Tom went through to ship the piano up the river and then drag it by oxen to your house." Rachel cuddled the baby. "But no one has ever seen it or heard you play. Why not?"

Jenny wiped the top of the ornate instrument with her dingy apron. Thick dust fell to the wooden floor. She hadn't touched the piano in months.

Rachel jiggled the whimpering baby. "I'd love to hear it."

"She wouldn't perform for her husband, why would she play for you?" Ma Duncan glared from the doorway. "Tom's foolery."

"If you'll take my basket to the kitchen, Mrs. Duncan, you'll find tea cakes. Perhaps you could brew us a cup of tea?" Rachel's dimples appeared in a pert smile Jenny remembered well.

Ma Duncan grumbled but hauled the basket into the kitchen on the other side of the stairs.

"Why don't you ever play this beautiful instrument?" Rachel asked in a low voice.

Jenny clenched her hands. After all this time apart, could she still trust Rachel? She released her fists, smoothed her skirt, took a deep breath, and spoke the truth out loud for the first time.

"Tom won it in a poker game. I can scarcely bear to look at it."

Chapter 4

When they reached the main road, Colonel Hanks paused to look over the property.

Charles halted his chestnut horse, Bet. "Pretty piece Jenny Duncan's got."

"One of the finest. Her father Sam farmed this land for twenty years." The colonel pointed to the cornfield where the boys were picking ears from the tall green stalks. "I don't think Caleb and Micah will be able to bring in the corn by themselves."

The hay was in, thanks to their help; Charles's muscles still remembered. "They'll use all that corn this winter."

"Yep, and they need to store it." Hanks nodded to the next field over. "Looks like Sam and Tom got the oats in before the fever got 'em. That's something. We'll ask the church and the neighbors to finish the harvest. Townsfolk liked Sam."

"How will Jenny manage with just these boys? Has she got any other kin?"

Hanks tugged his hat to shield his eyes. "If you met Tom Duncan at Fort Delaware, did you meet the Peck boys there, too?"

"Peck?" A cheerful face flashed in Charles's memory, laughing and covered in freckles. Another visage, grim and determined but with the same ruddy look, made his gut clench. "Asa and Ben?"

"Yep, Jenny's other brothers. They fought at Gettysburg with Hood's Brigade like all the Anderson County boys. Neither came home."

"No," Charles muttered. Asa had died of dysentery within months of their arrival. Charles didn't want to think about Ben's death. He touched the small cubes in his right pocket. "Were you at Gettysburg?"

Hanks shook his head. "My wife got ill early in the war, and I had twenty-one slaves needing oversight. I'd only signed up for one year. When my son died, I asked to be relieved. The Army needed our food crops, so they sent me home."

Bet stepped closer to Hanks's stallion. "Did the Pecks own slaves?"

The muscle tightened in the colonel's left jaw. "He rented three during the war, but afterward Sam was pretty strapped working the farm without the older boys. Tom came by to return their effects, took one look at Jenny and married her. Sam needed Tom's help on the farm. By the way, Moss. Forget we were ever here on a surveying job. This land belongs to Jenny." Hanks nudged his horse forward.

Charles glanced at the peeling white farmhouse as they trotted away. A pretty woman, strong and hard working, Jenny Duncan would be a draw even without her property. Charles just couldn't imagine the Tom Duncan he knew working on a horse farm. But then, war could change a man.

The countryside spread out before him as fine as Ben and Asa Peck had described it back at Fort Delaware. In the warming sun, he smelled field grass gone to seed. He saw indications of deer and other game. When they approached the pine grove where he now knew Jenny's family was buried, he spied the makeshift crosses through the green trees.

Hanks grunted. "Maybe you can help the boys carve better grave markers this winter at school."

"How can Jenny afford to send them?"

"The school board answers to me. They'll be there."

A broad man of sixty with square shoulders, Colonel Hanks had fair skin that was now blistered red in the summer's heat. He mopped his sweating brow, checked his county map, and kicked the stallion into a gallop. Riding hard after him, Charles appreciated the breeze on the fast track.

A half-dozen furlongs down the road they set up their equipment. Hanks used the compass, telescope, and other tools to calculate and record angles and distance while Charles held the rods and chains, moving them as the surveyor directed. They measured acreage, drew plot and topological maps, and also noted elevation and grade. Charles suspected Hanks, as the senior surveyor, was making other notations, possibly for a private interest like the railroads.

But he knew better than to pry.

Charles set up the leggy tripod and screwed on the telescope for the older man. When he reached for the rod the telescope sighted, Hanks grabbed it first. "You do the measurements today, you're faster than I am and I've got things to think about." He passed the map and notebook to Charles.

"Thank you, sir."

"You're good at the calculations. Just don't make me move the rod unnecessarily."

While the map gave a rough indication of boundary lines, Charles noted faint lines marked along level spots. Train track needed to be laid on the most level land available, and topography often determined the route.

Jenny Duncan's farm was among the most level in the area.

Charles worked swiftly, taking sights and jotting observations as he sketched the land. With its lakes, rivers and woodlands, Anderson County's weather had been humid during the summer but nothing like what he endured in Lexington, much less at Fort Delaware. The clean, healthy air and the sunshine felt good. Texas was an excellent place for Charles to start over.

They broke for the shade of a woodlot when the sun rose straight overhead. Hanks unstrapped a basket of food from his horse and they both carried Confederate Army canteens. The colonel spread a blanket on the grass.

"Roast chicken." Hanks handed Charles a slab of bread with meat. "Much better than hardtack."

"Your wife's cooking is superior to anything I ate in the army."

"My mother-in-law manages the kitchen. Louisa never learned to cook."

"Ah." Charles lounged on a corner of the blanket. "The servant problem."

"Louisa is expecting another baby, and we need to hire help. I pray society sorts things out soon and we can find a nurse," he sighed. "But I've been thinking about something else I need to discuss with you."

"Go ahead." Charles took a swig of spring water from his canteen.

Turkey vultures spiraled in the hot air above and mourning doves called from grasslands to the west. Heat ripples rose over the fields and the dirt road.

They'd seen no one since the horse farm, but town lay several miles in the opposite direction. For all Charles knew, they could still be on Jenny Duncan's property. He chugged more water.

"Stovall Academy is just another mile down the road," Hanks said. "I know you're a good surveyor and you sing well in church, but are you a trustworthy man with women?"

Charles sputtered. "What kind of question is that?"

"A straight-shooting one. Sam Peck wanted his boys in school. Jenny needs an experienced horseman on her farm or she won't last the winter. She's got a bunk room in the barn where you could live and take board with the family. I wouldn't suggest it if her mother-in-law weren't there, but this looks like a solution for both of you."

"What problem does it solve for me?" Charles set down his food.

"You can't live in your tent through the winter. You need to come indoors and be respectable. This way you can have a comfortable place to live and decent food. With you to help with the chores, Caleb and Micah are more likely to attend school. You'll have two more students."

"Does Jenny Duncan want a lodger?"

"If we put it to her the right way, I think she'll agree. She's got to get through the winter. Come spring things will change and she'll have opportunities. She just has to survive the winter."

"What opportunities?" Charles touched his pocket. "She'll have to prepare the fields for planting, and I'm not likely to have the time or interest to do the work. Has she got money to pay a hired hand?"

"You forgot about the horses." Colonel Hanks raised an eyebrow.

No, he hadn't. Charles never forgot about horses; that was part of the problem. Every fast mare, every strong stallion he saw caused the blood to course faster through his veins with racing possibilities.

Charles shoved the idea away. He was through with horse racing. He'd fled Lexington to avoid it. He had a new life in Christ and a desperate desire to undo some of the past by doing what God called him to in the present.

"A pretty widow and two orphans," Hanks mused. "If you don't want the job, I'm sure I can find an odd man or two to help. But I doubt anyone in Anderson County can help prepare the horses for sale as well as you."

Was a good Christian man, a justice of the peace, and the school board head supposed to tempt a man with a dare?

"I'll pray about it," Charles said.

"Fair enough. Pray fast. I'm going to suggest it to Jenny this afternoon."

Charles spent the rest of the workday hoping God would provide an answer when the time came.

They heard pianoforte music coming from the house when they trotted down the lane late that afternoon. The colonel nodded. "I knew seeing Rachel would do her good."

Charles, however, was looking toward the river where Caleb had coaxed Sal to help round up the horses. The dog barked in a halfhearted way as she plodded after the youngest foal.

Charles dismounted and whistled for the shiftless dog, who pricked up her ears. Her yellow tail wagged, but Charles narrowed his eyes and strode to her. "Round 'em up."

Sal whimpered but scurried over to the lagging horses and yipped near their delicate ankles. The horses picked up the pace and thundered through the gate Caleb had just opened.

The teenager gaped. "How'd you do that? She only obeyed Pa."

Charles gazed at him. What were the odds this kid could mature to do the necessary work without a grown man to guide him? "Dogs and horses are alike; you just have to prove who's in charge."

Colonel Hanks dismounted and entered the house, but Charles went to the barn with Caleb to settle the livestock. Micah tended a cow tied in a stall near the house end of the barn, where Charles saw two doors on either side of the long corridor down the middle. One was obviously an office. "That an extra room?" he asked about the other. "Mind if I take a look?"

The boy nodded. "We sleep there now, but Jenny wants us to move into the house."

A bunk bed, potbellied stove, square table, and two benches made up the furniture. Rumpled blankets covered the beds and worn clothes hung from pegs. Charles thumped the walls: solid. Much better than a tent.

"You gonna move in, Mr. Moss?"

Charles saw the hope in Caleb's eyes. "It depends on your sister."

They hitched the horse to the buggy and were ready when the colonel came out of the house with Rachel, her baby, Mrs. Duncan, and Jenny. Jenny hugged her friend good-bye but then bolted to the bushes at the side of the house.

"She's been throwing up a lot lately." Caleb's brow furrowed.

Rachel handed her baby to Colonel Hanks and went to Jenny.

The colonel cuddled the baby and shook his head. "I've seen this before. She's pregnant, isn't she?"

Chapter 5

Mid-September

Jenny stood on the porch to greet the dawn and braid her long hair before starting the chores. The fresh air soothed her sleepless worry, and she savored the early morning birdcall. "Where are You, Lord?" she whispered as the sky lightened over the top of the eastern hills. "Show me what I need to know."

Sal raised a sleepy head when Jenny slipped into the barn. She noted the closed door on the right. She'd told her brothers to sleep in while she handled the livestock. The day would be full of moving and sorting, and with all the emotions waiting to ambush them, they'd be more cheerful with plenty of rest.

The cow lowed and she blew it a kiss. "I'll be back soon." As she walked the length of the long barn, the friendly horses nickered from their stall doors. Chickens grumbled in their enclosure and the rooster tried a raucous greeting. The comforting grain and hay scents mingled with the other evidence of livestock. Jenny couldn't remember any other life.

That all might change, soon.

Jenny opened the double doors to the pasture and let the horses out, one by one. The yearlings kicked their heels and scampered as fast as they could to the water pond. The mares plodded after with their foals, a whisper of amusement tickling their muzzles.

Jenny released the sturdy geldings last and watched them saunter out. They were her only hope, the half-dozen chestnut horses her father had meticulously trained. She'd continued taking them through their paces as best she could, but already they had lost her father's fine tuning and they let her know as they ambled into the sunrise.

Jenny freed the cow and Ma Duncan's chicken flock, then straightened her shoulders. The barn had two rooms: the bunk room where her brothers slept and where Charles Moss would move in today, and the small office where her father had managed the farm's business.

That was the second part of the morning's chores: going through her father's paperwork.

Jenny stepped inside the stale room. Drifts of straw followed her, and she frowned. Pa never tolerated untidiness. She'd sweep when she finished.

The standing desk to the left held cubbyholes stuffed with papers. Shelves filled with ledgers, medicines, and tired horse-doctoring books covered the right wall. Jenny had taken money out of the locked cash drawer in the six weeks since her father's and husband's deaths, but now she needed to learn exactly where they stood financially. Jenny sat on the high stool and started at the top cubby on the left.

"Oh, Pa," Jenny whispered as she sifted through the papers, her heart contracting in sorrow at his precise handwritten notes. She'd walked in a daze, hardly knowing what to mourn first: the ache of her father's absence, the never-ending work, the guilt of feeling grateful she didn't have to worry about Tom anymore. The emotions overwhelmed her.

And now a baby.

Too much.

"Good morning, ma'am." Charles Moss knocked on the door, saddlebags and a rifle over his shoulder. Sal padded behind him wagging her tail.

Jenny flinched. "I didn't expect you until later, Mr. Moss."

"Call me Charles." He frowned. "Boys not up yet? The horses are out."

"They've been working so hard, I told them to sleep in this morning with school starting on Monday."

He laughed. "I bet they've been eating a lot, too."

"Constantly. It's a good thing they like oatmeal." She stared at him. "I hope you like oatmeal."

"Ma raised me on it. It makes good filling."

Jenny nodded. "We've been living on oatmeal, eggs, milk, and chickens, plus the vegetables from the garden."

"Then I've got good news. I shot a fat doe not far down the road. I'll leave my gear here and retrieve it." Charles dumped the heavy leather bags beside the door.

When was the last time she'd eaten chewy, flavorful venison? "Thank you."

Charles's face came alive with his bright grin. Jenny quickly looked down. She should not be so bold as to share the excitement with him. She was a married woman.

Her brain protested. Not any longer.

She heard him step away. "Do you have a smokehouse?"

"Behind the house near the garden."

"I'll hang it there," he said.

"Thank you, Mr. Moss. Roast venison will be a treat." Jenny's cheeks felt hot and probably were turning red. She peeked at him.

"Charles, remember?" He scratched Sal's ears. "This dog needs to run off some fat. Can I take her with me?"

"Sal hasn't run in ages," Jenny scoffed.

"No?" He raised an eyebrow at Jenny and whistled as he exited.

The dog loped after him.

Jenny stepped to the doorway to watch them go, the tall lanky dark-haired man with the yellow dog running behind. He spoke to Sal as he swung onto his horse in a fluid movement that bespoke years in the saddle. When he saw Jenny, he lifted his hat in salute and then clicked his horse and the dog toward the road.

He rode mighty fine.

Jenny returned to the office.

An hour later, she spread the papers from the locked drawer across the desk and slumped on the stool. "Oh, Pa, what were you thinking?"

Ma Duncan stomped into the small room. "That man is back, and he's butchering a deer. Them boys ever going to get up?"

Jenny blinked away the tears. "He's shot meat for dinner."

"That fool dog follows after him like he's a god. You mark my words, he's up to no good." Her shrill voice carried too loud for Jenny's ears.

"We need his help. Let's treat him well."

"Don't you get any ideas, you hussy. He may be easy on the eyes, but he's not one for you. You've got my Tom's babe to think about. You ain't even started your grieving yet. Why, you're not even wearing black."

"I don't have a black dress; that's why I sewed the black sunbonnet."

Ma Duncan's tight little face contorted. "I rue the day Tom ever did your family a service and brought the family your brothers' effects. Your family and friends were nothing but bad news for my boy. And now look what's become of me. Stuck in the middle of nowhere without any kin."

"You have us," Jenny said.

"Fat lot it's going to do me if 'n you starve me to death out here to save all your precious horses."

"Do you know anything about these papers?" Jenny handed three neatly written IOUs to her mother-in-law.

She backed away. "You know very well I don't got much learnin'. What do they say?"

"They say Tom loaned my father money. Do you know where Tom got cash?"

Ma Duncan's eyes gleamed. "That's one skill you never did cotton to. My boy came back from the war knowing ways to get money when he wanted it."

"By gambling?" Jenny asked point-blank.

The old woman cackled. "He knew when to take a chance, my boy did. He could spot a sucker a mile off."

Jenny's mouth went dry, and her stomach roiled yet again. "Why did he marry me?"

"You folks had a nice little place here, missy. And if them IOUs mean anything in a court of law, it now belongs to me."

Chapter 6

Charles hoisted the deer carcass onto a metal hook hanging from the smokehouse crossbeam. He cut off a sliver of meat and tossed it to Sal lying in the sun outside and still panting from her jog. The dog snapped it out of the air; a new trick.

The younger boy, Micah, came around the back of the farmhouse with a shout. "Did you really shoot a deer, Mr. Moss?" When he saw the bloody hide on the grass, he ran toward the barn yelling, "Steak for dinner!"

Charles stuck the butcher knife into one of the walls and closed the door on the small log house smelling of old smoke. Strips of jerky still hung on racks, and the remains of a ham, but this winter would be thin on anything except chicken if they didn't hunt more game. Charles wiped his hands on the grass. A man's job was never done when kids were around.

He pumped a tin cup of water and then joined the family at the barn. The boys were carrying their possessions from the bunk room to the main house where they were taking over Ma Duncan's former bedroom upstairs.

"Where will you be sleeping now?" he asked the crotchety old woman.

She thrust a boney finger at him. "Don't you wish you knew?"

"She's taking Pa's room downstairs." Caleb toted an armful of clothing. "None of us can bear to go in there."

"Finest room in the house," she crowed. "It's about time."

He located Jenny still in the office looking through paperwork. Frown lines crossed her forehead, and he saw dried tears on her cheeks. "That bad?"

When she didn't look up, he gently set a note from Colonel Hanks on the desk. She stared at it a moment before slowly unfolding the lined paper. Jenny gasped. "When did he give this to you?"

"This morning as I was leaving, why?"

"Horace Mitchell is coming to look at a horse this afternoon. I need to find him a suitable mare." She pulled a black ledger from the shelf and ran her finger down a page. The tip of her tongue stuck out, reminding him of a student calculating a math problem.

Slamming the book shut, she pushed past and hurried toward the south pasture. He grabbed three halters off a peg in the barn and strolled after.

"Did the colonel say why Mr. Mitchell wanted a mare?" The horses were at the far end of the paddock, and she sounded breathless.

"Riding horse, I thought, maybe for his daughter headed to school?" Charles hadn't paid any attention until the colonel handed him the note.

"Daisy might be a good choice," Jenny said, "though she's got a foal. Do you think he'd take them both?"

Charles heard Sal barking. A buggy turned off the road. "You can ask him yourself."

Jenny bit her lip. "I wish I knew which horse would suit. Willow is a fine saddle mare and we just weaned her filly."

"Go talk to him. I'll bring some mares over." Charles didn't know the horses by name, but he saw several possibilities. He whistled for Sal. Micah came with the dog.

Charles tossed him a halter. "We want an easy riding horse. What about the roan?"

The boy tripped. "Princess?"

"Sounds perfect for a girl. How does she ride?"

"Pa liked her best," the boy stuttered.

Charles stopped. "Princess was your father's horse?"

"Yes, sir."

"Show me Daisy."

They led three mares to the farmyard, one with a foal dancing behind. A well-groomed man wearing a white Stetson waited with Jenny. A thin girl in a yellow gingham dress clutched his hand.

"The colonel said you had quality horses, gentle enough for my Emma." The man peered at the selection.

"All three of these mares are excellent riding horses. I broke them myself." Jenny's face flushed. "You're welcome to take one out for a ride."

Mitchell pushed through the gate and ran his hands down the legs of all three horses. "Which one's the dam? I don't need another filly."

"Oh, Papa, the baby is so cute." Emma's chin just cleared the top rail of the fence.

"Any of these horses take a sidesaddle?" Mitchell asked.

"They all do." Jenny joined him to stroke the white blaze down the painted pony's face. Daisy whinnied in response.

Mitchell puffed out his cheeks. "I'll try the bay."

"We'll saddle her up." Charles nudged Micah toward the barn. The boy ran off, tugging the horse after him.

"What's the white one down there?" Mitchell pointed to one of the geldings. "Did your pa train it? I hear he was a good trainer."

"Not for sale. We're preparing him for the Army." Jenny crossed her arms.

"We'll get him for you," Charles said. "You'll want to escort your daughter while she rides the mare." At Jenny's look of protest, he shook his head. Caleb retrieved the horse to saddle him up.

Mitchell helped his daughter into the sidesaddle and mounted the gelding.

Charles grinned at the surprised satisfaction on the man's face and opened the gate. The two rode off together.

"You can always tell a mark," he murmured.

"Rover's one of the Army horses," Jenny hissed. "Mr. Mitchell can't buy him."

"A sale is a sale," Charles said. "He's one happy man."

Jenny shook her head. "I can't sell him Rover. I may need that horse."

"I thought you needed money." Charles leaned down to scratch Sal's ear.

Jenny bit her lip and stared at the barn. When the man returned wanting both horses, she wrote the bill of sale without a word.

"We'll tie them to the back of your buggy." Charles shook Mitchell's hand.

"You the new teacher at Stovall Academy? Emma will ride her horse to school Monday morning," Mitchell said as he helped his daughter into the buggy.

"Math and physical science. I look forward to teaching you, Emma."

"I'm glad to buy your pa's horses," Mitchell said to Jenny. "He had a good reputation. I'm sorry for your loss."

"Thank you." Jenny watched the Mitchells depart with the horses. She looked thoughtful as she returned to the office. Charles followed.

"Why are you here, Mr. Moss?" she asked as he slung his saddlebags onto his shoulder.

"Room and board, ma'am."

"Did Colonel Hanks send you out here to keep an eye on his investment?"

Charles frowned. "I don't know what you mean."

Jenny plucked a piece of paper from the desk. "The colonel has a lien on my land. I just wondered if he sent you out here as a spy."

"He told me you owned all this property."

She shut the door in his face.

Chapter 7

Late October

Every Sunday morning Charles Moss asked, and every week she demurred. Church held too many painful memories for her. Tom had forbidden her to go during their marriage, and staying home to read her Bible alone had become her preferred habit.

Besides, she couldn't bear to face the wagging tongues at her expanding waist. Posthumous child, they would call it.

Caleb and Micah, however, rode off happily with Charles Moss, just as they had when Pa was alive, resolute to defy Tom on Sunday mornings. Then they'd stay to eat a picnic dinner and often didn't return until halfway through the afternoon.

With the end of the harvest season near, Ma Duncan decided she, too, would attend church. "I need some socializing," she declared, and the four drove off in the buggy, leaving Jenny alone on the farm.

Charles was disappointed they only needed two horses to pull the buggy. He wanted to show "potential customers" their "merchandise" and always insisted the boys ride different horses to school every morning. It did get the ginger out of them, and Jenny suspected Charles used the opportunity to train both the horses and the boys. Which was all for the best, she sighed.

Jenny leafed through the Bible on her lap and tried not to be discouraged by the weight of responsibility. After helping her sell the horses, Charles took on the boys' skills, and their work was done more efficiently under Charles's directions.

The boys hardly mentioned Pa or Tom with Charles keeping them busy, but they needed boots for the winter, and both had outgrown their overcoats. Caleb's shoulders were broadening, just as she remembered Asa's and Ben's doing at the same age. She'd go through the old trunk to see if any of their brothers' old clothing would fit.

Or Tom's. He'd had a warm overcoat.

She frowned. Jenny hadn't seen it since the previous winter. Had he lost it in a poker game?

"I cannot afford to feed the seed root of bitterness," she said aloud. She rubbed her face with her hands. "But I'm so angry, Lord," she continued. "I don't even care he's dead. Now I don't have to worry about him cheating people and shaming us. But that doesn't feel very Christian."

She thought about Colonel Hanks and the lien he never mentioned. What were his motives? He and Charles had been very helpful, but could she trust them? Weren't all men out for their own objectives?

The Bible fell open to Psalm 20, and she read the words her father loved to quote: "Some trust in chariots, and some in horses: but we will remember the name of the LORD our God."

Maybe so, but the only thing keeping them afloat at the moment was the sale of those two horses last month. "Help me, Lord." Jenny closed the Bible. She had horses to train, even on the Sabbath.

As she did every morning once Charles and the boys left for school, Jenny removed her homespun dress and tugged on a pair of her father's riding pants and a full shirt. She threaded a piece of twine through the belt loops and tied it into place. They needed to make the Army sale soon; she wouldn't fit into these pants much longer. Jenny stepped into Pa's knee-high boots, secured the spurs, and headed to the paddock.

She paused at the black sunbonnet and left it behind. Her long hair would fly free this morning.

Ma Duncan grumbled daily about Jenny's training outfit. Jenny had become used to her fussing with the chickens while she groomed the horses. Her mother-in-law managed a sizeable flock that provided the eggs and meat they all enjoyed.

All of them included the boarder.

Jenny turned her mind away from thinking about her overly involved and handsome lodger. She couldn't trust him, even though she longed to depend on someone.

She caught the black gelding, Caesar, and saddled him up with the McClellan 1865 army saddle her father had purchased after the war. She led the tall horse out of the paddock to the mounting block and swung into the saddle. Jenny loved the rush of power that came from controlling the large horses.

A light touch of the left spur and Jenny began. She cantered Caesar along the cut hay field and toward the river. Stopping and starting the horse as applicable, Jenny turned him quickly with steps her father had taught the horses and her. They paused for a breather near the stubbled cornfield, where the cow gleaned with a friendly moo.

Jenny caught her breath and glanced at the sky. "Thank you for those good church people finishing the harvest for us."

She should go to church soon, if only to thank them. Jenny would think about that next week when Charles asked her again, as she knew he would.

Caesar danced three steps to the left. Jenny tightened her thighs to hold the horse in place.

He quieted.

She pushed with her legs and clicked three times.

He took three steps forward.

"Oh, you beauty!" she cried and spurred him. He galloped along the cleared riverside, leaving the fields, the house, the chickens, and the past behind. Jenny shrieked with joy to try to startle him. Caesar ran without a break.

She turned him at the end of their land and raced him back, exulting in his smooth gait. With wind blowing in her face and her long hair flying behind, she felt free. Carried away, she urged Caesar on. She slowed him to a mild trot as they reached the paddock fence, and kneed him to a walk, but he turned instead and cleared the fence in effortless flight.

How many times had she jumped a fence, landing with a give in her knees?

Her body did not respond as expected. The heaviness about her middle, some five months gone, hit the saddle with a thud of pain. Black and white stars prickled her vision, and she reeled to a stand in the stirrups.

The horse faltered.

"What are you doing?" Charles appeared out of nowhere and grabbed Caesar's bridle.

Ma Duncan screamed from the buggy with pointed finger. "Trying to lose my Tom's baby, that's what she's doing."

With the horse now under Charles's control, Jenny closed her eyes. Her forehead felt clammy, and she leaned far out the right side of the saddle to throw up. When she finished, she grabbed at her shirt collar, desperate for the cool fall air.

Her left boot caught as she slipped off the horse into Charles's arms.

"I'm okay," she mumbled.

He untangled her onto her feet, but when Jenny tried to shrug off his arm, his grip tightened. "Let's see if you can walk. You don't look well."

"I've got the horse," Caleb yelled.

"You going to be all right?" Micah's voice caught. Was he crying?

Her head spun, and the same stars returned. Deep inside, she ached.

"Lean on me. Let's take you into the house." Charles's voice came from far away, but she could feel him close. He half carried, half walked her into the house and up the stairs to her room.

"Tom always said I was too big a woman to tote."

"A smaller woman couldn't manage that horse," Charles grunted. He laid her on the bed and removed her boots.

"Baby'll be coming now. Too soon, too soon," Ma Duncan wailed.

Charles's blue eyes loomed over her, worry frowning his features. "How do you feel? Is the baby coming?"

Jenny laid her hand on her belly's slight mound. "It feels better to lie down."

Charles ordered Ma Duncan to get water and said, "Take your caterwauling out of here."

Lying on the bed and staring at the knotholed ceiling, Jenny's head started to clear.

"A fine rider on a glorious horse is a sight to see," Charles said. "But taking a fence, even as neatly as Caesar did, is dangerous in your condition. Surely you knew better?"

Jenny blinked rapidly, yet she felt a tear slip out of the corner of her eye. "It just felt so freeing to ride. Caesar ran like a dream."

"And you rode him like a dream," Charles muttered.

"What?" She tried to sit up. He gently pushed her onto the pillow.

"Have you been jumping them this whole time? I knew you'd been riding and training the horses, but I never suspected you jumped them."

"This is the first time I've jumped since"—she swallowed—"the baby."

He used his foot like Tom used to, hooking the cane-back chair to the bedside. Jenny grimaced at the memory.

"We need to sell those horses to the Army before you do something even more foolish. Good thing Colonel Hanks gave me this letter this morning at church." He reached into his coat pocket.

"A letter came?" Jenny closed her eyes again. "Thanks be to God."

Charles searched his outer pocket, his pant pockets, and even took off his hat. "Where is it?" He went to the stairs and shouted for her brothers.

Micah thundered up. "Are Jenny and the baby okay?"

"Stay here to protect her from Ma Duncan. I've got to ride back to church. Do you know what happened to the Army letter?"

Chapter 8

C harles called for Caleb when he got to the barn. When the boy didn't know about the letter, he asked him to saddle up a horse while he rifled through his Bible. Charles didn't recall sticking the thin envelope into its pages, but where was it?

He searched the buggy. Nothing.

When Caleb led out the mare Daisy, Charles climbed into the saddle and took off.

After all the trips to school, Charles knew the road well. He sped past the graves, rounded the hill, dropped down with the road to the river, and soon reached the Stovall Academy, a rough-hewn log cabin with two classrooms. All along, he scanned the road, but the countryside held no stray envelopes.

He stopped at Professor Stovall's door, but the man hadn't seen a letter. Charles continued on toward town and church.

No luck.

His heart sank when he reached the Methodist Episcopal Church and saw Colonel Hanks talking with Jack Willard, another former prisoner from Fort Delaware.

"I thought you went home," Hanks said.

"I'm trying to find the letter."

Hanks winced. "You lost Jenny's letter from the Army?"

Charles touched his pocket then sat up straight in the saddle. He'd suffered a powerful man's disapproval before. "Yes, sir."

"You're not doing well by her if you lose important mail." The colonel's eyes narrowed. "I suggest you solve this problem."

He caught his hand before he saluted. "Yes, sir."

Hanks shook hands with Willard. "I'll see you at the memorial wreath laying. Thanks for doing this. Good day, men." The colonel walked toward his house.

Charles replayed the envelope incident in his mind. Hanks had stopped him at the buggy following the service, reached into his coat pocket, and pulled out the letter. They'd spoken briefly about the potential contents and what it could mean to the family. Charles had examined the small red profile of Washington on the three-cent stamp. He'd agreed to give the letter to Jenny, set it beside his Bible on the buggy seat, and climbed in.

Surely he had put it in his pocket.

Or had he?

Ma Duncan had shrieked when the buggy started. Charles closed his eyes to think. Did Ma Duncan pick up the letter? Why?

"Huh." He turned the horse toward the road home.

Jack Willard called after him. "You joining us the last Friday of the month to remember our fallen soldiers?"

Charles halted. "What time and where?"

"In front of the cemetery, around four. My wife wants to lay a wreath to honor the men we lost, particularly the Peck boys and James Tubb."

"Should I bring Jenny Duncan?"

Willard spat tobacco juice into the dirt. "Maybe if we could forget her last name is Duncan. What are you doing out there? Does she know what Tom did to Ben when he tried to escape?"

"Not yet." Charles held himself steady under Willard's scrutiny.

Willard crossed his arms. "Tom Duncan wasn't a bad kid when he left here, but gambling turned his head. Maybe if there'd been no war and he'd stayed in Anderson County he never would have learned to gamble. But it got in his blood, and he lost all sense. What was he thinking betting against Ben like that?"

"Prison did strange things to men," Charles said.

"Really? What'd it do to you? Turned you into a holy roller."

"I bet for Ben that night, and it's haunted me ever since. I've never taken another bet since."

Willard squinted at him. "You've never taken another bet? I doubt it. Still carrying them good-luck dice?"

Charles pressed his lips together and suppressed the urge to touch his pocket.

"I figured so. It's in your blood, too, Moss. You gamblers never change." Willard spat again and stalked off.

What a miserable Sunday, Charles thought. Willard was right about the urge to gamble never leaving a man, which is why Charles carried the dice as a reminder.

He'd failed Ben Peck, a young man he'd liked, on a wild rainy Delaware night. How many times had he relived the night Ben watched Tom Duncan take bets on his chances of success? With the numbers running against the young man, Charles couldn't bear the discouragement on his face. He'd anted up for Ben, and a dozen others joined him.

Afterward, Ben shook his hand. "Thanks. I needed someone to boost my confidence."

Then he drowned.

Charles kicked and the mare took off, moving like the wind along the dusty Sunday road. Charles put his head down and raced for all he was worth, repeating, "If only, if only."

A flash past the school reminded him of the preacher's words that morning. "For freedom Christ has set us free; stand no more under the yoke of slavery to sin."

He'd confessed the sin. He'd been forgiven. He just wished he didn't see Ben's eyes in Jenny's face.

Charles focused on the horse. Fleet of foot, she galloped with a smooth stride. He'd love to see her racing against his family's stable in Lexington. She'd give them a run for their money. He groaned. Why couldn't he shake the racing lure? He'd vowed to never take a bet again.

Charles touched the reins to slow the fabulous mare to a walk. The farm was in sight, and he needed to prepare himself to reenter his payback prison.

Chapter 9

Late November

Jenny rolled to her side and stared out the four-paned window at the moon riding high on a frosty night. The barn loomed dark, but she could see a flickering light through the small bunk-room window. Charles was up late as usual preparing his lessons. She admired his diligence and work ethic.

She heard a creak on the stairs. Jenny curled around her full belly, and her body tensed. Even after all these months, she remained alert lest Tom return. Would the fear of him ever leave? She felt no relief when she climbed the hill to look at the graves. She missed Pa nearly every hour as the responsibilities grew. Ma was now a distant sigh, and for Asa and Ben, Jenny burned with disappointment they'd died alone.

Tom?

When she stopped at his grave, she begged God to forgive her for being glad he was gone. She hadn't wanted him dead, just no longer controlling every part of her life.

Of course he'd left a tiny visitor behind. Jenny rubbed her hand along her belly. She could hardly wrap her brain around what the baby meant.

Jenny had seen enough livestock give birth that labor and delivery didn't frighten her. Concern her, yes, which is why she would see the midwife when she went to town next week.

Jenny rolled over and stared at the door, now lit by moonlight. She couldn't fall asleep with worries hounding her. She had to deliver the horses to Fort Griffin. When? How?

They'd lost time waiting for Ma Duncan to admit she'd taken the letter and then produce it from the back of the chicken coop. Some days her mother-in-law was as flighty and senseless as a hen, but then, that was why Tom had wanted her on the farm where she couldn't get into trouble.

Since sleep wasn't coming, Jenny got up and pulled on the day dress she had discarded only an hour before. She'd reexamine the letter and check on Blossom. The cow would calve soon.

Jenny lit the oil lantern when she reached the barn. Blossom lay on her side in the straw.

False alarm. Jenny yawned and entered the office. She reread Quartermaster Stewart's offer of a fair price for six trained geldings. The money would supply clothing they all needed, items for the baby, and even pay off Colonel Hanks's lien, thus removing the fear she might lose the farm.

The only problem was getting the horses to him.

Quartermaster Stewart wanted them delivered by the end of the year to Fort Griffin, two hundred miles away. It could easily take two weeks to herd the six horses there and return.

Jenny rubbed her side. She, obviously, couldn't make the trip even in a buggy. Hiring someone would eat into her profit, even if she could justify sending Caleb along as the second rider. But did she have another choice?

She yawned and pinched the space between her eyes. What was she going to do?

Charles knocked on the door. "What are you doing out here?"

"Checking on the cow and reviewing this letter."

"Has her time come?"

She shrugged. "She looked fine a little while ago. I'll check her again."

Blossom swayed a little when Jenny held the lantern high over the stall door. "Let's toss in hay. She's due soon."

Charles picked up the pitchfork. "I'll go for water," Jenny said.

He took the bucket from her hand. "I'm not going to stand here while a pregnant woman hauls water. I'll fill the trough if you'll promise not to do anything."

With his eyes alight with a righteous fire and standing so close, Jenny dropped her gaze. "She's my cow. I'll take care of Blossom."

He walked away carrying both the pitchfork and the bucket. "Not if you don't have the proper tools."

Jenny hid her smile. "Then wake up Caleb. You're a paying lodger."

"Not in Colonel Hanks's book. He keeps quoting that Bible passage about helping widows and orphans."

"I don't need your sympathy," Jenny said when he returned with two buckets of water.

"Maybe not, but you need my help and I need to work. Too much time in the classroom will make me weak. Tending your livestock keeps me strong." He poured the water into the trough, and Jenny pretended not to watch his flexing muscles.

"So you're here under orders?"

He paused. "I'm here because you provide a comfortable room and Ma Duncan is a good cook. I'm still trying to get used to the easy life, but it's growing on me. Anything is better than being in prison."

"Where did you live before you came here?" Jenny watched Sal slip out the bunkroom door.

"In my tent. Living in a prison camp will put the desire for open air in you."

"But the war was over more than two years ago. You slept in a tent through two winters?" Jenny pulled her shawl closer.

"First winter I spent at home in Lexington sleeping in the barn with the horses. I taught school last winter in Florida where the weather is mild. Tent was fine."

Charles seized the pitchfork and tossed hay into the stall with such fervor, the cow bellowed. When he finished, Charles's look sharpened. Blossom rocked on her feet. "Cows don't like to be watched. Let's stand where she can't see us."

"I thought you were a horse expert," Jenny whispered.

"We owned cows, too." Charles stared at the cow, whose sides flexed with contractions. "They usually deliver pretty fast. I think she's having trouble. Stay here."

He spoke in a calm voice as he entered the stall. Sal slipped in after him. Charles scowled at the dog and pointed to the door. The dog hunkered down. Charles pointed again. Sal tucked her tail and joined Jenny. "Get me a bucket of water and soap," he ordered. "I need to check on the calf."

Jenny hurried to the well, wondering if she should awaken Caleb, but the boys' window was dark. She toted the full water bucket, grabbed the small pail of soft soap, and passed them to Charles. Blossom's lowing intensified.

Charles removed his shirt and tossed it onto a peg. Jenny looked away, but the gelding in the stall beside Blossom's poked his head over to watch. Charles shoved its head away. Jenny grabbed the nosy dog.

Blossom's tail stood straight out. Charles soaped up his left arm and slowly reached into the cow, his forehead furrowed in concentration. He closed his eyes. "She's bearing down. Ease up, old girl."

"What is it? What's happening?"

He grunted and twisted his arm. "One of the hooves is bent backward. I need to turn it forward."

His shoulder muscles tensed as he concentrated on the task. Sal whimpered at Jenny's feet. Several horses whinnied and woke up the rooster who crowed when he saw the lantern light.

Charles yanked his arm out of the cow.

A splat, a yell, and the warm scent of delivery filled the stall. Blossom nibbled at the mucous sac. Once the nose was clear, she nudged the tiny calf to its feet and licked it.

Charles picked up a handful of straw and thrust it into the calf's nose. The calf sneezed, and its sides expanded with the first gulp of air.

Jenny's heart turned over and tears slipped down her cheeks.

Charles grinned. "It's a girl."

She joined him in the stall to rub Blossom's neck. "We can always use another milk cow."

He examined his slimy arm, chest, and clothing messy from the delivery. "Any water left in the bucket?"

He tossed the remaining water against his chest and left the stall. Once at the well, he pumped more water and turned the bucket over his head, dousing his body and clothes. "Brrrr."

Sal bayed. Jenny laughed. "Maybe I should wash your clothes for you."

"Only if you want to," Charles replied. He held his shirt at arm's length. "I'm going in out of the cold now. Good night."

"Thank you for everything." Jenny rubbed her belly thoughtfully as she walked up the porch steps. She hoped her delivery wouldn't be so complicated.

Chapter 10

Charles handed the buggy reins to Jenny and climbed out with Caleb and Micah following. "The boys and I will join you in town after school. Don't leave without us."

Jenny laughed. "I'll be at Rachel's house sewing baby clothes. I'll meet you at the cemetery." She chirruped to the horses and they trotted away.

Charles watched until the buggy rounded the bend. Caleb nudged him. "She's not going to get lost, Mr. Moss."

He gulped. "I was admiring how well the horses are matched."

Micah snickered. "One is a roan mare and the other gray."

"Their steps are well matched, demonstrating excellent training." Charles knew he sounded absurd. "Time for class."

The Stovall Academy was the only coeducational school in the county. Charles taught the more advanced mathematical and science students—eight boys and three girls—first thing in the morning. He also took a turn at Greek and Latin—subjects he had learned during his two years at Fort Delaware. After lunch, he swapped classes with Professor Stovall and instructed younger students with simpler lessons.

Charles had enjoyed the last three months and got along well with the students, if not always his teaching colleague. Stovall was uncomfortable with unorthodox teaching methods, though he allowed Charles a free hand. He approved of Charles's Christian behavior—his regular church attendance, and the fact he daily helped two widows and two orphans. All the same, Stovall liked rules, so Charles struggled to obey them.

He carried his books and lunch pail in one hand and stuck the other hand in his right front pocket to touch his old talisman. Whistling an off-key version of "Dixie," he walked to his log cabin classroom where Stovall opened the door and followed him in.

The schoolroom smelled of pine already burning in the potbellied stove. Charles set down his books and hung his coat on the nearby peg. He picked up the school bell and wondered why Stovall waited by the door. "Sir?"

"You shouldn't whistle. It sets a bad example for the boys. Uncouth behavior."

"Sorry. Old habit."

"I've noticed you frequently have your hand in your pocket. Is there a reason for that?" Light from the window glinted off Stovall's wire-rimmed glasses.

"Am I breaking a rule?" Charles fought the urge to touch his pocket.

"I don't know. Are you?"

A verse he wrestled with about obeying those in authority flitted through his mind. He pondered the professor's character before answering. Could he trust Stovall with the truth? "I struggle with temptation. I carry a personal object to remind me I do not struggle alone. When the temptation rises, I touch the object and it helps me stay faithful."

Stovall's lips jutted out, and his eyebrows went up. "Very commendable. What is it?"

"It's personal, sir."

Stovall narrowed his eyes. "I'd still like to see it."

"It was a gift from my father and private."

Stovall stomped over and held out his hand. Charles sighed and dropped the two dotted cubes into the professor's palm.

Stovall dropped his hands as if the dice were made of fire.

Charles noted he'd rolled two sixes.

"Why have you brought gambling devices to school?" the professor demanded.

"I never pull them out of my pocket. I carry them as a reminder not to gamble. Those dice were the last things my father gave me when I went to war. He was dead by the end. I told you. They're personal."

"We advertise our school as a place of good morals and high refinement. We specifically tell the parents we do not condone betting of any kind. You have defied our authority by bringing gambling tools to school."

Charles had considered this argument when he accepted the job and more than once had resolved to leave the dice in his gear at home. But he needed to touch those cold dice when he felt the urge to bet come over him. Rather than encourage, the dice reminded him of what he never wanted to do again. He considered it a matter of personal pride he'd not gambled since the dreadful day Ben Peck died in Delaware.

"Have you nothing to say?"

"I've not gambled since November 12, 1863, more than four years ago. I don't plan to gamble again. I can see why you might not believe me, but it's true."

"Young man, do you not know the first time you defy temptation, you have put your feet on the path to destruction? The Bible does not tell us to resist temptation, it tells us to flee temptation. As best I can see, you have kept yourself in a continual state of resisting temptation."

"Which has strengthened my faith, since I haven't sinned with the dice," Charles said.

"Which has left you vulnerable to failing," Stovall corrected. "I'm sorry. I like you and you're a fine teacher, but the risk of moral failure is too high. I need to discuss your employment with the school board. Until then, you must not teach. You are suspended until you hear from us."

Charles felt as if he'd been slapped. "Just like that? You can dismiss me without the school board's permission?"

"You put us into a compromised situation. You cannot work until further notice. You should have thought of your students before you tried to resist temptation in this way. I will call upon the other two school board members, Colonel Hanks and Mr. Ezell. Good day."

He opened the door. Charles put on his coat in slow motion and gathered up his possessions. As he exited, Caleb ran up. "What's happening?"

"I'm not teaching today. I'll meet you and Micah as planned. See you later." Charles raised his collar and plodded down the road toward town. A crow cawed and flew ahead to land in a pine tree leaning over the road.

He stamped his feet in frustration as he walked. When he was guilty of gambling, he hadn't been caught. When he struggled and fought the demon using his father's dice as a touchstone, he hadn't failed. But when some nosy old man who didn't trust him accused him of something he hadn't done, he lost his job.

Unfair.

"Wait, Mr. Moss, I'm coming with you!"

Charles shook his head. "Go back to school, Caleb. You'll make my situation worse if you don't return."

"Go to Colonel Hanks. He'll help you."

"Good idea." But was it? He wasn't sure the colonel trusted him anymore after Ma Duncan stole the letter right out from under his nose. Still, Hanks was probably his only choice. Charles would seek him.

Unfortunately the colonel wasn't anywhere to be found.

Charles spent the afternoon at the dry goods store reviewing his books and watching for the colonel out the window. He caught up with him as folks gathered for the memorial ceremony.

Hanks frowned as he listened to Charles's story. "I wouldn't have hired you to even survey with me if I'd known you carried dice. You don't pack temptation around; you flee it. What else don't I know that will affect my opinion of you?"

"Nothing, sir. I've told you the truth about everything else. I haven't gambled since Ben Peck died."

"You told Jenny about Ben yet?"

"No."

The colonel stared at him. "I'll think you a better man when you tell her what happened to her brother."

Charles saw Jenny leaving Rachel Hill's home with a basket over her arm. "Right now she's looking for a trustworthy man to deliver her horses."

"Have you been tempted to gamble since Ben's death?"

Charles looked him in the eye. "Yes. But with Christ's help I've overcome the temptation."

"Throw the dice away, then I'll know you're serious. Jenny spoke to me earlier about needing a drover. Since you won't have a job for a while, maybe you should volunteer."

A laughing Jenny with red cheeks headed their way. Visiting her friend had done her good.

"I'm sure Professor Stovall destroyed the dice," Charles said. "How soon do you think it'll be before I can have my job back?"

Hanks shook his head. "I'll talk with the other school board members, but I figure it's probably a two- to three-week trip to Fort Griffin. I'd say you have time to ride there and back before you're needed."

The gray November sky loomed, and a thin breeze blew up. It would be a cold ride two hundred miles west through mostly empty land by himself, not to mention the return trip. He'd be doing business with bluecoats again, something he'd avoided since Fort Delaware.

"Would Tom Duncan have made that ride if he'd lived?" Charles muttered.

Hanks peered at him. "No. Sam Peck would have taken the ride for the good of his family. Why?"

Charles gave a curt nod. "I can do it for the Pecks."

He hoped.

Chapter 11

G ambling?" Jenny felt as if ice water had been thrown in her face. "You lost your job because you were gambling?"

"Not gambling," Charles said. "I carried dice my father gave me, and Professor Stovall suspended me until the school board can discuss my rules violation."

Rage roiled in her gut, and she wanted to scream, send him away, kick a barn wall, and demand God explain, one more time, why the only men she loved were untrustworthy.

Well, Pa had been honorable, but he was dead and couldn't protect her anymore. Ben and Asa had abandoned the family to war and never returned. Tom she couldn't bear to think about. She could, however, deal with this living man, this schoolteacher who had weaseled his way too close to her heart, probably following Colonel Hanks's orders.

She licked her lips and watched him through cat-slit eyes.

His jaw worked several times, but he faced her with his shoulders back.

The baby jabbed under her left ribs. Sal slunk up and leaned against Charles's tall boot. Tom's dog.

"I suppose you were part of Tom's gambling den at Fort Delaware," she hissed. "Is that how you knew him?"

"Yes."

The simple word silenced all other sounds in the big barn and sliced into Jenny's heart like a knife. She slumped onto the milking stool beside Blossom's stall. "Did you really know Asa and Ben?"

"Yes." Charles knelt on the barn floor beside her and spoke gently. "And I prayed with them before they died."

She lifted her head, tears flooding her eyes. "What?"

Quietly, in a calm voice, he told of meeting the Anderson County soldiers not long after they'd been captured at Gettysburg. He remembered Asa's cheerful grin, mirrored in Micah's face, and described how the young man, only twenty at the time, had succumbed to dysentery in his brother's arms.

"They weren't in very good shape by the time they got to Fort Delaware," Charles said. "Weakened from not eating well and fighting so hard. But Asa tried to see the positive side of things, and he asked us to take him to the prayer meetings every morning. I'd started to see war differently by then and went with him and Ben. We prayed together every day, and I carried him to the hospital."

"Where he died on October 22, 1863," Jenny whispered.

"Ben and I were there, and Reverend Paddock, the hospital chaplain, prayed over him. The Feds buried him in the Finn's Point cemetery across the river."

"Do you know where he's buried?" Jenny grabbed his arm.

"Yes, ma'am. After I was paroled at the end of the war, I stopped at the cemetery and saw his marker. Ben's, too."

Jenny took away her hand and sat upright. "Ben drowned. How could he be buried somewhere? How could you have prayed with him before he died?"

Charles took a deep breath and grimaced. "Ben drowned trying to escape with another man. I prayed with him before he snuck away, to give him confidence. I saw his body the next morning when it washed up on shore."

Jenny screamed and doubled over her belly. He put his arms around her. "I'm so sorry."

She paid no attention, rocking with her sobs. Ben had been only seventeen. Smart, determined, and always looking for a way out. Of course he'd tried to escape, no matter how slim the chances of succeeding.

A grassy whuff over her shoulder made Jenny turn. Blossom's brown eyes regarded her. Across the way three horses stood at their stall doors watching. She sniffed. "I guess I'm not alone."

Charles released her and stood up. "You don't have to be alone. Plenty of people care about you."

She brushed the tears off her face. "Why didn't you try to escape?"

"The odds weren't very good, and I'm not a strong swimmer."

"Strong swimmer? What does that have to do with it?"

"Fort Delaware is in the middle of the Delaware River. They escaped on a rainy night and tried to swim to the Delaware side. Their aim was to find the underground and return to Confederate lines. Ben was angry about Asa's death." Charles scratched Blossom's forehead.

Odds? Slim chances? Dice? Jenny's head spun. "If you prayed with him, why didn't you talk him out of it?"

He closed his eyes as if in prayer, and Jenny's voice rose. "He was a boy. You're a man."

"Ben was a proud warrior who had faced the guns of Little Round Top. Both of your brothers met their deaths as men." The dog whined at his feet.

He wouldn't meet her eyes now. Jenny stood. "What about Tom?"

Charles hesitated. "Why did you marry Tom? Did you honestly love him?"

"No," Jenny said. "What was he doing?"

"Jenny, I..."

Horror filled her with an anger that knew no bounds. "What was he doing?"

"He was laying odds of whether or not Ben would survive the swim. Once the men ganged up on him, I don't think Ben had a choice. I tried to intervene, but we were in a prison camp with brutal men." Charles peered at the dark shadowy ceiling of the barn. "When I saw how it was going, I bet Ben would make it. He needed to believe someone thought him capable."

The anguished cry burst from deep within. The baby kicked, and Jenny stalked down the length of the barn.

"I'm so sorry," Charles called after her. "Ben's death cured me. I've never bet again, and I never will. I'm sorry for everything."

She pushed open the barn door and stomped into the near-freezing night. Stars spattered the dark sky, and she let the grief flow until she could weep no more. "Why, Lord?"

A whinny from the barn, the hoot of an owl, and a shooting star across the universe.

"How can I trust You, Lord, when You've taken everyone away and left me with all this?"

Sal joined her and groaned at her feet. Tom's dog, who had changed her allegiance to another man.

But that man had accepted the responsibility of the dog and trained her, turning her into a sleeker, more helpful farm dog. That same man had been a better example to her brothers, all her brothers, than her husband. Like her father, Charles had a deft and steady hand with horses.

She longed to trust him, to take the burdens off her shoulders and hand them to a capable man not requiring her supervision. "But how can I trust him, Lord?"

The night lay silent with a chill hush across the land. A thin line of light crept from the barn door. Jenny bit her lower lip and tasted blood. His strong hands, his concern for her, and his skill with horses. How could she not trust Charles?

Had Colonel Hanks sent him? Or had God? Jenny sighed. There was only one way to find out.

Caleb was talking to Charles about a math problem when she returned. With steel in her spine, Jenny marched up to Charles. "Why are you here?"

Charles glanced uneasily at Caleb. "Room and board?"

"Why here, on this farm? How did you have the nerve to come here and face us?"

"What are you talking about, Jenny?" Caleb's voice cracked. "He's here to help us. God sent him, obviously."

Sal wagged her tail.

"Is that true?" Jenny demanded. "Did God send you?"

Charles scratched his ear, as if listening to something she couldn't hear. "Yeah," he finally said, "I think maybe He did."

Chapter 12

December

Charles strapped the final bag of oats onto Archer's back. Caleb brought the other five geldings over on their leads and climbed aboard Willow. Jenny handed up his filled canteen. "We'll be praying for you. Keep safe, and make sure you study your schoolwork."

Micah glowered from the porch. Stuck behind to care for the womenfolk and attend school, Micah clung to Sal, who wanted to go, too.

Ma Duncan brought out a bag of hot fried chicken. "This should keep ya going for a while."

"Thanks." Charles attached the bag to his saddle and faced Jenny. "Any last words?"

"I plan to pay you," she said.

"Micah, make sure Jenny attends church on Sunday, that's my pay."

"Don't be ridiculous." Jenny frowned. "You'll get a share from the sale."

"This is my payback for Fort Delaware. If Ben had come home, he would have made this trip."

Jenny glanced over her shoulder. Ma Duncan stood beside Micah. "If Ben had come home I never would have married Tom," she whispered.

"Then when I return, we'll be square."

"Can I trust you to come back?"

Charles laughed. "I'm taking your brother and leaving my dog. I'll be back."

"Sal's my dog, but it's a deal." She put out her hand.

Charles considered her outstretched hand. He then met her eyes and crushed her to his chest.

And kissed her speechless.

As Ma Duncan and Sal both howled from the porch, Charles released Jenny and swung onto Bet. "Let's go." He chuckled all the way to the road.

—⚬—

Charles and Caleb headed west by northwest following an old trail out of Anderson County. The boy's horse pranced with excitement, and Caleb's laugh rang out on the comfortably warm morning. Charles's spirits soared.

It had been difficult since the hard conversation in the barn, but the colonel, as usual, was correct. Confession had been good for his soul. Now that he didn't have to shield Jenny from his past, he could move forward into an honest relationship. Losing the dice meant he no longer had a physical object to touch, but he could always appeal to God for help.

"Think she'll go to church now?" Caleb asked.

"She said she would if we drove the horses to the Army. You got any reason to think she won't?"

"Naw. She's been wanting to go for a long time. Pride got in her way, and then you and Rachel forced her hand."

Charles stared at the kid.

"Rachel told her the church needed her to play the organ. She said Jenny was keeping her lamp under a bushel for no good purpose. Jenny won't break her deal with you. Besides, Ma Duncan's always nicer after church. She'll go."

They took the two hundred miles to Fort Griffin at an easy pace, twenty-five miles a day with plenty of stops for the horses to graze. During the stops, Charles drilled Caleb on his schoolwork. Colonel Hanks had sent word Charles could return to the classroom after Christmas. Leaving his father's old dice behind with Professor Stovall had convinced the school board he'd changed his ways.

Did he still want to teach? Charles considered the question as they rode through sunny days. He liked sharing the things he knew and answering his student's questions. He wasn't content, however, with the physical aspects of the job. It reminded him too much of prison—done voluntarily, but indoors.

Training the horses for Jenny reminded Charles how much he liked horse farms, especially without the pressure to produce a racing winner. He knew all too well this horse farm came with a very pretty and capable owner. He admired her more than any woman he'd known before.

She'd said she had never loved Tom.

Charles mulled over that news through the rolling hills of eastern Texas. Why had she married him then? He eyed his young companion.

"It's a shame Tom died. He could be making this ride instead of us," Charles said.

Caleb spit. "Tom never would have taken this trip. He hated horses unless he needed one to ride."

"Why did your sister marry him?"

"No one ever asked her before, and with so many men dead after the war, she was worried she'd be an old maid. She thought Tom was her only chance." Caleb made a face. "Why? You interested?"

Charles laughed. "I guess you're the man of the house. I'd have to ask you."

"Take her. You'd make everyone happy." Caleb's face flushed. "Except Ma Duncan, but nothing makes her happy."

"I'll take your words under advisement." Charles basked in the information the rest of the day.

They reached Fort Griffin on December 14 and made their way to the quartermaster's office. The blustery, red-faced Quartermaster Stewart inspected the horses and letter carefully. "Looking a little lean."

"We brought them two hundred miles. They'll fatten up soon enough," Charles said.

Stewart eyed him. "Where'd you get that scar?"

"Cave City, Kentucky."

"Looks like a bayonet cut. Morgan's men fought there. You one of them?"

"Yes, sir." Charles knew to keep his answers short when speaking with Union Army officers.

The man's eyes narrowed. "Were you on the great raid north into Indiana?"

"Yes, sir. I was captured in Ohio."

Stewart stared at him. "Did you learn anything?"

"I learned to be careful who I followed, sir."

Stewart examined the horses once more. "Where's your allegiance now?"

"To God and the United States of America."

He grunted. "Watch yourself tonight; not all these soldiers believe the war is over."

Charles sent Caleb outside the fort to water and forage Bet and Willow while he and the horse master spent time with the six geldings. Afterward, he collected the payment and sought Caleb. Once out of eyesight of the fort, they mounted and rode off at a gallop. Charles wanted to put as much distance as possible between the money and the fort. He'd learned the hard way not to trust a soldier.

Charles thought about the dreadful day Morgan's raid turned bad. Hounded by Union forces, they'd tried to forge the Ohio River too late in the afternoon. With darkness closing in and Union gunboats firing at them from the river, he'd urged his exhausted horse into the water, General Morgan riding hard behind him.

In the chaos of bullets, screaming horses, drowning men, and smoke, they nearly made it across. The general, however, turned back when it became obvious a large part of the command wouldn't make it. Charles tried to follow his leader and was captured.

Prison camp at Fort Delaware became his duty station for the rest of the war.

Had he followed the right man? Morgan was charismatic and bold, but he courted danger. A gambler, just like Charles was then. Or was Charles a gambler because of the company he kept?

Maybe Hanks and Stovall were right. Living in an environment and prone to gamble, carrying those dice might be too dangerous for him. He'd never considered that angle before.

Charles and Caleb arrived in Neches six days later, trotting down the main street on a slow Sunday afternoon. Colonel Hanks was locking up the church when they passed, and he waved them over.

"Success? Any problems?"

"A good trip," Charles said. "Caleb held his own very well."

"What'd you learn, Caleb?"

The boy opened his eyes wide. "The quadratic formula. Isn't that what I was supposed to learn?"

The colonel nodded. "School's not out until Wednesday; I think you'll fit in fine tomorrow morning." He and Charles both laughed at Caleb's surprise.

"Railroad men have been in town this week. They liked your work, Moss," Hanks said. "They'll hire you next summer if you want to do some railway surveying."

Charles couldn't read Hanks's face. "What route?"

"They've got two in particular to choose from." He nodded at Caleb. "One's across the Peck place."

"No," Caleb said.

"Your sister will need to make the call." Hanks looked pointedly at Charles. "She's been getting lots of advice."

"How's that?" Charles asked.

"The widow Duncan's been entertaining most of the unmarried bucks in the county now the news is out. She has until spring to choose."

"But she's pregnant," Charles said.

"With a baby and also the possibility of a lot of cash. A fellow might be willing to overlook another man's child if he wins a pretty woman and a pile of money, too."

"Jenny wouldn't marry another man for convenience," Charles said.

Hanks raised his eyebrow. "You're the gambler. You tell me."

Charles spurred Bet. "I'll race you home, Caleb."

And he took off like a shot.

Chapter 13

Late February

Watching the rain pour down, Jenny thought of all the changes in her life the last nine months. As her time approached, it grew hard to imagine the innocent woman she'd been last spring. With Pa gone and Tom, too, she'd lost her anchor but also her chain.

Which is why she shook her head over the three men who had been courting her since Christmas. Why would she settle for another marriage of convenience? She knew the would-be suitors were waiting for the railroad trustees to make their decision about the tracks. If the railroad wanted her land, she'd get three marriage proposals on the spot.

If the trustees picked the other route, she'd be on her own

The implications of both options troubled her.

The one man she respected had shut himself away since Christmas. Charles spent most of his free hours working on his lesson plans, hunting with her brothers, and training the yearlings. He'd even built Ma Duncan a new henhouse. The only person he avoided was her.

But that surprising kiss when he left with the horses lingered in her memory. She tried not to think about it when he spoke to her. Surely she hadn't imagined the warmth in his eyes when he smiled at her?

How would Jenny really know? She'd married a man who smiled at her, and that didn't work out well.

Charles, though, always came through with what he said he would do. He respected Jenny's judgment and discussed plans related to the farm and the boys with her. Surely she could trust him? Then why hadn't he commented on the men who came to court her? Why didn't he follow suit?

Could she have misread that kiss so badly?

The wind picked up from the southwest and howled around the wooden house, shaking the walls with an intensity that made Jenny fear for the roof. Out the window, a wall of rain separated the house from the barn, but she caught sight of dark figures dashing across the farmyard.

Caleb and Micah burst in the front door, rain dripping onto the floor. "What a gully washer," Caleb shouted. "It's turning cold, but we got the livestock in. They're watered and bedded down for the night."

"Even little Petal is tucked up tight next to Blossom." Micah had a soft spot for the three-month-old calf.

Ma Duncan hiccupped. "How my chicks doing?"

"Everything's buttoned up tight, ma'am," Caleb said. "They were nestled in their straw." He reached into the pocket of his slicker. "They even sent a gift."

"Coo." She cradled the fresh egg like a jewel.

"Strip off your wet clothes." Jenny draped their waterproof slickers over the chairs near the stove. "Where's Charles?"

"He'll be in at suppertime. He's got lessons to plan."

Jenny rubbed at a side twinge. "Let's hope he doesn't have to swim."

"He'll have to swim to school—the creek was riding high when we rode over it." Micah grabbed at hot corn pone fresh from the oven.

Jenny peered out the window again. She'd felt restless all week, but that day her bulky body refused to settle down. "Nesting instinct," Rachel'd said when she visited the day before.

Everything was ready for the baby: clothing washed, a soft basket prepared, medical supplies, gum sheet to cover the bed, hot water, and plenty of wood on hand. Rachel had even given her a bottle of whiskey, explaining, "It's medicinal."

She pushed at her aching back. "Bring this baby in the right time, Lord," Jenny whispered. "After the storm's gone."

"You're like a broody hen," Ma Duncan said. "If you can't sit still, why don't you play that old piano? Do something useful with your energy."

"How come none of your beaus have come out to see you today?" Micah snickered. "Afraid of a little rain?"

"If they're afraid of rain, they're not for me," Jenny said absently. Something felt wrong.

"You should tell them I'll own the farm when I turn eighteen," Caleb said.

Ma Duncan scowled. "It's mine."

"Colonel Hanks explained it to you," he said. "The farm belongs to Jenny since she was married to Tom."

"That's not what my Tom wanted," she slurred. "He wanted me cared for." Tears dripped down her face.

"You're here with us," Jenny said. "You're safe here on the farm. Tom wanted you to have a home." He may not have wanted to live on the farm, but he wanted his mother far from her temptations.

The woman hiccupped again and swayed.

Had Ma Duncan found the basket of birthing supplies while Jenny worked upstairs?

"Is that sleet?" Micah asked.

They crowded to the window. Sleet was unusual in eastern Texas, and snow hadn't fallen in ten years. Jenny shuddered.

The door banged out of Charles's hand, and frigid air entered with him. He rubbed his hands and joined everyone beside the stove. "Mighty bad night out there. The animals are restless."

"They're not the only ones." Ma Duncan pointed at Jenny.

She handed the plates to Micah and pulled the stew pot off the stove. If Jenny didn't look at Charles, she wouldn't have to answer any questions. She felt self-conscious as all four watched her move around the kitchen. Her large belly nearly hit Ma Duncan when Jenny turned to set the corn pone on the table.

"How are you feeling?" Charles's voice sounded far away, like she had cotton in her ears. Her face felt hot, and the front of her stomach tightened. She couldn't go into labor now; she'd just ignore the pain and it would go away.

Charles grabbed her right arm above the elbow. "Look at me. Are you having contractions?"

She waved her hand in front of her face. "I'm hot. I'll sit farthest from the fire so you can warm up."

She squinted at an ache far down and suddenly wondered if she had lost her bladder. A puddle gathered around both her feet and Charles's. "You're all wet," she said.

"I practically had to swim over from the barn," Charles said. "I may get stranded in here tonight like on Noah's ark."

"The animals are all in the barn." Another tweak. The baby could not come. It would be impossible to fetch the midwife.

Somewhere outside they heard a crack. "Must have been a tree falling. Cold wind blowing out there," Charles said.

For one second she allowed herself the luxury of really looking into Charles's face, and then she dropped her eyes away.

"Is it the baby?" he asked in a low voice. "Changes in weather patterns can bring on labor."

Jenny turned her head away. "I don't know. I don't feel quite right. Have you delivered a human baby before?"

"Of course not, but if you think you're in labor, I need to go for the midwife before the storm worsens, if that's even possible." Charles glanced at the window.

Rain pounded like pebbles against the glass.

"I'm sure it's nothing." Jenny wanted to believe her trembling words.

"I'm sure it's not," Ma Duncan cackled with a brightness Jenny had never heard before. "Baby's coming, and no one's here to help but me." She burped. "What do I know about birthin' babies? I like them best when they crack out of eggshells."

Charles stepped closer to Ma Duncan. "What did you say, ma'am?"

She repeated her words.

"I smell whiskey." Charles stared at Ma Duncan. "Where did you get it?"

"I found it. It's for my grandchild, but I knew he wouldn't mind if I took a nip."

"She's drunk?" Caleb's mouth dropped open.

Jenny waddled to the sideboard and peered into the birthing basket. The whiskey bottle was almost empty.

"Have something to eat, Ma Duncan, then we'll put you to bed." Charles pulled out her chair and sat her at the table.

She wept. "You don't want me around. But I'll be here for my grandchild. You mark my words."

Jenny took the chair beside her in dismay. The one person who had actually been through this experience could not help her. She looked around the table. Micah was too young. Caleb too rough. That left just one. Charles, at least, had delivered livestock before.

She felt her face flame and buried it in her hands. Jenny couldn't do this part by herself, but how could the midwife arrive in time? How would they get her?

"I'll wear both slickers. Good thing Bet knows the way to town even in the dark." Charles filled his bowl with stew. "I need to eat fast. Are we going to say grace?"

"Please. You pray," Jenny said.

His deep blue eyes held her with a question before he ducked his dark head and prayed for the food, for her, and for the wild night. "Bring everyone safely to this house who needs to be here. Amen."

"Is the creek fordable with the buggy?" Jenny asked.

"You're staying here," Charles said. "I'll go for the midwife. Good idea to take the buggy, but it will take longer."

Uncertainty tore at Jenny. Which man could she risk losing? Caleb or Charles?

Ma Duncan bobbed over the table then slumped across it, pushing dishes and cutlery away. Charles jumped up before his bowl landed in his lap. "To bed with this one." He slung her over his shoulder and stomped through the parlor to her room.

Jenny touched Caleb's hand. "Do you think you can ride to town in this storm?"

"You want me to go?" Excitement danced in his face.

If only she could ask Asa; he had been capable of anything. But Asa and Ben were lying in their graves. Caleb was the oldest brother she had now, even if he was eight years younger. "I want you to think about it. There's no loss if you don't want to or if you think it's too dangerous."

"I rode all the way to Fort Griffin. I can ride to town in the dark."

Sleet pelted the window. Micah's eyes were huge.

"What do you think, Micah? Should I send Caleb for the midwife or Charles?"

"I'll go if you need me."

He looked so worried, Jenny could only smile. "I need you here to keep the fire stoked and to pray. Can you do it? We may need you to go out to the barn before this is over to tend the livestock. I know you can help us."

He nodded.

Jenny waited through a spasm and then leaned toward her brothers. "You're my only kinfolk. You're the only ones I can ask. If it comes to it, do you have objections to Charles delivering my baby?"

"I'm going for the midwife," Charles declared from the doorway.

Caleb stood. He was as tall as Charles. "I am. My sister needs you here."

"Me?"

"I've never delivered anything before. Someone needs to stay with Jenny in case I don't return with the midwife."

Micah stood beside him. "You're a man of honor, aren't you?"

"What?" Charles glanced between them.

Micah's voice cracked. "We can trust you to help her, can't we?"

"I'm sure Caleb will return in time," Jenny said.

Charles opened and closed his mouth several times.

"Get your slicker, Caleb. Take the barn lantern, and go slow." Jenny caught her breath. "What other information does he need, Charles?"

Charles reached for his slicker. "I'll walk you out and help you harness up."

Jenny grabbed his hand. "Charles, please. Don't play any tricks. Caleb has to go. I need you."

He gazed at her. "Jenny, I'm not even a member of your family. This is so wrong. I can't help you deliver a baby."

She let him see the fear in her eyes this time. "You have to, Charles. You're the only person I can trust."

Chapter 14

Charles did not like the idea of sending a boy out to do a man's job, even a young man as competent as Caleb had proven himself to be. While he was familiar with anatomy and the birthing process, Charles knew this would be hard, even if he got past the intimate exposure of the woman he now realized he loved.

He shuddered just thinking about the embarrassment. She wouldn't want to see him after this, and he wasn't sure how he was going to face her even now. And what if she died?

"Jenny's right. You're the best choice. I give you my blessing," Caleb said.

What was it with this kid?

"Thanks, but you better get back here with the midwife," Charles said. "Take Bet, she's used to riding in bad weather."

"How will I bring the midwife here if I'm on your horse?" Caleb reached for the buggy whip. Charles watched him swallow. Hard.

"Go to Colonel Hanks first. The midwife's husband won't let her go out into such a wild night with just you, experienced though you are. Tell the colonel you need his help. He'll come."

Caleb stopped. "You don't think I can do it?"

The words echoed from his past. Ben had asked him the same question before he, too, disappeared into a wild and stormy night.

Sal dragged herself out of the warm straw and trotted over. Charles scratched her ears then shook Caleb's hand. "If I were still a betting man, Caleb, I'd bet everything on your ability to do this job. You've proved you got what it takes to complete a man's task. Let's pray, and we'll trust God to bring you and the midwife in time."

Caleb sniffed and swiped the hat off his head. Charles put his hand on the boy's thin shoulder and prayed. While Caleb saddled up Bet, Charles went into his room and found his flint and a candle lantern. It was so dark outside, he wished it would snow to lighten the night. On the long march to Tennessee during Morgan's 1862 Christmas raid, Charles had ridden through freezing rain, sleet, and snow. He preferred snow.

Caleb led Bet to the barn door and mounted. The sleet was thickening. "Snow will be good," Charles said. "Light the candle when you're confused, but I think Bet will be able to get you to town. Godspeed."

"And the best of luck to you," Caleb said. "Even though I don't believe in luck."

"Pray all the way for yourself and your sister." Charles slapped the horse's rump, and they left. He closed the barn door and carried the lantern into the office in the vain hope Sam Peck had owned a human anatomy book.

He returned through now-falling snow to the house twenty minutes later. Jenny sat at the cleared table while Micah polished off the final piece of corn pone. "Did he get off okay?" she asked.

"Yep. He should make it without any problems now it's snowing."

"How will the buggy manage with the snow?" Jenny asked.

"They'll figure it out." He hung up his soaked slicker and emptied his pockets. "We use willow bark for livestock. It's a pain reliever. I'll give you some if you need it."

"How much?" Jenny asked.

"I'll have to think," Charles said. "We usually give a whole twig to a cow."

"That should be enough for me," Jenny said. "I'm as big as Blossom now."

Micah swallowed the last bite. "No, you're not."

"I was trying to joke," she said.

Charles wasn't in a laughing mood. "Any pains?"

"Some tightening across the front. Rachel described contractions to me, and that's what this feels like. But maybe it's just false pains."

"Let's hope so." He stared at her belly straining against the housedress. He moved toward her with his hands outstretched. "Do you think the baby's in the right position? Do you mind if I try to feel?"

Cows and horses delivered on their own without problems as long as the foal or calf was in the right position, feet first. Humans? He shuddered.

"I hope you won't have to soap up your arm." Jenny tried to make light of her comment, but he could see the panic in her eyes.

"I'm not reaching into you."

"Let's hope you don't have to." Jenny swallowed. "Go ahead."

He laid his hands on both sides of her belly, feeling the ripples of contractions. He felt a push under his right hand and a shove under his left. Could this baby be breech? Then what would he do?

Sweat beaded Jenny's face, and a worried Micah followed her every movement. This would not do. They needed to be confident.

Thus began the longest night of Charles's life. All he knew was to keep her moving, just as a horse walks in labor. They pushed the table into the corner to clear a path, and Jenny paced the kitchen, across the entryway, and into the parlor. Once she tried the stairs, but the pangs grew in such intensity, she cried out and hurried down.

Through it all, Micah watched with large eyes, praying lips, and fear. Ma Duncan snored on her bed; Charles checked on her several times. He tried to distract Jenny with stories of his childhood, of the war, of his students.

She paced and breathed heavily.

When the clock in the parlor ticked past four, Charles peered out the window to the farmyard, now covered in a thin veil of white. The rain and wind had died. Micah slept with his cheek to the table, and Jenny walked against the pain.

"Do you want a boy or a girl?" he asked.

"Girl. I don't want this baby to remind me of Tom."

"Do you have a name picked?"

"Mary, for my mother. I sure wish she were here."

Charles asked for her memories, and they spent an hour talking about her dead mother, father, and brothers. The family had been close, and Jenny wept more than once.

"You never answered my question." Jenny leaned against the wall and tugged at her hair. "What made you come here?"

"I didn't know you were Ben and Asa's sister," Charles said. "Colonel Hanks said we were doing a survey for Tom Duncan."

Jenny closed her eyes. "Why did Tom want a survey?"

"The colonel said something about an IOU. I didn't pay much attention; I was doing my job."

"He probably wanted to sell Pa's note to the colonel," Jenny said, weariness dragging her words out.

"Possibly, but with Tom dead it didn't matter." Charles said.

"Colonel Hanks told me Pa paid off the lien on the property with our stud stallion. The colonel didn't tear up the note because Pa wanted to buy back the stallion when he had the money. If he'd ever have the money. Are all farmers gamblers?"

Charles shook his head. "Farming isn't gambling; it's taking a calculated risk. You work hard to earn your way. Gambling's just trying to get rich quick by taking money off fools."

"You overcame your gambling problem. Why couldn't Tom?" She sounded breathless.

Charles shook his head. "It took God's help to do it. I'm not sure it's completely gone, but I want to live my life right before God, and do right by you, Jenny."

"I wish this baby had a father like you, a man who faced up to his problems, took responsibility for them, and wanted to change. Instead, she'll have to live knowing her father was a gambler who thought only of himself." Jenny's face scrunched in pain.

Charles scanned the empty farmyard. Micah sighed in his sleep.

Charles swallowed. "The baby doesn't have to have a father like Tom. You could marry me. I'll be your baby's father."

She stood up straight and stared at him. "What are you proposing?"

"I know these beaus who've been around have made you offers. I've left you alone to figure out for yourself what you want."

She frowned. "You mean you've been avoiding me on purpose?"

"Yes," Charles said. "It was a risk, but I figured if you cared for me, it wouldn't matter what the other men did."

Jenny leaned against the wall before speaking. "But you made yourself indispensable. Everything you did made me love you. I can't imagine living here without you."

Charles took her hands. "Living here, or just living? I want to be with you always. I love you, Jenny, with or without your farm. Will you marry me?"

She smiled with all her heart and then gasped. "You've picked a curious time to ask."

He mirrored her smile "Will you?"

"Yes. But we've got work to do before I can get married."

Chapter 15

With Caleb leading the way on Bet, Colonel Hanks, Rachel, and the midwife drove a carriage into the farmyard not long after dawn. Charles ran down the stairs to greet them. His hand ached from holding Jenny's through the bone-wrenching pain.

Mrs. Gray, the midwife, hurried to her patient.

"How is she?" Rachel asked as she unwrapped her scarf.

"I'm very glad to see you," Charles said.

Rachel went upstairs, too.

Charles went out to the barn to clear his head and help with the buggy. Colonel Hanks slapped Caleb on the back. "Terrific job through difficult weather. Your father would have been proud."

Caleb nearly fell over in his exhaustion. "Is the baby here yet?"

"No," Charles said. "You're my hero."

Colonel Hanks laughed. "Let's go inside where it's warm."

Mrs. Gray was making tea when they entered the kitchen.

"Is she okay?" Charles asked.

"Fine, fine. It will be awhile yet, but she is doing very well." She poured the tea into cups. "We all need a little warming, I think."

Colonel Hanks and Caleb reached for a cup.

"Is the baby breech?" Charles asked. "Will Jenny survive?"

"No, the baby is head down and feet up as it should be. I think she'll do fine," Mrs. Gray said. "Large-boned women like Jenny usually deliver without too much trouble."

"How much longer?"

"Maybe an hour, why?"

Charles turned to Colonel Hanks. "You're a justice of the peace. Have you got your prayer book with you?"

The colonel laughed. "If you want what I suspect, I think I can manage without the book."

Charles indicated Caleb. "Her next of kin has already given his permission."

"Yes, sir!" Caleb shouted.

Micah stirred from the table. "What did I miss?"

"Nothing yet. Think you can do the honors before the baby arrives?" Charles asked Hanks.

"You're not wasting any time, are you?" Colonel Hanks stamped the snow off his feet and called for Mrs. Gray.

—⁓—

Sunlight shone through the window when Mrs. Gray placed Mary into her mother's triumphant arms. Jenny lay against the pillows and gazed into the little girl's tiny red face.

"This has been a very busy morning." She yawned. "The entire world is different today."

"You're a different person this morning, Mrs. Moss," Charles said. "When can I hold my daughter?"

"Are you sure you want to? Loving a girl can be a risky proposition," Jenny said. "You might lose your heart."

Charles leaned down to gaze at the newborn. "I'll take the chance, especially when she has a mother as pretty as you."

Jenny turned on the pillow to look deep into his eyes. "Did I ever tell you I love you?"

Charles laughed. "I think it's time, now, for me to kiss my bride."

ANGEL IN DISGUISE

by Darlene Franklin

Dedication

And all that believed were together, and had all things common;
And sold their possessions and goods, and parted them to all men,
as every man had need.

Acts 2:44–45 kjv

Chapter 1

San Antonio, Texas, June 1875

Rosie Carson sat in the circle of chairs gathered for the Young People's Society of the New Testament Church of San Antonio. She loved the Lord and she loved the Bible, even though she found it a little confusing at times. But if she heard any more people read the exciting stories with such droning voices, she'd fall asleep.

By the time Rosie caught up with the teacher in the second chapter of Acts, he was droning on about "tongues of fire" resting on the disciples. She screwed her mouth, trying to imagine a tongue made out of fire. Where did it rest on the head? Did it come out of their mouths?

There was a mention of the Holy Ghost. . .Father, Son, and Holy Ghost. She'd like to hear more about that. The teacher continued to read as if he were reciting multiplication tables. His voice didn't convey any of the excitement Rosie felt when she read the accounts of the early Christians.

Some of the witnesses said, "These men are full of new wine." A picture formed in her mind of church members so excited about the Lord that they were accused of being drunk. She giggled at the image of people with fire sprouting out of their mouths, like circus entertainers, talking in languages half the congregation didn't understand, staggering about the stage, hollering, "Praise Jesus!" She laughed out loud.

The leader stared at her, directing the attention of everyone in the group to her unfortunate outburst. "Miss Carson, would you care to tell us what you find so very amusing?"

Rosie gulped. Didn't these people realize how blessed they were, that they had read the Bible so often that it rolled over them like wagon wheels running through the same ruts?

"I'd like to hear what Rosie thinks about the day the church was born." Macy Braum, a pleasant contrast to her stuffed shirt of a brother, gave Rosie the courage to speak.

"It's the place where it says people were mocking the disciples and all, saying they were drunk. Here God was doing something amazing and wonderful and all they saw was drunks."

"Yeah, Braxton, maybe we should hold the next service at the saloon down the street," a young man Rosie didn't recognize said.

Laughter followed, although Rosie didn't think it was such a bad idea. Didn't Jesus eat with publicans and sinners and even ladies of the night? They were the people who knew they needed a Savior, not people who had grown up without ever wondering where their next meal was coming from.

"At least they took a risk in sharing their faith." A deep voice from the back of the room said.

Turning, Rosie registered his blond good looks while feeling a bone-deep fear of the authority shouting from every inch of his frame.

—⁂—

Ranger Owen Cooper smiled inwardly at the excitement generated by the young lady's comment. He almost quoted the verse from Ephesians, where Paul said, "Be not drunk with wine, wherein is excess; but be filled with the Spirit." He would love to hear Miss Carson's take on that verse. She might be the only one who noticed it said "in excess."

Since his parents' death, Owen hadn't been home to San Antonio for more than a weekend for several years. His work as a Texas Ranger kept him running from Texarkana to El Paso year-round. On the rare occasions he had time to himself, he stayed near the headquarters in Austin. The life of a Ranger, with open sky and an outlaw's trail to follow, appealed to him more than the closed-in feeling he had in town and in the congregation of the New Testament Church of San Antonio.

Miss Carson was a pleasant exception. The way the red in her cheeks matched the red leather Bible cover, brown curls bounced against her neck, and her expressive faith shouted her love for God's Word—she couldn't bore him if she tried.

The Bible study ended not long after that, leaving the sermon the apostle Peter preached at Pentecost for another lesson. How could a sermon that convicted over three thousand people when Peter preached it stir little more emotion than a recitation of the Apostles' Creed in the nineteenth century?

After the "amen" of the closing prayer, Owen's eyes sought out Rosie. She hung back from the crowd, taking a glass of lemonade before retiring to a quiet corner. Wanting to discuss her thoughts on the Bible study, he headed in her direction. Before he could make progress, Macy and two of her friends interrupted him.

"Ranger Cooper." Nancy Wilkerson, as vapid a woman as Owen had ever met, breathed his name as if the continuation of the state of Texas depended on it. "We were ever so concerned to hear about your injury at the hands of that awful outlaw Wilson. We have been praying for your recovery."

Owen looked for an escape but found none. The injury she mentioned, not to mention his upbringing on the treatment of ladies, kept him slow of movement. "Your prayers are appreciated. I hope to resume my duties soon."

"Not too soon," the third woman, whose name escaped Owen at the moment, simpered. "We are hoping you can stay in our midst for an extended period this time."

"That depends on the doctor's report." And whether Owen could sway his opinion to let him return to duty as soon as possible. He glanced again at Miss Carson, who sat by herself, responding on the infrequent occasions when someone spoke to her.

Miss Wilkerson turned in the same direction as Owen's gaze. In a stage whisper, she said, "You seem quite taken with our Miss Carson. But I must warn you, she isn't someone you would want to associate with, not at all."

Someone as experienced as Miss Wilkerson must know that kind of warning often served to send most men straight to Miss Carson's side. He simply lifted his right eyebrow. "Oh?"

"Nancy." Macy stopped her friend before she could say more. "Miss Carson is our sister in Christ. I especially invited her to come, and I won't have you gossiping about her past. In fact, I will go over there right now and say hello. Do you want me to introduce you, Owen?"

Rosie had moved. She returned her glass to the refreshments table and walked out of the house.

"Too late. She just left." He moved in the direction of the door, but another group of interested ladies, as his mother described them, blocked his path.

Owen sighed. If Miss Carson was a new Christian, he should have other opportunities to speak to her, away from curious stares.

He found his next opportunity at church on Sunday. New Testament Church offered a Sunday school class for the adults as well as for children. Owen spied Miss Carson in the back row of the sanctuary, where the class was held. By virtue of moving quietly during the final prayer, he reached her before she could disappear.

"Yes?" Lively brown eyes peered at him from beneath a fringe of curls.

"Perhaps I should introduce myself. My name is Owen Cooper." He didn't give his occupation or rank. "I find myself in San Antonio for a few weeks." He didn't like to mention the injury either, not wanting pity.

Recognition dawned in Rosie's face. Of course, his name had been placed on the church's prayer list. Miss Carson's mind was cataloging him, name, rank, and family.

"You're the Ranger." Her eyes clouded. "You were injured, chasing that outlaw Wilson."

"That's me." He wanted to get her mind off the subject that had drawn a curtain of some kind between them. "I confess I've spent several moments wondering about the reaction of the crowd to men who appeared drunk."

A bit of humor returned to her expression. "I went ahead and read the rest of the chapter. That was quite a sermon Peter preached! Although I do have some questions about—"

Before Miss Carson had a chance to voice those questions, Miss Wilkerson came up behind them. "Excuse us, please, won't you, Miss Carson?" Somehow she swept toward the doors, holding on to Owen's arm. She leaned in, closer than he liked, and whispered, "I wanted to warn you. Miss Carson is a thief. She's spent time in jail. She only started coming to church a month ago, after she came forward at a revival meeting."

—m—

"Miss Carson is a thief."

Nancy Wilkerson's words stung Rosie like the bite of a whip. Pastor Martin said to hold her head high; she was a new creation. The old, thieving Rosie had passed way, and a brand-new, baby Christian had taken her place.

At the pastor's urging, two weeks ago Rosie had shared her testimony in front of the church. Mostly she had done what she had to to get food and shelter for her family. But during that last robbery, the storekeeper had pulled a revolver. Rosie's brother struck first; the storekeeper was injured, but Jimmy died. Because of the physical injuries, to both the criminal and the victim, the judge had decided to send a strong message. She'd spent two years in jail, only getting released two months ago. When the police officer who'd taken an interest in her suggested she attend the revival service, she learned about a loving God, and the Good News transformed her life.

Most of the church people didn't know what to do with her. At best, they pitied her. At worst, they shunned her.

The first person who had seen the new Rosie, the woman who was hungry for God, and who considered her worth listening to, stood on the other side of the door. *God, You're up to some strange tricks if You think a Texas Ranger and a convicted thief can ever be friends.*

Chapter 2

"I don't understand why you have to go out again tonight, Rosie gal. You just got in from your job." Ma's quavering voice almost broke Rosie's resolution. Old before her time, bent, thin, and hungry looking, Ma depended on her daughter more than she let on.

"I'm going to a meeting of the Ladies' Aid Society at church. Seems to me like they're the ones who are supposed to help folks like us. I figure they must not know much about us, or they'd be doing more." Rosie added the winning card. "After they heard my testimony, they wanted to hear more."

"I just hope those church folk don't disappoint you too bad."

"I know, Ma." Rosie filled her mother's bowl with more beef broth. "You need to eat some more and regain your strength."

A few minutes later, Rosie left. Her mother's warning stayed in her head as she chased down streets that some people avoided. If only Ma didn't keep repeating the same warning. It made her suspicious of folks' intent. A few were spiteful, but most of them were nice enough. That would all change tonight, she hoped. Once they saw what the need was, why, they'd do the right thing.

As Rosie approached the homes in the King Wilhelm's district, her feet slowed. Even with Jimmy, she had never come to this part of town. Adobe homes that looked like they belonged to Old Mexico sat side by side with fashionable houses on parcels big enough for two or three apartment buildings, like the one Rosie lived in with her Ma. Whatever the style, they all spoke "money." Imagine her, plain old Rosie Carson, being invited to a place like this.

At the last street crossing, she started across the road without checking for traffic. The neighing of a horse, the shadow of a horse rearing over her head, warned her of danger, and she jumped back.

Bringing his horse under control, the rider of the horse dismounted and called her name. "Miss Carson?"

Ranger Owen Cooper, again.

—⁓—

Rosie Carson's presence didn't surprise Owen. Pastor Martin had advised him of her attendance when the Aid Society invited him to speak tonight. "That way, they figure they'll hear from two different sides of the same question. From a lawman and from, well, a lawbreaker. They want to help, but they don't quite know how or what's best."

Seeing her on this street, wearing what was probably her Sunday-best dress, she looked as out of place as a whale swimming in the San Antonio River. "I'm sorry for the way my horse nearly trampled you there." He held tight on the gelding's reins, and the horse snorted in resentment, as if to say, "I know when to stand still."

"That's all right." Rosie shook her skirts, stirring some dust from the ground. "It's my fault. I didn't look proper." She stopped, staring at the biggest house on the street. "That's it, isn't it? The Wilkerson mansion?"

Owen nodded, not commenting. The ostentatious nature of the house said it all. "Did Pastor Martin warn you that they invited me tonight as well?"

She shook her head.

He shrugged. "I'm sorry, but they asked me at the last minute. I confess, I'd hoped to meet you again when we might avoid interruption"—he tugged on the horse's reins and offered Rosie his arm—"I hadn't expected my horse to make it happen."

Rosie threw back her head and laughed, a carefree sound that represented what Owen had come to recognize as her usual good humor. "I heard Pastor Martin speak about a donkey that talked. And that man, Bal-something or other, answered! If that don't beat all." She looked suspiciously at the horse as he bared his teeth and pawed the ground. "You're not fixing to talk, are you?"

Owen laughed. "Let's get out of the way of traffic and head that way." He stayed on Rosie's left side, protecting her as another carriage rumbled past, Mrs. Terrell Braum aboard. She lived in a slightly smaller house a couple of streets away. Ever since he, Macy, and Terrell had been in school together, the laughter of children rang through its halls and on its lawns. His former Sunday school teacher, Mrs. Braum, took the children in her charge to her heart and into her home. The memories brought a smile to his face.

Rosie's head swiveled from side to side, those bright eyes registering everything. How a woman with such an expressive face ever made a successful career as a thief baffled him. She'd stand out in any crowd. "A penny for your thoughts."

Pink jumped to her cheeks. "I was wondering how many families lived in houses like this. Big places like this call for big families, seems to me, but I haven't seen any children outside. It's too pretty a day to spend inside, don'cha think?"

Owen stuffed his hands in his pockets and considered. "The couple who live in that house there"—he nodded to his left—"lost their two sons in the War between the States, and their daughter went and married a Yankee and moved away. Up ahead, they have children, three girls and two boys. But the children are inside doing schoolwork or some such."

He agreed with Rosie. At that age he'd spent every minute outside that he could. If he wasn't at play, he was helping around the livery that his father owned. Until this last visit tonight, the only family who had invited him to one of these homes was the Braums. Of course, the incident that made him a local hero and in demand in every debutante's home had changed all that.

Not a one of them had ever laughed at the thought of Christians sounding drunk on the day of Pentecost.

A stick landed at Rosie's feet, and a dog ran up to fetch it. He picked up the stick and lifted his paws as though to place them on her knees. The brunette bent over and ruffled the fur on his head. "Aren't you a good doggie." A young boy ran across the lawn, followed by a lumbering nanny. "Rover!"

The dog's tiny tail twitched, and he ran in circles, inviting Rosie to join in the play. He yipped in Owen's direction but stayed away from the horse's hooves.

"Here, Rover!" The boy had almost reached them, his little legs pumping as fast as they could go.

Rosie tugged the stick out from the dog's mouth and threw it overhand close to the boy's feet. The dog raced after it. "Thanks, miss!" the boy yelled before he fell on the ground, turning over and over with his pet.

"Andrew, shame on you, you'll get your clothes all dirty." The nanny bundled him away, the dog trotting along behind.

Rosie stepped back, sighing. "I'd like to have a dog someday." A wistful note crept into her voice.

Owen had grown up with animals of all kinds—even a snake one memorable winter, until his mother had managed to "lose" it after a few months. Later she assured him she had let the animal go in the wild, where it would be happier. Owen had walked the streets where Rosie probably lived. The only dogs he had seen were lean, mangy things, ready to bite for a share of his food. His heart went out to the young girl that Rosie Carson had been, wanting things he had taken for granted.

"That dog seemed to like you."

She shrugged. "It was my job to keep the dogs quiet when we went into a home. Some of them were pretty scary, but most of them were sweethearts, like that fella there." She looked across the lawn, keeping her gaze away from Owen. "Somebody's told you about my past, haven't they?"

"Only that you spent time in prison." He told himself professional curiosity drove his interest in the details, not an attraction to a vibrant Christian who had a rough start in life. He didn't ask any questions. She had a right to put that behind her.

They passed two more homes without comment. "I'll be sharing more of my testimony tonight. Why I started thieving in the first place. God saved me from all of that, praise Jesus. I wouldn't talk about it now, except I hope that the ladies will want to help once they learn how hard some children have it."

Owen doubted both whether the women would want to help and whether financial help would make a difference. Not every thief was poor, and not every poor person became a thief. One of the worst thieves he had ever chased, Gentleman Joe Brown, had grown up with a proverbial silver spoon in his mouth.

Before Owen could formulate a response, the shadow of a carriage passed over them, and the vehicle stopped beside them. Macy sat next to her mother on the backseat, behind the driver. "Ranger Cooper! Miss Carson! You must be headed to the meeting of the Ladies' Aid Society. Ranger Cooper, I see you have your horse. But would Miss Carson like a ride?"

Rosie threw a confused look at the mansion that lay only two blocks away, but nodded her acceptance when she looked at Macy's determined expression. The two Braum women scooted over, and Owen helped Rosie into the carriage. He tipped his hat at the three ladies. "I'll see you again in a few minutes."

—∞—

Rosie didn't see the carriage driver until he came around to help her step down. She'd seen him at church, sitting in the back row, head thrown back, his face wreathed with smiles while he sang praise songs to the Lord. "You're looking fine, Miss Carson. I'm praying for God to put the words in your mouth today." He winked at her and set her on the ground.

"Thank you." She followed the Braums into a parlor bigger than Rosie's entire apartment, chairs crowding every available space. The room was about half full. As they entered, the front doorbell chimed as more arrived.

If Rosie thought the Sunday congregation looked like a forest full of colorful birds whose voices rang in song to their Creator, this gathering of ladies looked like a garden filled with exotic flowers. She had never seen such finery before, not all in one place. For half a second she wanted one of those dresses. Then she dismissed the thought as unworthy. She was God's daughter, dressed as fine as any sparrow of the air, and that's all that mattered. Why, she bet that the family next door to her and Ma could feed their family for a month for what one of those dresses cost. That was why she was here today, wasn't it? To let them know of the need? If she had a fancy dress, they would question the truth of what she said.

Three chairs had been set at the front, facing the room. When Mrs. Braum led her forward, Rosie realized she had been given the seat of honor. The thought of all those people looking at her. . . God will give you the words to say. Rosie took the words to heart. The door chimed, and the butler opened it to Owen's tall frame. He looked every bit the gentleman in his frock coat, but somehow Rosie guessed he'd feel more comfortable in Levi's, a comfortable shirt, and a gun belt.

Mrs. Braum led him forward. "Miss Carson, you have made Ranger Cooper's acquaintance."

They both nodded. Owen held the back of Rosie's chair for her to sit down then took the third chair for himself, leaving the middle one open.

A maid brought Rosie and Owen cups on a tray. "Do you care for coffee or tea?"

"Coffee," they replied as one.

The maid stirred cream and sugar into Rosie's cup, and it tasted like nectar. However, Rosie refused the offer of cookies. She didn't want crumbs sprinkled on her dress. Owen accepted two and bit into one with relish.

When the maid left, Owen leaned forward. "I eat when I'm nervous. You must have a stronger constitution than I do."

"I doubt that." Heat crept along Rosie's cheeks at the compliment. Anyone who was a Texas Ranger could do almost anything. "Is there a third speaker tonight?" She touched the chair sitting between them.

"That's probably for our hostess, Mrs. Wilkerson. She's the president of the society," Owen whispered back.

If Nancy was like her mother, she wouldn't think kindly of Rosie. A smidgen of doubt entered her heart for the first time.

Chapter 3

Rosie thought speaking to the ladies tonight would be easier than when she'd addressed the entire church, with fewer people in a nice, homey room instead of a giant sanctuary. The experience had turned out to be harder.

For one thing, she wouldn't describe the big room as homey. For another, the furniture showed no evidence of use; no children could have climbed on it. She searched the audience for a friendly face, passing over those who looked bored or critical, at last finding a group of younger women who appeared interested and supportive. She rushed through her words, arguing the need to help poor people with food and housing and doctor bills and hiring them to work. She ended with what she considered her trump card: a Bible verse from the second chapter of Acts. She opened her Bible to verse forty-two, reading with the same degree of excitement as the words engendered in her. "Why, when I read verse forty-five, I felt like I had died and gone to heaven. It says right there, they 'sold their possessions and goods, and parted them to all men, as every man had need.'" She read it slowly, savoring every word.

A few women shook their heads, but she continued, her voice growing more agitated with her ideas. "It wouldn't even take that much money, just a place and people willing to help. Think about how many people like me you'll keep from going the wrong way if you share what you already have."

Polite applause greeted her remarks as she sat down. Next Mrs. Wilkerson turned to Owen. "Ranger Cooper, in your work, you deal with the criminal element. Do you believe education and aid are the answer to the growing problems we have in our city?"

Puzzled, Rosie stared at Owen as he stood. He spared her a quick apologetic glance before he cleared his throat and began to speak. "I'm sure education and aid will help some people. But like the Bible says, we're born sinners, and we choose to sin. All of us. Now, some of us do things like gossip and envy and harbor bitterness against one another."

Without peeking, Rosie felt the sting his words caused the women in the room.

"Others, though, take to robbing and fighting and killing." His eyes sought out Rosie, begging her to understand. "So, no, I don't think education alone will make a difference. Aside from new life in Christ, thieves will continue to be thieves and murderers will kill again."

Enthusiastic applause followed that comment. He hurried on without waiting for the applause to settle down. "But I'll tell you that thieves aren't always poor, and rich people aren't the only people who gossip."

That comment brought a smile to Rosie's lips, but no one else seemed to find it funny, so she covered her mouth with her hand.

"Thank you both for sharing on this important topic." Mrs. Wilkerson smiled. "I will meet with the board to discuss what God would have us do regarding the growing problem." She relaxed. "And now I believe Mrs. Braum has a letter from her cousins, laboring for the Lord in the heart of Africa."

Was that all, no more discussion? They seemed more concerned about the poor people over in Africa than those two miles away from the church. Maids circled among them, offering refreshments to any who wanted. Rosie almost grabbed cookies for the children in her apartment building, but she hadn't come prepared to carry anything home.

Conversation buzzed around Rosie and Owen, but most ignored the two guest speakers. Owen studied her quizzically. "I hope I didn't disappoint you by what I said." He quirked his right eyebrow, as if he was truly interested in her answer.

She shrugged her shoulders. "Rangers mostly work out in the country, don't they? On farms and ranches and such, like up in Mason County, but that's pretty much range wars, from what I read." The account of the tragedies taking place just to their north had rent her heart. "Were you involved in any of that?"

He shook his head. "And you're right, we don't do too much in the cities. We chase after outlaws that have built a reputation, like Wilson, the man I was chasing when I was injured. But it's not a country or a city problem. Nor poor nor rich. It's a heart without God."

"But the temptations for the poor..."

"'There hath no temptation taken you but such as is common to man...ye have the poor always with you.' That's what the Good Book says."

Rosie shut her mouth. She couldn't argue with Bible quotes. Not with someone who had learned the truth at his mother's knee. She knew her face must be bright red.

His blue eyes remained eerily calm. "Would it help you to know I didn't grow up rich? Not poor, either. But my brother is living among the robber's caves up in Indian Territory. We were both raised by the same parents. We don't tell many people, and not many folks at church know the whole truth. But there it is. My brother is a robber and a murderer several times over. And then there's me, putting my life on the line to put men like him in jail."

Rosie thought of her brother, but this wasn't the place to mention him. Would it be rude if she left? In any case, she had to leave before the night grew too dark. "Where did they put my coat?"

—⁓—

Owen looked at Rosie and made a snap decision. "Let me accompany you home. I'll get our coats."

"But your horse..." Even as she protested, she accepted his arm as she stood.

"I'll get him later." His broad shoulders made working their way through the crowded room easier.

The valet disappeared to get their overcoats while Mrs. Braum came to say goodbye. "Leaving so soon?"

Owen nodded. "Miss Carson needs to get home to her mother. And I offered to accompany her."

Mrs. Braum turned her kind expression on Rosie. "I know you were disappointed tonight, my dear. The wheels of this group take a long time to engage, but once we get started, we're hard to stop. Keep praying God will show us the right thing to do."

"But. . ." It took effort for Rosie not to protest further, and Owen noticed it. "I will do that."

How many times had Owen heard the same advice. "Pray, Owen, pray." His job as a Ranger called for a man of action. Often a call to prayer felt like a call to do nothing. He shook his head. One of the areas where he failed the Lord.

"Here." Mrs. Braum pressed a bag of cookies on Rosie. "My children were always fond of my snickerdoodles. I'm sure you will find homes for our leftovers."

The grateful smile on Rosie's face warmed Owen inside. He wanted to bring that smile to her face. Even in this tumult, he smelled the scent of cinnamon rising from warm cookies in the bag. Such a simple thing, to mean so much.

Now that she had finished her presentation, Rosie asked questions all along the route home. Who lived there? How many servants? How many rooms? She took particular interest in homes where members of the church had residences.

At the church, they changed direction and passed through less affluent neighborhoods. About five minutes later, Rosie stopped. "This is where I turn to go home. That way." She nodded with her chin down a street that headed toward one of the city's poorest blocks, where the streets crowded together and lamp lights were broken almost as soon as they were put up. "You don't have to come with me. I'll be fine."

"If you don't mind, I'll feel better if you're accompanied by me and Mr. Colt."

She winced at the mention of the revolver. "You won't—"

He shook his head. "Not unless our lives are in danger."

As they entered her world, they reversed the roles of interrogator and answer giver. First she told stories. "Mr. Rivera has a vegetable stand there. If he hears somebody's sick, why, he brings them some of the spoiled stuff so they can have a good broth. And sometimes Mr. Rosen adds some chicken wings to go with it, so we can have a good soup. It's helped more than one person beat the cold around here."

Such a simple gift. Spoiled vegetables and chicken parts no one wanted. No wonder the waste of the rich galled her so.

"That's the school I attended until I was eight." She pointed to a tiny building that wasn't nearly big enough for all of the children who lived around the neighborhood.

"Why did you leave?"

"I was lucky to go as long as I did. When my Pa died, I had to work to bring in money. We all did. Even children too young to go to school can earn a few pennies a day."

She continued the story after they passed the next building with its heartbreaking stories. "Ma said me and her and Jimmy were lucky when our Pa died. It was a lot easier to take care of three of us than some of the bigger families."

In nearly every case, at least one member of the family had been arrested, imprisoned, or even died, while breaking the law.

Owen didn't know what to say. If the ladies at the Society heard these stories, they might stay away for good, as if poverty were a contagious illness they might catch.

However, if they lived in the shoes of the poor for a week, they might change their minds.

Chapter 4

Rosie smoothed her apron over her maid's uniform, provided to her from the church's clothes closet. The pastor's mother had helped her to find a new, better-paying job to go along with her new life. Mrs. Braum, Macy's mother and Owen's Sunday school teacher, had taken Rosie in.

She thought she would be sent home when the butler opened the front door. He stared at her maid's uniform. "Help comes to the back." He sniffed.

Mrs. Braum swept past him. "Don't mind him, Miss Carson. Come on in. I'm so glad you were available. Good help is hard to find. We may have another opening later, if you think your mother might be interested. I'll call the head maid, and she can explain your duties."

Rosie lingered in the front hall, catching sight of a full-sized mirror. She had never seen what she looked like from head to toe. The pins she had stuck into her hair kept it off her neck and out of her face, and the toes of her boots were a shiny black, her apron snow-white and her dress a faded black. Inside she didn't feel nearly so black and white; she was bursting with joy in all the colors of the rainbow.

The head maid, called simply "Franklin" and referring to Rosie as "Carson," had the no-nonsense attitude of a schoolteacher. She wasn't cruel or mean, but she and Rosie would never become friends. She escorted Rosie to the kitchen. "When you arrive tomorrow, come around here."

Rosie peeked out the door and saw how the drive swept past the house, around the back on its way to the stables. "I never been in a house with a back door before," she said.

Franklin raised her chin, as if anyone should know at least that much. "Miller will undertake your training. This job requires that you work hard, but the mistress is fair."

Following Miller around felt like trailing a jailer. Do this, don't do that, be careful. When they were in one of the back bedrooms on the second floor, she explained her attitude. "I know your story. You say you've changed. I think it's just a pious coat for the old you, so you won't fool me. You'd better watch your p's and q's around me, or I'll see you're fired before the end of the day."

At that, tears jabbed Rosie's eyes, and she wanted to run away. She blinked them back; she didn't want to ruin her newly clean uniform with a childish fit. Mrs. Braum's house was almost as big as Mrs. Wilkerson's, and room after room stood empty. Miller said the Braums entertained a few times a year, and guests used the rooms at that time. With or without guests, Rosie's job was to keep the rooms clean and change and launder the bed linens at least once a month.

After lunch, Miller left Rosie to clean an indoor bathroom. Alone in the magnificent house, Rosie allowed herself to wander. She had never imagined such luxury in a chamber designed only to sleep in, not to mention a whole room just to take care of personal needs. Five pillows were piled on a mattress wide enough for three or more, but where most people slept alone. Even husbands and wives slept in different rooms, according to Miller, although a door connected them. That seemed downright odd to Rosie, against what God intended for man and wife. A ewer and basin to wash in waited on a small washstand, with a thick blue towel embroidered with pink roses draped over it. In the cabinet beneath the basin, she found a matching set. Did each room have its own bath? These folks didn't even need to share bathwater. Imagine that.

Rosie sat by the vanity and stared at her reflection in the three-way mirror. This room must be designed for a lady. Right was her best side, she decided, as she looked this way and that. Peeking in the drawers, she found combs and brushes and a can of sweet-smelling powder.

Rosie had to stand on tiptoe to make the high bed. One thick mattress lay on top of another. Imagine having extra mattresses, when some people she knew slept on the floor. She shook her head.

After she finished the room to Miller's satisfaction, Rosie cleaned two more bedrooms as well as an upstairs closet where she found a rack of coats and dressing gowns for guests who came unprepared to spend the night.

By the time she left at the end of the day, a kernel of an idea had taken root in her mind.

—⁓—

At Mrs. Abbott's invitation, Owen attended the next meeting of the executive committee of the Ladies' Aid Society. Pastor Martin was also in attendance. However, to Owen's disappointment, Rosie didn't attend.

Mrs. Wilkerson, who hosted the meeting, led the board members group past the large parlor where the Society had gathered to a small sitting room. Every item was perfectly placed—knickknacks sat on every surface with a precise design, and fresh flowers adorned an empty stand here and there. He sank into an imposing chair with a curved back, and when he was tempted to slouch he straightened his back and leaned forward, dangling his hands between his legs. The day he had put in had tired him out more than usual, thanks to his injury. But he fought fatigue. This subject required his entire attention.

The women who gathered were often in the society pages of the San Antonio Express, and their names guaranteed the success of many civic activities, from musicales to libraries to parks.

"You may wonder why I have called everyone here today." Mrs. Abbott's voice was rather like fingernails on a chalkboard. Owen cringed at the sound.

She looked straight at Owen, inviting him to respond. "I assume it has something to do with my speech the other night."

She nodded, as if she were approving a smart schoolchild. "Miss Carson's plea for help touched all of us, but I confess, we fear encouraging someone already committed to a life of crime."

Beside him, the pastor fidgeted in his seat. "The Bible tells us not to judge."

"But it also says not to throw pearls before swine." Mrs. Wilkerson smiled as if she had spoken the last word. Her smile urged Owen to agree to anything she had to say. She was a beautiful woman. "That's where you come in, Mr. Cooper. We hope you can help us identify the deserving poor."

And who decides who is deserving? Owen could hear Rosie's question as if she sat in the room with him. Any child who goes to bed with welts on his back and an empty feeling in his stomach is deserving, no matter what his parents do.

But his experiences told him otherwise. Some people, like Rosie, latched on to the truth and ran away from their pasts as God worked in their lives. Others heard and rejected the Good News, like the hard soil of Jesus' parable. As a Ranger, he encountered a lot more of their kind than the ones like Rosie.

But he'd heard that the outlaw Wilson himself had become a Christian. Owen swallowed a snort at that idea. He seemed as likely to leave a life of crime as Judas was not to betray his Lord.

He brought his thoughts back to the question at hand. "What do you have in mind? What kind of help are you offering?"

Mrs. Abbott spoke for all of them. "We thought we'd start with jobs. If someone is willing to put in an honest day's work for an honest day's pay, they're halfway out of the poorhouse."

Owen nodded agreement. With Rosie's help, he could show how far those salaries would have to stretch. She'd also know which men—some women, too—abused alcohol. He wanted to find a way to help the families of those who couldn't hold on to a paycheck between their job and their home. "Whom are you looking to employ? What kind of work?"

Mrs. Wilkerson took over. "Each of us is willing to employ another maid-of-all-work and a manservant, and I'm sure there are others in the Society who will join us."

Owen cataloged what he remembered about household staff. "Those are excellent opportunities for men and women joining the workforce. But do you have any opportunities for those who are more experienced, with families and responsibilities that require more income than what a maid would make?"

The committee looked at one another again, coming to a silent agreement. "No. We want to encourage these people to make responsible decisions for their lives, which includes not marrying or bringing more children into the world than they can care for."

Owen could hardly disagree, since those were the very reasons he had avoided marriage to this point. For him, it wasn't a lack of money, but a lack of stability. Some Rangers had found women who were up to the tough job of marriage to a lawman.

He had not found such a woman, but marriage to the right woman. . .someone like Rosie. . .was an attractive proposition.

His mind slammed down on that thought. Of all the women Owen could marry, a convicted thief didn't belong in that role, no matter what her conversion.

As they settled the details about the job, Owen hoped Rosie would help him. Without her assistance, he'd have about as much luck finding out the information he needed as a thirsty horse looking for water in a desert.

The butler came up to Mrs. Wilkerson, a slight quiver in his right leg betraying his nervousness. When she signaled Owen, he followed her into her husband's study.

Mrs. Wilkerson motioned for Owen to take a seat. "Terrible news. Terrible news." She shook her head and lapsed into silence, her eyes straying to the door, looking for her husband's entrance.

When Mr. Wilkerson came, a dozen worries wrinkled his brow, and he frowned at the butler. "Cooper, how provident that you are here tonight." He took his seat. "My butler here has quite a story to tell. Go ahead, Truesdale."

Truesdale focused his eyes on a spot on the wall, where a frame held the Wilkerson family motto. "There's been a robbery in this house today. We believe it happened this morning."

"This morning? Then why weren't we informed earlier?" Mrs. Wilkerson infused just the right amount of indignation into her tone.

"The thefts were only brought to my attention after supper, ma'am." Truesdale coughed. "Cook is waiting outside the door to explain the situation."

That comment left Owen confused, but he kept his face neutral. The Wilkersons' cook came in, dismay marring her pleasant face. "I am so sorry to trouble you, ma'am. When the things were first missing this morning, I thought I had misplaced them. I waited until this evening, when I could go through the pantry and china closet and check each item."

Owen frowned.

"You're saying kitchen items were stolen?" Wilkerson's question echoed Owen's thoughts.

Cook nodded her head vigorously, the curls on her head escaping from her coif. "Yes, sir, ma'am. I had just finished churning some fresh butter, and last week's mold disappeared. A cone of sugar, flour, cornmeal, canned jars, even some cracked plates that the missus told me to set aside."

Both the Wilkersons looked at Owen, waiting for words of wisdom to explain the strange situation. He cleared his throat. "And that is all that was stolen? Have you completed an inventory of the rest of the house?"

"Just a quick look, sir, but no one has reported anything. We run a tight ship here, sir. Few thefts happen because our staff understands what will happen if they take off with what doesn't belong to them."

Owen stood and went to stare out the window, looking at the doors into and out of the house. "Is the pantry empty?"

Cook hesitated. "No, sir. That's why I waited to do a thorough search. It's like they only took things we had at least two of. There's nothing missing that can't be replaced in a week's shopping."

"But someone stole from us! One of our employees, whom we trust with our secrets. Or even worse, some hooligan from off the streets." Mrs. Wilkerson spread her hands open. "Ranger Cooper, after this...invasion...I must ask you to wait before pursuing your search for suitable employees. Truesdale, Cook, you may leave."

Mrs. Wilkerson stayed still long enough for her picture to be taken before she spoke again. She turned burning eyes on Owen. "Ranger Cooper, this is exactly the kind of situation I feared would come upon us if we take these people into our homes. I'm sure I speak for the remainder of the committee when I say we will not pursue our plans until the perpetrator of this outrage is caught and properly punished."

Properly punished? What did the woman have in mind?

Owen didn't ask. He had been given his orders, and he must carry them out.

Chapter 5

Tonight Rosie ignored both her maid's uniform and her new Sunday-best dress, instead, returning to the shabby blouse and her worn black skirt. She tugged a black hood closer to her face and headed home.

Few people wandered the streets at this time of night, but this was her San Antonio, a place of quiet and stealth and creatures of darkness. Tucked beneath her cloak she held a heavy bag. This year her neighbors would have a celebration big enough for Christmas in time for Easter. Her bag held plenty of biscuits and eggs and even a few cookies for children who often had nothing at all for breakfast, even on the day Christians celebrated the resurrection of their Savior.

Some might consider what she had done wrong. But the more she heard Nancy and others talk about the new frocks they would wear on Easter Sunday, the more confused Rosie became. The early disciples worried more about taking care of the poor than buying new clothes. Why didn't her church do the same thing? All she had done was even the resources of the rich and the poor, taking from those who had twice as much—or more—than they needed and giving it to people without anything.

She had invested most of her first week's pay in a bolt of bright yellow cloth. Working in the semi-dark of her apartment while her mother slept behind a curtain, she cut the cloth into squares and debated how much to give each family. An hour tonight had finished the job. Now she was done. She had made sure the lamps in the hallways of her apartment house had gone out before she began her rounds.

Starting with the first floor, she left a large bundle for a family with eight children and another on the way, and the china for an old widow who had broken all her dishes as her eyesight deteriorated.

Rosie started to ask God to protect the gift from being broken before it could be received. The words stuck in her throat. Could she pray God's blessing on something she wasn't entirely sure was hers to give?

As Rosie headed for the staircase, someone opened a door. Rosie hurried away, knowing her black cloak hid her face and revealed nothing about her figure except that she was a woman. Young Freddy Hill traipsed after her. "Hey, miss. Stop, miss! Thank you!" he whispered after her.

Feet speeding at his enthusiastic words, heart pounding at the near miss, Rosie ran downstairs to the street. She waited in her usual hiding place behind the trash bin, where she and Jimmy used to wait for people to throw away something, anything, they could eat. After she decided she had waited long enough, she went inside and worked from the top floor down before returning to the third floor, where her apartment was. Each family received its share of food and dishes, according to their need. Last of all she placed a small bag outside her own door. Since there were only two of them, and Rosie had work, they were in the least need of anyone in this building. But if they didn't receive a bag, fingers would point straight at Rosie, and she couldn't afford that.

Once inside, she spread her cloak on the floor next to Ma's bed, and removed her dress. She intended to pray for each family who'd received a gift as she fell asleep, but her mouth and mind turned numb as soon as she stretched out. In four hours, she would start another full day under Iron Maiden Miller's nose.

—⁓—

"Rosie."

Rosie stretched, not wanting to wake to the day.

"Rosie gal. You'd best get to work." Ma shook her shoulder gently. Round eyes stared at her. "But look what your God provided for us last night. Real butter! And wheat flour! We'll have a feast on Sunday morning for sure."

Rosie stretched, a smile wreathing her face as Ma thrust the gift into her hand. "Where did this come from?"

"Someone left it outside our door! Mercy me, I never saw anything like this."

Ma's smile brought Rosie to wakefulness, and she forced herself into her maid's uniform. She only worked a half day on Saturday, and Mrs. Wilkerson gave her staff every other Sunday off to encourage them to go to church. The afternoon was special today, on the day before Easter. She had discussed a plan with Mrs. Braum, who had agreed to help make this celebration of Jesus' resurrection memorable.

Mrs. Braum called for Rosie as the noon hour approached. Two cartons of brightly colored eggs stood on the table, making her heart proud. When she told her employer that she had never colored boiled eggs, let alone gone on a hunt for them, the teacher took over. Showcasing the energy that made her such a favorite with children year after year, she insisted on organizing a hunt for the children at Rosie's building. "I'd best see what kind of homes these young ones live in for myself," she said in her simple way. "Don't you think?"

Rosie couldn't deny "her" children the opportunity. She hadn't expected others to get involved, but in the front hall, she heard a male voice with the rhythm of the open range in it.

Mrs. Braum had enlisted Ranger Owen Cooper to help with the games.

—⁓—

Helping the little ones and encouraging the older ones to hunt for eggs sounded like more fun than Owen had had since the Christmas before last. He had another two dozen eggs sitting in his wagon, compliments of Mrs. Martin, as well as a bag of cookies. "I know the way." Owen gave his hat to the butler and headed for the kitchen.

Rosie had removed her apron, and her hair was pinned up tighter than he had ever seen it. Tendrils still strayed from their grasp, and pink sang in her cheeks, whether from a day's hard work or high emotion or both. "The eggs look beautiful, Mrs. Braum."

"Oh, that was fun." Smiles wreathed Mrs. Braum's face like a nightcap. "And Cook let me in the kitchen." She laughed. "Owen, I'm so glad you could come. I believe you've already met Miss Carson."

Rosie curtsied, an action that seemed out of character for the feisty lady, Owen thought. He extended a hand in welcome. "Good to see you again, Miss Carson."

She colored at his formal greeting. "Please, it's Rosie. Just plain Rosie. Especially today, when we're going to be cavorting about like little children ourselves."

Mrs. Braum's laughter accompanied Owen's smile. "When you put it like that, Rosie." He winked. "And you must call me Owen."

Chapter 6

The smile on Rosie's face dimmed a tiny bit, so quick he wouldn't have noticed it if he weren't used to studying people's faces in case they betrayed anything. What could be bothering her on this day of celebration? Suspicion jumped to his mind, and he chased the thought away as unworthy.

Rosie went from door to door inviting the children to come to the party for games, food, and stories. Owen would never have guessed how hard hiding eggs in these conditions would be. So many likely hiding places held hidden traps like broken glass, rusty nails, or splintering boards. He and Mrs. Braum trudged up and down the worn carpeted stairs, leaving them in easy-to-spot places.

Rosie escorted groups of children down the stairs, keeping the hallways as hidden as possible from their sight. Every now and then Owen spotted a curious face peeking around her skirts. He smiled and waved. One precious little girl, with a thatch of red hair, giggled as she waved back. The older boys sauntered by as if unimpressed by anything going on today. . .or perhaps grown too far past hope to believe any good would come.

By the time they finished the sixth floor, Mrs. Braum was huffing and puffing. They hid the final few eggs. "Give me a minute to catch my breath. I'm not as young as I used to be, chasing after you young rapscallions." She bent over, placing her arms on her knees, and drew in deep, ragged breaths.

Whistling "Christ the Lord Is Risen Today," Owen took a moment to rest his injured leg. The climbing hurt worse than he liked. He studied the building more closely than he had before. Warm air gave testimony to the mid-afternoon hour, but the hallway was as dark as an alleyway in the nighttime. Conflicting odors clung to the walls, giving some idea of the floor's occupants: cigar smoke and alcohol, peppery spices and tomato sauce, soiled diapers and sweating bodies.

Mrs. Braum's breathing grew normal. Owen looked down the stairs, six flights of them to reach the street level. Several floors down, a black head bobbed. "Rosie!"

She looked up. "Are you almost ready?"

Owen looked at Mrs. Braum, who said, "I'm ready. Let's go."

Rosie trotted up the stairs to join them as if the number of steps didn't bother her, and she waited for them on the fourth-floor landing.

Owen's worries about an excessive number of eggs vanished when he saw the crowd waiting in the bright sunshine of a March afternoon. Children and even some youths had gathered, easily three dozen or more.

"They don't all live in this building." Rosie frowned. "But I hate to chase anyone away. I would've invited the whole neighborhood, but that would take more eggs than are laid in Bexar County in a single day."

Mrs. Braum laughed. "I expect you're right, Rosie. But that might be a problem. I hate to set limits, but if they hunt in pairs. . . ?"

Owen thought of the double batch of cookies Mrs. Martin had sent. "Maybe if any pair finds nothing, tell them they get an extra cookie apiece."

"That's a better idea." Rosie shook her head. "You tell some of these children to only take two and they might hide the extras away in their clothes."

Once a thief, always a thief. Owen chased away the thought as unkind.

Rosie worked her way to the center of the circle of children. "Thank you all for coming today! I heard about Easter eggs and this strange thing called an Easter egg hunt. All it takes is hard-boiling an egg." She held a plain white boiled egg high over her head. "And then you leave it in some kind of liquid that has color, like you get when you boil green tea or red beets. And the egg turns that color." She held up examples for everyone to see and then passed them around for inspection.

A startled cry replaced the oohs and aahs. "Watch out what you're doing, Liddy!" One of the bigger girls said to a toddler she held in her arms.

The cries became louder at that. "What happened, Alice?" Rosie asked.

"She dropped the egg, and it got all broken." She held up the red egg, a crack sneaking down from the crushed top halfway down the egg.

"That's nothing." Rosie held the egg for everyone to see. "After we find all the eggs, you can crack it wide open and pop the shell off." The shell cracked in half with a satisfying snap. "And then we can eat all the eggs. First we play a game, and then we eat. Now, ain't that smart?"

Rosie was as much at home in front of the children as Mrs. Braum ever had been. She had that kind of spirit, a quiet authority joined with a gentle touch that would make her a good mother. One who could handle the vicissitudes of a Ranger's life. Again the thought intruded, and Owen shook it off.

The children formed pairs, the oldest holding on to children who could barely crawl or toddle yet, then siblings and friends. Two were left, a boy and a girl, who stood apart from each other the way young children sometimes do. Owen smiled, remembering a similar occasion when he was a boy. You don't expect me to hunt with a girl, teacher, do you? He came forward and spoke to the boy. "Tell you what. I'll be your partner, and you get to keep all the eggs." He winked at Rosie. "And I expect Miss Carson will go a-hunting with your friend here."

The way the boy's eyes lit up let Owen know he had made the right choice. Over the boy's head, Mrs. Braum beamed at him. "Well done," she mouthed.

"When you're done hunting, come on back outside. We have another treat in store." Rosie waited until every child's eyes were on her. "And. . .go!"

The first pairs reached the eggs left around the perimeter of the building and picked it as clean as a bunch of buzzards. Rosie urged them on. "Go inside. We hid eggs in the halls, too."

The boy's eyes widened and he dashed away, dragging Owen along with him. In between steps, he said, "My name's Mr. Cooper. What's yours?"

"Freddy." At least that's what Owen thought he heard him say as he dashed away. "I see one!" He found a green-colored egg tucked into a crevice created by a torn patch of carpet. He started to hand it over to Owen. "Do you mind if I keep it?"

"I promised you could keep all the eggs we found." Owen closed the boy's fingers over the egg.

Freddy dashed off when he spotted another egg, red this time, tucked in between the railings farther up the stairs. "Whoopee!" He flew back down the stairs. "This one is yours."

Owen didn't want the egg. But this young man already understood fairness, and the way he clenched his jaw tight said he wouldn't take no as an answer for a second time. Owen gave in and accepted the proffered egg.

Before Owen had time to tuck it into his pocket, Freddy dashed away with another cry of delight. A different pair of children, older and bigger than Freddy, reached it first. The biggest boy held it high over his head and teased Freddy.

Freddy shrugged and glanced upstairs. "You already been up there?"

The older boy shrugged. "It's pretty much picked clean." He scanned the hallway and started down the stairway.

Freddy palmed his green egg and stared at it with big hazel eyes. "This is even better than this morning."

"Oh? And what happened this morning?" Owen asked, debating about whether or not to slip the second egg into Freddy's pocket.

"You didn't hear about it, mister?" Freddy held on to the railing and climbed on it, ready to slide down the slippery surface. "Somebody left gifts outside of every door. We all got something different. My ma made us fried potatoes for breakfast. I'm still so full I don't want much lunch, and now I got a whole egg for myself."

That did it. Owen dug the egg out of his pocket. "Then you take this home to your ma or someone else who didn't get an egg in today's hunt."

Freddy hesitated. "I wouldn't, but my ma's been sick." He wrapped both eggs in a dirty bandanna and held the bundle tight.

They had almost made their way to the bottom of the fourth flight of stairs before the significance of Freddy's remark sank in for Owen. "What kinds of things did other people get?"

"Flour. Sugar. Butter. Old Mrs. Strauss got some cracked china 'cause all of hers was broken." His eyes sparkled. "It was like Santa Claus came in the middle of the year."

Chapter 7

Rosie issued an invitation for each family to come to church with her in the morning for a special sunrise service. "They'll have some delicious breakfast treats called hot cross buns, with sweet icing and raisins and such." Mrs. Braum had promised her cook would bake extra, "hundreds extra," she put it, so that no one would be turned away hungry.

Last of all Rosie invited her mother. "I'd be right proud if you'd come with me tomorrow."

Like usual, Ma grunted and shrugged her shoulders. Rosie told herself not to expect much. If all of today's doings brought only one family, one child, to the Savior, she'd consider it a great success.

After talking herself into not expecting much on Sunday morning, Rosie woke out of a dream to a soft candlelight pushing at the predawn dark coming from the kitchen. Ma was already up.

"Rosie, is that you? Hurry up so's you have time to eat."

Sweet-smelling johnnycakes sizzled on the grill. Ma had stirred up enough batter to use up all of the eggs, but she had only cooked two apiece. They might have more of the corn cakes with beans for supper and lunch, but Rosie didn't mind. Sometimes all she had for breakfast was half a piece of bread with the crusty part of the end of a loaf. Ma wore a faded red apron over a navy-blue dress, one she only took out for special occasions.

"You're coming with me today?" Rosie squealed loud enough to be heard in the apartment next door.

"I'm curious, I admit." Ma plunked two johnnycakes onto a plate and took out a precious jar of molasses, drizzling a tablespoon over both cakes.

Rosie's mouth watered. Such a breakfast deserved extra time to savor every bite, but she had promised to meet anyone interested in attending church with her outside at quarter of five. After she chased the crumbs from her plate, Ma rinsed down the plates, and someone knocked.

Owen filled the doorway when she opened the door. He held his hat with two fingers. "If you don't mind, I thought I would escort you and your friends to church this morning. There's likely to be questions once we get there, and you might have trouble answering them all by yourself."

"I don't think there's going to be that many people coming with me." She hated to think of Owen walking on that still-sore leg. Although he tried to hide it, she had seen him wincing more than once.

Owen raised an eyebrow in that special way of his. "I guess you haven't peeked outside this morning."

She shook her head. "But we're ready to go."

Mrs. Strauss made her way out of her door as the three of them came out of the Carsons' apartment. She smiled in their general direction. "And you must be the handsome Ranger our Rosie has told us about." Her rheumy eyes almost sparkled.

Owen's ears colored, and he twisted his hat, as if wishing he could set it back on his head and cover up his embarrassment. Rosie smothered a smile.

"And you must be. . ." Owen paused as if recalling a list of names. "Mrs. Strauss." He tipped his hat to her. "May I escort you down the stairs?"

Rosie appreciated his kindness. On the first floor, they encountered a woman who was heavily pregnant lining up four toddlers and giving them a list of instructions.

Owen walked to the front. "May I?" He held the door open for the family, then Mrs. Strauss, and last of all, Ma and Rosie.

So many people waited before her, she could hardly see the sky. Although not as many waited as had come to yesterday's party, a solid two dozen had arisen to attend church on this day of resurrection.

A silent whistle squeezed between Rosie's front teeth. "Are you waiting to go to church with me this morning?" Heads bobbed in all directions. For a moment her heart quaked. She had expected to squeeze in a strange face or two, a small enough group to all sit on the back row and not raise a lot of questions. This many would capture attention. Suddenly she was glad for Owen at her side. He was her champion, and few in the church would fly in the face of his authority, both as a Ranger and as a Christian.

"Let's go then." Owen spoke to the crowd. "The church is about six blocks away." He gave precise directions. "The congregation will gather on the east side of the church building, where they can see the sun rise. We'll see them as we get closer." In a lower voice, he spoke to Ma and Mrs. Strauss. "Do you ladies feel up to walking that far?"

Ma sniffed. "I've walked farther than that to get to work for most of my life. I reckon I can make it to a church service."

Apology written on his face, Owen turned to Rosie. "Next time, I'll bring a carriage, or maybe a wagon, so at least people can ride."

He said "next time." Rosie smiled in answer.

Their company squeezed single file through the carriages gathered on the church's lawn. When at last Owen led them all to the right place, Rosie gasped in disbelief. Someone had covered an entire rose trellis with fresh flowers, turning the ordinarily unornamented lawn into the garden where Jesus was buried. She knew that, because a few feet away, someone had painted an empty crate gray, like the rocks covering the cave where Jesus was buried. She had read the story in all four Gospels this week, and each account washed over her in bursts of joy. "He is not here: for he is risen, as he said."

—∞—

Rosie watched her guests' reactions to the story Owen knew so well. He knew she did, because he watched her while she watched them. Yesterday she had displayed an understanding of the Gospel—Jesus died, was buried, and raised from the dead. Exact words from Corinthians—beyond her recent conversion. As far as he knew, she had never seen the story reenacted before. There was Nicodemus, asking for Jesus' body. The apostle John leading a weeping Mary away from the cross. Rosie placed an arm around her mother's shoulder and wiped at a tear in her eye through that part of the story. The trip of three grieving women through the early Sunday dawn. . . like Rosie and her friends traveled this morning, Pastor Martin mentioned, a gleam in his eye. When they arrived in front of the "grave," they discovered that the center rock had been moved, soldiers asleep on either side. The greeting by the angels. . .the women running with joy to tell the disciples. . .Mary Magdalene's encounter with her Lord in the garden when she didn't even recognize him.

When the congregation sang "Christ the Lord Is Risen Today," Rosie joined in on "alleluia!" with every verse.

All around him, Owen heard shuffling feet and muffled weeping. When the pastor offered a time of invitation, half of Rosie's guests went forward. Men, women, children, entire families.

Afterward, the ladies of the church directed those not involved in prayer and counseling to the tables laden with bacon, egg salad, and hot cross buns. Owen didn't know how anyone could eat. He had rarely seen God work in such an amazing way. What was it Jesus had told his disciples? He had food to eat that they knew not of, and they all thought he was talking about bread and water?

Mrs. Wilkerson took Mrs. Braum's place behind the tables as, no surprise there, Mrs. Braum went to counsel with a couple of women down front. Rosie was there, with her mother. How pleased she must be.

Dragging his attention back to the food tables, Owen spotted Mrs. Strauss. He helped her find a seat then fetched a plate with a good helping of everything. "Mr. Cooper, this is too much!"

Mrs. Wilkerson gestured for Owen to approach, and Mrs. Strauss excused him. "You don't need to stay with me, young man. Go ahead and talk to your friend."

Something told Owen he would prefer Mrs. Strauss as a friend over Mrs. Wilkerson, but he wouldn't say so. "I'll try to come right back."

As soon as Owen reached Mrs. Wilkerson, Nancy appeared. "I'll take over, Mother, so you and Ranger Cooper have a few minutes to talk in peace." She smiled an apology. "We weren't expecting so many people, you see."

Bless Mrs. Braum for her foresight. The Wilkersons might not have expected the crowd, but Mrs. Braum had, after the amazing response to yesterday's party and storytelling.

Mrs. Wilkerson led Owen a few feet away. She didn't even bother to lower her voice as she rasped at Owen, "What does Miss Carson think she's doing, bringing all this riffraff to our church!"

"Jesus Himself said He came to seek and to save the lost." Owen offered a mild reply.

Mrs. Wilkerson plowed over him as if he hadn't spoken. "For all we know, one of them is the thief who robbed my house! And now we've welcomed him into our bosom!" She heaved the aforementioned body part in indignation.

Owen tore himself away, worry fighting with anger over the effect such a diatribe would have on hearts Jesus had brought near. Mrs. Strauss dropped her plate, adding another victim to her collection of broken china. A tall man, who'd appeared to hold himself back during the invitation by only great effort, called his children. Owen's heart broke when he saw Freddy was one of the children. His father's rigid features told Owen the story. It would take a lifetime of blue moons before any of them showed up at church again.

—✺—

On the way home from church, Rosie floated along in the clouds where the pastor said Jesus would someday return. She'd bet her mother floated along with her. Not until they rounded the final corner did she realize a few of her guests were missing. Panicked, she turned to Owen. "There's people missing. We shouldn't leave them to walk back on their own." Owen's visible black mood dampened Rosie's happiness. "What is it? What happened?"

"Not everyone has as big a heart as you do, Rosie." His face sagged as he spoke. "Not everyone was happy when so many people showed up with us today."

Rosie's mouth dropped. The Bible talked about increasing the number of people who believed in Jesus each and every day. Three thousand in one day, she had read. She couldn't imagine anyone who'd already met Jesus would not want everybody in the world to believe. "Why not?" she demanded.

Owen hesitated even longer this time. "Let's not talk about it in front of the others."

She wanted to stop in the middle of the road and demand an answer, now. Maybe he was right. If something bad had happened, she'd rather learn about it in the peace and quiet of her apartment and not in front of people who might reject Jesus because of something an unkind person said. Her steps sped up, and tears of joy now mixed with tears of sadness.

A laughing group climbed the stairs to the various homes in the apartment building. When Owen followed Rosie into the apartment, Mrs. Carson looked at the table, which she'd set with their best dishes in preparation for the noon meal. "Mr. Cooper, I hope you will join us for our meal today." She fitted her actions to the invitation, adding a third plate on the table as quickly as she could. "Or are your parents expecting you home?"

"My parents are home with the Lord. I've been staying with the Martins." Owen blushed, a little. "Mrs. Martin told me to accept an invitation if it was offered. I would be honored to share your food." His voice dipping again, he said, "But I wish I had better news to contribute."

Although still consumed with a desire to discover what happened, Rosie put a finger to her lips. "If it's that bad, let's wait until after we've taken our fill of Ma's wonderful beans." From the aroma in the kitchen, she could tell Ma had added molasses to the beans as well. She poured three cups of milk from a small jar she had kept cool with a bit of ice. Rosie studied the amount of batter left in the bowl, and glanced at Ma and at Owen. Ma nodded. She would use all of the batter.

Did Owen have any idea how big a feast day this was for the Carsons? The molasses made it extra fancy. Ma only used it on special occasions like Christmas or a birth. The last time they'd had any was—a lump formed in Rosie throat—the day of Jimmy's funeral.

Owen's presence flustered Rosie. She'd never had a gentleman caller. Ma piled his plate high with extra beans and a johnnycake, adding a spit of the precious butter waiting on a saucer in the middle of the table.

Unlike Pa, Owen didn't dig in right away. He waited with hands folded in front of him while they finished serving their own plates. When both ladies had taken a seat, he asked, "Would you like me to return thanks for the food?"

Ma looked at Rosie, a question in her eyes. Rosie's thoughts flew to the Wilkersons' dinner table, where a reverent hush had reigned at the table and everyone folded their hands. Mr. Wilkerson droned on in a prayer that made even less sense, with all its thees and thous, than the Bible. She followed the Wilkersons' example of bowing her head and folding her hands, but Owen's prayer was a simple, heartfelt expression of thanks for the provision of food, for Jesus' resurrection, and for the new people in the kingdom of God today. He mentioned Ma by name.

Ma waited a bit after he said "amen" before looking up. "That was right nice of you to mention me to God."

Owen laughed. "God is thinking of you all the time, Mrs. Carson. He is always with you; the Bible says so." Owen ate half his beans before pausing, looking at Rosie, begging her not to make him tell the bad news that was coming.

His prayer had restored the joy Rosie had felt in the morning. "Go ahead and tell us, Owen. We're strong women. I doubt you can tell us anything that's worse than what we've already lived through."

His mouth twisted in a crooked smile, and he ate another bite of beans, together with a second johnnycake. Laying his fork on the plate, he sat back in the chair. "One of the women at the church approached me about the people who came with you. She didn't like it, not at all. Mr. Hill overheard her remarks and left." He stuffed in another spoonful of beans, as if fortifying himself to deliver bad news. "And that's not the worst of it. A couple of days ago, someone took food from the Wilkersons' pantry. Yesterday Freddy told me someone gave everyone in this building a special gift of food—the same things that were stolen." He glanced at the hands he had folded in his lap then looked back up. "Rosie, I have to ask. Do you know anything about the robbery?"

Chapter 8

Today Owen wished he were somewhere out in the open countryside, with space for his horse to stretch his legs and gallop through big, empty spaces, while Owen's mind filled with all kinds of thoughts. He did a lot of his problem solving that way.

Where did city dwellers go to do their thinking? Owen had tried walking down the street with his face turned to the ground. But he bumped into people, and complaints of "Look where you're going!" followed him. He wasn't much better off on horseback, since he had to watch for all oncoming traffic, whether people, wagons, or animals.

When he asked Pastor Martin where he might go for a few minutes of quiet, he suggested that Owen go to Mrs. Braum's house. She wouldn't object to Owen's presence, and the parcel of land where her house sat was big enough to give him the illusion of space.

The problem with Mrs. Braum's place was that he would find Rosie there. In her presence, he couldn't think straight. Mrs. Wilkerson also would allow him to roam her grounds, but running into Nancy would be even worse than running into Rosie.

When the Wilkersons had been robbed, a part of Owen chuckled. They so deserved it. He sobered quickly enough when the thief struck again. A member of Mrs. Wilkerson's bridge club described the same kind of robbery as the first. The thief only took things the owner had multiples of that could be of immediate benefit to people in need. The third strike differed a little. The victim had filled a closet with outgrown and out-of-date clothes she wanted to get rid of. The thief cleared out most of the extra clothing, leaving only a few fancy items, as well as taking a little bit of fresh food.

So far Owen hadn't visited Rosie's neighborhood since Easter Sunday. He feared seeing children clothed in things that should have been freely given from the heart of the previous owner. As the thefts continued, Owen hadn't quite known how to proceed. In the robberies he had solved, the thieves had taken obvious valuables like cash and jewelry. Usually it was simply a matter of learning who might have prior knowledge about the items taken and where they were kept.

That line of reasoning led him nowhere in this case. No thieves he knew bothered with perishable items like sugar and flour. Anyone could guess that food would be kept in the pantry.

He also had never encountered a robbery where the items stolen couldn't be returned. The food was consumed almost as quickly as it was dispersed. Freddy's remark focused Owen's attention on Rosie's apartment building. When he asked her about it, she'd admitted to the wonderful gift of butter and cornmeal that had given them his Easter Sunday johnnycakes.

Owen decided to visit the second victim. The maid, a woman who had attended church with Rosie's group on Easter, brought them tea and petits fours. If he didn't return to duty soon, he would have extra weight he needed to work off before he was at his prime again. Thinking about that was easier than considering the questions sure to follow.

"Have you discovered anything new, Ranger Cooper?" His hostess's blue eyes sparkled as she asked the question. Of all the members of Mrs. Wilkerson's circle, she did the most to help the poor. Like most other victims of a crime, she felt violated and frightened in her own house. "I can hardly go to sleep at night, for fear of someone coming in and causing harm while I lay abed. I'm all alone, you know, ever since my husband passed away. And my son lives down Galveston way. He's telling me I should move in with him, that's how worried he is. But my home is here." Her cheerful facade slipped. "Please tell me you know what is going on."

Her son had been a proper snob when he was in school, and Owen doubted he was all that worried. But he felt her palpable fear and wondered, once again, what to do. He had talked with God about a dozen times already, but if God was answering, Owen hadn't heard it.

"Take me through the day of the theft again." He hoped, prayed, for some fact that could turn the direction of his suspicions in a different way.

She repeated her story. Owen kept his eyes on the floor, fixing the facts in his mind. As she mentioned each member of her staff, he brought their faces to mind. Nothing gave him pause until she mentioned her new maid, Iris.

After she finished her recital, he asked, "Iris. Who is she?"

Blue eyes blinked. "The new maid, as I said. The one who brought in the tray just now."

The fear in Owen's chest formed a ball. Both this robbery and the last one were connected through Rosie Carson.

—⁂—

The group that gathered to go to church the Sunday after Easter was half what it had been. Most of the children came back, though, and Rosie couldn't stop smiling. The parents were more than glad to have the children away from home for a few hours.

Whatever the reason, Rosie was glad to have them. If these young people could hear and see and taste and feel the love of Christ, she couldn't wait to find out what would happen.

Only one tiny cloud hovered on her horizon. Make that two. She felt good and right when she left the gifts with people who needed them. The first cloud came in the shape of the dismay and anger rich people felt about the robberies. Why they missed a few things here and there when they had so much, she couldn't guess.

She hadn't expected the anger in Mrs. Braum's voice when Rosie had expressed the joy of the neighborhood about the gifts of extra food for Easter. "You should have seen their faces, Mrs. Braum. They were so happy. They ate on that food for a week. Not many of them go a week without being hungry."

Mrs. Braum had harrumphed. "I am glad the children had food to eat. Truly, I am. But, Rosie, people can't steal to get what they need. That's just not right."

Rosie couldn't understand that attitude. The pastor had preached about Ruth the other week. He said they were commanded to leave the corners of the fields unharvested, so that poor people could follow along behind and gather what they needed. She'd thought of the clothes packed to give away and extra food sitting in the pantry like the leftover wheat. But when even Owen said it was wrong, she was in a quandary.

Also, she had read the whole book of Acts. All the stories excited her, at least until she got to the fifth chapter and read the horrible story about God striking Ananias and Sapphira dead when they didn't give all the money they made to the church.

It didn't seem wrong to hold something back. If they gave everything, what would they live on? The words Peter spoke to them bothered her. "Why hath Satan filled thine heart to lie to the Holy Ghost, and to keep back part of the price of the land? . . . .why hast thou conceived this thing in thine heart? thou hast not lied unto men, but unto God." He didn't even give them a chance to repent.

Rosie didn't mind the thought of going back to jail, although she didn't think she deserved it, but getting God mad enough at her to make her die, that was something else.

She looked at the money purse where she kept all the coins she had picked up on the ground and saved from her salary and even a few she found lying loose in the pantry. It was a good amount, more than she had ever had at one time before. But she knew a child who needed an operation to make his leg straight. It would cost lots more money than she could make in a year.

No, Rosie, the angel in disguise, would have to strike one more time before she retired. Just this one time. She knew God approved. Didn't God want to heal the sick?

He had even showed her the right place to get that kind of money.

Chapter 9

T he Easter Angel seems to know exactly who needs what. She's treating people's personal property like a mercantile, where she can buy whatever she needs for nothing." Owen tried to inject humor into his remarks, but he knew he fell short.

Rosie hesitated a step. "I'm glad you asked me to come with you when you go to visit Iris. She'll be scared right out of her mind, and her father might tell her not to go back to work. And they need every penny she makes."

Fear was not what he wanted Rosie to feel, unless she needed to. She confused him in a hundred different ways. He stopped in his tracks. A neutral spot, away from places that engendered suspicions and made him believe in the honesty of the woman he admired, might restore a sense of balance.

"Do you mind if I put off speaking with Iris?" At her confused expression, he said, "Don't worry, I won't question her unless you are there. But for tonight"—he relaxed his shoulders and allowed a smile to pull at his mouth—"let's go somewhere different. Have you ever walked by the river? It's quite pleasant."

Her hands dropped to her sides, and she fingered the material of her uniform. "Can I go there, looking like this?"

"You look fine." He took both of her hands in his. "In fact, you look so fine, I'd be scared for you to go there alone. You'd have half the young men in San Antonio chasing you."

"Oh you." Red blossomed in her face as she pulled her hands away from his.

"You're pretty when you blush."

The color deepened at that comment. Owen couldn't wait to show her the river, and he decided to splurge. Walking by Rosie's side, he enjoyed the silent camaraderie until they reached a street where hansom cabs plied their trade.

"Is it far?" Rosie pointed to the darkening sky.

Owen spotted a cab headed in their direction. "It won't be for us." He lifted a hand to halt the cab.

"You're renting a cab?" Once again Rosie's hands strayed to her apron and tugged at it. "That's an awful extravagance."

"Don't worry. I have the money." He helped Rosie into the cab, where she raised the window curtain and stared at the passing street. "I tell you what I'll do. I'll match the cost of the cab and put it in the special offering box at the front of the church."

She brought her hands together. "That's a wonderful idea. I wish more people would do that. . . ." Her voice trailed off. "But they don't."

"You've made me think about things in a different way. Since I met you, I don't even think about buying a cup of coffee at the restaurant without setting aside money to give to people in need. Jesus said, 'For ye have the poor always with you,' but even with my job, I've ignored them. Blind to what was right in front of me."

He was in danger of talking about the very things he had promised himself he wouldn't discuss, at least for this night. But before he could stop, he felt he had to say at least one more thing. "Give people time. This is all a new way of thinking." He spotted the water ahead of them and tapped the top of the cab to let the driver know to stop. "And here we are."

"Look at that water!" Rosie raced ahead, pausing well above the edge of the river-bank. "It winds through the city like a ribbon in my hair."

She sounded like she was seeing the river for the first time. He wished he had a ball with him, or maybe a dog with a stick. He'd love to see Rosie chasing after a little dog. Was that what separated criminals from law-abiding citizens, a few chance hours in fresh air and sunshine? "You know, this would be a nice place to hold the Easter egg hunt next year."

"Do you plan to be here next year?" Rosie turned away from the river and looked into his eyes. Something about the intensity of her gaze said it was more than a casual question.

"Yes." Where did that answer come from? Owen hadn't bothered coming home during Passion Week until his injury forced him to this year. But he knew why he wanted to return: the woman standing before him. Rosie. An impossible question popped to his throat.

She had turned away from him, once again facing the river. "This would be a lovely place for a hunt. There are all kinds of wonderful places to hide eggs. But I don't know if we'd be allowed. . . ." She swallowed. "I still don't like disappointment. God is with me all the time, I know that, but it still seems there are places I'm not supposed to go."

"Aw, Rosie." The impossible question refused to leave Owen alone. "If you were with me, in the company of a Texas Ranger, no one would ever question you again."

At those words, she turned her body about, those bright eyes piercing his heart and soul. "What are you saying, Ranger Owen Cooper?"

He had come this far. He couldn't go back. "I'm saying I'd like to court you, Miss Rosie Carson. If you're willing."

—⁓—

Owen Cooper wanted to court her? Fear fought with joy in Rosie's heart. A good, God-fearing man wanted to court her, like she was any ordinary woman. He deserved someone so much better than she was. Imagine that, a Ranger asking to court a thief who had gone to prison for her crime.

But he didn't know about her latest exploits, did he? If he knew about her plans for a final strike... With her whole being, she wanted to say yes. But she must refuse. "If you knew me, you wouldn't ask me that question."

He blew his breath out and his cheeks collapsed into flat plains, a pale stubble covering his chin and hiding that marvelous mouth. "I may know more than you think I do, Rosie."

At that she expected him to march her to the Ranger office at Leon Springs, but he said no more. Overhead, a gray cloud scuttled by, obscuring the moon on the rise to the east. "It's getting dark. I'd best get you home."

Rosie's feet hurt, and if she walked all the way home, she might hurt bad enough not to go out tonight, for fear of the noise she would make creeping around a building with leaden feet. On this night full of the unexpected, Owen surprised her again by calling for another cab. "I don't know about you, but I'm tired. Do you mind?"

She shook her head, and the pressure of his hand on the small of her back as she climbed in gave her joy. His hands wouldn't be so gentle if he ever had to arrest her.

Again Rosie lifted the window. How different the familiar streets looked from this height, at this time of day. In this part of town, lamps kept the streets nearly as bright as day, only thinning out a little as they passed into a residential neighborhood.

"Mr. Abbott, the church's treasurer, lives down that street. He's a local banker. I hear tell he just received a large deposit that he brought home for safekeeping."

Rosie's insides rattled, but she fought to stay in place. "That's interesting. I wonder if he's Mrs. Abbott's husband. The president of the Ladies' Aid Society." She had already heard about the deposit from the servants' network that wove the city together. She glanced at Owen, but he had settled against the back of the seat, his face inscrutable.

When they stopped by her home, he stopped her from getting out. "I meant what I said earlier. I promise, if you ever need to talk, I'll listen without judging. You are too good a woman to let a few mistakes bring you down." He stepped out, helped her down, and walked her to the door. She waited in the doorway as he vanished with the cab into the darkness.

Rosie plucked a dandelion from the lawn. Some people called it a weed, but she'd rather think of it as a flower, one determined to grow no matter where the seed landed. She'd tear off the petals, she decided. It might not be the best way to make a decision, but she had used it before. God seemed to have stopped talking to her since she started her plan to make the church do God's will, whether they wanted to or not.

For each thought that sped through her mind, she pulled off a petal. If Mom is awake when I go upstairs, I won't go out again. She tore at the petal. If I accept Owen's request for courtship, I must quit. A second petal floated to the floor. If I don't go out tonight, I can never gather enough money for the operation. A third petal dug under her fingernail and turned it yellow before disintegrating. I will go. I won't go.

She made it halfway around the stem when she reached the top of the second flight of stairs. God, it's up to You. You can even add an extra petal if You need to. Should I go? Or shouldn't I go? She continued tearing the petals, dropping one on each step. By the time she reached the last stair, she saw how it was going to play out. Even so, she continued until she had stripped the stem of all the petals, almost hoping God would change the outcome. But He didn't.

"Very well," Rosie said under her breath. Ten minutes later she slipped out the same way she'd come in, so quiet even a dog couldn't hear her light tread.

—⁓—

"Are you sure this is necessary, Cooper?" Abbott patted the pocket of his suit, searching for a pipe. "No thief has ever cracked my safe."

I wish it wasn't. "It is best to take precautions. We sent out enough rumors that the thief will find it hard to resist the temptation. It's best if we catch"—he kept himself from saying "her" just in time—"them in the act, don't you think?"

"Then let me stay here with you. I don't want you risking your life on my account."

That was the one thing Owen didn't want. "I'll be fine. It's no contest, between an armed and experienced Ranger and this thief who relies on stealth as opposed to violent action to garner the goods. No, you take your wife out and enjoy your visit with your son."

Abbott had given the servants the night off and made arrangements to stay overnight with his son. The stage was set for San Antonio's Easter Angel to make an appearance.

Heavy curtains covered the walls in the study that held the safe, and Owen took his hiding place between the floor-length drape and the wall. He was prepared to stay until dawn if necessary; in fact, it's what he hoped for. Unfortunately, he suspected he would have company, and soon.

Owen had left his timepiece behind, not wanting the ticking seconds to give his presence away. For the same reason, he had allowed himself a fresh bath before going out with Rosie. The bearded stubble made up for his vanity with the bath, at least that's what he told himself.

By his calculations, two hours passed before he heard the door to the kitchen squeak open. Light steps ran down the hall, headed straight for the study door. Someone must have informed the thief about the layout of the house.

The door opened with a whisper of sound. Owen waited while feet crossed the room and pulled a small stool across the floor. Thin, metallic sounds testified to the use of a lock pick's tools on the safe.

God, help me. Owen sent up a final prayer before he stepped out from his hiding place.

The feminine figure dressed in black from the top of her cape to the tip of a booted foot turned with a gasp.

"Rosie, I told you I knew more than you thought."

Chapter 10

The hood of Rosie's cloak fell back, moonlight highlighting her pale features. "Owen." His name came out in a jagged whisper, and she stumbled forward, crossing her arms in front of her, ready for him to clasp handcuffs over her hands.

Owen's heart throbbed in his chest. Oh, Rosie. He closed the drapes so no one from outside could see them and lit the single lamp in the study.

She stood rooted in place, as if caught in a child's game of freeze tag. As gently as he could, he placed a hand on her shoulder. She jerked away. Sighing, he pulled a chair to the front of the desk and gestured for her to sit. She did, sitting on the edge, ready to spring away. Instead of sitting behind the desk and frightening her even more, he placed another chair in front, where he could look into her eyes, and sat down next to her. He waited, hoping she would speak first.

When at last she spoke, her words surprised him. "I never should have trusted a dandelion. They never brought me luck before."

Owen had no idea what she was talking about, so he ignored it. "I meant what I said earlier tonight. I'm willing to listen. What happens when we leave here depends a lot on what you do right now." His heart ached. He wanted to help her, but she had to take the first step.

"Is there money in that safe?" Her head jerked toward the heavy box. "Or was that a lie, too?"

"There's money there." Owen felt slapped. "And what I said is not a lie." He drew a deep breath. "I will admit that I asked Abbott to bring money home from the bank and to make sure all his servants knew about it. I promised to keep it safe. And so, I'm here tonight."

"Did you know it was me all along?" Her head hung low in shame. How he longed to lift her up.

"I was pretty sure. You were the strongest link between the robberies and the people who were helped. San Antonio has been abuzz with our own Robin Hood, our Easter Angel." He smiled. "Your heart was in the right place. But, Rosie. . .you just can't go around taking things from people without their permission. Not even clothes destined for the church clothes closet."

She slipped out of her chair onto her knees. "Oh, God, what have I done?" Tears slid down her face. Salty smears and pain-contorted lines marred her loveliness as she turned to Owen. "Go ahead and arrest me. I'm ready."

His heart contracted. "I'm not going to arrest you. All the people involved want is for the robberies to stop. I have a different idea. Are you willing?"

"Yes. I've been asking God what I should do. I have a feeling your plan is going to lead me in the right direction."

He outlined his alternative. "It will be difficult for you. Are you still willing?"

Peace eased the lines around Rosie's face. "Yes."

—ᴍ—

The original Easter crowd joined Rosie outside the apartment house on Sunday morning, along with several additional families. At her request, many of them wore the clothes she had distributed among the neighborhood. It was both a confession and a plea.

Owen, with the driver who worked for Mrs. Braum, arrived at the apartment house with two wagons. Every inch of floor space was taken as the horses lumbered in the direction of the church. As excited as ever, the children chattered and jumped up, standing by the rail to feel the wind whipping their hair and to lean out and try to touch the hands of someone in the other wagon. Rosie worried some might fall out, but their parents kept quiet, and she couldn't bring herself to fuss at them. She'd have to trust their safety to God, something she had neglected too much in recent days.

As if sensing her mood, the people around her kept silent. Only Ma and Iris knew what lay ahead this morning, and they sat on either side of her, cushioning her against her fears.

Mrs. Braum and the pastor's wife waited by the door to the church, walking forward to welcome them as everyone scrambled out of the wagon. "Freddy, why don't you show the children where our class meets. And today we've started a class for the little ones. They'll be going with Mrs. Martin."

The pastor's wife came forward. "Any children who are under five years old will be in my class." She passed down the line and patted the head of the first toddler she met. "Come with me. We have some special things planned for you today."

The child's older sister clung to his hand. "He's staying with me."

Mrs. Martin took a step backward but recovered quickly. "I understand. Maybe next week he'd like to check out my class." After a few minutes, two lines of children followed their teachers to the open spot on the lawn where they had started holding children's Sunday school.

The adults went to the sanctuary, where one of the deacons taught the weekly Bible class. Soon only Owen remained to escort Iris, Rosie, and her ma. "Are you waiting to make sure I don't run away?" Her laughter was only half genuine.

Owen shook his head. "I thought you could use a friend today. That is"—he gestured at the women on either side of Rosie—"another friend. Do you want to go on to class, or would you rather find a private spot?"

Rosie longed for a time of quiet and privacy, but she had invited her neighbors to church. What would they think if she didn't attend Sunday school? She shook her head. "I'd better go to class. But I'll sit at the back." She made it through the next hour by rote. She answered when people talked to her, nodded her head when appropriate, and even introduced a few of her neighbors to people from the church.

The start of the worship service relieved her of social interaction, but she froze as the hymns were sung. The time for the pastoral prayer had arrived. Her stomach knotted so tightly she thought she might look like a bow, tied in the middle.

"Today we are doing something different during our prayer time. Miss Rosie Carson, who shared her remarkable story with us a few weeks ago, has asked to address our congregation again."

Murmurs rippled across the sanctuary. Owen helped Rosie to her feet and walked with her to the first row. "Go ahead. I'm right here," he whispered and nudged her forward.

Light slanted through the windows, crossing the patch of floor she must cross to reach the pastor's side. Light and dark, freedom and imprisonment, acceptance and rejection. . .she had to walk those few short feet to reach her heart's desire. She took one hesitant step forward then a second. Light shone full on her face when she turned to face the congregation, and she felt as though she stood in the presence of God.

The pastor had already heard Rosie's confession. To the congregation, he said, "We all learned a lot from Miss Carson's first testimony. I believe today will be equally powerful, if we listen with open hearts." He nodded for Rosie to begin.

"A few weeks back, I bragged how God had reached down and saved and plucked me from the pit of crime I found myself in." She looked at the floor then looked back up into the light. "The truth is, I'm the one the newspaper's been calling the Easter Angel. The first time I ran into a problem, I turned back to my old ways."

Tears fell down her face, but Rosie didn't stop them. "It's okay if you cry," the pastor had said.

"I made excuses for myself. I thought I was helping the New Testament Church of San Antonio act more like the church I was reading about in Acts, where people who were rich sold things so everybody's needs were met. I didn't think anyone would even notice anything was gone." Her eyes had adjusted to the light, and she searched for Mrs. Wilkerson. "Mrs. Wilkerson, I have to ask for your forgiveness. You invited me into your home and asked me to share my heart. And I repaid you by taking your things. Please forgive me."

She and Owen had debated whether she should confess her plans to steal the money. They decided, no, she shouldn't.

"All along, I read some verses that talked about leaving the corners of the harvest for the poor, and helping widows and orphans, and giving somebody your coat if they needed it. God was showing me all those other verses, too, the ones about not stealing and how Christians shouldn't steal anymore. It's even on God's list of the biggest ten sins we can commit. I have asked for God's forgiveness, and now I ask for yours."

Not a page rustled in the silent sanctuary. The light obscured most faces in front of her, and she couldn't tell how people were reacting.

"I know I was wrong to take those clothes. But before we wash them up and return them, I wanted to show you who I gave them to. Ma, will you help our neighbors up here?"

Each person wearing an article of clothing from the robbery formed a ragged line. They came forward and talked about the clothes they had received. Rosie heard rumblings in the congregation as the parade of clothes finished.

"We can't give back the food, because we already ate it all. I'll work for free until I pay back the cost. And if I need to work more for the clothes besides giving them back, I'll do that, too." Exhausted, Rosie pushed herself to the last thing she needed to say. "You have every reason not to trust me or want me in your church. But don't blame my friends. Welcome them as you would welcome Jesus if He were here. And, I guess that's all." Her legs sagged as she took a step forward, and Owen rushed to her side. He walked with her to their seats on the back row.

When Rosie's senses returned, she heard quiet sobbing around her and low voices in conversation.

Pastor Martin took his place behind the pulpit, head bowed, waiting for a full minute without speaking. When he lifted his head, he didn't open the Bible but instead looked across his congregation. "God has opened a window for us at New Testament Church today. We can close the curtains of opportunity and continue to do everything the same way we've always done it. If we do, as God's shepherd of this flock, I warn you, we will not see the blessings God wants to pour down on us.

"But if we forgive Miss Carson the wrong she has done—and she freely confesses her sin—and open the doors God has placed to our community, we will see unprecedented growth. New Testament growth." He continued exhorting the church to love not only God with all their hearts but to love their neighbors as they loved themselves.

After the service, people flocked to Rosie. Many of them wished her well, even the lady she had stolen the clothes from. "Oh, Miss Carson, don't worry about those clothes. In fact, I'm sure I have some more garments to give away. If I get them to you later, you'll see about giving them to people who need them, won't you?"

Rosie could barely find a voice. After what she'd done, what she'd confessed, they would still trust her with the clothes? She nodded.

"An excellent suggestion." Mr. Abbott came last in the line. "Right in line with what the deacons are proposing. We just had a quick meeting"—he nodded at the men gathered behind him—"and we're in complete agreement. We have been remiss in our care of the people at our doorstep. It took you to show us that. And we believe you are the best person to take charge of our outreach. Are you willing?"

They were handing Rosie her heart's desire on a platter? But she had to say no. "As soon as I finish paying back what I stole, I gotta find work that pays. My ma's only got me to support her. I can only work on something like that part of the time."

Mr. Abbott blinked. "Miss Carson, we will pay you for your services. We'll help you work things out with the people you hurt."

Happiness welled up inside Rosie. "Then I say. . .yes!"

The last of the deacons filed out behind Mr. Abbott, leaving Ma, Iris, and Owen with Rosie. Ma winked at Iris. "Let's go out into the sunshine and leave these two alone for a few minutes."

"Owen—"

"Rosie—" They spoke simultaneously.

She broke into nervous laughter. "Well."

"I told you God had things under control." Owen's grin could have filled all of Texas. "Remember the question I asked you that night by the river?"

When you said you want to court me? How could I forget? "Yes."

"Do you have an answer for me now? I already asked your mother; that's why she left us alone."

"Will you ask me again?" she asked. Part tease, part a request for reassurance.

"I love you, Miss Rosie Carson. Will you allow me to court you, to shower you with my love, and marry me in due time?"

"Yes." But Rosie wasn't finished. "What about you, Ranger Cooper? Do you want to court a convicted thief, a sinner who returned to her old ways at the first opportunity?"

"Who is that?" Taking her hands in his, Owen looked straight through her. "The only woman I see here is a new creation in Christ, beloved of God and called to ministry. I am the one who is honored, if you will accept me."

For answer, Rosie stood on tiptoe and leaned forward, audaciously inviting him to kiss her. "Yes."

He brushed her lips with his. "Welcome home, angel."

REUBEN'S ATONEMENT

by Lynette Sowell

Dedication

This book is dedicated to CJ, my outlaw.
I love the trail we've traveled together.

Prologue

Denmark, Texas, 1867

Quit your bawling, Benjamin." Reuben Wilson didn't mean to sound harsh, not with his baby brother. But a six-year-old couldn't understand why they couldn't go home. Reuben didn't care to think about what he'd left behind in Wyoming. Otherwise he'd probably want to lean back and give a good howl like Benjamin.

Benjamin's round cheeks flamed red, his eyes swollen from a day and night of crying. "I want Ma!" A few passersby on the street glanced toward them but kept on their way. Reuben hoped they'd mind their own business. Colt should be back any moment with their supplies. That is, if he didn't lose his head and draw too much attention to them.

"You can't have Ma, not with the law after us." Caleb Wilson bent closer to Benjamin. "One day, I promise, I'll come back for you. Me, Reuben, and Colt."

"You p–p–promise?" Benjamin's sobs turned to hiccups.

"Yeah, sure do." Caleb chucked him on the shoulder.

"Y'all gonna stand there jawing with the boy, or can I show him where he's goin' to sleep?" Sadie stood in the doorway of the Gilded Lily. Her booted foot tapped like a woodpecker on the boardwalk. She shoved the short-capped sleeve of her flaming red dress over her bare shoulder. "I got customers waitin' to meet the girls."

"Yeah, go on, Benjamin." Reuben kept scanning the crowded street. He considered himself a man at twenty, and he took his responsibility for his brothers seriously. "Sadie's goin' to take good care of you. She'll even give ya some spending money once in a while for helping out." His gaze darted from faces to horses to weapons of passersby. They needed to leave, and fast.

"She will, will she?" Sadie's brow furrowed. "I don't recall agreein' to pay the boy just 'cause y'all are running from the law."

Reuben flashed his attention to Sadie. "Just give the boy a quarter once in a while. He's a good boy. My ma taught him. He can read a mite, even sweep floors and do dishes. Can you help 'er out, Benjamin?"

"Okay." Benjamin hiccupped.

"We can't go back to Ma now. But one day I'll come back for you." The promise made Reuben feel as if he'd swallowed an apple core.

Pounding hooves made Reuben look up. He touched the revolver on his hip. It was only Colt, riding up on a new mount. He had two more in tow. "Got our rides, boys. Let's go."

Reuben's eyes burned as he took one last look at Benjamin. If only Caleb and Benjamin hadn't tailed them from Wyoming. By the time he and Colt had discovered the boys following, they couldn't well turn back. Not with the sheriffs of three towns hunting for them. He said nothing and grabbed the reins of the nearest mount. The other horses had been ridden too hard, and they couldn't risk stopping for long.

Before Benjamin's tears began anew, Reuben led Colt and Caleb to the edge of town.

Reuben reined in his horse and faced both of them. "We go different directions. Y'all lay low, keep your noses clean, and get a new life if you can. A year from now we meet here, get Benjamin, and go back to Ma." Colt and Caleb nodded, then spurred their mounts and disappeared in clouds of dust.

Desperation now drove them apart, but Reuben hoped they'd all find their way back together somehow.

Chapter 1

Raider's Crossing, Wyoming Territory—February 1880

Thirteen years and a heart full of memories lay between Charlotte Jeffers and Reuben Wilson. That, and his mother's coffin being walked down the chapel aisle and out the front doors. Charlotte shivered at the blast of wind that whistled through and touched them all.

The man's heart had to be as icy as the late winter air to leave his mother for so long and return but a few days before her spirit left this earth. Charlotte knew Reuben had broken Elizabeth Wilson's heart. She shoved her own childhood pain aside and prayed silently that somehow the Lord could work good out of the whole mess.

Reuben removed his hat. His calloused hands traced around the band. Lines etched his face, partly from grief and partly from a life spent away from Raider's Crossing that Charlotte could only guess at. Propriety reined her in from stepping across the aisle and telling Reuben exactly what she thought of him.

He'd grown tall, as she'd guessed he would. Broad as a fence, with arms that looked strong enough to hold up a wagon by the axle. Walnut brown hair as untamed and unruly as its owner, and green penetrating eyes that held plenty of secrets. Reuben's well-kept mustache lent a maturity to his face. If he weren't one of the Wilson boys, she reckoned he'd be yet another eligible man in town. Which didn't interest her one bit.

"They say he's a changed man."

Charlotte started at the whisper in her ear. "We'll see about that, won't we, Mrs. Booth?" She should know better than to entertain conversation with the postmistress who happened to know all sorts of interesting tidbits about folks in town.

"I heard he killed a dozen men in Colorado and New Mexico. And he's got a red-skinned wife hidden somewhere." The older woman's voice carried in the crowded chapel.

"If he's made his peace with God, his past won't matter anymore." As for the wife? Well, that was Reuben's own business. Her words sounded trite and pompous. She dropped the conversation, hoping Mrs. Booth would fall silent. This would teach her to accept a ride from James instead of accompanying her parents to the funeral. "A fine young lady like you would do well to stay away from the likes of him. Good thing those brothers o' his aren't around, either. Scalawags, the lot of 'em." Mrs. Booth clucked and hissed, shaking her head. "Except for poor Benjamin..."

Charlotte wanted to distance herself from the gossip, but she was wedged shoulder-to-shoulder with the other residents who'd come to pay their respects. James sat on her other side, and she guessed he probably wondered if anyone had noticed his new buggy. She wondered where he'd gotten the money for it.

She forced her feet to keep still and clamped her hand on James's offered arm. He started rubbing slow circles on the back of her hand. Charlotte slipped her hand free from the unwanted demonstration of...affection? James's expression didn't exactly show affection. In fact, she couldn't quite put a name to the look on his face. It made her want to find her parents.

Other young ladies in town saw James as a fine match for an unattached female. He came from good, hardworking people and had made quite a name for himself in Laramie, or so he claimed, writing for the newspaper. Now he was back in town and writing for the *Raider's Crossing News*.

A good name was something to be proud of, unlike some names that sprang to mind. Like the one attached to the man across the aisle from her.

Charlotte glanced at Reuben and saw his expression boring into her. Her face tingled. She straightened her posture and refused to pull her gaze from his.

I know what you're all about, Ruby Wilson. No childhood loyalties will keep me from surrendering the land we bought from your mother. Leave Raider's Crossing, and we'll all be better off.

—∞—

A man could do only so much to make amends. Reuben sighed, the sound an echo of the prairie wind. He would never be able to make up for his ma's undeserved grief.

The tiny community had gathered for a brief service, but their faces were a blur to him among a sea of dark suits and dresses, showing respect to his ma. He would not look at them, only at the cross that hung at the front of the tiny church.

What do I do, Lord?

"Find your brothers, Reuben, and buy our old farm back." Ma's last request came to him again. "Make your pa's dream come true."

"I promise, Ma," he'd said. At that moment he would have agreed to anything, to see the glow of pride in her eyes.

Long ago, when life was simpler, he and Colt, Caleb, and little Benjamin had lived a joyous boyhood as they traveled west and helped their pa build a home. Pa had promised they would raise cattle and keep as many horses as they could.

Where had those days gone? When did joy sneak away like a bandit in the night?

Whispers drifted through the crowd after the closing prayer, and Reuben forced himself to look directly at the source of the voices. Mrs. Booth, the loosest jaw in town, and Charlie Jeffers. Reuben found himself locked in a battle of glares with the younger woman while memories dragged him away....

"Charlie! Girls ain't supposed to ride like boys!" Fifteen-year-old Reuben bellowed at a honey-haired girl with spindly arms. She rode astride a straggly pony as she gave Reuben and his brothers hot pursuit across the rolling hills. He reined in his horse and watched the pair approach.

"Can, too!" Her bonnet flopped around her neck. "I can do anything you or Colt or even Caleb can!" She set her jaw and gave him a look hot enough to fry an egg.

"Go home and help yer ma." Girls! Always getting underfoot. Arguing, then sniffling and bawling when they didn't get their way.

"Stop treating me like Benjamin." Her lower lip started to quiver. "B'sides, I'm your blood sister."

Reuben spat on the ground and glared at Colt. He'd been the one to let Charlie in on their little ritual. "Blood brothers—and sister—till the stars die," they'd promised.

Now Reuben felt the heat of the same expression. He and his two younger brothers had always been fascinated with the customs of the natives in the land, but it never occurred to them the silliness of proclaiming themselves blood brothers. The only one who'd really been bonded to them through the ritual was Charlie.

Did she remember? He let himself stare until a blush swept over her face. Her once-thin features had bloomed, and her awkwardness had transformed into curvy womanhood. A brief thought fluttered through his mind. Did she still wear trousers on occasion? The caught-up hair that still reminded him of honey in sunlight and the prim neckline of her dress told him she'd put childish notions behind her.

Reuben had come to town with money in his pocket, with hopes of one day buying back his family's land, but he wanted to test the waters before he plunged in with talking about a sale. The folks in Raider's Crossing held grudges, he discovered. They also took care of their own.

Just like the dandy who'd been eyeing Charlie like she was a prized possession. And eyeing Reuben like he was a fox trying to get into the henhouse. Reuben gritted his teeth. Courting Charlie Jeffers would be like expecting to rope the moon. Finding his brothers and getting the family land back would be nearly as difficult.

He barely remembered stumbling to the cold outside, shaking the preacher's hand, and thanking him for his words about Ma. Reuben wouldn't have been able to speak, and he didn't deserve to. He couldn't have spoken of the few happy childhood memories he owned. Just as well. He'd probably have cried in front of the town.

An older yet familiar man, who of a certainty had to be Mr. Jeffers, shook hands with Charlie's suitor. The suitor smiled at Mr. Jeffers then offered Charlie his arm. The couple left for a smart-looking buggy. Reuben seized the moment to approach Charlie's father.

"Mr. Jeffers, thank you kindly for coming." He touched the brim of his hat and nodded at Mrs. Jeffers. "Ma'am, thank you, too."

Sam Jeffers regarded Reuben's hand for a moment, then reached out to give a hearty shake. "Welcome back, son."

"Thank you." Reuben swallowed hard. "I—I've been meaning to ask you somethin' since I've been back."

"Yes?" Sam huffed through his gray mustache.

"I was wonderin' if you're needing a hand about your place. I've been working some ranches in Colorado, and I ain't afraid of hard work here." Reuben dwarfed the man by at least six inches, but somehow in his presence Reuben felt as if he were ten years old.

"I reckon I'll need some help with the horses, plus the barn needs patching 'fore a late storm sets in." Sam looked him straight in the eye. "You come on out at suppertime, and we'll talk some more."

Reuben nodded. "Yes, sir. That'll be fine, sir. I've got a room in town."

"Is that so? If you work for me, plan on staying in our bunkhouse. It's not much, but it's warm. Our other hired hands go home to their families, so you'll be on your own." Sam squeezed Reuben's arm. "Etta puts supper on the table at five, so bring your appetite."

"Thank you, sir, ma'am." Reuben watched them leave the churchyard, and he felt strangely alone.

He'd gotten used to his own company these past years after losing track of Colt and Caleb. Reuben moved back to the wooden coffin and squatted next to it on the hard ground. He had ordered a stone with honestly earned cash in anticipation of a burial come spring. But the man had accepted the money with a suspicious look in his eye.

"Lord, it's a beginning. At least Mr. Jeffers—Sam—will look me in the eye. Thank You for the chance to make things right again."

Reuben bowed for a few minutes more in wordless prayer, letting regret sweep through him until silent sobs threatened to wrack his body. He did not care that a couple of men stood nearby, waiting to carry his mother's coffin to be held with the others until the ground thawed.

"Mr. Wilson?"

He forced his face into a semblance of composure and glanced up. "Reverend. I was just takin' a moment—"

"You've walked a long road to get here."

Reuben nodded. He had arrived by stage and meant to buy a horse, but he figured the reverend was talking in a different sort of way. "Yeah, I have. I–I'm not the same person I was when me and the boys lit out years ago."

"People around here, they don't change much, I've noticed."

"I have, thanks to God and an old preacher named Reverend Mann. He told me I needed to start making amends for what I'd done." Reuben turned his focus to the wooden box before him. "It meant jail time, but Reverend Mann was right. A man sleeps easy with a clear conscience."

"Well, maybe in time people here will see the change in your life." Reverend Toms patted Reuben's shoulder. "Won't happen overnight, but you give them a chance, and they'll come around. God's grace covers all of us willing to accept it. I'll be praying you find your family."

"Thank you, sir." He watched as Reverend Toms left the yard to return to the parsonage. The preacher had been in Raider's Crossing since Reuben was a boy. He imagined the older man entering the tiny home he shared with his wife. Their children were probably grown and gone.

Would Reuben ever have the security of home and know the warmth of a family? Right now he felt as desolate as the grave. Warmth didn't linger among the dead.

He supposed he'd better get moving, back to the rooming house, and prepare himself to face the Jeffers clan. Maybe he could glean a bit of comfort from them. Although he didn't deserve any kindness, he hoped even Charlie would welcome him.

Chapter 2

H e's coming here?" Charlotte's voice cut off with a squeak. She set the kettle back on the stove and whirled to face Momma.

"Your pa's talking about hiring him to help out. You know we need an extra hand around here, especially with your brother gone." Momma matter-of-factly kneaded the bread dough a final time.

"I figured Pa had already hired someone." *Reuben Wilson, coming here?* Her thoughts swirled around; then a gnawing feeling settled in her stomach.

"Thirteen years can change a body."

"Yes, you're right." Charlotte handed the bread pans to Momma. "But how do we know for certain?"

Momma reached out a flour-covered hand and touched Charlotte's arm, stopping her from moving back to the stove. "Child, I'm not telling you to give him your heart. No one's asking for that."

"I know," Charlotte whispered. She managed a smile and hoped the subject would change.

He'd made her out a fool once, but not again. At thirteen she'd trusted him with her fragile heart, only to have it tossed at her feet in a million pieces two years later when he and his brothers disappeared. Then when he reappeared, she realized she'd only squashed the pieces together, and her whole heart threatened to crumble again. This "put her in a mood," as Momma would say.

James had left after a short conversation in the front parlor earlier in the afternoon, a fact for which she was grateful. No, maybe she wanted him here by her side at supper, at least to drive home to Reuben the fact that her life did not include him. *Stop it. You'll not use another man to prove a point to someone else.*

Charlotte started heating the grease to cook the beef her family reserved for special occasions. If Reuben was like the prodigal son in the Bible, she needn't act like the jealous older brother and begrudge him some Christian hospitality.

She'd been praying about acting more like a Christian outside of church. Therefore she would do her best to see Reuben as the reformed wanderer, in need of restoration and kindness. But she would make sure the walls around her heart held firm. When she put supper on the table, a knock sounded at the front door.

Momma said, "Charlotte, open the door for our guest."

"Of course." Charlotte placed the plate of meat on the table, smoothed her apron, and headed for the front room.

As she expected, Reuben waited, turning his hat over in his hands. His bulk filled the doorway.

"Please come in." Charlotte reached for his hat. A tangle of fingers made her catch her breath.

"Your ma and pa have a nice home. I think they were building it when. . ." Reuben's voice trailed off as he took in his surroundings with a somber expression.

"Yes." Charlotte glanced at the comforts she'd grown to love. Her momma's warm knitted throws, perfect to wrap up in on a chilly night, the hand-carved rocking chair from back East, an iron woodstove that kept the front part of the house warm. "Pa finished the house not long after you and. . .you and your brothers left." The words came out in spite of her reluctance.

Reuben winced as though she'd slapped him. "What about your brother? Is he still around? He should be about eighteen by now, right?"

Charlotte shook her head. "No. Momma and Pa sent him to school. Which is why Pa needs the help now. We lost a hand recently also."

She turned her back to lead Reuben to the warm kitchen, but his strong hand on her shoulder stopped her.

"Charlie."

Charlotte closed her eyes and murmured, "It's been a long time since anyone called me that." She allowed Reuben to turn her back around. What had happened to her head? Her feet refused to take her into the kitchen.

She opened her eyes and tilted her head back to meet Reuben's gaze. Her rebellious pulse now hammered in her ears. The last time they'd been this close was the night before Reuben and his brothers disappeared. She now saw a man's face instead of a mostly grown boy, torn between loving her and running from the sins of his youth. Well, she thought he'd loved her. The fingers of her free hand tightened into a fist.

"Oh, Reuben—" Her fingers tingled, wanting to touch his jaw, which tensed with emotion. The sorrow in his eyes struck her in the gut, making her feel like the time she'd taken one of the boys' dares to leap from the hayloft onto a haystack. She'd fallen down, down, down and landed on a shallow part of the stack. The air had left her lungs with a whoosh as she slammed onto the hay-covered ground. Just like now.

"I'm sorry, Charlie. We'd gotten in over our heads. I didn't want to lead the law straight to Ma. Turns out I broke her heart anyway. We all did." Reuben raked his hand through his hair. "I didn't want to break yours, either."

The old feelings of betrayal surged through her. "I loved you once. But that was a long time ago. We're both adults now, and I'm sure quite different people." The admission of her old feelings made her face flame hotter.

"I know I'm different now. Which is what I hope you and the rest of the town will see one day." Reuben expelled a hollow sigh. "And I thank you for coming today. Your family has done me a great kindness. I'm glad my ma wasn't all alone."

"No, she wasn't." Her emotions teetered between compassion for the man before her and anger at the years they'd lost. "She prayed for you, even up until the end."

"She prayed me home."

Charlotte fell into the river of anger. "A little too late, don't you think? Why are you here, anyway?" Two stray tears crept down her cheeks.

"This place is my home. I need to make amends for what I've done." He wiped away one of her tears with his rough yet gentle fingers.

Her stomach quivered at his presumptive gesture and stepped backward in the direction of the kitchen. "Come. Supper's on the table. Pa should be washing up after seeing to the animals, and then we'll eat."

So much for building up walls around her heart. As he had done in childhood, Reuben snuck around the back and caught her unawares. No matter what he said, some things hadn't changed, but she wouldn't tell him that. Her heart accused her of being a fool not to realize that James was a lesser man than Reuben.

—⁓—

All through the meal, Charlie avoided looking Reuben in the eye. Although Sam talked about the work he needed help with around the farm, Reuben felt as though he held an unspoken conversation with the woman across the table.

During the few moments in the front room before dinner, the feelings coursing through Reuben nearly overcame him. He wanted to shove through the years piled between them and take Charlie in his arms and kiss her, as he should have years ago, and promise never to leave.

What would have happened if he and his brothers had returned the money from the robbery in Colorado and come clean? Reuben imagined Benjamin, who was safe at home, and Colt, Caleb, and himself running the Wilson ranch after jail.

"So what do you think, Reuben?"

"Sounds fine to me."

"You ain't heard a word of what I've told you the last five minutes, have ya?" Sam chuckled. His molasses brown eyes glinted in the lamplight. "Ah, but you've had a lot on your plate. I can't pay you much—"

"That's all right, sir." Reuben downed the last sip of his coffee. "I'm here to figure out some things, maybe earn some respect back for my family. One thing I have learned is there's no shame in hard work."

Sam nodded. "Right you are. I was hoping Sam Junior would have wanted the farm one day, but he's got work of another kind. He's going to be a lawyer."

He appeared to change his direction of thought. "Another thing, around here we work every day except Sunday. We go to the Lord's house and worship. And you'll come with us, too."

"That's fine by me." Reuben didn't dare venture a glance at Charlie. "Another thing I've learned is a man isn't much of a man without living for God. I'm nowhere near the man I want to be, but with His help I'm trying."

That said, he picked up his coffee cup and raised it to his lips, then stopped. He'd forgotten it was empty.

"Charlotte, get our friend Reuben here another cup of coffee, would ya?" Sam gestured toward Reuben's cup, still held in midair.

A knock sounded at the front door. Sam glanced at his wife, then at Charlotte, who had moved to the stove.

"I'll answer that," she offered. Charlotte rounded the table, her skirts swishing.

She returned a few seconds later with a red flush on her cheeks. The young dandy who'd driven her home after the funeral followed close behind. Reuben didn't miss the challenge in the young man's eyes.

"I apologize for interrupting your supper, Mr. and Mrs. Jeffers. I happened to leave my hat here earlier and thought I'd retrieve it now." The man appraised Charlotte with a look that made Reuben want to wipe it from his face. Reuben found himself the focus of the mild-mannered gaze that masked anger held back like a wild bronc.

Reuben stood from his place at the table. "I don't believe I've made your acquaintance, but I want to thank you for coming and paying your respects to my ma. I'm Reuben Wilson." As if the man didn't know. Reuben extended a hand.

"James Johansson. I used to share a desk with your brother Caleb in school." James's hand clenched Reuben's in a wiry grip. "Mr. and Mrs. Jeffers, since you have company, I'll be off. But if Charlotte wishes and with your permission, may I return tomorrow evening to listen to her read?"

Sam nodded as Reuben took his seat.

"All right, tomorrow at seven. Have a pleasant evening." James put on his hat then left.

Reuben stared at his empty coffee cup and wondered if Charlotte could see that James was as slippery as a fish. From the corner of his eye, he saw her move to the stove for the coffeepot, her face now glowing crimson.

"Here's that coffee, Reuben." Charlotte was at his elbow. Her hand shook as she poured.

"Thank you. It's good coffee."

"Ma made it." She returned to the stove and kept her back to him.

Reuben ignored the barb. "Another thing, Sam. I'm going to start looking for my brothers. Part of my promise to Ma, you know. Has anybody heard from them?"

Sam shook his head. "Not since Caleb came through about five years ago. He looked wore out. Think he was pretty ashamed. Saw yer ma and left."

Etta added, "I remember talking with her about Caleb over tea. I think it hurt her again that he left, but she believed that somehow the words she shared would bring him back to following the Lord's ways."

"I'm grateful to you both for watching out for her. You gave her a fair price for the land, and she lived comfortably in town." Reuben sipped his coffee, feeling the all-too-familiar shame rising inside again. "You've been good neighbors. She said you helped her after Pa died." His throat tightened.

Etta patted his hand. "We take care of our own here, Reuben Wilson. Welcome home."

Reuben caught Charlotte's gaze. Her eyes glittered with unshed tears.

Chapter 3

Reuben this, Reuben that!" The wind tugged at Charlotte's hat, so she grabbed the brim with a free hand. She'd tucked her other hand around James's arm. "For two weeks now that's all I've heard."

He reined in the horse pulling the buggy. "And that's all I've heard from you." Though they were on the road leading from town to her parents' farm, James drew her closer and moved in for a kiss.

His face swallowed up her vision, and Charlotte pushed James away. "Don't! Someone might see us!"

"I don't mind if you don't. I'd rather the world know I'm courting you."

Charlotte sat up straight and as far away from James as she could. "Courting? I know you've been escorting me home, but my pa never spoke to me about courting."

"What do you think I've intended, if not to court you?" James took her gloved hand in one of his. "Then you needn't feel so shy about kissing me."

Charlotte didn't know about the shy part, but kissing James had been the furthest thing from her mind at the moment. What had been on her mind was Reuben. Every day of the week at every meal she'd seen him. In the sleepy hours before dawn she silently poured his coffee, and he smiled his thanks. Sometimes at the noon meal he'd return dusty and tired from his labors. In the evenings after supper he would listen to the family Bible readings. And at night, when she was supposed to be sleeping, she would find herself awake and wondering about the man asleep in the bunkhouse.

"Well, you're not saying anything. That doesn't bode well for me." James chirruped to his horse, and they continued down the frosty lane.

"I'm sorry." Charlotte shook her head. "I've been distracted."

"I can tell."

"Thank you for driving me home and for rescuing me from Mrs. Booth at the general store." Charlotte shook her head. "That woman tries to get news from people like a bee gathering pollen."

"I'm always glad to help a lady in a predicament. If I'd been a few minutes later, I'd have needed to rescue you from Reuben."

"No need. Reuben would never hurt me. . . ." Charlotte recalled seeing Reuben on the street. She wondered what business he had in town, especially on a workday when he should be helping her pa.

Reuben's face had lost some of its somber cast when he saw her, and she thought he might offer to escort her home, especially when she saw her pa's wagon hitched in the street.

"So what news was our Mrs. Booth attempting to wrest from you?" James's voice held a mild tone.

"Oh, if Reuben Wilson has stolen any of our valuables—things like that." Charlotte shook her head. "Of course he hasn't. He's worked hard. In fact, I don't think Pa's paying him enough for what he's doing."

"Sounds like you're going soft on him."

"It's not like that," Charlotte stammered. "I think he needs a fair chance, just like everyone. People can change. Especially since he's a Christian."

"Uh-huh. And a leopard can change his spots."

"Really, James, you sound like Mrs. Booth."

"Charlotte, Reuben and his brothers went bad. They tore all over the place, thieving and such. You remember that robbery at the mercantile, the one they pulled right before they disappeared with Benjamin?" James slowed the buggy. "Some people are bad news through and through. There's no changing that. I'm a newspaper man. I deal in facts."

"Facts change. People can, too." Charlotte was wishing more and more she'd stayed in town and let Reuben drive her home instead.

—⁂—

Reuben signed his name at the bottom of the telegraph form. "That should do it. You'll be sure to let me know if you hear back, right?"

"Check in with me next time you're in town, Mr. Wilson." The telegraph operator proofread Reuben's form and accepted his fee. "It may take awhile—depending on the records and how busy the lawman is—before you hear anything."

"I suppose I'll keep waiting then." Reuben put his hat back on. "Have a good day."

He left the telegraph office and entered the brisk outdoors. Raider's Crossing's hubbub of busy citizens crisscrossed the street. Reuben headed down the boardwalk to the rooming house where his mother once lived.

Reuben touched the bankroll nestled in an inner pocket of his coat. It would have taken him too long to write a letter that made sense, so he figured he'd telegraph sheriffs for information about his brothers' whereabouts. One of the first things he'd done was write to Sadie, but his letters had returned unopened.

Please, Lord, help me find my family. I need to stay here to get the land back, and I don't know where to look for the others.

Charlie and her persistent suitor had probably already left in his snug little buggy. He had seen her earlier across the street. She almost appeared as if she wanted to speak to him.

In fact, he'd borrowed Sam's farm wagon with an ulterior motive in mind. Not just to take his mother's and family's effects with him, but maybe even take Charlie home. She'd stubbornly walked the two miles to town, claiming she wanted to get the mail and some fresh air. Probably ruined her pretty boots in the frozen, muddy wagon tracks.

A reluctant smile tugged at his lips as he entered the boardinghouse. The smell of fresh apple pie made his stomach growl.

Mrs. Beasley, the boardinghouse owner, met him by the staircase. "Mr. Wilson, good day. You've come for your mother's things?"

"Yes, I have." His throat tightened. "I won't be long."

"No worries. Take as long as you like. Here's the key." She handed him the cold piece of metal.

Reuben went to what had been his mother's room, where she'd lived the past five years or so. As soon as he opened the door, he smelled the rosewater she used to wear.

The patchwork quilt on the bed was neatly tucked under a pillow. A brush and hand mirror lay near the bowl and pitcher on the washstand, as if waiting for his mother to return. He moved to the small wardrobe and opened a door to find several dresses, worn yet well cared for.

Maybe Charlie or her mother would like them. He removed the dresses from the wardrobe and placed them on the bed. The bureau contained a few ladies' undergarments. It was odd removing those; perhaps he would throw them away.

Reuben's throat swelled, and he dashed away the tears. He needed to finish this job fast before he set to bawling. The trunk at the foot of the bed came open easily, its lock broken. Reuben stuffed the dresses, the brush, and the mirror inside. He glanced around the plain yet tidy room. Nothing else was left for him to do except gather the contents of his family legacy into the trunk and head for the Jeffers farm. Having a family around him might help him squirrel through this box to see what to keep and what to give away. Reuben corrected himself. Having Charlie next to him would help. He could force himself to wait for the right time.

―⁓―

Charlotte's eyes burned. Even by the window in the front room the afternoon light didn't help illuminate her mending very much. But the chore was a welcome diversion that had sent James on his way. He'd unsettled her with his advance in the buggy. Before they parted, he promised he'd never make such an assumption again. Still, she didn't like the way he spoke of Reuben.

The front door opened. Charlotte didn't bother to look up when a familiar clomp of boots entered the room. They crossed the room and stopped near her.

"Could you help me, please?" Reuben stood before Charlotte, carrying a wooden trunk. "That is, if it's not much trouble."

"Help you?" He seemed to have no difficulty carrying the trunk.

"These are. . .were. . .my ma's things." His gaze dropped from her face to what he held. "Some things I want to keep, but I. . .I found a few things you might like."

Charlotte swallowed hard. She couldn't imagine having to complete such a task, didn't even want to think of it. To do so alone, with years of regret piled high. . .

"Of course I'll help." Her gentle tone surprised her. "Set the trunk beside the stove, and I'll put the kettle on for tea. It's cold outside."

"Thank you." Reuben deposited the trunk on the rag rug and sat on the chair across from Charlotte's.

She went to the much warmer kitchen and stoked the fire in the cookstove to a snappy blaze, then filled the kettle with water from the sink pump. Reuben's mere presence and humble request made her head reel, much more than James did.

Reuben needed a friend. Any romantic entanglements would only complicate matters further. Besides, Charlotte couldn't be sure that he wouldn't run again. She returned to the sitting room where Reuben knelt before the open trunk.

She found a spot on the rug next to him and lifted a simple gown and matching shirtwaist from the trunk. "What do you want to do with the dresses?"

Their gazes locked. In the harsh afternoon light, the scar on Reuben's face seemed deeper than usual. Instead of the sadness she'd seen since their reunion, she glimpsed a spark of hope in Reuben's eyes.

"You can have them. I mean, you and your ma might find them useful." Reuben turned his attention to the trunk's contents.

Charlotte folded the clothing and set it to the side. In the next layer of trunk items she found a rather large packet of brown paper tied with twine. "What's this?"

"Open it."

She untied the packet and unfolded the paper. A gown of soft silk, more than thirty years out of style, tumbled onto her lap. "Oh, it must be your ma's wedding gown."

"You can keep it if you want to. I know it's not the style ladies wear now, but maybe you can make something else from it. I don't know, but the fabric looks fine." Reuben rubbed his forehead and opened another paper packet, this one containing several daguerreotypes.

"Your ma and pa. And"—Charlotte smiled—"you and your brothers. So long ago. . ." Her eyes smarted as she wondered what had happened to the other Wilson boys.

"We were still in knickers." Reuben smiled, and Charlotte wished she could see that expression on his face more often. "I think I was all of fourteen. Benjamin was a baby."

His voice cut short, and Charlotte heard the sorrow in his tone. "Where are they, Reuben?"

"I don't know. I've written to—to the place where we left Benjamin. Never heard anything." Reuben put the daguerreo-types back into the packet and retied the string. "We were stupid, thinking we'd never get caught or that no one had wised up to what we were doing. And Benjamin? Benjamin thought we were having fun adventures without him."

Reuben settled to a seated position on the rug, and Charlotte forced herself to be quiet long enough for him to continue.

"He followed us, the little coot." Reuben shook his head. "We didn't know until it was too late. And we didn't want to risk leading a trail home to Ma."

"So you split up."

"Yeah. It wasn't supposed to be for long. Then months turned into years somehow." Reuben held up a pocket watch and let it spin on its chain. "Time moved fast."

Charlotte's heart surged with compassion. She couldn't imagine being alone in the world and knowing that somewhere out there she had kin. She placed her hand on Reuben's arm. "I want to help you. I'll write letters, do whatever we can to find them."

He covered her hand with one of his. "Thank you, Charlie. That means a lot to me."

"We're old friends. I suppose that hasn't changed."

Reuben picked up her right hand and turned it so the palm faced upward. He moved the cuff of her dress up a few inches, exposing her forearm. The simple action made her face burn. "Do you remember?"

"I never forgot." Charlotte wanted to weep out the sorrow of the lost years between them. *Lord, we can't go back.*

She stared at the faint scar from long ago when she and the Wilson brothers pledged to be blood kin to the bitter end. Back then she had no idea what that would mean. And now she had no idea if her heart was up to the challenge.

Chapter 4

The wind sliced through Reuben's thin and threadbare coat as he walked along the boardwalk in Raider's Crossing early Saturday evening. His stomach ached after enjoying an early supper in town. He'd bought a new horse, too. While in town he'd met a few more people, and the name Wilson meant little to them—other than wasn't that the older woman who had passed on sometime back? Then when they found out it was his ma, their tone changed. No questions asked, either. He supposed not everyone knew of his prodigal state.

Reuben shivered and turned down the side street to the livery. He paused once out of the wind. A warmer coat would be nice. Reverend Mann, though, had said he ought not to spend money on frivolous things like a new coat, not after how he'd squandered money in the past. To atone for this sin, Reuben waited awhile longer. He wondered when God would think it was long enough. Maybe he'd ask Reverend Toms. Reuben had no Bible, but he sure paid attention to the preaching, and Reverend Toms seemed to know the Book well.

A voice drifted down the side street and into Reuben's ears.

"Yessir, that pretty little Charlotte Jeffers comes with a fine package if I marry her."

Reuben curled his hands into fists at the sight of the dapper young man talking and laughing with other spit 'n' polished lads.

"You know her pa's going to throw in that old Wilson parcel."

His friend chuckled. "I tried to come courtin' once, but she's as cold as Raider's Pond in December."

Charlie's suitor clapped his friend on the back, and the men paused at the end of the alley with their backs to him.

"Well, my friend, the ice is beginning to thaw. I'm sure of it. If I have my way, she'll be begging her daddy to let her marry me. You know she's three years older than me?"

"She don't look long in the tooth."

The suitor—James, was it?—strutted like a rooster. "Nor the rest of her, either. People will pay good money for that land, and they're going to be paying it to me once it's mine."

Reuben turned and walked to the livery before he punched a wall or, worse, planted a fist into James's face. The man had practically sold Charlotte's dowry before he'd even married her. James had no knowledge of how to treat a lady, either.

Reuben had a right to buy that land, intended dowry or no. Soon he could make Sam Jeffers an offer. And wouldn't that throw a kink in James's spokes? He grinned at the thought.

Something didn't set right with Reuben about James. The man's expression reminded him of the sort of fellow who marked cards and hid his pistol under the table.

The warmth of the livery made up for Reuben's coat, and the scent of straw and animal swirled around him. Reuben went to the stall where his new mount, a roan mare named Checkers, waited. She had wise eyes and looked strong. One day she'd make a fine cutting horse. He'd need to get some cattle first, though.

"Come for your horse, have you?" Mac, the liveryman, stood holding a pitchfork at the end of the aisle.

"That I have, and I thank you for the saddle." After settling the matter of payment, Reuben swung up onto the horse's back and rode out feeling a mite taller—and not because of the mount.

He had arrived in Raider's Crossing by stage with nothing but the clothes on his back and a small sack of sundries. His pa's words came to him. *You take a trip one step at a time and build a life one day at a time.* He remembered not understanding their humble beginnings when they arrived in Wyoming Territory. He wanted the riches Pa had promised, and right away.

Reuben wondered if his dissatisfaction had led him astray. The old memories accompanied him back to the Jeffers farm as he rode Checkers along the trail out of town.

—m—

"Tell me about life on the trail," Charlotte ventured while she and Reuben sat in the parlor that evening. Ma and Pa remained in the kitchen, their soft after-supper conversation taking place as it had every night for many years. Reuben had missed supper, and Charlotte in turn had missed him. When he arrived after she put away the last clean dish, her stomach gave a lurch at his presence.

Now Charlotte knitted, or tried to knit, while Reuben sat across from her and kept her yarn from tangling. At least that was what he said he was doing.

"I don't like talking about those days." Reuben remained focused on the yarn. His eyelids drooped. Pa said Reuben put in a full day's work. Why, then, would he be here in the evening when he could be settling down in the bunkhouse for a well-deserved rest? Charlotte didn't want to think he meant to spend time with her.

"I'm sorry. I often wondered where you'd gone." She cast another loop of yarn over the needle and paused. "I'd ride out on Belle, hoping to see you coming over the ridge to our place." Her throat burned. She reworked her stitch. The blanket she was knitting for a new mother at church would never take shape at this rate.

"Well, we ended up in Texas and left Benjamin there with a. . .friend." Reuben set the mass of yarn on his lap. "Then I headed up to Colorado, got caught selling stolen horses." His face flushed.

"How—how long were you in jail?"

"Eighteen months." He cleared his throat. "The first time." The expression on Reuben's face made her think the yarn had turned into a pile of snakes on his lap.

"But you were sorry, weren't you?"

"The first time I was sorry I got caught." Reuben clutched the yarn as if it were a lariat.

"Why did you do it?" Charlotte's eyes burned. The Wilsons, she remembered, were not wealthy people, but neither were they destitute.

"The money and the challenge." Reuben sighed. "Money just ain't all it's cracked up to be. It goes too fast and makes people do crazy things only to lose it again. And challenges? Well, I could have found some better ones than stealing horses."

Charlotte didn't know what to say to the serious man who sat across from her. His shoulders slumped as if they bore a great weight.

"Reuben, I'm sorry you walked such a long road." She bit her lip. "But I'm glad you're home again."

"I'd like to say I'm glad, too." He held her gaze.

"Are you going to ask me what I've done these past years?" Charlotte tried to lighten the conversation.

"I can see you've grown up."

"Of course. What a feat that would be, to remain exactly as I was when you left." She smiled at him. There was so much she wanted to tell him—why she had never married, why in the last year she'd still looked for him when out riding Belle.

"I'm glad you're not the same. But I figured you'd be settled down with a family by now and have a posse of kids."

"Well, you can see I'm not. And I don't." Charlotte hadn't intended the words to sound so cold and brittle, but the ripe old age of thirty was two short years away.

"That young man coming around—do you think he's honorable?"

What a question. Charlotte could only say that James was polite, had some polish from schooling, and didn't seem to mind that she was a few years older than he was. Other possible suitors had no doubt been rebuffed by her deliberate disinterest.

"He has never led me to believe he isn't." At that her face flamed, but she dared not tell him about James's attempt to kiss her.

"I see." Reuben's stare bored into her.

"I'm not getting younger." She hadn't expected to be defending herself, although clearly Reuben enjoyed the focus being off him.

"I still care about you, and I don't want you hurt." The tender expression on his face surprised her.

"That means a lot to me. I still. . ." Charlotte swallowed hard. This conversation was not at all turning out as she'd hoped. A brief getting-to-know-you-once-again, not unspoken revelations of the heart.

Reuben leaned forward. "I have something I feel I ought to tell you—only I'm not sure you'll like it."

Her heart felt as if it had leapt into her throat. "You're not leaving again?" Here she was, come full circle as she knew she would. At first she wanted him to go, but now. . .

Reuben shook his head. "It's about James."

Charlotte scooted her chair a bit closer. "What?"

A flush swept over Reuben's face. "I don't want to be accused of tale-bearing, but. . .just. . .be careful about him, okay?"

He was close enough now that she could see flecks of gold in his green eyes. She wanted to make him smile, to see them twinkle as they once did. Reuben's beard was making an appearance, and Charlotte wanted to touch the stubbly growth on his jaw.

"All right."

Reuben stood and reached for his hat. "Promise me. Be careful, Charlie. Wise as a serpent, harmless as a dove."

Her head swam, and she sat back. James. Reuben had said something about James and being careful. But right about now what she wanted was for Reuben to kiss her, and James was the furthest thing from her mind.

Charlotte nodded mutely and watched as Reuben went into the kitchen. She tossed her knitting onto the floor.

—m—

Reuben stoked the embers in the bunkhouse stove and tried to coax some warmth into the old room. Mr. and Mrs. Jeffers had offered him their son's bedroom in the main house, but Reuben didn't think it was proper. He wasn't accustomed to living under a family's roof, not for a long time. In jail you did what you were told when you were told. The idea of being in the outside world, doing what you wanted when you wanted—well, it was hard getting used to.

"Lord, I still need Your help. I'm not sure how to behave among upright people," Reuben muttered as he folded his change of clothes. He placed them in the small trunk he had bought on a trip to town.

Had he done the right thing in telling Charlotte to be careful about James? Reuben dared not repeat the words James had used, soiled with their double meanings. He did know he would protect Charlotte, even if it meant losing her.

Reuben stared out the lone window across the stockyard and at the Jeffers home glowing with warm rectangles of light.

Losing her. He chuckled to himself. He had given up all rights to claim her heart when he rode away all those years ago. No matter what Reverend Mann thought, some things a fellow still couldn't make up for.

Chapter 5

Reuben clutched the receipt for his bank deposit, his heart pounding all the while. Now his money was safe in an account. He glanced about the lobby, but the other customers seemed to be minding their own business, even Mrs. Booth in the corner. Carved wood and iron bars proclaimed security. The bars also reminded him of days gone by, years lost and wasted. Not anymore if he could help it.

No, if God could, and would, help him. Reverend Mann would caution him in that singsong voice of his to take heed not to succumb to greed. God would help him pay if he truly showed repentance for his ways. Reuben hoped he had shown just that. Repentance.

He reread the piece of paper in his hand as he started for the front doors. If he kept all his new earnings for himself, the amount would have been larger. Paying back those whom he'd stolen from helped ease his conscience along the way.

Reuben collided with a short, squat man in a bowler hat. The man's head was tucked low against the blast of cold air that followed him into the bank. A sack fell from his hands. Paper money and coins scattered, the paper floating on air before settling on the floor.

"Oh, pardon me," Reuben said. "I wasn't paying attention." He bent to help gather some of the money.

"No harm done." The man squatted and scraped some coins onto his palm. "I was in a hurry, not paying attention myself."

"I think that's all of it." Reuben straightened.

The man stood, as well, and extended his right hand. "Howard Woodward, *Raider's Crossing News.*"

"Oh, you run the newspaper. I'm"—Reuben shook the man's smooth hand—"I'm Reuben Wilson. Pleased to make your acquaintance."

"Likewise. And next time I'll watch my step."

"And I will, too." They exchanged nods, and Reuben wondered if the man's words held a double meaning. He brushed off the idea like a pesky fly and pushed through the bank doors to come face-to-face with James, also on his way into the establishment. James gave him nothing but a glance.

Reuben tugged the collar of his coat more tightly around his neck and pocketed his receipt. The ice-tinged air bit into him, and Reuben shivered where Checkers stood tied outside the bank. He needed to hurry before the freezing rain began to fall, but he had to make one more stop first.

—⁓—

"Too bad we haven't seen any of the other Wilson boys," Pa remarked while he stabled the animals for the night after returning from town.

"It's sad, Pa." Charlotte paused while brushing Belle's warm flank. "I wish we could do something to help Reuben." The wind had already picked up outside with the promise of another ice storm. Charlotte wanted spring to come and breathe new life across the land.

"God can make something out of nothing. He knows exactly where those boys are. Even now their ma's prayers are at heaven's throne. Perhaps she's visiting there awhile, too." Pa leaned over the stall door. "I didn't want to worry you, but I ran into Howard Woodward today at the mercantile. He was asking about Reuben."

Charlotte's throat constricted; then she found her voice. "Why's that?"

"He's missing some money from his deposit today. Claims he and Reuben were at the bank, ran into each other. Reuben helped him pick up the money."

"You don't think Mr. Woodward's saying—"

Pa raised his hand. "Don't worry. He was only asking about Reuben since he heard I hired him. I told him I'd vouch for Reuben. We haven't had anything missing since he's been here."

"It's not fair." But Charlotte didn't blame his distrust. She didn't want to trust Reuben at first.

"I know, but that's how people are. Seems like there's a few who want to give him a fair shot. I'm going to talk to him tonight, warn him in case there's trouble in the future." Pa sighed uncharacteristically. "Well, you'd best finish up. Ma's laying supper on the table." He didn't chide her for not being inside the warm kitchen and helping, and Charlotte wanted to hug him for it. She had not taken refuge in the barn for longer than she could remember and now realized why she'd loved its peacefulness as a child.

"I will." She waved at Pa and watched him leave. The barn door groaned as he closed it behind him.

Charlotte started half thinking, half praying as she brushed Belle. This afternoon of solitude was meant to be a time of speaking with the Lord, away from distractions. But Reuben and his family had somehow followed her thoughts into the barn.

She could not imagine losing her brother and not knowing where he was. Last letter she had read, his first-year studies in Lincoln were going well. She knew her parents sacrificed to send him to school, and she was proud of him.

Her thoughts turned to James. Her parents neither encouraged nor discouraged the possibility of him calling. Charlotte moved to Belle's hindquarters and started working some snarls from the mare's tail. But what did she want?

All the prayers she'd sent heavenward so far about James had been met with a resounding silence. No yes or no, no warning sign. Or was it that she didn't want a warning? Or was it because her former love for Reuben and his subsequent rejection made her leery about opening her heart to another? The thoughts chased themselves around her head.

Belle shifted her weight and nearly stepped on Charlotte's foot. She moved away in time and patted her mare's neck.

"Sorry, Belle." She'd been brushing too vigorously, and the mare had sensitive skin.

Reuben had warned her about James. She wanted to drag the meaning out of him, but if he was as stubborn as when they were children, he wouldn't budge. Did she trust the warning? Reuben had nothing to gain. . .or did he? She thought about Mr. Woodward's questioning.

Charlotte tossed the brush onto the straw and placed both palms on her forehead. Her swirling thoughts reached a frenzied pace.

The barn door groaned open again, and a blast of air made Charlotte step closer to Belle, who snorted and moved to the edge of the stall. Another horse answered.

"Who's there?" *Please, not James inviting himself for supper.*

"It's me, Reuben." The sound of his voice made her feel warmer. And relieved.

Charlotte picked up the castaway brush and met Reuben outside the stall. He led Checkers into the barn. The young mare's ears twitched.

"Has she been a good horse so far?" Checkers turned at the sound of Charlotte's voice, and Charlotte touched her velvet nose.

"So far she's been smart and strong." Reuben grinned, a sight Charlotte hadn't seen in years. "She's the first of many horses that will run cattle."

"So you're planning to start a ranch then?"

Reuben nodded. "I want to continue what my father started. Or tried to start."

"Lots of opportunities here."

"That there are." He looped the reins over one hand and adjusted his hat.

"Where will you get the money?"

"I've got some put back. I'll save and work. I can make furniture to sell. I learned how to build tables and chairs in prison." Reuben's face flushed. Charlotte believed him and tried to calm the flutters in her stomach.

"The Ladies' Aid Society is having a box social." The words came out before she could stop them. As if he would be interested.

"Oh. When is that?"

"Saturday night." She was already fussing over her box, hoping to decorate it well. "The money is going to the children's home in Laramie."

"I will most definitely be there and bid high." Reuben swallowed. "I think about children like Benjamin and what he might have lost by not being in a proper home. I think the children need some place warm and safe to live where they can get good teaching."

Reuben turned from her and led Checkers to an empty stall. Charlotte followed.

"I hope Benjamin's all right, wherever he is. Have you heard anything yet?" She stopped and watched Reuben close the gate to the stall.

"No, nothing." The sigh he gave echoed the wind increasing outside.

Charlotte shivered. "Pa and I were talking earlier. If you need help. . ." She touched the sleeve of his coat and realized how thin it was.

He shrugged off her hand. "Thank you, but I'll be fine."

"Let me get you another coat then. You must be freezing in this one." Her breath made puffs in the air.

"No!" Reuben stepped around her.

She followed again, feeling like a puppy at his heels. "Why? Let me do something."

He whirled to face her, and she collided with him. She could scarcely breathe. He took her by the shoulders.

"I don't deserve your help. Work on your box for the social. I'll bid on that."

Charlotte nodded. "I wish, back then. . ."

He reached up to her face, then let his hand fall. "I know, Charlotte. I know."

—⁓—

Charlotte sat at the table and tried to fold the thick pasteboard to make her box. Thanks to Momma's coaching, she'd managed to cook some chicken and make biscuits that wouldn't break off someone's teeth. She already had a spare length of blue ribbon tied into a bow that would adorn the top of her box.

Momma came from answering the door. James followed her from the front room. Momma's eyebrows rose so high they were nearly lost in her hairline.

"Good afternoon, Miss Charlotte." James set his hat on the table although no one had invited him to stay.

"Hello." She tried to smile and focused her attention back on the box. Now that James had seen her box and the ribbon, of course he would know which box was hers. At lunch Charlotte had left the materials at the end of the table, hoping Reuben would notice it when he came in from work. If he had, he said nothing. Not since their moments in the barn together had they spoken, except for the usual everyday greetings.

"You're quiet today."

"Ah, yes, well, I'm getting ready for tonight."

"May I see you to the church?"

The question hung in the air while Momma lurked in the background. Charlotte looked up at James. His eyes brimmed with sincerity. She recalled Reuben's warning. Reuben would not lie to her for his own gain. At least she hoped he wouldn't.

"No, but thank you all the same. I'll be riding with my parents tonight."

James snatched his hat from the table. "I see. I'll call again sometime." He turned on his heel and left the kitchen. The front door banged behind him.

Charlotte released a long, slow breath.

"I'm so glad you said no." Momma fetched a clean cloth for Charlotte to place inside her box. "Your pa and I have been talking, and we don't think James is a man you should be spending much time with."

"Why didn't you say so? I would have told him 'no' sooner." Charlotte arranged the cloth.

Momma touched Charlotte's blue bow. "You were always the headstrong one.

I wanted you to see for yourself. Be patient. Your time is coming."

Charlotte tried to smile at Momma, but her eyes filling with tears surprised her. She didn't know how much longer to wait or what exactly she was waiting for.

Chapter 6

Reuben could see the white box with the big blue bow on the table at the front of the chapel. That box had to be Charlotte's. He recalled that the bow he'd seen on the Jeffers table at dinnertime was blue. He glanced in Charlotte's direction. Patches of red glowed on her cheeks.

"What am I bid for this fine supper, last box of the night?" Albert Booth held it up for all to see.

"Ten dollars!" Someone else's voice rang out. James, of course.

Heavenly smells drifted across the room. They reminded Reuben of Ma's cooking, and the memory panged him. If he wanted to eat tonight, he'd better get a move-on.

"Who else to bid on this fine meal? Remember—the money goes to Ladies' Aid." Now was his chance. "Fifteen dollars!"

Reuben ignored the gasps of the crowd and the sharp look from James. Surely the fellow didn't plan on going as high as Reuben, who had enough cash in his pocket to outlast Mr. James Newspaper Writer. He sure hoped Charlotte had learned to cook. Enjoying her company would be enough, though, regardless of the supper.

Albert Booth grinned over at James. "Any more bids?"

"Twenty dollars." James nodded.

Reuben's stomach growled. "Twenty-five."

Now came the whispers. "Where'd he get that money?"

"Thirty!"

More roars from the crowd. James had leapt to his feet. Charlotte went pale, and Reuben wanted to tell her she had nothing to worry about.

Albert Booth stared him down. "Anyone else?"

Reuben remembered the times he had stolen, once pilfering a donation plate such as rested on the table at the front of the room. Why the Almighty had shown him such great mercy, he didn't understand. He hoped tonight would go a ways to paying Him back.

"Forty-five!"

Whoops rose up around Reuben, and someone clapped him on the back. He saw James conversing with a friend, maybe the same one he'd been talking with about Charlotte. The man showed James empty pockets.

James faced Mr. Booth. "Fifty dollars."

The look in James's eyes told Reuben he'd come to the end. Maybe the fellow didn't have such a great poker face after all. Reuben stood a mite taller.

"Sixty dollars."

The room fairly buzzed. James threw his hat on the floor while Reuben went to claim his supper box. He didn't regret the money. But he hadn't counted on the ruckus when he withdrew cash from his inside jacket pocket. Mr. Booth shook his head while he counted the money. Mrs. Booth fanned herself and appeared as though she needed smelling salts.

Reuben didn't care. He searched for Charlotte, who had her back to him and was speaking with a few of the other women from church. One younger unattached woman giggled when he approached.

Charlotte's cheeks looked as if she'd spent an hour in front of the mirror pinching them. "Hello." Her glance darted from her friends then back to him. "I had some help with the cooking."

"That's all right." Reuben found himself grinning. "Ma'am, let's sit down and have us some supper."

He turned and nearly walked smack into James.

"Where'd you get all that money?" His brows furrowed. His dark eyes held a demanding glare.

"I earned it, fair and square." Reuben clutched the box instead of going with his gut inclination to shove the man out of his way.

Charlotte tried to step between them. "James, don't."

Reuben balanced the box on one hand and touched Charlotte's shoulder. "No harm done. He realized he was mistaken, didn't he?"

James leaned closer. "You think you've got people fooled, but you haven't fooled me. Wait and see. I'll make sure this whole town sees you for the fraud you are."

"I'm not that person anymore." Reuben's stomach growled. His expensive supper was waiting, and his temper was tighter to rein in the hungrier he got.

"Keep telling yourself that."

There came Albert Booth. "Gentlemen, is there a problem?" He stood as if ready to intervene. A few in the room had stopped dining to stare at the face-off.

Reuben waited for James to answer and gritted his teeth.

"No, sir." James kept boring into Reuben with those burning molasses eyes. "But I'd keep my wallet close by if I were you."

Only Charlotte's firm squeeze in the crook of Reuben's elbow kept him from taking a swing at the man. *Lord, I sure need Your hand to hold mine back right about now.*

James pushed past them both, and Reuben released a pent-up breath.

"Son, you did good." Albert gave him a nod, then went back to his wife.

"Let's sit down and eat, and you can tell me how wonderful everything tastes." Charlotte moved closer to his side, not releasing her grip on his arm.

"Thanks." Reuben found a quiet place at a bench in the corner. He settled onto the seat. The rest of the crowd seemed to be enjoying their meals. Would his past continually trail him like this? No wonder he had delayed coming home for so long. He removed his coat and laid it on the bench behind him.

He watched Charlotte unfold a pair of napkins. She handed one to him.

"Here. Wouldn't want you to muss that nice shirt of yours."

Charlotte had their meal spread between them quick enough. He asked the blessing and wasted no time tearing into the largest piece of chicken in front of him.

"I'm glad you won." She gave him a small smile that lit the corner of the room.

"I am, too," he said around a bite of chicken. "This is one more step toward atonement."

Her face flushed again. "What do you mean?"

"You see, after I made my peace with the Lord, I promised Him I would make up for as many wrong things as I could. To show Him I was sorry. Reverend Mann said it was needful that I do."

"Needful?"

Reuben nodded. "To make sure I was forgiven."

"I believe in making restitution when you can, but, Reuben, you can't atone for your sins." She touched his hand, an act that made his throat grow a knot. He hoped no one had seen the gesture.

"You don't understand." Reuben moved his hand away from hers. "I've done so many wrong things that the scales are heavy against me. God's scales."

"What about grace?"

"What are you talking about?"

Charlotte leaned closer, close enough that he could see the sprinkle of freckles remaining on her cheeks. "God's grace and the forgiveness He gives us tip the scales in our favor. Well, better than that. He knocks the weights off the scales, and we don't owe any more."

Reuben set down the chicken bone and grabbed a biscuit. He tried to think about her words. The scales knocked clean. Not owing anymore. The thought of weights being lifted from him sounded like a breath of fresh air, the kind a man inhaled when sitting on top of a mountain.

"You don't know what I've done, Charlotte." The flaky biscuit did little to soothe the churning Reuben felt inside his stomach. "It's easy for you. You haven't drifted off the straight 'n' narrow more than a few paces in your life."

"But I've still been wrong. I battle with—with pride, a sharp tongue, a bitter attitude. Quite often, in fact." Charlotte was trying to look him in the eye, but at the moment he found a second biscuit more interesting and wouldn't glance her way.

"Charlotte, I was an outlaw. I lived without thought of right or wrong. I don't think asking for forgiveness is all I have to do."

"Are you saying that what Jesus did for us wasn't enough?"

"Of course not." He didn't care if she saw the biscuit lolling around in his mouth. Tonight was not going as he'd planned. Not at all. He had wanted to see if there might be an inkling of love for him inside Charlotte, but instead he'd gotten tossed onto the grill over an open fire.

"Reuben, there'll always be people like James wanting to fling your past in your face. But as you told him, that's not you anymore."

He wanted to believe her, to kiss the lips on her earnest face. Right now, though, he felt as if the hangman's noose had settled around his neck.

"Miss Charlotte, I thank you kindly for the superb meal and your company." Reuben stood and nodded to her while reaching for his hat. He found his coat, which had slipped to the floor, and put it on.

"Where are you going?" Her eyes pleaded with him to stay.

"I reckon I need some air." With that he turned on his heel and walked away. If he could but step away from his past so easily.

Reuben paused at the door when he reached inside his outer pocket and felt a piece of paper. He slid it out and found a five-dollar note.

This was not his money. The cash he'd withdrawn from the bank for supper, he'd tucked inside his chest pocket. He did not recall anyone giving him cash, either.

Someone was out to smear him, and he had a pretty good idea who'd like to try. He stood outside in the chilly air and felt a long, slow burn inside.

"Reuben Wilson?" He turned at the sound of a voice at his elbow.

"I'm Ed Smythe. . .from the telegraph office?"

Reuben's heart leapt inside him. "Have you received word?"

Ed withdrew a folded paper from his pocket. "I was hoping you'd be in town Friday, but since you weren't, I thought I'd bring this tonight."

"Well, thank you." Reuben received the paper and watched Ed stride toward a waiting team.

He read the paper.

"Colt Wilson. Inmate at Texas State Penitentiary, Huntsville." The chief warden had replied to Reuben's inquiry.

Oh, Ma. I'm making good on my promise. Reuben needed to speak with Sam as soon as possible about leaving for Texas.

When Charlotte emerged from the chapel with her ma and pa, Reuben found Checkers and watched, hoping to speak to Sam without having to face Charlotte.

The last thing he saw before riding home was Charlotte talking to James, standing next to his buggy that gleamed in the lantern light.

—⁂—

"No, James." Charlotte shrugged off his attention and shivered. Her breath made puffs in the evening air. *Where did Pa go? He said he'd be right along with the wagon.*

"I'm trying to warn you." James took a step closer. "Reuben Wilson has not changed, and I'm going to prove it. One way or another."

"Whatever Reuben is, he is my friend, and I've known him practically my whole life." Charlotte glared at him as best she could. "Leave him alone." She saw Pa driving up with the team and moved away from James.

"You're not thinking clearly. Childhood fancies have—"

"I've never thought more clearly than now." The chilly air stung her hot cheeks.

"In fact, it's clear to me that I don't want you to come calling—or offer me rides anywhere—ever again."

Charlotte turned on her heel and joined her parents. This was what Reuben had meant. She felt like a young child bilked out of her small coins by a huckster's false promise. Relief soon followed, and she smiled at Pa.

"Everything all right?" he asked.

"Yes, it is. Or I hope it will be."

He helped Momma and then her onto the wagon, and they headed for home.

Reuben did not come to the house after the family returned from the box social. Charlotte didn't suppose he would, but for a while she held the remote hope that he might. She had so many things she wanted to say to him.

The poor man, all he'd wanted was a good supper, and she'd kept at him like a pecking hen.

A knock sounded at the door as if in response to her thoughts. Reuben stood there holding his hat. "Charlotte, I must speak with your pa." The urgency in his voice made her stomach turn.

"Of course." She opened the door wider for him. "What's wrong?

"Nothing, but I need to leave for a spell."

"Leave?" A dozen questions soared through her mind. She turned to the kitchen. "Pa, it's Reuben."

"Well, send him in here. Your ma has the kettle on."

Charlotte followed Reuben into the warm kitchen. He stood there, shifting his weight from one foot to the other. She tried to sit without drawing attention to herself.

"Sir, I've received word of my brother Colt. He's in Huntsville."

Pa nodded. "You must go to him."

"I'm real sorry. I don't like leaving you like this. But I promise I'll be back as soon as I can."

Leaving? Charlotte's heart sank. He said he'd return but. . .

"We'll send you with a parcel of food for your trip." Pa huffed through his mustache. "Charlotte, gather some things for Reuben."

Charlotte stood, glad for something to do. That way she could listen while the men planned. She began gathering provisions.

"I'll leave on the next stage out. Can't say as I know how long I'll be."

"You take what time you need, and we'll be home waiting for you, son." Pa gripped Reuben's shoulder.

"Thank you, sir." Reuben's voice was a bare whisper.

Home. Pa had called this place Reuben's home. Charlotte's vision blurred with tears. This time she wouldn't let him leave without a word. This time things would be different. They had to.

—m—

Reuben slid the piece of paper money from his pocket and showed Sam once Charlotte had left the room. "Sir, this isn't mine."

"Well, whose is it then?"

"I don't know. I found it in my pocket tonight."

"Do you think you miscounted?"

"No, sir, I don't. The bank clerk counted the money twice in front of me." Reuben sighed. "I counted my money twice when I paid for my box supper tonight."

"That doesn't explain the extra bill."

"It doesn't. I think someone put it in my pocket, intending to frame me for stealing it. I know it's only a five-dollar note, but I'm not going back to jail again."

"Now, son, don't think that." Sam scratched his chin. "I tell you what. Let me hold onto this until you get back. We'll get it straightened out. Go see your brother. Right now you going to Huntsville is safer than staying here."

Chapter 7

Reuben felt as if he moved in someone else's dream as Sam drove him to meet the stage. He had a sack of food, enough for two men, on this trip. He was not sure what would happen, nor was he worried about that at the moment.

Charlotte had not said good-bye to him that morning. He had hoped for a glimpse of her, but in the predawn hours, Mrs. Jeffers told him Charlotte was ill. A fine time for her to get sick.

"Well, son. Here you are." Sam drew the team to a halt. "You be sure and telegraph when you get there, just so we know. We'll be praying for you and for Colt, as well."

"I appreciate that, sir." He shook hands with Sam and climbed from the wagon. Approaching hoofbeats made him look back where they'd traveled from.

Charlotte rode up on Belle. Her hair streamed back in the wind, her cheeks flushed.

"You ought to be home in bed," Sam chided.

"No one woke me." She swung off Belle's back. Her face looked pale. "But I had to see you before you left."

Sam reached for Belle's reins. "Go on—you two talk. I'm not going anywhere."

Reuben couldn't believe he was leaving Charlotte again. But he would be back.

He escorted her a few paces away from the wagon. "Your ma told me you were sick."

"I don't care." Charlotte's cheeks blazed. "I couldn't let you leave without telling you. . ."

"I'll be home again as soon as I can. I want to see what I can do for my brother and hope to start making up for the past."

"Do you think you can do that in a matter of days or weeks?"

"I'm not going to stay there too long, but I want to make a start anyway." He studied her face and saw the fear in her eyes. "What are you afraid of?"

"That you won't come back this time."

He took her hand, which was as much as he dared. "Charlotte Jeffers, it about rips a hole inside me to think of not seeing you every day. When I get back again, I aim for a new start with you, too."

A smile crept across her face. "Well, I aim to hold you to that."

"Pray for me?"

"You know I will."

Her hair reminded him of those days long ago when she'd chase after them on her pony. She'd followed again, with the promise of love in her eyes. Now how could a fellow not return to that?

He released her hand and, without a backward glance, headed for the waiting stage.

—⁓—

Reuben stood before the prison in Huntsville, Texas. His heart pounded in his throat. He had vowed never to enter such a place again. After he was admitted and the doors clanged shut behind him, he had the inclination to turn around and run. Right now, though, he was about worn out after days of travel. The bath and shave, a hot meal and a good night's sleep helped some, but now that he'd turned a couple of corners past thirty, he felt the effects of traveling.

He found the man they told him was Colt. Reuben tried not to grimace at the odor in the cell block, the scent bringing back a flood of memories. No wonder he had inhaled deeply of the outside air once he'd been freed from prison.

"Can I help you with somethin'?" His voice sounded deeper, coarser than Reuben remembered. He sat up on the straw mattress that crackled and popped under his weight.

"It's. . .it's me, Colt." Reuben felt as if he'd swallowed an apple whole. "Reuben, your big brother."

"Well, if you don't say so." Colt remained seated. "Been a long time. Thought we were gonna meet back in Denmark and get Benjamin."

"I thought we were, too." Reuben's eyes burned, and he clutched the bar with one hand. The excuses and avoidances of the past thirteen years swirled within his head.

"You look good. You come into any money?"

"The hard way. By workin' for it."

"So. What're you here for?" Colt's dark gaze dropped to the floor. Reuben remembered the way it felt. Not to be free to speak, to move.

"I came to see you. I need to ask your forgiveness. . . ."

Colt's head snapped up, and his gaze bored into Reuben. "What're you talking about? I wasn't a spineless nitwit who followed you like a pup. If anything, you would've never done half the things you done if it wasn't for my gumption."

Now this was the Colt that Reuben remembered, already wanting to pick a fight after not five minutes. Reuben smiled and let the words blow past him.

"All the same, I'm sorry for my part in what happened to our family, and I want to make it up to you."

Colt shot across the cell until but inches remained between them. If it weren't for the bars and the watchful guard, Reuben supposed his brother's hands would be clamped around his neck.

"Make it up to me? That's real easy to say when you're on the outside looking all polished like you're ready to go to a church meeting." The air crackled between them as Colt ground out the words.

"Once I was right where you are. I know what it's like. And it's only with God's help that I'm about half the man I oughta be."

A crooked grin slid across Colt's face. "Got religion, did ya? It's not surprising. Many fellows do when they're on the inside. Say a prayer, cry like a mama's boy, and start singing hymns is all you've got to do."

Reuben's heart sank. But it wasn't as if he really expected Colt to greet him with any measure of brotherly love.

"I have to go now." Reuben glanced at the guard. "But I'll be back."

Colt ambled over to the bunk attached to the wall and sat. "Suit yourself. I ain't going anywhere."

—⁓—

Charlotte stared at the telegraph in her hands. "Arrived safe Huntsville. Pecan Street Hotel. RW." The seven days he'd been gone so far felt like seven years. She trudged along the boardwalk and saw her family's wagon. Her parents were still about, Momma at the mercantile and Pa on his errands. They never complained about having an old maid daughter, but today she felt as useless as a holey, worn-out dishrag. She might as well join Momma at the mercantile. She'd said something about purchasing some new fabrics for spring dresses.

The bell clanged over the shop's door as Charlotte entered. Momma looked up from the dry goods. She clutched a bolt of cloth to her chest and smiled.

"They have some nice-looking fabrics over here."

Charlotte nodded and joined Momma. "We got a telegraph from Reuben. He made it." She fingered the flower-sprigged navy blue. Normally the color would appeal to her, but today the prettiest pattern had no interest.

"I'm glad." Momma moved to the thread and gave Charlotte a glance. "You don't look too happy."

"I miss him, Momma."

"That's good. But is that all that's eating at you?"

She shook her head. "I'm afraid that he won't. . .he won't come back."

"He promised, didn't he?" Momma's pat on the hand wasn't reassuring. "You need to have faith in the man you love and faith that God will watch over him while he's gone."

"You. . .you can tell how I feel about him?" Charlotte touched her burning cheeks. "Is it obvious?"

"Like the sunrise on a clear day. To me and your pa, anyhow."

Mrs. Booth moved from her place behind the post office window. "Ladies, how are you today? Do you think spring is about here yet?"

No, but I think you're here to see if you can catch a tidbit about Reuben.

Aloud, Charlotte said, "We're fine, thank you. And I do believe a thaw is on the way."

"Oh, I certainly hope so." The older woman leaned closer. "I think if another ice storm came upon us I'd give up and move back East." Charlotte almost hoped she'd sensed a freezing bite in the air outside.

Charlotte felt the toe of Momma's boot press hard enough on her own to cause her to stifle a yelp. Same as always, Momma probably had her figured out.

"Mrs. Booth," Momma said, "do you remember how much the Ladies' Aid raised at the box social?"

"Over a hundred dollars, thanks to Reuben Wilson." Mrs. Booth's stare at Charlotte made her blink. "I hope that was some supper you fed him. Although, honestly, seein' him flash that money when he paid for his box got me a bit worried."

"Whatever for?" Momma placed her hand over Charlotte's as she spoke.

"Where'd he get that cash from?"

"He's been working hard," Charlotte interjected. "He was working his way home and saving money before he returned here."

Mrs. Booth nodded. "It wouldn't surprise me if he's trying to get his gang back together and rob us all blind. Didn't I see him leaving on the stage not a week ago?"

Charlotte glanced at Momma. Reuben had asked that they not tell the full nature of his errand so as not to get tongues wagging in his absence.

She let Momma speak. "Reuben is away seeing to a family matter." Then Momma's face closed up tight. A customer clanged into the store at that moment, and Charlotte wanted to breathe in relief.

Mrs. Booth humphed and stomped back toward the post window. "I think the sheriff ought to know. Forewarned is forearmed." Her boots clunked on the wooden planks as she moved to the postal window and put on a fresh smile.

Momma kept silent for a moment. Then, "I'm proud of you for not saying anything. Nearly every time I see that woman and speak with her, I find myself on my knees apologizing to God for something I said."

"Some people bring out the best in us, and, well. . ." Charlotte couldn't get her mind off Mrs. Booth's words. Reuben. Getting the gang together. He'd told her he promised his ma he'd find his brothers.

She hoped Reuben hadn't faltered in his desire to get back the family ranch. *What if he finds his brothers and they run off again?* Charlotte pushed back the idea. Have a little faith in the man you love and in the Lord, Momma had told her.

Help me, Lord, to do just that.

Chapter 8

Y ou're back." Colt still sat on the mattress in his cell. The other inmate snored from his bunk along the opposite wall. Reuben had arrived after supper, hoping to have a better visit than yesterday.

Reuben couldn't decide if Colt had asked him or told him. Either way, Reuben knew he wouldn't give up on building a bridge to reach his brother.

"Yes, I'm here."

"Why?"

"I...I promised Ma I'd find you." Reuben's throat caught. *He doesn't know about Ma.*

"Does she still care? Doesn't she know I'm here?" Colt almost sounded like a little boy again.

"She does care...well, she did." Reuben swallowed. "Ma...Ma passed in February. I got back to Raider's Crossing a few days before she..."

The Adam's apple bobbed in Colt's neck. "I'm glad she wasn't alone." He looked lost.

"No. She never quit prayin' for us, either." Reuben wanted to reach through the bars and hug Colt, but he figured he'd probably get slugged. "The Jeffers family bought Pa's land."

Colt nodded. "What about that little girl they had, the one always chasing you on her pony?"

"Charlotte? She's there." And Reuben knew he should be with her.

"I see. Guess she's plenty old enough now for you two to get hitched." A wry smile teased the corners of Colt's mouth.

"Yeah, she is. If she'll have me." Reuben's heart panged. "If she'll take a fellow with a past like mine."

Colt shrugged. "See—now that's what I meant yesterday. You pray a few prayers, dress right, sing some church songs—yet you still ain't fixed. I don't need that. I don't have the time."

"But God's forgiven me. I've turned from my wicked ways." Reuben found himself gripping the bars as he had yesterday.

In three steps Colt stood at the bars that separated them. "Then, big brother, tell me why you look like you're still carrying a sentence on your shoulders. Either this religion works enough for you to tell me about it, or it don't."

Reuben drew in a shuddering breath. "Colt, I want this to work. The way I did things didn't. I've got no other choice. I know I can't do this without God."

"Always the serious and responsible one. Ruby, there's some things a man just can't keep taking responsibility for. You need to learn when to let go." Colt ambled back to his bunk and sat down.

Colt's words slammed into Reuben like a well-planted fist. He would have welcomed the fist more than the words.

"Colt, how much longer do you have in here?"

"I get out real soon."

"You're welcome to join me in Wyoming. I'm going to get our land back, and I'd like your help building what our pa lost." Reuben felt like he was begging. "It won't be easy, but having family around will make the burden lighter."

Colt appeared thoughtful. "I. . .I can't. I've got somewhere else I need to be. You ain't the only one who made a promise."

Reuben had to leave it at that. "All right. But, Colt, if you need me, you get word to me. You're my brother, and that don't change."

With that, Colt hung his head. "You take care now, Ruby."

—∿∿—

That night Reuben could not sleep, alone in a strange town with his long-lost brother not far away. The late-night rumble of carriages, the sound of a piano somewhere, and laughter and muffled voices from downstairs reminded him of how much he missed Wyoming. He longed for the sound of the wind whistling in the bunkhouse eaves, the pop of burning wood in his stove, and the occasional call from one of the cattle. Even the mournful coyote. Most of all he wanted to hear Charlotte's voice.

Instead, he heard Colt's words that pierced into his soul. Since he couldn't sleep, he figured he might as well pray.

Kneeling on the hardwood floor as Reverend Mann had said a man ought to pray, Reuben began.

"Lord, I've been trying to do what's right in Your eyes, but I still"—he drew in a shuddering breath—"I still feel like I'm not good enough. I know I've done all those things Colt said, but the idea that You've forgiven me just doesn't add up."

Charlotte's words at the box social chased Colt's words around Reuben's mind.

"Now, Lord, I'm not saying what Jesus did for me wasn't enough. It was plenty for one thief on the cross. And I have a feeling he and I aren't much different."

Reuben paused and heard only the sounds of the traffic outside and hotel noises below. He touched his face, and it was wet with tears.

"Remember me."

The weight on Reuben's shoulders nearly suffocated him as he remained on his knees, his head bowed. Colt was right. He'd worn the past like his old coat and dragged it along behind him like a string of chains when it got too heavy. The bitter realization made a flood of tears burst from inside, tears he'd never let himself shed since that day in Denmark.

"Please release me from this, Lord." Now he was blubbering like a five-year-old.

"I'm not sorry about getting caught. I know what I've done was wrong."

A quiet breeze drifted in the window, and it held a hint of early Texas spring.

I make all things new.

The silent words wrapped around Reuben and swallowed up the weight that covered him. He felt as if he'd dropped a heavy load.

Reuben imagined he was out riding Checkers and had cast a burden on the trail. He could picture himself looking back at the heap lying in the dust. Sure, he'd owned up to it, but he wouldn't carry it any longer. Then another rider came up on a horse that glowed brighter than fresh cotton. This rider took up Reuben's load and slung it over his shoulder. His smile hit Reuben like the sun's glow.

Let's ride together.

Reuben opened his eyes to see the blanket on his bed in the hotel. It was time to go home.

—⁂—

Charlotte flung back the covers and rolled out of bed. The new dress with its sprigs of flowers hung on the dress form in her room. She and Momma had worked to finish the dress before Reuben returned home—today!

The simple telegraph lay on the washstand, and Charlotte had dreamed of the message the whole night:

"Returning. Arriving Wednesday on stage. RW." She hoped and prayed that Reuben's errand was successful.

She hurried through her simple chores and helped Momma make breakfast but didn't change into the new dress until it was time for them to leave for town.

Why had she doubted? For an instant, Charlotte wondered what dark thing lay in store for them.

"Sorry, Lord. I didn't mean to borrow trouble. Go before us today and guide our steps. Watch over Reuben on his journey." She stood before the looking glass that hung on the wall over the washstand and pinched her cheeks. Color sprang into them.

"You ready?" Pa called at her door. "Don't know exactly when that stage will arrive, but I'd like to be there. The team's waitin' outside."

"I'll be right there, Pa." Charlotte paused and glanced back into her bedroom. A spinster's bedroom. The room of a woman who waited for a broken promise to be fulfilled. No, not quite broken. Just delayed. She regretted the lost years she had spent, not in idleness certainly, but in waiting. But some things, some people were worth waiting for.

Momma was fastening the bow under her chin when Charlotte entered the kitchen. "Sam, I don't see why you're going, too."

"Etta, the other boys have things in hand around here till we get back. Besides, I need to speak with Reuben." Pa showed them a folded piece of paper money. "He asked me to keep this while he was gone—says he doesn't know how it came to be inside his coat pocket and didn't want to be caught holding this money."

Charlotte eyed the money. "You think someone might be trying to make it look like he's stealing again?" No, not Reuben. But all that money at the social and him at the bank—the idea made her blood boil.

Pa nodded slowly. "If Reuben's in trouble, he needs all the friends he can get right now."

She looked at Pa. "Why didn't you tell me?"

"Didn't want you to spend your time worryin' while Reuben was gone."

Charlotte grabbed her shawl and followed them into the late winter chill. Borrowing trouble? She suddenly felt as if they'd bought a whole pile of it.

—⁓—

Days spent on the stage left Reuben with a short scruff of beard and a weary heart. He hadn't expected his brother to rush to him with open arms. He hadn't expected his faith to be shaken to its crumbly foundations, either.

The buildings of Raider's Crossing loomed ahead. Home. For good or ill, Reuben would stay. He squinted from his place on top of the stage. Better on the outside freezing than inside below with a screaming baby and folks smelling of travel.

Reuben caught sight of the Jeffers' wagon, and his heart leapt when he saw Charlotte. The first thing he wanted to do, after getting a bath and shave, of course, then speaking with her pa, was take her in his arms.

Then he saw the fear on Charlotte's face.

Another sight made his heart fall. There stood the sheriff, Mr. Woodward, the newspaper man, and James Johansson.

Be my shield, Lord. I have no defense but the truth.

Reuben waited until the stage rolled to a stop. He climbed down, his heart pounding a drumbeat. Charlotte ran to him and wrapped him in a strong hug.

"I don't believe it. They're wrong," she whispered in his ear. "You should have told me about the money."

"I didn't want to worry you," he whispered back.

Fresh tears came from her eyes. "You sound like Pa."

"I consider that to be a compliment."

"Miz Jeffers," came the sheriff's no-nonsense voice, "you need to step aside."

She did so slowly, her hands curled into fists. "You've got no proof."

"Have I done something wrong, Sheriff?" Reuben looked him in the eye.

"That remains to be seen, Wilson." The sheriff nodded in the direction of Mr. Woodward and James. "You need to come down to my office and answer some questions. Mr. Woodward is asking that robbery charges be lodged against you."

Chapter 9

Reuben's eyelids drooped as he sat in the stiff-backed chair across from the sheriff. He didn't know how many times he repeated the same answers to the same questions.

"Like I said before, I only made one deposit and one withdrawal. Check the bank records."

The sheriff kicked back in his chair and leaned against the wall. "Mr. Woodward here says he started noticing money missing about the same time you arrived in Raider's Crossing. And he told me about the time y'all bumped heads at the bank, money going everywhere.

"I'm sure it's mighty tempting to a man in your position to see a month's worth of wages going across the floor."

Reuben curled his hands into fists at his sides. *A man in your position.* "Sheriff, I'm not that kind of man anymore. I've earned my money from hard work, not thieving."

James stepped forward. "And you have enough to throw down for a silly supper? What, were you trying to impress her father?"

It would take but one punch to fell this dandy.

Reuben sucked in a deep breath. "I don't recall the sheriff allowing you to ask questions. In fact, I don't know why you're here in the first place." He glared at James, who shrank back to the corner. "You've had it in for me since the day I came here. Wouldn't it be something else if you were the one causing all this trouble?"

James licked his lips. "Howard, tell him about the accounts."

Mr. Woodward began. "I've been missing money, here and there, five to ten dollars at a time, from the subscription receipts." He tossed a ledger onto the table. "Sheriff, start from the beginning of this year."

"I'm not a man of numbers, Woodward." The sheriff thumbed the pages. "What'm I looking at?"

"The missing amounts are circled, right here. Somehow between the newspaper office and the bank, the money goes missing." Mr. Woodward pointed to the last entry. "See here? Last Tuesday, five more dollars missing."

Reuben sat up straighter. "Mr. Woodward, I believe you've got a thief, and I know it's not me. I was in Huntsville visiting my brother in prison on that date. The Jeffers family has two telegraphs I sent, on my arrival and right before I left. And the prison has a record of my visits."

James's face had turned the color of paste. "Wh–what?"

Mr. Woodward turned to face James. "You told me you had seen Reuben that day in town. Unless he can work some kind of trick, I don't see as how he can be two places at once."

James bolted for the door, but Reuben stuck out his foot and sent the man flying. Not quite a punch, but at the moment it would serve the cause of justice.

—⁂—

Charlotte saw Reuben leaving the sheriff's office before Momma and Pa did. "He's coming out!" She picked up the hem of her skirt and ran for him. "What happened?"

He smiled at her, his green eyes alight in a way she hadn't seen in years. "It was James all along. Seems he had a hankering for a new buggy and other things. Figured a few dollars here and there would help. When I came to town, he started getting greedier."

"So that explains it. I wondered how he got that buggy." She shook her head. Reuben offered her his arm, and they walked along to her parents' wagon.

"He looked squeaky clean around me." Reuben shrugged. "Get enough rumors flying, people will look the other way at what's under their noses. Howard Woodward didn't quite suspect me, though. But he had an idea something was up when Mrs. Booth mentioned me being out of town on the same day James said he saw me on the street passing by the newspaper office."

Charlotte laughed. "Thank you, Mrs. Booth, for sharing information! I never thought I'd say that."

Reuben's chuckle made her go all warm inside. "Yes, and thank You, Lord."

"What about Colt? How is he?"

"About as well as you can expect in prison. I offered him a place here with me one day, but he's got somewhere else in mind. He showed me something, even though he didn't want to listen about God changing him." Reuben stopped and took Charlotte's hands in his. "He showed me I was wrong, thinking I could earn my forgiveness. Like if I did enough good, it would cancel out the bad. It's hard sometimes, still, thinking about what I've done, but I'm ready to start looking forward."

Charlotte smiled. "Me, too. And one day I'd love to see Colt and thank him."

"You two going to talk each other to death?" Pa's voice carried over the wind that held the hint of early spring. "In case you didn't know, it's freezing out here."

—⁂—

Reuben tied a knot in his necktie. He could never get used to feeling gussied up, but when a fellow proposed marriage, he couldn't take a chance at appearing in less than his best. Sam had told him to make sure he joined them for supper. Maybe he was a tad overdressed for a Wednesday night supper, but he figured he wouldn't be comfortable even in his everyday work clothes.

He crossed the yard to the main house where the scent of supper drifted from the kitchen door. Charlotte's and her ma's laughter joined the smells that made his stomach growl louder. After a week of jerky and stale bread, a supper of beef and potatoes would go down well. *Thank You, Lord, for true freedom.*

"There you are!" Charlotte stood in the doorway and drew him inside with her hand. Her smile made him feel warm to his toes. She squeezed his hand, and he raised her hand to his lips. The blush that swept over her face reminded him of the days in summer when they'd tear around on horseback and she'd leave her sunbonnet at home.

Sam entered the kitchen and surveyed the table laden with food. "Son, I almost feel like sending you away again so we can eat like this every night."

"Now, Sam," his wife chided. But she beamed, as well, when he tugged on her apron strings.

Sam asked the blessing once they were all seated around the table. "Lord, thank You for this food. Bless it to our bodies and our lives for Your service. We thank You for delivering Reuben from the snare of the wicked today. Thank You, as well, for bringing him home again. Amen." At that Reuben tightened his grip around Charlotte's hand.

"Sir," he ventured once they filled their plates, "I must talk to you about something important, before I lose my nerve and before I eat and lose my supper at the idea of speaking to you."

Charlotte's father set his fork down next to his plate. "Well, if it's all that important, I'd like to hear it before I eat."

"Two things." Reuben tugged at his necktie. "First, I love your daughter. I always have, and I always will." He could feel her face glowing from where she sat opposite him. "I haven't been a Christian man for many years, but I'm learning. Once I can provide for her properly, I want to marry her, and I'd like your blessing." His throat hurt after the long speech.

Sam nodded. "I appreciate you asking me first. I see Charlotte's answer on her face."

Reuben reached for Charlotte's hand. "I love you, Charlie Jeffers, till the stars die. I was stupid and selfish many years ago, but I promise you I'll never leave our love behind again. We were only children, but even then I knew. . ."

"I did, too." A tear slid down Charlotte's cheek, and she grinned as she dashed it away with her free hand.

"Now." Sam punctuated his sentence by slamming his palm on the table so hard his coffee cup jumped. "How do you propose to provide for my daughter?"

Reuben cleared his throat. "That's the second thing I'd like to talk to you about. I want to buy back the land my family used to own. I don't have enough money yet to make you a good offer, but I'm working on that."

Sam picked up his fork and stabbed a bite of meat on his plate. He swirled it in some gravy and popped it in his mouth. Reuben could almost see the man's mind working as he ate.

Reuben followed Sam's lead and popped a piece of meat into his mouth although his appetite had fled. He swallowed it without even noticing that it was so tender it melted in his mouth. Then he paused and smiled at Charlotte. They had so many things to talk about.

At last Sam broke the silence. "I can't sell you that land."

Reuben felt his shoulders sag, but he refused to let Sam see the dreams crumbling inside him. "I. . .I see."

"I'm going to give it to you."

"Sir—" Reuben's throat tied itself in a knot to match his necktie.

Sam raised his hand. "No. Cut that out. I know what you're goin' to say. You don't deserve that. Maybe not. But this is what we'll do." He took another bite.

"What's that?"

"I'm going to give you the pick of the spring calves this year, seein' as how you're going to help me with the calving. You raise those and add to the small herd I know you can buy." Sam sipped his coffee. "Then, for the next three years, all the female calves your herd bears will be mine."

The room seemed to spin around him. "You'd do that?"

"We both want the same thing. I want my little girl cared for. I want you and Charlotte to work that parcel. . .together."

"Oh, Pa. It's a dream come true." Charlotte squeezed Reuben's hand.

Sam smiled, a rare sight Reuben hadn't recalled since working for the man. "That it is."

Epilogue

Charlotte and Reuben rode out to their future home. The March breeze spoke of living things and new chances. The Wilsons' soddy would be snug until Reuben had completed repairs on the main wood-frame house, abandoned for years. Charlotte could hardly wait to make the place their own.

"Think we'll be courting for long?"

"I don't know," Reuben replied. "I think your pa knows we spent many years apart. I think a summer wedding is fine. Except I'd marry you tomorrow if I could."

"My dress isn't finished." Charlotte studied his expression. "I know you're wanting a short walk to the altar, but I'm not getting married in my Sunday dress. I've waited too long for you to take shortcuts now."

"I know." He smiled that Wilson smile she loved so well.

They halted the horses, and Charlotte swung off her horse. Reuben did the same, and Checkers and Belle strolled on long reins as they munched the new grass.

Reuben took Charlotte's hand. "I need to be getting back soon, but I wanted to have a few minutes of quiet. Promise me one thing?"

"Of course."

"Help me keep looking for Caleb and Benjamin."

"You can count on me." She would sprout wings and scout the land for the two men if she could.

"It doesn't matter if they don't want to come home. I want to know they're safe and well, and if they need help, I want them to know I'm here." Reuben blinked, and Charlotte thought she saw a few unshed tears.

"We'll find them together." She squeezed his hand tighter.

"That's how I always want it to be." He pulled her into his arms. "You and me, together."

"Till the stars die," Charlotte whispered just before Reuben kissed her.

THE PEACEMAKER

by DiAnn Mills

Chapter 1

Texas 1880

When Anne Langley became a widow, she vowed her children would know Jesus and never go hungry. She'd accomplished those things and more. Standing on the back porch of her white-stone home that faced east, she sipped from a mug of strong coffee and watched the sun slowly expand the horizon in shades of purple, orange, and pink. She inhaled the beauty around her—the kind of beauty that only God could paint. Morning had come to life with color and promise for the day. Heaven's beams gently illuminated the hundreds of acres Anne called the Double L.

All this gives me a reason to go on. Thank You for Your love and those mercies that are new every morning, just like Your book says.

The door squeaked open behind her, and the sound of boots tapping against the wooden porch revealed her visitor.

"Mornin', honey," Anne said without turning to greet her daughter.

"Another pretty one, isn't it?" Fourteen-year-old Sammie Jo leaned in close to her mother.

"I believe you're right." Anne wrapped her arm around the girl's shoulder. This winter Sammie Jo had shot up like a weed after spring rain, and her body had begun to look more like a young woman. Anne wasn't ready for that. In a few years, she'd be shooing away the young cowboys like flies on. . .on what comes natural.

"We're leaving right after breakfast?" Sammie Jo lifted a mug of coffee to her lips. She drank it black like her mother. The steam rolled off the top in a mystic dance before disappearing into the air.

"And not a minute later. Your sister doing all right?"

Sammie Jo nodded. "She hates not going. Says she feels better."

Anne chuckled. "Nancy should have thought about what those green dewberries would do to her stomach before she ate so many."

"Mama, those had to taste terrible, and she got so sick."

Anne shook her head. "Curiosity gets the best of Nancy. Reminds me of your daddy."

"Ever wish we were boys?"

"Never. But I do think some of the ladies at church believe I've turned you into them."

Sammie Jo laughed. "I feel more comfortable in my boots and jeans than dresses."

Anne kissed the tip of her daughter's nose. "Me, too, but we best keep that tidbit to ourselves. Let's see what Rosita has for breakfast. The sooner we help the others round up strays, the sooner you and I can do a little hunting."

"Is Clancy going with us?" Sammie Jo turned her head slightly, peering up with sky blue eyes that mirrored her daddy's. The look always caused Anne's heart to remember the man she'd loved.

"I don't think so. He's taking a few of the men to the upper ridge. Fence needs mending."

Sammie Jo frowned. "He's getting too old for all this hard work. Needs to settle down and spend out his days in a rocking chair. And his aim's getting bad. I beat him with my rifle in target practice last Saturday."

"Do you want to be the one telling him that?"

"No, ma'am. Clancy would chase me with a branding iron."

Anne hugged her daughter's shoulder again. They had a good life. For five years they'd worked hard and made the Double L Ranch the largest in this part of the state. And she intended to keep building it into an empire. Vast herds of longhorns and a line of fine quarter horses made her proud. A few eligible men had eyed her ranch and come courting. Didn't need a single one of them except Clancy, who was like a daddy to her and a granddaddy to the girls. Hadn't been a man since Will who interested her or could tame her stubborn nature.

Will used to call her *Mustang*. She smiled. Most women would have slapped a man silly for calling them a horse, but Anne took it as a compliment. Those traits helped make her strong when Will took sick and died. Her girls would have a good life ahead of them with money for education back East, and they'd not be dependent on a man to survive.

God had smiled on the three Langley women, and she prayed He'd continue for a long time. Two tragedies in a lifetime were enough.

—⁓—

Colt Wilson could taste the freedom. It lingered on his tongue like thick honey, and when he swallowed, his whole body felt the excitement. His fingers trembled like a kid with a fish on a hook. For six years he'd worn chains and worked like a fool to pay his debt to the state of Texas in Huntsville Prison. Now, as he placed one foot in front of the other, he could see the steel door that led to sweet liberty's sunshine. No more bug-infested food and bedding down with rats, and best of all, no more jumping every time the man jammed a rifle barrel in his ribs.

"Good luck to ya," the guard said. "You're a smart man, Wilson. Don't get yourself in here again."

Colt nodded and offered a grim smile. Prison life did that to a man: made him slap on a fake smile when he wanted to fight, laugh when he wanted to cry, and respect those who held his life in their hands. Years like what he'd endured made a man take stock in what he stood for—and what he'd do and not do when he got out.

The heavy door swung open, creaking like the gates of Hades releasing one of its own. Colt inhaled the freshness of life. Air so pure he gasped to make sure he hadn't died and gone to heaven by mistake. He'd shaken off the shackles that had physically bound him, but he couldn't shake the memory of the man who had allowed him to be turned in to the law. Those shackles tightened around his heart, and the key lay embedded in bitterness. The hate threatened to overtake his good sense, but Colt had long since promised himself never to set foot in a jail again. He had no future unless he got rid of the past.

He knew the right way to live, and he'd abide by the law. But first he had a matter to settle.

Inside of a week, he found a job with a rancher. He enjoyed the hard work, especially when he got paid for it. The solitary life with a few ranch hands for company settled well with him. The sound of bawling cows was like music, certainly better than gunfire or fighting men.

Summer heat sent sweat dripping down his back, but he'd take these sweltering temperatures above the stench of heat fused with filthy men any day. His mind drifted to the days ahead, and the more he pondered on ranching, the more he realized he could do a whole lot worse than punching cows for the rest of his life.

Two months later, Colt had a few dollars in his pocket, a good horse, and a worn saddle. With a Winchester strapped to his saddle and a saddlebag full of provisions, he headed toward a little town outside Austin called Willow Creek. Before he could get on with his life, Colt needed to see a man face-to-face.

Heading back home to Wyoming needled at him. Seeing his brothers again might be good, but he didn't know where to begin. They were a sorry lot. All of 'om bent on breaking the law. That most likely had been part of what killed Ma. Maybe his brothers would turn around their way of thinking before their pasts caught up with them. At least Reuben had learned from his mistakes, even if he did get religion. Colt remembered his eldest brother visiting him in prison. Colt had no desire to listen to Reuben's God-business, but it did grieve him to learn of Ma's passing.

Colt rode into Willow Creek and headed straight for the general store. Storekeepers always knew the goings-on and could give him directions. He lifted his hat and banged the trail dust from it on his jeans before stepping inside.

"Howdy." He grinned big at the balding man behind the counter.

The man greeted him, and they talked a bit about the dry weather and the sore need of rain.

"Say, I'm looking for an old friend of mine. Haven't seen him in years, but I know he was from these parts," Colt said.

"What's his name?"

"Will Langley."

The storekeeper rubbed his whiskered chin. "I hate to give you the bad news, but Will's been dead nigh on to five years."

Colt pasted a sorrowful look on his face. "Sorry to hear that. What happened?"

"Accident at his ranch. An ax went through his leg. Got gangrene and died."

"What about family? Anyone I can pay my respects to?"

"His widow owns a ranch not far from town. I can tell you how to get there."

"I'd be obliged," Colt said. "It's the least I can do."

Colt took note of the road to the Langley ranch and headed back to his horse. Disappointment snaked through him. Will's widow probably didn't have anything but a rundown piece of no-good property. He'd ridden all this way, though. Might as well take in a few more miles. Hard to make a man pay when he was dead. Bad luck had dealt Will Langley a rotten hand, but he felt sorry for the widow. A woman always seemed to suffer for loving the wrong man.

Revenge is bad for the soul. He could hear his daddy lecturing him, although he'd been dead for years. Unfortunately, whatever folks told him, Colt had a habit of doing the opposite and usually with a heavy dose of temper. Even Reuben had been afraid of him. Colt's ugly disposition was what got him behind bars in the first place.

No matter what he ended up doing, he had to stay to himself, keep his temper in check, and be careful not to rile anybody. Colt clenched his jaw. Will Langley being dead was probably good. Colt would most likely have lost his temper and ended up back in Huntsville prison for life or in a hangman's noose.

Colt followed the storekeeper's directions and rode straight onto a ranch so wide and green he wondered if he'd made a wrong turn. Herds of cattle grazed over rolling pastures, and when he strained to look again, he saw some of the finest horseflesh this side of the Mississippi. *Will Langley's widow owns this ranch? This may be my lucky day.*

Colt rode right up to a ranch house that was about the fanciest he'd ever seen. This part of the country was known for its abundance of stone, and the Widow Langley's ranch used lots of it. He dismounted about the time a young girl stepped onto the front porch with a rifle in hand. She wore a tattered hat pulled down over her eyes. Couldn't tell what she looked like.

"What's your business, mister?" the skinny, half-sized woman said.

"I'm here to see a Mrs. Will Langley."

"What for?"

"Business. What's your name, little girl?"

"I'm no little girl, and you haven't any right riding on my land and asking me who I am." She raised her rifle and aimed straight at him.

"Be careful. Do you know how to use that thing?"

"No matter, since I'm about to blow a hole right between your eyes if you don't ride on out of here."

"Sammie Jo, put down that rifle before I take a switch to you." A woman's voice rose above the quiet. "That's no way to treat a man just riding in off the trail."

Colt expelled a ragged breath. For a moment, he thought he'd meet his Maker by way of a girl. He swung his attention around to a woman dressed like a man. A very pretty woman, tall and with hair the color of deerskin. She must work for the widow.

He yanked off his hat. "Thank you, ma'am. I'm looking for Mrs. Will Langley. Her husband is an old friend of mine."

The woman lifted her chin and eyed him curiously.

"I'm Mrs. Will Langley. What can I do for you?"

Chapter 2

The color drained from Colt's face, and sweat dampened his back. He'd had a better reception at Huntsville Prison on his first day. This was Will's widow and his daughter? In Colt's opinion, Will was the one who needed sympathy. Whatever happened to defenseless women? If Will died of gangrene in his leg, these two probably offered to cut it off.

The girl called Sammie Jo lowered her rifle and propped it against the side of the porch. A younger girl dressed in jeans and boots slipped through the door and stiffened to about four feet tall. She placed her hands on her hips and scowled.

"I smell him clear over here," the smallest girl said. "Doesn't he know what a Saturday night bath is?"

"Hush, Nancy. You mind your manners," Mrs. Langley said.

What is this? Have I died and gotten what I deserve?

"State your business, sir. I have a ranch to run." Mrs. Langley crossed her arms over a green plaid shirt. She nodded toward the girls. "Meet me in the horse barn. We'll talk about your punishment for treating this man shamefully. Right now, you two apologize."

When the girls hesitated, she repeated her request—a little louder.

"I'm sorry," the two girls echoed and hurried toward the barns.

Colt dragged his tongue over dry, cracked lips. He'd never done well talking to women. "Your husband, ma'am, was a friend of mine."

"He's been gone for five years."

"Yes, ma'am. I've been drifting."

"In prison, no doubt. What's your name?"

He started. "Colt Wilson."

"A friend of Will's, you say?"

"Yes, ma'am." Alarm—the strength of a tornado—twisted through him. He best be riding out of there before she questioned his business with her departed husband. If Will had told his wife what he and Colt had done, she most likely would have killed him on the spot.

"Are you wanted?"

"No."

"What were you in prison for?"

Didn't your husband tell you? He shifted from one foot to the other. "Bank robbery."

"Kill anyone?"

"No, ma'am."

"Ever kill anyone?"

"Only to defend myself."

"Likely story." She glared at him. "Need a job? From the horse you're riding, you must not have stashed away the money."

The question caught him by surprise. "Why would you give me a job since—?"

"Since you just got out of prison? Because you knew Will and because I just lost two hands."

Did he want to work for this woman? For that matter, did he want to spend five more minutes with her? Unpredictably, he heard himself saying, "I'd be grateful."

She pointed to the bunkhouse. "Take your stuff over there and ask for Clancy. He'll show you where you'll sleep and what he needs you to do." She whirled around to follow the girls. "Don't waste any time. I'm short-handed and have too much work for you to dillydally."

"I'll do a fine job for you, Mrs. Langley."

She stopped in her tracks and turned around. A little cloud of dust spun up from her heels like a miniature dust devil. "Don't make me regret hiring you, or I'll be the one squeezing the trigger."

A lady boss? Why had he taken this job? He came looking for Will's widow, thinking she might be in a bad way and know a little about her husband's past dealings. Instead, he'd been waylaid. Sure, she had a pretty face and owned a large ranch, but this was downright degrading. Colt swung a look after her. Mrs. Langley might dress like a man and give orders like a man, but she didn't walk like a man.

— ∞ —

Anne studied her two daughters inside the shadows of the horse barn. Some days she wondered if she'd done the right thing by making them strong and feisty. After seeing their behavior toward Colt Wilson, she realized she'd stepped over the boundaries between strength and inhospitality.

Sammie Jo crossed her arms over her chest and tapped her foot. Nancy had her familiar stance of planting her chubby hands on her hips.

"I'm ashamed of both of you," she said. "What have I taught you about manners?"

"I didn't like the way he looked," Sammie Jo said.

"And I didn't like the way he smelled," Nancy said.

"Hmm. Is that what the Bible teaches?"

"No, ma'am," they chorused.

"Look around you." Anne pointed toward the horse stalls. "Do you like what you see and smell?"

"Not really." Sammie Jo wrinkled her nose. "Needs a good cleaning."

"And you two are going to do that very thing." Anne almost laughed at the horrified looks on their faces.

"Mama, that's too hard a punishment." Nancy's eyes widened, mirroring the same shade of blue as her sister's.

"I'd rather take a whippin'," added Sammie Jo.

Anne shook her head. "That's too easy. You can think about good manners and what the good Lord requires of us while you're cleaning stalls." She nodded at her precious daughters and headed toward the sunlight filling the doorway. "You can watch the horse-breakin' before you start your work."

Giggles broke from behind her, but she dared not turn around or she'd relinquish the stall cleaning. Anne had shoveled them a man-sized job, but she hoped it taught her sassy girls a lesson.

Colt Wilson. She searched the cobwebs of her mind for the name. Nothing tore through the many memories of Will and their countless hours together. Near the end he'd told her many things, but a wayward man by the name of Colt Wilson wasn't one of them. Maybe he followed the law back then. Given time, she'd find out the truth. If she'd learned anything over the past five years, it was how life dealt every man and woman a bushel basket of mountains and valleys. How people handled those happenings made them who they were today. She'd hardened through it. . .maybe too hard.

Anne shuddered. Where were her brains in subjecting Sammie Jo and Nancy to an outlaw—or rather a past outlaw? And what about the good hands who worked for her? Some men never shook off the habits that had thrown them behind bars. Still, a nudging at her heart had told her to offer him a job. And she sure hoped it was the Lord and not stupidity.

"Mrs. Langley, are you riding?" Thatcher Lee asked.

She surfaced from her reverie and waved at the young man standing with the other three hands. She laughed at the seriousness on his face—barely eighteen years old and her self-proclaimed protector. Or maybe he had his eye on Sammie Jo in a few years. That thought curdled her stomach.

"Ah, yes, I am. In fact, I want that bronc you're afraid of."

"The sorrel stallion?" Thatcher Lee asked.

"You bet. I see you have him ready. About time I showed you men how to ride."

Clancy strode up to the corral with Colt beside him. "Anne, that horse is mean. You could hurt yourself real bad. Why not let me sell him?"

"Are you kidding? How many times in the past few years have you seen me back down from a good fight?" She laughed again.

"When he tosses you on the ground I'm not helping you up." Standing with his back against the sun, Clancy's shoulder-length silver hair glistened, his Apache heritage evident from every inch of him.

She opened the gate and headed toward the stallion, which snorted and pranced. Clancy might be right. Thatcher Lee held the reins and tried to settle the horse. Oh, this one would cause her to taste dirt more than once.

"Be careful, Mama," Nancy called. Sammie Jo knew better than to object.

Fearfulness ruined Anne's concentration.

Lord, I have a foolish streak, and I know it. Seems like I always have to prove something.

She grabbed the reins, stepped into the stirrup and swung onto the saddle. As if stung by a swarm of bees, the horse reared. Anne dug her knees into his sides and held on. Her heart raced, pumping excitement through her veins. That quickly, his head touched the ground, and his rear legs aimed for the sky. If she hadn't watched the stallion's habits, she'd be lying in a heap of bruised flesh looking up at the sun—and listening to Clancy scold with an "I told you so." It could happen yet.

About the time that thought emptied her head, she lost balance and hit the hard ground. Thatcher Lee headed her way, but she waved him off and spit out a mouthful of dirt. The young man grabbed the stallion's reins, and she mounted the horse again.

With a twist of powerful muscles, the horse jerked and twisted in midair. She heard nothing, saw nothing, and concentrated on the massive animal beneath her in an attempt to sense its every move. After several minutes, the stallion began to slow. Good thing, for she was ready to give the job to the nearest ranch hand.

Some days she didn't have a lick of sense.

Finally, the stallion ceased its rearing and snorting and allowed her to walk him around the corral. The others shouted her on. She tossed them a smile. *This is the last time I'm doing this.*

When she finally dismounted and handed the reins to Thatcher Lee, she thought her legs had turned to matchsticks.

"You all right?" Thatcher Lee whispered.

"Yeah," she said. "If I mention doing this again, remind me I have two daughters to raise."

From beneath his hat he nodded and grinned.

Anne glanced at Clancy, who narrowed his eyes. No doubt he had his lecture all worked out. She deserved it. Her gaze swept to Colt. Curiosity rested in his dark eyes. Usually admiration greeted her from the ranch hands.

Pride goeth before destruction. That's why she wasn't breaking any more horses.

Anne glanced at her girls standing on either side of Clancy. Nancy's face had turned ashen. She'd apologize to her baby girl. Shame had made its point. She walked over to her girls.

"Good job, Mama." Sammie Jo lifted her chin.

Anne nodded and cupped Nancy's quivering chin in her hand. "I won't be breaking any more horses, darlin'."

The little girl swallowed hard and swiped at a single tear rolling over her cheek. "Thank you."

She caught Colt Wilson's gaze again. This time he offered a thin-lipped smile.

"Young'uns have a way of setting us right," he said.

Fire burned her cheeks. "I'd appreciate it if you'd keep your remarks to yourself."

"Just making an observation, ma'am."

"I can take care of my girls just fine."

"I reckon so."

His words were like kindling on a crackling fire, but she dare not lose her temper in front of the girls or Clancy. What made matters worse was that he'd spoken rightly. To prove herself equal to a man, she'd risked her life, but she didn't need him pointing out the truth. And that's what made her even angrier.

Chapter 3

Three days later, on Saturday night, with a belly full of smoked ham and beans, Colt brushed down his mare in the ebb of daylight. He'd already decided to take an evening ride and think through the mess he'd gotten himself into. Decisions needed to be made soon, because his idea of a good job didn't mean taking orders from a woman. He'd looked up Will for a reason, and those reasons still needled at him.

The sound of sloshing water snatched his attention. He watched a couple of the ranch hands hustle about heating water over a fire and adding it to a watering trough in the middle of the barn.

"What's going on in there?" he asked Thatcher Lee.

"Bath night," the muscular young man said.

"Why?"

" 'Cause we smell. Mrs. Langley demands it."

"Why?"

Thatcher Lee scowled. "For church. We all go to church on Sunday morning with Mrs. Langley and the girls."

Colt laughed. "Not me. I haven't set foot in a church since my ma carried me on her hip."

"Well, on the Double L, you either get to church or hit the road."

Irritation bubbled up inside Colt, but he swallowed it. This wasn't the first time he'd heard strange notions coming from Anne Langley. The more he thought about the Double L, the more he realized she had to know about what he and Will had done. Where else had she gotten the money to build up this ranch? He'd learned from Clancy that Will had purchased it about a year before he had the accident.

That meant a portion of this fine acreage was Colt's. All he had to do was convince her of his partial ownership. Except every time he considered Anne Langley as a business partner, his insides shook.

"What if I don't have any clean clothes?" Colt asked.

"We have extras."

"I'd rather take a bath in the creek."

Thatcher Lee tossed him a cake of soap. "Me and Clancy feel the same way. I'm on my way now. You might as well join us."

"Since I don't have a choice, I reckon so."

A bath and church. This woman would drive him crazy. He nearly laughed aloud. The sight of the Langley women stepping into church with their jeans and boots instead of dresses and bonnets must amuse the locals. No matter. He'd catch up on his sleep during the sermon.

Sunday morning he dressed in clean clothes and stomped the dirt and manure off his boots. He mounted up with the rest of the hands, thinking his brothers would never let him live this one down. Clancy had a Bible. No wonder the old Indian didn't curse or tell a good story now and then. As far as drinking, he doubted if Clancy did that either, since the boss lady didn't allow it on the ranch.

Up at the house, Colt did a double take. The Langley women sashayed onto the front porch dressed like fine ladies. Why, they looked quite fetching—especially Mrs. Langley. All three had ribbons in their hair and wore shoes instead of boots. But what he noticed the most was how Mrs. Langley curved out nicely in a corn-colored dress, and her walk still took his breath away.

Stop it, Colt. You'll get shot for such thoughts. He lifted his hat and brushed back his hair, hoping no one could hear what raced through his mind. Every time he considered Will and the boss lady married, he simply couldn't picture it. Will's take-charge nature and the strong-willed woman Colt secretly called "Boss Lady" would have been like fire and dynamite. And he wouldn't have wanted to be around for the explosion.

Oh, he should be fair. The boss lady did have her gentle moments; he'd witnessed her tender side with the girls and Rosita—and even Clancy.

The small church stood out in the middle of nowhere with plenty of room for wagons and horses to crowd around the wood-framed building. He expected folks to be solemn, but they were laughing and calling out to each other as if they were on a picnic. Peculiar. Real peculiar.

He swung over his horse and watched Clancy help the boss lady and her daughters down from the wagon as if they'd break in two. Mrs. Langley sure played the part well.

Colt waited as long as possible before he mounted the wooden steps to the church. Spending his morning with Bible thumpers didn't appeal to him. Not at all. He took his place on a bench with the other hands while Clancy sat with the Langley women. The arrangement made it easy for Colt to sleep and her not to know.

The preacher stepped up to the front. "Open your hymn books to 'Shall We Gather at the River?'"

Colt grinned. The man must have been at the creek last night when he, Clancy, and Thatcher Lee took their baths. In the next instant he closed his eyes, and that was all he remembered.

—⁓—

Anne could barely hear Preacher Rollins for the snoring behind her. A quick glance told her it was Colt Wilson. Later she'd tell him what she thought of desecrating the Lord's day by sleeping in church. Heathen. She must have been touched in the head to hire him on the spot last week.

But that day she had no choice after firing Hank and Thomas for pulling their guns on Clancy and Thatcher Lee. The two had been caught red-handed cutting a few head of cattle from the herd. Since then, the other hands tried to keep up with the work, but it was nearly impossible. A week later and ten more longhorns were missing. She'd filed a report with the sheriff, but the man had laziness written across the seat of his pants and a nagging wife that wanted him at home.

Hank and Thomas held their own with a gun, and the thought frightened her a bit—not for herself, but for the girls and the other men. Anne blinked. Surely Colt wasn't working with them on this. He'd known Will, but Hank and Thomas had never met her dearly departed husband. Colt's riding in must have been a coincidence. Anne didn't believe in coincidences any more than she did in fairytales. God must have purposed Colt Wilson to arrive at the exact time. He looked like neither an angel nor a saint—and he didn't snore like anything heavenly, either. Why God might have brought him into her life was beyond her thinking.

This morning when Anne caught sight of Colt all cleaned up, he looked right handsome. And he did have those big gray eyes with flecks of gold. . .and eyelashes a girl ought to have. Too bad he was an outlaw, and most likely he wasn't worth the lead to send him to kingdom come.

She inwardly scolded her wandering thoughts and focused on the preacher. God knew how she felt about all this, and He'd handle it. But, oh, how she wanted to take off after those two cattle thieves herself.

—⁂—

Colt sprang from his bunk. Rifle fire cracked a second time. In the dark, he grabbed his pants and rifle then tore through the bunkhouse with Thatcher Lee right behind him. In the light of a full moon and a sky filled with stars, Clancy leaned against the side of the bunkhouse, fully dressed. Before him stood Sammie Jo.

"What are you shooting at this time of the night?" Clancy asked. "You could have been killed by one of us."

"I got him." Sammie Jo's voice rose in the stillness. She held up the tail of a coyote. "He won't be stealing any more of our chickens."

"Well, I reckon you did." Clancy laughed.

"Rosita was carrying on something awful yesterday with another hen gone."

The excitement in Sammie Jo caused Colt to burst out laughing. The Langley women never ceased to amaze him.

"You hightail it back to bed, and I'll get rid of that coyote," Clancy said.

"I want him skinned."

"Sure thing. You and I'll do it tomorrow."

"Can we make a hat?"

"I suppose. Now get going before your mama finds you missing."

Sammie Jo gave the old man a hug and raced toward the main house, but Thatcher Lee caught up with her. Colt watched them disappear into the darkness. That gal acted just like her mama.

"I'll never understand women," he said in the stillness.

"You mean Sammie Jo or Anne?" Clancy asked.

Colt shrugged. "Neither one of them is like any woman I ever knew. I never had sisters, and my ma acted. . .well, normal."

"She hasn't always been this way," Clancy said. He studied Colt. "I hear you knew Will."

"We had some business together."

"You best keep that business to yourself. Anne doesn't need to hear any of it."

"I figured so."

Colt gazed out into the night, as though staring after Thatcher Lee and Sammie Jo. His thoughts narrowed in on what Clancy must know about Will, and what the boss lady didn't know.

"How fast are you with a gun?" Clancy asked.

"Fair. I prefer a rifle."

"Stick around here until a few matters are settled. Anne's going to need all the help she can get."

"Trouble? What kind?" Colt asked. An image of Huntsville settled on him like a bad case of the backdoor runs.

"The kind that can get a body killed. I buried Will, and I don't plan to bury her or them girls." Clancy released a heavy sigh. "She may look and act tough, but that's a cover for something else. And"—he turned and stared at Colt face-to-face—"we didn't have this conversation."

"Why me?"

"I see more in you than I reckon you do. This might be your one chance to straighten out your life."

Colt bristled. "What do you mean?"

"I'm no fool. You ride in here looking for a dead man, which means you've done time. No family. No money. No purpose in life. No relationship with the Lord. But I do see a shred of decency."

Colt swallowed hard and was grateful for the darkness hiding him from humiliation—and anger.

"No need to answer," Clancy said. "Will you stick around until the trouble's gone?"

"I need to know what kind of trouble."

"Let's take a walk." Clancy headed out into the blackness toward the corral, and Colt followed. More out of curiosity than interest.

"Thatcher Lee and I caught two of Anne's men rustling cows. They would have killed us if Anne hadn't ridden up and surprised them. She run 'em off, but they threatened to burn her place to the ground with her and the girls in it."

Those words did set off Colt's temper. The two men needed a hangman's noose.

"What about the local law?"

"Aw, the sheriff says those two are long gone, but I don't believe it for a minute. Besides, ten of our cows are gone."

Colt let the silence filter his thoughts. He didn't much care about getting shot or interfering in someone else's trouble, but threatening womenfolk wasn't right. Another thought entered his head. By helping the boss lady with this problem, she might feel grateful enough to give him what was rightfully his. That thought pricked his conscience. He didn't have any business taking advantage of a woman, even a woman like Anne Langley.

I've gotten mean and hard. But if I don't look out for myself, who will?

"What do you say?" Clancy asked.

"Yeah, I'll stick around to help," Colt said.

He made his way back to his bunk and tried to go to sleep. His mind sped ahead about his predicament. He kept learning new things that interrupted his original plans. Anger surfaced again toward any man who would threaten a widow and two little girls. At least they weren't defenseless. Those two hands who'd rustled cattle might have had other things on their mind. Maybe they got wind of Will's activities before he died. Maybe stealing a few cows was to cover up for something else.

A short while later, Thatcher Lee eased onto his bunk beside Colt's.

"Took you long enough," Colt whispered.

"We were talking."

Colt nearly came out of his bunk. "That gal is fourteen years old. Too young for you to be thinkin' on courtin' matters."

"You ain't her pa."

"No, but I knew him well enough to figure out what he'd have done to a young whippersnapper after his little girl."

Thatcher Lee mumbled something under his breath.

"Give her about three or four years, and let her grow up proper. Filling her mind with woman things instead of letting her find out about life on her own is downright wrong." With those words, Colt turned over away from Thatcher Lee's bunk.

From Clancy's bunk, he heard a muffled laugh.

Chapter 4

olt leaned against the corral fence and pumped the well over the watering trough. The day had been a scorcher, and his mouth tasted as dry as the dirt beneath his feet. He'd been working at the Double L for more than three weeks, and not one more cow had been stolen. His fears about the two men using thievery as a cover for something else were unfounded. He had no doubt they'd long since left the territory.

Water began to flow from the spigot, and he cupped his hands for a cool drink. Once he doused his face, he stood and glanced up at the house. Why did he stay? Was it the money, or was it about being a decent man?

With no answers, his gaze focused on Nancy high up in a live oak tree. How did she get herself up there? And how did she plan to get down? He walked over there until he stood beneath the branches of the tree.

"Miss Nancy, how did you get up there?" he asked.

He saw the little girl rub her nose. A faint sob escaped her lips.

"Are you stuck?"

"I think so."

Colt shook his head. "Did you climb up there?"

"Yes, sir. I tried and tried. Then I got the ladder and finally made it. It fell, and I couldn't figure out how to get down."

He wanted to chuckle but thought better of it. "Can you make your way to the lowest branch?" On the far side of the tree, the ladder rested on the ground.

She nodded and slowly descended until her bare toes touched on the branch.

"Jump and I'll catch you," he said.

"Promise?" Her lips trembled—a trait he'd seen when the boss lady had ridden the bronc.

"Promise."

"And you won't tell my mama or Sammie Jo or Clancy?"

"I promise."

She took a deep breath and jumped right into his arms. Made him feel real protective.

"Are you hurt?"

"No, sir. Would you put me down before someone sees?"

He grinned. "Sure, and I'll keep our little secret."

He set her on the soft ground, and she scampered off. Shaking his head, he picked up the ladder and headed to the barn. His swaybacked mare awaited him to join the others.

"Thank you."

Colt swung around to find the boss lady speaking to him from the back porch.

"You're welcome." He waved and continued on.

"Got a minute, Colt?"

Great. Wonder what he'd done wrong. The tongue-lashing over sleeping in church had kept him awake the past two Sundays. Bored, but awake.

"Is there a problem?" he asked.

"Not at all. Do you have time to take a ride with me?"

His heart felt like tumbleweed in a windstorm. "I imagine so."

He put away the ladder while she retrieved her horse, and he helped her saddle it.

"Will used to saddle my horse," she said. "He always took the time to make sure it was tight." She tilted her head, looking real pretty. "Then I decided I needed to do everything myself."

He handed her the reins. She'd never talked to him before like he was a human being. But he'd wanted her to.

"I can see Will taking good care of you," Colt said.

"That's what I want to talk about."

This must be it. She wanted to settle up on the money owed to him.

As they rode out across the pasture, Colt searched for conversation. His dealings with women in the past hadn't been proper, and the women hadn't been real ladies.

"I understand you told Thatcher Lee to stay away from Sammie Jo until she grew up."

"Yes, ma'am. Sorry if I spoke without asking you first."

"Not at all. I appreciate it. She wasn't listening to me or Clancy. Of course, she's a lot like me."

Colt smiled.

"Tell me about Will and the times you spent together."

How much dare he say? The man lay buried on his ranch. His wife did better than any woman he'd ever met, and his daughters weren't afraid of anything—except Nancy and tall trees. Still, defaming the dead seemed wrong, even if it meant Will went to his grave with the knowledge of Colt's money.

"What do you want to know?"

She hesitated as though carefully choosing her words. "I know my husband didn't live according to the law. He confessed a lot to me while dying."

Like the whereabouts of what belongs to me?

"And if you came here looking for money, you might as well turn around and head out of here, 'cause I don't know anything about it."

Colt's spirits sank to his toes.

"What I want to know about is the man," she said.

"Mrs. Langley—"

"The name is Anne."

"All right, Anne. This is real difficult for me. Will and me did things I'd rather not discuss with a lady."

"I'm your boss—and Will's widow."

Sweat streamed down the side of Colt's face, and it had nothing to do with the heat. "He had a way of leading out in a situation that showed real guts. I mean, he didn't ask a man to do anything he wouldn't do."

She nodded. "Go on."

"He never lied or killed anyone that I knew about."

"How much money did you two steal?"

He was afraid she'd ask that. "Twelve thousand."

"I never saw any of it. My folks left me money to buy the ranch."

They rode on in silence while Colt contemplated his miserable existence. No future.

"Did he speak to you about his family?" she finally asked.

"No. Didn't know he had one until I looked you up." He pondered over his conversations with Will, then turned his attention her way. "But he wasn't unfaithful to you."

A faint smile greeted him. "I'm glad to hear that. He always said he loved me and the girls. Thanks."

"You're welcome."

"I have another matter to discuss with you."

Dread inched over him. The last topic nearly drained him.

"Do you think any other men might be looking for him because of money—or revenge?"

"I honestly have no idea."

"If you think of anyone, would you let me know? I have my girls and my ranch to protect."

"Why did you give me a job?"

"God told me to hire you."

"God?"

"Yes, the one we worship on Sunday mornings while you pretend to listen."

He laughed. "That must be the one."

"Someday when you least expect it, God is going to grab your attention."

"Yes, ma'am. He'd have to shake me good."

"Oh, He can, Colt. And it wouldn't hurt you to be talking to Him now and then."

—∾—

Anne kissed Nancy's cheek, then watched her slip into dreamland. Her daughter had confessed to the tree adventure, not realizing her mama had seen the whole thing.

Nancy had sighed and folded her hands over her chest. "Mr. Colt helped me down out of that tree and held me like I was a baby kitten," the little girl said.

"He must have thought you might break."

In the lamp's light, Nancy's face grew strangely solemn. "I thought I might.

Mama, I just kept looking up in that tree and wondering what it would feel like to sit in its branches like a bird. I couldn't stop myself. Then the ladder fell, and I was scared."

"Sweetheart, curiosity is good, but you have to back it up with a little common sense."

"I'll try, but it's hard."

Anne blew out the lamp. "Ask Jesus to help you."

"I did—for the next time."

"I'm proud of you. Now close your eyes. I'm going to sit right here until you go to sleep."

Anne never tired of watching her precious daughters sleep, and she did so tonight until darkness concealed Nancy's features and Colt's face took over.

Buried beneath the hardened man was a soft heart. She'd seen it with Nancy today and heard about it from Clancy. All of Anne's frettin' hadn't deterred Sammie Jo from chasing after Thatcher Lee, but Colt had handled Thatcher Lee quite nicely. Today he'd chosen his words carefully so as not to mar Will's image. Anne liked that.

Her husband might not have obeyed the law, but he'd loved her and the girls. And she'd loved him, too. The times he'd been gone on business must have been the times he robbed banks and other folks who had money. She hated that part of his life. It made her feel dirty. The girls should never find out about their daddy—no reason for them to learn the truth.

Until recently Anne hadn't looked at another man. Strange that Colt Wilson had captured her attention, but she liked his rugged looks and quiet mannerisms. Her heart must lean toward lawless men. He was rough and tough, and his language hadn't been graced by the inside of a grammar book, but he had some good in him. She prayed the Lord would touch him for heaven before he got himself into trouble and was killed.

Anne made her way to the open window where a slight breeze swayed the curtains. Her gaze trailed to the bunkhouse. Loyal men lived there—men who respected her and worked hard. Had it all been worth the struggle of just day-to-day living? As she turned to leave Nancy to peaceful slumber, she caught the silhouette of a man staring up at the stars. She studied him and wondered if it was Colt contemplating the future, maybe thinking about her.

Odd that she should care.

—※—

Clancy, Thatcher Lee, and Colt rode around a grassy ridge and along a thick forest north of Double L land. Clancy had something on his mind, and twice he'd dismounted to look at the ground. Obviously his part-Indian eyes detected a trail.

"Where are we going?" Colt lowered his voice to speak to Thatcher Lee. He knew better than to worry a concentrating man.

"My guess is that he has an idea about those missing cows."

"Glad I'm packing my rifle," Colt said.

"I never killed a man."

"Here's hoping you don't have to. But I tell you this, if it's them or you, you'll squeeze the trigger."

Colt scanned the area around them. Between the woods and the rounded hills, unseen men could be watching their every move. He pulled his rifle onto his lap. Thatcher Lee did the same.

Clancy halted his horse and raised his hand, signaling for them to stop. For long moments, he observed the terrain and waited. Finally he motioned Colt and Thatcher Lee to see what he'd found. At the foot of the hill below them were Double L cows.

"Where're Hank and Thomas?" Thatcher Lee asked.

"Not where I can see 'em." Clancy slipped off his horse and led the animal into the woods.

The two men followed. Colt admired the old man's skill and confidence.

"Thatcher Lee, you stay here while Colt and I do a little scouting."

The young man frowned.

"You heard me. Colt and me have done this kind of thing before. I don't want to be taking you back full of bullet holes." He didn't give Thatcher Lee a chance to argue but took off toward a path that led around the hill. Vultures circled overhead.

Neither man spoke. Their bodies blended into the sights and sounds of nature. Peacefulness always masked the stalking of trouble. They moved hunched over through the woods and crawled through the low-lying areas until they were within several feet of one of the grazing cows.

"I didn't see a sign of anyone," Clancy whispered. "But that doesn't mean they aren't ready to ambush us."

Colt pointed to a clump of trees adjacent to where they lay in tall grass. Clancy nodded. A cow bawled. Squirrels chattered. Birds sang. A sultry wind blew around them. The old sensation of excitement flowing through his veins swept over Colt as he made his way alone. All thoughts left his mind except the task before him. Once he made it alone to the other side, he drank in the surroundings.

His eyes narrowed. To his far right he saw a man sprawled face down on the ground. The grass was stained red. A few feet beyond him was another man on his belly. Brush hid the second man's upper body. Two vultures picked around the area.

Colt studied the two men for signs of life. He motioned to Clancy and crawled closer. Once he joined him, they'd figure out what had happened here.

"Hank and Thomas," Clancy said a short while later.

Both men had bullets in their heads, their hands tied.

"This is worse than what I thought," Clancy continued.

"You and I both know about Will," Colt said. "It's been over five years since he died, but I can't help but think this is related."

A bullet whizzed past his ear. A second caused a gasp from Clancy as it ripped open flesh in his shoulder. A third lodged in Colt's thigh.

"If you ever thought about praying, now's the time," Clancy said.

The fire burning in Colt's leg fueled his temper. He yanked his rifle to his shoulder and fired repeatedly into the brush where the shots had come from.

"You go ahead and talk to God," Colt said. "Ask Him to send Thatcher Lee our way and cover us while we hightail it back into those woods."

Clancy aimed and fired. "That's a start."

Chapter 5

G od was looking out for you two," Anne said once she'd yanked the bullet from Colt's thigh and wrapped clean bandages around his leg.

"I know He was." Clancy winced as she dabbed whiskey on his open flesh. "That hurts as bad as the bullet tearing across my shoulder."

"Don't complain," Colt said. "You weren't the one she dug into with a knife."

Sammie Jo peered over her mama's shoulder. "That looks real bad, Clancy. Makes me wonder if you and Colt might up and die on us. Daddy's leg didn't look any better than you two."

"Sammie Jo." Anne whirled around to face her daughter. "I thought I asked you to pray for these two men, not bring death knocking at our door."

"Yes, ma'am."

Colt's leg throbbed, but he managed a nervous chuckle. "Sammie Jo, are you afraid of anything?"

"No, sir."

He studied her young face, so stubborn and innocent. "Life's hard, Sammie Jo. One day you'll find what you're afraid of. When you do, face it."

She frowned at him. Oh, that gal had a lot to learn.

"Sammie Jo, you run along and draw water for Rosita," Anne said. "I need to talk to these men."

Once the girl had left the bunkhouse, Anne turned her attention to doctoring Clancy.

"We didn't see anyone," Clancy said. "If it hadn't been for Thatcher Lee, we'd have been as dead as Hank and Thomas."

Anne studied Thatcher Lee. "Did you see them?"

"No, ma'am. They were like ghosts. I kept firing into the brush where the shots came from while Clancy and Colt crawled away."

"I'm not sure what to think about this," she said. "Those men need burying but not at the risk of getting our men shot."

Colt squeezed his eyes shut and tried desperately to forget the pain in his leg. Drinking the rest of that bottle of whiskey was mighty tempting, but Anne didn't permit drinking—for any reason.

Colt cleared his throat. "We need to keep our eyes open until this is settled. I

318

wonder about Hank's and Thomas's enemies and why they didn't take the cattle." He wasn't about to mention Will's name with Thatcher Lee standing there.

"Maybe this will get the sheriff off his lazy backside and doing his job," Clancy said. "We'll see him tomorrow morning at church."

"Neither of you is going to church." Anne wrapped a clean bandage around his arm. She nodded at Colt. "You can snore right through the sermon."

"And I don't have to take a bath?" Colt grinned through the pain in his thigh. He found himself captured by her deep blue eyes.

Anne shook her head. "No, you can smell like a dirty barn for another week."

"Good," Clancy said. "I have the whole morning to preach to Colt. High time that man knew about Jesus."

"No rest for a wounded man?" Colt asked.

Anne laughed. "You two can pester each other for the next week. Because neither of you can smell trouble, I've got to help the other hands."

Clancy chuckled. "I love your kind heart."

Colt fixed his gaze on her. Was she lingering a little on him? Or was it his imagination? Maybe he'd grown weak in the head with the bullet wound. But for now he'd enjoy Anne's special treatment.

The seriousness of the situation hit him hard. Anne and those girls were in danger. He knew it as well as he knew his own name.

Anne left the two alone to go help Rosita with dinner. Colt glanced at Clancy. Without asking, Colt understood the old man felt the same way. And here they were shot up like two mangled coyotes.

"Are you still praying?" he asked Clancy.

The old man nodded. "Wouldn't hurt for you to do the same thing."

"I'm not ready for religion, but I'm glad you're on speaking terms with God. I'm worried about Anne and the girls."

Clancy nodded. "She likes you, Colt. I can see it in her eyes. She hasn't looked at a man like that since Will."

"Naw. She's just glad I wasn't killed today, and she doesn't have to go looking for another ranch hand."

But Colt wondered. He didn't deserve as fine a woman as Anne. Neither did he deserve two spunky girls like Sammie Jo and Nancy. But the thought made him feel good—real good.

—⁕—

Anne tried to concentrate on helping Rosita with dinner. Instead, her thoughts raced with the shooting—Hank and Thomas dead for no visible reason. . .Clancy and Colt shot. . .and why?

She'd never had any trouble like this. Hard work was one thing. Raising two daughters and running the ranch left her tired and oftentimes grumpy. But murder downright scared her.

Had Will left enemies who just now decided to whip out calling cards? Her husband had confessed to so much law breaking. At the time, she hid her fright and focused on keeping him comfortable. A dying man usually had a wagonload of regrets and things he wanted to say. He hadn't given her names or mentioned that her life and the girls' lives were in danger. Five years had passed since then. Surely this was something completely different from Will's acquaintances seeking revenge. She hoped so. She prayed so.

A twinge, like a knife twisting in an open wound, startled her. The trouble began just before Colt arrived. Was he a part of this? She shook her head to dispel the frightening thought. He'd been in prison before coming to the Double L, which caused her to suspect him, but today he'd been hurt worse than Clancy. She refused to believe he'd taken part in what happened. Perhaps God had sent her an outlaw to run off outlaws. Peculiar thought. For certain, she wasn't in the business of second-guessing the hand of the Almighty.

"Mama, do you like Mr. Colt?" Sammie Jo asked.

Anne turned the soft biscuit dough in her hands. "He's a good worker, and he helped save Clancy's and Thatcher Lee's lives today."

"I mean, do you like him?"

"Sammie Jo, I'm not sure what you mean." But Anne understood exactly what her daughter meant, and she had no intentions of answering.

"Do you like him the same as Daddy?"

Anne's heart pounded like an Indian drum. "Why ever would you ask me such a thing?"

"Because I see the way you look at him and the way he looks at you."

"I think your dreamin' on Thatcher Lee has gone to your head." Anne hoped her words sounded gruff.

Sammie Jo giggled. "You answered my question. How would Daddy feel about you takin' up with an outlaw? Especially one who's a heathen? The way I look at it, you two could marry up and then have other outlaws at the ranch looking for work and free food."

"Child, I'm going to take a switch to your backside if you don't stop pestering me. Do you understand? No more such foolishness."

"Yes, ma'am."

Out of the corner of her eye, Anne saw a grin spread over her daughter's face. Mercy, did the whole world see her interest in Colt Wilson?

—

"We're having church," Clancy said.

Colt wanted to sleep. His leg hurt. Clancy's arm had to hurt, too. Irritability inched through his veins like a slow-rising flood.

"Can't do that," Colt said. "Anne told us to sleep. We need to heal and get back to work."

"God said to honor His day."

"Still can't. We didn't take our Saturday night bath."

"Fine. I'm reading from the Bible, and you can lay there and listen."

Clancy fumbled under his bunk while Colt rolled over to head back to sleep.

"Doesn't your arm hurt?"

Clancy chuckled. "Yeah, but when I think about what our Lord did on the cross for me, it makes no difference."

Colt moaned. *Here it comes.* Preaching with a one-man congregation. Next Clancy would be asking him to confess and head to the creek to wash away his sins.

"This morning the good Lord's leading me to read from Genesis, the story of Jacob and Esau."

"And who are they?"

"Brothers who never got along."

Colt blew out an exasperated sigh. "I have three, and we fought all the time we were growing up."

Clancy cleared his throat. "Lord, we ask Your blessing on the reading of Your Word. Make sure Colt listens. I'm beginning in Genesis chapter 25, verse 19."

Colt half listened, half dozed through the story about twins named Jacob and Esau. One was his daddy's favorite, and the other was his mama's. Colt had been a part of such a family. He hadn't been anyone's favorite. All of a sudden, Clancy had his attention.

"You mean Esau sold his inheritance for a bowl of soup?"

"Yep. He must have been powerful hungry."

"More like a fool." Colt opened his eyes. He'd listen a little more. "How did those two get in the Bible? One is a fool, and the other lies to his own daddy."

"The Bible is full of sinful people. I know you've heard the preacher say how none of us is perfect. Now will you hush and let me finish?"

So Colt listened. Jacob had to take off because Esau threatened to kill him for getting the inheritance. His mama sent him to live with her people. Then Jacob fell in love. Colt was beginning to understand how that felt, too. "None of those fellers is decent," he said. "Jacob worked seven years for Rachel, then got stuck with her ugly sister and had to work seven more years." He started to say more, but Clancy shot him one of those "shut up and listen" looks.

The story went on, and Colt started to drift off to sleep until Clancy got to the part about the angel breaking Jacob's leg and how he limped to meet Esau. Jacob was scared his brother was going to kill him, and Colt understood those feelings, too. He'd been a horrible bully to his brothers. It worked out for Jacob and Esau, but those men had been real bad.

"What do you think?" Clancy asked.

"I'm thinking on it. Jacob wasn't much better than an outlaw until he wrestled with the angel. He turned himself into bein' a decent man after that."

"What about you?"

Here comes the confessing-your-sins part. "What about me?"

"Looks to me like you're changing into a different man from the one who rode in here. God must be wrestling with you, too."

Colt didn't say a word. Clancy closed his Bible and placed it back under his bed.

"I'm going to rest a little," Clancy said. "My arm's on fire."

"And my leg feels like someone branded it."

Me, wrestling with an angel? The only thing I wrestle with are all the things I've done in the past—and if I'd ever be good enough for Anne and the girls.

Chapter 6

Waiting for his leg to heal gave Colt plenty of time to think about what had happened the day he and Clancy were shot. Repeatedly he walked his mind back through every moment of that day. He recalled the way the wind blew and questioned if the birds he heard were actually calls made by men. Sights and smells lingered in his thoughts. When he'd crawled through brush and grass, he'd seen no signs of men.

The mystery of it all puzzled him, and he and Clancy filled their waking hours talking about who could have done the killings.

"If I believed in ghosts, I'd say they fired on us," Colt said.

"Does seem real strange, and I was quite a tracker in my day." Clancy rubbed his whiskered jaw. "I even wondered if a small band of renegade Indians could have done it. But nothing I recall showed any signs of 'em."

"I've laid here three days thinking about this and haven't come up with a thing," Colt glanced around. "I'm fixin' to use the crutch Thatcher Lee made for me and get out of this bunkhouse for some fresh air."

"Walkin' around helps. At least I can get out of here. I imagine the bunkhouse feels like pris—." He stopped himself. "I'll help you the best I can."

"We've turned into a couple of helpless old men," Colt said.

"Speak for yourself. I've got another twenty good years left in me."

Colt glanced at the old man's silver hair and weather-beaten face. "How many lines can your face hold?"

"As many as it takes to make sure Anne and the girls are safe and you find the Lord."

"He doesn't want me, Clancy. I don't like church, and my singing sounds like it came from a hollow bucket."

"Oh, He wants you powerful bad. You just don't have sense enough to realize it." Clancy stood and grasped the makeshift crutch. "I don't always like the preacher's sermons, either, and my singing sounds like a hurt wolf. It ain't about that at all. It's about realizing you need something you don't have. Something that is more powerful than what any man can get on his own."

Out of respect for Clancy, Colt kept his thoughts to himself because he wasn't in the mood for preachin'. The pain in his leg felt like liquid fire. Truth be known, he'd been thinkin' on God and the stories Clancy had read to him from the Bible. The story about Jacob and Esau had hit close to home. Clancy said they were true, and lately Colt hoped they were.

Sweat streamed down Colt's face by the time he hobbled out of the bunkhouse and made his way to a shady tree—the one Nancy had climbed. He sat beneath it and stretched out his burning leg. Frustrated with the time it was taking to heal when he wanted to ride out to where the shooting took place made him want to tear into the first man who crossed his path.

"Can you leave me alone?" he asked Clancy. "I need time to think about a few things."

"Sure. When God is working on a man, he needs time by himself."

Clancy made his way to the barn, and Colt felt a little guilty for letting the man think he had religion on his mind. Leaning against the oak tree, he closed his eyes and willed the throbbing to end.

"Mr. Colt."

Nancy's sweet voice didn't irritate him at all. That little girl had stolen his heart.

"What can I do for you?"

"That's what I wanted to ask you." She sat in the grass beside him, her bare feet caked with dried mud.

"You been wadin'?"

She nodded. "I was looking for frogs. I found a little one." She reached inside her overalls and pulled it out. "I'm going to feed him some tasty bugs."

He chuckled. "I always thought little girls played like they were grown women."

"Sometimes I do. I like both."

"What about Sammie Jo?"

"Mama makes her learn cooking stuff, but she'd rather be ridin' or explorin'."

Alarm weighed on Colt's mind. "Promise me something."

She gazed up at him with huge, trusting eyes.

"Promise me you and Sammie Jo won't go explorin' very far from the ranch."

"Why? Because of what happened to you and Clancy?"

"That's right. This leg of mine hurts powerful bad, and I wouldn't want you to hurt, too."

She nodded. "I promise. Sammie Jo's braver than me, so I'll tell her what you said."

"Would she listen to anyone besides you and me?" Colt recognized the older girl's stubbornness and figured she'd do the opposite of what he or Nancy asked.

"Maybe Thatcher Lee. She's still sneaking around and seeing him." Nancy stared into Colt's face. "He's a grown man, Mr. Colt. Mama would whip her good if she knew."

"I'll say something to Thatcher Lee." As if he hadn't before.

"Thank you." Nancy grinned. Her attention focused on the utmost tree branches. "I sure appreciate you helping me down out of this here tree. Sammie Jo laughs at me getting scared easy."

"Takes a real smart gal to stay away from danger, and you and Sammie Jo are real smart."

Nancy wrinkled up her nose. "She thinks she knows everything."

Colt frowned but kept his thoughts to himself. He feared Anne's oldest daughter might need to learn a few of life's lessons the hard way.

—⁓—

Anne lifted the canteen to her lips and drank deeply. She worked sunup to sundown to take up the slack until Clancy and Colt were healed. Bone-tired, she prayed God would give her strength to continue on. Sammie Jo enjoyed helping, but Anne believed her enthusiasm had a lot to do with Thatcher Lee. Twice Anne had caught her talking to him when they thought no one was looking. Thatcher Lee knew better, especially if he wanted to keep his job. Anne would have cut him loose a long time ago except he was a good ranch hand and she needed help. No matter that her daughter looked older. Sammie Jo had a few years of growing and maturing before Anne allowed a young man to come courting.

The object of her frustration rode toward Anne with Thatcher Lee alongside her. Sammie Jo's face flushed red—and Anne knew it had nothing to do with the heat.

"Where have you two been?" Anne asked.

"Roundin' up strays." Thatcher Lee tipped his hat. Always the mannerly one, which kept his body free of buckshot when it came to Sammie Jo. "Won't take long to move the herd into the upper pasture, Mrs. Langley."

Anne screwed the cap back onto her canteen. "That job took both of you?"

"Yes, ma'am. Sammie Jo had a lot of questions about ranching."

Anne focused her attention dead center on Thatcher Lee's eyes. "She has a mama for that. If I don't have the answers, I'll find them. Do you understand what I mean? She's fourteen years old, not eighteen."

"Yes, ma'am." Thatcher Lee's lips turned up slightly.

Anne bit her tongue to keep from using words a good Christian woman had no right to use. But this was her daughter, and she'd work this ranch without Thatcher Lee if he didn't stay away from Sammie Jo.

After dinner when the sun had slipped just beyond the horizon, she stopped by to see how Colt and Clancy were doing. Clancy had been cleaning out stalls one-handedly, most likely to chase away boredom.

"I need to talk," she said to Colt. "Do you feel up to limping outside?"

He grabbed his crutch and made his way beside her. She caught a few looks from the other hands as though they suspected something going on between them. Right now she wasn't in the mood to ask what they were gawking at.

"Thatcher Lee and Sammie Jo are sneaking around." She blurted out the words in a mixture of anger and near-tears. Not at all as she intended.

"From what Nancy said to me today, I don't doubt what you're telling me. Looks like that little talk I gave him went nowhere. You want me to have another one?"

"I told him earlier to stay away from her. I hate to fire him. He's a good hand, but I'm not risking my daughter's future on a two-bit cowboy."

"Maybe he needs to know what you're thinking. I don't mind telling him he's looking at getting fired."

"Thanks. The only reason I'm asking you is because Thatcher Lee respects you, and he and Clancy have had their problems in the past." She feared her request made her look like a whining female.

Colt smiled, and it spread across his face. She could get used to his smile and the way he seemed to care about her daughters.

"Were Hank and Thomas friends with Thatcher Lee?"

She crossed her arms over her chest. "Always. He was real angry when those two were caught with Double L cows. He and Clancy tried to talk them out of cattle rustling, but it didn't do any good. Sure glad I rode up when I did, or he and Clancy would have been dead."

Colt appeared to take in her every word. That made her feel a little uncomfortable but in a special way. Mercy, she'd gotten as bad as Sammie Jo with Thatcher Lee.

"Why do you ask?"

He shrugged. "He's young. Maybe what Hank and Thomas did—and later finding them dead—makes him want to talk to someone who'll listen."

"Maybe so." She sighed. "I'll talk to him—see if I can be that ear instead of my daughter." She laughed. "Raising daughters is hard, but I guess raising boys wouldn't be any easier. Any suggestions?"

He hesitated. "I think if my ma had taken the time to rein me in when I bullied my brothers, maybe I wouldn't have ended up in prison. She worked hard and didn't have time to listen when we needed to talk. But girls? I don't have nary an idea."

"No sisters?"

He shook his head. "One of my brothers took up with a woman who had a little girl. The woman did anything he asked, and it nearly got her killed. That's what worries me about Sammie Jo and Thatcher Lee. She's so young and. . . Excuse me. Sammie Jo is none of my business."

She glanced at the house. A lot of wisdom rode under Colt's hat. And she understood exactly what he meant about Sammie Jo. Anne hadn't spent time with another man except Clancy since Will died. Her head warned her not to lose her heart. Colt was a strange man. His eyes were hard, but sometimes she saw a spark of genuine decency.

"There's some milk cake left over from dinner. Would you like a piece and some fresh coffee?"

"Sounds real good, Anne. Do you mind if I check on Miss Nancy? She found herself a friend today—a frog."

Anne smiled. "She's taken with you, Colt." *And so am I.*

Chapter 7

Three weeks after the shootings, Colt climbed on his horse and attempted to do his share of the work. The longest three weeks since prison. Strange how he'd always taken walking for granted. Now he counted the days until he could make his way around the ranch without limping. Nancy said he looked "grumpy," but some of the other ranch hands had more colorful words to describe his aggravation.

He had a few suspicions about what was going on at the Double L. With nothing to do but think and read, he'd watched the men to see if any said or did anything out of the ordinary. One man stayed foremost in Colt's mind, but until he found evidence, he'd keep his mouth shut and his ears and eyes open.

During the fourth week, Colt, Clancy, Thatcher Lee, and two other hands rode together for fence mending. It wasn't one of Colt's favorite chores, but he was just glad to be in the saddle instead of flat on his back. Anne and the girls joined them in a wagon with the fixin's for a noon meal. Already the sun beat down hard. They needed rain, and the cracked, parched earth proved it. Midsummer in Texas gave a whole new meaning to *fire and brimstone*.

Anne smiled and waved from several feet away. Nancy called out to him. Even Sammie Jo waved—a first since she'd made it known how she felt about him interfering with her and Thatcher Lee. Lately Anne made sure Sammie Jo stuck to her side. Colt had talked again to Thatcher Lee and told him their boss was ready to fire him. So far the young man had steered clear of Sammie Jo.

Clancy had done nothing but grin all morning.

"What's so funny?" Colt asked.

"Oh, I'm in a good mood. Thanks for returning my Bible," he said.

"Yep, I saw you readin' it," Thatcher Lee said. "Next you'll be preachin' like Clancy."

Colt laughed. "I'm not getting religious, so you two can wipe those holy looks off your faces. I like the stories."

"I'm right tickled you're reading it," Clancy said.

"Yeah, it shows." Colt wasn't about to comment on his interest in God. But interest was all he had. Anne took a lot of stock in a man who knew God, and he wanted to know why.

Sitting in his saddle, listening to the familiar creak of the leather, and taking in the surroundings lifted his spirits; he felt a rare sense of peace. He'd grown to care for these people, something he never thought would happen. Before his release from Huntsville Prison, he hadn't cared about anyone but himself. His life had changed, and he believed it was for the better.

Glancing to the right of him, he saw Anne slow the wagon until she drove beside him. He'd resolved to stay clear of her, but this morning it was real hard. He dug his heels into his mare and caught up with Clancy.

"You doin' all right?" Clancy asked. Sweat dripped from his forehead.

"Yeah. I'm glad to be earning my keep again."

"Good to see you on a horse and your face not all screwed up in pain. Any other ideas about what happened?"

"A few."

Clancy glanced around. "So do I. Got my eyes on him."

Colt nodded. Whether they suspected the same man or not didn't matter. They both were anxious to find out who'd done the killings—not to mention who'd shot the two of them—and get 'em handed over to the law. He'd feel better when all of this trouble was settled.

Anne. She made an ordinary day fill up with sunshine. Colt sensed his heart had taken a plunge well-deep. While waiting on his leg to heal, he'd considered collecting his pay and riding out. Seeing her every day and realizing he'd never be good enough for such a fine woman depressed him. She'd loved one outlaw and ended up a widow. What more did he have to offer? Sure, he'd left the past behind, but what he'd done surfaced in his mind every time he thought they might have a good life together.

The day's work nearly wore out Colt—not so much the fence mendin' but the heat. His leg ached as he limped to the corral with Clancy. He sensed the old man had things to say. At times it seemed like the two of them had the same mind.

"Neither one of us is men who talk much about what we're thinking." Clancy leaned on the fence. "I enjoy teasin' you and pushin' you to think on the things of God. But accusing a man of murder is different."

"I agree." Colt sighed. "I'm still not sure if I should say what I suspect."

"Don't blame you, and I've known him longer than you."

"Ever have any problems with him?" Colt asked.

"You know the answer to that."

"What kind of trouble?"

Clancy shrugged. "Not enough to pin murder on him. He slacks when it comes to working unless Anne's watching. Don't like 'im. Never did. And I try to look for the good in a man."

"Did you ever see him slipping away?"

"Sure have. He stuck close to Hank and Thomas until I caught those boys stealing cattle."

"I thought both of you caught them." Colt's mind raced with accusations.

"Nope. Just me, and then he rode up."

"He isn't getting out of my sight."

"Mine either. Although I can't figure out why he would have murdered Hank and Thomas."

Colt hesitated. Recollections of what he and Will used to do settled in his mind. "Maybe they knew too much about Will's business, or he just got greedy."

Clancy glanced behind them. "Hey, Thatcher Lee."

The young man joined them. He placed his foot on the fence rail. "I'm real worried about Mrs. Langley and the girls."

"We are, too, son." Clancy stared out into the ever-darkening shadows. A few horses made their way toward them.

"I want whoever has caused this trouble found," Thatcher Lee said. "I think the only reason the women went with us today was because it left no one there to defend them."

"This is their home," Colt said. "I know our boss can handle herself, but she shouldn't have to tote a rifle to protect what's hers."

"Well, count me in on what needs to be done," Thatcher Lee said. He stroked the head of one of the horses. "I wonder about our good sheriff. He's never around when you need him, and he's plum lazy." With those words he turned and strode off toward the stables.

"What do you think?" Clancy asked.

"Nothing's changed. I just want to know why."

—⁂—

In her bedroom, by the light of the kerosene lamp, Anne counted the money in the cash box, the money she used for payroll. Last month it all balanced out, but this month she was two hundred dollars short. Where had it gone? No one knew where she kept it. Someone would have to search her room to find it. She kept it at the bottom of the leather trunk with the girls' baby clothes and her parents' Bible on top. Rosita? The sweet lady never set foot in Anne's room. No, Rosita had not taken the money. But who had?

She shivered. Cattle rustlers. Murders. Money gone. Hard work and sleepless nights she could handle, but this shook her. Will would have known what to do. He'd have strapped on his Colts and cleaned up this mess.

Strapped on his Colts. The Peacemaker. Colt Wilson.

Her mind must be slipping to linger on a man who was most likely as rotten as her husband.

Anne shoved the cash box back into the trunk and eased down onto her bed. It squeaked, as it always had. She lay back on the quilt, the one her mother had given her on her wedding day—one of the few memories of Will that didn't hurt. He'd lied to her and broken the law, and maybe he'd brought down this trouble on his family. Betrayal stalked her day and night, and she didn't want to love a man who'd do the same thing again. Why couldn't she fall in love with a man who wasn't an outlaw?

Burying her face in her hands, she cried until not a single tear was left. *Oh, God, what am I to do? I have Sammie Jo and Nancy to raise. Someone is murdering my ranch hands and stealing my cattle and my cash. A near-man has my Sammie Jo's attention, and*

Colt Wilson is too good-looking and so very kind.

"Mama."

Anne blinked, wiped her face, and took a deep breath. "Yes, Nancy."

"My frog's gone."

"Come on in, honey." Anne stood from the bed.

The door opened, and Nancy broke into tears the moment she saw her mama. "He's run away. I just know it."

"Are you sure?" For certain if the frog had died, Rosita would have taken care of the matter.

"Can we go find Mr. Colt? He'll know where to look for Mr. Frog."

Anne sensed the color drain from her face. "Honey, we can't bother Mr. Colt. He's worked very hard today."

Nancy sniffed. "But he's my best friend. He never laughs at me, and he talks to me like I'm all grown up."

Oh, Colt has stolen more than one Langley woman's heart. She bent to her daughter's side. "Perhaps we can find your Mr. Frog. I'll help you."

Nancy wrapped her arms around her mama's neck. "It's no good, but we can try."

Anne grasped her daughter's hand and the lamp. Together they made their way through the house, looking here and there for one lonely frog. Satisfied it wasn't inside, they stepped onto the porch.

"Mr. Frog," Nancy called, "you don't have to hide. I'm here."

"Miss Nancy, did you lose your frog?"

At the sound of Colt's voice, Anne's legs felt like quivering matchsticks.

"Yes, sir. He's run off."

Colt mounted the back porch steps. He bent down to Nancy. "I'll look, but you know what?"

She shook her head.

"I think he's missing his frog friends. I know you take good care of him, but I bet he wants to be with his family and friends. What if you lived with him? Wouldn't you miss your mama and Sammie Jo?"

"I would, sir. And I'd miss you, too." She swiped at her eyes. "I want him to be happy. I'll let him be free."

"Your daddy would be proud of you." Colt stood and shoved his hands into his jeans pockets.

Alarm took over Anne's senses—the missing money and all the trouble at the Double L. "Nancy, why don't you run along and get ready for bed?"

"Good night, little one," Colt said. "Don't forget to tell your sister good night."

Nancy started to protest, but with a lift of her mama's chin, she disappeared inside. A few moments later, Anne stared into the shadows at Colt.

"You have a good evening, ma'am."

When he turned to leave, curiosity got the best of Anne. "Were you needing to talk to me?"

He shrugged. "No."

"Then what were you doing up here?"

"I'd rather keep that to myself if you don't mind."

Anger simmered to a fast boil. "You're snooping around my house, and you don't want to tell me why?"

"That's what I said." He stiffened.

"Maybe you know more about what has been going on than you're telling."

Colt said nothing.

"Are you keeping something from me? Or are you involved?"

His fists clenched. "If that's what you think of me, then I'm clearing out of here tonight."

Regret washed over her. She rubbed her shoulders. "I don't think you're against me," she said softly. "Colt, you know something you're not telling me, and I don't like it at all."

"I'm not in the habit of accusing a man without proof."

"What did you see here tonight?" she asked, barely above a whisper.

"Nothing."

Clancy appeared from the shadows. She held her breath.

"Anne, Colt won't tell you what's going on, but I'll tell you. In fact, I'm part of it, too."

"I want to hear all of it." She whipped her attention to Clancy.

"We've been keeping watch on the house and barns at night. One night I do it, and Colt does it the next."

Anger smoothed to near tears. She grabbed the porch post. "I'm sorry. I thought...I thought..." She swallowed the lump in her throat. "If I'm to trust anyone, it's you two."

Colt stepped forward then back. He raked his fingers through his hair. "I'm heading back to the bunkhouse. Enough for one night."

"That's what I came to tell you," Clancy said. "He's missing."

"Who?" Anne asked. "You have to tell me." Her voice rose higher. "Please tell me."

Chapter 8

Anne trembled in the shadows, a different side for Colt to see. In all of the times they'd been together, she'd been strong and fearless—bossy and full of spirit. He wanted to reach out and hold her, take care of the situation and put her mind at ease. But he couldn't.

"Anne, I don't have proof," Colt said. "I spent too many years in prison to accuse an innocent man. Clancy and I suspect one of the hands, and we're watching him. I can't say anymore."

Her shoulders lifted and fell. "I'm sorry, and I understand. Don't know what's got into me."

"I do," he said. "You have a family and a ranch. It would make a person question everyone around 'em—especially someone you trusted."

She nodded. "Thanks." She peered around him to Clancy. "After Will died, it took that feisty old man behind you to toughen me up."

Clancy chuckled. "You had it in ya. You just didn't know it."

"What can I do to help?" Her attention focused on both men. "Won't do any good to tell me 'nothing.' I can't sleep or think right, and I won't until this is settled."

Colt wished he'd spent more time with his mother so he'd know how to convince Anne of her foolishness. "I guess keep your eyes open. Nancy and Sammie Jo wander off a lot. Might be good if you'd make sure they stick around the ranch." He forced a laugh. "Although Sammie Jo can handle herself, there's no point in her walking into a snake pit."

"I agree," Clancy said. "Both girls have a streak of stubbornness when it comes to telling them they can't do something. Kinda like their mama."

"I'll make sure it sounds like it's their idea—and include Rosita with this, too. She could find things for them to do. I want the girls to be cautious but not afraid."

Colt thought about Will. He should have been more careful and held on to this woman. Any man would be proud to. . .

"Cattle's missin', too," Clancy said. "We brought back the ones Hank and Thomas stole, but now there's twenty or so gone."

"So we're looking at a real greedy man." Colt glanced toward the bunkhouse. "If you two don't mind, I'm going to take a little look around."

"Got your rifle?" Anne asked.

"Yes, ma'am. I've used it a time or two."

"I'd still like to know who you two suspect."

"If you run him off, then we don't have a chance to catch him. At least this way Clancy and I can make sure he or they are stopped." He hoped his optimism reassured her.

"I'll be along in a bit," Clancy said. "I want Anne to take a look at my shoulder."

Colt stepped down from the porch steps and headed toward the bunkhouse and barns. Leaving Anne with Clancy gave him an opportunity to back away from her soft voice and the yearning in his heart. She made his senses go loco.

Studying the shadows, he doubted if anyone would be stupid enough to do anything with him and Clancy out checking on things. Usually it was just one of them, like he was taking off to the outhouse or couldn't sleep.

The full moon helped light the corral and the surrounding buildings. He walked to the back of the barns, along the fences, and then to the bunkhouse. The beds were occupied except his and Clancy's. Had their suspect guessed what was going on and crept back to his bunk? This cowboy was one clever *hombre*.

He eased onto his bed and stared up at the ceiling, not really looking but pondering the situation. While in prison he thought he'd done enough thinking for a lifetime. Obviously not, 'cause he couldn't figure out what was going on at the Double L.

"You and Clancy all right?" Thatcher Lee whispered.

"Yeah. Clancy's shoulder is botherin' him, and I made sure he got to Miss Anne's before changing his mind."

Colt listened to the snores around him. Tonight, like so many nights before, he pretended to sink his toes into the boots of the murderin' cattle rustler who had made life miserable for Anne and tried to figure out how to stop him. He remembered the days when his own mind wrapped around the best way to deceive innocent folks. Odd—now he was on the other side. He understood how folks felt when robbed of their property or when someone they knew was killed.

Whoever had been up to no good would slip soon. His confidence would overcome his good sense, and he'd start making mistakes. Colt planned to be right there when it all broke loose.

"Too bad," Thatcher Lee said. "She'll fix him up. G'night. Big day tomorrow."

———

Anne examined Clancy's shoulder by the lamplight in the kitchen. She thought it had been healing fine, but infection oozed from it.

"Why didn't you tell me about this sooner?" She blew out an exasperated sigh, remembering the infection in Will's leg.

"I was taking care of it myself. Used some aloe leaves on it, and it does look better." Clancy sat at the table while Anne poked at his sore arm.

"It needs to look a whole lot better." She held the light over his shoulder for signs of red streaks. "Lucky for you I don't see any blood poisoning."

"What can you do for me?"

"I'll clean it up and use some whiskey to burn out some of the infection. Probably wouldn't hurt for me to squeeze a little aloe on it. In the morning I'll take the wagon into town for medicine. I need supplies anyway. Nearly out of sugar and coffee."

"Can't do that. We need the wagon to haul feed for the cattle."

She opened the pie safe and pulled out a bottle of whiskey. A clean towel lay on the kitchen table. "Then I'll ride in by myself. Faster that way."

"With all the trouble we're having around here?"

She tapped her foot against the wooden floor then dabbed the wound with the whiskey, watching him wince. "Do you want to go with me?"

"Oh, I'd be a lot of good with a hurt shoulder."

Concern mixed with fear shadowed Anne's calm composure. Clancy was running a fever and needed more than she could do. A woman in town knew a lot about herbs. An extra day made a lot of difference. "I'll ask Thatcher Lee to ride along."

"I'd rather you take Colt—in case of trouble."

All the way to town with a man who leaves me tongue-tied? "What about one of the other hands?"

"What's wrong with Colt? He's good with a gun, and I won't have to worry about you. Is it because you've got feelings for him?"

Anne sensed her face aflame. If Clancy had guessed her secret, had anyone else?

"Don't worry. I haven't told a soul. But I do think it's a good idea to have him go along with you."

She realized he'd backed her into a corner. No way out but to ask Colt to escort her. "All right. I'll ask him first thing in the morning."

"No need. I'll do it when I head back to the bunkhouse."

Barking orders seemed the easiest way for Anne to cope with trouble. "Don't go out with the men tomorrow. Stay here and keep Rosita and the girls company."

"I did toughen you up, didn't I? Before Will died, you'd have packed up the girls and left for the city."

"Times change." Her voice softened. "I love you like a father, don't you know that?"

Clancy nodded. "I'm a bit partial to you, too." He peered at his shoulder. "The aloe is helping a lot. In another day it'll be fine. I only asked for you to take a look at it 'cause I can't see what it looks like. You don't need to go to all this trouble."

She forced a smile through her weariness. Clancy's shoulder just added to more of her worries—like a stall no one wanted to clean. At least she could do something about Clancy in the morning.

Spending the day with Colt tomorrow would cause her a sleepless night tonight. A handsome man had no room in her head or her heart.

———

Colt had given up on any sleep tonight. If he hadn't enough on his mind, now he had to ride into town with Anne. She made him nervous with all the men around. What would happen during the several hours alone? He'd most likely fall off his horse.

He glanced at Clancy and doubted if he slept, either. His shoulder probably throbbed each time his heart beat. And it had to hurt powerful bad for him to ask Anne for help.

Lord, would You heal Clancy's shoulder? He's an old man who works hard. I'd rather him go see You years from now.

Colt nearly jolted out of bed. Was he praying? When did this happen? His heart pounded like thunder rumbling on the prairie. Taking a deep breath, he eased back onto the bunk. He must believe in God, or he wouldn't have prayed. When he thought through the last few days, he realized his trust in God had grown while trust in himself had slipped away.

This must be what Clancy had been talking about. God would reach out and snatch him when he least expected it. In the middle of frettin' over Anne and the ranch, Colt had shaken off his independence and depended on God—not his rifle, his mind, or anyone around him.

Do I feel any different? He touched his chest as if God might have made him a new heart. According to what he'd read in the Bible and from listening to Clancy talk, if he believed and died this very minute, he'd live with God.

Heaven was a whole sight better than the other place, and he'd been real close to that. Reuben would be real pleased about this, but his other brothers would laugh good and hard about this one. Colt didn't care what any man thought. Strange how his mind had moved from thinking on himself to thinking about God.

He'd been hooked like a fish on a line and didn't mind a bit. He thought men found God when trouble had them next to death—like in the middle of a shootout or with a body full of holes lying next to 'em. This was an ordinary night. Nothing special, except Clancy's shoulder needed doctoring.

Telling his friend crossed his mind; Clancy would want to know. And Anne. . . wonder how she'd take the news? Or was he supposed to keep quiet?

Guess he should pray a little more and do it right. From what he'd read, Jesus took the blame for his ornery soul, and he needed to thank Him and ask Him to take over his rotten life.

Chapter 9

C olt took a glimpse at Anne's saddle to see if she'd brought two canteens of water. The day promised to be another scorcher. Once assured she'd be fine, he swung up onto the saddle.

"This will be a hot one," he said. "Sure you don't want me to take care of business in town? You could stay here and tend to Clancy."

Anne shook her head. "I'd feel better if I could talk to the woman who knows herbs. Could be we're doing all we can for Clancy, but I'm hoping for a remedy to bring down his temperature and stop the infection." She turned in the saddle to view Rosita. "It'll be late when we get home. The horses will need to rest a bit in this heat before pushing them the fifteen miles back."

"We'll have a good day." Rosita wrapped her arm around Nancy's shoulder and kissed the top of her head. "Expect a berry pie when you return."

Anne adjusted her hat beneath her chin and nodded at Colt.

He waved at the girls and Rosita, but Nancy threw him a kiss and giggled. That little gal sure had his heart—just like her mama. Sammie Jo, on the other hand, looked like she'd just as soon blow a hole through him.

They'd ridden for about thirty minutes at an easy gallop when they slowed the horses in the heat. Colt considered some kind of conversation, but his tongue wouldn't form the words. This was hard. Real hard. He wanted to tell her about makin' a decision for the Lord, but the words stayed in his head.

"Do you see storm clouds gathering, or is it my imagination?" Anne finally asked, relieving Colt of the worry of talking.

He peered to the north and studied them. "Sure looks like it, and we sorely need the rain."

"I don't mind getting wet."

"Me either. But I hate riding out in the open during a thunderstorm."

She laughed—that musical ring that sounded like a sweet song. "Why, Colt Wilson, have I found something you're afraid of?"

"If you're referring to thunder and lightning, then you're right. I don't relish the thought of getting fried up like a slab of bacon."

She laughed again. "So what are you going to do when we're caught in the middle of it?"

"Pray." The moment the word slipped from his mouth, Colt thought better of it. She started, and a wide smile spread over her face. "When did this happen?"

He sensed his face heat up. "Last night, thinkin' on Clancy."

"Does he know?"

"Naw. Not sure if a man's supposed to tell folks about these things. Like I was bragging or trying to look religious."

"Colt, I'm so happy for you."

She sounded like she was going to cry, which made Colt more nervous than before.

"Huh, thanks."

"Do you want to talk about it? Did it happen after we talked?"

What had he gotten himself into? "It happened later, and I do feel right uncomfortable. I have to get used to this a bit."

"Oh, I'm sorry. I am proud of you, and Clancy will be so happy." She took a glance at him. "All right. We'll talk about something else."

Good. He'd rather get caught with bolts of lightning jabbing on all sides of him than talk about finding God in a smelly bunkhouse.

"Are you going to tell me who you and Clancy suspect? It's making me crazy not knowing which one of my men is a thief and a murderer."

He wished she'd run out of words. "No. Can't do it."

"Even if it makes me so mad I can't see straight?"

"Yep."

Long moments followed, but he refused to give in.

"How about your thoughts on bringing in some fine quarter-horse stock?" she asked.

For the next several minutes, Colt told her everything he knew about horses, anything to keep her off the subject of God and the trouble at the Double L.

"Nancy sure likes you," Anne said.

He chuckled. "She asked me to marry her when she grows up."

"Oh, my. What did you tell her?"

"That we'd wait and see how she felt then."

"She said to me, 'Mama, Mr. Colt is right handsome; don't you think so?'"

He sensed her peering at him.

"Colt, you're blushing."

"No, I'm not." But he felt plum silly, even if it was little Nancy making the claim. Truth be known, he wondered if Anne thought he was pleasing to look at. Not that it mattered.

"Colt." She spoke quietly as if something might be wrong.

"Yeah."

"Have you been avoiding me lately? I mean, I said some ugly things to you last night, but for days now you've acted like I offended you."

He scratched his jaw. "Well, some of the others were saying a few things that weren't, uh, proper."

"Like what? You and me together?"

Had she not heard the jeering? "Yes, ma'am."

"I appreciate your gentlemanly ways, but I wish you'd have said something to me about it instead of acting like I'd made you mad."

"You're my boss."

"I'm still a woman."

Colt whipped his attention her way. Tears were streaming down her face. What had he done wrong? "I didn't mean to make you cry."

"I can't figure out why I'm crying anyway."

What was he supposed to say now? "Do you need my handkerchief? It's a clean one."

She shook her head and pulled out one from her shirt pocket. "Sorry. This is new to me."

What's new to her? Him finding God? What the others were sayin'? "I don't understand. What the ranch hands were saying made you cry?"

She glanced at him and blinked. In the next instant, she spurred her horse and raced away.

For sure Anne had him confused. He hesitated and hurried to catch up. The remaining miles into town were spent in silence, and that made him real glad.

—◆—

The longer Anne and Colt spent in town, the darker it grew until thunder cracked and lightning flashed in the distance, but Anne sensed it was coming closer. Within minutes a torrent of rain pelted the dusty streets.

"Sure glad I already have the herbs for Clancy." Anne pulled her slicker over her head as they stood under the overhang of the general store. "I'm ready for it to rain like this for three days, but I want to get back to the ranch, tend to Clancy, and make sure my girls are fine."

Thunder crashed down around them, and lightning streaked across an angry sky. They were dry, but water poured off the roof in buckets.

"We're staying right here until the storm lets up," Colt said. "It's moving toward the ranch, and we can be right behind it."

"I hope the girls' outing didn't get ruined."

"I thought you were keeping them close to home."

His voice held a twinge of alarm. She appreciated this man; he reminded her of Clancy in many ways. Since Colt had found the Lord, he'd taken on more of those traits. Her heart was betraying her, and if she didn't mask her feelings better, he'd know for sure.

"Don't worry. Rosita took the girls berry-picking, and I sent Thatcher Lee along to keep them safe. Rosita won't hesitate to tell Sammie Jo to keep her distance from him."

Colt punched his fist into his palm.

"What's wrong? They're probably within shouting distance of the Double L."

"Who'd hear? Clancy? The rest of 'em took feed to the cattle."

"Why are you so upset?" Suddenly realization hit her hard. Anne's stomach churned. "It's Thatcher Lee," she whispered.

"We only suspect him."

"But you have to be wrong. He's always been a hard worker, and he and Clancy tried to stop Hank and Thomas from running off with my cattle. And. . .and what about when you and Clancy were shot? He rode in and saved you." By now, she fought the sobs choking her throat.

Another clap of thunder shook the roof above them as if a bad omen had taken root in her fears.

"I don't have proof." He lingered on every word as if trying to convince himself.

"Tell me why you think it's Thatcher Lee."

"Here's what Clancy and I think. Thatcher Lee, Hank, and Thomas were good friends. They often rode off together, but no one ever questioned where. Clancy said the three were hired on at the same time."

She nodded and clenched her fists.

"Clancy was the one who discovered what Hank and Thomas were doing. Thatcher Lee simply rode up and stopped it. When we were shot, he stayed behind. He told me he'd never shot anyone before, and so we thought it best for him to stay clear of danger. When we were fired on, one man was doing the shooting. When Thatcher Lee joined us, the shooting stopped. And the bullet taken out of my leg was from a revolver like the one he carries." Colt paused. "Do you really think he's interested in Sammie Jo, or do you think he has something else on his mind?" He shook his head. "I'm sorry, Anne. I should have put that a little more delicately."

Anne gasped. "My babies. Thatcher Lee has my babies."

An ear-piercing burst of thunder drove her into Colt's arms. He held her tight, and she stayed there.

"I'll ride back and make sure everything is all right," he said.

"I'm going, too."

"I could be wrong about Thatcher Lee. That's why I didn't want to accuse him."

Anne swallowed hard. "But everything you told me is true. I wish I knew why or what he wanted. I'll blow a hole clean through his skull if he's hurt one of my girls." *I wonder how the good Lord feels about that.*

"Do you know where he came from?"

"He never said; neither did Hank or Thomas. They needed jobs, and I needed hands."

"Doesn't matter. He wants something you've got, and he's not afraid—"

"To kill for it." Anne despised her own words. *Nancy, Sammie Jo. Her beloved Rosita.*

Colt pushed her at arm's length. "I'm heading to the ranch."

She nodded. "Let's go." Hesitation stopped her. "Colt, you don't have to do this. You could be hurt if you're right about Thatcher Lee."

"I care too much for those girls—and you—to stand by and do nothing."

Anne sank her teeth into her lower lip. Later she'd ponder over his words, but not now.

Amid nature's fury, the two rode toward the ranch with the understanding that man's fury was often harder to reckon with.

Soaked clear through to their clothes with water dripping from their slickers, Anne and Colt raced toward the ranch. In what seemed like the worst storm he'd seen in a long time, Colt finally saw the outline of the house and barns. How he prayed those girls were safe inside with Rosita. His spurs dug into the mare's sides.

He jumped from his horse and hurried up the back porch steps before Anne could dismount. He threw open the door and called for Rosita, then Sammie Jo and Nancy. Nothing but the sound of the rain on the roof met his ears.

"Are they here?" Anne asked from the doorway.

Colt turned slowly. "No. Where do they normally pick berries?"

"Near the edge of the woods on the eastern side."

"I'll start there. They could be taking shelter from the storm." He refused to comment on the rain washing away their tracks or what Thatcher Lee might do to the womenfolk. "We need to check on Clancy. He might know something."

Clancy rested on his bunk. All he could do was apologize for not keeping a better watch on the house. "Get on out of here. You're wasting time." He patted his shoulder. "I'm doing fine. Now go."

In the next moment, they were on their horses again and riding toward the eastern section of the ranch. If Thatcher Lee did have them—and he meant harm—Colt knew he'd forget the faith he'd garnered the night before.

No, I won't. For once I'm listening to God.

But Colt feared the worst. He'd been among desperate men too long, and he didn't trust Thatcher Lee at all.

Chapter 10

A nne pointed to where the girls often did their berry-picking. She attempted to calm the raging fears threatening to overtake her. Her mind recalled all the times Thatcher Lee had been overly polite and the way the other hands avoided him. Why hadn't she seen through him? *Oh, God, please keep them safe.*

A rush of memories from those days when she lost Will and the tragedy after his death washed over her like the rain blinding her vision.

"I can't lose my girls," she said as the horses made their way along the outer edges of the woods. The tracks she wanted to find weren't there.

Colt swung his attention her way. "I may be wrong about Thatcher Lee, and if I am, you'll probably fire me."

Emotion poured from her heart and eyes. "I could never fire you, Colt. I love you." There. She'd said it.

His eyes widened.

She must confess her heart. "I'm not sure what will happen here today. Only God knows. But I sent Will to his grave without forgiving him and telling him I loved him. I won't make that mistake again." She took a deep breath. "It cost me more than losing my husband. It cost me his son."

"Anne, I'm so sorry."

"It was my own fault. I couldn't pull myself from the guilt and grief when Will died. I was expecting, and the baby came early. If it hadn't been for Clancy, I'd have been buried alongside the baby and Will." She studied his kind face, the face she loved.

"Clancy has helped us both."

She realized Colt didn't know what to say, and she had no idea how he felt about her. "That dear man made me get out of bed, forced me to eat, and read to me from the Bible about God's strength. He lectured me about taking care of my girls, and that was only the beginning."

Colt offered a nervous grin. "What else?"

She met his smile with one of her own. "Taught me how to shoot and give orders, and all about ranching. Riding broncs was my idea."

"He did a good job." Colt glanced away, then back again. "I'm not good enough for you, Anne. Look at what I've done."

"Look at what you've become—a new creation in Christ."

He paused. "Maybe so." His gaze returned to the ground, and he dismounted. "They were here. Must have left when the rain started. We can follow these tracks."

"How many?" she asked. If more men were involved, she and Colt were outnumbered.

"Rosita, the girls, and one man. I pray I'm wrong about Thatcher Lee. I really do."

—∿∿—

Colt followed the trail through the mud. The small band was on horseback and headed to the place where the shooting had happened. What Thatcher Lee had done to Hank and Thomas settled on him hard. He glanced around—lots of rocks and trees to hide behind—easy for Anne and him to be ambushed. He turned his mare and circled behind where he thought Thatcher Lee had gone.

"Isn't this where you and Clancy were shot?" Anne asked.

"Yeah, and I don't understand why he brought them here. This would be the first place I'd look." He hesitated. "He wants us to follow him. He's planned this for a while." Colt refused to say what else he feared. He prayed Thatcher Lee had gotten too sure of himself and had made a few mistakes that would help Colt free Rosita and the girls. "We have to walk from here. Are you sure you want to do this?"

The look she threw him left no question about her determination. Colt loved this woman. Maybe when this was over, they'd have a chance.

The rain beat down harder, causing him and Anne to slip more than once in the mud. But if they were having a miserable time in the weather, so was Thatcher Lee. The man had a short fuse; this might not be good.

At a spot he believed gave him cover behind Thatcher Lee, Colt motioned for Anne to stop. He bent low and covered the next several feet alone. Over a slab of overhanging rock sat Thatcher Lee, Rosita, and the girls. From Colt's stance, he could see that the captives' hands were bound. Colt assessed the terrain and crawled back to Anne.

"I need you to follow me, no talking, and move as quietly as you can. When I motion to you, stay put. Cover me while I circle in around Thatcher Lee."

"So he does have my girls?"

"I'm afraid so." His mind raced with the best way to seize Thatcher Lee without endangering the others. But one thing needed to be resolved with Anne. "Remember what you said about Will dying and not telling him how you felt?"

She nodded and swiped at the tears.

"I'm telling you now that I—I love you." He spun around and crouched through the brush with Anne behind him.

At the designated spot, Colt pointed to where Thatcher Lee held his captives. Without another sound, he crawled to where he prayed God would give him an advantage over the man in the distance.

The closer he crept, the louder he could hear Thatcher Lee.

"My mama and Mr. Colt and Clancy will get you," Nancy said.

"Shut up. Your mama and Colt are gone into town, and Clancy can't do a thing with his shoulder. By the time they get back to the ranch, they'll find the note in the kitchen."

Note? He hadn't seen one. Knowing Thatcher Lee's intentions would have helped.

"Why do you want us?" Rosita asked. Through the brush, Colt could see a huge bruise on the side of her face.

"Well, Rosita, Anne's husband has hidden a sizable amount of money on this ranch, and I want my share. I figure she'll give all of it to me in exchange for you ladies."

"You're a liar," Sammie Jo said. "And to think I stole money from Mama because you said you cared about me—wanted to run away with me. You're worse than a rattlesnake."

He laughed. "Your daddy was a no-good thief. He's got money stashed all over this place."

When Sammie Jo protested, Thatcher Lee told her exactly what he planned for her—and it wasn't pretty.

Dirty animal. I'll tear him to pieces for what he's saying to that sweet, innocent girl.

Colt inched closer. He trusted God for guidance and to keep everyone safe. No matter what he had to do, Colt would not let Thatcher Lee hurt those girls or Rosita any more than he already had. Huntsville Prison sounded like a good place for him.

A stick snapped. Even in the rain the sound rang out like an alarm. Thatcher Lee whipped his attention toward Colt and took aim. Sammie Jo jumped from where she sat and pushed him off balance. Colt bolted into Thatcher Lee and pinned him to the ground. In the next breath, Colt wrestled the revolver away from him. He wasn't sure how Sammie Jo managed to get her hands untied, but the moment Colt had the revolver fixed on Thatcher Lee, she flew into his arms.

"I was so afraid," Sammie Jo said. "He lied to me and said horrible things about my daddy."

"It's all right." Colt patted her back with his eye on Thatcher Lee. "I've got Thatcher Lee, and your mama is right behind me."

"I'm sorry for all the things I said and did to you." Sammie Jo cried the way he'd seen Nancy do that day in the tree.

"No matter." He heard Anne thrash through the brush and head for her girls.

Colt shook his head at Thatcher Lee. "You are one stupid man. Now you're going to find out the hard way what it means to break the law."

"I see what you're doing," he said. "You're playing up to Anne for the money."

"There's no money," Colt said. "I don't know where you got your information, but Will Langley didn't leave a cent behind when he died."

Anne touched Colt's back. Her hand felt soft and warm, and he intended to get used to having this woman around.

Epilogue

"Papa Colt, I don't want to go back East to finishing school." Tears brimmed Sammie Jo's sky blue eyes. She was so pretty that he wanted her to pack a derringer.

"Yes, you do," Colt said. "You're going to learn how to be a fine woman. Oh, I know you can ride and shoot like a ranch hand, but your mama and I want you to learn all the things that will make you a lady."

"But who will take care of little Stephen and Nancy and Clancy?"

"It'll be hard, but we'll manage."

"But I'm scared."

Colt stifled a chuckle. Since the incident with Thatcher Lee, Sammie Jo had found more than one thing that scared her. "Nancy's growing up just fine. Your little brother has me and your mama, and Clancy would never want anyone else to take care of him."

Sammie Jo reached up and hugged him tightly. "Take care of everyone while I'm gone."

He laughed. "We'll just pray the good Lord gives me wisdom."

Colt felt an arm around his waist and knew it was his beloved Anne. How he could be blessed with the love of this fine woman still amazed him.

"Let her go, honey. She needs to catch the train," Anne said.

Colt took a deep breath and escorted Sammie Jo to the train steps. "I love you, little lady. We'll see you soon." He waved and watched the train until it disappeared out of sight.

"You have tears in your eyes," Anne said.

"Yes, Papa Colt, big ones," Nancy said with a giggle.

"Oh, I just love my family," he said and winked at Anne.

"And we love you," Anne said and planted a kiss on his cheek.

Strange how he amounted to nothing until the good Lord slapped a wanted poster on his hide and taught him how to love. Life was good. Very good.

OUTLAW SHERIFF

by Kathleen Y'Barbo

Dedication

To my nephews Daniel, Brian, and Ben Y'Barbo,
DJ Holman, William and James Heintschel, Jeremy Bodden,
Craig and Blake Adams, and Brant and Drew Goss.
May God bless you in mighty ways!

The Gentiles shall see thy righteousness, and all kings thy glory:
and thou shalt be called by a new name,
which the mouth of the LORD shall name.
ISAIAH 62:2

Chapter 1

Dime Box, Arizona—March 1881

Caleb Wilson tilted his hat down over his eyes then thought better of it. No, he'd ride into town head held high. If the Lord saw fit to give him a clean heart and a new start on life at the age of twenty-seven, the least he could do was act like it.

Even if it might get him thrown in jail—again.

He tasted trail dust and smelled the result of two straight weeks of going without a decent scrubbing. The heat of summer wasn't yet upon them back in Texas, but out here in the Arizona Territory there seemed little change between the seasons.

In the past his westward wanderings wouldn't have taken him any farther than Tombstone, where he would find a spot at the Crystal Palace Saloon and drink his dinner before encountering trouble, usually in the form of a woman. Not wishing to come across any of the Clantons, his former partners in crime, Caleb pushed farther west until he found the tiny town of Dime Box. He'd never heard of the place, and he hoped they'd never heard of him.

A trio of respectable folk looked up from a wagon filled with supplies as he passed the mercantile. Caleb hesitated before tipping his hat at the men.

The nearest to him, a skinny fellow not far out of knee britches, called out a "howdy" while a man of a few more years lifted his hand in a wave. The look on the older gentleman's face, however, reminded him he was a stranger here.

If he were still a drinking man, he'd be reaching for his flask about now. Instead, Caleb tightened his grip on the reins and reminded himself that a healthy dose of the Good Book was better for him than a round of gut-burning refreshment.

His mount trotted easily down the rutted road, oblivious to lesser horseflesh whose tails fought the flies and dust without success. The livery loomed ahead, and Caleb aimed the horse in that direction. The animal had done him proud on the trail to this place, and tonight she'd be rewarded with a better place to rest and a pail of oats. It was the least he could do considering she'd saved his life more than once in the past month.

His bad leg ached as if it still had a bullet in it, and he grimaced as he sat up a little higher in the saddle. Soon as he got where he was going—wherever that was—he'd have to give some serious thought to ending his trail-riding days.

Caleb sighed. If only it were that simple.

From a fellow inmate in Texas he'd heard tell that Reuben was looking for him, no doubt to put the gang back together. Well, he'd have none of that.

Even if Mama had gone on to Jesus, he still had the thought of her disapproval weighing hard on his mind. If only he hadn't gone back to see her one last time. Hadn't made the promise that led to his meeting the Savior and taking Him to heart. Oh, he was grateful the Lord met him at his mama's bedside back in Raider's Crossing, Wyoming.

Nothing could compare to the moment when his mama led him to the Lord.

He'd promised her then that he would make something of himself. That he wouldn't come back to Raider's Crossing until he'd become a new man, someone she could be proud of.

So far the only part of that promise he'd fulfilled was the first half. Some days he'd wondered how things were faring with his brothers. More often than not, he wondered about little Benny. He'd be a man now, having grown up with no men to show him the way unless the Lord had intervened.

Yeah, and you put him in that spot, Caleb. You and your brothers.

That knowledge pricked his conscience. Dropping him off at Miss Sadie's place had seemed the right thing to do at the time. Looking back with the eyes of a new believer, Caleb knew differently. But then that went for most every decision he made before he started involving the Lord in his business.

If only he could go back in time and make the changes he longed to make. If only he could start everything over.

The scent of greasy meat beat out the other odors that trailed him, and Caleb's stomach complained. Scratching the spot where his beard itched him most, he gave a full minute's thought to parking his mount in front of the source of the grub and satisfying his belly before he cleaned his hide.

He gave the source of the smell a second look. Set between a dry goods store and a doctor's office, the building looked as if it were about to fall down under the weight of the dust and grime it wore. Blistered paint was peeling from warped boards, and the front door listed to the left. Second-floor windows were half-covered with shutters that were missing most of their slats, and a tattered curtain covered in faded roses hung from the one in the middle. Just below, a hand-lettered sign proclaimed the place as MA's KITCHEN.

If the woman standing in the doorway was Ma, he'd have to pass. More than a few years past her prime, she wore faded calico and a frown and carried a black iron skillet like a prized weapon. From inside came the faint sound of breaking glass followed in quick succession by a man's raised voice and a barking dog. Ma, however, never flinched.

As Caleb rode by, the woman lifted the skillet in his direction. Whether in warning or greeting, he couldn't say. Just so as not to get on her bad side, he called out,

"Top of the mornin', ma'am."

She responded with a shrug before disappearing inside. *So much for charming the ladies.*

At that thought Caleb had to chuckle. The first thing he'd asked the Lord after his baptism in Cane Creek was for Him to take away the skills he'd possessed at wooing women. Wouldn't you know He'd answer that prayer right away?

He reached the livery and turned the mare over to a boy of no more than nine or ten. Thoughts of Benny returned, and he shook them off as he tossed a coin in the lad's direction.

"I'll double that if she's fat and happy with a good brushing when I return," Caleb told him.

"Thanks, mister. I'll take good care of her." The boy took the reins and tipped his cap before turning toward the stable.

"Say, there," Caleb called. "What's your name, young fellow?"

The lad stopped short to give Caleb a toothy grin. "Edmund, sir. Edmund Francis Thompson Junior."

Caleb returned the smile. "Well, Edmund Francis Thompson Junior, my horse and I thank you."

He watched them until the horse disappeared into a stall at the back of the stable. A moment later the boy emerged, then quickly returned with a brush, a blanket, and a bag of feed.

Satisfied that his horse was cared for, Caleb headed for a bar of lye soap and a shave.

—⁓—

Caleb walked out of the barbershop a good while later feeling like a new man. His complaining gut was the only remnant of the man who had ridden into Dime Box, and he could fix that in no time.

The barber told him about a boardinghouse a block off the main road where a man could fill his belly and rest his head on a clean mattress for a reasonable price. The proprietor, he'd been told, ran a respectable place. No drinking and no carousing. And no tobacco.

As he stepped onto the broad boards that made up the porch of the nameless rooming house, Caleb noticed an old shingle hanging next to the front door.

"No drinking, no carousing, and no tobacco." Caleb chuckled. "Least I was prepared. Not that any of that would be a problem."

"Well, I'm glad t'hear it. I run a respectable place. Don't cotton to no one but law-abiding citizens."

Caleb's grin was genuine as he met the gaze of a red-haired woman. She looked to be around his mother's age, with laugh lines etched at either end of her broad smile.

"The name's Wilson." Giving thanks for having such a common name, Caleb reached out to shake the woman's hand, surprised that she grasped his fingers in a strong grip. "And I reckon I qualify as a law-abiding citizen. I haven't broken a law in nigh on to two years. Does that pass muster with you?"

She looked him up and down, and for a minute he felt like a prized piece of horseflesh. "Pleased t'meet you, Mr. Wilson. Round here they call me Widow Sykes. Now come on in here and set yourself down. That growling stomach of yours is bad for business."

Caleb tipped his hat and followed his hostess inside. The dining room was sparse but tidy with a long table down the middle and benches running along each side. He estimated that during mealtime the place could easily seat two dozen hungry folks. Since it was the middle of the afternoon, Caleb was the only diner.

When the widow came through the door with two platters of food, Caleb rose to help her. "Set yourself down, young man. I've been doin' this since before you were even thought of." She met his gaze, and her expression softened. "I do appreciate it, son. Your mama ought to be proud she raised such a gentleman."

Caleb swallowed hard and rubbed his freshly smooth jawbone. Well, he'd fooled her, hadn't he? "Thank you, ma'am," he managed as he tied the red-checked napkin around his neck.

Twenty minutes later Caleb had feasted on beef stew and rock-hard biscuits and was contemplating whether to wash his pie down with cold milk or buttermilk when the door swung open. The man who walked in looked as if he'd ridden longer than Caleb and hadn't quite met with the soap bar yet. Of course he planted his dusty bones within spitting distance of Caleb.

"Howdy," the fellow said, and Caleb responded with a tip of his head.

He stabbed at the pie with his fork and kept his attention focused on the plate. Last thing he needed was a confrontation with a stranger. Caleb knew he'd probably be run out of town on a rail once the good citizens of Dime Box got wind of his past. He just hadn't expected it would happen before he had a good night's sleep.

The Widow Sykes came back through with buttermilk and poured him a glassful without asking. When she disappeared into the kitchen, Caleb set down his fork.

"Me, I hate the stuff," the stranger said. "I hear tell they make it from sour milk. Now, you tell me who wants to drink sour milk when there's fresh to be had."

Just to be ornery, Caleb took a healthy swallow. He'd gotten used to the vile drink at his mama's table. Now he had it for old times' sake. Never, however, had he learned to like it.

The fellow watched Caleb set the glass back on the table, then shook his head. "Name's Thompson." He stretched across the table to shake Caleb's hand. "Ed Thompson. When I'm not on the trail, I've got the Lazy T Ranch just north of here. Oh, and I'm the mayor around these parts."

"Pleased to meet you, Mayor Thompson. You wouldn't be kin to the young man at the livery, would you?"

Ed chuckled. "Depends on what he did. Oh, and call me Ed."

"He's a fine young man." Caleb removed the napkin from his neck and took a swipe at his lips. "Good with horses, too, far as I can tell."

"Well, I'm right glad t'hear it. I never know if he's gonna behave for his mama like he does when I'm around." He glanced down at the trail dust on his shirt, then back at Caleb. "I apologize for the way I look. I'm hungry as a bear, and wouldn't you know I'd come home the day of my wife's quilting bee? I'm not about to show up to a hen party. Better I fill my belly here, then slide in the back door once the ladies are gone."

Caleb muttered an agreement, then reached for his hat.

"Hold on there, stranger. I don't believe I caught your name."

Caleb froze. His breath caught in his throat. His name? As with the Widow Sykes, he said, "The name's Wilson."

For a moment Ed said nothing. Then something akin to recognition seemed to cross his face. "Did you say Wilson?"

"I did." Caleb took a step back, eyes narrowed. If the Lord saw fit to allow trouble with the first man he met in Dime Box, then so be it. He'd just have to take it as a sign to move on and start his new life elsewhere.

Ed rose and rounded the table to grip Caleb's shoulder. "*You're* Cal Wilson?"

Cal Wilson? He did ask the Lord for a new name just as it said in the book of Isaiah. Still, setting the man straight seemed the right thing to do, even if it meant having to hightail it out of town before sunset.

"Well, my mama named me Caleb, but you got the Wilson part right."

Ed Thompson took him by the shoulders, all the while grinning like he'd just found gold. "Well, now this *is* a surprise. I been looking for you nigh on a week."

Caleb swallowed hard. So there was another bounty on his head. By turning himself in back in Texas, he thought he'd gotten out from under all the trouble he'd put himself in.

"You don't look nothin' like I expected. You sure you're Cal Wilson?"

"Like I said, Mama named me Caleb, sir. That's generally the name I go by."

"Guess I got it wrong then, but you're definitely the one we been lookin' for."

Caleb thought a minute before responding. "What for?"

"You're an odd fella, Cal. It's all in the telegram from Dodge City. I believe I've got it somewhere back at the house. You want me to fetch it and show you?"

He exhaled a long breath and set his hat back atop his head. "Reckon we ought to mosey on to the jailhouse and get this over with then."

Ed Thompson shoved the last of his biscuit into his mouth, then washed the crumbling mess down with a healthy swallow of coffee. When he finished, he rose and swiped his palms on the front of his shirt. With a nod in Caleb's direction, he said, "Reckon so."

The man spoke with such happiness that the old Caleb would have slugged him for sure. But then the old Caleb would have been on the fastest horse out of town. Rather, Caleb found himself slowing his stride to keep pace with the sheriff as he headed willingly to jail.

Again.

Chapter 2

New Orleans, Louisiana—May 1881

Lydia Bertrand glanced around her room one last time, then allowed May, her mother's maid and now hers, to help her down the stairs. Were she capable of tears at this moment, she might have shed them.

If only Papa were here. Surely he would stop this madness. Surely he wouldn't allow Mama to ship me off as if I were some package headed for the Western frontier.

They stepped into the courtyard. The fountain gurgled, and the leaves dripped with sparkles of raindrops from a rain shower Lydia hadn't even noticed. Beneath her feet, the centuries-old bricks shone as if freshly painted. It seemed as if God had washed the courtyard clean in anticipation of her arrival.

She stopped short and grasped May's hand. "Mama said Papa's in New York." She whispered lest Mama be nearby. "What say we turn in our tickets for passage north? I'm sure once he hears what Mama has done he will overrule her."

May gave her a sideways look. "First off, chile, New York City's bigger'n any place you or I's ever been, and we don't know where your papa done gone there. Ain't no way to find a man lessen you know where he's done gone." She paused. "Second, your papa loves your mama more'n either of us can understand. They's put together by the Lord, and they fit like hand-in-glove. Your mama, bless her heart, was a strong-willed chile. Your papa, he lets her have her way, now don't he? You really think he gonna overrule your mama on somethin' she's so set on doin'?"

Unfortunately, Lydia couldn't disagree with anything May said.

"That's right. You know I'm tellin' the truth." She looked as if she wanted to say more. Instead, she turned her head and made a soft clucking sound.

"Go ahead and say it, May."

"All right, I will." She paused. "I wonder iffen the good Lord ain't behind this." At Lydia's incredulous look, May shook her head. "The Bible said we reap what we sow. You done sowed a whole bunch of trouble dancin' in that fountain at school, Miss Lydia."

Again she couldn't deny it. "So what do I do, May? This is serious."

May seemed to consider the statement for a moment. "Chile, how big is your

God? 'Cause my God is bigger'n any human plan."

Nodding, Lydia felt the beginnings of hope stirring.

"Well then." May placed her dark wrinkled hand over Lydia's, then squeezed. "If it's the Lord's intention that your mama get her way, there's nothin' you can do about it less'n you intend to jump outta His will. You wantin' to do that, Lydia Bertrand? You wanna go against the Lord Almighty?"

Lydia's heart sank. Disobedience had always come so easily. "No," she said softly. "Not this time."

"I didn't think so." May looked past her, presumably to the coachman. "She ready to go." Returning her gaze to Lydia, May smiled. "You the spittin' image of your mama. Difference is, by the time she was your age, you were runnin' around makin' trouble and she had lost your two brothers to the yellow fever." Her face softened as if remembering all over again. A moment later she stiffened her spine and blinked hard. "It's time you left here and made your own way in the world. What you think about that?"

Lydia glanced back at the house, and something sharp twisted in her gut. Was that Mama who let the lace curtain fall in the window above the door, or had the breeze caught it?

"I think she's banishing me."

May released her hand to envelop Lydia in a hug. "She not banishin' you—she sendin' you forth. Now let's us get a-goin'. Ain't no use to tarry when the Lord's got plans for both of us."

"May I help you in, Mademoiselle Bertrand?"

Lydia sighed as the same coachman who had handed her out of the carriage this morning now helped her back in. Two trunks and a carpetbag later, they rolled out of the courtyard onto Rue Royale with May seated beside the driver.

This time Mama definitely was nowhere to be seen.

Lydia reached for her journal to record the moment, then thought better of it. Whatever the Lord had for her, it was better she not speculate in her current frame of mind. Nor should she dwell on the feelings she now found raging inside her.

Instead, she cast her gaze down to the travel voucher in her hand and tried to pray.

When her jumbled hopes and cares refused to form a coherent thought, Lydia settled for leaning on the assurance that the Holy Spirit had taken her mutterings to the throne. As she glanced up front to where May sat, Lydia saw the older woman bow her head.

The rest of the trip to the train station seemed to go by quickly, as did the first leg of Lydia's journey west. By the time she and May landed on the doorstep of the Menger Hotel in San Antonio, Texas, she'd almost gotten used to the idea of being sent forcefully into the world.

Lydia slept soundly and might have missed breakfast to linger beneath the covers except for the noise from construction on the hotel's new east wing. This time when she prayed, she found the words to ask the Lord for a way to escape her current situation. While He did not respond immediately, Lydia had no doubt He was behind the plan she began to concoct.

As she handed the cream-colored letter to the gentleman behind the front desk and bade good-bye to the Menger Hotel, Lydia felt her heart grow lighter. Mama might hold the key to Lydia's immediate future, but eventually Papa would prevail. As soon as he heard of her troubles, he would surely come to her rescue.

All she had to do was bide her time until he arrived. She held that thought all the way across the rest of Texas and into New Mexico. By the time the train came to the end of the line and they transferred to a stage for the rest of the trip, the thought had become a prayer that she took to the throne every time they lurched over a rough patch of trail.

When not in prayer, Lydia contemplated how best to spend her time. Papa had long ago listed pertinent scripture verses in the front of her Bible, and she turned to them now. Chief among them was the one she called her life verse.

From the sixty-second chapter of Isaiah, she ran her finger over Papa's bold backward-slanting script. "And the Gentiles shall see thy righteousness, and all kings thy glory: and thou shalt be called by a new name, which the mouth of the Lord shall name."

To Lydia's surprise, May began to giggle. When a stern look did not silence the older woman's mirth, Lydia closed the Bible and shook her head.

"What's so funny, May?"

"Read that verse again, Miss Lydia." When Lydia complied, May doubled over in laughter. A moment later she gathered her wits. "I'm not laughin' at you, I promise. It's just that. . ." She pointed to the Bible. "Well, the good Lord, He do have a sense of humor."

The stage jolted to a stop, and Lydia braced herself. "What are you talking about?"

"Well, now, He say right there that you gonna be called by a new name. You see it?"

The coach lurched into motion once more. "Yes, I see it, but I repeat: what's so funny?"

"It's just that in all the years you were claimin' this verse as your own, did you ever think God would be doin' exactly what He says there?"

Lydia set the Bible aside and massaged her temples. The dull ache that had begun in New Mexico threatened to bloom into a full-fledged headache now that they'd left the state behind.

She closed her eyes and sighed. "Honestly, May, I have no idea what you mean."

May touched Lydia's sleeve. "You gettin' a new name now, aren't you, chile? Maybe you need t'stop blamin' your mama and start thankin' your Lord for makin' good on His promise."

When the reality of the statement hit her, Lydia could only groan.

"You know He goin' with us, now don't you?" May grasped a handful of Lydia's traveling frock and blinked hard. "I been prayin' for protection for you since you been borned, Miss Lydia, same as my mama did with your mama. The good Lord, He listen then, and He's kept you safe in spite of yourself, now hasn't He?"

When Lydia nodded, May continued.

"So when your mama told me what she had a mind t'do, I says to myself, is this of the Lord or is this somethin' else? Well, I set to prayin' and askin' for Him to stop the foolishness of this if it wasn't where He wanted you to be." She leaned forward. "Next thing you know, she gets word from that woman at the school that you'd done a dance in the fountain. Well, that's when I knowed for sure this was somethin' that had to happen."

Lydia leaned against the seat until the broken spring caused her to shift positions. She looked out at the passing landscape, so different from her New Orleans home, as she contemplated May's words. They made no sense.

"You can't mean that my mother planned this *before* I got myself sent home from school, May. That just isn't possible."

May sat back. "Oh, it's more than possible. She been pondering on this plan for more'n a year. She say she was worried about your future. Your papa, he knowed about it, too, and he thought it was a bad idea, but only because he wanted you close by. I know he was much aggrieved by what might happen to you after he and the missus was gone."

Lydia let May's words sink in. "If that's true, then why did he let me be sent off to Georgia to Miss Potter's?"

"He thought you were being sent off to learn how to teach the young'uns. The reverend, he figured that'd be a good trade for you, what with your talent takin' care of the little ones in the church nursery. When he found out your mama had lied to get you into that fancy boarding school instead of sending you to the teachers' college, well, he 'bout hit the roof."

So Papa wasn't behind sending her off to Miss Potter's school. That much she could believe. "Why didn't he come get me when he found out?"

She shrugged. "Well, he never said so to me, but I figure your mama convinced him it would all work out just fine. She's got a way of doin' that with your papa."

"Yes, she does." Lydia studied her hands for a moment, then lifted her gaze to meet May's stare. "Do you think Papa will come after me this time?"

May seemed to be considering the question. "I don't rightly know," she finally said. "But if I was you, I wouldn't count on him comin' right off. He gonna be in New York for two weeks—that's what your mama said. We been gone a week now, so that means he ain't even home yet. Far as he knows, you're still up in Georgia gettin' refined."

"But once he comes home, do you think he'll fetch me back then?"

May looked away. "I just don't know, Miss Lydia."

"Well, I do, May, and I'm just going to have to bide my time until he does."

She gave Lydia a look. "What have you done?"

Lydia shrugged. "I wrote my father a letter and mailed it back at the Menger. I'm sure as soon as he reads it he'll be on his way to fetch me back."

"Miss Lydia, when will you learn?" She shook her head. "Your papa, he don't disagree with this. He gave you a chance, and you didn't take it. If he comes at all, it'll be to see that you go through with it."

The words struck fear in her heart. Then on second consideration she dismissed them. "You can't be serious."

"I can't?" The older woman gave a tired sigh. "Think, chile. What does your papa want more than anything for your future?"

Trail dust swirled into the tiny coach. "That I be taken care of," she said before giving in to a fit of coughing.

May nodded. "And how has he tried to do that?"

Lydia blinked the dust from her eyes and swiped at them with the backs of her sleeves. "By raising me in a Christian home and seeing that I developed a relationship with the Lord."

"Uh-huh. And what else?"

She pondered a moment. "Well, by sending me to school and, oh. . ." Her eyes filled with tears. "I've done this to myself, haven't I?"

May patted her hand again but said nothing.

Lydia lifted tear-filled eyes toward her former nursemaid. "What am I going to do now?"

"Only thing I know is if the Lord wants you home in New Orleans, He gonna stop all this foolishness, not you."

The coach rolled past a sign announcing their destination. Any moment the coach would stop, and her new life would begin.

"Yes, but what do I do in the meantime?"

"You do what the Lord tells you, Miss Lydia. That's always the right thing."

They lurched forward as the coach halted before a primitive wooden building with a hand-lettered sign above the first floor. In a series of movements that felt like walking through water, Lydia left the coach and stood on a dust-covered walkway made of rough boards and marked by the occasional hole or missing board. To the right was an old woman staring at her from the doorway, her demeanor less than friendly. To the left a trio of roughs eyed her curiously before the coachman shooed them into the saloon.

She glanced down at the instructions Mama had given May, then up at the hand-lettered sign. So this was to be her new home, at least for now. According to Mama, her rent was paid for exactly two weeks. After that she was on her own.

As the driver hefted the first of her trunks onto the boardwalk, a panic like she'd never known before gripped Lydia. After she prayed, she covered the rising fear the way she always had—by squaring her shoulders and walking straight into it. Or, in this case, walking straight into the path of a cowboy who wore a black hat and a crooked grin.

Chapter 3

"S cuse me, ma'am." Caleb took a step backward and helped the little lady back onto her feet, then removed his hat and gave her a nod. "I'm real sorry. My mind was elsewhere."

"As was mine. I do apologize."

She was a pretty thing, no bigger than a minute, but with a voice as smooth as silk and a pair of big brown eyes that could cause a man to forget his troubles.

Well, most men might. Not him, though. His troubles were impossible to forget. Then again, something told him so was this gal.

"You comin', Cal?"

One more look at the big-eyed gal, and then he nodded and replaced his hat on his head. "Be right there, Ed. Pleased to make your acquaintance, ma'am."

He trotted across the street, then took another look at the lady. A force of nature, she'd already disappeared, leaving a stack of trunks and a dark-skinned maid in her wake.

"Probably best you didn't tangle with that one," he said under his breath, although the sentiment didn't reach his heart.

Not that he'd want a gal who looked so fragile. No, he liked a woman with a little meat on her bones. And while dark hair was nice, he'd always fancied blonds.

"What are you thinking, Wilson? Remember that prayer you prayed? There isn't a woman alive who'd be interested in you, leastwise not until the Lord changes His mind."

Then there was the issue of his freedom.

Caleb shrugged off his miserable self-pity to step into the sheriff's office. The smell hit him first, then the dust. He reeled backward trying to sneeze and cough all at once and nearly tripped over a pile of lumber that looked to have once been part of the roof.

When he recovered, he saw Ed standing in the door. "You okay, Cal?"

Straightening, Caleb swiped at his mouth with the back of his hand. "Name's Caleb, Ed, and I'm fine. Just wasn't prepared, that's all."

"Yeah, looks like we got some cleaning and fixing to do in there." Ed shrugged. "To tell you the truth, ain't nobody been in there since Sheriff Merritt passed on last winter. The skunks must've moved in 'bout the time the sheriff moved out. The roof, well, you got me how that whole thing fell down like that. Must've happened when we had that big wind back in January. See, there's an old piece of roof. I reckon we must've had some rotten timbers that didn't cotton to being pounded."

Caleb let his gaze sweep the office and adjoining jail cell. No sheriff or prisoners since last winter?

That surely told a man what sort of town Dime Box was. Even if he weren't about to be the guest of the jailhouse, he might have considered staying around of his own accord. What were a few skunks when the townsfolk were a law-abiding sort? Compared to Tombstone, this place was paradise.

A thought occurred. "If the sheriff passed on last winter, who's been keeping the peace?"

Ed leaned against the door frame and crossed his arms over his chest. "Oh, we mostly been doing it ourselves, the menfolk, that is. Once in a while we get a tough customer who has to be taken over to Millville. Mostly, though, we see a few drunks and the occasional mischievous lad."

"I see." Caleb paused. "Well, then, I suppose we ought to be heading out. Millville's a half day's ride."

The Thompson fellow looked at Caleb as if he'd grown an extra ear. "What would we be wantin' to go to Millville for?"

"Well, I just figured, what with the jail not being usable you might want to put me over there."

To Caleb's surprise, Ed began to laugh. At first he chuckled; then he doubled over in full-fledged laughter. When he straightened, he had to wipe his eyes before he could speak.

"You're a real hoot, Cal." He gestured toward the place where they'd just come from. "I reckon you can head on over to the Widow Sykes's place and set yourself up in a room there. Last I heard she had two empty ones. Once we get the jailhouse back in shape, we can move you in here. That to your liking?"

To my liking? Caleb searched Ed Thompson's face for signs he was pulling a prank. What he saw looked to be concern. "Anything wrong?" Ed asked.

"Wrong? Well, I guess I was wondering if you're serious or just pulling my leg."

There was that look again. "Why would I be pulling your leg? Don't you like the rooming house? I mean, I know things are fancier where you come from, but I figure a clean bed and a good meal's the same no matter where you get 'em."

"I reckon you're right." He reached out to shake Ed's hand. "I appreciate your trust in me, Ed, and you've got my word as a law-abiding man that I won't leave town."

"You're too much, Cal." His amused expression turned serious. "I wonder if we ought to keep this under our hats, though. I mean, once the townsfolk get wind of who you are, well, you and I won't have a moment's peace."

Caleb said a quick prayer of thanks for the reprieve, then beat a path to the rooming house before Ed changed his mind.

Caleb spent four nights at the Widow Sykes's place and five days at the jailhouse helping Ed repair the ceiling damage and remove all traces of the skunk family that had spent Christmas in the lone jail cell. When questioned as to his reasons for taking on such a task, Caleb had an easy answer: "If I'm going to be spending my time here, the least I can do is make it livable."

That response satisfied Ed, and just before sundown on the fifth day, they completed their work.

"I best go get cleaned up," Ed said. "The missus is particular about smelly menfolk at her supper table." He scratched his head, then glanced over at Caleb.

"Why don't you join us tonight, Cal? Evelyn sets a fine spread, and I know she'd welcome you. She's been after me to fetch you home, but I figured with you working yourself to the bone here the last thing you felt like was socializing of an evenin'."

Along the way he'd met quite a few of the townsfolk, most of them arriving carrying a baked good of some sort. They welcomed him like an honored guest rather than the inmate he was to become, and they all called him Cal, which struck him as odd. Still none of them had invited him to socialize.

He met Ed's gaze. "You sure about this, Ed? I mean, I'm a—"

"Pa, you still in there? Mama said to tell you she's buttering the corn bread."

Ed grinned. "Looks like I'm being called to supper. You comin' or what?"

Caleb pondered the invitation for a moment before shaking his head. He sure did like a good piece of buttered corn bread. In fact, he loved to eat.

"I really ought not to get used to such luxuries. You tell your wife I appreciate the invite, though."

Ed studied Caleb a moment, then shook his hand and headed out the door. A moment later he returned. "I know you're tired and all, but we need to talk about getting you moved in here. What say you fetch your things from the Widow Sykes's place after breakfast and meet me here? Say eight o'clock?"

"Eight it is." Caleb straightened his hat and walked out into the dying rays of the last sunset he would see as a free man—at least for quite a while.

"Lord," he said under his breath, "I sure would like another chance. If You'd see fit to let me get a clean start, I'd be much beholden."

Bypassing the dining room, Caleb made his way upstairs and kicked off his boots. It would be a shame to spend his last free night alone, yet he felt no need to go any farther than the table where'd he left his Bible.

A sound drifted up and pulled Caleb toward the window. There below, in the sliver of dirt and rocks the Widow Sykes called her garden, the dark form of a person huddled against the far wall. Upon closer inspection he could see skirts.

The sound found him again, and this time he knew it was the sound of a woman crying. While he watched, she doubled over, then sank to her knees.

His first instinct was to leave her be. A woman's tears were a more dangerous weapon than a gun or a knife, and he generally steered clear of a female packing a damp hankie.

But what if she's hurt? What if she's hiding from someone looking to do her harm? Despite what Ed said about Dime Box's low crime rate, plenty of bad guys were lurking out there, and they could just as likely be hiding here as anywhere.

Caleb ought to know. He used to be the worst of the worst, and his favorite hiding places were where the decent folk went. That's how he'd learned to pass himself off as a gentleman.

Some days he felt like he was still playing that game: an outlaw pretending to be a man of character. Then the good Lord would give him some reminder He had settled the score and wiped away the past.

Caleb waited a moment longer, then made his decision. "Nothing like spending the night before I go to jail doing a good deed."

Shoving his feet into his boots, Caleb headed outside. He might not be able to do much with his immediate future, but the least he could do was help a woman who was obviously in some kind of distress.

Chapter 4

Lydia's breath came in gasps, and her eyes stung from the tears she'd held back all day. So much for making the best of the situation. The moment May fell asleep, the strong facade Lydia had kept all week crumbled.

Try as she might, she hadn't managed to believe the Lord intended her to be here. In this place.

Doing what her mother insisted she must do.

A sob tore from her throat, and Lydia silenced it by taking a deep breath. The spot she'd chosen was private enough, with only one darkened room having a view; still she worried someone might happen upon her.

Funny how she had no trouble making a spectacle of herself to get sent home from all the finishing schools she'd attended over the years, yet she couldn't shed a single tear in front of a witness.

She dabbed at her eyes with her handkerchief. Always she had found a way out of her predicament, a way to get back home. This time, however, her situation seemed a bit more. . .dare she even think it?

Permanent.

Tears sprang afresh, and this time she gave them free rein to flow down her cheeks and soak her frock. To think Papa knew of this and still—

"Anything wrong, ma'am?"

Lydia scrambled to her feet, then reeled backward and thudded against the wall. Her head banged against the rough stones, and she cried out. A pair of strong arms lifted her off her feet.

"What are you doing? Put. Me. Down."

As if he hadn't heard her, the stranger whirled around with her in his arms and headed for the boardinghouse.

"Put. Me. Down!"

The man froze. A slice of moonlight cut across chiseled features she might have thought handsome had the oaf not just hauled her around like a sack of potatoes.

"What do you think you're doing?" she demanded.

He cocked his hat back, revealing more of the face she knew must have caused more than a few women to take notice. "I thought I was helping a lady in distress."

"The only distress I'm feeling is because I'm being tossed about by a complete stranger. Put me down before I call for the sheriff."

This time he complied, setting her feet on the rocky ground, then taking a step backward. "Go ahead."

Lydia gave him a look. "I mean it. I will."

The cowboy leaned against the side of the rooming house and crossed his arms over his chest. "Like I said. Go ahead. There's just one problem."

"What's that?"

He shrugged. "Far as I know, there's not a sheriff in Dime Box. Leastwise there wasn't one this afternoon."

No sheriff? This was interesting. Dare she hope?

"Since when is there not a sheriff?"

Another voice spoke up. "Ed says the sheriff is going to be sworn in tomorrow morning." The Widow Sykes turned the corner. "You ought to know that, Cal." She turned to Lydia. "Everything all right out here, Miss Bertrand? I was takin' a pie out of the oven and thought I heard some commotion."

She gave the stranger a look, then turned her attention to the innkeeper. "Yes, I'm fine. Will you excuse me? I'd like to return to my room."

"Let me go with you." The landlady gave the man named Cal a nod, then reached for Lydia's arm. "What say I walk with you just to be sure you're all right?"

"That's not necessary, really." A light breeze blew past, bringing the scent of something delicious in its wake. "What sort of pie is that? It smells wonderful."

"It's my mama's recipe. She called it a Jeff Davis pie. She was from Savannah, you know."

"Might I have the recipe?"

The older woman stopped short. "You like to cook, do you?"

"Very much," Lydia said, "although I haven't had the chance to do so in far too long."

"Now isn't that interesting? I was just asking the Lord for some kitchen help this mornin'. I can pay in wages or free rent. You interested?"

—⁂—

The dark-haired gal reminded Caleb of his mama's banty rooster, and he would've told her so except he intended to leave there in one piece. He watched the Widow Sykes usher her out of sight, then lifted his gaze to the heavens. The stars shone bright.

Somewhere beyond them was his real home. Knowing this made what he faced tomorrow seem a little less awful.

It occurred to him that in all their time together Ed hadn't mentioned anything about the charges against him. Of course he hadn't asked, either, but then neither he nor Ed cared much for idle chatter. They'd worked most days in silence.

By the time Caleb climbed under the threadbare blanket and laid his head on the pillow, he'd come up with a sizable list of possible crimes he'd committed. Some he'd already confessed to, and a few others he might have forgotten.

Still others might have been blamed on the Wilson boys but committed by others. That happened occasionally.

A spark of hope rose. *What if I can prove I'm innocent? What if Ed's mistaken?*

He winced when he thought of the man he was. The Good Book said the Lord could wash a man clean and turn his scarlet sins to pure white.

If the Lord said it, Caleb believed it. Understanding it—now that was another matter.

But then, come tomorrow he'd have plenty of time to study on the idea.

That night he slept in short doses and met the Lord in His Word well before sunrise. Dressed and ready before six, Caleb wandered downstairs with the intention of taking one last walk around Dime Box before meeting Ed.

Passing the dining room, he turned down good coffee, then thought better of it and sat down to let the widow pour him a cup. One cup turned into two, and before he knew it, he had a plate of eggs and bacon sitting before him.

He stabbed a fork into his eggs and took a hefty bite, then washed it down with black coffee. Before his mug could hit the table, Widow Sykes wandered in from the kitchen and set a pan of biscuits on the table, then disappeared with a promise to bring more butter and some honey.

He grabbed three biscuits, then set one back on the plate. No sense being greedy, even though he sat alone in the dining room. Two more bites of eggs and he was ready for that butter and honey.

Once the bacon was gone, Caleb began to wonder if she'd forgotten. The biscuits smelled too good to ignore, so he decided to taste one plain. It was so good he had another.

Caleb winked. "They'd be even better with butter and some honey."

He thought to call his landlady's name just to see if she was heading this way, then decided he'd amble into the kitchen and help her find that butter and honey. One push on the door and he found it stuck. On the second try, it almost felt as if the door pushed back.

He gave it a good shove, and the door cooperated, swinging open to reveal the Widow Sykes standing at the black cookstove.

The door slammed against the wall, and a woman screamed. Caleb took a step forward, then tripped.

About the time he landed on his posterior, he found the source of the roadblock—and presumably the caterwauling. There in all her honey- and butter-covered glory was the dark-haired gal from last night.

Chapter 5

Caleb tried to right himself under the glare of the sputtering woman but found nothing but slick floor boards beneath him. He tried rolling onto his stomach to push up from the floor but landed on his face.

A few more maneuvers, and he managed a sitting position. The pretty gal looked as if she wanted to wring his neck, and he fully expected the first words out of her mouth to be directed at him.

Instead, she surprised Caleb by looking past him. "Might I trouble you for a length of toweling, Mrs. Sykes?"

A length of toweling? She certainly wasn't from these parts.

She met his gaze, and her eyes narrowed. At that moment Caleb felt about as welcome as a wet dog at a church picnic.

"What are *you* doing here?"

It was more of a demand than a question, really, and with her glaring like that, Caleb had to think hard to remember how to respond. "I came to fetch the butter and honey," he finally managed.

She seemed less than impressed with his answer. Of course, with honey smeared across the front of her dress and a streak of butter running from the corner of her mouth to her nose, she probably wasn't paying much attention.

"I thought I was helping," he decided to add. "Best batch of biscuits that ever come out of the cookstove, ma'am," he said to the widow.

Widow Sykes looked like she was about to double over laughing. "I appreciate that, Cal, but I'm not the one who mixed up that batch." She gestured to the dark-haired gal. "You've got Miss Bertrand to thank for that."

Caleb dared a sideways glance at Miss Bertrand. "Them's prize-winning biscuits, ma'am."

She lifted the corner of her apron to swipe at her cheek, smearing the butter in the process. "Glad you liked them," she said without much enthusiasm.

"Miss Bertrand's gonna be cooking for us. Least until she says her 'I-dos,' that is."

"Is that right?" When she didn't respond, he tried again. "So when's the hitchin'?"

"Hitchin'?"

"Your wedding. When's the wedding?" He reached for his hanky, clean as of this morning, and handed it to Miss Bertrand.

She dabbed at the butter, then handed it back. For a moment her expression softened. "I'm not exactly sure." Soon as the words were said, the temper returned. "I'm thankful it's not today. This was my only clean dress."

"Bein' as I'm not your intended, I'd rather not imagine you without a clean dress, ma'am."

His joke fell flat. Rather than smiling as he hoped, she deepened her frown. "Just what are you suggesting, sir?"

"I'm not suggesting anything, Miss Bertrand. It's just that you've unintentionally given me an image of you that a gentleman doesn't need to have."

Caleb dabbed his finger in the honey and tasted it for effect. Yes, it would be mighty fine on those biscuits waiting for him back in the dining room. From the look of his clothes, however, he probably ought to eat on the run.

Dare he hope the widow might see fit to send a meal or two his way while he was a guest of the jailhouse? He'd have to ask once he knew exactly how long a term he faced.

With that thought weighing on his mind, Caleb struggled to his feet and reached to offer help to Miss Bertrand. When she declined, he made his way back upstairs to step into the last set of clean clothes he owned: his Sunday suit.

He knew he looked ridiculous wearing it to jail on a Tuesday morning, but it was better than parading over to the jail in his long johns.

—∿—

"Be still, Miss Lydia, or I'm never gonna get that honey outta your hair."

Lydia leaned farther over the basin while May poured yet another pitcher of water over her sticky hair. She gritted her teeth and entertained a few unsavory thoughts as the icy water splashed onto her neck then began to trickle down her back.

"That Wilson fellow is the most irritating man I've ever met. I mean, the nerve of him. Last night he hauled me around like a sack of potatoes. A sack of *potatoes*, May. Do you hear me?"

"Um-hum." May began to work lavender soap through Lydia's tangles. "Potatoes. I hear you."

"And today. If you'd been there, you would have seen what a cad the man is. Can you feature that he would actually be amused by causing me to spill butter and honey all over myself?"

May stopped scrubbing and reached for the pitcher.

"And of all the nerve. Do you know what he said to me? He said he was a gentleman, and he didn't want to imagine me in my—." Lydia yelped as icy water cascaded over her head. "Warn me next time, May."

"Cold water ain't what you need to be warned about, chile." She set the pitcher down. "You all done. Now let's get you dry."

Lydia stewed until May finished the process of drying and braiding her hair. When the last pin went in, she could stand it no more.

"What exactly do I need to be warned about, May?"

May pressed the wrinkles out of the skirt of the yellow frock Lydia had worn the day before, then held it out toward her. "I don't believe you really want an answer to that question, Miss Lydia."

She stepped into her dress and frowned. "And why not?"

"Why, indeed." Whirling Lydia around, May began fastening the row of buttons that ran down the back of the dress. "It most certainly wouldn't be to your likin'."

Lydia stepped away and turned to face May. "Try me."

The older woman shook her head. "Chile, you are as stubborn as your mama sometimes. When are you gonna learn that the Father knows what's best, and it ain't no use to run from Him or put off what He's a-wantin' you to do?"

"What do you mean?"

"I mean there's no use frettin' and fussin' when the good Lord brought you here for a purpose. You know why you're here—now you need to go present yourself."

Lydia swallowed hard. "You mean, just walk up to him and say, 'Hello, I'm Lydia, the bride you ordered'?"

May rested her hands on her hips. "That's exactly what I mean. Now you scoot outta here and do just that, or I'm gonna start worryin' you're gettin' sweet on that fella who 'bout ran you down in the kitchen."

"That man?" Lydia grimaced. "Trust me, May. He'd be the *last* man I'd ever be sweet on. I can promise you that."

"Oh, I don't know 'bout that." May made a soft clucking sound as she turned her back to empty the basin out the window. "I got me a feelin' 'bout you and that fella."

She pointed to the letter her mother had sent along with the one she'd written. The man who paid her way to Dime Box had penned this. The man who bought her lock, stock, and petticoat.

Lydia took one last look in the mirror. "Your feelings aren't worth anything when compared to that letter over there. Fetch it and let's go get this over with."

"How 'bout we take him a pie, Miss Lydia?"

She stopped short. "A pie? Whatever for?"

May shrugged. "Ain't nothin' a man likes better'n a good fresh-baked pie, and you done made an extra this mornin'. I doubt Miz Sykes'll mind."

"Oh, all right. But if this fellow's awful, I'm heading for the hills. You understand?"

May chuckled. "Oh, I been speakin' to the Lord, and I believe He's got a nice surprise for you."

Lydia squared her shoulders and refused to comment.

Chapter 6

Caleb had already reached the porch when he thought to go back inside and make his apologies to the landlady. He found her clearing the last of the honey from the floor with a mop. The room smelled of cleaning fluid and pie crust.

"I'd be obliged if you'd let me help," he said.

"It's nothing but a little spill." She shook her head and leaned up to give him an appraising look. "Now don't you look sportin'?"

"I suppose." He glanced down at his suit, then back at the Widow Sykes. "Let me pay for the dry goods I ruined."

"Oh, no, I wouldn't think of it." The widow climbed to her feet and gestured toward the stairs with her cleaning rag. "What with the answer to my prayers staying right under my roof, nothing bothers me today."

"The answer to your prayers?" Caleb chuckled. "That feisty gal?"

"Let me tell you something about feisty gals." She slung the rag over her shoulder, then crossed her arms over her chest. "I'm of the opinion that behind most feisty gals is a little girl crying for attention. I figure once she settles down, so will her temper."

Caleb laughed out loud. "For the sake of her poor husband, I certainly hope so."

He chuckled all the way to the sheriff's office, then sobered his expression when he walked through the door. The room had been cleared of the tools they'd left last night, and someone had put a pie on the corner of the desk. Upon closer inspection, he decided it was a Jeff Davis pie.

"Just like Mama used to make," he said as he inhaled one more time.

Situated between close buildings, the office was darker than it seemed it ought to be. An old Regulator clock chimed, and he took note of the time. Fifteen minutes early. At least no one could accuse him of procrastination.

He gave the jail cell a wide berth, searching instead for some way to light the kerosene lamps in the dark corner of the office. A search produced a match, and soon enough he had sufficient light to see the wanted posters stuck up on the wall.

Right off he recognized three fellows he and his brothers had ridden with. Two were back home in Missouri, having retired to become gentleman farmers, and the third owned a dry goods store in Kansas City. Last he heard, Reuben made the place his favorite hideout when the law got too close.

Reuben.

The reminder of his brothers sliced like a knife to his gut, so he squared his shoulders and stepped away from the posters. Last thing he wanted was to see one of them up there.

Not that it would have surprised him.

"You're early." Ed stood just behind him, proof positive that Caleb's outlaw instincts were rusty.

"No sense putting off what I can't change." He walked over to the desk and removed his pistol, then set it and his holster on the desk. Without a word, he walked over to the cell and placed his hands on the bars.

"I'd be much obliged if you'd let the Widow Sykes know I appreciate her hospitality. I know I won't be takin' my meals at her place for a spell, but I left her some money in my room just the same." He turned to look Ed square in the eye. "I wonder if I might have her good home cooking carted over here every once in a while. I'd pay, of course."

"Well, I don't see as how that would be a problem. Although you could just as easily go fetch it."

Caleb shook his head. "But, Ed, I'll be—"

"There's the man of the hour." A burly redhead lumbered in and parked himself behind the desk. "What say we get this started?"

"Are you the judge?" Caleb asked.

"Judge?" The man slapped the surface of the desk with his open palm, then laughed. "I like that idea, Ed. Since you're the mayor, why don't you make me the judge?"

"Wouldn't that be like putting the wolf in charge of the henhouse, Elmer?"

The men shared another laugh while Caleb stood and watched. It was all well and fine that the fellows enjoyed one another, but did they have to do it while he waited to hear his crime and receive his sentence? He was about to ask them when Ed held up his hands and stopped his chuckling.

"Elmer, I don't believe you and Cal have been formally introduced. Cal Wilson, meet Elmer Wiggins. He's the barber and the undertaker. Guess you could say Elmer gets you comin' and goin'."

"Pleased to meet you, Mr. Wiggins." Caleb rubbed his chin. "I got a fine shave and haircut over to your place. Wasn't you who did the job, though."

Elmer shook his head. "No, that was my brother-in-law Pete. He generally only works on the corpses, but I let him try out his skills on live folks every once in a while."

Ed clapped his hands, then rubbed them together as if he actually looked forward to what was about to happen. Elmer looked more interested in the pie than anything else.

Neither of them seemed to give a second thought to the prospective inmate.

Caleb felt his temper rise, then reminded himself he was no longer that sort of man. "Let's get on with it then."

Elmer rose and pushed away from the desk, giving the pie one last look. "That from your wife?" he asked Ed.

"The Widow Sykes, actually." Ed gestured to the door. "I got a surprise for you, Cal."

A surprise? Outside?

That's when he heard it. The sound of people. Caleb leaned toward the window and lifted the red-checked curtain. Sure enough, half the town was waiting for him in the middle of Main Street.

If the good folks of Dime Box, Arizona, wanted to lynch him, they'd have to find him first. His gaze darted around the room in search of a back exit.

Finding none, he contemplated a different means of escape. In the old days, he would have shot his way out, risking any number of innocent lives in the process.

A hand clamped down on his shoulder, and Caleb looked around to find Ed had joined him at the window. "Cal, as mayor, I want to be the one to—"

The door burst open, allowing the sound of cheering to drift in from outside. Miss Bertrand practically fell into the room, followed by the same dark-skinned maid he'd noticed with her earlier.

Oblivious to Caleb's presence, Miss Bertrand addressed Elmer. "I need to speak to the sheriff."

Her voice sounded as if she'd run all the way from the boardinghouse. Under her arm she carried a tin of what he hoped were more of her biscuits. While the feisty gal irritated him to no end, she sure could cook.

"Hold on there, girlie," Elmer said. "The menfolk are carrying on important business here. Is this here an emergency?"

"Emergency? You could call it that." She set the tin on the desk beside the pie, then caught sight of Caleb. "What are *you* doing here?"

Ed released his grasp on Caleb's shoulder to slap him on the back. "Haven't you heard? Cal here's the new—"

The Widow Sykes came bustling in. "Ed Thompson, what's taking so long? You got everyone in town out there waiting. If you're not gonna make the announcement, then leastwise go and tell them so." She shifted her attention from Ed to Caleb. "Hello there, Mr. Wilson. What're you doing here?"

"That's what I asked." Miss Bertrand inched forward and swiped at the spot on her cheek where butter and honey had been only an hour ago. "Did the law finally catch up with you?"

A few responses came to mind, none of which was particularly nice. He settled for ignoring the question.

"In a manner of speaking," Elmer said with a chuckle. "You might say he's gonna make the jailhouse his home now."

"Hush, Elmer, you old fool." Ed pressed past the ladies to reach for the door knob. "Come on, Cal. Let's get this over with."

Irritation turned to white-hot anger. Now both of them were grinning. Meeting his Maker was one thing, but enduring ridicule was another.

"Now hold on a minute, Ed," Caleb said. "I got some rights here, and before I go out there, I'd like to know exactly what you're charging me with."

"What we're chargin' you with?" Elmer guffawed. "We're chargin' you with being the new sheriff."

"Sheriff? Hold on." Caleb shook his head. "You got the wrong man, Ed. I'm Caleb Wilson."

Ed slapped Caleb on the back and pushed him toward the open door. "That's right. You're Sheriff Caleb Wilson."

"I'm who?" He shook his head. "Is this a joke?"

While Elmer guffawed, Caleb took a step backward to try to make some sense of the situation. Somehow he'd obviously been mistaken for a man whose name was similar to his. In nothing flat, he'd gone from inmate to jailer.

Caleb took a deep breath. He ought to set them straight, ought to say right out that he was Caleb Wilson, not Cal Wilson, and that six months ago he'd been cooling his heels at the Huntsville prison. Then he had another thought. Had God heard his prayer and given him a chance at a new life?

"*He's* the sheriff?" Miss Bertrand looked as if she might fall down right where she stood. "*You're* the man I'm supposed to marry?"

"Sheriff Wilson, I knowed it, I did." The dark-skinned maid waved a paper in Caleb's direction. "It's all right here in your letter. You the one who sent for Miss Lydia."

"Say somethin', Cal." Elmer pointed to Miss Bertrand. "Tell these women who you are."

Caleb took the paper and unfolded it. There on the top were written the words that nearly sent him to the floor.

"Contract to marry?" He looked up at the maid who nodded; then he shoved the paper back at her. "You've got the wrong man."

She gave him a look that would chase off a polecat. "You the sheriff, ain't you?"

Under her scrutiny he almost cracked. Almost told the whole town they were about to pin a badge on the wrong man. Then he looked over at Miss Bertrand and couldn't say a thing.

Elmer answered for him. "Sure he's the sheriff. Tell her, Cal. We been waitin' for Cal Wilson nigh on six months. We was beginnin' t'think he'd run off with our travelin' money, so Ed went lookin' for him, and here he is." He returned the maid's scathing stare. "Who'd you think he was, one of the prisoners?"

Chapter 7

The next thing Lydia remembered was waking up in a jail cell. May dabbed a damp cloth against her forehead, and a man with red hair paced nearby.

Someone called, "She's awake."

Another said, "Fetch the bride out to meet the folks."

The bride.

It all came tumbling back. The contract to marry, the conversation with May, and her first look at her groom-to-be. Then the realization hit that she was to wed the man who plowed her down in Mrs. Sykes's kitchen.

At this reminder she groaned.

"You hit your noggin, hon?" This from May who ran her hand across the back of Lydia's head.

Mrs. Sykes stood in the door of the cell shaking her head. "To think I had both of you under my roof and I didn't know a thing."

Lydia climbed to her feet and shook off May's attentions. "Well, I didn't know, either."

Without bothering to explain, she straightened her shoulders and rose. Putting one foot in front of the other, she headed for the door and her intended—or maybe she'd just keep walking until she'd shaken off the dust of Dime Box, Arizona.

Whichever choice she made, she first had to make good her escape. With the only exit being the front door, she took a deep breath and stepped through. The claps and cheers should have stopped her, but they didn't. Rather, she walked all the way to the end of the sidewalk before she turned to see Cal Wilson staring at her.

By pausing, she was well and truly caught, for several ladies reached her and began to talk about dress fabric and wedding dates. She might have been there indefinitely had Mrs. Sykes not made her apologies to the ladies, taken her by the arm, and led her back down the sidewalk.

"There she is, folks." The red-haired man pointed to Lydia. "She's a little shy. Let's make the sheriff's intended feel welcome. Folks, welcome Lydia Bertrand, soon to be the new Mrs. Wilson."

Lydia's stomach did a flip-flop, and tears sprang to her eyes. The crowd parted to reveal the new sheriff standing by his side. Odd, but the lawman looked as miserable as Lydia felt.

Could it be that the goods he purchased had not met his expectations? Had he decided she wasn't all he hoped her to be?

Well, of all the nerve. What was wrong with her? Why, half the boys in New Orleans of marrying age had been trotted through their parlor, and not a one of them had made *that* face at her.

Why him? Why now? Eyes narrowed, Lydia strode over to the man to ask him.

Before she could take two steps, May intercepted her. "Now don't you go making a spectacle of yourself, Lydia Bertrand. You done been raised better than that."

Lydia pasted on a smile and aimed it at the lawman. "Well, of course I have, May. That's why I'm going to go over there and show my intended just how glad I am he's chosen me."

May whirled her around and stared at her hard. "And how do you intend to do that?"

"I'm just going to go over there and be polite." She shrugged. "If he's going to marry me, he needs to meet me proper, don't you think?"

May gave her a sideways look. "I didn't think you wanted to marry him."

"I don't." She upped the smile and aimed it in Sheriff Wilson's direction. "I just want *him* to *want* to marry *me*."

"That don't make no sense," May muttered. "That just don't make no sense."

She left her maid shaking her head on the sidewalk and headed for the spot where the mayor of Dime Box was introducing Cal Wilson as their new sheriff. Something gleamed in the sun as she approached. The badge, she realized.

"Would you like to do the honors, Miss Bertrand?" the mayor asked.

"I'd be delighted, Mr. Mayor."

⁓

The crowd cheered as the Bertrand woman flounced over to give the mayor her biggest smile. As she drew near, badge in hand, Caleb instinctively put his hand over his heart. From the look in her eye, she'd either stab it or steal it.

She lifted up on tiptoe, then met his gaze. For a moment she almost smiled. Then the woman looked down and went to work fastening the tin star on his shirt. Her fingers trembled, he noticed, and he couldn't help but wonder if his old charm had returned.

Then she looked into his eyes. She looked more determined than smitten. But determined to do what?

"So when's the date, Sheriff?"

He looked over at Elmer, who seemed to take great pleasure in Caleb's discomfort. Ed, however, looked as if he might come to the rescue any minute.

"Honestly, we haven't discussed a date." Miss Bertrand's smile could have lit a room.

"That's right," Caleb added as he plotted how to get himself out of this fix.

All he had to do was admit he and Cal Wilson were two different folks. That would get him out of the marriage contract. It would also set the townsfolk straight. The only trouble with the truth was that it didn't seem to fit with the answer to prayer he so clearly felt he'd received.

He'd asked the Lord to give him a second chance, and here He'd gone and let a reformed outlaw become sheriff. By speaking up now, he could very well ruin the plans the Lord had made for him.

Something in that logic chewed at his conscience, but Caleb ignored it. Instead, he smiled and shook hands and made small talk with the people he'd been entrusted to protect. He noticed the Bertrand woman was doing the same thing. She might be as pretty as a newborn calf, but he'd have to find some way of getting out of this contract.

The last thing Caleb Wilson needed right now was a wife.

Finally, the mayor stepped up and put his hand on Caleb's shoulder. "Folks, let's leave these two alone for a spell. I'm sure they've got some catchin' up to do."

A few hoots and hollers later, the people of Dime Box went back to their business, leaving Caleb to attend to his. He shook Ed's hand and stepped inside to take his place behind the big wooden desk.

Caleb and Ed had cleared the mess off the top of it, but he'd never looked to see what was inside. He did that now, starting with the top right drawer. Inside he found a layer of dust and a stack of papers. He lifted them out and set them on the desk. Topmost on the pile was a letter written on the stationery of the Wentworth Hotel in Wichita, Kansas, promising that one Cal Wilson's arrival would fall somewhere between the end of January and the middle of February.

No wonder Ed and the boys were getting impatient. He set the letter aside and, two posters down in the stack, found a familiar face staring up at him from a wanted poster: his brother Colt.

Caleb tore it in half and wadded up the pieces. He knew for a fact that Colt had done his time on this charge. He'd just missed seeing him in Huntsville.

The temptation to dwell on family pressed hard on him, and Caleb had to force himself to ignore it. He had more than enough to worry about, what with a feisty gal with marriage on her mind and a new job on the other side of the law.

He leaned back in the chair and set his boot heels on the desk. Given time, he'd find a way out of that predicament.

"A moment of your time, Sheriff." The object of his thoughts barged through the door, her maid following in hot pursuit.

"A moment?" He looked her up one side and down the other. She had her feathers ruffled for sure. "Looks like you aim to take more than that." He pushed two chairs up to the desk. "Set yourself down and speak your piece."

Both women spoke at once, leaving Caleb to shake his head and call for quiet. The maid clamped her mouth shut and handed over the paper she'd showed him earlier. Right there on the bottom line was the signature of a man named Calvin Wilson. Proof positive it couldn't be him.

He was about to say so when the Bertrand woman cleared her throat and aimed her attention in his direction. She wore yellow, an idiotic thing to notice considering the situation, but it did make her look pretty as a picture.

"Mr. Wilson," she said in her prim and proper way, "you and I have a contract. We also have a situation."

Caleb nodded. "Yes, indeed, I'd say we do."

"You got a *situation*, all right," the maid said. "The situation is you brought this gal all the way out to this place, and you are goin' to marry up with her right and proper—or I'll know the reason why."

Miss Bertrand placed her gloved hand on the maid's arm. "Let me handle this, May." She addressed Caleb. "As May said, I've traveled from New Orleans to fulfill my end of the contract, Mr. Wilson. I am interested as to whether you intend to fulfill yours."

"Well, now, just a minute here." Caleb's mind raced through the possible excuses for holding off on a wedding, coming to a stop at the most likely one. "You and I, we barely know one another, Miss Bertrand. I suspect you don't relish the thought of being married to a total stranger. Besides, we haven't exactly had a good start, have we?"

Her look gave him the impression she didn't relish the idea of being married to him at all. If he hadn't been so set on getting out of the deal himself, he'd be offended.

"This is true." She shifted positions and cast a quick glance at the maid. "But the townsfolk are calling for a wedding date, sir."

"I'm aware of that." Caleb set his boots on the desk again and tried to look as if he hadn't a care in the world. "What do you think of a summer wedding, Miss Bertrand? Say June?"

"June? Why, that's several months away." Her tone signaled displeasure, but the twinkle in her eye told him she felt otherwise.

"It is indeed," he said slowly. "But don't you think we need the Lord's blessing on this? You *are* a God-fearing woman, aren't you?"

"I am," she said. "And I think your idea is an excellent one. There's just one problem. I was not prepared for such a lengthy engagement."

He crossed his legs at the ankle. "Meaning?"

"Meaning we will be in need of a place to stay. I'm sure Mrs. Sykes won't be pleased when we have no more funds to pay for our room."

"Well, now, that is a problem. Let me ponder on it a spell." She rose, and Caleb set his feet on the ground and did the same. "I suppose I ought to come calling now that we're going to get hitched, Miss Bertrand."

She looked less than pleased at the idea. To her credit she recovered quickly. "That would be lovely, Sheriff. Please, call me Lydia."

"Lydia." He looked past her to see the maid frowning at him. "I'm Caleb."

The maid's frown deepened, but she said nothing.

"The mayor and his wife are having me to supper tonight. What say I fetch you round about six and we walk over together?"

Lydia aimed a smile in his direction. "Are you asking me to supper, Caleb?"

He hitched up a grin. "I reckon I am."

"Then you'll have to do better than that. I'm used to spending time with gentlemen."

With that she swept out of the office like the queen of England. Rather than follow, the maid leaned toward him.

"I'm on t'you, Sheriff," she said softly. "But I'm gonna speak t'the Lord afore I say another word t'anybody."

"While you're talking to Him, would you mind mentioning that I'd take any help He might want to send my way?"

She lifted a dark brow. "If'n you're gonna have anything t'do with that 'un, you're gonna need all the help He can send."

Caleb watched the swirl of yellow skirts disappear from sight and sighed. "Ma'am, I believe you're right."

Chapter 8

For some reason unknown to him, Caleb showed up at the boardinghouse at a quarter to six. Hat in hand, he had Widow Sykes announce his presence in the parlor. Courting came about as natural to him as breathing before he met the Lord. Now he seemed to be sadly lacking in the fine art of wooing a lady.

Not that he intended to woo Lydia Bertrand. Rather, he sought to pass the time until the Lord got him out of the mess he'd gotten himself into. In the meantime, it didn't seem proper to ignore the woman the whole town thought he was to marry.

He practiced his speech a couple of times while he waited. He'd tell her he was sorry they'd gotten off on the wrong foot, sorrier still he'd brought her all the way to Dime Box just to find out the wedding wasn't going to happen.

Sure, he'd said June, but after giving the matter some thought, he'd figured she would see the logic in holding off on getting hitched. Then she stepped into the room, and every word he planned scattered like dust on a stiff breeze.

This time she wore green, and it occurred to Caleb that he'd never once noticed the color of a woman's dress before today. Proof positive he had to steer clear of Lydia Bertrand.

"Mrs. Sykes said you wanted to speak to me."

"I did, actually," he said, hat in hand. "I felt like I had some apologizing to do, and now seemed as good a time as any." He shook his head. "What I mean to say is, I know you and I didn't get along right off, but I was wondering if you might consider putting that aside and accompanying me to the mayor's house for supper. I didn't ask right the first time, and for that I do apologize."

She seemed to consider his offer. "I'm not sure I have the time, Caleb. It's rather bad form for you to come waltzing in on short notice and expect me to jump at your command."

The woman certainly didn't intend to make his apology an easy one. "Yes," he said, "I do appreciate the problem here, but I believe if you'll think on it, you'll see that I did mention it earlier in the day. I just didn't use the right words."

Caleb straightened his shoulders and took a deep breath. He'd learned much about being humble over the past year, but he did have his limits.

"I can see I've made a mistake in coming here." He set his hat on his head and pressed past Lydia to head for the front door. "I'm sorry I wasted your time. Do have a good evening, Lydia."

He hadn't even reached the street before the Bertrand woman caught up with him. "My, but you walk fast, Caleb."

"I thought. . ." He looked down and saw all the fire had gone from her expression. "My mistake, Lydia. I assumed you'd be dining with the Widow Sykes tonight."

"It was an option," she said as she gathered her shawl about her shoulders. They walked in silence for a bit; then she spoke up again. "Apology accepted," she said softly. "Would you accept mine, as well?"

Caleb nodded and kept walking. The less they talked, the more he liked it.

With the mayor's house in view, Caleb stopped short and reached for Lydia's hand. "What say we start over, you and me? I mean, long as folks think we're a pair, we might as well be civil."

"About that." Lydia studied the ground for a minute, then swung her attention up to meet his stare. "I should have said something sooner, but if I had my way, I'd be back home in New Orleans. I really don't want to marry you, Sheriff."

"You don't?" Caleb's shock rendered further words impossible for a full minute, maybe longer. When he recovered, he shook his head. "If you're telling me the truth, you're the first woman I've ever met who wasn't looking to snag a husband."

Her giggle surprised him. "I suppose that makes me one of a kind then, doesn't it?"

The mayor's wife called Lydia's name, and he watched her wave and pick up her pace in response. Caleb caught up with Lydia and grasped her wrist, halting her progress.

"Wait a minute," he said. "You really *don't* want to marry me?"

Lydia's smile lit her face. "Not in the least."

—⁓—

Dinner seemed to last forever. Making small talk with Amanda Thompson didn't hold a candle to besting Caleb in a discussion about weddings. While Amanda ladled gravy over the roast, Lydia recalled the entire conversation in the street. Every time she thought about telling the sheriff she had no interest in marrying him, she smiled.

"Penny for your thoughts, Miss Bertrand," the mayor said.

"I'm sure she's planning our wedding." Caleb leaned over to squeeze Lydia's hand. "Her face just lights up when she's thinking about getting hitched."

Lydia kicked Caleb under the table, then she watched with satisfaction as he winced then propped his smile back into place. "Oh, yes," she said to the mayor as she extricated her fingers from Caleb's grasp. "I do so love to think of my Caleb. He's such a fine catch, don't you think, Amanda?"

The poor woman seemed at a loss for words. The mayor, however, offered a quick blessing over the food, then asked for the corn bread to be passed in his direction.

"So when is that wedding, Caleb?" the mayor asked.

Caleb stabbed his fork into a slab of beef and unloaded it onto his plate. "Lydia and I were just talking about that today. Why don't you tell them, dear?"

She gave Caleb a smile, then turned to face Mr. Thompson. "Caleb's a gentleman, you know, and so protective of me." She patted Caleb's hand. "He suggested a June wedding to give me time to adjust to living here in your lovely community."

"June?" The mayor shook his head. "That's thinkin' positive. We usually don't get a parson in here till late summer."

Lydia nearly dropped her fork. "You mean you don't have a preacher in town who can marry us? What about the fellow who's been doing Sunday services?"

"Elmer Winslow?" The mayor cut a swipe through the air with his hand. "He's nothin' but a farmer from north of here. He offered to fill in until we got a full-time preacher. He's right good at carrying on a Sunday service or speaking at funerals, but he don't have no marryin' abilities."

Relief shot through Lydia. Perhaps there was a way out of this mess after all. "And you say you expect a preacher in July?"

"Or August," Amanda said. "That's when the circuit riders come through. 'Course, it could be sooner."

Caleb looked in her direction and smiled. "Well, dear, looks like you'll have to wait longer than you wanted to get hitched."

"Oh, I don't know," she said in her sweetest voice. "For you I'd wait forever." She leaned close to Caleb. "Actually, forever sounds like just the right amount of time to wait."

The evening stretched on until Lydia thought she'd never see the end of it. After supper the men headed out onto the porch to talk politics while Lydia followed Amanda into the kitchen to help with the cleanup.

"You didn't wash many dishes back in New Orleans, did you, Lydia?" Amanda asked.

"Truthfully I didn't." She dabbed at the plate in her hand with the towel. "How could you tell?"

Amanda took the plate from her and finished the task, setting it on the drain board. She turned to Lydia and removed her apron. "If I'm being nosey, you just go ahead and tell me."

Lydia folded her apron and set it atop Amanda's. "Of course."

She leaned against the edge of the cabinet and dried her hands, then looked up sharply. "I was a mail-order bride, too." She held up her hand. "Ed and I haven't shared that fact with anyone in Dime Box, so I'd appreciate it if you'd keep this to yourself."

"Of course."

Amanda led her to a chair by the fire, then settled in the rocker beside her. "My first husband passed on and left me with my son to raise. Ed here is a fine man, and he never held it against me when his mail-order bride showed up with a mail-order baby." She chuckled at the joke, then grew serious. "I'm telling you this because I want you to understand that God engineered the circumstances. Remember He does that. Often He does it in spite of us."

"Yes, I'm reminded of that frequently," Lydia said.

Amanda nodded. "Please know that I understand you're afraid, and you have every right to feel that way. You're far from home without a mama or papa to advise you, and now you're about to gain a husband."

Tears clouded Lydia's eyes, but she refused to allow them to fall. Rather, she took a deep breath and let it out slowly.

"Cal Wilson's a fine man," Amanda said. "My Ed says he comes highly recommended, and after working beside him nigh onto a week getting that jailhouse back in shape, he claims Cal's a hard worker, too."

Lydia shifted positions, suddenly uncomfortable. "I wouldn't know."

"I've seen him in worship, Lydia. That man loves the Lord. It's plain on his face when he's singing the hymns."

"You make him sound like a saint, Amanda."

"Oh, honey, none of us are saints." Amanda set the towel across the clean dishes. "Remember that when you go judging the man the Lord gives you."

"But I'm not judging," she protested. "It's just that I don't want to be married to a man who. . ." Lydia found she had no words to complete the sentence. She hung her head. "Yes, I suppose I am judging him. It's just that every time we're together something happens to irritate me." She sighed. "I can't explain it."

Amanda patted Lydia's shoulder and smiled. "There's a fine line between irritating and interesting."

"Are we being spoken of, wife?" Ed Thompson rounded the corner and embraced his wife, who merely grinned. "I was tellin' your intended that we're lookin' at buildin' a new Sunday go-to-meetin' place. One of our parishioners donated her property before she left to go back East. Now all we have to do is figure out how to turn it into a proper place of worship."

"Anything would be better than the little place we use now. Why, it's so small we barely have room to squeeze everyone in. But you know all about that, don't you, Cal?"

"I do indeed, ma'am." From where she stood, Lydia could feel the sheriff staring. She braved a glance and saw Caleb leaning against the doorpost, hands crossed over his chest. His grin took her by surprise.

"I'm going to send a bowl of cobbler to your landlady, Lydia. I promised I'd send some next time I made it."

While Amanda spooned dessert into a bowl, Lydia noticed Ed studying Caleb. She watched the mayor for a moment before turning her attention to the sheriff. To her surprise, he walked over and placed his hand atop hers. Lydia swiftly removed her fingers from his grasp and reached for the cobbler.

"It's been a real pleasure," Caleb said to their hosts before taking Lydia's elbow. "Once Lydia and I set up housekeeping, you're going to have to teach her how to make that delicious roast, Mrs. Thompson."

Chapter 9

I want a recipe for roast?" Lydia walked two steps ahead of the sheriff, stalking off her irritation. "Do you think I can't make a roast?"

Caleb shrugged, a grin forming. "Can you?"

She made her way around a puddle, then turned to head for the boardinghouse. "That's beside the point."

He came up beside Lydia, then stepped in front of her. "What *is* the point, Lydia?"

Lydia stopped short then tried to walk around him. The persistent sheriff caught her elbow and whirled her around. This time when she looked into his eyes, she saw no hint of teasing.

"That contract—is it real?" He blinked hard. "What I mean is, did you actually come all this way to marry me?"

Her heart thumped against her chest. "You're not funny, Caleb. Not at all."

The moonlight cut a slice across his face. "I wasn't trying to be."

"You're the one who sent for me," she managed. "I never asked to be here."

Caleb's expression softened. "Care to explain?"

"No." She turned to go, then thought better of it. What did it matter if she told him?

"What's your story, Lydia? I'm not going to ask again."

"Miss Lydia, that you, chile?"

She glanced over her shoulder to see May sitting on the porch. "Yes, it's me. I'll be right in."

"See that you do. You ain't hitched t'this man yet, and your mama would have my hide if'n something were to happen."

"I was just leaving." Caleb turned his attention to Lydia. "You let me know when you're ready to finish this conversation."

———

As it turned out, the next day Caleb was too busy to finish any conversations. His first full day as sheriff was spent helping Ed Thompson and Elmer Wiggins fetch a wagonload of supplies from Millsville. The lengthy trip gave them plenty of time for conversation, much of which Caleb only listened to.

Occasionally Ed would ask a question of him or make a comment that required an answer, but most times Caleb drove the wagon and let the older men do their jawin'. Round about an hour from Dime Box on the return trip, Elmer fell silent.

Caleb glanced over his shoulder to see the red-haired man sound asleep leaning against the pile of supplies.

"Mind if I join you, son?" Ed asked as he climbed up on the seat beside Caleb. "I'm of a mind to give some advice. You of a mind t'listen?"

"I suppose," Caleb said.

Ed stretched his legs out in front of him and leaned back against the seat. "I'm wonderin' something, Sheriff Wilson."

A dry wind blew dust across Caleb's face, and he lifted his bandanna to cover his mouth and nose. "What's that?"

"I'm wonderin' what your intentions are toward Miss Bertrand."

Caleb gave Ed a sideways look. "What set you to wondering about that?"

The older man shrugged. "You didn't fool me," he said slowly. "I know you and that girl are complete strangers." He clapped a hand on Caleb's shoulder. "Oh, don't worry. Amanda and me are the only ones who've figured it out."

"Figured what out?"

"Figured out you mail-ordered your bride from back East." He shook his head. "Now there's nothin' to be ashamed of. Why, that's how I got my Amanda."

"It is?"

He nodded. "They's some fine women who start married life as a stranger to their husbands." Ed paused. "And they's some husbands who don't cotton to gettin' hitched to the gal they paid for. I reckon they figure they can do better elsewhere, but I say you stay with what God brings ya."

"What are you trying to tell me, Ed?"

"If I ain't makin' myself clear, then I don't figure I ought t'keep talkin'." He crossed his arms over his chest and got comfortable. "Wake me up when we reach town, would ya?"

"Yes, sir, I will." He chuckled. "And, Ed?"

He lowered his hat, then lifted one eyelid to regard Caleb with a sleepy gaze. "Yep?"

"You're making yourself crystal clear." He tightened his grip on the reins. "And thanks for saying what I needed to hear."

"Question is, what're you gonna do about it?"

"I don't rightly know."

He crossed his legs at the ankles. "Well, maybe I ain't done with my advice. Maybe you got some wooin' t'do with your bride-to-be."

Caleb shook his head. "Ed, I don't even know if I want her to be my bride. She's the most exasperating woman I've ever had the displeasure to know."

"Well, that settles it then." Ed straightened up and set his hat back on his head. "Marry her. That's love if I ever heard it."

"I don't think you were listening, Ed. That woman drives me to distraction."

Ed tipped his hat back down over his eyes. "I don't think you were listening to me, Caleb. If a woman drives you to distraction, it's a sure sign the Lord must've put her in your life. I don't know why that is, but that's how I've seen it work out."

Caleb pondered on Ed's words for four days straight. Rather than face Lydia directly, he took his meals at the office or out on the work site. Each time he saw her, he pretended he hadn't. He felt pretty sure she did the same.

Every time one of Dime Box's citizens addressed him as Sheriff Wilson, he felt a little more uneasy. He jumped whenever someone called his name, because he figured someone had found him out.

Each night he pestered the Lord about his predicament. What he got back scared him.

God wanted him to have a new start, but Caleb had taken the timing into his own hands. Clean hands didn't come from a life built on lies.

Caleb chewed on Ed Thompson's advice almost as hard as his situation with the sheriff's office. Much as he hated to admit it, Ed's words mostly rang true.

The only thing he couldn't figure was whether Lydia had been sent by the Lord or had become his punishment for not telling the truth. In either case, he had a woman on his mind and a serious danger to his heart. If he kept the truth to himself, he'd get to keep her without a doubt. If he told the truth, she might get away.

Trouble was, Caleb didn't know which way he preferred things to go. He decided to do as Ed said and take to wooing his bride-to-be. That way, if the Lord released him from his obligations, at least he could part ways with Lydia knowing he'd done his best.

The next evening, Caleb arrived at the boardinghouse with a handful of penny candy he'd picked up in Millville. He'd thought to keep the sweets in his desk and savor one or two when he felt the urge. Instead, he'd gone against good sense and made a present of them.

"I hope you like them," he'd planned to say when he saw her. "I brought them from Millville," he might add.

But when she swept into the parlor smelling like flowers and wearing a dress that made her look fresher than springtime, he lost all ability to be clever. He thrust the handkerchief he'd carried them in toward her, then took a step backward.

"For me?"

He nodded.

"Thank you."

Again he nodded.

Lydia popped a sour into her mouth, then made a face. A puckering face. At that moment Caleb was horrified to realize he wanted to kiss her square on her puckered lips.

Chapter 10

Lydia offered Caleb a piece of candy, but he couldn't look at anything except those pretty puckered lips.

"No, thank you," he finally managed. "In fact, I can't stay. I just thought you might like a sweet."

"Thank you."

She took his hand to shake it, but he brought her fingers to his lips instead. An awkward moment passed between them until Caleb released his grasp.

She walked to the window and lifted the lace curtains. "A lovely evening for a stroll, don't you think?"

Caleb rocked back on his heels. "Stroll?"

"Do I need to spell it out? I'm going for a walk, and I'd like you to accompany me." She paused to let the curtain fall back into place, then turned to face Caleb. "That is, if you'd like to. I'm quite capable of going out alone." Without waiting for his answer, Lydia reached for her shawl and wrapped it around her shoulders.

"Hold on there, darlin'." Caleb grabbed his hat and set it back on his head. "You don't have to be in such a hurry."

"I do if I don't want to lose my nerve."

"Your nerve?" The screen door slammed behind him, and Caleb hurried to catch up. "What're you talking about?"

She pointed to the garden, the same place where he'd seen her crying what seemed ages ago. "I'll be honest. I lured you out here to tell you my story without fear of being overheard."

Caleb nodded. "I appreciate that you trust me enough to share it."

Lydia stopped short and looked up into his eyes. "It's not you I trust. It's God." She swallowed hard. "I need to tell you about me, Caleb. About why I'm here in Dime Box."

He gave her a sideways look. "All right. Why's that?"

She took a deep breath and prayed the right words would come. "I'm an only child and quite a disappointment to my parents. You see, I—"

"Who's out there?"

Lydia saw Mrs. Sykes standing at the garden wall in her dressing gown. "It's me—Lydia. I'm with the sheriff."

Mrs. Sykes waved and disappeared inside the rooming house. Lydia stepped away from the wall, and Caleb followed. Somewhere between the garden and the street Caleb slipped his hand around hers.

She walked beside him in silence, allowing Caleb to lead the way. Before long they were strolling down the sidewalk toward the sheriff's office.

"We can keep walking or talk in here," he said.

Lydia peered inside the office, then nodded. "Here's fine."

Caleb bustled around lighting lamps and putting on a pot of coffee while Lydia watched. Before she knew it, he sat across the desk from her with a pair of mugs in hand. He set one in front of her, then leaned back in his chair.

The time had come. Lydia watched the steam rise from the black coffee, then began. "As I said, I'm an only child." She lifted her gaze to meet Caleb's stare. "I'm sure my father expected more from his daughter. My mama, well, I know she did."

To his credit, Caleb remained silent.

"Mama was from a distinguished family. Old money, I guess you could say. Papa, well, he is a preacher. He loves the Lord and my mama." She paused to take a sip of the best coffee she'd tasted since leaving New Orleans. "He loves me, too, but I'm afraid I disappoint him regularly."

Caleb looked concerned. "How so?"

"Silly things to you, I suppose, but to Mama my antics have been an embarrassment."

"Antics?"

Lydia felt the heat rise in her cheeks. "Yes, you see I've been in boarding schools since I was ten. Mama felt it would be good for me to broaden my experiences, but all I wanted was to go home." She sighed. "I soon learned that fine line between misbehaving and things that could get me sent home."

Caleb leaned forward. "Like?"

She shrugged. "Like dipping my slippers in the punch bowl or dancing a jig in the town fountain." Before he could speak, she held up her hand to silence him. "I was modest about it, I promise."

His grin disappeared. "So how did you end up in Dime Box?"

"Well, actually, this was Mama's doing. With Papa's approval." She blinked back tears. "She—or rather, they—felt it in my best interest to send me away to find a husband."

"I see." He steepled his hands and stared hard into her eyes. "And how do you feel about this?"

Lydia let out the breath she'd been holding. "I feel like God must've sent me to marry Cal Wilson, so that's what I am supposed to do."

Caleb rose abruptly and set his mug on the desk. He walked around to her and reached for her hand. Rising, Lydia found herself dangerously near to the sheriff.

"Is that what you want to do, Lydia?"

She looked up into eyes that glittered with emotion. They were gray, she noticed, the color of the New Orleans sky just before a storm.

Before she could answer, before she could manage to put together a thought as to how she felt, Caleb Wilson kissed her. Lydia stepped back, touching her lips.

No man had ever been so bold with her. No kiss had ever been so welcome. With all her heart, Lydia knew God had led her to this place, to this man. Fear slipped away, and peace took its place.

"This changes everything." Had she spoken or merely thought this?

"Yes, it does." Caleb stepped back and leaned against the desk. "I'm not who you think I am, Lydia. I believe it's time you heard my story. You see, I'm not Sheriff Cal Wilson. I'm Caleb Wilson, outlaw. Well, reformed outlaw, that is."

"This sounds like quite a story. Do you mind if I sit down?"

Lydia settled back on the chair while Caleb paced the room and told her of his life as part of the Wilson gang. When he finished, he had his back to her and his attention focused on the wall of wanted posters.

"I know personally more than half the men on this wall." He turned to face her. "But I know one man who makes all this not matter anymore. See, I found Jesus behind the prison walls. I was locked up, but He set me free. I wanted to do something good for Him, but I haven't gone about it the right way. I need to go talk to Ed and make this right."

"Would you like me to come with you?"

Caleb shook his head. "I need to do this alone."

Chapter 11

Caleb stole another kiss before he left Lydia at the boardinghouse. Any other time he would have whistled his way home, but tonight he felt like he was walking in lead boots. He knocked on Ed's door and prayed he would be able to handle whatever punishment he got after he spilled his story.

Amanda Thompson let him in, then called for her husband. She left them in the kitchen with a plate of cobbler and two glasses of milk.

Ed shoveled a healthy amount of dessert onto his plate, then regarded Caleb with a frown. "You look like you're heading for the gallows, Cal. What's the problem?"

"In a way I might be." Caleb refused Ed's offer of cobbler. "I'm not who you think I am, Ed."

"I wouldn't be so sure about that, but go on and tell me about it."

Caleb started at the beginning. When he finished his tale, exhausted after repeating it for the second time in one night, he sat back and waited for Ed to react.

To Caleb's surprise, the man continued to eat his cobbler.

"Did you hear me, Ed? I'm Caleb Wilson. I'm an outlaw, or rather I was until Jesus got hold of me."

Ed set his spoon down and reached for the milk. After taking a healthy swig, he set the glass on the table. "I reckon we all got a story, Caleb. Yours, well, I'll grant you it's not like most." He leaned forward and rested his elbows on the table. "I 'preciate you comin' clean with me. Now, I wonder if you're gonna be at the church house tomorrow, because it looks as if we're gonna need a few extra hands. We're shorin' up the ceiling, and we're gonna have our hands full with keeping it from fallin' in around our heads before we build the new one."

Caleb shook his head. "I don't believe you heard me. I'm a criminal. An outlaw. It just happens my name is similar to the man you were expecting. Doesn't that mean anything to you?"

" 'Course it does." Ed met Caleb's gaze. "It means the Lord works in mysterious ways. But then we both knew that."

He pushed back from the table and stood. "I need to come clean with this, Ed. I've got to admit to the folks of Dime Box that I'm not the man you all were expecting."

Ed rose and straightened his lapels. "You know Elmer Wiggins?"

"I do."

"You respect him, do you?"

Caleb scratched his head. "Yes, I heard him preach last Sunday, and he did a good job. I'd say he's a fine man."

"No, he's a reformed horse thief. Ben Mulligan over t'the general store? He used t'rob stages until he got a good shot of the Holy Ghost." Ed shrugged. "I could tell you stories that would curl your hair. The Widow Sykes, well, suffice it t'say she can pick a fine lock if she still had a mind to. There's a reason she don't live in Savannah anymore. And Ma, the gal who owns the restaurant?"

He nodded. "Now she's a rough-looking character."

Ed chuckled. "And yet she gives just about every penny she makes to the orphanage back in Dallas where she grew up. Nobody in town but me knows this, so I'd appreciate you keepin' it quiet. She brings me the money every month and has me send it 'cause she don't want the man at the bank t'know she's the one makin' the donations."

Caleb hung his head. Of all the things he'd thought about Ma, picturing her like this was not one of them. "I guess you never know about people."

Ed clamped his hand tight on Caleb's shoulder. "No, you don't. Folks don't come to Dime Box, Arizona, for the good weather and fine food. They come, most of 'em anyway, t'forget who they were and concentrate on bein' who they ought to be. Ever wonder why there ain't hardly no crime?"

"I guess I hadn't."

"Well, I have a theory on that. I figure the Lord's got His hand on this place. I don't know for sure, but I'd like t'think maybe He created Dime Box as a place where sinners are forgiven."

Ed's son burst into the room nearly out of breath. "Pa, there's a coach a-comin'."

"A coach?" He looked up at the clock. "It's a quarter of nine. You sure it's a coach?"

"Sure as can be," he said.

Ed nodded. "Looks like I've got work t'do down at the livery. Son, you head on down there and light the lamps." He waited until his son had gone, then thrust his hand in Caleb's direction. "I 'preciate you comin' clean, son, but I have to confess I figured out who you were right off."

Caleb shook his head. "You knew who I was from the beginning?"

"Sure," Ed said. "You told me."

"I did?"

Ed made his way to the door as the sound of a team of horses drew near. "I called you Cal Wilson, and you corrected me right off. Did that a couple of times. So you never did deceive me, boy. Whilst I was jawin' with you that day, I felt the Lord tell me you were the one we'd been waitin' for. Now I've got work to do. I believe you need to go home and study on what I told you."

Caleb walked out with Ed and watched as a stage halted outside the livery. The driver jumped down to open the door. Two men spilled out into the semidarkness.

"Welcome to Dime Box," Ed said. "They's rooms at the boardinghouse across the street and a good meal to be had there, too. Where you all comin' from?"

As Ed continued his mostly one-sided discussion with the weary travelers, Caleb walked away with his heart light and his conscience clean. Before he did anything else, he went straight to the garden beside the boardinghouse and picked up a small rock. He lobbed it against the darkened window of Lydia's room, then waited for her.

"Who done been throwin' rocks?" The maid appeared at the window. "It's you. What you want?"

"I'd like to speak to Lydia."

"What you want with Miss Lydia?"

"That's enough, May." Lydia appeared at the window. Her hair hung loose, and she appeared to have been sleeping. "I'm here."

"I need to talk to you. Can you come downstairs?"

She leaned forward as she began braiding her hair. "To the garden? Now?"

"No, to the parlor. I'll wait on the porch." Without allowing her to say no, he made his escape from the garden.

He watched the activity at the livery until Lydia opened the door. "This is highly irregular," he heard the Widow Sykes call from somewhere upstairs. "So speak your piece and go on home so decent folk can get their sleep."

Decent folk. Caleb swallowed hard. Indeed, tonight he felt as if he could be counted among the decent folk. "Yes'm," he called back. "I thank you for allowing the interruption."

"Anything for a man in love."

A man in love? Yes, that just might fit him.

He followed Lydia into the parlor. While she chose to sit, he knew he couldn't. "I'll stand, thank you."

"So how did Mr. Thompson take the news?"

Caleb began pacing. "He said he knew all along who I was. Said it was the Lord's will I showed up when I did. He told me I was meant to be here." He stopped to look down at Lydia. "What do you think about that? Or, I guess the better question is, what do you think about me? Will you still have anything to do with me now that you know about me?"

Lydia rose to fall into Caleb's embrace. "Don't be silly. Of course I will."

Caleb held her tight. She was a pretty thing, no bigger than a minute, but with a voice as smooth as silk and a pair of big brown eyes that could cause a man to forget his troubles.

And she was all his.

Or she could be soon as he asked right and proper.

Caleb let her go and dropped to his knee, taking her hand in his. "Lydia Bertrand, I'd be right proud to wake up to your biscuits every morning for the rest of my life. Will you do me the honor of—?"

"Lydia? Oh, sweetheart, is that really you?"

His intended let go of his hand and sprinted past him as if he hadn't said a word. Caleb scrambled to his feet and watched as Lydia fell into another man's embrace.

"Hold on here," Caleb said. "Who is this man?"

The fellow stared back at him with a surprised look. "I might say the same thing. Who are you?"

"The name's Wilson," Caleb said. "I'm the new sheriff 'round these parts."

"You're a liar, sir. I just rode into town with Sheriff Wilson. He's at the livery at this very moment."

Chapter 12

Lydia slipped from the man's embrace to reach for Caleb's hand. "Caleb, I'd like you to meet my papa, Reverend Augustus Bertrand." She turned to the older man. "Papa, this is Caleb Wilson, and I don't care who you rode in with—*he's* the sheriff of Dime Box. He's also going to be my husband."

If he weren't in such a sudden fix with her papa at that moment, Caleb would have kissed her for sure. Instead, he tried to think of a way to get out of this mess. He had no doubt the older man had ridden in with Cal Wilson. It would be about right to have the real sheriff finally show up when he'd made his peace with keeping the job.

Caleb felt her squeeze his hand, and he squeezed back before offering his palm to Reverend Bertrand. "Pleased to make your acquaintance, sir. I assure you I am Caleb Wilson."

"He is who he says he is, and I'm here to vouch for him." Ed Thompson walked into the parlor and shook hands with the pastor. "He's a fine, God-fearin' man who's been helpin' with the church when he isn't busy keepin' the peace." He turned his attention to Caleb. "I'd like you to meet someone, Caleb. This here's Cal Wilson."

A portly fellow tipped his hat at Caleb. "I hear tell you took my job."

"I suppose I did."

The fellow reached over to shake Caleb's hand. "I'd just like to thank you."

He shook his head. "You want to what?"

"You see, I was headed this way to take the job when I come across the loveliest gal a man ever set eyes on. Suffice it to say, I made the gal my wife in short order, which left me with two problems: the job and the woman I'd sent for from New Orleans."

The pastor gestured toward Lydia. "That would be my daughter, Lydia."

Lydia smiled in his direction. "Pleased to make your acquaintance."

"Likewise, I'm sure." He turned to Caleb. "I'm not here to take your job, but I do need to set some things to rights." He looked at Ed. "First off, I need to repay you for the money you wired, Mr. Thompson. The whole hundred dollars is in there. You count it and be sure." He handed the mayor a thick envelope. "And then there's the matter of my betrothed."

He took a step toward Lydia. "My dear, you are lovely. I deeply regret any trouble

I've caused by sending for you and then failing to be a gentleman and fulfill my end of the contract."

"Actually, I'm grateful for how things turned out." Lydia looked past him to where Caleb stood. When she smiled, his heart nearly turned over. "At least I think I am. Caleb was in the middle of an important question earlier, and he never did finish asking it."

"Reverend Bertrand, I'd like to do this right and proper. Would you do me the honor of allowing me to marry up with your daughter? I'll see she never wants for a thing as long as I draw a breath."

"Is this what you want, daughter?"

When Lydia nodded, Caleb dropped to his knee again. "Will you marry me, Lydia Bertrand, and not in June but as soon as your papa's willing to perform the ceremony?"

Lydia looked down at the man who'd stolen her heart and smiled. Tears began to fall, and she didn't care who saw them.

"I'd be honored to become your wife."

Caleb rose to embrace her, then kissed her quickly before shaking hands with her father. Only one thing kept the moment from being perfect.

"Papa, where's Mama?"

Her father smiled. "She's out in the coach. She was afraid to come in until I checked things out. For some reason she thought you might be a bit miffed at her. It was her idea we make this trip."

"It was?" A thought occurred to her. "Papa, were you offered the position in New York?"

He nodded. "I was, but I turned it down."

"You did?"

Papa smiled. "I had a better offer, but I'll let your mother tell you about it."

He stepped out and returned with Mama, who cried and professed love and apologies all in the same breath. "There's nothing to forgive, Mama," Lydia said. "Meet Caleb Wilson, the man I intend to marry."

Her handsome husband-to-be charmed Mama in no time flat. She knew Mama approved when she looked over toward Lydia and nodded.

Mrs. Sykes called from the kitchen that coffee and a hot meal awaited the travelers. The portly former sheriff headed off, but Mama and Papa lingered behind.

"So what's this about a new assignment?" Lydia asked.

Mama smiled. "Yes, your father has taken a prestigious assignment with an up-and-coming church. I'm so very proud. He will be the first pastor to preach in their new building."

Lydia turned to her father. "Where is it?"

"Right here in Dime Box, dear. Mr. Thompson was very kind to allow me to break the news. You see, Lydia, I've been plotting this ever since I returned from New York. Rather, your mother has been. Isn't that right, dear?"

Mama kissed Papa, then nodded.

Caleb shook Papa's hand. "Welcome to Dime Box, sir." He gathered Lydia into an embrace, then kissed the top of her head. "I know from experience that when you're where the Lord wants you to be, there's not a better feeling."

A GAMBLE ON LOVE

by Tamela Hancock Murray

Dedication

*A father to the fatherless, a defender of widows,
is God in his holy dwelling.*
PSALM 68:5 NIV

Chapter 1

Denmark, Texas—Summer 1882

A nother round for the boys, Pearl." Balancing his chair on its back legs, a sober Benjamin Wilson kept his facial expression unreadable and studied the playing cards he held.

"I already knew what you were thinking, darlin'." With an oval-shaped fingernail, Pearl tapped the half-empty bottle. She batted her eyelashes and swayed her hips in Benjamin's direction, motions that always left him wishing he could be alone with her instead of sitting at a card table surrounded by cowpokes, whiskey, and tobacco smoke.

Benjamin winked at her. Though Pearl said she loved him, she spurned his advances beyond an occasional kiss. But at the moment, Pearl winked back at him as she tipped the bottle toward the dry glass of a young self-proclaimed cattle rustler, a man they knew only by the name of Owen.

"No more for me." Owen looked up at Pearl and placed his flat hand over the top of his glass. "Or cards, either. I'll hold 'em." He pulled on his mustache.

"Are you sure you don't want another round, Owen?" Pearl tilted the bottle, hovering it over the empty glass. "There's plenty."

Benjamin didn't take his gaze off the cards. "Plenty" was a code word. His hand was better than Owen's. With seventeen dollars on the table, Benjamin didn't want to lose this round. Pearl lived up to her name, all right. She was a jewel.

Another habitual card player, Cyrus, threw his cards on the table. "I'm out."

Benjamin held back a smile. *If I can just hold on, I'll get a good take.*

He caught Sadie studying him from her perch on a settee near the front door. No doubt her silent observations went something along the lines of how foolish his companions were to fall for his tricks—again. Blue-eyed and baby-faced, with dark blond stubble that matched longish blond hair, Benjamin knew his innocent-looking demeanor misled many players into thinking they could beat him at the card games he had long since mastered.

Pearl's coded talk interrupted his musings. "There's plenty more here for you, too, W.C."

With a nod, W.C., a man whose wealth derived itself from suspicious origins, accepted the drink. "I'll raise you." He tossed some coins in the pot.

Since W.C.'s hand also lacked the cards to win, Benjamin kept the game going. "I'll see you and raise you."

A look from Pearl told him he'd done the right thing—according to the rules of a cheating gambler. But in the world beyond Sadie's, Benjamin was doing wrong, according to what they said at church. That's why he seldom attended worship.

If the preacher had his way, he'd take away whiskey, cards, and tobacco and even shut down Sadie's business. While whiskey and tobacco didn't impress Benjamin, he realized those threats didn't touch his penchant for cheating. But he let the boys win once in a while so they had their fun. Just often enough so the local gamblers and out-of-towners passing through wouldn't catch on to Benjamin's guile. He knew he should feel guilty, but he couldn't. He'd been cheated in life when his brothers dumped him off at Sadie's at the age of six. Why shouldn't he be rewarded now?

Benjamin had begged to go along with his older outlaw brothers, but they would have none of it. The last remembrance he harbored was watching them ride out of town. Only Reuben looked back at him. Having been thrust unceremoniously into manhood, he never whimpered or complained after that, but the hole his brothers left in his heart had never healed. He tried to fix the hurt by gambling, but no amount of money soothed his wounds.

At least on this night he'd get a temporary lift from winning. According to Pearl's signals, Benjamin had the best hand at the table. He held out until the call, showed his hand, and watched as his gaming companions threw down their cards in defeat, snorting and frowning.

"I'm gonna be in a right nice fix with my wife tonight. That was her egg money." Luke, a young farmer with a wild streak, rose from his seat.

Benjamin resisted the urge to sympathize. No one had forced Luke to join the game. Every man who played knew the chances of losing were greater than those of winning. As for Luke, well, he'd spent over three quarters of his wife's egg money on whiskey before he even sat down at the table.

"You know," W.C. said with a menacing tone that gave Benjamin pause, "you seem to have a powerful lot of good luck at cards."

"His luck will run out soon. I'll be here next week to win my money back." Wagging his finger, Owen seemed more cheerful, his mood no doubt brought on by one shot too many of libations.

"Sure, we'll play next week. I'm not that hard to find." Benjamin looked around, but he didn't see Pearl. Wisely, she had disappeared from view. He smiled to himself. Pearl wasn't that hard to find, either.

—⁂—

Pearl drew two silk frocks from the narrow oak wardrobe occupying the small room she had called home for the past year. Colorful dresses, fashioned to flatter, were part of the allure that first brought her to Denmark, Texas. But fancy clothes couldn't compensate for disappointment. Life at Sadie's hadn't been glamorous or exciting, as she imagined when she first left Pa's ranch in a misguided attempt to earn easy money. Why she had listened to grand promises from the loose girls back home, she never knew. Their advice had proven dismally wrong.

Pearl should have known earning money was never easy, but back then she wanted to try. Pa had died and, with him, Ma's dreams of making the ranch go. Most of the livestock were sold off, and only the garden crop, one cow, two pigs, and some chickens remained. Pearl's fantasies were grander. She wanted to make the ranch a going concern. Not only that, but she dreamed of sending money to her favorite sister, a young widow with five small children, living in Abilene. Both efforts required money.

She thought back to her entrance at Sadie's only a few short months before. When Pearl eyed Benjamin, she thought herself fortunate. But not all the men were like gentle and handsome Benjamin, and on that first evening there, she hadn't been talking to one of the cowpokes ten minutes when she realized what she had done. She ran upstairs to the shelter of her room, crying. Sadie demanded that Pearl pack her bags and leave. But when Benjamin offered her a chance to help him win at cards, she took it. She knew cheating was wrong, but the alternatives—including returning home in defeat—seemed worse.

Returning to the present moment, she remembered the letter she had tucked away in a little box where she kept correspondence from home. In the box was a missive from her sister Rachel letting her know that Ma needed Pearl, and so she had to go back to the ranch. Pearl was ready to return. If only she didn't have to leave Benjamin.

A tear dropped down her cheek. She let it flow.

<hr />

Benjamin found Pearl in her room. Little red veins appeared in the whites of her brown eyes, and the lids were red, too. Her skin, though still creamy, looked splotchy. He'd caught her crying before and surmised she was thinking about her home. At least, that's what she always told him when sadness overcame her.

She looked up from folding a dress and gasped. "Benjamin! What are you doing, sneaking up on a body like that?" When she looked away from him and resumed folding, he understood she wanted him to ignore her saddened state.

Leaning against the door frame, he dressed his face in its best smile. "Gettin' ready to go to a party later?"

She shook her head but didn't look at him.

After ascertaining no one would overhear them, he approached Pearl. "You must be plannin' on something important. You haven't even asked me how much the take was." He kept his voice low in volume.

That got her attention. She regarded him. "How much?"

"Here's your share for the week." He handed her twenty dollars.

"Not bad." She inspected the bills and then hid them in her bodice. "Now you wouldn't cheat me, would you, Benjamin?"

"Never. Not you." He smiled as if he meant it, and he did. He and Pearl always joked about how they would cheat gamblers, but never each other. Stroking her cheek, he noticed her gardenia perfume. "And even if I did, you could forgive me, couldn't you?"

"Maybe." She smiled. "But you better not try."

He laughed and stepped back. "You'd better not try any fast maneuvers on me, either. Even though I could forgive you anything."

"Could you really?" She cocked her head.

"Yes. I do believe I could."

"Maybe you better watch what you say," she advised.

"Oh? How come?"

"Because you won't like what I'm about to tell you." Her coy manner evaporated as she took in a breath and let it out. "Today was my last with Sadie, and with you. I'm leaving tonight."

"What? What do you mean, leaving?" Anger overtook shock. "You can't do that to me."

Pearl flinched and covered her face.

"Now you know I would never haul off and hit you, Pearl. But I tell you, you can't do that. Don't you see what you're losing? We have the perfect business. Why would you want to leave?"

"It's my ma. She's sick. Real sick." Pearl cried anew.

His heart softened, and he took her into his arms. As soon as he did, her sobbing increased, tears wetting his shirt. "I'm sorry. I didn't realize. But you know what? I'll wait for you to come back. Why, I'll even take a vacation, a little break. Maybe I can visit Reuben's family in Wyoming. How does that sound?"

"I—I don't want you to wait for me. You don't need to worry. Plenty of other women would be glad to take my place." He could tell by her anxious expression the suggestion pained her.

"But I don't want anyone else to work with me. We're a team, Pearl."

"I know it." Her sobs increased. "But Ma needs me. I gotta go. You—you can make do without me."

"No, I can't."

"Sure you can. You're skilled—and lucky—at gambling. Why, I think you'd win most every time even without me."

"It's not just the gambling, Pearl. You know that. Don't you? Without you I'd have no heart left at all."

She drew back and sniffled.

He reached in his pocket and handed her his red bandanna.

She accepted the kerchief and wiped her eyes. "Neither will I, Benjamin. Neither will I."

"Then don't go. I know you love your ma, but can't one of your brothers or sisters go to her?"

Pearl shrugged. "You know I'm the youngest of ten. They've all long moved on to their own broods. I'm the only one who's not tied down to hearth and home. So I'm the one who takes the responsibility now."

Seeing Pearl's pretty face lined with care saddened him. He knew what he was going to do. And no one would be able to stop him.

Chapter 2

The next day, hoping no one would see him, Benjamin strode toward the front door of Sadie's. She was the only person who knew he planned to leave. He wanted to keep it that way.

He had only a few more paces to the exit when a familiar female voice stopped him. "Say, Bennie, whatcha doin'?"

Letting out a sigh, he turned to face Eliza. "Why are you up at ten in the morning? Aren't you usually in bed at this hour, still getting your beauty rest? Not that you need it." He sent her the sardonic grin he knew she loved.

She drew closer. "Flattery will get you everywhere, except out of answerin' my question. Are you thinkin' of leavin' us?"

Benjamin looked down at the trunk that housed every possession he owned. Their number was not great. He hadn't ever needed much. His life hadn't been one of fond memories tracked by souvenirs, so two changes of clothes and some toiletries were all he ever needed.

"You won't answer. You must be leavin'."

He twisted the heel of his boot into the floor. "Matter of fact, I am."

She placed her hand on her hip. "Where?"

"Out of town."

"For how long?"

"Don't rightly know. Not sure if I'll ever come back."

Eliza's painted face fell. "Not sure if you'll ever come back? Whatcha mean by that kind of crazy talk?"

"It's no crazy talk." Benjamin didn't want to admit he planned to follow Pearl because he couldn't stand to be without her—and because he saw a new opportunity in relocating. "I need to leave town, to—to—help out a friend."

"Pearl." Eliza grimaced and crossed her arms.

He didn't answer but looked at the pine floor.

"Don't try to fool me. I know she left yesterday. Something about her ma dyin'. But she didn't say nothin' about you goin', too."

He looked into Eliza's face. "That's because she doesn't know."

Eliza shook her head. "This gets crazier by the minute. If Pearl didn't invite you, why are you goin'? There's plenty of us around here who'd love to take her place."

When Eliza swayed her hips, the motions had no effect on his heart or emotions. The realization only made him long for Pearl.

Eliza persisted. "I'll bet Sadie doesn't like that you're leavin'."

"No. She doesn't like it at all," Benjamin admitted. "And Pearl might not like it, either. But I'm a man who's hard to stop once I set my mind to something."

"That I know. But don't stay too long."

Benjamin didn't make such a promise but tipped his hat as Sadie had taught him and left.

As he made his way to the corner where he was supposed to meet the coach, he tried not to look back. Leaving the familiar house presented new opportunities, but he hadn't remembered feeling so anxious since his brothers dropped him off there years ago. He wondered what awaited him at Pearl's family ranch.

Minutes later, to his surprise, among the crowd Benjamin saw Pearl approach the corner of Main and First. Like him she had only one trunk. But instead of her familiar red rouge, darkened lips, and black lines around her eyes, she had left her face bare. He studied her countenance, hoping his admiration wasn't obvious. Her cheeks contained natural color, a soft pink rather than the red circles to which he was accustomed. Even without paint accentuating her eyes, their chestnut color stood out, dotting skin the color of cream. Red color no longer covered her lips, but her full mouth still looked appealing. Pearl had always possessed beautiful black hair. The sun caught reddish highlights he had never before noticed. He hadn't thought it possible, but she looked more ravishing on that day than she ever had at Sadie's.

Feeling curious and amused stares upon him, he remembered they stood amid three others awaiting rides out of town. Apparently he had been observing Pearl too long, and his fellow sojourners had taken notice.

At that moment, Pearl's glance caught his. Her mouth slackened, and he watched surprise turn to vexation. "What are you doing here?" she asked, keeping her voice just above a whisper.

"Waiting for a coach. What are you doing here? I thought you left these parts yesterday."

"I was planning to, but the coach I was supposed to be on broke down. So they said I could ride out on the next one."

"But I didn't see you at Sadie's last night."

Pearl shook her head. "I'd said my good-byes. I couldn't return. I stayed at Mrs. Hoffman's."

"Mrs. Hoffman's?" He started to say more, then thought better of it.

"I know what you're thinking. She wouldn't want a woman like me in her place. But without my face paint, I'm not sure she realized who I was." She averted her eyes. "But that doesn't explain why you're here. You aren't leaving because of me, are you?"

He took her aside, out of earshot of the others. "I decided on my own to leave town. To start a new life. Time to move on before the gamblers around town catch on to my tricks." Remembering W.C.'s veiled threat, he held back a shudder.

"I wouldn't worry about that. They have their fun. Where would they be without you to offer them a challenge?"

"I suppose. Sort of like trying to outgun a sharpshooter. Haven't been caught yet. Well, except for that one time when that traveler caught on and landed me a pretty good punch in the jaw." Benjamin rubbed the now-healed spot. His account attracted the attention of one of the ladies. She clutched her bag closer to her, apparently afraid that Benjamin might be interested in her cash, too.

"Yes, you do present a challenge," Pearl conceded and smiled.

He liked her familiar smile, even though it wasn't painted on.

Soon the coach arrived, jangling to a stop. Minding his manners, he acted the gentleman, letting the ladies board before him and taking the least desirable seat by the window. Dust always came through there the most, especially landing on those who faced forward. Pearl's posture relaxed, and he felt comfortable.

After five hours of riding down bumpy trails, away to another world Benjamin didn't know anything about, the coach finally stopped for dinner at a town even smaller than Denmark. The inn in question wasn't much better than a bunkhouse. The meal offered was a watery soup of beans and carrots.

He stuck near Pearl, glad to have her as a dinner companion until he sat beside her at a corner table.

"What is the meaning of all this?" she hissed.

"All this?" Peering around her, he noticed no one else was nearby. No wonder Pearl didn't mind speaking freely. He didn't like the ire he saw in her flashing brown eyes. Clearly she had saved her wrath just for his ears. "Why the change in attitude? You seemed fine before."

"I only seemed fine. I don't like making a public spectacle of myself. Now that we're alone, I want to know what you mean by following me like this. You have no right. I'm finished with that life—for good. I don't ask or expect you to change for me. Why don't you go back to the life you know? The life where you have plenty of money and more than enough eager women." She rose from her seat. A fresh tear dripped down her cheek. "You can start by eating dinner by yourself."

Her angry words notwithstanding, Benjamin knew he had made the right decision to join her. The tear told him all he needed to know. Desperate to stop her, he blurted, "I'm changing my ways, too."

She stopped in midmotion, nearly spilling her soup before returning to her seat. "You are?"

He crossed his fingers behind his back. "Yes."

She looked at him cockeyed. "I hope you really mean that, because I have news for you. If you go home with me, you're going straight whether you like it or not."

"Oh?" He looked at her without flinching or blinking, a skill garnered from years of gambling.

"Ma won't allow any illegal or immoral activities on her ranch. In fact, she might not even let you stay since she knows you're a link to a part of my life she doesn't approve of."

He stirred his soup as he clenched his back teeth under closed lips. His plans to convince Pearl to help him win a few dollars from bored ranch hands looked as doomed as a man holding a hand of twenty-two in blackjack. But he wasn't giving up that easily. Not with his way of living at stake. "If she doesn't approve of your past, why are you running back to her now?"

"Because she's my ma, that's why. Not that I can expect you to understand that." He hadn't seen that coming. This time Benjamin winced.

"I'm sorry," Pearl blurted. "The way you were brought up isn't your fault." She reached across the table and placed a comforting hand on his arm. She swallowed. "Truth be told, out of all my sisters, I'm not Ma's first choice. She's only letting me come back home because she's desperate for help." Her crying had slowed as she spoke, but now fresh tears poured down her cheeks unabated.

Benjamin reached into his pocket and pulled out his red bandanna. "Here you go."

She accepted the gesture, and they heard the driver calling out the room assignments for the night's lodging.

Benjamin took the opportunity to embrace Pearl, not caring about the stares and odd glances they received. "I know your ma has been judgmental and condemning of you in the past. Don't worry. You can always come to me for a shoulder to cry on. I'll protect you," he murmured into her ear.

She pulled away. "I don't need protection. Not from you, not from anybody."

When pride tugged at Pearl, arguing was useless. Benjamin tried another tactic. "If you'll let me tag along, I'll consider it a personal favor. You can do a good deed for an old friend, can't you?"

"I—I don't know."

He searched a satchel he carried and found the bottle of perfume he'd been saving for just the right time. The tuberose scent was Pearl's favorite and one the shopkeeper didn't always have in stock. Benjamin had been lucky to get the last bottle.

She gasped when she saw the pink glass vessel.

"This sweetens the deal, wouldn't you say?"

She uncorked it and inhaled. A dreamy look entered her eyes, and she indulged by dipping the bottle upside down so the cork would absorb some of the scent and then using it to apply a drop behind each ear. Before she closed the bottle, she took another whiff.

"I'm glad you're enjoying your gift already."

"I'd better while I can. Ma won't abide the scent of perfume around her. Says virtuous women don't need any aroma other than soap."

Benjamin wondered how good business would be at Sadie's place if the women didn't keep themselves painted and smelling pretty, but he decided not to make reference to the life Pearl was leaving. "You'll just have to wear it when she's not around."

"Maybe." She slipped the bottle into her dress pocket. He had a feeling she'd hold on to it the whole trip.

"So you'll consent to me following you?"

"Against my better judgment," she agreed.

Benjamin grinned. "Whether your judgment is good or bad remains to be seen."

Chapter 3

Pearl didn't say much during the second day of the trip. Worried, she fiddled with her skirt, a simple brown cotton affair she had worn on the day she first went to Sadie's and hadn't donned again until that morning. Ma would be glad to see her in a drab house dress, even though the hem had muddied from the trip. If she tried to approach her mother while wearing silk, despite Ma's desperate illness, she'd throw Pearl out faster than a gunslinger could draw his pistol.

Why she hadn't given the silk frocks in her trunk to her friend Eliza, Pearl didn't know. Why were the dresses—a literal outward show of the past she wanted to shake—so hard to shed?

Musing, she realized the dresses symbolized another link. To Benjamin. She was thankful he'd followed her, even though she pretended to be mad at him about it. She could only hope he wouldn't buckle under the pressure of Ma's discipline and insistence that everyone in her house walk the straight and narrow. Though Ma was ill, she'd find a way to control them. She didn't know how she could stop it.

Lord, I know I haven't talked to You much, but I pray You'll keep me strong now. I'm teetering on the edge of the new life and the old. Don't let me fall off the fence and land in the muck.

———

They reached Rope A Steer, Texas, that afternoon. Pearl hired a buckboard to carry them to her mother's place.

"The ranch sure is beautiful," Benjamin remarked as they approached an unpainted gate. The sign said "M&H," which stood for Milk and Honey. Pearl had told him the name represented the Bible's promise and her father's hope. The horse pulled them past a stand of brush, over a shallow creek, and down a fenced field. The simple frame home looked to be missing a few roof shingles. The house wasn't much, but he hadn't expected to be so taken with the acres upon acres of flat land stretching as far as he could see. Nearby a cow grazed on more land than she needed, rich green grass offering a veritable feast.

"I've always thought it was beautiful out here." A wistful look covered Pearl's face. "You should see the fields in spring when the bluebonnets are at their peak."

"I can only imagine how pretty that must look." Benjamin noted that Pearl couldn't seem to take her gaze away from the land. From the moment she had stepped into Sadie's, Benjamin knew Pearl wasn't meant for that kind of life. Now she was back home, and the radiance in her face showed she had landed right where she needed to be. "You really missed the ranch, didn't you?"

"I suppose I did." Pearl cleared her throat as she put her hand on the front door latch and looked him in the eye, much like Sadie used to do when she was about to lecture him on how to be a gentleman. "Now Ma isn't expecting you, so you need to be real quiet and let me handle her, you hear?"

"I hear."

Pearl straightened her shoulders and crossed the threshold. Her surefootedness surprised him, considering Pearl had said Ma was quite a character. Perhaps since Pearl no longer bore the marks of one of Sadie's girls, her ma could overlook her brief mistake, and they could start anew. At least that's what he hoped for Pearl. He set down both of the trunks he carried—his and Pearl's—on the kitchen floor.

"I'll go ahead and put on some coffee. You can help yourself to a cup while you wait for me to greet Ma," Pearl instructed. "I'll let you know when you can meet her."

Benjamin nodded and took a seat at the rickety oak table. Seemed a mite small if they were expecting to serve a number of ranch hands their meals. He shrugged. Maybe the hands ate in separate quarters. Smiling to himself, he fantasized about easy pickings from bored gamblers. He'd seen that the nearest town, Rope A Steer, offered an inn, a blacksmith shop, and a tiny dry goods store. Not much in the way of entertainment. Surely the men here would be more than happy to go a round or two of cards. He'd make sure to hit them for a game on payday.

—⁂—

Pearl said a quick, silent prayer for courage before she entered the sickroom. No matter what Ma said, she was determined to be as cheerful as any paid nurse or companion. Even more so. She remembered how Ma's favorite daughter, Rachel, conducted herself. Rachel's sweet demeanor and radiant peace brought life to her plain features and made Pearl wish she could be more like her. Pearl decided she'd do her best to emulate her older sister.

Opening the door, Pearl found Ma lying in the finely carved four-poster bed Pa had built out of pine years ago for his new bride. Though her eyes were shut and she lay in repose, Ma's face looked haggard and pale. Had she really aged ten years when Pearl had been away only a few months? Her mother's mortality, and her own, struck her.

Before Pearl could ponder her new role as a nursemaid in silence, Ma opened one eye then the other. "Well, look what the cat dragged in."

Pearl had been prepared for a cool greeting, so her heart didn't twinge, nor did she draw near to her mother for a kiss. She summoned her best impression of Rachel. "I'm happy to see you, Ma."

"Sure you are."

"I'm pleased to hear your voice sounding strong even though you look a mite peaked."

"Of course my voice is strong. It had better be if I have any intention of convincing a sinner like you to stay out here in God's country. Sure would have been easier on me, not having to preach while I'm sick. If Minnie had come, I'd never have to say a word to her. And Emmie would open the Bible right along. I don't suppose you have a Bible with you, do you?"

She flinched. "No, ma'am."

"Never mind. Mine's right here on the table. You'll be reading at least a chapter a day to me, you know. Maybe you should start with the tale of the prodigal daughter."

"You mean son."

Ma's eyes narrowed. "You would know, wouldn't you? Guess I can't expect to bear ten children and not have one turn out to be a black sheep." Ma pulled herself up on her elbows.

"You sure you're up to sitting?"

"Sure I'm sure. Wouldn't try it if I wasn't."

Pearl rushed to her side, placing pillows so the older woman could situate herself in comfort.

Ma inspected Pearl with sharp brown eyes. "I see you're wearing the same dress you wore when you left."

Pearl winced. "You won't be seeing any colorful silks around here, Ma."

"That's good. You know red's not a good color to wear around a bull. Maybe it works real good around a two-legged bull, but not one with four legs. Did I tell you our bull died?"

"No. I'm sorry." Pearl pursed her lips. The bull's death had no doubt been yet another setback for her mother and the struggling ranch. She was sure the event had only added to Ma's agitation, which was greater than Pearl expected. She didn't want to break the news about Benjamin's arrival to her mother. "I'll be fixing supper shortly. Maybe I can fry up one of those cheese omelets you like so well."

"That's one thing you can do, is make a cheese omelet. And I've got some cheese and a few eggs in the house—what I was able to gather before I got so sick I had to send for you." Ma let out a labored sigh. "I'm mighty tired of livin' off the atrocious food Mrs. Wilkins brings by. Not that I'm not grateful for whatever that good Christian soul is willin' to do for me. She's mighty obedient, livin' the Lord's commandment to love your neighbor as yourself. But her cookin' is somethin' awful."

Pearl laughed out loud in spite of herself. "Now, Ma, you're mighty picky for someone so sick."

"A sick person needs edible food." Ma crossed her arms, but Pearl detected the slightest upward curve to her lips.

Since her expression was the closest to congenial she'd seen in the few minutes she'd been there, Pearl decided to broach the subject of Benjamin. "I—I didn't come here alone."

All pleasantness evaporated. "What are you sayin', child?"

"Someone followed me here. Benjamin."

"Benjamin? Who is that?"

"I didn't ask him to follow me, but he did." Pearl decided she might as well tell the whole truth. "He's the man I love. And he loves me, too."

"Is that so?" Ma eyed Pearl's left hand. "Then why don't I see a weddin' band on your finger?"

Without meaning to, Pearl inspected her ringless hand. "Maybe you will one day."

"That's what he wants you to think."

"I don't ask you to approve of Benjamin, but I do ask you to meet him," Pearl said.

"Fine. Stuck in bed as I am, I have no other choice." Ma looked down at her night shift. Though the garment was fashioned from opaque cotton and the collar covered her neck, she grabbed her bed jacket from the foot of the bed and donned it, fastening the buttons with quick expertise that reminded Pearl of how Ma used to dress her.

After a nod from Ma, Pearl went to the door and motioned at Benjamin. Without hesitation he set down his coffee and made his way into the room.

Ma tilted her head and peered at him through narrowed eyes. "Well, well, lookee here. Cat's been busy today."

Benjamin was obviously taken aback by Ma's odd greeting. "Come again, ma'am?"

"Ma's just being Ma," Pearl said, rushing to intervene before she made the introductions.

Ma looked Benjamin up and down. "You must think a mighty lot of my daughter to follow her all this way. Though only the good Lord can understand why."

Benjamin shot Pearl a distressed look before he answered. "I think your daughter is a fine woman, Mrs. Hubert."

"You do, do you? Turn around and let me see you."

Benjamin hesitated.

"Go on, boy. What's the matter with you—got some sort of defect you don't want me to see?"

"Ma!" Pearl objected. With his fine features and strong physique, Benjamin had nothing to be ashamed of in his appearance.

"Now, you shush. I want to see what kind of man would follow you all this way." Benjamin, looking stunned, complied.

"I think you'll do." Ma nodded. "You'll do just fine working here on the ranch."

"What?" Benjamin and Pearl said in unison.

"You came all this way. What else were you plannin' to do?" Ma's tone feigned innocence.

"He didn't come out here to be a ranch hand." Pearl looked at Benjamin. "Did you?"

"No, I've never worked the land a day in my life."

Ma sniffed. "I won't bother to ask how you do make a living."

Pearl decided not to enlighten her. "I'm sure Benjamin wouldn't mind doing a little work around here in exchange for room and board."

"Room and board? No, that won't do. I can't have a man livin' here with you the way you are and me too sick to stop whatever it is he plans to do. No, he'll live in Rope A Steer and report to work every day just like he was a paid employee."

"You can't expect him to work for free," Pearl said.

"I suppose you're right about that," Ma conceded with a sigh. "We'll pay what we can."

Pearl turned to Benjamin. "You don't have to work here."

Benjamin set his gaze on the open window that offered a view of the land, land that appealed to him. Though the idea of winning money from the ranch hands crossed his mind, Pearl was more important. He wanted to stay near her. How could he refuse her ma's invitation?

"No, I don't have to work here," he answered Pearl. "But I will." He looked toward the older woman. "I accept your offer, Mrs. Hubert."

Chapter 4

Later that evening, after Pearl had served her mother the omelet she promised, she sat with Benjamin at the table. She took delight in how he savored every mouthful of omelet and the satisfied grin that accompanied each bite. Though it was much too soon to entertain such thoughts, she couldn't help but dream about dining with Benjamin every evening. His presence lifted her spirits and soothed her mind in the face of Ma's criticisms.

Pearl didn't want to consider the possibility that he regretted promising Ma he'd work at the ranch. Yet she felt she had to offer him a way out, just in case. Courage to broach the topic arrived over after-supper coffee.

She cleared her throat. "I know Ma must have taken you aback today with her offer of a job. Truth be told, it surprised me, too. I have to ask, are you sure you want to work here?"

He didn't hesitate. "I'm sure. The idea's kind of grown on me." He swirled his half-full cup in circles with more enthusiasm than was required to melt the two lumps of sugar he took. "Uh, I realize I won't get treatment this good every night. Reckon I'll be eating with the ranch hands from here on out. Living with them, too." He looked up. "You don't mind showing me the quarters after supper, do you?"

"The—the quarters?" She set down her cup and patted her lips with her napkin.

"Uh-oh. Are you telling me you don't have an extra bed?" He shrugged. "Well, I can sleep on the floor if you can spare a blanket." He downed his coffee. "How many hands do you all employ, anyway?"

She stiffened. "Employ?"

A chuckle escaped his lips. "Yeah. You know. Like a man works for you, and then you pay him. We have this here paper in the U.S. of A. that we call money. The same paper we used to win at our games." He winked.

Instead of consoling her, his wink made her uneasy. Because she knew Benjamin's schemes, her mind didn't take long to form an unhappy conclusion. "Games, huh? I hope you weren't thinking you'd win the ranch hands' paychecks. Now you wouldn't be thinking that way, would you?"

His lips twisted into a little grin. "You know me too well. All right. I admit it. I confess I followed you out here because I couldn't stand the thought of being without you." He placed his elbow on the table and set his chin in his palm.

Pearl knew him well enough to realize the blue-eyed puppy dog look he gave her was contrived to melt her heart. Though it was working, she decided to remain steely. "But?"

"But." The puppy look disappeared, replaced by a mischievous light as he retreated by leaning back in his chair. "In the back of my mind, I thought maybe I could rustle up a few extra dollars from the ranch hands."

"Benjamin! You'd take advantage of our ranch hands?"

"I wouldn't call it taking advantage. Gambling's a form of entertainment, the way I see it. Everybody knows there's a risk. But for your sake, I wouldn't have taken too much of their money." Sincerity coursed through his voice.

"I believe you," she answered.

"I must say, things have changed a little since your ma hired me. So I'll go you one better. Now that you've got me working, eating, and living with them, I won't be taking any of their money by cheating. I'll win every game fair and square." He lifted his forefinger to emphasize his point.

"Are you sure?"

"Of course. Why would I lie to you?"

"I don't think you're lying. I just think you don't possess the conviction to keep your promise." She sighed. "Maybe you'd see the real need to be an honest man if you knew God. I wish you weren't so mad at Him."

"I'm not mad at God. I know He's there. He must be, for all those people to pour into church every Sunday morning. He just hasn't showed up a whole lot for me, that's all." Benjamin's voice betrayed sadness and defeat.

"I reckon He's not too easy to find in a place like Sadie's. I know I didn't see much of Him there. Not that I looked too hard." She let out a breath. "Lately I've been thinking a lot about my life."

Benjamin surveyed the room. "Being out here does that to you, doesn't it?"

"Yes. Not too much music and talk to distract you." Pearl let out a little laugh.

"You know, I thought I'd miss all the noise, but I don't. Isn't that strange?"

"Strange in a good way. Maybe the good Lord's telling you how you don't need all those distractions after all."

"Maybe. But I interrupted you. What have you been thinking?"

"Oh." Pearl got her thoughts back on track. "When I left home, I was hoping for a lot of things. I wanted to help Ma by sending money to her and my widowed sister, too. I thought living in a bigger town would be exciting and talking to men would be an easy way to get money. After all, Ma kept reminding me how I attracted too many men for my own good. And I have admitted to the Lord that a part of me wanted to get away from Ma's strict rules. But I didn't know until I got to Sadie's how high the cost of escaping Ma's domineering ways would be. These past months away from home were the worst I've ever had. I wouldn't have survived if not for you. I'll always be grateful to you for being there during my darkest hour. But now it's time for me to see the light and to try to walk with God once more."

Benjamin didn't answer right away. Pearl gave him time to absorb all she had shared. "Where does that leave me?" His voice was quiet.

She placed her hand on his knee and gazed into his eyes. "Walking beside me, I hope."

"But I am right with you, by working here. Right?"

"There's more to it than that." When she hesitated, the silent air seemed to oppress the room. "I–I'd like you to start going to church with me."

His eyes widened. "Church?"

"Is that so bad?"

He chuckled and nodded at once. "I don't reckon so. You know you can make me do almost anything when you look at me like that."

Pearl laughed. "I hope so. But I'm leaving the heavy work up to the Lord."

"You're going to need Him to convince me to repent. Churchgoing and all is nice for a lot of folks, but you know it's not something I'm used to. Maybe things would have been different if Pa hadn't died. But my outlaw brothers had plans for me that didn't include God."

"They did the best they could."

"I know it. And I understand they've changed—although I haven't seen them in years to find out one way or another." He leaned closer and, with his blue eyes, searched her face. "You don't think I'm like them, do you?"

"I—I never thought much about it."

"Well, I'm not. I might cheat a little at cards, but I never stole outright from anybody. I never robbed a bank and sure never shot anybody over money or anything else. And how many other men would live at Sadie's and still resist the ladies?"

"You—you have?" Though she'd never seen him act un-toward to any of the women there, she didn't realize he had maintained his virtue. In her eyes he was becoming more and more heroic.

His face reddened, and he pulled away from her. "Don't tell anybody what I told you. Some of the men would never let me live it down."

"I wouldn't tell anybody if my life depended on it," Pearl promised. And she meant it. They were silent for a moment before she spoke once more. "I won't even tell anyone if you decide to go to church." She smiled.

"Do I have a choice? I'll bet your ma makes all the ranch hands go to church every Sunday, doesn't she?"

Sorry he had returned their conversation to a raw topic, she took her hand off his knee and didn't look him in the eye. "I have to tell you. We—we don't have any ranch hands out here. This is a small enterprise. My parents ran it themselves. Ma owns a few acres, but she and Pa just subsisted."

His expression took on a confused light. "What? You mean you don't own all this land I see?"

"Not all of it by any means. No, most of it belongs to Oliver O'Connell, proprietor of the Double O Ranch next door. Now that's a man who owns some acreage."

"Then why do you insist on calling this place a ranch?"

"That's what they planned for it to be one day. Pa hoped to buy more land in the future. But he became ill soon after he settled our little parcel, so he was never able to bring the ranch up to its potential. Now Ma doesn't even farm except for keeping a little livestock and growing a few vegetables to eat. When she's well enough, which isn't often, Ma takes in sewing and laundry and sells eggs to make enough money to buy the dry goods she can get by on. Of course, I've always sent her a good part of the money I made at Sadie's. Now don't you mention it to her, because she'd never admit it. She thinks my money is dirty." Pearl slumped in her seat, and her voice grew quiet. "Maybe it is."

"You need money to live, though, don't you?"

"Yes, but maybe we'd all be better off with a little less money and a little more ingenuity. Although I was glad for what I earned with you. I sent a good part of it to my widowed sister. With four boys and a girl, she needs all the help she can get."

He could do nothing but shake his head in amazement and admiration. "I had no idea. I thought all your money went to pretty dresses and perfume."

"Had you fooled, didn't I? I'm pretty good with a thread and needle, so I managed to keep myself in fancy costumes." She looked down at the plain gray house-dress she wore at that moment. "Truth be told, I'm happier wearing this."

Benjamin studied her. He remembered how she once looked in low-cut, beaded gowns fashioned from silks in colorful hues. The way she looked now, with a simple kitchen as her backdrop, made him comfortable. Pearl presented the vision of a strong woman, capable of hard work. "Truth be told, you look even better dressed like that than the way you looked at Sadie's."

"Now you're just funning me."

"No, I'm not."

Pearl looked beyond him through the open window. "The sun's getting low. You'd better be going. Why don't you use one of our horses for a ride into town? Get yourself a room at the inn."

———⁓———

A half hour after he left Pearl's, Benjamin rode a gentle horse into Rope A Steer. His second look at the dust-ridden town revealed that his first impression had been right. The place felt dead. He spotted only one sign of promise—HOOT N HOLLER INN. Not that the wooden structure, in dire need of paint, looked like anything to hoot or holler about.

The inside didn't offer much more promise. An old man sat behind a tall counter boasting a sign that read NO PAY, NO STAY in bold letters. The rack housing three rifles on the wall behind him indicated he planned to enforce his policy.

"Got a room I can stay in for a couple of months? Maybe more?" Benjamin asked.

"I got something for a dollar a week if you're not too picky."

"I'm not."

The innkeeper held out his palm. "That'll be two weeks in advance."

Benjamin peeled two dollar bills off his roll of cash and relinquished them.

"You can call me Mr. Dimsbury." He handed Benjamin a key. "Third floor. You won't have trouble finding it since it's the only one up there."

The idea of an attic room hadn't occurred to Benjamin, but considering he hadn't seen any other inns, he figured he'd best take it without complaint. Once he navigated the narrow stairs, his fears of a tiny room with a pointed ceiling proved true. The bed looked no larger than a coffin, and there wasn't even a desk. He figured it was a good thing he wasn't much of a writer or scholar.

Unpacking, he was almost grateful he couldn't stay at Pearl's. Had he remained on the ranch after work hours, she might have sensed his mood and realized how distressed and shocked he felt. He'd come all this way only to find a pathetic little enterprise with no ranch hands to cheat? The idea of leaving suddenly seemed fine. But if he did, what would life be like without his Pearl? Making money by cheating a few ignorant and bored ranch hands appealed to him, but Pearl appealed to him more. He couldn't leave her. He was going to stay, even though that meant rooming in a hole in the wall in a tiny speck on the road that considered itself a town, where no one knew him.

As soon as he set himself up in his new quarters, Benjamin looked for a saloon. He didn't see much prospect of being paid to work at the ranch no matter how noble the Huberts' intentions. Sure, Pearl had decided to walk the straight and narrow, but even without her he could make money. Why, maybe even better money than before. With that thought he allowed himself a triumphant smile.

He hadn't been in the Drunken Steer Tavern a moment before he attracted the attention of a woman wearing a revealing dress. "Hey, handsome, you new around these parts?"

"Sure am. Thought I might set up a little card game." He cocked his head toward an empty table.

She shrugged. "I don't mind, but Bart might want a cut of your winnings. He's the owner."

Benjamin hadn't thought of such a possibility. Then again, Sadie had always been his friend and knew Benjamin's card games attracted customers. At least this woman hadn't asked to be his partner. If she had, he'd have turned her down. No one could take Pearl's place.

That fact became more evident as he played that night. He won, but not as handily as usual. Without Pearl's help, Benjamin wasn't gambling in the fine form to which he had become accustomed. He had to convince Pearl to change back to her old ways. And fast.

Chapter 5

The following morning Pearl opened the door to her mother's sickroom, expecting her to be asleep. Instead, Ma sat in bed, looking outside through the open window. Her Bible rested in her lap.

"You got my bed jacket?" she asked Pearl.

"Yes, ma'am. All nice and clean, fresh off the clothes line." Pearl walked toward the bed and handed the garment to her mother.

"Took you long enough." Ma brought the article of clothing to her nose and inhaled. Pearl expected to be complimented on how fresh it smelled, but Ma had other ideas. "This is still damp."

"It is?" Pearl reached for the bed jacket and squeezed the cotton until she felt a tinge of dampness on one edge. "I suppose I could have let it stay out there a little longer, but I thought you wanted it back."

"I know you're tryin' real hard, and I appreciate it, but you burned my bread and forgot to put the sugar in my coffee this morning," Ma pointed out. "You haven't been yourself ever since you got back. It's that man, isn't it?"

"You mean Benjamin?"

"Of course that's who I mean. Who else? He's all you can think about, isn't he?" Ma didn't wait for an answer. "He's a handsome one, all right. But he ain't no good for you. Not until he gets right with the Lord."

"I know. I'm worried about him finding trouble in town. Even though Rope A Steer is hardly as sophisticated as I imagine a big city back East is."

"True. I know what you're thinkin', young lady." Ma wagged her forefinger at Pearl. "The answer is no. He ain't staying here with us overnight. There's too much temptation for that. I can see in the little time you've been here that you're tryin' to do better. And, sick or not, I'm your ma, and it's up to me to help you get back where you should be with the Lord. That means avoiding temptation."

"But, Ma—"

"Now don't you sass me." She held up her palm. "I can look into your eyes and his and see that. I might be old and sick, but I remember what it's like to be young. Just barely do I remember, mind you, but I remember. You know what your grandpa would say if he was still kickin'? He'd say we ought to work Benjamin so hard he'd be too tired to think about anything else at night but sleepin'. And speakin' of work, where is he, anyhow?"

Benjamin was indeed late, but Pearl didn't want to dwell on that subject. At that moment, they heard a horse's hoofbeats. Pearl looked through the window to see Benjamin approach, looking like a fine gentleman on his borrowed horse rather than the gambler he was. Her heart beat harder upon eyeing Benjamin. Ma was right. He offered her nothing but temptation. Temptation she didn't need.

"Is that your man?" Ma asked. "It's about time that he showed up."

"It's Benjamin." Pearl noticed the trotting horse stirred up red dust. "I'd better get the rest of the clothes off the line before they're ruined."

She hurried out the front door to greet Benjamin. She noticed the wind blew in the opposite direction of her clean clothes, so the dust would have little effect. Watching him hitch the horse, she summoned all her willpower to keep herself from running. Only a day had passed since he had last been to the ranch. Why did it seem more like a month? Or a year?

"Did you miss me?" he teased.

She felt her cheeks warm up. "What's the matter? Do I look like a forlorn coyote or something?"

"Nope. You look better than that. Much better."

She laughed. "You're full of flattery today. You aren't seeking shelter, running from the sheriff, are you?" She realized her question, made in jest, held a hint of fear and seriousness.

He didn't seem to be offended. "Naw, I stayed out of trouble so far."

"You found a room at the inn?"

He shrugged. "More like a broom closet. But it will do."

"What were you expecting in such a small town? A fancy hotel?" She motioned for him to follow her into the house. "I promised you breakfast every morning. I'll scramble you some eggs. Unless you've already eaten."

"Not yet." He rubbed his stomach. "Breakfast sounds good."

Soon they entered the kitchen. "Go on and wash up now."

"Yes, ma'am," Benjamin said with good humor.

"I've already milked Pansy this morning, so she won't need attention until this afternoon. So probably the best place for you to start your day after you eat is to see if all the fences are in good repair. Our land runs up through the creek on the south side."

"You've gotten mighty bossy." His tone sounded teasing.

"Have to be. I'm the boss." She squared her shoulders and broke an egg into the frying pan. "I've got some cured bacon, too. You'd better eat a slice or two. You'll need to keep up your energy if you want to put in an honest day's work on a ranch, even if it isn't much of a ranch."

"You seem to be enjoying being bossy." He dried his hands on the plain white towel that hung from the side of the basin.

She peered out the kitchen window and thought about how much a coach ride had transformed her. From a life where she was subject to the whims of others, to telling Benjamin what to do. The change felt good.

"So you don't want to answer me. I reckon that dashes my hopes."

"I'm sorry. I was caught up in my own thoughts. What hopes are you talking about?" Pearl scooped up the eggs onto a plate.

"I was hoping maybe you'd like some excitement. How about coming to town and being my partner again?"

"Benjamin, you know I can't." She set his plate before him. "Give me a moment and I'll slice you some bread."

"You mean you're happy serving me breakfast and tending to your ma? What kind of life is that?"

"The kind of life I'm leading now." She slackened her posture. "You wouldn't be asking me to abandon my own ma, now would you?"

"No. I just was hoping you might be a little tired of your ma's preaching by now. I know I was after I was with her only ten minutes. Not that I mean any disrespect."

"I know. Ma takes some getting used to." Pearl sat at the table. "But now that I'm home, she's softening up a little. Why, just this morning she told me how much I'm trying." Pearl decided to omit the criticism of her cooking that accompanied such faint praise.

"Well, that's fine, but you still do a lot of work. Wouldn't you like to get out of the house one or two nights a week? You could put on a fancy dress like you used to. Paint your lips pretty. Don't women like to do those things?"

The persuasion in his voice made the prospect sound almost too good to pass up. Without meaning to, Pearl studied her hands. In a short time they had grown pink. Not too much, but enough that she could tell she'd been scrubbing pans, washing clothes, and tending to livestock. She could only guess what they, once soft and pretty, would look like in no time at all.

On second thought, she didn't have to guess. They'd look like Ma's. Coarse, with blue veins evident. And in years to come irregular brown spots would appear on the backs of her hands and grow larger and larger. Soon the skin was destined to deteriorate to the point where wearing a ring or bracelet would only call attention to her age and the facts of what was turning into a hardscrabble life.

Pearl shuddered.

"You didn't answer me." Benjamin picked up a slice of bacon.

She turned her gaze from her hands to his face. "Sure, I like pretty clothes. But this dress I have on is a lot more comfortable."

He snorted. "That doesn't sound like the Pearl I know."

"The Pearl you know isn't around anymore."

"Is that so?" He leaned toward her, close enough that she could take in his clean yet manly scent. His nearness made her want more. But Benjamin represented a life she had left behind. A life to which she could not return.

She rose from her seat and made much ado about pouring herself a cup of coffee and him one, as well. "I know that. But I can't live with my ma and act one way in the daytime, just to go out with you and cheat men at cards every night."

"I'm not asking for every night. Just one or two nights a week." His mischievous eyes were impossible for her to resist. Nearly. But she had to resist.

"No. I can't."

"So you're going to bargain, are you? Can't say that I blame you. Fact is, I admire you for getting smarter so fast." She was only half surprised when he withdrew a box from his satchel. "Here you are. I got this for you before I left Denmark."

Returning to her seat, she remembered the bottle of perfume he gave her at the station. "Just how many gifts did you get, Benjamin? Looks to me like you might have bought out every store in Denmark."

"I'd do that if I thought it would make you happy. I just wanted to be prepared, Pearl. And I'm glad I had that foresight. The general store in town has mighty slim pickin's."

"Our needs out here are simple."

"Judging from the goods that Simpson fellow carries, I'd agree."

"I know adjusting to life here must be hard for you, Benjamin. Out here, our way of looking at life is different. Our lives revolve around church, not saloons. At least, my life does." She swallowed and looked at her napkin on the table.

"So you don't miss Sadie's at all?"

Pearl shook her head. "But I would have missed you if you hadn't followed me out here. I sure am glad you did."

He looked toward her ma's room. "I don't think everyone shares that opinion."

"Ma wants me to find a churchgoing man." She looked at him plaintively. "What do you say, Benjamin? Would you give church a chance? Maybe you and I could go together next Sunday."

"I don't know, Pearl. I've done a little Bible reading, even been to socials at church a couple of times."

"Really? You went to church?"

"Once or twice. When I was younger."

"I always thought the people in church were nice. Don't you think so?"

"Yep. Even nicer than most, I reckon," he admitted.

"So what made you stop going?"

"Gambling. Whenever I stepped near any church, the preacher man would try to make me give up gambling."

"And that made you mad."

"No. Not really. I knew the preacher had to say such stuff and nonsense. He had to make a living just like everybody else."

Pearl laughed even though she wasn't sure she agreed with his logic.

"Laugh all you like, but I don't know any other way to make a living."

"Now you're the one talking stuff and nonsense. You sure do know how to make a living."

"How's that?"

"Why, you can make a living right here, earning more than the pittance we can pay you now. You don't realize it, Benjamin Wilson, but I have big plans for this place."

Chapter 6

Benjamin looked into Pearl's shining brown eyes. For the first time since he'd met her, they sparkled with joy. He propped his elbow on the kitchen table and stroked his clean-shaven chin. "What are your plans? And, uh, do they include me?"

"They can if you want them to." Pearl averted her gaze, then looked back up at him. "If you really do want to get away from life at Sadie's. I mean, I think you do. You followed me out here. And so far you haven't hightailed it back to Denmark in spite of Ma's preaching."

He leaned back in his chair. "Her preaching must not bother you much. You're still here."

Pearl shook her head. "And I want to stay here. Listen—I know Ma must seem peculiar to you. She's not at all like the women who raised you. I know she takes some getting used to; but she's my ma, and I love her."

"You're a fine daughter."

Pearl's grin looked wry. "I'm trying to improve."

Her words stung. In the solitude of the country, he could see where he needed to improve, too. Maybe it would be nice to take a break from his life of gambling. Sleeping in late every day, up all night—what kind of life was that? Besides, maybe taking a new turn would elevate him in Pearl's eyes. Funny, he had come out here to talk her into changing her life back to the way it was, and instead, she had convinced him to try a new way of living.

"So do you think you can help me realize my dream of making this a real ranch?" Pearl asked.

"I'd like to, but what use do you think I'd be around here? I don't know anything about ranching, and anyhow, it seems to me there isn't much of a ranch to handle. You told me your ma only grows enough vegetables to keep herself fed."

"Yes."

"I've seen your stable. You don't have horses to break, and even if you did, there's not much room for them to run. You do a pretty good job on your own of taking care of the chickens, and how much work is it to take care of two pigs, a few chickens, and one cow? Even your ma could do that much on her own before she got sick."

"True. But I have plans, and you can be a part of them. If you joined us here on the ranch, we could buy more livestock and eventually hire more people and make this ranch a real going concern, not just a little farm where one or two people can barely eke out a living."

"Sounds ambitious. You really do have dreams for this place, don't you?"

"I suppose so. I didn't realize it myself until I came back." She leaned toward him. "What do you say? Will you help me?"

Those eyes held too much interest for him to refuse. "All right. I will."

—⁓—

That afternoon Benjamin reentered the house, and Pearl joined him in the kitchen.

"How's she doing?" he asked.

Pearl shushed him, though not in an unkind way. "She's asleep."

He nodded and lowered his voice to just above a whisper. "Everything looks to be in good repair, except I saw a few places where the chicken coop could use some work. I should be able to get to that this week."

She nodded. "Thank you."

The absence of food on the table told him he'd finished his chores well before supper, much to his regret. According to his rumbling stomach, he could use a bite to eat. He could only hope the inn would have something good on their menu. "I'd best be getting along. See you tomorrow."

Raised eyebrows indicated Pearl's surprise. "You milked Pansy already?"

Pansy! He'd forgotten. And he wished Pearl had forgotten, too. Afraid of failure since he'd never milked a cow, he was desperate to escape the chore. He looked out a window to the sky, hoping the sun hadn't settled too far. "It's a little early for milking, isn't it?"

"No. In fact, your timing couldn't be better. You'll find the bucket and milk stool in the barn."

Instead of expressing gratitude for her guidance, Benjamin shuffled his foot from one side to the other and stared at the tip of his brown leather boot. "Oh."

"What's the matter? Has the sun gotten to you? Are you feeling too poorly to milk Pansy?" She peered into his face, her expression much like that of a concerned nurse. "My, but sweat is just pouring down the sides of your face. I reckon the sun can get pretty hot out there when you're used to being inside all day." Pearl glided to the kitchen counter and picked up a transparent pitcher. "Here. Let me get you a glass of water. That might cool you off."

Benjamin wanted to lie and tell Pearl that indeed he felt sickly and wanted to go back to his room at the inn right away. But he realized that excuse would only buy him that afternoon. The next day he'd have to tell her the truth. Besides, if he was going to be more like the man Pearl wanted him to be, he couldn't start out by lying to her now.

He cleared his throat. "A glass of water would be nice, but I'm right as rain physically."

Pearl handed him the water. "That's good to hear. But you seem hesitant. Why?"

Stalling for time, he took a gulp of water. Never could he remember feeling so stupid. "I—I don't think I can milk Pansy."

"Why ever not?"

He paused. "Truth be told, I don't know how."

She opened her mouth as if to say something, then burst into laughter.

This time it was Benjamin's turn to shush her. "Do you want to wake your ma? Besides, I don't see what's so funny."

"I'm sorry. It's just that it never occurred to me you wouldn't know what to do. But why would you? You've never had to tend livestock before in your life." Pearl looked toward her mother's open door and back. "I think Ma should be fine. Come on. I'll give you a lesson."

Embarrassed that Pearl had to discover his ineptitude but grateful she was willing to help him learn, Benjamin watched her lure Pansy to the barn with the ease of a woman familiar with the task. Soon they were situated. A honey brown creature with big brown eyes, Pansy chewed her feed while regarding him with what seemed to be nonchalant disdain.

"I'll be gentle, Pansy," he assured her.

"She doesn't look too worried." Pearl placed a bucket underneath the animal's udders. She set the stool beside the cow and sat down.

Benjamin noticed the cow's bag looked plenty big, and he wondered how long the process of extracting the milk would take.

"Here's how it's done." Pearl reached for a teat, gripped it, and squeezed a stream of milk into the pail as though the motion were the most natural thing in the world. The cow remained unperturbed, chewing and swishing her tail. Pearl drew two more streams of milk into the bucket, the liquid hitting the bottom of the metal bucket with force.

"You make that look easy enough."

"It is easy. You'll learn in no time." She rose from the stool. "Now you try."

"I was hoping you were having so much fun you'd keep at it yourself," he only half jested.

Pearl smiled and pointed to the stool.

Benjamin took the seat. He chose the nearest udder and gripped it gently. For some reason, the animal's warmth, conveyed through thick pink skin covered with sparse but coarse white hairs, took him aback. He let go.

"Everything all right?"

He nodded. "Yep." Taking a breath, he tried again, forcing himself to become accustomed to the cow. This time he pulled. No milk resulted.

"You have to pull a little harder," Pearl advised. "Try an udder on the other side. Don't be scared. Pansy can sense your fear."

His manly pride took a blow at such a term, but he knew Pearl meant well. He nodded and yanked. This time a stream of milk came at him, and good. The milk missed the bucket and landed on his thigh.

"Don't get discouraged. Happens to all of us." Pearl grinned, looking as though she'd held back a big guffaw.

The idea that Pearl was amused by his clumsiness left him in ire. Determined to succeed, he grabbed a back udder and aimed it at the bucket. He yanked.

He heard Pansy's angry moo, then felt a kick. With a sharp hoof the animal struck him in the leg with such force that Benjamin fell off the stool and yelped.

"Benjamin!" Pearl knelt beside him, all traces of mirth absent from her expression. "Are you all right?"

He righted himself though pain reminded him of the encounter with Pansy. "I reckon so." He grimaced.

"Don't try to stand up. Not yet. Just stay there for a moment."

Benjamin didn't argue. Intense pain left him with little choice.

"You don't think your leg is broken, do you?" Fear penetrated her voice.

Benjamin shook his head. "I'm just bruised, that's all."

"You'll have a right good bruise, I'm sure," Pearl speculated. "Do you feel like getting up yet?"

He nodded and, with some difficulty, rose in stages.

Pearl nodded toward a bale of hay. "You sit on down."

He hobbled to the hay, wishing he'd been gentler with Pansy. He'd let his foolish pride irk him and was suffering the consequences.

Meanwhile, Pearl consoled Pansy, patting the cow and rubbing her. Soon the beast breathed more slowly and resumed feeding.

Benjamin imagined Pansy was calmer than he was. "I'm sorry I made Pansy mad."

"You didn't mean to." Pearl gave the animal one final pat then nodded toward the house. "Come on. Let's go back. I'll tend to you and then come back here and finish up later."

If Benjamin were prone to blushing, he would have at that moment. He had proven a colossal failure. How could he ever expect to be of any use to Pearl?

"Don't worry," she consoled him. "You can try again tomorrow."

Benjamin didn't answer. He wasn't sure he ever wanted to see another cow.

Chapter 7

Weeks later, Benjamin rose early on Sunday morning to escort Pearl to church. After long days of physical labor, he looked forward to an hour or so of sitting on a pew, listening to Preacher Giles, and praying and singing. Since he was running late, he hurried with shaving and dressing and soon retrieved the Huberts' buggy, which he had borrowed since he'd be taking Pearl to church. Trotting toward the ranch, he thought back on his time there, being part of Pearl's new life. The first few days after he agreed to help bring the ranch up to its potential, he didn't think he would survive. Pansy's kick had been a setback, and his injured leg had impeded his progress as he tried to learn the ins and outs of ranching. But once he and Pansy became friends, he learned to milk her with as much ease as Pearl. He found that such a chore, along with the other labor, brought its own sense of pride in accomplishment. Even in the past, when he had outwitted other gamblers and taken home their money, he never felt proud of his day's labor. On the ranch he did.

Pearl had said the ranch was small, and he reckoned it was by Texas standards, but the amount of work it entailed made it seem gigantic to him. First he had invested some time in making sure the fences, barn, and chicken coops were in good repair. As he approached Milk and Honey Ranch, he admired his handiwork.

He admired Pearl even more when he saw her waiting for him. Nearly unable to control himself, he took in a breath. Her Sunday dress, though simple, made her appear even more radiant than usual. He had barely called the horse to a stop before Pearl ran toward him and jumped into the buggy.

Benjamin marveled at how she managed to maintain a grip on her Bible while leaping into position. "Good morning!" He twisted his mouth into a wry grin.

"I hope it's good. We're late." She looked straight ahead.

"I know. I'm sorry. I overslept a mite."

"I hope that means we'll only be a mite late."

He pulled the buggy out of the drive with more force than he intended. Pearl jostled and grabbed her hat.

"Sorry."

"Never mind. I can take a little bump if it means not being late for church."

"How's your ma this morning?"

"Not so good. She didn't eat breakfast. Just turned back over and went to sleep.

I almost decided to skip worship service, but I figured that would upset Ma more than me leaving."

"I'm sorry she's still feeling poorly. But you can't do anything to help her when she's sleeping," Benjamin consoled. "That's probably the best thing. Did Dr. Spencer have anything much to say when he saw her yesterday?"

Pearl shook her head. "There's nothing he can do. I think he just wants me to make her comfortable."

Benjamin didn't respond. The idea of watching Pearl's ma wither away wasn't a happy one. Pearl remained silent for a moment. He wondered if her thoughts were similar to his own.

She changed the subject. "I do have some good news. News I think has cheered up Ma, too. It's about the ranch."

"Oh?"

"Remember the Angus bull and two cows I was thinking about buying? Well, I took the leap. They're all mine." Excitement colored her tone.

He let out a low whistle. "You must have saved more money than I thought."

"Ma had a few dollars hidden away, and I drove a hard bargain with our neighbor." She smiled and nodded once, a sure sign of triumph. "Now your job is simple. Make sure they stay healthy so we can expect to deliver some calves soon."

Benjamin wasn't sure he was up to the job, but he wanted to do right by Pearl. "I'll do my best."

"And I have a few other chores to keep you busy. I'd like to procure a few more chickens, so do you think we can build another coop?"

"I reckon." He tried to sound enthusiastic but failed.

Pearl didn't seem to notice. "Good!"

"I'm glad we're in sight of the church. If it was too much farther away, you might find other things for me to do."

"Oh," Pearl jested in turn, "we haven't ridden home yet."

Later, as they entered the sanctuary, Benjamin didn't feel apprehensive. Weeks ago, the first time he darkened the door of the little frame building that also served as the schoolhouse, he'd felt like a speckled sheep among a lily white flock. Jittery since he wasn't sure how to act in such a holy place, he tried not to notice curious glances thrown his way. But the glances had melted, and he greeted people he had come to know.

That day he didn't squirm in boredom as Pastor Giles preached about the Ten Commandments. Benjamin couldn't recite but two by heart—the ones on lying and covetousness—but he decided to memorize all ten that week.

"Now I ask you, my friends," Pastor Giles shouted, "do you want to be thrown into the pit? Into hell's fire?"

Several answers in the negative resounded.

"Then you must obey these commandments!" With each word the pastor touched the Bible he held with his forefinger. The pastor was so fired up that Benjamin thought he could almost see the flames of hell.

Choruses of "Amen!" filled the sanctuary.

Benjamin knew he hadn't been obedient, especially about bearing false witness. And he reckoned that coveting other people's goods had led him to cheating. Not so long ago, the thought wouldn't have worried him. But now that he had seen a better way to live, sorrow visited him. He realized that each time he attended church he'd become more certain he had to change. For good.

Pastor Giles preached. "Now I ask you today, do you know where you are going when you die?"

The pastor looked right at Benjamin. He tried not to wince. But Pastor Giles was right. Benjamin didn't know where he'd be headed when he died.

"Some of you young folks might think you have all the time in the world to repent," the pastor said. "But you may not. For tonight your very life might be required of you."

Benjamin shook his head in surprise and regret. Such a thought had never occurred to him.

"You don't believe me?" Preacher Giles's stare focused on Benjamin, who responded by looking at the back of the pew in front of him. The pastor continued. "Turn in your Bibles to Luke chapter 12, verse 16, and read along with me the words of our Lord Jesus Christ."

They read:

And he spake a parable unto them, saying, The ground of a certain rich man brought forth plentifully: And he thought within himself, saying, What shall I do, because I have no room where to bestow my fruits? And he said, This will I do: I will pull down my barns, and build greater; and there will I bestow all my fruits and my goods. And I will say to my soul, Soul, thou hast much goods laid up for many years; take thine ease, eat, drink, and be merry. But God said unto him, Thou fool, this night thy soul shall be required of thee: then whose shall those things be, which thou hast provided? So is he that layeth up treasure for himself, and is not rich toward God.

The words shook Benjamin. He had no reason to think God would take him any-time soon, but what if He did? Farm work offered plenty of chances for accidents. He remembered Pansy's kick. What if the blow had landed on his head? He shuddered.

Pearl laid a gloved hand on his arm and whispered, "Are you all right, Benjamin?"

He wasn't sure.

"Are you like this man? If you are, I ask you today to come to the altar and make a proclamation to God. Ask Jesus to forgive your sins and make you clean."

Benjamin felt so drawn to the altar that he had no other choice. He had to go. Rising from his seat, he walked to the front of the sanctuary and knelt at the altar. Pastor Giles kept preaching, and he heard shouts of joy from the congregation; oth-erwise, all was a blank to Benjamin. He just prayed. Tears rolled down his cheeks unabated.

He had come home.

Throughout the ride back to the ranch and even as she prepared Sunday dinner, Pearl didn't hold back her expressions of joy. "Oh, Benjamin! I'm still stunned about the day's events. I never expected you to take the altar call. I've never been happier!"

"Me, neither." Though he spoke the truth, he didn't want to admit he felt scared. The new life he promised God sounded hard to live. But he could try.

"I wish I had planned something more special for dinner than my same old fried chicken."

"Your fried chicken is special any day," Benjamin assured her. "Besides, now that I've come to Jesus, I'll bet every day will be special regardless of what I eat." He flinched. "Oh, I reckon I shouldn't use the word *bet* anymore."

Pearl laughed. "I know what you mean." She picked up a silver tray that held a small meal and an abbreviated glass of milk. "As soon as I take this in to Ma, I'll set ours on the table."

"Sure you don't want me to help?"

"Thanks, but you do enough around here. But you can come on in and talk to Ma. She'd like to hear your news."

Benjamin nodded. For the first time, he didn't feel fearful about seeing Pearl's mother.

Pearl poked her head through the sickroom door. "Ma? You decent?"

"Yes," a weak voice responded.

Benjamin followed Pearl.

"I've got lunch," Pearl announced. "I'm hoping you'll eat something."

"I'm not hungry right now. Leave it on the nightstand, will you?"

"Would you rather have an omelet?"

Pearl's mother barely shook her head.

Pearl set down the tray and drew closer to her mother. "Ma, I've got news. It's about Benjamin. He accepted the altar call at church today."

Ma opened both eyes. "He did?"

"I sure did, Mrs. Hubert," Benjamin assured her.

"Well, praise God." Her voice sounded stronger although she didn't sit upright. "So when is the baptism?"

"Baptism?"

"You mean, you've already been baptized?" Pearl's mother asked.

Benjamin hesitated. "If I have, I don't remember."

"Well, we'll have to take care of that," Pearl said. "Don't you worry about a thing, Benjamin. I'll take care of everything."

Later that week, Benjamin arrived in Pearl's kitchen for his usual breakfast. When he entered, bacon and eggs awaited.

"Sure smells good, Pearl."

"Me or the food?" she asked.

Her playful mood offered a pleasant surprise, and Benjamin decided to play along. "Both."

"I have a feeling this time of morning the bacon and eggs take precedence over the smell of my soap."

"I notice you don't wear the perfume I gave you much." He pulled up a chair and sat at the table. "Kinda hurts my feelings a mite," he teased.

"I'm saving that perfume for special occasions. Besides, didn't I tell you Ma doesn't allow perfume around here? Thinks it makes a woman smell—well. . ." Pearl looked into the frying pan and seemed to concentrate a little too much on dishing four thick slices of bacon and two eggs sunny-side up onto his plate. She buttered a slice of bread to go along with the food. He noticed a splotch of red on each cheek.

"The scent makes your ma think of your past, doesn't it?" he asked as he took his seat.

She nodded and set his plate before him. "And me, too. I don't want to go back."

"Neither do I."

"Oh, that reminds me. Pastor Giles says he'll baptize you in Trinity River whenever you're ready. But he doesn't want to wait too long."

"I know. But there's something that would mean a lot to me, if we can get it to happen." Benjamin's voice became quiet. "I'd like my brothers to be there to see it."

"Are you sure?"

"Part of getting my life where it should be is forgiving them. Isn't it?"

"Sure." Pearl fetched the coffeepot.

"You're afraid of them, aren't you? Afraid because they're outlaws?"

Pearl nodded. "I wish I could say different."

"I understand. But they won't do any harm around here. They might still be outlaws, but they always made sure I was protected. So will you help me find them?"

"If it means that much to you, sure, I'll help," Pearl said as she poured coffee. "I wonder if they'll recognize you."

"They might not—it's been so many years."

"I hardly recognize you myself. Your skin isn't as sallow as it used to be, and you walk with more vigor than you ever did at Sadie's."

He chuckled. "Vigor? I wonder how, considering how tired I am every day."

Pearl laughed as she served the coffee. "Physical work is a challenge, isn't it? I find it rewarding. Don't you?"

"Yes, I reckon I do."

She took her seat. "We need to say a blessing."

Chastened, Benjamin set down his fork. He'd already taken a bite of egg. "If it's not too late."

"As long as we're living and breathing, it's never too late to be thankful."

She bowed her head, and Benjamin knew she expected him to offer the prayer, a practice to which he still hadn't become accustomed or comfortable. Nevertheless, he managed to utter a few words, and they proceeded with breakfast.

"So you haven't been tempted to gamble?" she asked.

He shook his head. "Not so far. Nobody in town knows me as a card player, so that helps, I think."

"I would venture you sleep easier at night knowing you haven't cheated anybody."

"I'd have to agree with that." He chuckled, then turned serious. "I'm glad I put the past behind me."

"You mean that?"

An idea occurred to him. "Yes, I do. Do you want to see how much?"

"Sure, but I don't know how you'd show me."

"Go get that bottle of perfume. And you'll see."

"Now I am wondering what you've got up that sleeve of yours," she said, then disappeared into her own room.

Benjamin was just finishing the last of his eggs when she returned.

"Here you go." She set the perfume on the table.

Benjamin picked up the bottle. He imagined the squat shape, with a little bulb on top to spray out the fragrance, would seem pretty to a woman. He'd spent a lot of money on that bottle of tuberose scent for her. Money he'd risked a lot to earn.

"So why did you want to see the bottle of perfume?" Pearl persisted.

"I'll be right back. I have to go get something." He picked up the bottle. "Meet me outside."

Benjamin hurried to the shed to retrieve the hammer he'd been using to make repairs. For a moment he indulged in the luxury of examining the tool, thinking about what he planned to do. The smooth metal felt slightly chilled, warming quickly under his touch. He never thought he'd think in such a way, but the worn wooden handle fit his fingers as if it had been fashioned for him. He marveled at how the hammer, instrumental in creating buildings and fences and maintaining their usefulness, would now be used for destruction. He slipped the tool into his back pocket and made his way back to the stoop where Pearl waited.

"What are you doing?" she prodded.

"Would you set the bottle down for me?" He pointed to a step.

Pearl shook her head ever so slightly but didn't argue.

"Stand back." As she stepped backward, he retrieved the hammer and showed it to her. "Take one last good look at that bottle of perfume. In a few seconds it will be history."

She gasped. "But you paid a lot of money for that perfume. Are you sure you want to do that?"

"I'm not going to think about the money now. I'd ask you to give the perfume to a friend, but I doubt any respectable woman around these parts would wear it. Am I right?"

After the briefest interlude she responded. "You're right." She looked at the bottle and gulped.

"Sure you don't mind?" Benjamin asked.

Pearl took in a breath that broke the morning stillness. She nodded. "Oh, I mind, but I think you should do it."

Benjamin nodded. Before Pearl could have a chance to reconsider, Benjamin took the hammer and gave the bottle a good, hard strike. The bottle split into several pieces, spilling tuberose perfume. The pungent, sickly sweet odor, so lovely in small doses, sent both of them to coughing with the power of its unabated volume.

"I sure hope Ma doesn't smell that, for a lot of reasons." Pearl furrowed her brow with a concern Benjamin hadn't seen in some time. "The scent will remind her of my venture to Denmark, but even worse, it might make her physically sick."

"Really? Tuberose can be a bit strong, but—"

"No, it's not that." Pearl shook her head. "It's just that Ma's been feeling even more poorly lately. Odors, even nice ones, seem to bother her an awful lot. And when she's not flushed, she looks more pale and sickly. She's not eating much. I'm really worried."

Benjamin didn't know what he could say. When Pearl left Denmark, she knew her ma was near death's door. "I suppose you're never ready for the death of a loved one, even when you've been expecting it."

"I'm not ready," Pearl admitted. "I wish I had been a better daughter."

"I think you've been a wonderful daughter. Probably better than she deserves."

"I doubt that, but thank you." Pearl's voice was just above a whisper, and she kept her gaze on the shattered bottle.

They remained quiet for a time. Benjamin contemplated the broken bottle and everything it had meant to them both. Judging from the faraway look in Pearl's brown eyes, she shared his thoughts.

Finally, he broke the silence. "Are you going to be all right, Pearl?"

She nodded. "Benjamin, I never thought I'd say such a thing about a broken bottle of perfume, but you've made me glad. I feel like you've unlocked shackles from around my feet."

He understood all too well what she meant.

Chapter 8

The next week, Benjamin arrived as usual at the inn, tired even though his body and spirit had grown accustomed to the physical work the ranch required. He had planned to go straight to his room, wash up, and go to bed since Pearl had seen to it he enjoyed a good supper before he left her place. They had lingered over coffee. He treasured those times with her.

When he entered the small area that passed for the inn's lobby, he halted. Leaning on the counter toward the proprietor was a tall, lean man Benjamin recognized as Owen. Back in Denmark, he'd cheated Owen at cards many a time. He wondered if he was in town trying to get Benjamin to pay back some of the money. If so, was he willing to draw pistols over it? Or maybe Owen's errand was something else altogether. A terrible thought that Sadie might be ill entered his mind.

Worried, Benjamin debated whether to duck from Owen's view or to approach him with a warm greeting. Maybe Owen was traveling through town and merely looking for a place to stay for the night. He hoped he was on his way to somewhere else and that somewhere else was California. A long, long way from Benjamin and Pearl.

Summoning his courage, he strode toward Owen. Suddenly he became aware of how loud his heels sounded clacking against the worn wooden floor.

Owen turned toward him, and recognition flickered upon his features. "Benjamin!"

He tipped his hat. "Evening, Owen."

Owen excused himself long enough to get a key from Dimsbury.

"You two know each other?" the innkeeper asked.

"Sure do. We were friends back in Denmark," Benjamin said.

"Well, just make sure the two of you stay friendly," he warned. "I don't want no trouble around here."

"You won't have any trouble," Benjamin assured him.

Owen nodded, which seemed to satisfy Dimsbury. He'd put up a sign saying he'd be away a spell, then disappeared as he always did at that time of day. Benjamin always assumed he took dinner next door since it was the right time and he was always punctual about leaving for an hour.

Owen turned to Benjamin. The two men walked a few steps away from the counter before resuming their greetings.

"What are you doin' here?" Owen asked. "I knew you were somewhere in these parts, but I didn't think I'd find you like this, in a speck of a place out in the middle of nowhere."

"If this is such a speck in the road," Benjamin quipped, "then what are you doing here?"

"I'm passing through on my way to California. My aunt died, and she left me a house in San Francisco."

Benjamin chuckled. "You want to live way out there in a city?"

Owen shrugged. "I figure I can at least go and see the house. At the worst, I can sell it and make some money. Maybe replace some I lost to you." He folded his arms. "Speaking of that, I don't have anything to do tonight. I noticed there's a saloon next door. How about we get up a game of cards?"

Benjamin hesitated. What could he say to Owen that his former gambling buddy would believe?

Owen drew closer. "I'll bet you already know most of the saloon girls by now and probably have a set of regular card players, don't you? Just like back home."

He squirmed for a response. "This isn't the same place."

"Of course not. But women are the same everywhere. They all swoon when they see a handsome fella. If I looked anything like you, I'd be married with ten kids by now."

"You'd be married if Ellie had her way." Benjamin grinned.

"I know it. Maybe if I like this house out in San Francisco and I don't see no other woman that looks better, I might send for Ellie. She's not the best-looking woman in the world, but she'd make a good enough wife."

Benjamin didn't want to agree that Ellie was one of the homeliest women in Denmark. Considering the likelihood Owen would find another woman in San Francisco, Benjamin visualized Ellie's slim chances with Owen evaporating.

A sly grin covered Owen's features. "Seeing as how we don't got any women to worry us, what about that card game?"

Benjamin shook his head. "I'd better not."

"Aw, come on now. You must know a few men who'd like to play a hand or two."

"Nope. I haven't visited the saloon but once since I first got here."

Owen's mouth dropped. "Come again?"

"You heard right."

"I don't believe it."

Benjamin shrugged. "I can't help whether you believe it or not. It's true. I've been working on a ranch."

Owen whistled. "You've been getting your hands dirty? That's a switch for you."

Benjamin knew he deserved Owen's disdain. "It's about time I started to make an honest living, don't you think?"

"Men who make an honest living during the day often don't mind a little bit of what they call 'recreation' at night. Time's a-wasting. Let's go get up a game."

As much as he hated to admit it, even to himself, Owen's offer tempted Benjamin. He hesitated. "I've changed since I've been working on Pearl's ranch."

"I can't imagine you lifting a finger outdoors." Owen eyed him. "But I have to say, you do look a mite tanned. But that don't mean you can't play cards."

Benjamin shook his head.

"What's the matter?" Owen scoffed. "Scared Pearl might find out? Pshaw, she's no better than we are."

Such words sent Benjamin's blood raging. Without thinking, he laid his fist into Owen's jaw. Owen reeled but recovered.

Benjamin heard chair legs on the front porch shuffle, wood meeting wood, making a scratching sound. Two men rushed into the front room.

"What's wrong, Benjamin?" inquired a boarder Benjamin knew only as Harry. "This here stranger bothering you?"

"We don't take much of a hankering to that kind of thing here in these parts," Harry's friend added.

"He's not bothering me," Benjamin rushed to explain.

"More like he's bothering me," Owen said. "Laid a mean punch on me over a misunderstanding."

The two would-be rescuers regarded Benjamin, then glared at Owen, then returned their gazes to Benjamin. "You sure about that? 'Cause we can beat him up pretty good if you need us to."

"I'm sure," Benjamin confirmed. "But all is well here."

Owen looked whipped, but Benjamin wanted to be sure a sour word about Pearl never again crossed Owen's lips. He spoke to the man in a lowered voice. "Pearl has more goodness in her little finger than you and I have in our whole bodies and souls put together."

Owen rubbed his jaw and stared at Benjamin. "Whatever you and your friends say."

Benjamin wanted to point out that the two men were always looking for a fight and weren't really his friends and he could have taken care of himself. But he decided to omit all three statements. The fact that he had resisted Owen's suggestion to go back to his old ways—an easy way to make money, to be sure—was victory enough.

Benjamin smiled at his friend from Denmark. "Look—I'm sorry I flew off the handle like that. Punching someone never solves anything. And I know you wouldn't even be standing here still if we hadn't known each other a long time."

"You got that one right," Owen said.

"How about I get you a cup of coffee?" Benjamin offered.

"No, I'm not in the mood for coffee. I think I'll go to the saloon and try my luck there to find a night's entertainment." Owen studied Benjamin. "You really have changed. Never thought I'd see the day."

"Like Preacher Giles said in church last Sunday, with God all things are possible."

Owen put his hands on his hips and looked at Benjamin cockeyed. "Is that from the Bible?"

"I think so. I'm not entirely sure. But if Pastor Giles said it, it's pretty close."

"So you're a pew-sitter now? Either you've gone crazy, or I have."

Benjamin laughed. "Maybe you ought to try it sometime. Maybe you'll find yourself a pretty girl."

A week later Pearl and Benjamin had just entered the house when Ma called.

"Pearl?" Ma's weak voice sounded from her room.

Pearl sighed and sent Benjamin a look and set down the tomatoes she had picked. Just as quickly she regretted her show of impatience. Her mother couldn't help being sick. But some days she was more demanding than others. On this particular day, she had called Pearl five times in the span of an hour.

Pearl softened her expression and set her voice to a happy pitch. "Yeah, Ma?"

"Can you come here? And bring that man of yours with you."

So Ma wanted Benjamin? Pearl wondered what could be the matter. She motioned to Benjamin, who was just finishing breakfast. "Come on."

Without delay he complied.

"We're here, Ma. What's the matter?" Pearl noticed that Ma had consumed all the water in the pitcher in her night table. "Do you need more water?"

"I will, but not now."

Pearl sat on the side of her mother's bed. Strands of the older woman's hair clung to the sides of her face, saturated with sweat. Wet droplets marked her forehead. Her cheeks looked flushed, and she was thrashing. Pearl hadn't seen such a sight since one of Sadie's girls died of consumption, spreading fear throughout the house. Pearl remembered that was the one time she had asked the Lord to spare her, though she didn't deserve His mercy after traveling away from His protection for so long. Yet He had seen fit to answer her prayer. In a flash, she wondered if the Holy Spirit had brought that remembrance to her mind. Was it time to pay Him back?

Pearl noticed her mother's sheets had twisted and turned. "Here. Let me smooth these for you." She set about her task.

"You would have made a good nurse if you hadn't of. . ." Ma regarded Benjamin. "I'm glad you're here, too. I'm in desperate need of prayer, and I'll take petitions from anyone with a voice."

Pearl dried her mother's forehead with a clean cloth. "Your head is as hot as a branding iron." Pearl's throat tightened.

"I know it. And I feel mighty puny."

It wasn't like Ma to admit she didn't feel well. The confession worried Pearl.

"I don't want to die. Not yet."

Die! "You're not gonna die, Ma." Pearl hoped her words would prove true.

Ma took Pearl's hands. "Please. Please pray for me."

"I will, Ma. But first there's something we need to do." Pearl turned to Benjamin. "Fetch the preacher. If he's not at church, try the parsonage next door."

Benjamin nodded. "Right away."

Ma's voice rang out in the room. "No!"

"Ma! Don't you want the preacher?"

"There's not enough time. I know there isn't. You'll have to do."

Ignoring her mother's veiled insult, Pearl dropped to her knees and set her elbows on the side of the sickbed. "Lord, I pray You'll see fit not to take my ma. I know the mansion You built for her in heaven is much better than anything she can have here, but she's not ready to leave us yet. She feels so bad, Lord. Can't You see her tossing and turning, doing her best to sweat out the fever? I know she has a lot of life left in her, and she wants to live it. Please grant her a few more years with us. Please." Pearl felt tears drop down her cheeks.

She kept praying, not keeping track of time. During that spell, she noticed Benjamin's presence beside her. He had joined her by the bed and was on his knees, too. Though he didn't speak, his nearness consoled her. The fact that he had joined her in prayer made her sob.

She felt Benjamin's arm around her. "Shh. You'll wake her up with all that boo-hooing."

"Wake her up?" Pearl studied her mother. Indeed, she had fallen sound asleep.

Ma's aged features had softened far beyond anything Pearl could have imagined only a few moments ago. Deep wrinkles, brought on by years of toiling in the sun, weren't as apparent as usual.

Unwilling to rise from her knees, Pearl scooted along the floor until her hand could reach her mother's forehead and cheeks. When she touched her mother's face, Pearl was relieved to find that her skin didn't feel nearly as heated as it had before they prayed. The redness had left her cheeks, leaving in its stead the soft pink color she was accustomed to seeing in her mother. The woman's breathing had become even. An occasional rattle that could once be heard in Ma's chest had left. It was as if the years had floated away and a youthful Ma was taking a nap while her little children played.

Benjamin took her hand and lifted her to her feet. "Let's go," he whispered. "There's nothing more we can do."

Chapter 9

A few minutes later Benjamin and Pearl returned to the kitchen.

"I can't believe Ma is resting so well." Pearl kept her voice low.

"After the way she was acting so sick before, I can't believe it, either. Let's just hope she stays that way. Restful and feeling better." Benjamin took his usual seat at the table and then looked at the entrance to the sickroom. "God sure acted fast, didn't He?"

Pearl joined him at the table. "He sure did. Not that He always works that quickly. But I'm glad He did this time. Ma was suffering."

Benjamin looked back at Pearl. "So you think our prayers had something to do with your ma's fever breaking?"

"What else could it be? She begged us to pray for relief. As soon as we did, the fever broke."

"We've been here awhile now. Wonder why she picked that moment in time to ask us?"

"I think she was too sick and desperate not to."

Benjamin was thoughtful. "Maybe God does help people, after all."

"Of course He does." Pearl remembered Benjamin's bitterness over how his brothers had deserted him at Sadie's. "Just because you had a tough childhood doesn't mean God wasn't there."

"But how could He expect me to find Him at Sadie's? I didn't go there on my own. But when I ended up there, I naturally fell into the gambling life. What else could I have done? If I'd had my druthers, I'd have done something else with my life if God hadn't abandoned me."

"Like what?" Pearl kept her voice gentle. She wanted to challenge him to think, not to alienate the only man she had ever loved.

Benjamin shrugged. "I don't know. I might have been a blacksmith's apprentice. Or worked at a shop in town. Or maybe even been a rancher."

"You're a rancher now. Of sorts."

"I suppose I am." Benjamin crossed his arms. "But it's taken me an awful long time to get here."

"Maybe God had a reason for you to take the long way around."

"You took the long way around, too," he pointed out.

"I'd like to think of my time in Denmark as a mistake. I learned a lot from straying off the path. I never will stray again."

"I'm glad," Benjamin said. "I don't mean any disrespect against your ma, but I can see by the way she talks to you that you haven't always had it easy. You never have had it easy, really."

"Maybe not. But I haven't had it as hard as some people. At least I do have a ma, and she does love me enough not to want me to suffer for an eternity out of the presence of God. I don't want you to suffer, either," Pearl said. "I want you to know God, but not because you've made some sort of bargain or deal with Him. You must seek His face because you want to know the Lord and because you want the Lord to be part of your life through all times, not just bad times."

"Things have gotten better since I stopped gambling and cheating people out of their money. I feel much better now in my heart. I can see now, by the way things have turned out in my life, that God never abandoned me while I was at Sadie's. But I sure can see a difference in my life now compared to then."

"I can see the difference in you. And I can feel the difference in me, too. That was no life for me. Or you," Pearl added.

"I do want a new life, Pearl. Pastor Giles said I can get baptized. I think I want to do that."

Pearl gasped and touched Benjamin's arm. "You do! Oh, Benjamin, I'm so glad to hear you say that. You've made me so happy!"

Ma called from the next room. "Pearl!" Her voice sounded strong.

"Ma!" Pearl jumped from her seat and rushed into her mother's room. "How are you—?" She stopped. "Ma!"

The older woman was sitting upright in her bed without her back touching the pillow. Sickness had melted from her being. A smile decorated her face.

Pearl gasped. "Ma! What happened?"

"I—I feel better than I have in weeks. Why, I do believe the Lord cured me! Hallelujah!" Ma lifted her arms in praise. "Thank You, God, and thank you both for your prayers." She threw back the covers and started to exit the bed.

Pearl hastened to stop her. "Don't leap out of bed just yet. You might not be as strong as you think."

"What do you mean? I should be able to get up and fix supper. Remember Peter's mother-in-law in Matthew, how Jesus healed her of a fever? 'And when Jesus was come into Peter's house, he saw his wife's mother laid, and sick of a fever. And he touched her hand, and the fever left her: and she arose, and ministered unto them.'" She shook her head at the young couple. "And if there's anybody who needs ministering to, it's the two of you."

Pearl let out an exasperated sigh and watched her mother try to bound out of bed. As soon as she did, she sat back down.

"I'm a bit dizzy. Must be the vertigo," Ma conceded.

Pearl helped Ma position herself back into a reclining position. "I'm not sure it's vertigo. What I am sure of is that you've been in bed a long time, and you're still weak.

That's nothing to be ashamed of. You'll be as well as Peter's mother-in-law was soon enough. Then you can minister to us all you want. And cook supper, too."

"I'd like that."

"Let me bring you some hot soup in the meantime."

"I'd like that, too." Ma's voice sounded gentler than usual. She placed her hand on Pearl's. "Thank you, Pearl. And thank you, Benjamin."

Pearl nodded, unwilling to say anything that might discourage Ma's gentleness. Perhaps her healing marked the beginning of a new era. A new era for them all.

—⁓—

"Now won't you have another helping of chicken, Benjamin?" Ma asked him two weeks later as she served supper.

Benjamin set a clean drumstick bone on his plate. "Don't mind if I do, Ma." She'd asked him to call her by that name, but it still sounded strange to his ears. "It's mighty good chicken."

"I know I'll never cook chicken as good as Ma can," Pearl conceded, though she declined a second piece.

"Sure you can fry up a bird as good as I can," Ma protested. "I'll show you how. Again."

Benjamin cut Pearl a look and tried to withhold a grin. Ma's acerbic tongue would outlive her, most likely. "Pearl cooks just fine, Ma. No husband of hers would ever starve to death."

"Is that so? Well, then, why don't you find out?"

"What do you mean?" Benjamin knew exactly what she meant, but he wanted to hear her put her feelings into words.

"I mean, what are you waitin' for, boy? Do you think a woman as pretty as my Pearl is goin' to sit around here forever and wait for you?"

"Now, Ma," Pearl protested, "you're embarrassing me!" Reddened cheeks confirmed her statement.

"I thought you were long past the point where anything could embarrass you, Pearl. Although I must say, you do seem more modest than you used to."

"I reckon I should thank you?"

"That's a compliment. But if you're lookin' for an insult, I can give you plenty of those, too."

"Ain't that the truth?" Pearl asked no one in particular.

"Now, if you keep on talkin' that way, I'll tell Benjamin here that he can forget about asking you to marry him. He can go on about his business, and I'll get Zeke Callihan to work for us in his place."

"Zeke?" Pearl scoffed. "Now, Ma, I know you mean well, but I don't want Benjamin to ask me to marry him just because you say he should. You wouldn't do that, would you, Benjamin?"

He grinned. "I think you know the answer to that."

With her fork, Pearl played with her mashed potatoes and didn't look up. Benjamin had delivered the quip without the least bit of hesitation. Maybe he wasn't planning to ask her hand in marriage after all. Not that she could blame him. She had asked an awful lot of him, that he come to a saving knowledge of the Lord and change his ways. From all appearances, he had done both.

Lord, You know what's best. If Benjamin isn't the one for me, let me know quick. I can't stand the idea of waiting and wondering. But if he's the one You have picked for me, please let him ask me real soon.

"What are you daydreamin' about, Pearl?" Ma asked. "Never mind. You'd best get goin' on your chores. You took on a powerful lot more work while I was sick, and now you've got to be sure it all gets done."

—⁕—

Leaving the general store in Rope A Steer, Benjamin reached into his pocket and fingered the little ring he'd bought for Pearl. He wouldn't rest until he got it safely on her beautiful finger.

Walking to the inn, he contemplated his life. Never would he have guessed that he'd marry Pearl, the woman who once helped him cheat at cards. But now he expected she'd help him in a better way—God's way. She would be the person who walked beside him, making a go of the ranch with him, bringing it up to its full potential. He imagined a full herd of dairy cattle in his future and plenty of money from the milk, cheese, and butter he could sell. He'd earn every penny. The hard work of farming already told him that. But each fiber of his muscles pulsated with energy and vigor. Sunshine hit the part of his face not sheltered by his brimmed hat, tickling his skin. After the harvest, Pearl would put up their food for the winter, and fall would begin in full force.

He could only hope the river wouldn't be too cold on the day of his baptism. After he broached the topic with Pearl the day Ma was healed, he hadn't mentioned baptism again. Thoughts of such a momentous event left him ecstatic and fearful. A new life of walking in the Lord's path presented a challenge for the reformed gambler, but the rewards of an honest living and a clear conscience seemed worth it all.

Not to mention the best prize. Pearl. She would be his forever. And not in the shadows, but in the full light of day, as his wife.

If she'll have me.

Crossing the inn's threshold, he fingered the ring again. He'd ask when the time was right. He knew when that would be. The day he proclaimed once and for all that his life belonged to the Lord.

—⁕—

On the day of the baptism, Pearl fanned herself more than she usually did during church. Nervousness, not just the heat, spurred her to take such action. She had a surprise for Benjamin. Today that surprise would come to fruition. She tried to restrain herself from looking out the window too much, but self-control wasn't easy. Every once in a while she cut her gaze to the sunshine outdoors without moving her head.

Ma knew about the surprise. And, though Pearl could feel nervous energy emanating from her, too, Ma watched Pearl and poked her in the ribs so she'd pay attention to the sermon on new beginnings. Meanwhile, Benjamin appeared to keep a close and anxious eye on Pearl, as well. No doubt in his own excitement he didn't realize they had something planned. A good thing, too, because any other time he would have caught on to their nervousness and wormed the information out of them.

Noon approached, and the last hymn was sung. Pearl didn't linger to talk with her friends. Instead, she hurried Benjamin outside. She couldn't wait any longer for what was to transpire.

In the churchyard, as planned, three men awaited. Pearl didn't have to ask who they were. She would have known them anywhere because she could see traces of her beloved Benjamin in them all.

"What? What are they doing here?" Benjamin stopped in his tracks and studied his brothers.

Pearl could hear murmurings from the other congregants behind her, but she wasn't about to answer questions. She wanted to savor the reunion she had planned for Benjamin.

He let out a whoop and ran to each brother, embracing him in turn. Slaps on the back and happy greetings resulted.

"Do you know what's happening today?" Benjamin asked them.

Reuben nodded. "Pearl told us."

"Pearl?" Benjamin gasped and turned toward her. "I guess I'm not surprised." He strode over to her, then took her by the arm so he could guide her closer to his brothers.

Since they were outlaws, Pearl half expected lusty looks and whistles, but each man, while looking at her approvingly, took off his hat and greeted her with respect. The love they had for their youngest brother showed in their eyes, even though their demeanor was stiff since the reunion had been a long time in coming.

Preacher Giles joined them. "Are these the brothers you've talked about before, Benjamin?"

"Sure are, preacher." Benjamin introduced Colt, Caleb, and Reuben.

The pastor nodded and shook hands with each brother. He knew all about their past, but no judgment expressed itself on his face or in his demeanor. "I'm looking forward to knowing you all, but we have a baptism to get to now."

"That's a fact," Pearl agreed.

Preacher Giles grinned. "You ready, Benjamin?"

"I sure am. Now more than ever."

Benjamin squeezed Pearl's hand, and then they walked back to church together. Benjamin needed a few moments to change out of his Sunday suit and into attire more suitable for being drenched in water. After the baptism, a churchwide picnic was planned as a celebration.

Before he left her side, Benjamin embraced Pearl. "You kept your promise. I never doubted you would try, but I can't believe you found them all. And you never said a word."

"It wasn't easy, but I tracked them down with a little persistence and a whole lot of prayer."

"I didn't think this day could get any better, but it sure has." Benjamin's eyes misted. "Thank you, Pearl."

—⁂—

Later Pearl watched Benjamin rise from the water. Drenched in water and prayer, he'd never looked better.

People in church congratulated him. Many had developed a genuine fondness for Benjamin. He glowed amid their friendship and support. Time with Benjamin's brothers had been brief, but Pearl knew they would have a few days to get to know them before they returned home. After that, she planned to be instrumental in never letting Benjamin lose touch with them again. She made this resolution with no fear or trepidation.

Instead of the outlaws Benjamin had described to her, the three men had changed. Caleb was a sheriff out in Arizona and happily married with a baby on the way. Reuben stood with quiet confidence, unlike the outward bravado she had expected because of what Benjamin had told her about him. Pearl wished she could have met his wife, but she had stayed behind in Wyoming because she, too, was in a family way. Colt had a beautiful wife and two daughters who adored him, plus a little one. Pearl could see the baby was the spittin' image of his daddy. Surely the Lord had touched them all, even as He had touched her Benjamin.

Pearl waited for everyone, including Ma, to convey kind words to Benjamin before she took her turn. By the time she approached, the sun had almost dried him. "Oh, Benjamin, I'm so glad you got baptized."

"Me, too, Pearl. I never thought the day would come." He set his gaze on the ground and spoke softly. "Can I talk to you for a minute?"

"Why, sure, Benjamin." She could tell by the excitement in his eyes that something was urgent. But what?

He led her underneath a tree outside, where they had sought shade many a time. His expression conveyed tenseness, but he didn't seem unhappy.

Pearl couldn't stand the suspense. "What is it, Benjamin?"

He cleared his throat. "I have something to tell you. Or to ask you, that is."

Her heart beat faster. Was it finally time?

Benjamin reached into his trousers pocket and pulled out a little box. "I—I was hoping you might take this as a gift. You've been so good to me." He opened the box and showed her a brilliant garnet ring.

She gasped. "Oh, Benjamin! It's beautiful! But I—I can't accept something so expensive!"

"Sure you can."

"But where did you get so much money? Surely not from what I'm paying you."

"I had some left from my gambling days. In fact, I spent all that money on this ring for you. I want you to think of it as a symbol of what God did for us—protecting us through our dark times and staying with us until we found Him again. So please accept it." He paused and looked into her eyes. "If you're planning to be my wife."

"Your wife!" The phrase sounded so good falling from her lips.

He smiled shyly. "If you'll have me."

"Have you? Why, I'd be a fool not to say yes!"

Benjamin chuckled and placed the ring on her finger. "I don't know about that, but I do know I've loved you ever since I first set eyes on you."

Pearl looked into his eyes, which shone brighter even than the stunning garnet. "And I've always loved you, too. Isn't it something how God used that awful detour I took to bring me to you, and you to Him?"

"He sure can do a lot of things, Pearl."

"Yes. Yes, He can."

Benjamin took her in his arms. "I'll always be grateful to Him till the day I die, for giving me you."

As his lips touched hers, affirming the true love they shared, the love that would last a lifetime, Pearl knew Benjamin meant every word.

ABOUT THE AUTHORS

Darlene Franklin

Bestselling author Darlene Franklin's greatest claim to fame is that she writes full-time from a nursing home. She lives in Oklahoma, near her son and his family, and continues her interests in playing the piano and singing, books, good fellowship, and reality TV in addition to writing. She is an active member of Oklahoma City Christian Fiction Writers, American Christian Fiction Writers, and the Christian Authors Network. She has written over fifty books and more than 250 devotionals. Her historical fiction ranges from the Revolutionary War to World War II, from Texas to Vermont. You can find Darlene online at www.darlenefranklinwrites.com.

DiAnn Mills

DiAnn Mills is a bestselling author who believes her readers should expect an adventure. She combines unforgettable characters with unpredictable plots to create action-packed, suspense-filled novels.

Her titles have appeared on the CBA and ECPA bestseller lists; won two Christy Awards; and been finalists for the RITA, Daphne Du Maurier, Inspirational Readers' Choice, and Carol award contests. *Library Journal* presented her with a Best Books 2014: Genre Fiction award in the Christian Fiction category for *Firewall*, the first book in her Houston; FBI series.

DiAnn is a founding board member of the American Christian Fiction Writers; the 2015 president of the Romance Writers of America's Faith, Hope & Love chapter; and a member of Advanced Writers and Speakers Association and International Thriller Writers. She speaks to various groups and teaches writing workshops around the country.

DiAnn has been termed a coffee snob and roasts her own coffee beans. She's an avid reader, loves to cook, and believes her grandchildren are the smartest kids in the universe. She and her husband live in sunny Houston, Texas.

DiAnn is very active online and would love to connect with readers on any of the social media platforms listed at www.diannmills.com.

DARLENE MINDRUP

Darlene has written over thirty romance books, her Biblical and Viking stories being her favorites. Her love of history has been her inspiration through the years. She now lives in Montana with her husband where she can be close to her kids and grandkids.

TAMELA HANCOCK MURRAY

Tamela Hancock Murray is the author of over thirty novels and nonfiction works. She feels honored and humbled that her books have placed her on bestseller lists and that one of her Barbour titles, *Destinations*, won an RWA Inspirational Readers' Choice Award. Tamela has been a literary agent since 2001 and is with The Steve Laube Agency.

Tamela lives in Virginia with her husband of over thirty years. They are the parents of two lovely daughters. Tamela enjoys church, reading, and spending time with her immediate and extended family and friends.

Tamela is passionate about edifying and encouraging other Christians through her work. She always enjoys hearing from readers. Please visit her on Facebook and Twitter.

LYNETTE SOWELL

Lynette Sowell is an award-winning author with New England roots, but she makes her home in Central Texas with her husband and a herd of five cats. When she's not writing, she edits medical reports and chases down stories for the local newspaper.

MICHELLE ULE

Michelle Ule is a direct descendent of the Col. James Hanks featured in *An Inconvenient Gamble*. A California native, she's the biographer of *Mrs. Oswald Chambers: The Woman Behind the World's Bestselling Devotional,* and the bestselling author of five historical novellas. Her full-length historical novel, *A Poppy in Remembrance,* releases in fall 2018. You can learn more about her at www.michelleule.com.

KATHLEEN Y'BARBO

Bestselling author Kathleen Y'Barbo is a multiple Carol Award and RITA nominee of more than eighty novels with almost two million copies in print in the US and abroad. She has been nominated for a Career Achievement Award as well a Readers' Choice Award and is the winner of the 2014 Inspirational Romance of the Year by *Romantic Times* magazine. Kathleen is a paralegal, a proud military wife, and a tenth-generation Texan, who recently moved back to cheer on her beloved Texas Aggies. Connect with her through social media at www .kathleenybarbo.com.